The Anarchist
Who Shared
My Name

Pablo Martín Sánchez

Translated by Jeff Diteman

DALLAS, TEXAS

DEEP VELLUM

Deep Vellum Publishing
3000 Commerce St., Dallas, Texas 75226
deepvellum.org · @deepvellum

Deep Vellum Publishing is a 501c3
nonprofit literary arts organization founded in 2013.

ISBN: 978-1-941920-71-8 (paperback) · 978-1-941920-72-5 (ebook)
Library of Congress Control Number: 2018936728

Cover design by Anna Zylicz · annazylicz.com
Typesetting by Kirby Gann · kirbygann.net

Text set in Bembo, a typeface modeled on typefaces cut by Francesco
Griffo for Aldo Manuzio's printing of *De Aetna* in 1495 in Venice.

Distributed by Consortium Book Sales & Distribution.
Printed in the United States of America on acid-free paper.

ACKNOWLEDGMENTS

Jeff Diteman wishes to thank Christiana Hills, Grace Nowakoski, Maria Tymoczko, Pedro Cano, Martín Espada, Paul Fournel, and Craig Florence; and to dedicate this translation to Donna Diteman and Florence Josephine.

PROLOGUE

THERE IS SOMETHING EXCITING AND AT the same time terrifying about the idea that chance can govern our lives. Exciting, because it is part of the very adventure of living; terrifying, because it produces a dizzy feeling of lack of control. When it comes to writing, chance tends to play a smaller role than most people think—although some authors have made it the protagonist of their whole body of work. The story you hold in your hands, however, would not have been possible if chance had not knocked insistently at the writer's door. Or, to put it more accurately: this story would not exist as it is retold here. Most of the facts can be dug up in archives and periodicals libraries, those flowerless cemeteries of memory. But an untold story is a story that does not yet exist: someone has to weave together the thread of the events. And chance or coincidence intervened in my path so that I would be the one to do so. Because this is the story of someone who may have been my great-grandfather. It is the story of an anarchist who shared my name. It is the story of Pablo Martín Sánchez, a story that is perhaps worth telling.

IT ALL BEGAN THE DAY I googled my name for the first time. Back then, I was a young, unpublished author who blamed his failure on the ordinariness of his name. And the search engine proved me right: I entered "Pablo Martín Sánchez," and the screen vomited up hundreds of results. References to me did show up here and there, amid the motley list of surfers, chess players, and reckless drivers facing prosecution. But there was one entry that particularly grabbed my attention, perhaps because it was written in French:

"International dictionary of anarchist militants (from Gh to Gil)," said the title, followed by this stub: "Captured, condemned to death and executed with other participants in the action including Julián Santillán Rodríguez and Pablo Martín Sánchez…" Intrigued, I opened the page and discovered that it was an article about the anarchist Enrique Gil Galar, with a passing mention of Pablo Martín Sánchez. I then tried to access the letter M for Martín, but the dictionary was under construction and only went up to G. However, the entry on Gil Galar shed a bit more light on the text of the stub: "Member of an action group, Enrique Gil Galar participated on November 6 and 7, 1924, in the Vera de Bidasoa expedition in which one hundred comrades coming from France penetrated Spain."

I was unable to find any other references online, but for a few months I kept going back to the anarchist militants page to watch the progress of their dictionary. Unfortunately, their pace of work was hopelessly slow, and it seemed it would take years for them to reach the letter M. Finally, I wrote to them asking for more information about Pablo Martín Sánchez. Their polite reply, which I have kept, reads: "Hello and thank you for your letter. However, I do not have any more information about Pablo Sánchez Martín [sic]. Perhaps you should look in Spanish newspapers from the time and in the legal archives. Sincerely yours, R. Dupuy." And that is exactly what I did: I tracked down periodicals from the time at the National Library, consulted dozens of books about the events in Vera de Bidasoa, and traveled to the very site of the incidents. Only then did I understand that I had to write the story of this anarchist who had stolen my name.

However, it didn't make much sense to limit myself to recounting what had happened in 1924. Other, more prominent writers had already done so, including Don Pío Baroja in *La Familia de Errotacho*, written in his study in the farmhouse of Itzea, with a view overlooking the path that the revolutionaries took on November 6 and 7. What I needed to do was something that no one had ever done before: reconstruct the biography of Pablo Martín Sánchez. But the task was not going to be simple, because, although his participation in the events in Vera was well documented, little was known about his previous life, perhaps due to having been unremarkable, like the lives of the vast majority of people, although his end made its way into the newspapers. In fact, one of the few pieces of information I had was that he was born in Baracaldo, so I decided to start my search at the beginning: the civil registry. And that's where I went one rainy autumn day.

There was a line at the registry. I waited impatiently for my turn. When I reached the window, I asked for the birth record of Pablo Martín Sánchez. "Date?" asked the young woman behind the window. "I don't know exactly," I replied. "Well, without the date of birth, we can't do anything." Then I remembered that the chronicles of the events stated that Pablo was 25 years old at the time of the incursion. "Around 1899," I ventured. "I'll go check," said the woman, and she stood up to consult an enormous binder. She came back, shaking her head: in 1899 there was no one registered with that name. "What about 1900?" I asked. But although the woman looked in all of the volumes between 1895 and 1905, the closest match she found was a certain Pablo Martínez Santos, who died from respiratory collapse just a few days after being born. When I noticed that the people in the line were starting to grow impatient, I said thank you and left, without paying much attention to the face of the woman who had helped me. That's why I didn't recognize her when, that same night, she walked up to my table at the bar Txalaparta, where I was ruminating on the strategy I would use the next day, and, with a mischievous smile, snapped me out of my reverie, saying, "I didn't think you'd survive till evening." Seeing my confused look, she continued, "Man, you left the registry so depressed, I thought you were going to commit suicide as soon as you got home." I invited her to sit down, but she was celebrating a birthday with some girlfriends, so she said she would only linger a few minutes. I told her the story that had brought me to Baracaldo, trying to explain my frustration that morning, and she told me to look at the parish baptismal records, which were sometimes more reliable than the data in the registry.

She wished me luck and said goodbye with a pair of cheek kisses. Only then did I realize that I hadn't even asked her name.

The next day, I went back to the registry, but instead of the young woman with the mischievous smile, I was assisted by a chubby, sweaty guy. I asked after her, and he told me she was ill. So I wrote a note on a piece of paper, signed it with my email address, and asked him to leave it somewhere for her, if he would be so kind. Two days later, after running around to all of the churches, I returned to my hotel room empty-handed. I didn't know where to look next. Just when I was about to give up, a message came that renewed my hope: it was the woman with the mischievous smile (I will keep calling her that, out of respect for her desire for anonymity). She said that she had taken an interest in my story, and since the hours at the registry seemed interminable, she had been poking around in the archives and had found a certain Pablo Martín Sánchez born on January 26, 1890. She didn't think it was the person I was looking for, but who knows, maybe it was. In addition, she had told the story to her grandfather, making him promise that he would ask around at the community center to see if anyone had heard of him. I wrote her back immediately, thanking her and thinking that, once again, chance or coincidence had crossed my path. If, instead of going to the Txalaparta that night, I had gone to the Tempus Fugit, it is quite likely that you, dear reader, would be holding a different book in your hands right now, instead of mine.

The information that the woman with the mischievous smile had found in the civil registry was correct: it was the Pablo Martín Sánchez I was looking for, born quite a while before what was stated in the chronicles of the time (a generalized error, which there will be time enough to explain). In addition, the woman's grandfather put the word out at the community center, and got some results. One of the elders of Baracaldo who met every afternoon to play the card game mus knew someone from a nearby village who had a cousin whose father had been in France during the Primo de Rivera dictatorship, participating in some of the secret meetings where they plotted to overthrow the regime. The man had died a few years before, almost a centenarian, but his son still remembered some of the stories he had told. The problem was that he lived in Boston, Massachusetts, and I could not afford the luxury of traveling all that way to interview him; the most I could do was write him a letter, which never received a reply. But the elders of the community center refused to give up; excited by this story that seemed to give them back the energy of youth, they kept putting the word out all over Baracaldo. The woman with the mischievous smile sometimes went to see them and kept me informed of their progress, amused by the stories that these "geriatric bloodhounds," as she called them, were telling her. So I barely had to do anything; they cast the net all by themselves, and one fine day I received word that they had found someone who could tell me a lot about the story: a niece of Pablo Martín Sánchez, over ninety years old and a notorious misanthrope, who lived in a senior citizens' home in Durango, about thirty kilometers southeast of Bilbao.

You might think, dear reader, that I ought to have felt overjoyed at that moment, but I must confess that all I felt was fear. Yes, an inexplicable fear, a vague fear. Fear of looking into the story only to learn that it was boring, fear of finally speaking with this niece and having to accept that there was no story there to tell, fear of discovering that my namesake the anarchist had been an insignificant person or a second-rate delinquent who signed up for the Vera mission with petty intentions. For a moment I thought about staying home and forgetting the whole thing. But my curious side ended up winning over the cowardly part that was holding me back, and I undertook another trip, this time to Durango. On a cold but sunny Saturday at the end of January, I went to the Uribarri retirement home. They made me wait for a few minutes and then accompanied me to the garden, where the niece of Pablo Martín Sánchez was waiting for me on a bench, half dozing. Her head barely emerged through the collar of the thick green coat she was wrapped in, which gave her the curious appearance of a tortoise sleeping in the sun. The nurse gently rubbed her shoulder, and the old woman stretched her neck out toward us, unhurriedly opening her eyes behind thick glasses. She scrutinized me for a few moments before smiling. From her shell emerged a wrinkled hand gleaming with a strange, T-shaped ring, and she extended it to me in a friendly manner, saying, "Teresa, at your service." Without pause, she continued in the same soft voice: "Please, do sit down."

This encounter inaugurated a series of visits that extended into the following autumn: the first Saturday of every month I went up to Durango to listen to Teresa, the niece of Pablo Martín Sánchez, and the woman to whom I owe at least half of this book, because practically everything I know about the life of her uncle up until the moment he decided to enlist in the revolutionary expedition comes from the inexhaustible fountain of her memory, which was sparkling clear at first, although it grew foggier with each of our sessions. And thus, completely giving the lie to the misanthropic reputation some had pinned on her, she offered me, in nearly perfect chronological order, the story of the life (or what she remembered others having told her about the life) of her uncle the anarchist.

The last session was scheduled for All Hallows' Eve. At the previous visit the nurse had informed me that Teresa's health had been worsening a lot recently, and that the efforts of memory that my visits required might be harmful. I went to the home in the early afternoon, with a box of chocolates in my hand and a knot in my stomach. I was seized by a strange mixture of sadness and relief: sadness at the idea of putting an end to these pleasant meetings, and relief at being about to complete the puzzle of a story that would turn into a book. The life of Pablo Martín Sánchez had turned out to be one of the most fascinating I had ever heard, and the old woman had promised me that at our final meeting, she would tell me one "last surprise," smiling mischievously and half-closing her eyes behind her thick glasses. But when I asked for her at the reception, the unexpected news of her death struck me such a blow that I feared I would lose my balance. Despite her age and her declining health, I had believed her to be indestructible. "She died last week," they told me, "Peacefully, in her sleep." They regretted not having been able to let me know, but they did not have my telephone number. I thanked them and left the residence home, with the box of chocolates in my hand. Crossing the threshold, I heard someone say my name. I turned around. It was the nurse, with an envelope in her hand. On the back, it said "For Pablo." "We found it in Teresa's bedside table," said the nurse. "I think it was for you." I looked in her eyes, and I don't know why, but all I could manage to do was hug her. Probably because I couldn't find any words.

On the street, I sat down on a bench and opened the envelope. Inside, there was an old photograph, very well preserved, as though someone had kept it carefully for a long time. It showed three people: a handsome man, a dark-haired woman, and a teenage girl, embracing each other and leaning against a stylish delivery truck from the 1920s, which showed that the phenomenon of advertisement had already arisen: visible over their heads was a drawing of a large cow's head with earrings, along with the brand name: "*La vache qui rit.*" Studying the picture, I discovered that this man was the same one I had seen in the National Historic Archive, on one of the anthropometric files compiled by the police after the Vera incident: none other than Pablo Martín Sánchez, my namesake the anarchist. I did not recognize the mother or the teenager, but I supposed they were his sister and his niece, Teresa herself, although she looked nothing like the old woman who had opened up the bounty of her memories to me. Upon returning the photograph to the envelope, I discovered that there was also a scrap of paper, on which she had written, as if at the last minute: "Thank you for everything, Pablo. My uncle would have laughed out loud if he knew he would end up being the protagonist of a novel."

The least I can do is dedicate this book to Teresa, and offer her my gratitude for having made it possible for you, dear reader, to bring to life once again the story of her uncle the anarchist.

PART ONE

— I —

Today, the only Spain is a cynically materialistic one, which thinks only about vulgar, immediate concerns; it doesn't believe in anything, doesn't expect anything, and accepts all the wickedness of the present moment because it lacks the courage to engage in the adventures of the future. The land of Don Quixote has turned into the land of Sancho Panza: gluttonous, cowardly, servile, grotesque, incapable of any idea outside the range of its blinders.

Vicente Blasco Ibáñez

Una nación secuestrada

THE STORY BEGINS WITH TWO LOUD KNOCKS at the door of the printing office that employs Pablo Martín Sánchez, who, startled, upends his composing stick and scatters to the floor all the letters he's aligned for the title of the next issue of the weekly *Ex-Ilio*: "Blasco Ibáñez Stirs the Conscience of Spanish Immigrants in Paris."

We find ourselves in the French capital, in the year 1924, at the start of a rainy autumn that has not washed away the memory of the summer's successful Olympic Games featuring swimming champion Johnny Weissmuller, Hollywood's future Tarzan. The sun came out unexpectedly today, Sunday, October 5, but now it is already sinking; Pablo was concentrating on his work when the knocks at the door disturbed his concentration. His employer is a small, dilapidated press called La Fraternelle, located at 55 rue Pixérécourt, in the middle of Paris's Belleville neighborhood. This is one of the most lively working-class areas of the city, and the one with the most Spaniards. Pablo is employed as a typesetter, but in reality he also does the work of an editor: he corrects, designs, and lays out all the Spanish content, which is no small amount since Primo de Rivera's coup d'état and the growing influx of immigrants to Paris from the other side of the Pyrenees. Since then, La Fraternelle has been printing *Ex-Ilio: The Spanish Immigrant's Weekly*, a four-page publication that all summer long has been reporting the breaking news on the Spanish team's Olympic standings, from the star role of the boxer Lorenzo Vitria to the disappointing performance of the soccer team, which, led by Zamora and Samitier, was eliminated in the first round by Italy, after an own goal by the defenseman Vallana.

Pablo's salary barely covers the thirty francs a week he pays for the hovel he lives in, since he only works at La Fraternelle from Friday afternoon to Sunday: during the rest of the week, the press is reserved for publications in French, overseen by the owner, Sébastien Faure, an old anarchist, well respected and short-tempered, bald as a cue ball and with great skyward mustache-tips, usually busier with litigation than with monitoring his employees' work. This arrangement is quite suitable for Pablo, who can do as he likes without running much of anything past "*Monsieur Fauve*," "Mr. Savage," as some call him behind his back in reference to his wild temper. In any case, Pablo only crosses paths with him on Friday afternoons, since the boss is equal parts anarchist and bon vivant, and it would never occur to him to come by the print shop on a weekend. The drawback is that some other employees take advantage of Monsieur Fauve's absence, and it falls on Pablo to pick up the slack. One such incident occurred last night, when he had to cover a protest meeting marking the first anniversary of Rivera's coup d'état—held three weeks late, as if to confirm the well-earned Spanish reputation for tardiness.

The event took place in the legislative chamber of the Community House on the avenue Mathurin-Moreau, adjacent to Parc des Buttes-Chaumont and about twenty minutes' walk from La Fraternelle. In attendance were people from the most diverse backgrounds, though nearly all united by two common interests: being Spanish and living in exile. The majority were anarchists and left libertarians, Paris being the hotbed of Spanish anarchism, but there were also many communists, republicans, and Catalan separatists, as well as various syndicalists and intellectuals, including fugitives and deserters—all those who, for one reason or another, had to seek refuge in France, fleeing persecution and torture by the Spanish Civil Guard. Some of the great political figures of the time were also there, such as Marcelino Domingo or Francesc Macià, and even Rodrigo Soriano—the politician and journalist who fought a duel a few years ago against Primo de Rivera himself—showed up, despite his bitter enmity toward Blasco Ibáñez. Renowned intellectuals were sure not to miss the event, such as José Ortega y Gasset, who had to seek refuge in France for having shouted "*Viva la libertad!*" upon hearing the announcement of Miguel de Unamuno's banishment to Fuerteventura. Unamuno, for his part, seated in a corner, seemed to be keeping himself busy drumming his fingers while he waited for the meeting to start, probably counting the syllables of some poem. Also in attendance were men of action who have been fomenting revolutionary sentiment in the Parisian henhouse, such as Buenaventura Durruti, with the stern countenance of a lazy-eyed gunman, or Francisco Ascaso, who insists, with his Andalusian charm, on denying the rumored half-secret that he was the one who shot Juan Soldevila, the Archbishop of Zaragoza, one year ago. Finally, discreet and evasive, Ángel Pestaña, the dapper new general secretary of the National Labor Confederation, appeared, having come to Paris expressly for reasons intimately related to the course of this story.

In fact, Pablo had planned to attend the meeting as just another exiled Spaniard, but in the end he had to do it for work reasons as well. In the last hour of the workday, when he was already getting ready to close the press, one of the writers of *Ex-Ilio* came running in, a thin, dapper man, with his hair slicked back and a recently trimmed little mustache:

"Listen, Pablo, you're going to the General Meeting tonight, right?"

"Yes," he replied, instantly regretting that he hadn't bitten his tongue.

"The thing is, it's my turn to cover the meeting—you know that Vicente Blasco is going to give a speech commemorating the anniversary of the coup. They say it's to promote the pamphlet he's planning to distribute halfway around the world…and, thing is, see, I have a date with a lady friend to go see Raquel Meller tonight, and the event goes on a long time, you know. So, I was thinking, since you're going anyway, maybe you could take the notes yourself, and tomorrow I'll come in first thing in the morning and write the article."

"It's fine, don't worry," said Pablo.

"*Merci, camarade*," the writer said as he exited the building smelling of cheap patchouli.

So there he was, the typesetter of La Fraternelle, playing the role of a journalist amongst the thick smoke of cigarettes and Cuban cigars, when Vicente Blasco Ibáñez, with his shirt starched for the occasion, took the podium to deliver his keynote address. Pompous as a peacock and sweating like a pig, he cleared his throat audibly, raised his hands a few times to quiet the crowd, and adjusted his monocle to read the careworn papers that he had taken out of the pocket of his blazer. Pablo opened his notebook and leaned against a column at the back of the room, next to a poster announcing the very same concert of Raquel Meller, the great Spanish cabaret singer of the Parisian stage. The poster showed Meller dressed in black, with the traditional *mantilla y peineta* head covering. Someone had drawn a large mustache on her face.

"My Spanish brothers working in France," the Valencian writer began his exhortation, "our reasons for meeting here today are rather unpleasant. As you all know, last September 13 marked one year of government (or, I should say, misgovernment) of our dear country by the tyranny and idiocy of a handful of bastards unworthy to call themselves Spanish. This is why, from exile, we find ourselves obligated to raise our voices to the world in protest of the dire situation our country is going through. Fortunately, in other places, such as here in sweet France which has taken us under her wing, it is still possible to express oneself freely without fearing that the henchmen of General Martínez Anido will take off their masks and come out from the crowd to brutally arrest us—"

At this point, someone shouted "Down with Anido!" and Pablo took advantage of the interruption to take a few hurried notes, before the applause died down and Blasco Ibáñez aimed his poison darts at Alfonso XIII and Primo de Rivera:

"These two court jesters, wagging their tongues, cause more harm to the nation than all the weapons of our enemies. For Alfonso XIII, poor Spain is a box of tin soldiers, and the whoremonger Miguelito has been trying to imitate Mussolini, but daftly, like a buffoon, proclaiming denunciation to be a public virtue and tampering with the mail, condemning citizens for what they've written in their letters. This is why I declare, with pain and with shame, that Spain is at this time a nation in bondage: it cannot speak, because its mouth is stopped by the gag of censorship; it cannot write, because its hands are tied."

The devoted crowd listened attentively to the writer's words as he modulated his speech with the bravado of a classical orator or one of those American actors he met in his time as a Hollywood screenwriter. Next, he laid into the war in Morocco, and started spewing his bile against the army:

"And what do you think of this worthless army that's using up most of Spain's resources and invariably gets defeated in every action it takes outside of our borders? You might say that the word 'army' is not quite appropriate. It might be better to call them military police, because the only victories they manage to win are in the streets of our own cities, where they use machine guns and cannons to threaten the masses, who have at most a lousy pistol in their pocket."

A few angry shouts went up: "Hear, hear!" And so Blasco went on pontificating for nearly half an hour, until he had condemned every imaginable enemy. When he stepped down from the podium, sweaty and clammy, he went directly to the venue's exit, where Ramón, his private chauffeur, was waiting for him, ready to take him in his Cadillac to the Hôtel du Louvre, where he lived comfortably in a spacious suite on the top floor with excellent views of Paris.

But all this happened yesterday, and today in the morning, the mild-mannered writer did not show up to the print shop as he had promised, so Pablo himself has had to write the story so it can come out tomorrow in the weekly *Ex-Ilio*. It is not the first time he has written an article, although Monsieur Faure has explicitly forbidden him from doing so. While he is composing the headline, "Blasco Ibáñez Stirs the Consciences of Spanish Immigrants in Paris," two loud knocks at the door make him jump and spill the type he had been lining up.

"Julianín!" shouts Pablo, collecting the characters scattered on the floor, "Julianín, the door!"

But Julián, the seventeen-year-old boy who has been the shop's assistant since summer, does not appear.

"Julianín, damn you!" the typesetter shouts, unexpectedly losing his temper. His irritability might be due to an incident from last night, when, at the end of Blasco Ibáñez's speech at the Community House, someone approached him while he was taking his final notes. He was concentrating so hard on what he was writing that he did not realize until he heard the offer:

"You want some?" said a raspy voice at his side, as a little tin of snuff entered his field of vision.

"No, thanks," Pablo replied, lifting his eyes from the notebook. The voice belonged to an extremely thin man with a pocked face.

"Interesting speech, huh?" the man continued, taking a sizable pinch of snuff between his finger and thumb, "Blasco knows how to hit where it hurts. I saw more than one person squirm to hear him criticize Spain. Some people would rather keep their blinders on, don't you think?"

"Well, nobody likes to hear a mother insulted, even if the one doing it is a brother—even if the brother is right."

"Yes, I think that's exactly what it is," the man conceded, before clarifying, in a quieter voice, "especially if you're an infiltrator."

Pablo stared steadily into his eyes. The other man returned the gaze for a few seconds. Then, moving closer and lowering his voice even more, he added:

"That's why it's better not to speak of certain things here. Come by afterward to the café La Rotonde and join our discussion group—"

"I'm sorry, I can't," Pablo cut him off, excusing himself, "I have to wake up early tomorrow for work."

"A shame. What's the world coming to when not even *la France* respects the day of rest?" And with a hint of a smile, he bid Pablo farewell, giving him a card with the address of the café La Rotonde. "Come by one of these days, but don't wait too long."

That last bit sounded more like a threat than an invitation, thought Pablo as he watched the man rejoin a group dominated by the voice of the secretary general of the National Labor Board, Ángel Pestaña. Pablo slipped the card along with his notebook into the inside pocket of his coat. Making his way through the smoke and the crowd, he left the building and went out into the street. His trusty bicycle, an old secondhand Clément Luxe, was there waiting for him. He pedaled furiously under a threatening sky, and only upon arriving home did he realize that someone had written on the back of the card: "We need your help, friend. Contact us immediately."

"The door, Julianín, for God's sake!" Pablo shouts desperately, while trying to pick up the type. "Where the hell have you run off to?"

Receiving no response from the kid, Pablo wipes his hands on his typesetter's coveralls, crosses the distance to the door with long strides, goes up the two steps, and looks through the peephole. His surprise could not be greater: upon opening the door, he embraces his childhood best friend, Roberto Olaya, known to all as Robinsón, whom he has not seen since the end of the Great War, back in 1918, when they went their separate ways at the Gare d'Austerlitz with lumps in their throats.

I

(1890–1896)

No. PABLO MARTÍN SÁNCHEZ WAS NOT BORN in 1899, as the newspapers will claim several decades later, but on the night of January 26, 1890, the feast day of Saint Timothy and Saint Titus, Saint Theofrid and Saint Theogenes—all bishops—as well as Saint Simeon the hermit. The thermometer in Barcelona marked four degrees centigrade, and the humidity was 82%. However, the sky was clear, and Julián Martín Rodríguez could see the stars of the constellation Cassiopeia glowing in the celestial canopy, as he firmly squeezed his wife's hand hoping that their newborn son would lift his head and take his first gulp of air.

At that time, King Alfonso XIII was barely four years old, so it was his mother, the regent María Cristina, who held the nation's reins. The presidency was going back and forth between liberals and conservatives, according to the shameful arrangement they had reached in the Pardo Pact, and now the turn of the liberal Práxedes Mateo Sagasta was over. Who cares who's in charge of the government, Julián thought as he looked at the stars and waited for the birth of his first child. We'll still be the poorest country in Europe. All he had to do was look at the view through the window, faintly illuminated by the moonlight: the inaptly named neighborhood known as the Desert, a chaotic conglomeration of unsanitary residences that had been piling up on the left bank of the Nervión River since 1876, when, at the end of the Third Carlist War, the area had undergone a rapid process of industrialization and population growth, without it ever crossing the mayor's mind to come up with an urban development plan. The hard, dangerous work in the iron mines, the local population's primary means of sustenance, had driven the life expectancy of Baracaldo to one of the lowest in Spain; at the time of Pablo's birth, it was only twenty-nine years.

Julián heard his wife's moaning announcing the end of the labor, but still he did not dare to look. He noticed her hand gradually slackening, and he heard the midwife spanking the newborn. He waited to hear the cry, and, hearing nothing, closed his eyes angrily and gnashed his teeth, fearing a stillbirth. Only when he felt his wife's hand on his back did he dare to turn his head. It was a boy. And he was alive. But, incomprehensibly, he wasn't crying; or, more accurately, while he made a face like he wanted to cry, nary a sob escaped his throat, as if this were one of those silent films that would arrive in Spain a few years later. The three adults in the room looked at each other worriedly in the candlelight, but at first no one said anything. Then, the old midwife wrapped the child in a towel and placed him in the arms of his mother, wiped her hands on her skirt and left the house in a hurry, without finishing the job, making the sign of the cross and murmuring spells, taking the silent crying as a bad omen. "*Lagarto, lagarto,*" were the last words the midwife pronounced before her shadow disappeared through the doorframe. My God, thought Julián, that witch is known to tell stories—we're going to go from undesirables to pariahs. But something more urgent demanded his attention, and he pushed the bad thoughts out of his mind. He took his knife from his pants pocket and in one movement cut the umbilical cord, which had already stopped pulsing. No one would have said it was his first time.

Julián Martín Rodríguez and María Sánchez Yribarne had met three years beforehand, a few months after the royal birth of Alfonso XIII. She belonged to the new Biscayan bourgeoisie, not the class of landed gentry fallen on hard times, but that of the visionaries who at the start of the century had hopped on the industrialization bandwagon and managed to get rich overnight, such as her grandfather, the mythical José Antonio Yribarne, founder of one of the country's most powerful industrial dynasties. Julián, for his part, came from an extremely humble family of Zaragoza, was the youngest of nine brothers and the only one who had been able to go to school, thanks to the fathers of Escuelas Pías, who had welcomed him into the seminary with an enthusiasm that was quick to raise suspicions. He excelled in algebra, physics, natural history, as well as Latin, Greek, and modern languages; however, theology, history, and philosophy stymied him from the start. When he felt he had learned enough, he left the seminary without saying goodbye to anyone and took off traveling all over Spain offering his services. And so it happened that at the end of 1886 he reached Baracaldo and was hired by the Yribarne family as a tutor to their young, misbehaving daughter, María.

Love took a bit longer to blossom than it tends to in the pulp novels from the time, but Cupid finally showed up with an ample quiver full of arrows. And when he came, he came with a vengeance. Even the couple themselves did not know if it was while practicing declensions, memorizing the list of Gothic kings, or speculating about the transubstantiation of the soul, but what is certain is that one fine day they found themselves kissing passionately on the table, crumpling quadratic equations and the poems of Victor Hugo. When María's parents got wind of it, they threw the shameless tutor out into the street with no severance pay. What they did not expect is that their daughter was prepared to follow him to the ends of the earth.

The wedding took place early in the spring of 1889. Only one member of the bride's family attended: Don Celestino Gil Yribarne, the black sheep of the family and María's favorite uncle, who had always treated her as the daughter he'd never had. People in Baracaldo whispered the most outlandish slander against him, accusing him of everything from bestiality to practicing Satanic rituals in his mansion at Miravalles. None of this was true, however. The only eccentricity he allowed himself—not without some trepidation—was collecting the pubic hair of the women he slept with, classifying it in a fetishistic, methodical manner, like a lepidopterist with his butterflies or a numismatist with his coins. As for the groom's family, no one was able to afford the cost of the journey, so all they could do was to send their best wishes by mail, in the form of a collective letter covered in grease stains and spelling errors.

The nuptials were held in the old church of San Vicente Mártir, with a very austere ceremony, although Julián had passed the qualifying examination for the title of teacher and was giving classes at a public school in Baracaldo. María, for her part, in an act of carelessness or brave defiance, had sought work in steel factories not belonging to her family, such as those in Santa Águeda or Arlegui y Cía. But as soon as they found out that she was the disowned daughter of the Yribarne family, no one dared hire her, and one after another they invented excuses to show her the door. Fortunately, Don Celestino defied the family patriarchs and helped pay for the costs of the ceremony, which the young lovebirds' scant savings could not cover. As if that were not enough, he also gave them a magnificent wedding gift: a trip to Paris to attend the opening of the World's Fair commemorating the centenary of the French Revolution. Hearing this, the newlyweds could not contain their excitement, and they recited in unison the famous lines of Victor Hugo that had been crumpled under their first kiss: *"Oh ! Paris est la cité mère ! / Paris est le lieu solennel / Où le tourbillon éphémère / Tourne sur un centre éternel !"*

The train that was to take them to the City of Light left Bilbao on the fifth of May, the night before the start of the fair. At the border, there was a transfer to get on the French track gauge, and from then on a horde of passengers pushed into the train at every stop, filling all of the cars—not only first, second, and third class, but also the freight cars. No one wanted to miss the great event. When they arrived at the Gare Saint-Lazare, the day was starting to clear up and the passengers exited the train hoping to be welcomed by the gleaming, massive skeleton towering a thousand feet high, designed especially for the occasion by a certain Gustave Eiffel, who was still ruminating on how to get out of having to take the tower down after the Fair, as had been planned. Unfortunately, the buildings surrounding the station blocked the view, and a slight disappointment spread through the crowd. The newlyweds went first to the Hotel Español, conveniently located on the Rue de Castellane, where Uncle Celestino had reserved them a room, because what could be better than staying in a hotel of compatriots? However, they soon realized that the only thing Spanish about the hotel was its name, apart from a few old copies of *El Imparcial* and *El Liberal* scattered around the lobby. The room had no closets, no shelves, not even a measly wash basin, nor a candle on the bedside table. But all this nothingness was costing ten francs a day.

Julián and María went to the Champ de Mars, where the Eiffel Tower served as the main entrance to the fairgrounds, which held over 120 acres of pavilions. On the way they ate French fries sold in a paper cone and drank glasses of sugar water flavored with orange blossoms. The streets of Paris were decked out in their Sunday best, adorned with wreaths of flowers and golden garlands, along with a vast, inebriated crowd waving patriotic flags. Now that's what I call iron—thought an astonished Julián when they arrived at Place de la Concorde and got their first view of the impressive tower—a far cry from what they dig up in the mines of Baracaldo. Then, walking along the bank of the Seine, they arrived at the Pont d'Iena, just when the president of the republic and his wife were getting ready to cross it in an official carriage pulled by four horses and flanked by a peloton of bodyguards. Sadi Carnot looked impeccable, dressed in the trappings of high ceremony, but it was the first lady who received the highest praise, with a bold tricolor dress designed for the occasion: a blue silk skirt, a white bodice of Alençon lace, and pale red trim. When the carriage passed under the giant arch of the Eiffel Tower, the bands struck up the Marseillaise, making way for the French president's predictable speech to officially inaugurate the World's Fair. Who then would have thought that five years later the Italian anarchist Santo Caserio would take the president's life, stabbing him with a knife and shouting "Long live anarchy!" Fortunately, the young couple enjoyed a peaceful and pleasant afternoon, and that same night, in the bare room of the Hotel Español, while the Parisian sky turned into a bacchanal of fireworks and multicolored lights, a sperm bearing the seal of the Martín Rodríguez family jubilantly united with an ovum produced in the Sánchez Yribarne factory, to create an embryo destined to bear the name Pablo Martín Sánchez.

"It's strange that he's not crying," said Julián when he had finished tying the umbilical cord.

"He is crying, but silently," replied María with a sigh, as her contractions continued, working to expel the placenta.

The very next day, with no time to lose, Pablo Martín Sánchez was baptized at the church of San Vicente Mártir, the very place his parents had been married nine months before. Again at the baptism he did not cry, not even when the young priest Ignacio Beláustegui put the holy water on his head, accompanying the gesture with three loud, poorly timed sneezes to complete the baptismal ceremony. What a brave Christian, Don Ignacio seemed to say to himself, without imagining that decades later he would find himself seeking a pardon for this brave child.

This act of silent rebellion marked Pablo's first steps in this world, and soon word spread around Baracaldo that the Martín baby was incapable of crying. The rumor was false, of course, because while it is true that the child wept rarely, he did indeed cry from time to time, but so subtly that only a keen observer could detect it. What was true, on the other hand, was that Pablo did not seem to be in any hurry to start speaking: he turned one year of age, then two, and when he reached the age of three years he still had not uttered a single word, despite his parents' desperate attempts to get him to say papa and mama. Until the day his sister was born. This was in 1893; in Saint Petersburg, Tchaikovsky was composing his *Pathétique* Symphony No. 6, while in Madrid the National Meteorological Institute was producing its first weather maps; María Sánchez Yribarne gave birth to her second child in the same room where little Pablo had been born three years before, but this time her husband did not have to get out his knife: the new midwife took care of everything. A beautiful, energetic sister was born and was named Julia, apparently intent on making up for all the crying her brother had not done. When the infant was finally asleep in her mother's arms, they let Pablo come into the room so he could see her. He approached the bed, looked wide-eyed at the newborn, and pronounced his first word out loud, to everyone's surprise:

"Pretty," he said nonchalantly.

The little girl changed Pablo's life. All the words he had not been saying before started gushing out of his mouth, like a river after the spring thaw. He would spend long hours telling Julia the most extravagant stories, in a language full of invented or incomprehensible words that the weary parents found both entertaining and worrisome. However, when his sister was not nearby he retreated into a strange muteness from which no one could extract him, so in the minds of misinformed or malicious neighbors the child who didn't cry transformed into the child who didn't speak, although both claims were strictly false. In addition to all that, there was an episode that would end up revealing a real deficiency in the firstborn, one that would impact his immediate future.

It happened in the spring of 1896, when Pablo was six years old and little Julia was about to turn three. The industrialized countries were starting to emerge from the economic depression, and, although Spain would soon lose its overseas colonies and plunge into a crisis with uncertain consequences, new winds of bonanza appeared to be blowing in the West. The Martín Sánchez family's economic situation had improved significantly, despite the fact that Uncle Celestino was no longer able to help them: a sudden aneurysm had ended his life while he was collecting butterflies at his little castle at Miravalles, and the Yribarne family had conspired to keep María from receiving her share of the inheritance. However, Julián's lucky star was still looking after him, and he had obtained a position at the Escuela Normal Elemental of Bilbao, where he spent most of his day trying to alert the aspiring educators to the importance of reducing the number of illiterates, which stood at over ten million in Spain at the end of the century. For her part, María stayed home to take care of the children. One midday in early April, while the woman was making food in the coal-fired kitchen, she heard the knife sharpener go by, his horn whistling its unmistakable melody. She looked at the knife she had used to peel the potatoes and decided it was time to have it sharpened.

Look after Julia, she said to Pablo, I'll be right back.

She took twenty cents from a jar and left the house with her knife in her hand, leaving the food on the fire. In the street, she saw the sharpener turning at the next corner, dragging his wheelbarrow. He took no more than five minutes to do the task, but when María took the newly sharpened knife and came back around the corner toward home, a speeding carriage caught her by surprise. She managed to avoid being trampled by the donkey, but could not duck quickly enough to avoid being struck in the head by the edge of the carriage seat. She fell to the ground unconscious, and the driver and the sharpener tried to revive her. A neighbor brought her inside, refreshed her face with wet cloths, and called a doctor. When María regained consciousness, she had been out at least half an hour. She had a lump on her temple and a terrible headache.

"What about my children?" was the first thing she managed to say. When no one responded, she went running home. Already from outside she could smell the smoke. She entered the house screaming and found Pablo sitting calmly in front of his sister, trying for the umpteenth time to tell her the story of the three-eyed snail. The house reeked of scorched food, but the child seemed not to have noticed anything; his sister, on the other hand, was wailing at the top of her lungs. María ran into the kitchen and yanked the pot from the fire. There was nothing left inside but a carbonized mass stuck to the bottom, giving off an unbearable stench.

"But, Pablo," the mother scolded her son, "didn't you smell the food burning?"

"I don't smell," said the boy, laconically.

And so it was that his parents discovered that he did not possess the sense of smell. The local doctor described it as "anosmia or olfactory dysfunction," and, in addition to prescribing miraculous Climent Hypophosphite Syrup (whose maker claimed it cured all illnesses, including insomnia, pallor, and brain softening), recommended getting him away from the wet climate of the North and bringing him to the drier regions of the interior, where he would probably be able to recover the smell he had never had:

"Don't forget that the devil's best trick is convincing us he doesn't exist," he offered as a way of saying goodbye, leaving the parents somewhat disconcerted.

Julián and María decided to follow the doctor's advice. Anything for the child's health, they said to each other, and started thinking about how to relocate. In a few days the news arrived that Madrid would soon be testing candidates for the Primary Education Inspectors Corps, as three positions had just opened up in the provinces of Albacete, Badajoz, and Salamanca. The writing seemed to be on the wall, so Julián sent in an application to take the test. Two weeks later, he received a convocation to a test that would be held in the capital of the kingdom on the thirteenth and fourteenth of May.

"Why don't you bring the boy with you so we can see if the dry climate of Madrid does him any good?" María proposed.

"Woman, it's only going to be two days."

"But at least he can keep you company."

"Fine, as you wish," Julián acceded.

The one who did not welcome the idea was Pablo, who did not want to be separated from his sister Julia, even if it was only for two or three days. But the decision was made, and on the twelfth of May, at eight o'clock in the morning, father and son took the Express Train to Madrid's North Station. Making their way between the passengers laden with saddlebags and chickens, men and women shouting, smoking, shoving, and spitting on the floor, the two Martíns managed to reach their third-class seats. On the platform, mother and daughter waved their hands, while Pablo pressed his nose against the window of the compartment and quietly repeated the first word he had ever said: "Pretty, pretty, pretty." A silent tear ran down his cheek. Then the train whistle blew, and the boy understood that this was the start of a great new adventure.

You, my people, whom they kill with work in the factories, in the fields, in the mines or in the war, seek justice. Endure no more the tyranny of the executioners who oppress you. Rebel. One life is worth nothing, even less when it is predestined to vegetate and to feel only animal plea-sures. Rise up, for it will only take one gesture from you to make those who seem so brave and boastful run away. The military are cowards, as are all those who need to be armed to live.

España: Un año de aictadura, a manifesto published by the Grupo Internacional de Ediciones Anarquistas.

NOW SIX YEARS HAVE PASSED BETWEEN their farewell at the Gare d'Austerlitz and this afternoon in early October 1924, when Roberto, known to all as Robinsón, crosses the threshold of the printing house where Pablo works, limping slightly from a childhood bout of polio, and sporting long red hair and a beard worthy of his namesake. He is still wearing his perennial suit with its elbow patches, his shirt cuffs stained with chalk, and a bowler hat that some suspect to be stitched to his scalp, because he never takes it off, even on entering a church, where he goes from time to time not to take communion, but to seek the cool air and take a nap. The bowler is an integral part of Robinsón's physiognomy, and he will readily tell anyone willing to listen the story behind his passion for a hat more appropriate to the bourgeoisie than to the proletariat: in his youth he belonged to a naturist commune that chose the bowler hat as its emblem and standard, and since then he has been faithful to it in honor of that group of friends, with whom he passed some of the best moments of his life. Behind him, tail wagging, comes Kropotkin, his faithful wiener dog.

The two friends look at each other for a few moments, with their arms extended and holding each other's shoulders, as though evaluating the changes time has wrought over the years since they last saw each other.

"You haven't changed a bit," says Robinsón. "You still look like a twenty-year-old boy."

"Those gray hairs in your beard almost make you look intelligent," says Pablo.

And with smiles like two gondolas, they pounce on each other, half-hugging and half-sparring, while Kropotkin barks confusedly, perhaps from joy, perhaps envy.

"How did you manage to find me?" Pablo asks.

"Pure luck," Robinsón answers. "I thought I saw you last night at the Community House, talking with Teixidó at the end of the meeting, but when I went over to talk to you, you had already disappeared. I asked him about you and he told me your name was Pablo, that you work in a printing house on Rue Pixérécourt and that you'd left in a hurry because you had to get up early today. I was sure that it was you. Actually, I thought you were still in Spain. Otherwise I would have tried to find you sooner."

"And I thought you were still in Lyon. Now I understand why you didn't answer any of my letters—"

"No, that's because I moved to a new house, I had problems with the landlady. I only arrived in Paris about a month ago."

"And where are you living?"

"Well, you know how I love nature," says Robinsón with an enigmatic tone, "and since the Parc des Buttes-Chaumont is so lovely and welcoming, and we're still having such fine weather..."

"Fine weather, you say? But it hasn't stopped raining for weeks! Tonight you're coming home with me. I have a little loft on Rue Saint-Denis. Also, I go out of town during the week, so you can come and go as you like. But where's Sandrine? Didn't she come with you?"

Robinsón wrinkles his forehead and says:

"Apparently she took the free love thing quite seriously. And Angela? Have you found out anything about her?"

Now it is Pablo who twists his face:

"She's gone with the wind. Forever."

The two friends look at each other, and take some time to build up another smile.

"Come on, let's get something to drink and you can tell me what's brought you to Paris," Pablo finally says, "I'm up to my ears in work, this damned weekly is coming out tomorrow and I have to finish it today. But it's not every day you get to see your blood brother... Hold on a second, Robin."

Pablo goes down to the basement and finds Julianín snoring in peaceful slumber atop a few crates of books. He wakes him rudely and leaves him in charge of the print shop and Kropotkin, then heads out for a glass of wine with Robinsón at the Point du Jour, on the nearby Rue de Belleville. His friend Leandro works as a waiter there. Leandro is a tall, heavyset Argentinian from the city of General Rodríguez, always keen for a joke or a prank. Seeing them enter the bar, which is strangely empty at this hour, he exclaims:

"Check you out, buddy, you found Jesus Christ. I hope ya brought along a crowd of thirsty apostles."

"Stop messing around, Leandro. We'll have two glasses of wine. This is Robinsón, my childhood friend. Robin, this is Leandro, an old friend I met in Argentina when he was still a kid dreaming of becoming a soccer player."

"*Enchanté*," responds Robinsón, mimicking a perfect French accent, "but no wine for me, thanks. I'll be happy with a glass of water."

Robinsón is a teetotaler, in addition to being a vegetarian, environmentalist, and naturist. A rare breed, a man ahead of his time, a practitioner of a mystical, even pantheistic sort of anarchism, a special way of understanding the world and relating to his surroundings. He is one of those who believe, for example, that all of humanity's ills come from wiping our asses with toilet paper rather than lettuce leaves. He has come to Paris on an assignment from the Spanish Syndicate of Lyon, with the aim of helping to organize a revolutionary plot to overthrow the dictatorship of Primo de Rivera. But Pablo still knows nothing of all this.

"I see some things never change," Pablo says. "You drink his wine, Leandro. We have to celebrate this reunion."

"Nonsense. I'm not participating if he's gonna toast with water."

"*Merde alors*, so let's not toast then, if you don't want to, but drink the wine, for the love of God."

"You mean for the love of our friend Jesus here," says Leandro.

So it is that the strange trio of Pablo, Robinsón, and Leandro sip their respective glasses, while the abstemious anarchist starts to tell them what has brought him to Paris, after making sure the big lackadaisical Argentine can be trusted.

HOWEVER, IN ORDER TO UNDERSTAND THE story Robinsón is now recounting, we need to know a little back story. The movements against the dictatorship of Primo de Rivera started shortly after the military uprising, both in France, where many syndicalists, communists, anarchists, and republicans of all stripes have immigrated, and in Spain—mainly Barcelona, where Catalan separatists have managed to foment a significant clandestine movement. At the end of 1923, various meetings took place on the French side of the Pyrenees and, shortly thereafter in Paris, the *Consejo Nacional de Trabajo* (CNT) and other syndicalist groups founded the Committee of Anarchist Relations, in charge of promoting and preparing an insurrection against Primo de Rivera's Directory. At the start of May, the Committee appointed an executive commission comprising the so-called Group of Thirty, including former members of known anarchist groups such as El Crisol, Los Justicieros, and Los Solidarios, responsible for some of the most famous actions of Spanish anarchism in the last several years, including the assassination of the archbishop of Zaragoza in retaliation for the death of Salvador Seguí, known as "Sugar Boy," who was riddled with bullets in Barcelona in a plot organized by the Machiavellian Martínez Anido, a proponent of the scandalous *Ley de Fugas* authorizing authorities to use a prisoner's escape as a pretext for a summary execution. Other members of this Group of Thirty include the young Buenaventura Durruti, Francisco Ascaso, and Gregorio "Chino" Jover, whom the French police have taken to calling "the Three Musketeers," and other, less well-known but equally enthusiastic members such as Juan Riesgo, Pedro Massoni, Miguel García Vivancos, Ramón Recasens, Mariano Pérez Jordán (known as "Teixidó"), the brothers Pedro and Valeriano Orobón, Augustín Gíbanel, Enrique Gil Galar, Luís Naveira, and Bonifacio Manzanedo, some of whom will end up departing for the border and playing a decisive role in the attempted revolution.

Contrary to what is happening in Spain, since last summer much of Europe (with the exception of Mussolini's Italy) has been experiencing moments of leftist euphoria: the socialists are in charge in France, the communists in Russia; in Germany the Republican Democrats have put the young Adolf Hitler in jail, accusing him of high treason; and in England the Labour Party has taken power for the first time in its history. In Spain, on the other hand, the CNT is virtually banned, and its general secretary, Ángel Pestaña, has traveled to Paris to renew the dialogue with the Committee of Anarchist Relations, which has cooled in the last few months due to disagreements regarding the planning of the revolutionary attack, and to personally learn how the preparations are going. The committee has assured him that they will be able to mobilize up to twenty thousand men ready to enter Spain and participate in the overthrow of the regime, provided that they can count on the necessary organization and support on the Spanish side of the border. Pestaña does not seem to have been very convinced by these optimistic predictions, but he has nevertheless agreed that preparations should continue, with fundraising efforts and attempts to obtain weapons, as well as propaganda campaigns among the exiled population. He has even given his support to the International Group of Anarchist Editions, founded by Durruti and Ascaso with the idea of publishing the pamphlet *Spain: One Year of Dictatorship*, which claims that the country is prepared for regime change and that all that is needed is a trigger to set off the revolution. But the pamphlet still has not been printed, because that will require the involvement of a young typesetter named Pablo Martín Sánchez, the very man who is now listening attentively to what Robinsón is explaining at the Point du Jour:

"They sent me from the Spanish Syndicate of Lyon to serve as a liaison with the Committee. But the truth is that the comrades in Paris view us with suspicion."

"Why is that?" asks Pablo.

"Because of Pascual Amorós."

"Ah, that."

As Leandro's face indicates that he does not understand, they explain the matter to him. Pascual Amorós was a syndicalist from Barcelona who had to run away to France a few years ago, supposedly fleeing prosecution. He started living in Lyon with a few of his comrades in arms, and soon began collaborating with the Spanish Syndicate. But one day someone discovered that he was actually the right hand of Bernat Armengol, known as "the Red," an infiltrator from the police who had worked in Barcelona on orders from the impostor Baron of Koenig and Bravo Portillo, the ringleaders of a band of gunmen on the bosses' payroll. The slogan "*Viva la anarquía*" tattooed on his arm fooled no one: with his life threatened by his own comrades, he had no choice but to return to Spain, where a few months later he was condemned to death by garrote for robbing a bank in Valencia.

"And since some of his old friends are still members of the Syndicate of Lyon," Robinsón concludes, "Durruti and company don't trust us. All in all, it's understandable; things being the way they are, you can't take any risks."

"But, then, why'd the guys here agree to have you come?" the Argentine asks, somewhat lost.

"For money."

"For money?" Pablo and Leandro both wonder at once.

"Yes, for money. Even an anarchist revolution requires money, as much as it pains us. The Committee is not doing well in terms of financing. The French comrades are still recovering from the war and the Spanish expatriates have a hard enough time just trying to feed themselves, let alone contributing money to the cause. The Solidarios haven't got a cent left from the robbery of the Bank of Gijón, even though that brought in more than a half-million pesetas... between the rifles they bought in Éibar and the creation of the Group of Anarchist Editions, they've spent it all, so most of them have had to find work in Paris. The fact is that in Lyon the Spanish Syndicate is doing well at the moment, and at the start of the summer Ascaso and Durruti came to ask us for money for the publishing project. We told them we were sorry, but in Paris we had already made donations to the newspaper *Le Libertaire* and to the International Bookstore on Rue Petit. So they had no choice but to tell us the truth: they needed the money to finance a revolutionary movement to overthrow the dictatorship of Primo de Rivera. We reached an agreement: we gave them the money and in exchange they accepted our collaboration in the mission. This is why I came to Paris, to join the Group of Thirty."

The three men sit pensive for a few moments, until the silence is broken by two regulars who come in laughing loudly, say hello and sit down at a table at the back of the tavern. While Leandro goes to wait on them, Robinsón lowers his voice and confesses:

"I didn't just come to visit you, Pablito: I also came to ask you to work with us."

"…"

"We need help from people like you."

"…"

"Our future is at stake. And that of millions of Spanish people—"

"But it's been years since you lived in Spain, Robin."

"True, but I would like to be able to return someday without feeling ashamed to look people in the eye. Think about your mother, think about your sister: are you going to let them rot while you're here, safe and sound?"

Pablo looks his friend in the eye, while his mind fills with images of his mother, sister, and niece, the women he abandoned to their fate when he left in exile. He thinks that perhaps yes, perhaps he's right, perhaps the time has come to try to change things. But he immediately thinks no, what business does he have getting involved in some crazy plot? Primo de Rivera will soon fall under his own weight, and a failed coup would only serve to reinforce his power.

"In any case," Robinsón interrupts Pablo's thoughts, "I'm not asking you to sign up for the mission, only to help us by printing a few posters."

"Are you going to go?"

"Yes, it seems crazy, but it's as if I feel an internal voice telling me to go. If Spain rises up in arms against the bandits in charge, I'm not planning to stand around doing nothing. If they need me, I'll be there. The more of us there are, the better our chances of success."

"But is the operation ready?"

"No, goodness no, there's still a lot to do. For now, we're only getting ready for when the comrades in the interior give us the signal, it would be crazy to go in to liberate Spain if the people in the country aren't ready to go through with the revolution. I don't think the thing will be ready until the end of the year. But when the moment arrives, we'll need to have everything well organized. So, what do you say, can we count on you?"

"I don't know, I'd have to discuss it with old Faure, the owner of the print shop, to see what he thinks."

"Don't bother, we've already spoken with him."

"Really?"

"Yes, he came yesterday to the back room of the International Bookstore on Rue Petit, a windowless little hovel we use for meetings. We wanted him to print an eight-page pamphlet for us called *Spain: One Year of Dictatorship*, which we're planning to distribute for free among the Spanish expatriates here in Paris. A good print run, a few thousand copies. At first the old man didn't catch on, but we finally convinced him by telling him that we're also planning to publish a trilingual review and an anarchist encyclopedia—"

"So what do you need my help for?"

"For the revolutionary broadsides we want to print for the incursion. When we cross the border, we want to bring posters to distribute among workers and the civilian population, a direct call to revolution against the dictatorship. It's safer to print them here than there, and the comrades in the interior already have enough difficulty just trying to hold meetings without getting arrested. But old Faure told us no way, he didn't want to hear another word about it. That he has enough problems in France, he doesn't need to go looking for them in Spain, and that he didn't want to lend his press for crazy revolutionary projects. You know that since the Great War he's become a pacifist, especially since he got to know Malatesta and published his manifesto *Toward Peace*. I say it's nothing but the paranoia of an old, washed-up anarchist, because you tell me what has he got to lose publishing the broadsides if he's going to publish the pamphlet?"

Leandro has now returned to his position in the trench behind the bar, and as he casually prepares two absinthes, he asks:

"Did I miss anything important?"

"No, nothing," says Pablo, pensive, and when he finishes off his wine with a final gulp, he bids farewell: "I'm sorry, but I have to get back to work. The old Minerva has left me stranded and I don't want to abandon Julianín too long with the Albatross..."

The Minerva is an old pedal-operated press that, having worked for over thirty years, is ready to retire. The Albatross is not much younger, but it is still capable of printing eight hundred sheets an hour.

"See you later?" Robinsón asks.

"Yes, of course, come find me at the end of my shift so we can go home."

And, touching his brim with his index finger, Pablo takes leave of his two friends. In the street, night has already fallen, and emaciated specters are silhouetted in the light of the streetlamps. These are hard times in Paris, the euphoria of the Olympic Games having given way to a period of economic recession. The franc is in freefall, but the exiled Spaniards have other worries to fill their bellies. The wheel of the revolution has started to turn, and it seems intent on catching Pablo in its vortex.

II
(1896)

HE COULDN'T. FOR ALL THE MANY TRAIN voyages he would later make, Pablo could never forget that first trip between Baracaldo and Madrid. Neither the asphyxiating heat, nor the tobacco smoke that permeated the train cars, nor the terrible smell of feet that seemed to bother his father so much, was enough to undermine the fascination that this first journey produced in the boy. With his nose pressed against the windowpane he watched objects go by with dizzying speed: trees, houses, and cows; farms, hills, and telegraph poles; workers with faces furrowed by a thousand wrinkles and children running along with the train and waving at the passengers. And all of this enlivened by the uncontainable logorrhea of one of the fellow passengers in the compartment, a retired railroad crossing keeper who narrated the passing scene, telling the most outlandish stories, full of exaggerated facts and figures:

"The net weight of a train car," he was explaining to his patient companions in the compartment, with the excitement of someone recounting the life of a famous bandit, "is thirty-six tons, and that's when it's empty! It has a length of eighteen meters and a height of three and a half. The beams are mahogany, holm oak, and white oak, and it is covered with paneling made of teak, a wood that comes from Northern Europe and is immune to atmospheric changes—"

"And is it true that the last car is the safest?" Pablo interrupted him, producing a look of disbelief in Julián, taken unawares by his son's unexpected loquacity.

"Who told you that, my boy?"

"My papa."

"Well, your papa couldn't be more right. Do you think a gatekeeper like myself would travel in third class if it weren't because it's the last car?"

In Miranda de Ebro and in Ávila they changed locomotives, and Pablo was able to observe, eyes wide open, how the operators performed the process of decoupling and recoupling the cars. But what excited him most on this first trip was the loud voice of the stationmaster, who at the end of every stop would shout "All aboard!" at the top of his lungs, and the throng of passengers would push to enter the cars, hoping not to get left behind as the train departed with all their belongings inside.

While the journey was full of emotions and discoveries, the best part was waiting for them when the train reached its destination. Night was coming on when they pulled into Madrid's North Station, which at the moment was overrun by a multitude going from one end to the other like frenzied ants in a trampled anthill. Pablo had never seen such a large, diverse crowd. Men with frock coats and top hats mingled with withered old ladies begging for alms and boys shouting the morning newspaper headlines or selling travel blankets to the passengers going to the trains. The outside of the station was also seething, and above the froth of voices rose the shouts of the drivers of buggies, popularly referred to in Madrid at the time as *simones*, after their inventor. When Julián and Pablo exited the station dragging the suitcase, two of these drivers had come to fisticuffs competing for clients who could afford the luxury of hiring a cab. One was leaking blood from his nose and the other was trying to recompose the damaged burlap toupee intended to conceal his unconcealable baldness.

The Martíns ran away from the station as if fleeing the plague, got onto a streetcar, and crossed the city toward the neighborhood known as Injurias, by the river Manzanares, to stay at a humble inn that a friend in Baracaldo had recommended. They shared a bed with squeaking springs and a mildewed mattress, and fell deeply asleep beneath the watchful eye of a reproduction of the Holy Christ of Lepanto hanging somewhat askew over the head of the bed. The next morning, they got up early, at six tolls of the bell of a nearby church, and ate at the inn in silence with the other early risers, who were more concerned with keeping the cockroaches off the tables than with making conversation with the other diners. Not a bad breakfast for a fleabag hotel, thought Julián as he dipped the strange little donuts in his coffee, pastries the innkeeper had called *tontas* as she served them.

The competitive examination for the Primary Education Inspectors Corps was to be held at the address 80 Calle de San Bernardo, in the building of the Central High School, and that is where father and son headed: Julián, reviewing in his mind the list of the Gothic kings, in an attempt to calm his nerves; Pablo, mouth agape and feeling distressed in this city of more than half a million. Leaving the inn, they took Calle Toledo, went through the gate of the same name and arrived at the Collegiate Church of San Isidro, whose entrance was thronged with people, despite the parish priest's attempts to get them to form an organized line. Father and son kept a safe distance, curiously observing the scene.

"What's going on?" asked Pablo.

"I don't know, Son," responded Julián, also surprised by the religious fervor of the Madrileños.

"It's for the saint," said a voice behind them.

The Martíns spun around to find themselves face-to-face with a miniature donkey covered in roses, carnations, and geraniums. At its side, holding its lead, a flower seller smiled affably.

"They have Saint Isidore inside," he continued explaining, "and at seven o'clock the church will open so the faithful can come venerate him. Care for a carnation for your lapel, sir?"

"No, no thank you," Julián replied, snatching his son's hand forcefully and making off toward Plaza de la Constitución, which a few years later would become known as Plaza Mayor.

They skirted the square via the Cava de San Miguel and shortly arrived at the Plaza de Santo Domingo, where the Calle de San Bernardo has its origin, showing that it is possible to cross Madrid by jumping from saint to saint. It was half past seven in the morning, and there was a market.

"Listen closely, Pablo." said Julián, holding the child's shoulders. "This isn't Baracaldo. This is Madrid, *la Villa y Corte*. So be careful here. Don't talk to strangers, don't wander too far, and be careful for cars and horses. And, if anything happens to you, come find me at 80 Calle San Bernardo, which is the street that starts right here. I don't know how long I will take, but wait for me in the square. If I take too long and you start to get hungry, buy some fruit at the market. Here," he said, giving the boy a one-*real* coin, "Don't lose it. And wish me luck, son."

"Good luck, Papa," whispered Pablo obediently, as his father adjusted his felt hat and set off for the Central High School.

The market stands were overflowing at this early morning hour, and if Pablo had somehow recovered his sense of smell for a moment, he would have felt dizzy from the mixture of odors coming from the square. He would have especially noticed the smell of roses, jasmine, and gardenias, as this market had been a flower market since the War of Independence. However, since the nearby San Miguel market was cramped, the vendors who could not find a place there had set up their stalls here, so he would also have noticed the sweet aroma of strawberries, the stench of sardines, or the sour smell of recently tanned leather. At first, Pablo remained seated at the edge of the square, watching the laziest of the vendors finish setting up their merchandise. Then he got up and walked distractedly amongst the people, following his curiosity wherever it led him. At the meat stand, the butcher was praising the color of his steaks. At the vegetable stand, the grocer was extolling the flavor of his tomatoes. At the chicken stand, the poultry dealer was celebrating the freshness of her eggs. And at the clothing stand, the vendor was saying to a customer:

"No, madam. It's not the blanket that warms you, but you who warm the blanket! So what matters isn't the thickness of the wool, but the tightness of the knit, so the heat can't escape … Anyway, madam, summer is just around the corner, by God!"

Pablo continued strolling around the square, and what he saw on the other side left him even more surprised. In a small alleyway, all the vendors who had not managed to find a place in the square were crammed together in disarray. On one side, there were smugglers selling black market goods, and on the other, there were gypsies offering rosemary to ward off the evil eye, doing tarot readings, and predicting the future by reading the entrails of animals. There were also wandering vendors selling pickled beans and candies to fill children's mouths with cavities. In addition, there were charlatans on improvised stages made of overturned fruit boxes, selling more outlandish products: miracle hair-growth tonics, cure-all potions, whitening creams, and talismans to fight trichomoniasis. Of all of them, the most noticeable was an impeccably dressed man in a top hat and spats. Perhaps it was his high, nasal voice, or his foreign accent, or the fact that he stood a bit apart from the others and had managed to gather a small group of onlookers, but Pablo felt drawn to him and walked over.

"The Lumière Cinematograph! The Lumière Cinematograph!" he shouted in an unmistakable French accent. "For the first time in Spain, the magnificent, the incredible, the extraordinary invention of the Lumière brothers: moving pictures, life itself! Can you afford to miss it, ladies and gentlemen?"

Intrigued by his words, Pablo mixed into the crowd of idlers listening to the man.

"Forget once and for all about dioramas, cycloramas, cosmoramas, kinetoscopes, and magic lanterns," the man shouted at the top of his lungs, "and don't be fooled by the animatograph of the Circo Parish—this invention of the Lumière brothers is completely revolutionary!"

A dog approached to sniff his spats and received a kick in the nose.

"Buy your tickets now, ladies and gentlemen, because tomorrow it will be in all the papers, and then it might be too late! Tonight we will present the first projection at the Hotel Rusia for the press, the authorities, and special guests. But starting tomorrow, from ten to noon, from three to seven, and again at eleven o'clock in the evening, just a few blocks from here, at 34 Carrera de San Jerónimo, you can see something never seen, never thought of, never imagined before. And all that for just one peseta!"

Hearing the price, the crowd dispersed. All except for one: a six-year-old boy named Pablo.

"Half-price for children…" the man muttered, dejected to see his clientele disappear.

Pablo instinctively stuck his hand in his pants pocket and felt the cold metal of a coin. The man in the top hat got down from his box and sat on it, as the ruckus of the square grew louder. If one peseta is four *reales*, then half a peseta is two *reales*, Pablo said to himself, proving that having a teacher for a father was good for something. So he still needed one more *real* to buy a ticket. With the same dejection as the Lumière barker, he turned around with his tail between his legs.

"Hey kid, where you going?" he heard someone behind him say. When he turned around, he saw that it was the man with the top hat. "Are you mute, or what?"

Pablo shook his head no.

"Don't tell me you wouldn't like to see a projection of the Lumière Cinematograph," he said with forced sweetness.

Pablo nodded his head.

"So tell your papa to give you half a peseta!" shouted the Frenchman. Clearing his throat, he climbed back up onto the box and laid into his spiel with renewed gusto: "The Lumière Cinematograph! The Lumière Cinematograph! For the first time in Spain, the magnificent, the incredible, the extraordinary invention of the Lumière brothers…"

Cheerful music started up on Calle de Leganitos, and Pablo began walking toward it, with the word "cinematograph" echoing in his ears. After walking a hundred yards, he discovered the origin of this melody:

a trio of Gitano musicians were making a goat dance on a wooden chair. The one in the middle, who was tall and thin, was playing the accordion and smiling, unashamedly displaying the only tooth that populated his mouth; the other two, much shorter but equally scrawny, were playing the flute and the violin. The people passed by without paying much attention to them, although every now and again the sound was heard of a penny falling in their coin box. Pablo sat down on a bench in front of them and fell asleep to the sound of the music. When he woke up, the sun was high in the sky and the gypsy trio had been replaced by an old hobo drinking red wine. Pablo wanted to go back to the market square, but he went the opposite direction and walked along the Calle de Leganitos until reaching a large esplanade, where an enormous building under construction seemed to be trying to scrape the sky. Completely disoriented, he tried to walk back, but wound up getting lost in the intricate maze of the streets of Madrid. Realizing that he was lost, he started running from one place to another, until he collapsed in a doorway and began silently crying, with his head between his knees. Five minutes had not passed when he heard a donkey braying. He lifted his eyes and saw the same flower seller from that morning walking in the middle of the street. The man was trying to drag the donkey along, but the animal, now relieved of his load of roses, carnations, and geraniums, thought it was time for a well-deserved nap.

"Come on, you filthy beast!" the man shouted, pulling on the rein. "You can rest when we get to the square!"

Pablo rose to his feet and, guided by a premonition, took the same path as the stubborn ass and his desperate master. After five minutes he was at the Plaza de Santo Domingo. The vendors were packing up their remaining merchandise or selling at a discount the foods that would not keep until the next day, as flies, cats, and dogs prepared to have a field day on the trash piles. The man with the donkey approached the flower stand and negotiated the price of the last stocks. Pablo sat down at the same place where he had left his father in the morning and prepared to wait for him. After a little while, his father appeared, coming up Calle de San Bernardo, waving his hat and smiling broadly.

"Passed the first test!" Julián exclaimed, kissing his boy's forehead. "Did you spend the coin I gave you?"

Pablo nodded his head yes, lying to his father for the first time in his life.

"Fine, it doesn't matter, let's go eat. I'm as hungry as a wolf!"

THE NEXT DAY, THE EVE OF Saint Isidore, the Martíns repeated the same routine. The previous evening, they had strolled around in the vicinity of the Plaza de la Constitución and had returned to the inn happily exhausted. They dined on a stomach-warming soup and lay down on the creaking bed, where the Christ of Lepanto again bid them goodnight. They awoke to the same bells again at six o'clock, enjoyed the same breakfast of *tontas* and *café con leche*, and again walked up Calle de Toledo until they came across the same parishioners pushing and shoving for a chance to venerate Saint Isidore. Finally, at Plaza de Santo Domingo, Julián gave his son the same lecture as the day before, along with another *real* in case he got hungry. He adjusted his felt hat and left Pablo at the same place as the day before, walking up Calle de San Bernardo ready to claim his post as provincial inspector.

This time, however, there was no market, and not a soul was in the square at this early hour. Even the smugglers had not shown up yet, nor had the little gypsy ladies with their sprigs of rosemary, nor the hair tonic hawkers. But the one Pablo missed the most was the Frenchman with the top hat who had announced the Lumière Cinematograph. The previous afternoon, while his father was showing him the thousand wonders of the capital, Pablo had not stopped thinking about the unthinkable, imagining the unimaginable, seeing in his mind the never-before-seen: moving photographs. A few months before, he had attended a magic lantern show in a tent in Bilbao, and it had burned in his memory its enormous projected images, with their commentary by the master of ceremonies, accompanied by festive music that appeared to put them in motion. But the Lumière Cinematograph promised to be something really extraordinary! The very word captivated him, and as his eye roamed the Plaza de Santo Domingo in search of the dream peddler, his lips could not stop pronouncing that strange and wonderful word: "ci-ne-ma-to-graph."

An hour later, Pablo had lost hope of finding the man in the top hat. The two *reales* were burning a hole in his pocket, and for the life of him he could not remember the name of the street where the projections were being held. Then he saw a newsboy crossing the square, shouting:

"*La Época*! Buy *La Época* and read the news of the day for only fifteen cents!"

And like a distant echo, Pablo remembered these words: "Buy your tickets now, ladies and gentlemen, because tomorrow it will be in all the papers, and then it might be too late ..." So Pablo leapt to his feet and marched with determination toward the newsboy, who was making his way out of the square. He could not have been over twelve years old, but he was already tall and sturdy, with brownish skin suggesting Roma roots. When he caught up to him, Pablo sidled up and walked a few paces alongside him.

"Hey, what's your deal, kid?" the boy asked when he noticed Pablo's presence. "Go on, take off. This here's grown-up stuff."

"Does it say anything about the cinematograph?" Pablo asked in response.

"What?" replied the newsboy, surprised by the question.

"I said, does it say anything about the cinematograph?"

"Why, of course it does! *La Época* explains it all!"

Resting his sack of newspapers on the ground, the boy took out a copy. The front page had an article by the writer Miguel de Unamuno, with the curious title in English, "The Last Hero," but since neither boy yet knew who Unamuno was, they continued scanning the columns. Finally, on the third page, under the section "Public Entertainments," they found the information that Pablo was looking for.

"Look, here it is, listen up," said the paperboy with unconcealed pride. He began reading the announcement: "'Starting last night, Madrid is being treated to a spectacle that is both novel and attractive. The *cinematograph*, otherwise known as the moving picture, is truly noteworthy, and represents one of the most marvelous scientific advances of this century. The exhibition of images and panoramic views is being held in a spacious room on Carrera de San Jerónimo, number 34, which last night was crowded with the many distinguished guests invited to the inauguration...'"

Pablo etched this information into his memory as he listened agog to the newsboy, who continued reading:

"'The projection of animated photography onto a white screen could not be done with greater perfection, reproducing all of the movements of persons and objects in the scene. The program, which was repeated several times last night, includes ten parts, of which it is especially worth mentioning the arrival of a train at the station, a stroll along the seaside, the Avenue of Champs-Élysées, the horse races of Lyon, and the demolition of a wall. The public will be able to admire this spectacle starting today, from 10 to 12 in the morning, from 3 to 7 in the afternoon and from 9 to 11 in the evening.' See, what'd I tell ya? *La Época* tells it all!"

Pablo put his hand in his pocket and heard the siren song of his two coins clinking together.

"And where is that street, the Carrera de San Jerónimo?" he dared to ask.

"Not far from here, near the head office of *La Época*. I'm going that way, you want me to show you?"

Pablo affirmed shyly as he memorized the name of the square where he had left his father.

"You're not thinking of going to see the cinematograph, are you?" the newsboy asked as he gathered up his papers.

To which Pablo merely nodded his head.

One result of the propaganda produced on French soil was that it won over a vast number of the wretches residing there, most of them anarchists, communists, syndicalists, and others, who, incited by the idea of returning to their various points of origin or dragged along by the dictates of their self-regard, which for some was more ideologically driven than for others, but all of them sneering at their duty toward their mother Spain and their fellow citizens, volunteered, having acquired quantities of cash, weapons, munitions, and methods of transportation, to come to Spain in order to execute the plan laid out by their inciters.

Diario de Navarra, 13 January 1927

THE WHIRLWIND OF REVOLUTION APPEARS TO be intent on sweeping Pablo up, but he will be the last to realize it. After the conversation at the Point du Jour with his two friends, he returns to the printing house, where Julianín has made fewer errors than usual. Pablo works until well into the night, with the help of Robinsón, who substitutes for Julianín after the young apprentice's shift has ended, putting on coveralls and rolling up his sleeves like a real professional. They forgo sleep to make sure that the weekly *Ex-Ilio* can be distributed starting first thing in the morning.

When the work is finally done, they make the difficult but exhilarating journey home mounted together on Pablo's bicycle. It takes constant effort to keep their balance as they careen down the steep slope of the Rue de Belleville, enjoying the air whipping their faces and ringing the bell like hooligans, as if transported back to their childhood on the Castilian Plateau. Frenzied and trailing his tongue like a streamer, Kropotkin chases

them down the hill, but cannot catch up until Faubourg du Temple, where
the grade is less steep. Arriving at Place de la République, the two friends
dismount the bicycle and walk the rest of the way to Pablo's cramped
hovel. There, the makeshift host takes a mat from beneath his rickety bed
and unrolls it, then puts an old blanket on top.

"I don't know if I can handle such luxury," says the visitor.

"Sorry I can't offer you the comforts of your palace on Buttes-
Chaumont," his host responds, and they both have a good laugh. Humor
is the balm of poverty.

They spend the night chatting and remembering stories from the old
days. From time to time they hear Kropotkin whining in his dreams outside the door, where they have left him to sleep on the *Bienvenue* mat.
When they finally take note of the time, dawn is coming on. Only then do
they fall asleep. And, since Pablo does not use an alarm clock, it's a miracle
when he opens his eyes two hours later, just in time to go to the station to
catch the train, leaving Robinsón to enjoy his bed for a few days.

Pablo works from Monday to Thursday in Marly-les-Valenciennes, a
tiny village north of Paris, near the Belgian border, where he takes care
of the country house of the Beaumont family, to make sure it is in order
when they come for the weekends. He watches the house, cares for the
garden and the pond, keeps the buildings clean, makes occasional repairs,
and feeds the two boxer dogs that Madame Beaumont spoils in a manner unconscionable to Pablo's working-class mind, a situation that once
prompted him, in a sudden act of class justice, to let the boxers starve for a
day, giving their food to the local strays. To tell the truth, the job is a sine-
cure: scant responsibilities, good pay, and board included, in a little house
next to the pond. For this reason, Pablo goes up every week, and plans to
keep going up until he finds something better to complement the miserable salary he receives from old Faure.

He takes the train from the Gare du Nord, passes through Amiens, and
arrives in Lille, where the ticket collector wakes him from a deep sleep;

from there he still needs to take another train to Valenciennes and then walk for twenty minutes to the Beaumont estate. The days in the country pass without any major disruptions, and Pablo takes advantage of the free time to read and go for walks, or to go down to the village for a glass or two of wine. Sometimes he surprises himself by smiling for no reason, which he attributes to the happy arrival of Robinsón in Paris; however, at other times he finds himself furrowing his brow, and this too he ends up blaming on his childhood friend, or, more precisely, on the conversation he had with him at the Point du Jour on Sunday afternoon. The drums of action have started pounding again, and he does not know whether to join the orchestra or run away before it's too late.

When he arrives back in Paris on Friday at noon, he goes directly to the print shop. There he finds Monsieur Faure, redder and angrier than ever, who greets Pablo with loud shouting as usual:

"Goddammit! I've been waiting for you all morning! Where the hell have you been?"

"But Monsieur Faure, I'm scheduled to start at two in the afternoon, and it's not even one yet ..."

The Savage's eyes widen until they are nearly bursting from their sockets, and he starts to puff up like a balloon, going from pink to red and then purple in a matter of seconds. Finally, he lets out a grunt and starts deflating, little by little.

"It's fine," he says, smoothing down his mustache tips, which are already greasy from so much handling, "let's go to the Point du Jour, I'll buy you a drink and we can talk."

There, he tells him about the print shop's new orders: the pamphlet against the Spanish dictatorship, the trilingual review, and the anarchist encyclopedia. Pablo pretends not to know anything about the matter and listens attentively, interjecting a question or suggestion every now and again.

"Listen well, Martín. The pamphlet needs to be published immediately, and I don't want to hear any excuses about the Minerva, because it's been fixed. So you better plan to have it ready for Monday—it's only eight pages. If not then, have it done by the time I arrive next Friday."

The review and the encyclopedia are not as urgent, he explains; they are medium- and long-term projects, so they will not mean too much extra work for Pablo. Just the same, the old anarchist asks him if he would be available to work on Friday mornings as well.

"But, Monsieur Faure, the print shop is packed to the gills on Friday mornings."

"Fine, you're right. What about Mondays?"

"I don't know, I'd have to check. Look, maybe it's better if we leave things as they are for the time being, and we'll see later. Julián is making great progress, maybe between the two of us we can take care of all of it. Of course, the ideal would be to get new machines; if we could invest in a Roto-Calco, which can print almost two thousand sheets an hour—"

"Over my dead body!" shouts Sébastien Faure, his anger returning. "Have you still not understood that this is a printing house, not a sausage factory like you have in your country? Watch your step, Martín. Don't piss me off."

And he leaves the bar without paying for the drinks.

WHEN THE PRINT SHOP CLOSES THAT night, Robinsón appears, walking Pablo's trusty, rusty Clément Luxe, with a smile from ear to ear and his bowler jauntier than usual. That's the great thing about Robinsón: he never loses his smile for any reason. It is obvious that, whatever happens, he is always in communion with nature.

"While you were gone I took the liberty of using your velocipede," says the vegetarian by way of greeting, chewing the last word with a certain smugness.

"Good for you," Pablo replies, "but if you don't mind, I'd like to walk the rest of the way home."

"But of course."

Kropotkin wags his tail in gratitude, clearly in harmony with his master's spirit. During the walk, as Robinsón pushes the bicycle, he tells his childhood friend what he has been doing these last few days in Paris.

"I have been chosen to recruit people who are ready to go through with the revolution. Workers, syndicalists, anarchists, communists if necessary; any Spanish expatriate with enough courage to drop everything and take up arms."

"Sounds like the Committee has finally given in to your messianic gifts," Pablo says sarcastically. "And have you managed to win anyone over?"

"A few, yes."

"And what do you say to them?"

"'Brothers,'" Robinsón begins reciting, projecting his voice theatrically, "'the time has come to overthrow the dictatorship. In Spain, the unions and workers' associations have been shut down, and the jails are filled with prisoners from among our ranks. We cannot close our eyes. Revolution is the only choice. We are preparing an insurrection at the border that will inspire the rest of the country to rise up. When we finally enter Spain, the people will unite with us and an extreme left government will take power. Anyone who enlists will receive some money and a train ticket; you will receive your arms at the border, so they won't get seized by the French police during the trip—'"

"I can't believe you managed to recruit anybody with such a sloppy pitch," Pablo interrupts.

And although Robinsón says nothing in return, the truth is that in his role as Pied Piper he has already recruited a few dozen collaborators, many of them from the Renault auto factory where Durruti works, where his evangelism was quite effective among those workers most dissatisfied with their situation in France. In the union locals as well he has rounded up some malcontents ready to enlist in the mission, as well as at the Community House and the labor exchange. Even in the Spanish

Theatrical Lyric Group he managed to seduce a few volunteers at the end of the show, with the priceless help of Felipe Sandoval, a member of the Committee and a regular at the theater who got up on stage to rally the attendees and to reassure them that the revolution would bring amnesty to prisoners and exiles, to deserters and all those who had to leave Spain to save their necks. His passionate speech ended with the crowd chanting "*¡Viva la revolución!*" Furthermore, Robinsón plans next week to tour the neighborhoods with the highest concentration of Spanish exiles, such as Saint-Denis or Ménilmontant, and the bars and cafés most frequented by anarchists and syndicalists, such as the Café Floréal on Avenue Parmentier, and those on Avenue Gambetta and Rue de Bretagne.

"Of course," says Robinsón hesitantly, "at the Point Du Jour there were a few interested people, and for a moment I had the impression that your Argentine buddy was going to tell me that he wanted to get on board."

Pablo says nothing, but something stirs in his guts.

"And since I eat every day at the vegetarian restaurant on Rue Mathis, I have also been able to light a fire in two or three of the Spanish regulars there. There's a Galician who is rather convinced that he wants to enlist, a guy with an intellectual look, who gives talks in Esperanto on naturism and free love. I suppose that's why he's called 'El Maestro.' You should come eat with me one of these days, I'll introduce you to him."

But the recruiting work they have assigned Robinsón is only one part of the array of activities going into the revolutionary plan. As he explains to Pablo while they go down Rue Faubourg du Temple, the group works in a collective manner, although in practice the main ideologues of the operation are Buenaventura Durruti and Francisco Ascaso. The two men complement each other perfectly: Durruti is a man of action, the charismatic leader who knows how to inspire the masses with his drive and his words; Ascaso provides reflection and calculation, cold logic and strategy. Both have the same idea of what revolution and anarchist struggle should be; an idea that is of course rather far from Robinsón's, who, whenever someone asks him what anarchism is, responds: "Anarchism? It's the doctrine of universal love," and leaves it at that.

Apart from Robinsón as lead recruiter, Durruti and Ascaso have appointed various trusted individuals to more specific tasks. Pedro Massoni has been chosen as manager of finances; he is a man with good contacts, accustomed to working with numbers and money since Bravo Portillo's henchmen left him one-eyed and limping in Barcelona in 1919. His first initiative was to organize an internal pool to buy weapons: thirty francs per head, which could be recuperated by selling a few "Pro-Liberation of Spain" stamps to sympathizers.

Miguel García Vivancos, one of the members of Los Solidarios who participated in the attack on the Bank of Gijón, is the man responsible for obtaining weapons, for which he has three open fronts: first, the Russian Bolsheviks living in France, always ready to provide top quality materiel for their communist comrades, but more hesitant to negotiate with anarchists; secondly, the arms traffickers of the Moroccan War, although they already have a reliable market and are reluctant to make deals with Spanish exiles hoping to overthrow the regime that is giving them fat benefits; and finally, and this appears to be the most economical and feasible way, are the small groups of French smugglers who root around in the old battlefields of the Great War looking for abandoned arsenals and selling any weapons they find in working condition.

Ramón Recasens (also known as Bonaparte, since he has a Napoleonic streak, with his short stature and his knack for military strategy) and Luís Naveira (a smart type who was a nurse or doctor at Santiago de Compostela and who is known as "El Portugués," even though he is in fact Galician) are those responsible for counterfeiting the documents and passports for the members of the Group of Thirty, since many of them have police records and could endanger the expedition if they were to travel under their real names.

Gregorio Jover, nicknamed "El Chino," another former member of Los Solidarios who escaped a few months ago from a commissariat in Barcelona by jumping out a window, has been designated as Committee representative and is taking care of communications with the various groups involved in the movement, both those from the south of France, who have the mission of drafting new participants who will unite with the groups coming from Paris, and those inside Spain, contact with whom is more difficult and dangerous.

Finally, Mariano Pérez Jordán, alias "Teixidó," the man with the raspy voice and an affinity for snuff, has been chosen as the manager of propaganda, which is why he approached Pablo the other night after Blasco Ibáñez's meeting, as publishing the broadsides is one of his main missions. No one in particular is responsible for the rest of the activities; those are being doled out as the project proceeds.

"And what's the plan for the expedition?" Pablo asks as they cross Place de la République.

"I'll tell you later," Robinsón whispers as he notices a squad of policemen emerging from a side street.

But we can skip ahead a few minutes as the two friends walk in silence through the intricate streets of the third arrondissement. The idea is that two large groups will leave from Paris for the border, one heading to the west end of the Pyrenees and the other to the east end. The first will amass in Saint-Jean-de-Luz until the order comes to liberate Spain, attacking the border posts and taking Irún, finally to reach San Sebastián, where some sectors of the army appear ready to rise up; the second will set up in Perpignan, to cross the border at Portbou, head toward Figueres to liberate the comrades being held in prison and then to advance on Barcelona, where the definitive uprising should take place with the support of social movements and sympathetic members of the military from the Atarazanas barracks. In order for the plan to work, both expeditions need to be perfectly coordinated, both between each other and with the revolutionary movements on the interior, whose mission is to attack the barracks and set up barricades, putting the squeeze on the security forces and inciting the rest of the civil population to rebel against the dictatorship, with the consent of the more progressive elements of the armed forces and liberal-leaning politicians. According to some rumors, it is also possible that, to the west and south of the Iberian Peninsula, other revolutionary groups will come in, made up of Spanish exiles in Portugal, Algeria, and Latin America, as well as some rebel factions from among the ranks of military stationed in Morocco, tired of a war that they consider absurd and unnecessary. Of course, Durruti and Ascaso are aware that the success of the operation depends on the revolution taking hold simultaneously throughout the whole country, as if it were a kettle placed on a flame, in which all the drops of water must start boiling at the same time.

This is more or less what Robinsón tells Pablo when they arrive at Rue Saint-Denis and sit in the frame of the carriage door to share a cigarette, before ascending to Pablo's loft.

"So, Pablito, when are you going to decide?" he asks after an awkward silence.

"When am I going to decide what?"

"You know, to work with us."

"I don't know. If old Faure says no, we can't do much. You fellows are crazy if you think I'm going to be able to convince him."

"We don't want you to convince him. Just print the broadsides without telling him."

"That's impossible."

"Why?"

"Because the old man isn't stupid. How many copies are we talking about? A few hundred, a few thousand?"

"More like a few thousand."

"Think about it. I can't make thousands of sheets of paper disappear

63

without him noticing. Also, all the sheets bear the press's letterhead. He'd end up hearing about it, even if they were only distributed in Spain."

"What if we bring the paper ourselves?"

Pablo takes the last drag from his cigarette and flicks it toward the far gutter with his thumb and middle finger. Kropotkin runs to look for it, thinking it is a game.

"No. I don't want you finding a way to convince me."

And the two friends go upstairs to bed, each wrapped up in his own thoughts.

ON SATURDAY AND SUNDAY ALIKE, PABLO gets up at dawn and rides his bicycle to the printing house. He spends the whole day doing piecework, since in addition to correcting, laying out, and printing the material left for him over the week by the various writers for *Ex-Ilio*, he has to do his own work with the eight pages published by the International Group of Anarchist Editions, *Spain: One Year of Dictatorship*, written by Durruti and the elder of the Orobón brothers, Valeriano, who, despite his youth, is already making a name for himself as a writer and translator (his adaptation of the Polish "Song of Warsaw," *A Las Barricadas*, will be a rallying cry in the Spanish Civil War). There is so much work that Pablo has had to invent a clever trick to incentivize the lazy Julianín: the boy will be paid five cents for each error he finds in the galleys; however, for each one he misses, he will lose ten. The bonus tends to be a pittance or even negative, but at least Pablo manages to keep him motivated and working.

After the hard day, the typesetter returns to his loft and smokes a cigarette with Robinsón before going to bed. For his part, the vegetarian takes advantage of Pablo's intense hours to get a bit of extra sleep on the mattress when his friend leaves for work, at which point he opens the door and lets in Kropotkin, who slides between the sheets like a little lord, as if to confirm the words of the Englishman who gave the dog to Robinsón:

"Take care of him, boy, this *perro* is a direct *descendiente* of Queen Victoria's last teckel." However, this noble lineage does nothing to prevent the dog from leaving the sheets littered with hair, which Pablo of course notices, but says nothing. Robinsón also takes advantage of the weekend to meet with the Committee at the International Bookstore and inform them of his progress in recruiting. It is decided that once the pamphlet is ready, Robinsón will take care of distribution in Paris, using his recruiting work as an opportunity to distribute pamphlets and using the pamphlets as a tool to draw in more recruits.

On Monday morning, October 13, *Spain: One Year of Dictatorship* starts circulating from hand to hand through the City of Light, while Pablo sleeps in the train on his way to Marly, after an exhausting weekend that finally ended on Sunday at the cusp of midnight.

III

(1896–1899)

"THE LUMIÈRE CINEMATOGRAPH." AND UNDERNEATH, IN smaller letters, the price of entry: "One peseta." Pablo and the newsboy had arrived at 34 Carrera de San Jerónimo with their hearts racing, after passing the offices of *La Época* on Calle Libertad, and now they found themselves standing in line to see the never-before-seen, the unthinkable, the unimaginable: moving pictures. The first session was going to take place at ten o'clock and they did not want to miss it for anything in the world, even if they had to spend everything they had in their pockets. When their turn came, the older boy asked:

"Children pay half price, right?"

The ticket man shot them a grumpy look through his monocle. "If you're less than ten years old, yeah," he said curtly, stroking the thick beard sprouting from his cheekbones.

"Ten years between the two of us, or ten years each?" the boy asked.

The man was so surprised by the question that he said, "Go on, give me a peseta and get inside before I change my mind."

Pablo placed his two *reales* on the counter while the newsboy rummaged in his pockets producing small coins until coming up with half a peseta. The clerk gave them two tickets and muttered a few incomprehensible words, while the sky suddenly went overcast, envious of the two boys' happiness.

Inside the building, a few men and women were discussing the virtues of the new gadget. The optimists claimed that the cinematograph would improve people's lives and contribute to the development of human thought. The pessimists seemed to be convinced that it would never be anything more than a sideshow gag, like so many others that had appeared and disappeared with more pain than glory. The doomsayers predicted that it would shrink children's brains and end up another petty entertainment like the theater and the opera. But there they all were, expectant, impatient to attend the event of the year. Soon, a side door opened and a sharply dressed little man entered; he walked beneath the great white cloth dominating the end of the room and sat down in front of a splendid German Spaethe piano. Only then, with rigorous punctuality, did the room lights go down, and everyone ran to get a seat. In the darkness, the thick cloud of cigarette smoke appeared to condense and the spectators all held their breath when a humming sound started up behind them. Almost immediately, a spotlight illuminated the white cloth and before the spectators' eyes appeared the image of a Parisian street, with its cars, its houses and its inhabitants frozen, immobile. A murmur of disappointment spread through the room, but then, suddenly, the crowd all hushed at once, a shiver running down their many spines as the image began to move, like a black-and-white version of real life. The carriages traveled from one end of the screen to the other; people got into and out of the cars and disappeared beyond the white cloth; some children were playing with a dog, which barked silently and leapt wildly in the air; a few cyclists passed in front of the camera, smiled, and waved at the astonished spectators in Madrid, who instinctively raised their hands to return the wave. All of this enlivened by the joyful music of the sharply dressed little man.

"Oooohh!" said a few voices when the reel was finished, after running barely a minute.

But there was not much time to discuss the clip, because immediately, another gray image took over the screen and started moving. This time it was a train, approaching the spectators at high speed.

"Aaaaahh!" shouted some, ducking their heads or holding tightly to their chairs.

Fortunately, the train passed by, disappearing to the left side of the screen, and those who had been most startled breathed a sigh of relief. Finally, the train stopped, and several people got into and out of the cars. After a few seconds of darkness, an image appeared of a gardener watering some flowers, followed by a street urchin who entered the scene silently and stepped on the hose without realizing it, cutting off the flow of water. The gardener, surprised, looked into the end of the hose and at that very moment the child lifted his foot and the man received a gush of water full in the face.

"Ha! Ha! Ha!" some spectators laughed, including Pablo and the young newsboy.

After the gardener, there appeared three men playing cards around a table. Then, various people walking by the sea. Later, there were lithe horses galloping in an equestrian show, followed by workers coming out of a factory. Finally, the spectators of Madrid were treated to an idyllic family breakfast: a father and a mother feeding an adorable infant, who smiled like an angel, cheeks bulging with porridge.

The lights suddenly came on, as the final notes from the Spaethe piano faded out. But the moving images lingered on in the retinas of the spectators; for some, like Pablo, this would end up being their fondest childhood memory.

"Wow!" exclaimed the newsboy as they left the room.

Pablo responded with the most eloquent silence. The screening had lasted barely five minutes, but his eyes were now shining in a new way. Outside, the clouds had lost their composure and it was raining violently.

"How do I get back to Plaza de Santo Domingo?" Pablo asked when he regained the ability to speak.

"This way. I'll show you," the other boy replied.

And they took off running in the rain, their heads filled with moving images. By the time they reached the square, it had stopped raining and the sun was shyly peeking through the clouds.

"What's your name?" asked Pablo.

"Holgado. Vicente Holgado," the newsboy replied. "What's yours?"

"Martín. Pablo Martín."

And they shook hands like men, without suspecting that they would meet again years later.

When Julián returned to the square, he found his son huddled in a corner, shivering badly but with a gleam in his eyes that his father had never seen. He placed his hand on the boy's forehead and felt that he was burning up. They took a mule-drawn taxi back to the inn. Julián gave Pablo some quinine tonic to drink and put him to bed. The fever subsided overnight.

The next day, the feast day of Saint Isidore, they returned to the teeming North Station and boarded the train for Bilbao: the adventure in the capital had come to an end. The Martín Sánchez family spent the next few days waiting impatiently for the results of the competitive examinations. Meanwhile, in Madrid, the Lumière Cinematograph made a huge splash—such an impression that the royal family requested a private viewing, attended by the boy king Alfonso XIII and his sisters, the teenage *infantas* María Teresa and María de las Mercedes, as well as their mother the Queen Regent María Cristina of Austria. Finally, in early June of 1896, the much-anticipated letter arrived in Baracaldo: Julián Martín Rodríguez had obtained the position of Inspector of Elementary Education in the province of Salamanca. Although it was only a third-rank position, it paid three thousand pesetas a year.

"We can't turn it down," said María.

"We can't turn it down," Julián repeated.

"Also, it might help Pablo's condition," María added.

"Yes, it might help Pablo's condition." Julián echoed her again.

And so it was that the Martín Sánchez family agreed to the following: the two males would move to Salamanca to start the new path while the mother and daughter would remain for the time being in Baracaldo, since the life of a provincial inspector involved constant travel, from town to town, hotel to hotel. Later on, in any case, if Julián managed to save up enough money, all four would be able to set up home in the city of Salamanca, although he would have to continue migrating all over the province. The summer passed, September arrived, and Pablo and Julián packed their bags, preparing for the hard winter of the Castilian Plateau. At the train station, as though repeating the same scene from three months before, Julia and María waved their handkerchiefs while Pablo pressed his nose to the window and silently murmured, "Pretty, pretty, pretty." This time, however, it would be a longer wait before he would see his sister again.

The first thing that the Martíns did when they arrived in Salamanca, after taking a room in a humble little hostel near the new railway station, was to visit the former inspector, Don Cesáreo Figueroa. This man, a widower, was living in retirement in Villares de la Reina, a tiny village abutting the capital. He welcomed them inside, wearing sandals and constantly spitting gobs of mucus due to the chronic bronchitis that had plagued him for years.

"Those damned Filipinos are getting out of line," he said by way of greeting, brandishing a copy of *El Adelanto*. "And it's all because of the damned Cubans, setting a bad example! But please, please come in."

Don Cesáreo Figueroa led them into the sitting room and offered them a glass of red wine, which Julián politely declined.

"The first thing you need to do," the old man said, speaking to Julián while Pablo busied his mind staring at the spots on a cowhide that served as a rug, "is buy yourself a donkey or a mule to get from town to town, because the longest road between two points is usually the right one."

Julián nodded politely, without really understanding those last few words.

"If you want, I can sell you mine, since I don't need him anymore. What's more, he already knows the way!" he added, erupting in a great laugh that then transformed into a coughing fit.

When he recovered, Don Cesáreo brought them to the stable at the rear of the house.

"Careful on those steps," he warned, "they're so old that they whine like strangled cats every time I go down to feed Lucero."

The mule lifted its head to greet its master as he arrived with the two strangers.

"I bought him three years ago at the fair in Béjar. He's smart as a whip," he said as he stroked the beast's mane. "Lucero, please meet Señor Martín, and—" But the introductions were cut short as Don Cesáreo burst into another coughing fit.

Two hours later, Pablo and Julián were on their way back to Salamanca mounted on Lucero the mule.

THE FIRST FEW YEARS WERE DIFFICULT. For work, Julián had to travel around to schools all over the province, including those of the capital, and monitor the work of the primary school teachers. This included both phases of primary school: early education, mandatory for all children between six and nine years of age, intended to teach reading, writing, and arithmetic; and advanced education, not mandatory in those days, where children learned history and geography, as well as specialties such as surveying and geometry for boys and domestic skills for girls, and of course lessons on Christian doctrine. Since most schools were not mixed (mixed schools were allowed only in the tiniest towns), Julián had to leave Pablo at the inn when he went to inspect girls' schools, but brought him along to the boys' schools so he could play with kids his own age while Julián spoke with the schoolmaster, reviewing him using a questionnaire covering seventy guidelines that were meant to be followed scrupulously. If they were found to be out of compliance, he noted it in his inspection log, a large notebook with a green cover, feared and loathed by the schoolmasters. He would then warn them:

"I hope that by the time of my next visit, you will have found solutions for these minor deficiencies."

After the end of the workday, Julián devoted the late afternoons to Pablo's own education. Pablo avidly absorbed his father's knowledge, undeterred by having to receive it one day in Ciudad Rodrigo and the next in Cantalapiedra, Alba de Tormes, or Guijuelo. So, for the first few years, he learned grammar and spelling, mathematics and geography, a little Latin and bit of French, a notion of natural sciences, and the four basic rules of the catechism, but that was as far as the theology lessons went. Deep down, Julián was anticlerical, and always found an excuse to put off teaching Catholic doctrine. If the weather was fine, he took Pablo out to the country and taught him to distinguish between a *Lactarius deliciosus* (the delectable saffron milk-cap) and a *Lactarius torminosus* (the poisonous woolly milk-cap), or between a starling and a blackbird:

"Look, pay close attention. Starlings don't build nests. They sleep wherever they find shelter, usually in holes in trees. Blackbirds are different, they take advantage of anything they can find to build their house: roots, branches, leaves, fur, even chestnut shells if they have to, and then they reinforce the whole nest with mud so it will be stronger. What would you rather be, Pablo, a blackbird or a starling?"

If the weather was foul, they would stay at the inn and Julián would teach his son to play chess or build castles out of toothpicks, or tell him fantastic stories, often inspired by the biography of historical characters:

"Have I ever told you the story of Évariste Galois?" he asked as he prepared an herbal tea or stirred the logs in the wood stove. As Pablo sat silent, he began for the hundredth time retelling the tale of that mathematical genius who had died in a duel in 1832, at only twenty years of age. "Poor fellow, to think what he might have accomplished if he hadn't had such bad luck. He tried twice to get into the École Polytechnique, which was the most prestigious mathematical academy in France, and both times they annulled his examination. Years later, there was a great French mathematician, and do you know what he said? That he had failed the test because he was smarter than the judges. Apparently, when they rejected him, Galois said: '*Hic ego barbarus sum quia non intelligur illis.*' Since they can't understand me, to them I'm a barbarian."

Pablo always listened attentively to his father's stories, as if they were Aesop's fables.

"By age seventeen he had already made some fundamental mathematical discoveries, so he wrote a thesis with all of his theories and sent it to the Academy of Sciences. And do you know what happened? They lost the manuscript! But that wasn't the worst thing: two years later he submitted another work that he hoped would win the top prize in mathematics of the Academy of Sciences. The secretary of the academy took it to his house to review it, and he died that very night! When they tried to get the manuscript back from the dead professor's house, they couldn't find it anywhere. So Évariste Galois, disappointed with the world and the stupidity of humanity, gave up on mathematical glory and decided to start a revolution. 'If it takes a corpse to wake people up, I'll give them my own,' he said."

"And what happened?" Pablo would ask, impatiently, although he already knew the story.

"What do you think happened, Son? They put him in prison. And when he got out, his political enemies were waiting for him. Someone challenged him to a duel and Galois couldn't, or wouldn't, or didn't know how to refuse. Maybe he wanted to die, after all that failure. He spent the night before the duel writing like a madman, recording all of the mathematical discoveries he had made in his life. Every now and again he wrote in the margin: 'I don't have time, I don't have time.' And when the dawn light entered the window, he wrote a goodbye letter and addressed it to his mother. But I've already told you all this, haven't I?"

At such moments, Pablo would shake his head to say no, and his father would take the opportunity to stir his tea or the fire.

"It was a duel with pistols, at twenty-five paces. The two men turned at exactly the same moment, but only one shot was heard. Galois fell to his knees, shot in the intestines. They left him for dead, and there he lay until someone found him and brought him to a hospital. Evaristo still had time to talk to his younger brother before he died. 'Don't cry,' he said, 'I need all the courage in the world to die so young.' And do you know the best part? Those equations he wrote during his last night on earth are still being studied today by the world's greatest mathematicians."

In summer and at Christmastime, father and son returned to Baracaldo to spend their vacations with María and little Julia, who was growing by leaps and bounds from one visit to the next. On these occasions, Pablo would spend hours and hours with his sister, telling her what he had seen and learned over the last few months, but mixing equal parts reality and fantasy. His sense of smell never improved, so his parents took him to the doctor again.

"What this boy needs is the dry climate of the interior," the doctor repeated again and again, sending them off with the same words every time: "Don't forget that the devil's best trick is convincing us he doesn't exist."

So father and son returned to their itinerant lifestyle on the Castilian Plateau, while the nation was rocked by its overseas wars: in February 1898 the United States declared war on Spain and that same summer they lost the colonies once and for all, an event the prime minister, Antonio Cánovas, did not live to see, having been assassinated by the Italian anarchist Michele Angiolillo during a therapeutic visit to the spa at Santa Agueda.

"What's an anarchist?" Pablo asked, hearing this word for the first time.

"I'll explain it when you're older," his father replied. "You're still too young to understand."

But shortly thereafter, another Italian anarchist, Luigi Lucheni, assassinated the Empress Sisi in Geneva by stabbing her with a stiletto. Again Pablo asked:

"Papa, what's an anarchist?"

And Julián did not know how explain it, so he changed the subject or poked his head out the window and launched into the names of the constellations:

"Look," he said, pointing to the sky, "That one shaped like a carriage is the Great Bear. And that smaller one is the Little Bear. And over there, the one shaped like an M is called Cassiopeia. That's right, Son. An M, like in Martín."

And so they passed the days, weeks, months, and years, and despite the nation's troubles and the difficulties of homesickness and travel, if anyone had had the crazy idea to ask the Martíns if they were happy, in all likelihood they would have responded that indeed they were. However, deep down, sometimes unconsciously, there was something that Pablo longed for. Something that always came up in the adventure novels he read at night. Something that he had never had, and that the continual movement made even more difficult to find. Something that could be summed up in a single word: a friend. Julián could not fill this role. Nor could Lucero, though Pablo often found himself in conversation with the mule. But what the boy needed was an Athos, a Porthos, an Aramis. It is true that when they stayed in one town for a few days, Pablo ended up getting to know the other children his own age, sometimes joining them in their games in the town square or chasing grasshoppers on the riverbank. But when they returned again a year later, the other children usually did not remember him, so he preferred to stay at the inn reading his adventure novels. And so it would have continued if it had not been for the occasion when, at the end of 1899, shortly before Christmas vacation, he met Robinson Crusoe.

− 4 −

The hub of Unamuno's life in Paris was the Café de la Rotonde. With regard to this establishment, all of the chroniclers of that period repeat the same line: La Rotonde is the café of rebellions.

EDUARDO COMIN COLOMER,

Unamuno, libelista

"EXCELLENT WORK," SAYS THE RASPY-VOICED, pock-faced man, as he holds out a copy of *Spain: One Year of Dictatorship*, "really excellent. In one week we've inundated Paris with pamphlets. It's been a total success, and not just in the Spanish enclaves—the French are starting to come around, too. Between the meetings and this, it's all bright red. I just heard that Blasco Ibáñez already has a French translator for his leaflet, and Juan Durá, his Spanish editor, can't wait to put it out. It seems Vicentito is really serious about it, and they're gonna translate it into English too, and distribute it in America. A million copies in all, they're saying, sponsored by the Russian communists, who want to export their revolution to all of Europe. Some say they sent fifty thousand francs to defray the printing and distribution costs, but Blasco won't confirm or deny it. Want some snuff?"

"No," Pablo shoots back, a bit ill at ease in this improvised meeting in a reserved room at the Café de la Rotonde.

Of course, the man who won't stop talking is Teixidó, the Committee's director of propaganda, the same one who approached Pablo a couple of weeks ago after Blasco Ibáñez's speech. At his side is Vivancos, tasked with obtaining arms for the planned revolution. And next to him, Robinsón, with an angelic smile that Pablo doesn't find at all reassuring.

"Durruti and Massoni will be here soon, I think," says Teixidó as he lifts a pinch of snuff to his nose and inhales deeply. "Let's wait five minutes, and if they're still not here, we'll tell you ourselves. In any case, I'm glad you've decided to work with the Committee."

"Look, I was just doing my job. The guy to thank is old Faure."

"No, I'm not talking about the pamphlet. I'm talking about the broadsides we want to print to send to Spain. It's a good thing we can count on your help, because don't think it's been easy ..."

"What? No, no. I haven't promised anything about the broadsides."

"No? But Robinsón told us ..."

Six eyes now turn in unison to a man hiding under a bowler hat.

"Hey, we've got to talk if we're gonna understand each other, right?" the vegetarian begins in his own defense, under the threat of being devoured by three carnivorous gazes. But before anyone can answer him, the door opens and Durruti enters, hastily removing his usual blue mechanic's cap, followed by Massoni, looking like an out-of-place banker. The murmur of Don Miguel's salon is audible from upstairs.

Today is Saturday, the eighteenth of October, 1924, and the fine, stubborn rain keeps falling on Paris, soaking into clothing and dampening hearts. Pablo has already been to Marly and back. And tonight, he has let Robinsón convince him to come to La Rotonde, the café par excellence of rebellions and conspiracies, located at the corner of the boulevards Raspail and Montparnasse. It was here that Lenin started incubating his own crusade, while playing chess with his nihilist compatriots; here that, between tirades, Trotsky slurped coffee as thick as the silt of the Seine. The café was also frequented by writers: Rubén Darío would come here to empty bottles of cognac and then to slog, hung over, through the writing of his journal *Mundial*; Pío Baroja would often show up in sandals and a scarf, lamenting that Paris was much more boring than his Bidasoa River valley; even Josep Pla, looking like an angry peasant, would come and sit in a corner to rant against anything that moved.

But La Rotonde didn't just thrive on hack writers and revolutionaries: for many years, it was also a melting pot of artists, bohemians, students, transvestites, police informants, petty criminals, and an unending stream of people who spent hours conversing, drinking absinthe or contemplating the paintings that cluttered the walls. The models for these paintings would pop by every now and again and surprise the clientele, baring their garters and putting on lipstick in public.

La Rotonde was also, inevitably, the place chosen by many of the Spaniards living in exile to combine their forces and their words of resistance against the dictatorship of Primo de Rivera. Shortly before the coup d'état, the freemason Carlos Esplá, personal secretary of Blasco Ibáñez, founded an interesting discussion group here, called the "Spanish Club." This club went on to become notorious, not so much for the quantity and quality of its participants, but rather for the amount of noise they were able to produce despite their small numbers. The café could be full of shouting people, and only the Spanish would be heard. With the ascent to power of the Military Directory, the group started to fill up with VIP expatriates, such as Marcelino Domingo, Francesc Macià, or the former minister Santiago Alba, but the ones who really brought glamour to the group were not the politicians, but the writers and intellectuals, such as Ortega y Gasset and, most notably, Miguel de Unamuno, who became the undisputed star of the meetings, to the point that the "Spanish Club" was renamed "Don Miguel's Club." Indeed, the very epicenter of the exiled professor's Parisian life was here at La Rotonde, where he came every day to compose the sonnets of his book *De Fuerteventura a París*, one of which ended up being inspired by the young man who, just now, in a private room in the same café, is standing up to shake hands with Buenaventura Durruti and Pedro Massoni:

"Good evening, comrades," says Durruti, extending his thin hand to Pablo, and squeezing firmly, "Nice to meet you."

"Hello," Pablo replies, squeezing back.

Massoni sits down without saying anything and starts to leaf through some papers. Out of superstition or maybe just caution, Durruti remains standing, since the only free chair has its back to the door.

"Have they told you what's going on?" he asks.

"Well…" Teixidó starts to excuse himself, rubbing his nose, "the thing is… Look. It seems there's been a misunderstanding."

"What's the problem?" Massoni asks, lifting his eyes from his papers. With a frank look, he says to Vivancos, "If it's a question of money, we don't have a red cent."

"The problem is that he doesn't want to collaborate," says Teixidó.

"Wait, look," Pablo defends himself, "it's not that I don't want to help, but it's not as simple as that. I already told Robinsón—" and here, he shoots Robinsón a dirty look "—that we can't print the broadsides without Faure's consent, and it seems that Faure flat refused."

"Yeah, exactly," Durruti huffs, "and that's why we thought of you. Knowing your militant history, we thought that you wouldn't mind giving us a hand, particularly in a moment like this, which is so difficult for us. We'll provide the paper, you don't have to worry about that, we already ordered ten thousand sheets…"

Everyone looks at Pablo, except for Robinsón, who is busy picking a bit of lint from his bowler, while in the next room, Unamuno receives applause after reading his latest sonnet.

It should be noted that Unamuno does not come to La Rotonde just to garner applause: from day one he realized that this place is an inexhaustible source of stories, and anytime he can, he takes advantage of it to listen and snatch bits of conversation out of the air: secrets revealed, rumors and jokes recounted; the inimitable raw materials he turns into his articles in *Le Quotidien*, which light up the minds on the other side of the Pyrenees and make Henri Dumay wring his hands—Dumay being the director of the newspaper and the one who organized Unamuno's rescue in Fuerteventura. The razor-sharp, vulgar wit of the ex-rector of

Salamanca has grown so famous in Paris that a French journalist said that he uses ink to frustrate his enemies, like an octopus or squid. The crowning moment came in late summer, when Primo de Rivera himself wrote an angry letter to Dumay denying the accusations Unamuno had heaped on him. The letter was published immediately, on the front page, three columns wide, along with the implacable image of the ex-rector. *Le Quotidien* has been strictly banned in Spain since then.

The power that Unamuno has acquired in the salon is so great that he has allowed himself the indulgence of tacitly expelling Rodrigo Soriano, who was rescued along with him from Fuerteventura. The trigger was the publication, in *Paris-Soir*, of an article by Soriano, in which he criticized "armchair revolutionaries," in clear reference to Unamuno. Since then, the ex-rector never grows tired of repeating, while fidgeting with his bread and reminiscing about his time imprisoned in the Canaries, that "The dictator didn't punish me by banishing me to Fuerteventura. The real punishment was making me live with Rodrigo Soriano—and that's what I can't forgive," and then, gathering momentum from the laughter in the peanut gallery, he goes on: "I know Don Rodrigo is nothing but a mosquito, but the thing is that mosquitoes sometimes get into an animal's ears and annoy them till they drive them crazy. But he doesn't annoy me, the little mosquito." One of the biggest fans of these speeches is Blasco Ibáñez, Soriano's well-known enemy, who, even though he has his own salon at the Café Américain, never misses a chance to pop by La Rotonde to take advantage of Don Miguel's popular draw in order to spout a few of his own diatribes, usually followed by a bit of self-aggrandizement. Such as now, when he has just arrived at the salon with an elegant, slightly cross-eyed lady on his arm, while Pablo is meeting in the private room with the vanguard of the Committee of Anarchist Relations. The first person he sees is José María Carretero, the young, prolific Spanish writer who signs his works with the somewhat immodest pen name "*El Caballero Audaz.*"

"Come to my arms, Carretero!" exclaims Don Vicente, with his enormous rain-barrel gut. Carretero lets himself be embraced, to the point of almost disappearing.

"How are you, Don Vicente?"

"Fine, fine, thanks. Have you read the *Quotidien*?" he asks, not bothering to introduce the woman on his arm.

"Yes, I've seen the interview. It seems you're in revolutionary mode. Is that so?"

"Absolutely."

"And what are you thinking of doing?"

"Why, what must be done: the revolution!"

"And how is that done, Don Vicente?" asks the Audacious Gentleman, with a certain disingenuousness, as if to belie his pen name.

"Don't you play innocent with me, Carretero, open your eyes. Spain can't go on like this, any way you look at it. And that's just the problem: the people who should be doing something prefer to close their eyes and look the other way. What we need in Spain are more Strogoffs, you get me? People who are capable of weeping for their nation and saving the whole country's sight, despite the hot irons that the bastards want to shove in their eyes. We have to wake people up, Carretero, get 'em jumping. And I'm planning to do it, no matter what. I'll hold the necessary meetings, I'll write articles in the newspapers, I'll distribute my pamphlet myself, if I have to …"

"And you haven't thought about taking up arms?" the young writer interrupts.

Blasco pales a bit, and then bursts out in a great peal of laughter, which silences everyone around him. Then, becoming suddenly serious, he replies:

"Look, sir, you're making a big mistake if you think I'm some kind of Capitán Araña, who's going to embark a crew and then stay on the land. No, no, my dear friend. No, I'll be on the front lines, you hear me? I'll be the first to take a bullet in the chest!" Raising his voice, he concludes emphatically: "I've lived enough, and I don't care if I die. I'm not afraid of them! I'm not afraid to fight, and I'm not afraid of death!"

A flurry of applause accompanies his closing words. Carretero excuses himself and goes to dine upstairs with a more cautious group of Spaniards, having decided to write a biting little exposé to take Blasco down a notch, which he will end up titling, "The Novelist Who Sold His Country Out." But let's leave Blasco, the *Caballero Audaz,* and their dialectical battles for now. Let's go down these two flights of stairs, which lead, at the bottom and to the left, to the private room, where we've just heard the conversation between Pablo and Durruti and company. Because let's not forget that La Rotonde is not just a haven for politicians and intellectuals who fight their revolution using letters to the editor and rhetorical devices, but also for true men of action, erudite anarchists who cherish more than anything the elegant lines of a Browning semiautomatic, the impossible beauty of a harmonica pistol, or the understated grace of a *cachorrillo*, the pocket pistol Larra used to commit suicide. So, while Unamuno and his ilk wage their paper war, the next table is usually talking about incursions, attacks, offensives, and putsches. But when things get serious, or there's concern that a snitch or informant is in their midst, they go downstairs to meet in the private room at the bottom left.

"Fine, okay, I'll do it," Pablo finally gives in, although he's still not very sure that a revolutionary incursion is the best available option. "When do you need it?"

"The date of the expedition hasn't been finalized yet, it doesn't depend so much on us but on the comrades in the interior, but the broadsides can be printed now. Well, as soon as we get the paper, of course."

"And the money," Massoni interjects, "Since, between Vivancos and Teixidó, we've spent everything."

The accused try to protest, but Durruti nips the conversation in the bud:

"Please, friends, we've come here to make plans. Let's leave the dirty laundry for some other time. Pablo, thank you for your cooperation, doubtless you will be a great help. I don't need to tell you that this matter calls for the utmost discretion. We will keep in touch with you through Robinsón, if you like."

And so, after shaking hands with everyone present and casting a dire look at Robinsón, Pablo makes his exit from La Rotonde. Meanwhile, in Don Miguel's salon, someone's just told a joke and the room erupts in strenuous laughter.

Safe to say, Pablo has now been inducted into the Orchestra of the Revolution.

IV
(1899)

"MY NAME'S ROBERTO OLAYA. BUT YOU can call me Robinsón," said the boy, lifting his eyes from a book with all its pages cut.

Pablo and his father had arrived ten days beforehand in Béjar, one of the larger villages of the province of Salamanca. About fifty miles south of the provincial capital and surrounded by mountains, the village was often cut off from the rest of the world by deep winter snows, as was the case at the time of the Martíns' visit.

"My name is Pablo Martín. But you can call me Pablo."

The two boys looked at each other in silence. Robinsón was slightly younger, but he looked older.

"What's that book you're reading?" the boy from Baracaldo asked.

"*Robinson Crusoe*," replied the boy from Béjar.

"Will you let me read it?"

"You can have it when I'm done with it. But don't let my papa catch you."

The boy's father was the owner of the inn where the inspector and his son had taken a room, located at the uphill end of Calle Flamencos, next to the church of San Juan Bautista. This man had been a syndicalist in his youth, but an accident at work in the textile factory had left him without his left hand, and he had had to open the inn to make a living. He had a reputation in the village as an atheist and freethinker, and those really in the know whispered that he was a Marxist, a word that tended to put people ill at ease.

"Why can't I let your papa see me?" Pablo asked.

"Because he doesn't like this book. He says it defends slavery. But I've already read it three times!"

"Are you almost done with it?"

"Yeah, almost," said the innkeeper's son, showing Pablo the pages he had left to read.

Béjar was the last village that Julián Martín had to inspect before returning to Baracaldo to spend Christmas with his family. The municipality had eight primary schools (four for boys and four for girls) and the provincial inspector was planning to visit all of them before going home for vacation, leaving the schools in nearby towns such as La Calzada, Ledrada, and Candelario for the next trip. However, he did not plan for the tremendous snow that would fall just before his departure, leaving them cut off from the rest of the world, a snow that would take many days to melt and decades to fade from the memory of the people of Béjar.

"In any case," said the boy called Robinsón, "with this snow I don't think you'll be able to leave the village until after Christmas, so you'll have plenty of time to read the whole book."

Julián sent a telegram to María to tell her about the situation, with the hope that he would soon be able to take Lucero across the mountain pass of Vallejera on the way to Salamanca. But the next day was already Christmas Eve, and it would be very difficult for them to reach Baracaldo in time for Christmas treats. The other guests at the inn were all in the same situation, so they decided to celebrate Christ's birth together, telling themselves that sometimes it is better to be in bad company than alone, despite what the proverb says. When the word got around that there was a provincial inspector staying at the inn, he was appointed master of ceremonies, and Julián had no choice but to fulfill his duty and officiate the evening's modest festivities. And it was that very night, a few hours before dinner, that the inspector's son found the innkeeper's son in the attic reading a book called *Robinson Crusoe*.

"Why are you hiding up here?" asked Pablo, who had arrived in the attic by following a pregnant cat strolling through the inn like she owned the place.

"This is my temporary lair. With all the snow I can't get to my hideout," Robinsón replied, mimicking the language of an adventure novel.

"And where is your hideout?"

"I can't tell you that. At least, not right now."

The two boys observed each other attentively in the dim light of the tallow lamp illuminating the attic space, a skeletal room filled with beams and rafters that to Pablo looked like the hold of an old pirate ship. Robinsón was sitting on an enormous, worn-out trunk, with a plaid blanket covering him from the waist down and the pregnant cat curled up on his lap.

"And when will you be able to tell me?"

"When you pass the test."

"What test?"

Robinsón closed the book he was reading and released a sigh.

"What test do you think? The friendship test."

"What's that?" asked Pablo, who was not much of an expert on friendship.

But Robinsón did not reply, because a voice was calling from the stairs:

"Roberto! Where have you run off to, Roberto?"

The boy made a sudden hushing gesture. Surprised, the cat leaped from his lap and disappeared behind pile of wooden posts in a corner of the attic.

"Roberto! Robeeeeertoooo! If you're in the chicken coop again, I'm going to take off my shoe!"

Robinsón tossed away the blanket and stood up, exposing the orthopedic device the doctors had placed on him to try to build the muscles of his left leg, which were atrophied due to a recent bout of polio.

"Here, get inside and make room for me," he whispered, opening the trunk and putting out the lamp, "if my mama finds us here, she'll thrash us good."

They nestled into the darkness of the chest and heard footsteps coming up the stairs. Both boys held their breath when the door's hinges creaked.

"I know you're up here, Roberto!" the mother exclaimed. "Do you think I can't smell the tallow smoke? But I'm not a fool, I'm not going to wear myself out poking around in the dark up here trying to find you. If you're not in the kitchen in five minutes helping me peel potatoes, there'll be no Christmas dinner for you!"

That said, she slammed the door as she headed back downstairs. Inside the trunk, Pablo and Robinsón could not contain their laughter. When they came out from hiding, it was as if they had been friends their whole lives.

"Sorry, I have to go help my mama," said the innkeeper's son as he opened the door to let in a little light.

"What about your hideout? When are you gonna show it to me?" the inspector's son asked, his curiosity unabated.

"First you have to pass the test, Pablo. Don't forget. Here, you can borrow the book for a while if you want. Anyway, I know the whole thing by heart."

"Thanks, Roberto."

"Robinsón, call me Robinsón," the boy corrected him, and started down the stairs dragging his lame leg.

That Christmas Eve thirteen people dined together at the inn, a number no one failed to notice. Surrounding the oaken table that dominated the dining room, there was a traveling pharmaceuticals salesman, a livestock dealer built like a wine barrel, a pair of newlyweds trying to get to Lisbon to see the Atlantic Ocean, and four comic actors from a traveling company who livened up the evening with jokes and songs, as well as the hosts Don Veremundo and Doña Leonor, and the provincial inspector, Don Julián Martín Rodríguez. Even though both boys had already taken their First Communion, they were seated at a separate table, and they left off chatting for a while as they slurped their cabbage soup and heartily devoured the duck, which, truth be told, no one refused, despite Catholic doctrine's prohibition against eating meat on Christmas Eve. Only the traveling salesman dared to object, albeit timidly, that Our Lord would not be happy to see this footed animal served at his table, but Doña Leonor gave the excuse that due to the snow no fish had been delivered to Béjar that week and they weren't going to celebrate Christmas Eve with vegetable soup. That settled that.

"Salamanca has an excellent climate for raising duck," said the livestock dealer, his mouth full of food. "There are a lot of chestnuts growing around here, and that's what ducks love most. But you have to roast the chestnuts first, of course—"

"I've heard," one of the actors interrupted, his booming theatrical voice hoarse with revelry, "that they also eat walnuts."

"Yes, it's true," the dealer avowed, wiping the grease from the corners of his lips, "But that gives the meat an oily taste. In other regions they feed them a slurry of potato, wheat flour, and milk. But I'm telling you: nothing beats chestnuts."

"And how did you make this delicious sauce?" the newlywed bride asked the hostess.

"Secret recipe," Doña Leonor replied with a half-smile.

"Well, it's scrumptious," said one of the actresses, licking her fingers.

"Chili peppers these days don't have the punch they used to," the traveling salesman tried to interject, but no one paid him any mind.

At the children's table, the conversation took a few unexpected turns:

"Do you know how many hairs there are on a human head?" Robinsón asked, stroking his own hair which was wiry as a bristle brush.

"No," replied Pablo, who had never really given the matter much thought.

"A hundred thousand!" said the innkeeper's son, opening his eyes wide as if he had found a treasure. "And you know what else?"

"No, what?"

"You know how snakes lose their skin and grow a new one? We do the same thing with our hair! D'you know how long it takes to replace all the hairs on your head?"

"No, how long?"

"Three years!"

"And what happens if they fall out but no new hairs grow?" Pablo asked.

"What do you think? You end up bald!"

When there was nothing left of the duck but greasy bones and fond memories, the time came for sugar cookies and *zambomba* drums, sweet wine, and caroling. Don Veremundo offered cigars to all the men, and everyone took one graciously except the fussy traveling salesman, who first wanted to make sure they were not from Cuba. The actors recited some lines to great applause from the improvised audience, and Julián finally took the floor, after some urging.

"Chance or Providence has decided that we would all spend this special night together, though just a few hours ago we were all strangers. I'm not going to lie to you: I would have preferred to spend Christmas Eve with my wife and my little Julia, and not just with my son Pablo and all of you. But since God wanted it this way, let's enjoy the evening!"

"Give us some good advice for the new year, Inspector!" the livestock dealer requested, chewing his words and a sugar cookie at the same time.

"I'm sorry, I don't give advice," Julián said. "You'll have to excuse me, but usually when people ask for advice, they don't follow it, and when they do it's to have someone to blame when it doesn't work out."

Everyone laughed at this remark except the livestock dealer, who did not expect such a response. He finally washed down the sugar cookie with a big swig of sweet wine and, turning to the innkeeper, asked:

"And will there be a midnight mass, despite the snow?"

"Of course," replied Don Veremundo, wiping his nose with his stump,

"The townsfolk have spent all day clearing snow off the streets and scattering salt, so anyone who wants to can go to the church of San Juan, it's not far from here."

"What, you're not planning to come with us?" the traveling salesman implored.

"No, you'll have to excuse me, I suffer from indigestion and I don't do so well with big meals like this—"

"There's nothing better for indigestion than Parodium Tonic," the traveling salesman interrupted, always eager to turn a sale.

"But my wife and son would be glad to go along, wouldn't they?" Don Veremundo continued, looking at his wife.

"Of course," replied Doña Leonor, knowing that what her husband really could not stand were the rites and robes. Julián also had little appetite for such things, but his duty compelled him to certain sacrifices, though he would need to follow it with a good dose of spiritual bicarbonate in order to get to sleep.

As midnight approached, the retinue prepared to leave for the church, with Doña Leonor leading the way and the actors singing silly folk songs. However, when they stepped outside, the frigid air quickly silenced their warbling. A few snowflakes were falling, and the men turned up the collars of their overcoats, while the women clutched their dress skirts in one hand and used the other to keep their shawls from blowing away. The two boys straggled a bit behind, slowed by Robinsón's limp. His orthopedic device made it difficult to find footing amid the snow and salt.

"Go on ahead with the rest, I know the way," said the innkeeper's son, proudly.

But Pablo did not leave his side until they reached the church. The crowd waiting outside was agitated, everyone having run out of small talk. A man with a cane and patent leather shoes was getting down from a carriage, followed by a woman wrapped in a mantle of Persian lambswool, while the panting horse tried to keep warm by urinating on the snow, creating a cloud of vapor like incense smoke. Seeing the elegant couple arrive, the beggars huddling around the parish door took their stiff hands from their pockets and begged for alms. Inside, the people thronged and the organist got ready to play the celestial notes of the *Puer Natus Est Nobis*. The sanctuary was dominated by a vague shadow favorable to contemplation, but also to dissolution, especially for those who had imbibed too many spirits with dinner. The twinkling light of the tapers could not penetrate the far corners of the church, and some congregants took advantage of this for some decidedly unecclesiastical necking. When the organ went tacit, the priest lifted his voice over the gathered faithful and, adjusting his embroidered chasuble, began to recite the Epistle of Saint Paul to Titus.

"Follow me," someone whispered to Pablo, and he turned to see Robinsón disappearing into the shadows. He looked up at Julián to seek permission, but the inspector seemed to have fallen asleep listening to that velvety voice speaking of piety and hope. He made his way through the crowd and followed Robinsón to the retrochoir, where an altar boy was manning a little wooden door hidden in the shadows.

"Hi, Juan," Robinsón whispered.

The altar boy nodded his head and looked around.

"I brought a friend," he added, pointing to Pablo.

"That wasn't part of our agreement," said the altar boy with a gangster-like tone.

"I'll give you double, if you want."

"Alright then, enter," and he opened the way for them, extending his hand surreptitiously.

Robinsón passed him an elongated packet, which immediately disappeared as if by magic, and signaled to Pablo to follow him. A few steep, narrow staircases led up to the organ. The priest recited the last few words of the Epistle, and the instrument roared to life again, startling the two boys.

Over here, Pablo read on his friend's lips.

Two or three meters from the imposing organ, just behind the big man pumping the instrument's bellows, there was a small gap in the balustrade. From there, hidden from the far-off eyes, the two boys could see out onto most of the church: in the pulpit, the chaplain was getting ready to read the Gospel of Saint Luke, while the parishioners, rich and poor, young and old, monarchist and liberal, were piled up on the benches, in the side aisles, and around the baptismal font, and the most fervid were squeezing together against the railings of the main altar.

"What did you give him?" Pablo asked, intrigued by the scheming.

"Who, Juan? Nothing, just a couple of my dad's cigars. Look, do you see that man there, leaning on the confessional booth?"

Pablo turned his gaze in that direction and could make out, well-lit by a nearby taper, a man of about fifty years of age, repeatedly nodding off.

"That's Don Agustino Rojas, my schoolmaster. I bet you anything he's drunk. And do you see that woman in the first row kissing her prayer book? That's the mayor's sweetheart. He's that guy over there, who keeps looking over at her whenever his wife isn't watching..."

Pablo tried to discern in the crowd all of these people who Robinsón seemed to know like family, as silence fell and the priest started to read the passage on the birth of the baby Jesus:

"And so it was, that, while they were there, the days were accomplished that she should be delivered. And she brought forth her firstborn son, and wrapped him in swaddling clothes, and laid him in a manger; because there was no room for them in the inn..."

Pablo let his eyes wander around that sacred space commemorating a birth that had happened 1,899 years ago, and though the plumes of incense were indifferent to his nonfunctioning olfaction, a strange calm came over him. He fit his head between two balustrades, while Robinsón went on telling him stories, and his gaze fell on a girl wearing a festooned blue dress. He could not see her face because she was directly beneath them, but she captivated his attention. To her left, a man dressed in colonial style was holding her hand firmly.

"That's Angela," Robinsón whispered, seeing that Pablo could not take his eyes off of her. "She's only been here in Béjar for a year. Her parents went to Cuba before she was born, and now they had to come back. They live just across from me."

"And who is that man holding her hand?"

"That's her father, Don Diego Gómez, Lieutenant Colonel of the Spanish army in the war overseas," said Robinsón as if reciting from memory a refrain he had repeated a thousand times. "He was General Weyler's right-hand man. Now he's retired, but they say that he has fought three duels, and he lost a finger in one of them. That's why he always wears gloves."

"And what happened to the others?" Pablo asked without taking his eyes off of Angela, perhaps thinking about the history of the unfortunate Évariste Galois, the intrepid mathematician whose story fascinated Pablo's father.

"What others?"

"The ones who fought duels with him."

"They're all pushing up daisies."

At that moment, a boy approached Angela and whispered something in her ear, but she appeared to ignore him.

"Who's that?"

"That's her idiot cousin. I've fought him seven times. His name is Rodrigo, Rodrigo Martín."

"Wow, that's my last name."

"Yeah, it seems there are a lot of Martíns."

"And did he come from Cuba too?"

"No, no. He was born in Béjar. His family was one of the richest in town, but his parents died when he was little."

At that very moment, when the priest finished his reading and the organ came back to life, the girl in the blue dress, the daughter of Don

Diego Gómez, without really knowing why, lifted her eyes upward, where they met the eyes of Pablo, the son of the provincial inspector. She stayed like that for a few seconds, with her mouth open and her neck craned uncomfortably, trying to figure out who the boy was looking at her from the bars of the balustrade. He too held there, paralyzed, unblinking, blushing in the darkness. And so they would have remained until the Nativity Mass or maybe even until New Year if Rodrigo Martín had not wanted to know what his cousin was looking at. Robinsón pulled back from the railing, dragging Pablo with him.

"Damn it," he murmured. "If he saw us, we're doomed."

"Why?" Pablo asked, when he had recovered from the surprise.

Robinsón took a moment to respond, but his response was a double confession:

"Because I've fought him seven times and never won once. And because Rodrigo is in love with Angela."

Pablo felt a strange constriction in his chest, as if he were suffocating. The organ music went on majestically, inundating the church with notes and many congregants' eyes with tears. A few days later, the new year would arrive and, after it, the new century. The streets would fill with automobiles, the skies with airships, and the cities with cinematographs, while Pablo was filling his heart with love and dreams.

— 5 —

The publishing and distribution of anarchist literature during those months corresponded to the International Bookstore at 14 Rue Petit, which served as the headquarters of the International Anarchist Publishing Group, under the direction of Férandel; as the publishing house of the trilingual bulletin *Revista Internacional Anarquista*, founded in November; and, finally, as the residence of the Spanish Committee of Anarchist Relations.

ANTONIO ELORZA,
El anarcosindicalismo español bajo la dictadura

"WHAT A DIRTY TRAP," PABLO REPROACHED Robinsón as they were leaving La Rotonde last night. As they were arriving at home, he added, "You deserve to spend the night on the floor with Kropotkin." But Robinsón's only reply was his most innocent smile.

Today he has come to invite Pablo out to eat. Having worked hard all morning, Pablo eagerly accepts the invitation, making an effort to forget the dirty trick at La Rotonde.

"Today I'm going to take you to the vegetarian café on Rue Mathis," says Robinsón, tugging at his beard with delight. "It's time to celebrate, because since last night, we're in the same boat."

"We've always been in the same boat, Robin, but until now you never seemed so intent on making sure I drown with you. Do you really think this revolutionary movement is going to succeed?"

"If I didn't think so, I wouldn't be doing what I'm doing."

"Well, I'd wager that in Spain even the rats have figured it out, with all the ruckus you're making. Martínez Anido must be licking his chops."

"That's the paradox of any revolution, Pablito. On the one hand, you have to shout so that the people can hear about it and get on board, and on the other hand, you have to whisper so that the ones you want to take down don't hear about it. Of course they're aware in Spain that over here we're getting ready to overthrow the government; they've known it since day one of their coup. And they're afraid of us—of course they're afraid of us, because they can control the people on the inside, but not us, especially since the French government is protecting us more than they'd prefer. Look what happened with the repatriation of Cándido Rey: the prime minister fired the guy who authorized it for not respecting the right to asylum. And now it seems that Primo is going to have to suck it up and send him back to us. In any case, the important thing is keeping the plan secret, so they don't know how or when or where we're going to arrive. And of course they don't know that, since we don't even know ourselves!"

The two friends smile as they leave La Fraternelle and head toward Place des Fêtes to catch the metro. As they walk past the Point du Jour, they hear shouting inside. They turn their heads and see Leandro going berserk, cursing as he tries to strangle the café's owner, Monsieur Dubois, who, pinned against the bar, is trying to defend himself by feebly kicking at his attacker. Pablo and Robinsón run inside and release the prey from Leandro's clutches. Dubois falls on the floor panting, while the two friends try to shove the Argentinian giant out the door. The latter finally goes out, leaving in his wake a string of the worst French insults he knows, which are not worth listing here: just go ahead and think of the nastiest curses that come to mind, and with a little luck you'll be halfway there.

"What the hell is wrong with you?" Pablo shouts while making the final effort to get Leandro out of there. "Have you gone mad, or what?"

The Argentinian is still out of his head, hollering in the direction of the Point du Jour like a man possessed, until Pablo, who has never seen him like this, smacks his face, leaving him agog mid-insult. There is a brief moment of silence and uncertainty, until Leandro lifts his hand to his cheek, spits on the ground and steps on the sputum, which is more of a compulsive tic than a sign of disgust (he once accidentally spat on a dog and had to chase it for several blocks until he managed to step on it).

"Come on, let's get out of here before Dubois calls the police," Pablo says, and after a few seconds he adds: "You like vegetarian food, Leandro?"

"Are you kidding?" the Argentinian barks, still smarting. "In my country eating plants is against the law."

"Then today's the beginning of your life of crime. Sorry."

And the three young men descend into the metro, headed for the vegetarian restaurant.

"Damn, che, even my daddy never smacked me like that," Leandro complains, rubbing his chubby cheek, while he asks for three second-class tickets.

"Maybe he should have," Pablo replies.

Since today is Sunday, the metro is less busy than usual and there are a few seats free, which would be unthinkable during the week in a city where hundreds of thousands of people take the underground every day. The advertising industry has taken note of the business potential, and the station walls bear brightly colored posters, such as this one for Dubonnet liqueur, an image that many Parisians are talking about: a cat behind a bottle that bears a label depicting a cat behind a bottle, which in turn has a label depicting a cat behind a bottle, and so forth until you can no longer make it out. Leandro plops himself into the second-class seat, which protests bitterly, its wooden bones creaking; perhaps it envies its colleagues in first class, covered with leather upholstery to soften such assaults.

And while the metro snakes around underground, with a roar that reinforces the feeling of speed, Leandro tells them what happened. Monsieur Dubois accused him of stealing money from the bar's register, to which he responded that that's a very serious accusation and that he should apologize. The old man told him that he was the boss and that he didn't have to apologize to anybody, and that, furthermore, he could prove it. The Argentinian yelled, did he have witnesses, and Dubois responded that his only witness was the new cash register, more efficient than the best snitch. Then the giant from Buenos Aires filled with rage and started insulting his boss, calling him a bourgeois exploiter and a bloodsucker, and saying that if he believed a cash register over an honest worker, he was more rotten than Rockefeller. Dubois told him he was fired. And the next thing Leandro remembers is being slapped by Pablo—

"You were strangling him," Robinsón refreshes his memory, "and the cash register was dumped on the floor."

"He deserved it, the son of a bitch," Leandro harrumphs. "You should have let me finish the job. The old guy thinks he's so smart...but if it hadn't been for that damned cash register, he never would have noticed!"

Pablo and Robinsón shoot astonished looks at their newly unemployed friend as they exit the train at the station Louis Blanc to connect with the line to Crimée.

"What're you all lookin' at?" Leandro says in his own defense, shrugging. "Do you really think that I could get by on what that bastard was paying me?"

The three friends continue on their way, laughing. The vegetarian restaurant is in the neighborhood of La Villette, one of Paris's most dangerous in the eyes of the moneyed bourgeoisie, but where you can eat like a king if you leave your prejudices behind, which will soon become evident to Pablo and even to Leandro, following the advice of Robinsón, and that of the Esperanto-speaking Galician and the two other vegetarians who sit at their table, and who claim to have decided to join the revolutionary mission.

THAT NIGHT, WHILE PABLO IS CLOSING up the print shop and getting out his bike, he hears a whistle behind him, accompanied by the barking of Kropotkin: at the end of Rue Pixérécourt, the silhouetted outline of

Robinsón's bowler is visible, along with his slight but unmistakable limp. Pablo goes to meet him.

"You've become my shadow, Robin. Are you afraid I'll leave you for another?"

"Absolutely. There's no better shadow in all of Paris. Listen, the Committee wants to talk with you."

"Have they obtained the paper?"

"No, it's something else."

"What?"

"I don't know, they didn't want to tell me."

"Fine, but they can wait until I get back from Marly, can't they?"

"Mmm, I don't think so, it seems urgent. They're meeting at the shop on Rue Petit. I told them that I'd come fetch you ..."

Pablo makes a bitter face.

"Come on, Pablito, with the bike we'll be there in no time. And the meeting's sure to be short."

"Look, Robin, you're starting to get on my nerves with your ideas. If, someday, I decide to sign up for your crazy expedition, you'll be the first to know it, don't worry. In the meantime, stop nagging. And don't give me that sad puppy-dog face ..."

But Robinsón is making the sad puppy dog face. And so is Kropotkin.

"Fine, here, get on," Pablo finally caves in. "The sooner we get it over with, the better."

They cross the Rue de Belleville and go down the precipitous Rue Crimée, pass alongside the Parc des Buttes-Chaumont and then arrive at Rue Petit. Up high on number 14, a streetlight illuminates the International Bookstore sign with its peeling letters. Through the dirty panes one can see shelves full of books, along with several copies of *Le Libertaire*, a weekly published here by the French comrades of the Anarcho-Communist Union, under the supervision of Séverin Férandel and his partner Berthe Favert, who some say is the lover of Francisco Ascaso.

"No, around back," Robinsón points, when Pablo heads for the main door. "Kropotkin, you stay here and guard the bike."

"Around back" means that they have to go to Rue du Rhin, climb over a six-foot wall, cross a thicketed little wasteland, and knock on a door that is halfway hidden in the wall. One, two, three knocks; then, after a pause, two more knocks. Then the door opens as if by magic. On the other side there is the little room where the meetings of the Group of Thirty take place, dominated by a vast table that takes up almost the entire room; around it, a few chairs and boxes of books serve as places to sit. The upper echelon is there in a meeting, but when Robinsón and Pablo enter, some of them excuse themselves and leave, including Durruti. The only ones who remain are Vivancos, Ascaso, and Massoni. The room stinks of tobacco, and moisture has drawn maps of other worlds on the walls. A bad climate for books.

"Sit down, Pablo, please," chirps Vivancos, who at last night's meeting at La Rotonde didn't deign to open his mouth. He has a soft, soothing voice, almost a whisper, contrasting with his appearance, which is like that of an executioner or an abbot, and he drags out his esses a bit when he speaks. "We won't keep you long. Robinsón has told us that tomorrow you are taking the nine o'clock train to Lille."

"Well, not exactly," says Pablo. "I'm going to Marly, but the train stops in Lille before that, yes."

"And in Amiens."

"Yes, in Amiens as well, of course."

"So, we would like to ask you to do us a little favor, not much effort on your part, but of great importance to us."

"Look, if it's up to me—"

"It merely involves passing a letter in Amiens. You don't even have to get off the train. While the train is stopped there, our contact will enter the last car. He will be carrying a doctor's bag, which will be slightly open. When you see him enter, you stand up and act like you're crossing the aisle. Then you drop the letter in the medical bag."

"And that's all?"

"Yes, that's all. Well, wait. When are you returning?"

"Friday morning."

"Will it be possible to get ahold of you in Marly?"

"Yes, I'm going to look after a country house. It has a telephone."

"No. No telephones. In any case, when you return on Friday, keep an eye out for the doctor again in Amiens. If he enters the train, it means he has something to give you. Same game in reverse, and that's it."

Pablo looks steadily at Vivancos, then at Massoni and then Ascaso.

"Just one question. Why me? I mean, if this letter is so important, why don't you deliver it yourselves instead of entrusting it to me, someone you barely know? Amiens isn't so far away—"

"You're right, but this is the safest method," this time it is Ascaso who speaks. "You've been making this trip every week for a while now, I imagine that the agents and conductors recognize you, so you won't raise any suspicions. We, on the other hand—the police know us."

"And can you tell me the contents of this letter?"

"For your safety, it's better if you don't know. It is highly confidential; the only ones who know are those of us who were here when you walked in."

"Yeah, I figured; otherwise, you'd just stick the envelope in the mailbox. And what happens if there is a checkpoint before I get to Amiens and they confiscate the letter?"

"Let's hope that that doesn't happen," Ascaso replies emphatically. "In any case, if you see anything strange or suspicious, the best thing to do is get rid of it. Tear it up and throw it out the window."

"Got it. Anything else?"

"Yes: thank you for your assistance."

"Good luck," Vivancos adds, in his velvety voice, offering a handshake and the envelope.

"I hope I won't need it," Pablo responds, putting the letter in the hidden pocket in the lining of his jacket. He leaves, accompanied by Robinsón, resigned to his new role as a guinea pig.

THE NEXT MORNING PABLO WAKES UP with a start, after a night of insomnia, with the impression of having fallen asleep with the last breath. But no, it's not an impression, it's reality: you did fall asleep, Pablo, and if you don't hurry you will miss the morning train. So jump out of bed and run to the station, but be careful not to step on Robinsón, who is still peacefully snoring at your feet.

Pablo puts on his pants and shoes in a hurry, grabs a bag and stuffs it with his four necessities, and runs out of the house in such a hurry that he treads on Kropotkin's tail, and the dog starts barking hysterically. He leaps down three stairs at a time, and running out into the street he realizes he's forgotten his jacket. With the letter he's supposed to pass in Amiens in the pocket. He runs back up the seven flights of stairs and discovers that Kropotkin is no longer on the landing but in bed with Robinsón. They both look at him with the same face, a mix of guilt and sleep. Without saying anything, Pablo grabs his jacket and runs out the door. Entering the Gare du Nord, the train has just started rolling, but he manages to catch it on the run. He finds a seat in the rear car as Vivancos instructed, remembering what his father used to say: in case of a crash, the last car is the safest. In any case, it's the car he always chooses and would continue taking even if it were the most dangerous, because it's the only third-class car, with its stiff wooden benches lined up two-by-two. But try as he might to distract himself thinking of other things, the letter is burning in his jacket pocket. And if he knew its contents, it would burn him even more.

The contact in Amiens is Juan Rodríguez, a somewhat posh expatriate from Extremadura better known as *El Galeno*—"the Physician"—although he never completed his medical studies. In Amiens, nevertheless, he works as a barber in the back room of a drugstore behind the cathedral. His assistant is another Spanish expatriate, Blas Serrano, said by gossips to be his lover. Times have really changed, and the village barber no longer extracts molars, provides abortions, or applies mustard plasters; now he busies himself trying to round up money for the anarchist movement among the Spanish workers residing in this region of northern France known as Picardy. The letter Pablo is carrying in his pocket, written on a gridded sheet, is signed with the initials M.G.V., and it as brief as it is dangerous. The smooth, elegant handwriting does not mask the bitterness of the words, which complain of the anarchist movement's lack of resources and the scant cooperation of the French comrades, informing Juan Rodríguez of the importance of continuing the fundraising effort among the Spanish workers living in Amiens, and lamenting the slavery we are subjected to by "that powerful gentleman known as Don Dinero, that treacherous opiate invented by the bourgeoisie to dirty our hands and spirit."

The script becomes a bit more hesitant when the letter gets into material matters, as though the words were afraid to say more than necessary when asking El Galeno to engage a mission of "the most absolute transcendence": obtaining weapons, in great quantity and at low cost, because the medical student-cum-barber has good contacts among the workers of the region employed in the recovery of war materiel, who have a habit of trafficking their spoils even though the regulations require all weapons to be turned over to military engineers for destruction. Further on, the words again complain of the movement's financial problems, and give way to numbers quoting the prices Rodríguez can offer the traffickers: a maximum of thirty francs per rifle and fifty for each case of "*bombillas*," revolutionary slang for grenades; no point buying "pieces," as there is a surplus of pistols at this time. The last thing El Galeno will read will be a few curt words of closure and thanks, and advice to destroy the letter as soon as he's done reading it.

Finally, the imposing cathedral of Amiens appears in the distance, announcing that the train is drawing close to the city. Pablo has not taken off his coat, and sweat is starting to run down his back. He is suddenly seized by the apprehension that he is attracting too much attention by keeping his coat on. He looks around and it seems that everyone is watching him, silently appraising his behavior. A little old woman in front of him, nose and cheeks covered with warts, makes a face that says you'll see when you get off, you'll catch your death of cold. Fortunately, the train starts to brake as it arrives at the Amiens station, slowing with light jerks. Pablo stands up, lowers the window and pokes his head out; when the train stops, a few travelers get off. Then he sees the man with the medical bag helping a pregnant woman with her luggage. His heart racing, Pablo leaves his position at the window and makes his way to the back of the car, toward the door the man has just entered. In the aisle, he subtly takes the letter from his inside coat pocket and nearly crashes into the pregnant woman; one second later he is next to the supposed doctor, whose medical bag is slightly open. Passing by his side, Pablo drops the letter in and continues on his way. No eye contact. Returning to his seat, Pablo still has time to catch a glimpse of the man with the medical bag leaving the station in the company of another man. Before he sits down again, he finally removes his coat, and the wart-faced woman shakes her head as if to say: it's about time, son, it's about time.

V

(1899–1900)

ROBERTO OLAYA WAS NOT MISTAKEN. AS he had predicted, the inspector and his son were unable to leave Béjar for the entire Christmas holiday. He was wrong, however, about one thing: Pablo did not have time to read *Robinson Crusoe* during the stay. In fact, he only got through the first few pages, so preoccupied was he with the thrilling discovery of true friendship and true love. The port at Vallejera did not reopen until the new year, practically the end of the vacation—a fateful vacation in the life of Pablo Martín Sánchez.

That Christmas Eve of 1899, after the midnight mass—known in Spain as *la misa de gallo*, the "rooster mass"—the two boys left their hiding place behind the balustrade and went to find the rest of the crowd from the inn.

"Where did you run off to?" Julián asked his son.

Pablo gave no answer. His eyes were shining with a glow Julián had only seen once before: the day, now long past, when he found him shivering at Plaza de Santo Domingo in Madrid. The four actors, the livestock dealer, and the newlyweds decided to prolong the night a bit, so the group returning to the inn was reduced to Julián, Pablo, Doña Leonor, Robinsón, and the traveling salesman, who spent the whole walk trying to convince them of the benefits of Palleschy Ointment, a surefire cure for chilblains. When they had nearly arrived back at the inn, Robinsón whispered in Pablo's ear:

"Look, see that house down the side street? That's the Gómez house. That window up there is Angela's room."

Pablo looked up.

"Of course," Robinsón added casually, "Our attic skylight is just across from her window."

Pablo had a hard time falling asleep that night. He tossed and turned in bed, unable to slow his mind down. At his side, Julián snored in deep slumber, his head topped with a nightcap with a tassel at its tip. The bell of a nearby church, probably San Juan Bautista, marked the passage of the hours with its metallic clang. Two bells, three bells, four bells...and when the church bell marked five, Pablo was still awake, still obsessing. It was as though Angela's eyes were staring at him from the interstices of sleep, enormous and unsettling. He finally got out of bed and exited the room on tiptoe, without bothering to put on a pair of slippers. He ascended the attic stairs and pushed on the door, which squeaked in protest at being forced into action at such an ungodly hour. He walked toward the faint glow of the skylight and sat in a chair that was directly below it, as though someone had placed it there intentionally. He opened the window and stuck his head out, receiving a gust of icy wind and a light dusting of snowflakes that quickly melted on his face. The Gómez house was just across the way, and he easily identified Angela's bedroom, as Robinsón had indicated. Her window was no more than four yards away, and he could see the light coming from behind the closed curtains. Maybe she can't sleep either, thought Pablo. Suddenly, as if in response to his thoughts, a voice spoke behind him:

"She always sleeps with a light on."

Pablo jumped in his seat, tipping it over and falling to the floor with a clamor.

"Sorry!" said Robinsón, unable to contain his laughter. "I didn't think you'd come back up here."

"I almost died!" Pablo stuttered.

"From surprise or from falling?" Robinsón asked, sarcastically.

"From both, I think."

And they both smiled in the darkness.

"You like Angela, don't you?" Robinsón asked.

"I don't know," replied Pablo, blushing. "I guess so."

"Well then we better be careful from now on."

"Why?"

But Robinsón was already dragging the trunk that had given them cover the night before and placing it under the skylight.

"Here, hop aboard," he said, without answering his friend's question. From up on his watchtower, he repeated, "She always sleeps with a light on."

"You said that. Why?"

"Because she's afraid."

"Afraid of what?"

"The dark, I think."

"How strange."

"You won't believe it, but it happens to me too sometimes. But you know what my papa says?"

"No, what does he say?"

"That only brave people can be afraid. People who don't feel fear can't be brave, because brave people are the ones who know how to overcome their fear."

The two boys sat in silence, staring at Angela's glowing window and trying to understand the deep meaning of these words, until the cold made their teeth chatter.

"Come on, let's go back to sleep, the sun's coming up," Robinsón yawned. "And if I was you, I'd forget about Angela, unless you want her cousin to make mincemeat out of you."

But there are times in life when there's nothing to do but jump into the meat grinder and see what happens.

PABLO DID NOT SEE THE GIRL in the blue dress again over the next few days, despite spending long hours watching her window from the inn's attic. Robinsón accompanied him, replacing him when his legs fell asleep or when he had to go to the toilet. But Angela did not appear to want to be seen behind her curtain. They also did not see her in the street, or at the Nativity Mass, or at the New Year's party at the Casino Obrero. They did, however, see her father, always dressed in the colonial style, with his long sideburns that went all the way down to disappear under his shirt collar. They also saw her mother, and two of her older sisters, and even her cousin Rodrigo Martín, who shook his fist at them from a distance. But Angela did not appear anywhere, as though, following the fleeting encounter at San Juan's, the earth had mysteriously opened and swallowed her down. So New Year's Day came and went, and with the new year came the end of the vacation, and with the end of the vacation came an improvement in the weather, and the roads were finally cleared so that the inspector and his son could once again climb onto Lucero's back to continue their route beyond the port of Vallejera.

"Tomorrow will be our last day here," Pablo said to Robinsón on the eve of Epiphany.

A thick silence filled the attic, which neither boy dared break.

"You know what?" said the innkeeper's son, scratching his arm. "The path to my hideout is clear now. We can go tomorrow, if you want..."

Pablo could not keep his eyes from lighting up.

"But before that, you have to pass the test, of course. The friendship test."

"What do I have to do?"

The question floated in the air for a few seconds.

"We have to each tell a secret and swear on our blood that we'll never tell anyone else," Robinsón said finally, taking a pocketknife from his pocket. "You first."

Pablo looked at the pocketknife and felt a squirming in his belly. It was time to show that only those who feel fear are truly brave. They were sitting facing each other on the trunk, and night had fallen a good while ago, although some twilight filtered in through the skylight from the unclouded sky, making silvery glimmers appear on the polished blade of the knife. The pregnant cat rubbed up against the boys' legs, seeking warmth or petting. After a few seconds that passed like hours, Pablo took the knife with a trembling hand, without really knowing what to do with it.

"This is the first time you've ever done this, huh?" Robinsón asked in a whisper.

Pablo nodded yes.

"Give it back then. I'll go first."

And, taking the pocketknife in his left hand, he made a tiny cut on the tip of his right index finger. A dark drop of blood appeared almost immediately.

"Now you," he said, offering Pablo the knife.

Pablo took it back, pressed the blade into the tip of his right index finger and closed his eyes. He breathed deeply, and when he looked again, the blood was already starting to flow from the cut.

"Press your finger to mine," Robinsón said, "And now swear that you'll never reveal my secret to anyone."

"I swear I'll never tell anyone," said Pablo, pressing his finger firmly against his friend's.

"And I also swear that I will never tell your secret to anyone," replied Robinsón, and he then put his finger in his mouth.

Pablo did likewise and tasted the sour-sweet flavor of blood, his own and another's.

"Now the secrets," said the boy from Béjar.

So the boy from Baracaldo told him that he had no sense of smell, that for him a rose and a fart smelled exactly the same, and a rotten egg had the same odor as freshly mown grass, which is to say none at all. This appeared the very height of mystery to Robinsón, and he answered with a confession equal to the circumstances: he told him that Juan, the altar boy, had found a tin full of photographs of naked women in the sacristy.

"When he showed them to me," he said, "I stole one of 'em when he wasn't looking. Want me to show you?"

Pablo had never seen a naked woman before and he nodded his head yes, feeling excited and fearful all at once. Robinsón went to the corner of the attic, where there was a big pile of broken-down furniture, and returned with a photograph. In the faint light of the tallow lamp Pablo saw the image of a young woman with small, firm breasts, gracefully leaning against a ladder, her arms in the air, her gaze lost in the distance, her face engraved with a smile, and her crossed legs meeting at an ample triangle of pubic hair. Only her feet were covered, with shiny boots and wool socks leaving just a bit of her calves visible. Pablo was stupefied, fascinated by this image, which would linger in his mind for a good long while, while Robinsón smiled as he watched Pablo's face.

"Alright, that's enough," he said after a moment. "If you look at it too long, you wear it out."

And he went back to hide the photo among the old furniture in the corner. When Pablo was able to speak again, he asked, "Have you done it before?"

"Done what?"

"The friendship test."

"Yes, once."

"Who with?"

Roberto Olaya peered out through the skylight at the starry night, and turning again to look at Pablo, said, "With Angela."

THAT YEAR THE THREE MAGI DID not bring him a tin drum or lead soldiers, but Pablo was about to receive a far better gift. He got up early on Epiphany and let his father take advantage of the holiday to sleep as late as he wanted. He washed his face in the washbasin without making a sound, dressed in a hurry and went downstairs to have breakfast with Robinsón in the kitchen, as if he were another son of Don Veremundo and Doña Leonor. The night before, he had passed the friendship test, and today he was going to receive his reward. He could still feel a slight sting in his fingertip, but that was nothing compared with his excitement at the prospect of visiting his new blood brother's hideout. Their breakfast was milk curds sprinkled with cinnamon and Robinsón's father's old war stories. Between spoonfuls, the innkeeper told them about his glory days as a syndicalist:

"I was in the Second International," he explained proudly, stretching the truth a bit. "My comrades from the textile syndicate sent me to Paris, to represent the Spanish workers. There I met Friedrich Engels and I was there when they chose the first of May as International Workers' Day."

When they were done with breakfast, they slipped a hunk of bread and a big piece of chorizo sausage into a leather pouch in case they got hungry later. They put on gloves and woolen caps and left the inn. The sun was emerging from behind the snowy mountains, announcing a splendid day. They walked down Calle Flamencos and, when they reached the side street that led to the front door of the Gómez house, Pablo lifted his eyes, almost instinctively, with the vain hope of seeing Angela. And it happened. It actually happened. Just at that very moment, the window opened and a head covered in unkempt, chestnut-brown hair peeked out. Seeing the two boys, she shouted:

"Roberto! Hey, Roberto! Where are you going?"

"To my hideout," he replied.

"Can I come with you?" the girl asked.

Robinsón looked at Pablo, but he didn't need to ask.

"Of course! We'll wait for you at the fountain."

Five minutes later, Angela arrived at the fountain and Pablo lost his composure. She had pulled her hair back into a ponytail, and her skin was so brown that she almost looked like a mulatta; for this reason the gossips of Béjar murmured that she was the fruit of an illicit affair between her mother and some Caribbean negro. Of course, no one dared say such a

thing in public, lest it reach the ears of Don Diego Gómez, lieutenant colonel of the Spanish army in the war overseas, who would be apt to blow
his top and challenge the insulting party to a duel.

"Angela, this is Pablo," said Robinsón. "Pablo, this is Angela."

"Hi," they both said at once, their voices mingling in the air. The girl
smiled as Pablo stared.

"Where have you been?" Robinsón asked. "I haven't seen you all
vacation."

"I had the flu," Angela replied with aplomb, unaware that influenza
would kill more than ten thousand people in Spain that year. "Today is the
first day that my parents let me out. Shall we go?"

They crossed the village and set off on the road to Candelario. The
snow was starting to melt, though ice patches still remained in the shadows. After five minutes, before arriving at the textile factory of Navahonda
where Don Veremundo had lost his left hand, they abandoned the main
road and went down through a steeply sloping oak grove. It smelled of
moss and wet earth. Shortly, they arrived at the Cuerpo de Hombre River,
blocking their way.

"It's frozen," said Robinsón after exchanging a look with Angela,
which Pablo could not interpret. "I don't know if it will hold our weight,
we should go one at a time. Do you want to go first, Pablo?"

Pablo had never crossed a frozen river before—he didn't even know
a river could freeze. But he didn't want to seem like a chicken. He swallowed and nodded.

"Be careful not to slip. Try to go in a straight line and keep looking
ahead," Robinsón advised.

Pablo put one foot on the frozen surface and noticed how the layer of
ice strained under his weight as the water flowed beneath it. If I pull my
foot back now, he thought, I won't dare put it there again. So he stepped
forward with his other foot, and found himself crossing the Cuerpo de
Hombre, with fear and wonder, like Peter walking on the water to meet

Jesus. For a moment he felt like he was losing his balance, that the world was trembling beneath his feet, but he lifted his arms and steadied himself like a tightrope walker, recovering equilibrium. He then proceeded forward with determination and reached the other side. Smiling, he turned around, but his smile froze on his face: Robinsón and Angela had disappeared. Then, upstream, someone shouted his name, and turning he could see his two fellow adventurers crossing a small wooden bridge, laughing hysterically. Pablo stayed put until the others reached him.

"Don't take it wrong," said Robinsón, wrapping his arm around Pablo's shoulders. "It's just the initiation ceremony you have to go through before you can visit my hideout. Right, Angela?"

"Yeah. And you were lucky," she said to Pablo, smiling. "I tried it in the springtime, and I got sopping wet."

"Let's go," said Robinsón, setting off walking. "We're almost there."

They went a few yards and then stopped. Their mouths emitted a dense fog, like the smoke from the textile factories that were the lifeblood of Béjar. The sun came filtering between the branches, and Robinsón approached an oak with a thick, majestic trunk, and pointed toward the top. There, hidden among the branches, Pablo could make out a little wooden house.

"My hideout," said the innkeeper's son, proudly, as he walked to the other side of the tree, where a series of branches, cut and nailed to the trunk, served as a ladder. He climbed up these steps and pushed on the door of the hideout. Angela went up behind him, with the agility of Tarzan, who a decade later would replace Robinson Crusoe as the idol of intrepid and adventurous children. From on high, they signaled to Pablo to join them. The tree house was small, but there was enough space for the three of them. The floor was covered in straw and there was a candleholder hanging from the ceiling with a stub of a candle. In a corner there was a sackcloth blanket, a brass canteen, a box of matches, a damp book, and a few basic tools, slightly rusted: a hammer, a handsaw, a box of nails.

"My papa built this place when I was born," said Robinsón, "Before he lost his hand."

It was cold, but they covered themselves in the blanket and gradually warmed up.

"What do we play?" Angela asked.

"We can tell jokes," Robinsón suggested, "Here, I've got one. What do you call a girl with a frog on her head?"

"Mmm, I don't know," said Angela.

"Me neither," Pablo gave up.

"Lilly!" said Robinsón, triumphant. "What vegetable is a dog that smells good?"

"Easy," said Angela, sticking out her tongue. "Collie-flower! My turn. Here's a joke they tell in Cuba, that everybody thinks is funny: On the street corner I met a little man. I pulled down his pants and ate the best part."

Pablo and Robinsón found this hilarious, without even waiting for the punch line. When they stopped laughing, Pablo asked, "Alright, alright, who was he?"

"A banana!" Angela shouted, giggling. "Here's another one: what do you call a deer that can't see?"

"No eye-deer!" Robinsón replied, laughing. "My turn: between two big rocks there's a little man who talks—who is he?"

"Mmm, I dunno," said Pablo.

"Umm, the wind?" Angela ventured.

"No, a fart!" Robinsón shouted, buckling over with laughter.

"Nasty!" Angela shouted, giving him a smack on the head. "What about you, Pablo? Don't you know any jokes?"

Pablo sat thinking for a moment, and finally said:

"As long as you keep me captive, I exist, but the moment you set me free, I die. What am I?"

Seeing that the others had no guesses, he gave the answer: "A secret."

And so they spent the morning, goofing around and telling jokes, playing jacks, "I Spy," and slaps, which helped them keep warm. Then they climbed down from the tree house and played the stick game *hinque*, and hide-and-seek, and even found a patch of wet earth where they drew a hopscotch and Robinsón showed that he was unbeatable at hopping on one foot. Then they went to the ravine to find some snow and built a snowman, but this turned into a snowball fight, and the half-built snowman ended up in a crossfire of laughter and snowballs hurled with too much accuracy. They looked for frogs on the bank of the frozen river and searched for mole and rabbit dens. When they got hungry, they went to get the canteen and filled it with water from the river, after breaking the ice with the hammer, and ate the bread and chorizo. Angela ate heartily after ten days of nothing but soup, eggs, and milk mixed with sherry. Then they went back up to the tree fort, lay down on the straw, and started telling stories. Robinsón told a scary story that he had heard from Juan the altar boy. Angela told stories from her life in Cuba, and her old Caribbean accent crept into her speech here and there. Pablo told them about the Lumière Cinematograph that he had seen in Madrid, which left them speechless. But, little by little, fatigue got the best of them and they fell asleep. When Pablo woke up, Angela's head was resting on his chest, as if she were trying to hear his heartbeat. When she noticed that he was waking up, the girl looked at him with her enormous eyes. She lifted her head and was about to say something, but then thought better of it and pressed her ear back down on the left side of Pablo's chest. Then, she sat up and asked Pablo the strangest question he'd ever heard in his life:

"You're a vampire, huh?"

Pablo didn't know what to respond, because he had never heard of vampires.

"You don't know what a vampire is? Vampires don't have hearts, that's why they have to drink blood. And you don't have a heart."

"Yes I do," said Pablo, disconcerted.

"No, you really don't. I was listening and I don't hear anything. You're a vampire."

"I'm not a vampire!"

"Yes you are, Pablo. Look, put your hand here," said Angela, pointing to the left side of his chest. "Feel that? No heartbeat. But you can feel my heartbeat, see?" she said, bringing Pablo's hand to her chest.

"What the heck are you jokers doing?" Robinsón asked, waking up.

"Um, nothing," said Pablo, taking his hand quickly from Angela's chest.

"Pablo doesn't have a heart," said the girl. "He's a vampire. Look, feel."

"Well I'll be. You're right," Robinsón said in surprise.

"You guys are crazy," said Pablo, standing to his feet. "I'm not a stupid vampire!"

"Yes you are," Angela insisted, "but it doesn't matter. I like vampires."

Pablo felt a burning in his stomach, as if his guts had burst into flames.

"I do too have a heart!" he shouted, putting his hand again to the left side of his chest. Feeling nothing, he grimaced and left the tree house.

"Pablo, don't go!" shouted Angela and Robinsón.

But Pablo was already running toward the river. After crossing the wooden bridge, he arrived at the road to Candelario and went running back to the inn, where he went directly up to the attic and hid in the trunk—not knowing that he was imitating a common vampire behavior. Enclosed in there, he could finally hear his heart, pounding with his distress. But when he searched for it with his hand, he discovered that it wasn't beating on the left side of his chest, but on the right.

Pablo did not know then, nor would he ever know, but this surprising fact was due to a congenital abnormality that produces a lateral inversion of the internal organs, which years later would be named *situs inversus*, although it has been documented since at least the seventeenth century, with the death of an old soldier in the army of Louis XIV; upon opening his chest the doctors found his heart on the wrong side. This abnormality has a high correlation with another very rare condition: anosmia.

6

Miguel García Vivancos learned the mechanic's trade at the age of 13, before emigrating to Barcelona in 1909, where the death of his father left him orphaned. He was a founding member of the group Los Solidarios, started in 1922 along with Buenaventura Durruti, Francisco Ascaso, and Juan García Oliver, among others. After the attack in August 1923 on the Bank of Spain in Gijón, he was arrested and incarcerated for three months, but he managed to foil the police investigations and was set free. He then departed for Paris with several members of the group and was given the task of procuring weapons for the rebellion against the dictatorship of Primo de Rivera. After having negotiated with a Belgian trafficker for the purchase of rifles and ammunition, he participated in the operation at Vera de Bidasoa on 7 November 1924.

International Dictionary of Anarchist Militants

AFTER A FEW RATHER QUIET DAYS in Marly, Pablo returns to Paris on Friday, October 24. As the train passes through Amiens, he peers through the window of the rear car to see if the man with the medical bag is in the station again. He does not see him, so he goes to the aisle to check the rear platform. Not a trace. He returns to his seat and waits to arrive in Paris, watching the landscape go by. A few drops fall, but the sun manages to climb through a crack in the wall of clouds, resulting in an unusually beautiful sight: a rainbow, glowing with the deceptive clarity of illusion. For a moment, Pablo believes he is in the fields of Castile, riding Lucero and clinging to his father's belt. He closes his eyes and falls into a reverie for several minutes. When he opens them again, the sad spectacle of the shabby houses of the Parisian outskirts—known, with a certain disdain, as the *banlieue*—snap him out of his daydream and back into reality. Arriving with a little time to spare, he decides to stop by home before going to the print shop. When he enters, something catches his attention. The mattress is still on the floor, and there is a suitcase in the corner that was not there when he left for Marly. And on top of the table, a hollow gourd, the one Leandro the Argentine giant uses for his yerba maté. Only then does he discover a note on the bed cover. It is from Robinsón and reads: "Pablo, the police are looking for Leandro. Seems Dubois ratted him out. They searched his house and put out a warrant for his arrest. It's best if he hides out here for a few days, don't you think? In any case, the nut says that if they don't want him here in France, he'll come with me to participate in the revolution in Spain. I will see you soon and tell you when things have settled a bit. Robinsón." Pablo lets out a sigh and tears the note into little pieces.

But the weekend will be calmer than expected. First, because Sébastien Faure is traveling in Switzerland, giving a series of talks trying to demonstrate the nonexistence of God. Second, because the Committee of Anarchist Relations has still not obtained the paper for the broadsides. And third, because Robinsón and Leandro are going on a trip, of which they inform Pablo that evening when they go to find him at La Fraternelle. That is, when Robinsón shows up with a giant man dressed in a black trench coat to his knees and a wide-brimmed hat that hides his face.

"You coming from a costume party or what? Pablo asks mockingly when he sees them appear at the door.

"Che, don't you know that the cops are looking for me? The old man reported me."

"Yeah, I know. But dressed like that you'll attract even more attention. You'd have a better chance of going unnoticed dressed as a woman."

But Leandro is in no mood for jokes, something's not right with him. Exhausted, he flops onto a chair, which cannot sustain the burden and collapses like a house of cards.

Pablo and Robinsón try to contain their laughter as they help him to his feet.

"Look, Leandro, what you ought to do is hide out for a few days here in the hovel," Pablo proposes as he gathers up the pieces of wood and tries to put the chair back together, "or, better yet, you should take a little visit to the country, you could come with me to Marly and hide out in the villa. What you cannot do is keep on wandering around Paris like this."

"That's what I said on the way here," Robinsón interjects, "in fact, we were thinking about heading south together tomorrow. The Committee has asked me to go supervise the recruitment down there. Seems they don't much trust the guy responsible for recruiting in Bordeaux, Bayonne, Biarritz, Saint-Jean-de-Luz, and the other towns and cities in the region."

"I thought the ones they didn't trust were you and your buddies from the Lyon syndicate. That's a lot of distrust to make a revolution, don't you think?"

"Well, situations like this one involve certain risks."

"And what do you think, Leandro?" Pablo asks.

"About what?" asks the Argentine, a bit distracted.

"About traveling, about what's going to happen?"

"It suits me just fine. That way I won't have to keep wearing these clothes. Anyway, I'm sick of this damn city, it can go to hell."

The impetus for Robinsón's trip was a telegram that the Committee of Anarchist Relations received earlier this week, sent from Bordeaux, in which the comrades of the Syndicate of Spanish Expatriates stated that they would not be continuing the work of propaganda and recruitment they had been assigned: "Sorry, cant handle matter. Saint-Jean-de-Luz person taking over. Name Max Hernández. Sncrly Syndicate Spanish Expatriates." The Group of Thirty was not at all pleased with this news. They met yesterday at the center on Rue Petit and made the decision to send someone to the region to supervise the work performed by this Max, who went by the sobriquet "El Señorito." And it was Robinsón who drew the short straw.

"That's enough talk," said Robinsón. "Tomorrow we're going to get some southern sun, it's already frightfully cold here. That way we'll give dear Pablo a little peace. Even he needs some privacy from time to time," he adds with a wink.

But that will not be until tomorrow. Tonight, the three of them will be sharing the hovel. Or, to be more accurate, the four of them; it's starting to be too cold on the landing for Kropotkin, poor fellow.

THE WEEKEND PASSES UNEVENTFULLY AND, AS if trying to contradict Robinsón, the weather is generous to the Parisians, offering them an unexpected warm spell for Saint Martin's feast day. Everyone seems to agree that they have to take advantage of it, and they go out en masse, wearing expressions of confused joy and rare good humor. At the Jardin de Luxembourg, a few young women are even trying to sunbathe, emulating Coco Chanel, who introduced the fashion of tanning two years ago by visiting Cannes with a garish bronze look. But Pablo knows that all this is an illusion, the calm before the storm. Not only because news of torrential rain keeps coming from the north of the country, but also because he has a premonition that his life is about to take an unexpected turn.

On Monday morning, Pablo goes to the Gare du Nord to take the train toward Lille. The sky has already gone overcast, and before getting into the train he buys *Le Quotidien* from a newsboy, one of the many who have proliferated in Paris since the end of the Great War. The front page shows a photo of the English swimmer Zetta Hills, who is planning to swim across the English Channel, wearing a specially designed rubber suit. There is also a headline stating that a professor from the University of Barcelona, Dr. Dualde, has been arrested in Gerona for reading *Le Quotidien*. Inside there is an article by Unamuno, in which, after fiercely attacking the Spanish Government and Primo de Rivera, he finishes by announcing his partici-pation in a meeting at the Salle des Sociétés Savantes (together with Blasco

Ibáñez and Ortega y Gasset), which he hopes will be attended by everyone with enough dignity to lift up their voices against Rivera's Directory, which is the shame of old Europe and of the whole world. But Pablo still has not finished reading the article when he gets into the rear train car and sits in the window seat, at the very moment when Vivancos, thin as a rail, passes on the platform wearing a monocle and a top hat. Their gazes meet, and Vivancos makes a barely visible gesture, but an eloquent one. Better if we're not seen together, he seems to say, and he makes off for the first class cars, because he knows that the best way to be left alone is to wear fine clothes and appear wealthy.

Pablo tries to read Unamuno's article, but he can't concentrate. It does not get any easier when, at the stop prior to Amiens, two policemen board the train, packing pistols and billy clubs. "Routine inspection," they say as the train starts moving again. "Please have your papers out." They go to the front seats and start inspecting IDs, followed closely by the conductor. Seconds later, Vivancos appears in the third class car, with a suitcase in hand, and gestures to Pablo to follow him to the rear platform, where no one can hear them. In fact, they can barely hear each other over all the racket.

"Listen," says Vivancos, his smooth voice dissimulating his anxiety, "those gendarmes give me the creeps. Take this briefcase. If anything happens to me, get off in Amiens and give it to El Galeno, the guy you passed the letter to the other day. He will be there waiting on the bench next to the cafeteria. Then get back on the train as though nothing happened. You have your papers in order, right?"

"Yes, of course."

"Great. Now go back to your seat and act normal."

Pablo returns to his seat with his guts in a twist and a burning object in his hands. That makes two hot items in the last two trips, first a letter and now a briefcase. Fortunately, once again he doesn't know what it contains, because if he did, he would be pale with panic. He places it on the floor, hiding it under his seat. From where he sits he can see the rear platform, but not Vivancos, who is outside his field of vision leaning on the rail. When the gendarmes reach his seat, Pablo greets them with the best French accent he can muster.

"*Espagnol?*" the younger one asks, after looking at his ID.

"*Oui, bien sûr,*" Pablo replies.

The young officer looks at him suspiciously and whispers something to the other gendarme, who shakes his head, pointing at the bottom of the ID card where it says that Pablo Martín Sánchez resides in Marly-les-Valenciennes. This appears to allay their suspicions, but just to be sure they call the conductor over. He drags his feet as he approaches. Stuttering, he explains to them that this is a regular passenger who makes this trip every week. The younger gendarme seems perturbed, but he gives Pablo back his papers. They continue on with their inspection, and when they are finished they exchange a few words without coming to an agreement. Finally, the younger one returns to the head of the train, while the other takes a cigarette from a case, lifts it to his mouth and walks to the rear of the car and goes out onto the platform. From where Pablo sits, he can see the gendarme's surprise to discover Vivancos, as he removes the cigarette from his mouth and asks him something, perhaps requesting his documentation. The policeman makes another surprised face and speaks again, with a gesture that says, "Follow me, sir." For a moment, nothing happens. Then he lifts his hand to his belt in a threatening manner. Suddenly a fist emerges into view and strikes the gendarme square in the face, knocking him down. When he manages to get up, he takes his pistol out and begins firing, not toward where the fist had come from, but toward the rear, into the distance, where Vivancos has tumbled to the ground after jumping from the moving train.

The nearby passengers shriek at the sound of gunshots. They crowd the aisles and peer out the windows. A woman at the rear of the car faints, and her companion shouts for a doctor. The young gendarme comes running, pistol at the ready as his colleague reenters the car with blood gushing from his nose. "Stop the train!" he shouts, cursing the fugitive's mother and family, but the train is already braking for its arrival at the Amiens station. When it comes to a halt, the two gendarmes leap down. "Don't let anyone off this train!" shouts the younger cop, as he starts running back to the spot where Vivancos disappeared. The other one goes to the cafeteria to ask for a towel and some water to clean up the blood, and a few passengers, half-frightened and half-intrigued, take advantage of his absence to get off the train, ignoring the stuttered warnings of the train agent, who tries in vain to remind them of the police's orders. Someone gets out a bottle of pastis to try to revive the woman who fainted. Others whose final destination is Amiens take the opportunity to leave, not wanting to waste their whole morning over the incident. Pablo exits the train just in time to see El Galeno leaving the station. Feeling as though he's carrying a ticking time bomb, he runs after him without thinking twice. He finds him in the street hailing a taxi, sidles up to him and puts the briefcase on the ground. El Galeno looks at him sideways, and either recognizes him or at least understands the situation. He picks up the briefcase and gets into the taxi, which speeds away. When Pablo returns to the train, the crowd is still in a frenzy, though the young woman has finally regained consciousness. The injured gendarme returns from the cafeteria with two pieces of cloth stuffed into his nostrils, and orders everyone back onto the train. He makes a telephone call to the gendarmerie of Amiens to request backup. His colleague returns drenched in sweat, boots covered with mud. "*Rien de rien*," he says.

Within a few minutes, five more gendarmes arrive. Two of them get on the train and give the engineer the go-ahead to continue the journey. From this day forward, Pablo Martín Sánchez will have a record with the French police, as will another eighty-three passengers, all as innocent as him. Or perhaps slightly more innocent, you might say, considering that the briefcase Pablo has just passed to El Galeno contains fifteen thousand francs intended for the illegal purchase of contraband firearms.

As the train is leaving Amiens, the first thunderclap resounds. Shortly, a furious rainstorm erupts.

VI
(1900–1904)

"SEE, I DO HAVE A HEART!"

After his discovery, Pablo had returned to Robinsón's hideout to show his friends that he wasn't a vampire.

"Only, it's on the right. Can you guys keep it a secret?"

Angela and Robinsón both kissed their thumbs, ceremonially tucked between their index and middle fingers, by way of promise. Then all three walked home in silence, saddened to think that they would soon be separated.

"Don't worry," Pablo said, trying to cheer them up as they parted ways, "we'll see each other again soon, I promise."

Indeed, he was true to his word; the Martíns would return to Béjar many times. In fact, from then on, every time Julián had to inspect the south of Salamanca, he went out of his way to make sure they spent a few days at Don Veremundo and Doña Leonor's inn, knowing that Pablo had forged a strong friendship with the innkeepers' son. So, after that life-changing Christmas, Pablo managed to keep the fires of friendship and true love burning. Like a bellows, every new encounter stoked the bonds between Pablo, Robinsón, and Angela, despite Rodrigo Martín's attempts to keep his cousin away from the two "suckers," and despite the changes inevitably taking place in the boys as they approached adolescence. The first time the Martíns returned to Béjar, Robinsón was no longer wearing his leg brace, although he was still noticeably limping, and Angela was half a hand taller, and from this new height she carried on observing everything with those big, sparkling eyes. At the next encounter, Robinsón had learned to smoke cigarettes and Angela to play the flute—so while the former was practicing his inhalations, the second was working on her exhalations, and torturing her friends with her efforts to emulate the Pied Piper. On another occasion, Robinsón had abandoned his adventure novels for books on the natural sciences, was diligently practicing the art of drawing, had taken up the hobby of raising silkworms, and had a water spaniel named Darwin. For her part, Angela had developed a new way of speaking, interjecting a "tay" between every syllable, and when she saw Pablo she said: "Hetayllotay Patayblotay, it'stay beentey suchtay atay long-tay timetay." At a subsequent visit, inspired by history's first Tour de France, Don Veremundo had bought a bicycle and Robinsón had become an avid cyclist, because when he rode a bicycle no one noticed his limp. Over a couple of days, he taught Pablo to ride, as well as Angela—though hidden from her parents and the parish priest, who had condemned all indecent women who would put a bicycle seat between their legs. The last time the inspector and his son arrived in Béjar astride Lucero, in February 1904, Angela's breasts had grown, and so had Robinsón's mustache, though he was in no hurry to shave it, preoccupied as he was with becoming a vege-tarian, a fashion that was timidly starting to catch on in Spain.

"I don't want to eat animals anymore," he explained to his friends. "Did you know that there have been people who didn't eat animals throughout history? Pythagoras, for example. And Jesus Christ himself! But my parents force me to eat it. They say I'm growing and I'll end up scrawny if I don't eat meat. One of these days I'm going to get away from here, and then they'll see, mark my words."

"I've heard," Angela interjects, "that there are places where people eat human flesh."

"That's called cannibalism," said Pablo, playing the know-it-all. "Not long ago, an English ship wrecked on an island in the South Pacific, and the cannibals killed the whole crew and ate them with potatoes. So if you're gonna become a vegetarian, Robin, I think I'll become a cannibal."

"Laugh all you want," said Robinsón, whose facial hair was on its way to being worthy of his nickname, "but I read in *Blanco y Negro* that meat isn't good for your heart."

"What do I care, since I don't have one ..." Pablo replied, and all three laughed at their shared secret.

"But do animals have feelings?" Angela asked, intrigued by the topic.

"Of course they do!" replied Robinsón. "Humans are descended from frogs! Do you know that a fish in a fishbowl can die of sadness if it's forced to live alone? But all you have to do is set a mirror next to the bowl, and it will be happy—"

"No way!" said Angela and Pablo in unison.

"I swear it's true!" Robinsón protested.

When Pablo left Béjar on Lucero's back for the final time, he had just turned fourteen, and the old mule was suffering beneath the load, which was growing heavier every day. Julián had already warned that sooner or later they would have to put an end to this itinerant life and settle down in Salamanca with Mother and little Julia, and find Pablo a job that would help contribute to the family's expenses, because tough times were ahead. In nearby Valladolid there had just been an altercation between the Civil Guard and a group of women who were protesting to demand "bread and work," which ended with the forces of order firing on the crowd, resulting in several women injured, two dead, and an increase in the proletarian resentment against the *Benemérito Instituto*.

But things took an unexpected turn for the Martíns when, on the road from Béjar to Ciudad Rodrigo, they were caught unprepared by a terrible storm. The sky suddenly darkened, and the purple clouds fiercely discharged all their ammunition, with terrible timing—just as Pablo and Julián were crossing a desolate scree field, without even a measly tree for shelter. The inspector kicked the old mule, but Lucero just brayed indolently. Soon, they thought they saw a distant light, and they made their way toward it, abandoning the main road. However, the surging waters of a creek cut off their way. Julián tried to look for somewhere to cross it, but the storm doubled down its forces and he could barely see farther than twenty or thirty yards.

"Hold on tight," he said to his son, and he whipped Lucero to prod him across the current.

The mule resisted at first, with prophetic stubbornness, but he finally gave in to the whip's insistence. The creek was rising by the second, and at the deepest point the water reached Lucero's crop. A lightning bolt lit up the sky and struck quite nearby, to judge by the swiftness and volume of the thunder. The frightened old mule tried to rear up, lost his balance, and the torrent swept him away, taking Pablo and Julián along with him.

"To the bank! Get to the bank!" shouted the inspector, but his son's leg had gotten stuck in one of the stirrups and the current was taking him downstream with the mule. Julián reached the far bank just in time to see Pablo's terrorized face lit up by a flash of lightning as the water swallowed him. The father ran alongside the torrent, hoping to see his son's head emerge again, while the sky went on wringing itself like an inexhaustible sponge, and Lucero brayed and kicked, trying to resist the force of the deluge. Suddenly, the stirrups came loose from the animal's body and, after a few moments of uncertainty, Pablo managed to come to the surface.

"Over here!" shouted Julián, stepping back into the deluge and stretching his hand toward his son. As Pablo reached the riverbank, the old mule ran out of strength and was swept away forever. Father and son collapsed in an embrace beneath the rain, bodies still tight with fear, and bid farewell to that companion who had traveled with them to every village in Salamanca.

"We came this far, Lucero," Julián mused as he watched the mule disappear from sight. And they carried on toward the distant light.

The rains lasted a whole week and caused flooding in much of the country. Some towns were literally submerged beneath the waters, many harvests were lost, several boats sank in the Cantábrico, and the press called the storm a "horrendous national tragedy." By the time the storm had abated,

Julián had already rented a tubercular little shanty on an anemic back alley of Salamanca (to use the sickly adjectival style that Miguel de Unamuno used to describe the urban complexion of the city), where the whole family would soon settle in. He sent Pablo to Baracaldo, and during the Easter vacation they made the move. Of course, he would have to continue traveling from town to town, inspecting schools all over the province, but at least he would have his loved ones nearby and a home to return to from time to time, as well as the two months of the year that he had to spend in the provincial capital in order to inspect the more than fifty schools in the city and its outskirts. He was also thinking toward the future, sure that, with the new trend in automobiles, any day now he wouldn't need the mule to get from town to town. And he wasn't all that wrong.

Pablo was the one who had the hardest time adapting to the situation. They had been eight years of itinerancy, eight years of continuous pilgrimage, eight years of wandering from place to place. Not just any phase, it was a phase of formation, in which the child discovers the world and turns into a person. The adventure on the Castilian Plateau had not cured the boy's anosmia, of course, but it had caused him to grow up like a nomad, and now the sedentary life caught him off guard. Of course, he did enjoy the daily company of his mother and little sister Julia, the familial warmth and the comforts of a decent home, but his happiness was bittersweet, because deep down he missed the travel and freedom of life on the road. Also, Béjar now seemed very far away, although the actual distance was only seventy kilometers. And Béjar meant Robinsón. And Robinsón meant Angela, and her big brown eyes. But there was no time for lamentations: within a few days of moving to Salamanca, Pablo found a job at the newspaper *El Castellano*, which at that time was directed by the blind poet Cándido Rodríguez Pinilla. His job: errand boy. His hours: from three in the afternoon to midnight, seven days a week. His salary: one peseta per day, plus a hot meal. But before starting work, he asked his father for money for a train ticket to Béjar to say goodbye to his friends.

He arrived at the station at midmorning and crossed the city at a full sprint, climbing the steep grades toward Calle Flamencos. At the door to the inn he encountered Don Veremundo, enjoying the spring Sunday and calmly smoking a cigar.

"Well, who do we have here?" muttered Robinsón's father. "And what about Don Julián? He didn't come with you?"

"No, sir, this time I came alone," Pablo responded, panting from exertion.

"I say, little man," he smiled and blew a smoke ring, "you going to stay a few days?"

"No, I'm headed back to Salamanca this afternoon. We have a home there now, with my mother and sister."

"Yes, so I've heard. But I suppose you didn't come here to chat with me ... Everyone's at mass, including Roberto and the Gómez girl."

"Thank you, Don Veremundo. Have a nice day," said Pablo, and he took off running toward the church of San Juan. When he arrived, the most impatient of the faithful were starting to exit the church, including Robinsón and Doña Leonor. The moment they saw each other, the two friends leapt on one another and began punching each other's backs, as if in a boxing match. But in mid-embrace, the inspector's son was left paralyzed: Angela emerged from the church, along with her family. Their eyes met and Pablo's heart skipped a beat. Robinsón turned around just in time to give Angela a signal before her cousin Rodrigo noticed him: he brought his two index fingers together, forming an inverted V, and said to Pablo, "Come on, let's go."

"What about Angela?"

"We'll see her at the hideout, don't worry."

Half an hour later, the three were reunited in the tree house.

"So I don't know when I'm going to be able to come back," Pablo was saying, after explaining his new situation. "But I'll write to you, you can count on that."

"What address are you going to put on the envelope? Roberto Olaya's hideout, first door on the left?" Robinsón joked.

"So you're going to be a journalist?" Angela asked, with admiration.

"Who knows?" Pablo replied mysteriously, unaware that he was going to spend more time with a broom than with a pen in his hand.

"I'm going to be a spelunker, like Robin," said Angela.

"That's impossible," said Robin.

"Why?"

"Because there are no woman spelunkers."

"Well, I'll be the first, you'll see."

And so they spent the rest of the morning making future plans, as a person ought to do when they have their whole life in front of them.

"Alright boys, I have to go home to eat," Angela finally said. "What time does your train leave, Pablo?"

"Six thirty."

At six thirty, Angela was at the station to say goodbye to her vampire. When the train started rolling, she walked along outside Pablo's car, while Robinsón remained standing on the platform waving his hat with enthusiasm.

"Angela," said Pablo, sticking his head out the window.

"What?" she asked, adjusting her stride to keep up with the train, which was gaining speed with every passing moment.

"I'll come back for you," he said, as she started to run. "Will you wait for me?" he added desperately, as the train left Angela behind, her eyes sparkling for the last time in the distance.

The last thing Pablo saw was the way she stopped at the end of the platform, nodding her head in affirmation, her arms now fallen against her body, unaware that a wise man once said that while the wind carries words away, gestures are the devil's affair, and that there can be more difference between two silent yesses than between a yes and a no uttered aloud. But what wise men say is not always true.

AT THAT TIME, SALAMANCA WAS A city in the grip of vice and poverty, with narrow, winding streets, squalid tenements often lacking running water, inhabited by people and animals in unsanitary cohabitation, with scant light and an outdated sewage system, all of which made the provincial capital one of the places with the highest mortality rates in all of Spain. Salamanca was publicly known as Little Rome or Little Athens for its monumental buildings and its famous scholastic past, but in private it was known as the City of Death, because of the periodic outbreaks of smallpox, diphtheria, or influenza, in addition to the frequent violent deaths that scandalized the populace and filled the pages of the newspapers. It's no wonder, then, that the editors of *El Castellano* were besieged with the most horrifying stories imaginable, although the city's newspapers, under pressure from the ruling class, had agreed to undertake a campaign of hygienic and moral sanitization.

Pablo started working in the middle of April of that year, 1904. The first day, before he left home, his mother kissed his forehead and tried to cheer him with the worn-out refrain that work gives a person a sense of dignity. But the Martíns' firstborn did not take long to understand that, while it's true that work brings a sense of dignity, it also brings a sense of mortality: on his very first day on the job, he would meet two peculiar people who would suddenly launch him into adulthood. If he had read Freud, who was in vogue at the time, he would have been able to put names to these people: the first would have been called Thanatos, the second Eros.

With the maternal kiss still wet on his forehead, Pablo departed from home, crossed the train tracks, and reached Alamedilla Park, one of the most disreputable spots to be found in turn-of-the-century Salamanca. The office of *El Castellano* was located on the main floor of number 28, Calle Zamora, next to the Plaza Mayor. Stepping through the door, Pablo was taken aback by the great hubbub and the asphyxiating tobacco smoke, which irritated his throat and eyes. The center of operations was a large space full of tables, chairs, wastepaper baskets, and spittoons, presided over by a stuffed owl mounted at the corner desk, monitoring everything with bulging glass eyes. There were about ten people in the room, talking, smoking, writing, or typing. For a moment, no one noticed Pablo's presence.

"You, boy, come here," he finally heard a voice calling him. Through the thick smoke, a bald man with a tawny face beckoned him closer.

"My name's not 'boy,'" said Pablo as he approached the man's desk, making a ploy for respect.

"Ah, no? Then what is your name, might I ask?"

"Pablo. Pablo Martín."

"Very well, Pablo Martín, listen up: from now on you're going to forget your name. We're going to call you 'boy' around here, you got that, boy?" the man barked, his cigar swinging up and down with each syllable. His eyes were red and his pupils were dilated as if he had taken belladonna.

"Understood," the newcomer finally replied, resolving to compromise with the new authority. After all, it wouldn't do to get fired on the first day.

"That's what I like to hear. Alright, now take this article to the printer. You know where that is, don't you?"

Pablo shook his head.

"You'll have to pay attention."

"I'll show you the way," said a female voice from the next desk over.

The bald man turned toward his colleague, a curvy woman with her hair coiled like a snail upon her head: the director's secretary.

"If you wish, Obdulia. But don't get distracted. I know your ways," said the man, winking at her.

"You're such a swine," Obdulia replied. Rising from her seat, she motioned to Pablo to follow her.

"Thank you," said the boy as they exited the office.

"No, thank you," Obdulia replied offhandedly, winking. Apparently winks came cheaper than day-old bread around here.

The print shop was located on the same street, Calle Zamora, in a cramped basement with no natural light occupied by two old Marinoni machines working at full tilt. The scene was completed by a plate, a guillotine, a stereotype, a glazing machine, several rolls of paper, galley prints, proofs, casts, and a diminutive man in coveralls with inkstained hands. Obdulia introduced the two of them, shouting over the noise of the machines. Pablo gave the printer the article, and then he and Obdulia made their way back to the writing office, where they found some of the writers in a heated discussion:

"No, damn it, it's not my turn today," said one.

"Mine neither. Last night I got stuck with the mess at the brothel," said another.

"I've been on the beat all week," said a third.

"So let's draw straws and be done with it," said the one with the dilated pupils, grabbing four pencils from his desk. "Whoever draws the shortest one has to go."

But it was he who drew the short pencil.

"Fine," he said, disappointed. "But I'm taking the boy."

And that is how Pablo came to gaze into the face of Thanatos. At the bottom of the river Tormes, near the Roman bridge, two corpses had just been found in a state of putrefaction, their feet lashed together and attached to a small anvil. When the representatives of *El Castellano* arrived, the Civil Guard were trying to disperse the onlookers, who were clogging the bridge trying to get a closer view. At the center of the action, a little boat equipped with a winch was raising the bodies of a man and a woman.

"Suicide or homicide?" the journalist asked a guardsman after identifying himself as a writer for *El Castellano*.

"We don't know, we don't know," the officer replied.

"Surely it was a suicide. The way things are these days, people prefer to die with their lungs full rather than live with their stomachs empty.

Write that down, boy," he said to Pablo, tossing a pebble into the river. But Pablo wasn't listening, hypnotized as he was by the two bodies swinging in the air. Although they were in an advanced state of decomposition, there was no doubt that they belonged to a young man and woman, practically adolescents, to judge by their clothing. And the most curious thing was that they appeared to have died consoling each other, as rigor mortis had left them locked in an eternal embrace. Suddenly, Pablo had a vision of Angela and he felt an acute fear of never seeing her again. At that moment, he promised himself that one day he would return to Béjar to marry her.

But the day's emotional trials were far from over. As they made their way back to the newspaper office, night had already fallen and the electric lamps recently installed in the city center gave it an unearthly appearance like a theater stage. Pablo and the journalist arrived at Calle Zamora, but they stopped in front of number 11, at the door to the Casino de Salamanca:

"Come on, let's have a drink before we go back to hell," said the writer.

"I don't have any money," replied Pablo.

"Don't worry, it's on the house. Manolito! Two cognacs!"

"Right away, Don Ferdinando!" shouted the waiter.

This is how Pablo learned the name of the writer with the dilated pupils.

"Here, boy, a toast to your first day on the job, and your first pair of corpses. Cheers!"

"Cheers," muttered Pablo, lifting his cup, and he let the golden liquid burn its way down his throat.

"Of course," Ferdinando warned him as they left the casino, "watch out for Obdulia. She has a thing for youngsters." And he emitted a cackle that echoed against the paving stones.

Back at the office, Pablo soon found out that what he said was true. Obdulia kept staring at him in a manner that anyone with more experience would not have hesitated to call lustful. She lowered her eyelids and shot looks at him through the cloud of cigar smoke. He could be emptying a wastepaper basket, or grinding coffee, or filling an inkwell; always in the corner of his eye he was aware of the persistent gaze of the voluptuous secretary of Don Cándulo, the blind poet who directed the newspaper from his home. When the clock at City Hall rang nine, the writers stood up in unison, as if spring-loaded, and leapt for their hats and coats to go to dinner.

"Boy, you stay here with Obdulia. If any urgent news comes in, you come tell us," Ferdinando said to Pablo. "We'll have the waiter wrap up our leftovers for you." He let out another of his cackles.

"Don't take it the wrong way," Obdulia said once they were alone. "Deep down they're not bad guys, you'll see. Why don't you come over here and tell me about your afternoon?"

Pablo approached and started to tell her about the suicides of the river Tormes, but soon the woman pressed her finger to his lips and hushed him. Then she caressed his face, his neck, and his head. She stood up and dragged him to the back of the room, where a green glass door led to the "Management Office," as indicated by the large gothic letters meticulously painted on it. The last thing Pablo saw before disappearing through the door was the glassy eyes of the stuffed owl, which appeared amused to see Señorita Obdulia up to her old tricks. "Come along, my little pepper sprout," whispered the secretary, in a tone attempting sweetness but which left Pablo feeling only dazed, "I'm going to teach you how to manage a newspaper."

Without turning on the light, she closed and locked the door and led her prey to the sacrificial altar. Then, as if in a dream or a nightmare, Pablo found himself fondling two extraordinary breasts, while a viscous tongue entered his mouth and turned it to an aquarium full of fish. His taste buds discovered the metallic flavor of a stranger's mouth, and his undershorts were suddenly too tight. A hand slid into his trousers and pulled out his virginal telescope, crowned by a red, swollen glans that appeared to be watching everything with a Cyclopean eye. A petticoat fell to the floor, sighs caressed the air, a wooden table creaked under the strain, and Pablo found himself being absorbed by a mythical creature, half jellyfish and half woolly goat. Finally, he found his body erupting as an electric shock ran from his feet to his head. He bit his tongue to keep from shouting out loud, and his strength abandoned him like Samson after his haircut.

Outside the door, breathing on the windowpane, Eros looked on, buckling with laughter.

7

"From Paris and Soissons new details have been received regarding the purchase of weapons in France. A few weeks ago, the police were informed that a Spaniard who worked as a barber in Amiens had made an agreement with various workers employed in the Red Zone in the recovery of war materiel, negotiating with them the purchase of any weapons and ammunition they might find. Two Spaniards were detained; their stated names were Serrano Blas and Rodríguez Juan, and they declared that they acquired these munitions in order to sell them on the black market in Morocco. However, the police believe that these individuals are working for Spanish revolutionary forces."

El Pensamiento Navarro, 16 November 1924

TODAY IS THURSDAY AFTERNOON, AND IN Marly, Pablo is recovering from three days of hard work. Torrential rains have destroyed the small dock on the pond, inundated the better part of the garden, and torn away some of the house's roofing tiles, causing leakage indoors. Luckily, by Tuesday it was already starting to clear up, and Pablo has had a few rainless days to fix the damage. Also, the work has helped him keep his mind off what happened on the train, although he hasn't been able to resist the temptation to go into town every night to see if he hears anything. But the name Vivancos doesn't come up in any conversation or in any newspaper, so no news is good news, as his father used to say. It is already starting to get dark, and Pablo, after bathing in the pond and changing his clothes, walks down the road toward town with the idea of calming the rumbling in his stomach. He'd like to eat something hot and have a good glass of red wine—back home he would have called it "tinted wine," *vino tinto*, which goes to show that reality depends on the lens through which you view it. What Pablo doesn't know is that this metaphor will soon come back to haunt him.

Madame de Bruyn's bistro is full of people at this hour, mostly workers who have finished their work day and are making sure to get in some elbow exercises before they go home to find dinner ready. Most are crowded around the bar, trying to stretch out the best moment of the day. But at the back of the place there are two large wooden tables, with benches on both sides, where a few diners with no one to make them dinner at home are stuffing their faces with the delicious fare that Madame de Bruyn serves for a song.

One such dish is this gargantuan *hochepot* the waiter has just placed in front of Pablo: a stew of various meats and vegetables, identical to the plates in front of the two guests sitting opposite and talking enthusiastically. At first, the typesetter pays them no mind, busy as he is allaying his stomach's urgent complaints, but as his hunger subsides, his brain starts working and a few words filter in through his ears. One of them is "*Amiens.*" Another is "*police.*" And when the term "*anarchistes espagnols*" is muttered, Pablo almost chokes.

The two diners don't know all the details of the story. All they've heard is that yesterday afternoon near Amiens the police thwarted an illegal arms deal, catching two men *in flagrante delicto* trying to buy a war arsenal from a couple of workers from Reims. When they were arrested, they claimed that they wanted the weapons to sell them as contraband in the war in Morocco, but the police suspected that it was more likely part of a plot hatched by Spanish anarchists. In this, they are onto something: the two men detained near Voyennes, on the road between Amiens and Reims, are Juan Rodríguez, aka "El Galeno," and Blas Serrano, his constant companion, assigned to the task of obtaining weapons for the revolutionary expedition.

The fatal outcome was set into motion last week, when El Galeno received Pablo's handoff of the letter assigning him the task of procuring weapons. Within a few days of setting about the task, he found the first offer—a Belgian war salvager had just found a German cache near Damery containing several rifles, cartridges, and grenades in decent condition. They were prepared to sell the rifles and grenades at the requested price, and would throw in the cartridges for free since some were damp and the powder was probably bad by now. Rodríguez contacted Vivancos and they decided to make the buy immediately so as not to lose this great opportunity. So Vivancos traveled to Amiens on Monday to pass El Galeno the money, an operation that the police very nearly thwarted and which only succeeded because Pablo happened to be on that train. Some people thought that the gendarmes' intervention was not a coincidence, and the rumor gained momentum yesterday afternoon, when a patrol unexpectedly showed up at the planned site of the swap.

The meeting had been planned for seven o'clock in the evening. Rodríguez and Serrano were leaving Amiens in a meat truck, a rattling Renault. They arrived half an hour early at the meeting place near Voyennes. The salvager, a man of few words, so blond that he looked like an albino, arrived twenty minutes later. With a gesture he invited them into the truck, and they accompanied him along a dirt road leading into the woods. Soon they reached a house in ruins. El Galeno and Blas Serrano exited the vehicle and entered the house behind the albino, who lifted a few planks from the floor and opened a trapdoor to the cellar. Down there, in crates, there were over one hundred Mauser rifles, several dozen grenades, and a few boxes of ammunition. They assessed the inventory by flashlight and handed over the corresponding money. Without saying a word, the three men started loading the truck. It took several trips. When they stepped out of the house with the final load, the police were waiting for them, pistols drawn.

Pablo still doesn't know the whole story, but he leaves his stew half-eaten and asks for the check. The diners' conversation has ruined his appetite, because he suspects that the arrests in Amiens have a direct relationship with the Committee of Anarchist Relations, and more specifically with the man on the train to whom he has passed an envelope and a briefcase in the past two weeks. Pablo doesn't know what the former said, or what the latter contained, and he still doesn't even know the name of the man with the medical bag, but if it turns out that he's one of the two who have just been arrested, and he ends up singing, Pablo's future looks very dark indeed. The police took his information on the train, and it's possible that his name is already circulating around the commissariat. But one needn't be so pessimistic! It's also possible that the man from the train won't squeal, that he'll take the fall. Because, as the two diners at Madame de Bruyn's bistro said, the arrested men claimed that they wanted the weapons to sell on the black market in Morocco. You'll just have to wait until tomorrow, little Pablo, when you get back to Paris and can learn more about what has happened. For the time being, though, everything seems to indicate that the authorities are hot on the heels of the revolutionary movement.

That night, Pablo has trouble falling asleep, and not only because of indigestion brought on by the stew—though that doesn't help. When he finally manages to fall asleep, nightmares disturb his rest. He dreams of railroad tracks beneath his feet and leading off into infinity. At the start of the journey, he sees a sign reading "Salvation, after all." He starts to walk, first slowly, then faster and faster. Along the way he sees more signs: "Hurry. Salvation is in your hands," and "Not much farther. Salvation is up to you." Pablo starts to run. Another sign: "Salvation, 2 km ahead." Then another at 1 kilometer, then 500 meters; he's choking, he can't take it anymore; then 100 meters, then 50, 20, 10 ... Then there is a sign that says "We're sorry, Salvation has been postponed," and he turns just in time to see a train coming straight at him. He wakes up screaming and drenched in sweat. He goes out of the house and washes his face in the pond. The nearly frozen water jolts him, but still he goes back inside to try to get some sleep, suspecting that troubled times are coming. In this, he is correct: he will never return to Marly or to the pond house.

THE NEXT DAY, PABLO FALLS ASLEEP as soon as he boards the train. He makes the transfer at Lille and again falls into a stupor. After a while, the conductor wakes him up, the same man who defended him against the suspicions of the gendarmes. Pablo feels tempted to ask him what happened at the end of the other day, but at the last moment he bites his tongue. Arriving in Paris, he buys a newspaper as soon as he exits the Gare du Nord, but before he can even read the headlines, he is attacked by a wiener dog who sullies his trousers with mudprints.

"Damn it, Kropotkin!" Pablo complains, waving the newspaper. "What are you doing here? Where's Robinsón?" he asks, fearing the worst. Kropotkin makes to pounce on him, but this time Pablo manages to dodge the attack with a pirouette worthy of a toreador. "What is it? What do you want?"

Kropotkin runs off toward a narrow street that disappears behind the station. Pablo follows, but by the time he turns down the little street, the dog has disappeared from sight. When he's about to give up and turn around, he hears someone talking to him, though he still sees no one.

"Psst, Pablo, over here!" It's Robinsón's voice, and it seems to be coming from behind a pile of trash at the end of the street, next to a half-built house. On approaching, Pablo sees a head poking out through a window on the second floor, half-camouflaged by a wooden scaffold. The head belongs to Robinsón, with Kropotkin by his side.

"What are you doing up there?"

"Shut up and get up here, quick! Climb the right side of the scaffolding."

Pablo climbs up to join his friend, who is acting like a conspirator, which, truth be told, is exactly what he is.

"What's going on?" Pablo asks as he climbs through the window. The building looks like it's been under construction for a long time, as if the work had been interrupted due to lack of funding. Inside, someone has set up a bench made of a plank and two bricks.

"A lot of things," says Robinsón, making room for Pablo on the bench.

"Good or bad?"

"Mostly bad. We're going to have to proceed with more discretion now."

"Oh, great. They've caught Vivancos, haven't they?"

"No, hell no. He almost killed himself jumping off the train, but he managed to get away. Of course, the Committee thanks you for everything you did. Too bad it won't amount to anything."

"Why not?"

"Because they nabbed Rodríguez."

"Who?"

"El Galeno. The guy you passed Vivancos's briefcase to."

Robin tells Pablo the whole story of the detention of the barber from Amiens and his companion.

"But do you know if they ratted?"

"Everything seems to point to no, that they're holding up under the police pressure and maintaining the story that they wanted the guns to sell in Morocco. But we don't know how long they're going to hold up. So you can imagine how morale is in the Committee."

"Yeah, I can imagine."

"And on top of all that, there's the matter with the telegram."

"What telegram?"

"The one that arrived yesterday from Spain. From Barcelona, to be precise. It said, 'Everyone to the border. Revolution about to explode.'"

"No way."

"Yeah, you can imagine the situation. We tried to have a meeting at the International Bookstore, but word of the telegram had gotten around, and we couldn't fit everyone there. In the end we held the meeting in the basement of the Labor Exchange. Some people wanted to head off to the border right away, but others said that the telegram was very suspicious, that our people in Spain would never have been so explicit. Finally, after a tremendous debate, the cautious voices won out, and this morning Jover and Caparrós left for the border to find out what's going on firsthand. Jover went to Portbou and Caparrós to Irún. From there they'll send a coded telegram to inform me of the situation."

"What's the code?" Pablo asks, more automatically than out of real curiosity.

"My, don't you have a lot of questions, Pablito!" Robinsón replies with a mischievous smile. "In theory, only those of us on the executive committee are supposed to know the code. Actually, it's really simple: if the telegram says 'Mama stable,' it means that the comrades on the interior aren't yet ready to start the revolution; if the message is 'Mama serious,' it means that they are ready and that we need to go to the border and wait to start the incursion, and if the telegram says 'Mama has died,' it means that the revolution has started and we need to go to Spain as soon as possible."

"Slim pickings," is Pablo's terse reply. "How do you plan to have a revolution without weapons?"

"Well, the cock-up in Amiens doesn't mean we don't have any weapons. The Committee has its own reserves, and there are still a few unspent rounds. If it comes down to it, we can risk trying to bring the thousand rifles that Los Solidarios bought in Eibar after hitting the bank in Gijón. They're stored at a secure location at the port in Barcelona. But it would be best if we didn't have to play that trump card yet. It seems that there's a Spanish gun runner here in Paris who's prepared to sell us a decent arsenal, and tonight we're going to approach Vicente Blasco to ask him for money. Also, the comrades in the South are working on obtaining equipment. That's one of the things I've been talking about with Max lately."

"Who's Max?"

"The guy in charge of propaganda and recruiting in the southwest. They call him 'El Señorito.'"

"I see. So the Committee's suspicions about him haven't been confirmed?"

"Well, he didn't give me such a bad impression, despite his aristocratic pretensions and his cocaine habit. Got to admit it's the best disguise to keep the police from thinking he's an anarchist, no doubt about that. Also, the way things are, we can't afford to be too fussy about it. Beggars can't be choosers."

"Well, I don't like the sound of it. I met a guy in Barcelona during the Tragic Week; he claimed to be a sculptor named Emilio Ferrer, but turned out to be a police informant." Pablo sighed, rubbed his eyes. "Hey, so whatever happened to Leandro?"

"He stayed in Saint-Jean-de-Luz. He says he's fallen in love with the village, but I have a feeling the real story is he's fallen in love with a village girl."

"And what's happening with the broadsides we were supposed to print?"

"I have no idea. I suppose that Teixidó still hasn't rounded up the paper."

"So if the telegram comes saying you have to go, you're going to leave without the posters."

"That's true. Hey, couldn't you print them with the paper at the printing shop? Just black out the letterhead." Seeing Pablo's sour face, he says, "Hey, don't take it like that! Anyway, will we be seeing you tonight at Blasco and Unamuno's shindig?"

"We'll see, Robin, we'll see," says Pablo, disappearing through the window to head to La Fraternelle, as Kropotkin wags his tail and lets out a pair of woofs: bye-bye.

VII
(1904–1906)

WHEN THERE'S NO BREAD, CRACKERS WILL do. If bread is passion, crackers are mere stand-ins: some are given to gambling, others to drink; some devote themselves to God, some to lost causes. Pablo was inclined to writing love letters and cultivating revolutionary ideas. The former grew ever more daring and received ever more fervent responses. The latter, ever more dangerous, were nurtured as the work at *El Castellano* put him in touch with "the reality of the present moment," as Ferdinando put it, in a stupendous pleonasm. It was there, on Calle Zamora, as he was emptying wastepaper baskets and trying to dodge Obdulia's attentions, that he first began to hear about workers' rights and about the law that had just been passed in Spain guaranteeing a day of rest on Sundays.

"Maybe someday it'll apply to us," said Fulano, the optimist.

"My eyes will never see the day," said Mengano, the pessimist.

"Well, the *Times* doesn't come out on Sundays, and it hasn't led to any weeping or gnashing of teeth," Zintano chimed in on a hopeful note.

It was also in the office of *El Castellano* that Pablo became familiar with the ideas of communism and followed Russia's 1905 revolution with great interest, from the terrible events of Bloody Sunday to the October Manifesto and the creation of the first soviet in Saint Petersburg, presided over by a young Leon Trotsky.

"Those Russians have lost their minds," muttered Mengano, who was a Carlist.

"They're more dangerous than you think," warned Zutano, who was a liberal.

"We'll see if that revolution doesn't spread through all of Europe," said Fulano, who was elated. But the revolution went up in smoke; while the tsar had agreed to create a constitutional government, the truth is that he reserved for himself the power to veto any law and limited the vote to the most privileged classes. This was enormously disappointing for Pablo, who had been rooting for the revolutionary side as he followed the Russian conflict with the eager anticipation of Spanish soccer fanatics or people who obsessively track the changing fortunes over the stages of the Tour de France. Feeling dejected, he traded his red jersey in for a black one the day Ferdinando appeared at 28 Calle de Zamora and spoke to him about anarchism.

"Berkman has been released from prison," said Ferdinando, his spotty cheeks stretching with the syllables, as he entered the room and made his way through the cigar smoke. "Do you know who Alexander Berkman is, boy? No? Then grab a pencil and paper, this *New York Times* article needs to be translated and my eyes are tired."

Alexander Berkman had become one of the most famous American anarchists after his failed attempt in 1892 to assassinate Henry Clay Frick, the bloodthirsty executor of the program developed by Carnegie Steel Company to repress its workers' strike; now, after fourteen years of incarceration, he had been released onto the street, having turned into a veritable icon of the libertarian left, whose most radical arm advocated tyrannicide and regicide as the straightest path to their objectives. If you don't believe me, just ask the twenty-fifth president of the United States, William McKinley, assassinated at the start of the century by the anarchist Leon Czolgosz.

"You know what Berkman says, boy? Before being a man, he is a revolutionary, and the only love a revolutionary can allow himself is the love of humanity. And do you know the first thing he did when he got out of jail? He ate the bouquet of flowers his girlfriend had brought him."

But it would not be until the young Catalan Mateo Morral got into action that anarchism started showing up on the front page of all the national newspapers, coinciding with the Royal wedding between Alfonso XIII of Bourbon and Victoria Eugenia Julia Ena de Battenberg on May 31, 1906. It was a year of great political and social upheaval in Spain, as was noted by the famous writer and countess Emilia Pardo Bazán, who reflected apocalyptically in an article published in *La Ilustración Artística*: "Goodbye, 1906! Year of calamities, attacks, eruptions, floods of hot lava and muddy water, fires, shootings, murders, bombs exploding from Russia to Madrid, earthquakes that destroyed entire cities, typhoons and hurricanes that devastated whole regions, crop-destroying droughts, death duels, crime waves, suicides, daily train crashes and derailments, shipwrecks in which hundreds of people drowned, and dire threats of leprosy and oriental plagues. The only thing missing was war." It was precisely one such calamity, which Pardo called "horrifying," that was about to derail the whole nation.

One hundred foreign reporters and more than fifty Spanish journalists had registered with the Ministry of Governance to cover His Royal Highness's wedding, and among them there was a fox in the henhouse: a certain Ferdinando Fernández, of *El Castellano* in Salamanca. Accompanying him was the young Pablo Martín, who had become his faithful sidekick since the day they attended the dredging of the suicides from the river Tormes. It had been ten years since Pablo had set foot in the capital of the kingdom, but he still distinctly remembered that morning in the spring when he had visited another kingdom, as Maxim Gorky called it: the kingdom of the cinema. He also had etched in his memory the face and name of the newspaper hawker who had accompanied him on his adventure: Vicente Holgado. What he didn't expect was that, in a city of more than half a million people such as Madrid, he would meet him again.

The other thing that Pablo didn't expect was that Madrid would so enthusiastically welcome the arrival of a new animal in its menagerie, soon to become the king of the jungle: the automobile. When they arrived at the capital on Wednesday night, on the eve of the wedding, he still had time to see a few motorized coaches. He had heard talk of them in Salamanca, but he had never seen one, and now handfuls of them were circulating around the capital. Of course, only the most comfortable classes could allow themselves the luxury of acquiring a Panhard 12 CV like that of the Duke of Alba, but even a proletarian conscience like Pablo's could not help being fascinated by those roaring monsters of gleaming metal.

"Close your mouth, boy," said Ferdinando, "You look like you're about to eat the world."

The spectacle came to an end when they arrived at the filthy inn that Obdulia had reserved for them on Calle de Barcelona, just a stone's throw from the Puerta del Sol, where the Royal Procession was to pass on its way to the Church of Saint Jerome.

"Four smackers for this fleahouse?" Ferdinando complained when the proprietress showed them the room, decorated with moisture damage on the walls and furnished only with two rickety cots and a beat-up bedside table.

"Yes, sir," said the woman, in the lisping accent of Cádiz. "But if you don't want it, don't worry, there are plenty of people standing in line to find lodging for tonight."

Indeed, according to official estimates, the city's temporary population had risen by more than one hundred thousand souls for the occasion of the royal wedding, and the hoteliers of Madrid, nobody's fools, had raised their prices without thinking twice. Fortunately for Ferdinando and Pablo, *El Castellano* was footing the bill. Ferdinando declined the dinner option and took Pablo to eat at the Café Pombo, on the nearby Calle Carretas, famous for its bookstores, jewelers, and the good wine of its taverns, but especially for its orthopedic shops, with their windows decorated with jointed arms, wooden legs, glass eyes, artificial dentures, and every kind of gizmo imaginable for the replacement of human body parts. The gas lamps lent an inviting glow to the café, which was formed of a small central salon and five separate rooms, which nevertheless were connected to each other by old stone archways. In one of the reserved rooms, a few Spanish journalists were making bets about the location the anarchists would choose to attack Alfonso XIII, because word had gotten around that Madrid was infested with men ready to blow the royal carriage sky-high and make good on the failed assassination attempt exactly one year before in Paris, where a bomb disguised as a pineapple nearly cut short His Majesty's life as he was leaving the Opera. Some even said that the city was full of graffiti announcing the attack and that on a tree in the Retiro someone had carved the words "Alfonso XIII will be executed on his wedding day," illustrating the threat with a skull and crossbones. It's no wonder, then, that security measures had been reinforced like never before, and that the Royal Guard had been augmented with staff from the army, the Civil Guard, and the mounted police, in addition to the English detectives that the bride's family had brought in specifically to protect her.

FERDINANDO APPROACHED THE GROUP OF REPORTERS who were raising their bets as they emptied their glasses, and he greeted a few men he knew. Then the server came, and Ferdinando ordered a plate of sherried kidneys, two steaks with potatoes, and a bottle of red wine.

"Eat up, boy, we're going to need to gather our strength. Tomorrow's going to be a bitch of a day," he told Pablo as he started laying into his plate of kidneys. By the time dinner was finished, the journalists had gotten into an argument between monarchists and republicans that seemed ready to end up like the Haymarket Riot. The most excited was a sickly looking lad who was vociferating and jutting his neck out like a plucked duck while threatening his interlocutor with a felt hat, the band of which had been replaced by a plaited cord, giving it a most ridiculous appearance.

"C'mon boy, let's get out of here, the ambiance will be better over on Ceres."

At that time, the Calle de Ceres was the haunt of Madrid's cheapest prostitutes, frequented by the lowest lowlife, the gutter bohemia of destitute painters, alcoholic musicians, and desperate writers who dedicated Alexandrines to it, in bad meter and worse taste:

> The hookers along this street so quiet
> Show their witchy faces in the streetlamp's light
> And the streetlamp girds them in milky white:
> Here's La Pepa, La Moños, La Rosa, and La Maruja.

The street would end up being razed to clear the way for the Gran Vía, but at the start of the century it was still a gathering place for the purebred *Lumpenproletariat*. Ferdinando and Pablo crossed the Puerta del Sol, glutted with people admiring the public lighting or trying to get a last-minute ticket to the royal bullfight; then they took Calle de Arenal, where a few laborers were still working to get the platforms ready for the next day; and they wandered to the Plaza de Santo Domingo, the same square where Julián Martín had left his son ten years before while he took the test to become a provincial inspector.

"I know this place," said Pablo.

"Don't tell me you've already visited the paradise of Calle Ceres," said Ferdinando with surprise, pointing toward a side street a little way ahead.

"No, I mean the square. I came here with my father when I was a boy."

"And he didn't bring you to see La Moños? What a thoughtless father!" exclaimed the reporter, shaking his head. "Come on, let's go. We don't have all night, boy."

"No, you go on ahead. I'd rather just walk around," Pablo excused himself.

"Listen, if you don't like tuna, I know a place where you can get some sausage," said Ferdinando, making an obscene gesture. Seeing that Pablo was no more tempted by this prospect, he bid him farewell: "Fine then, suit yourself, boy. I'm gonna get my rocks off, can't babysit you all night."

Emitting his signature cackle, he disappeared into the dusk.

Pablo went to sit at the same spot he had all those years ago. The square hadn't changed much, but the evening shadows gave it a ghostly appearance. How I'd like to go back in time, thought Pablo, standing up, and be here again listening to that man announcing the Lumière Cinematograph. It was a splendid night, and he started walking aimlessly, letting his legs take him where they would as his mind traveled to the past, to visions of trains in motion, hoses shooting jets of water, horses running races, and parents feeding their happy sons. The festive streets were hung with garlands and paper banners, resting in the dim light, saving their vibrancy for the next day. There were people camped in doorways, to the chagrin of the night watchmen, who brandished their nightsticks impotently, aware that they were far outnumbered. At eleven o'clock, Pablo decided to return to the hostel. It wasn't difficult to find Puerta del Sol, where there was still some hubbub and various unfortunate visitors dragging suitcases around and looking for shelter for the night. Then he took Calle Carretas and, passing in front of the Café Pombo, he again saw the passionate young journalist who a few hours before had been jutting his neck out like a duck and ridiculously threatening his interlocutor with a felt hat. The man took a watch from his vest pocket, looked at the time, and headed off toward Atocha, looking hasty and suspicious. Without really knowing why, Pablo followed him for a while, keeping his distance, until he saw him disappear into a building. He approached the entrance and his jaw dropped as he saw the marquee announcing: "IMPERIAL COLISEUM. The most perfect cinematograph. Followed by the remarkable works of the illusionist Canaris, with the beautiful Madame Albani and the ventriloquist Sanz." The ticket cost fifty céntimos, half of what it had cost ten years before, and there was a late show at half past eleven.

"One, please," Pablo asked, completely forgetting the man he had been following.

When the lights went down, a pair of newlyweds appeared on the screen, arriving at a hotel. But it wasn't just any hotel, it was a mechanical hotel, where everything worked as if by magic: the suitcases went up to the rooms all by themselves, the clothing folded itself into the dresser drawers on its own initiative, brushes polished shoes in the absence of a bootblack, and logs traveled single file like a train toward the fireplace, to burn in a fire lit by self-striking matches. Without a doubt, the illusion was better than anything a magician could do with mirrors, false floors, hidden pulleys, or invisible strings, and Pablo was astonished to see how the cinema had evolved in those ten years: no longer content to represent reality, now it was trying to change it. Then he remembered that a few months beforehand he had heard people in Salamanca talking about a movie depicting a man who traveled to the moon, and he wondered if the Lumière brothers' invention was an window to the future, a machine that could travel forward in time to see what future generations would see.

When the projection came to an end and the illusionist Canaris leapt to the stage planning to hypnotize a volunteer from the audience, Pablo got up and left the room, certain that no prestidigitator could possibly outdo what he had just seen. He was so wrapped up in his thoughts that, leaving the hall, he almost ran headlong into two men who were talking next to the entrance. One was the sickly, pale journalist he had been following, and the other was a sturdy, swarthy young man, one of those handsome ruffians who take women's breath away. He immediately looked familiar to Pablo. It had been many years, but there was no doubt about it—that defiant gaze, that swarthy complexion, that cocky tone in his voice...

"Vicente Holgado?" he asked.

The two men abruptly cut off their conversation and the one whose name had been called lifted his hand to his flank, indicating he was ready to answer with a Browning semiautomatic.

"Who's asking?" spat the man in the felt hat, stretching his neck out like an ostrich.

"Pablo Martín, from *El Castellano* in Salamanca," replied Pablo in his most professional tone, not taking his eyes off Vicente Holgado.

"Holy shit," said the latter, recognizing him. "Don't tell me you're that snot-nosed kid who went with me to see the Lumière Cinematograph."

"No, I was the snot-nosed kid who *took* you to see the Lumière Cinematograph," Pablo corrected him with a smile.

Vicente hesitated a moment, looking back and forth between Pablo and the sickly hack reporter like someone plucking daisy petals or flipping a coin to divine whether his love was requited. It must have come up heads, because he squinted at the exit and said, "Let's go. Come with us."

And that's how Pablo first came into contact with the anarchist movement, although it would take a few more hours for him to discover just how dangerous it could be. For the time being, they merely took him to a tavern on the corner and made the perfunctory introductions. The journalist from Café Pombo was working for the *Diario Universal* and had been a writer for *Tierra y Libertad*, the anarchist weekly founded in Madrid by Juan Montseny, aka "Federico Urales," a teacher from Reus who had become a syndicalist, journalist, and frustrated dramaturge. Vicente, for his part, said he was unemployed and didn't care to give any further explanation. Nevertheless, it was he who paid for the wine, with a wrinkled 100-peseta note that elicited protest from the waiter.

"Either you accept Quevedo or you make the round on the house," said Holgado, scowling and leaving the bill bearing the famous writer's countenance on the bar. Then, speaking to Pablo, he apologized: "I'm sorry, but we have to go. Tomorrow's going to be an intense day. I hope to see you again sometime, somewhere."

"I hope so too," said Pablo. And he meant it.

When he arrived back at the inn, Ferdinando was snoring profoundly, as only innocents and madmen can.

The next morning, they woke up early, washed in the grimy basin, and went to Café Pombo to breakfast on a well-deserved *chocolate de tres tantos*—cocoa, sugar, and cinnamon in equal proportions—as well as a few sweet, greasy churros that fell apart in their hands. Only then did they feel ready to start the work day, which was destined to last until the wee hours of dawn. At the Church of Saint Jerome, where the wedding was to take place, a special booth for journalists had been set up, but Ferdinando preferred to stake out a spot at Puerta del Sol to watch the royal procession pass.

"Weddings are all the same, boy. The interesting stuff is in the street."

In reality, he was annoyed at the thought of going to the church, and he had decided to set up his base of operations right there at the intersection of the four main streets of the wedding parade.

"Look here," he said, taking out a map and tracing an exaggerated figure-8 with his finger. "This is the route the parade will take: Calle Arenal, Puerta del Sol, and Calle Jerónimo going out, then Calle Alcalá, Puerta del Sol, and Calle Mayor coming back. Understood?"

"Understood."

"So here's what you're going to do: I'll wait for you here and you'll follow the royal carriage, writing down everything you see, hear, feel, suspect, or smell. Understood?"

"Perfectly," said Pablo, not mentioning that the last order would be a bit more difficult.

"And if anything out of the ordinary happens, come running and tell me. Got it, boy?"

"Absolutely, Your Highness," said Pablo with exaggerated courtesy, as he set off for Calle del Arenal, happy to get away from the dilated pupils of the domineering Ferdinando.

Passing in front of number 22, he saw a sign that read, "Great success of the voiturette Clément, designed for the highways of Spain. Climbs any hill. Easy handling." This was the dealership belonging to the Santos brothers, pioneers in automobile sales.

Sadly, there was no time to lose, since the correspondents of *El*

Castellano weren't the only ones who had gotten up early: when Pablo arrived at the Marine Ministry, Calle Bailén was already full of people. The shopkeepers had improvised little platforms in their windows for a better view of the parade, and now they themselves appeared to be for sale. The onlookers had also started to congregate on the balconies, and some had set up makeshift lean-tos and awnings, risking their lives to witness the passage of the hemophiliac Victoria Eugenia of Battenberg and the prognathous Alfonso XIII. Finally, at half past nine, the monarch emerged from his palace, flanked by coaches, automobiles, and mounted guards. He was wearing the dress uniform of a captain general and he saluted from the royal sedan with the solemnity of a marionette, accompanied by the *infante* Carlos and his little brother Don Alfonso María. To his right, never taking his eye from the king, rode Don Rodrigo Alvarez de Toledo, first footman to His Majesty, as the unquiet crowd shook their signs and threw hats in the air, shouting "*Viva el Rey!*" One woman fainted, and a child nearly suffocated, but the fate of the nation transcended such trifles. It was ten thirty by the time the future queen's entourage came out from the Marine Ministry. At the time, Pablo was perched on the statue of Neptune, watching Alfonso XIII's stately sedan turn toward Los Jerónimos.

The wedding went without a hitch, although the tension in the air was palpable, like a volcano about to erupt. The church had been combed by security a thousand times, but until the bride and groom said "I do," people were afraid there would be an attack. As if, once they were married, divine grace would immunize them against fire and dynamite! Inside the parish, the cream of the Spanish and European aristocracy had gathered, as well as the highest public officials, from the Archduke Franz Ferdinand of Austria to the Count of Romanones, as well as Maura, Caralejas, and the princes of Belgium, Sweden, Greece, and Portugal. When Victoria Eugenia of Battenberg entered, clinging to the arm of her mother-in-law-to-be, all in attendance stood in unison, as a murmur of excitement traveled among the pews and galleries set up inside the temple. The electric lamps hanging in the great altar appeared to glow more intensely, dazzled by the princess's white gown, fringed in silver and dotted with lilies and orange blossoms. The reverend Cardinal Sancha, Primate of Spain and Archbishop of Toledo, officiated the ceremony, and the fiancés became spouses, until death should have the caprice to part them. When they left the church and started walking down the red-carpeted stairs, the Royal March played for the umpteenth time, and madness swept through the feverish crowd, who stirred and shouted, tossing anything that came to hand in the direction of the royal couple. More than one of the female fans was tempted to take off her petticoat and throw it at the studly king, whose member was rumored to be as long as his sword.

Perched up in a tree, Pablo contemplated the scene from a certain distance, awestruck by the queen's beauty, as she waved her graceful gloved hand at the crowd of admirers, while the sun glinted golden sparkles on the tiara that crowned her wavy coiffure. Suddenly, he felt guilty. Guilty to be enjoying this decadent spectacle, while people were dying of hunger in half the villages of Spain. Guilty for having admired the beauty of a queen who symbolized the might of the powerful and the marginalization of the oppressed. Guilty for working to document this event rather than working to combat it, as the anarchists were doing.

"We are what our father taught us in his free time," he heard an old man behind him saying. "When he wasn't trying to educate us."

For a moment, Pablo thought the old man was talking to him, but when he turned around he saw that the man was blind and babbling. Nonetheless, he started mulling over these words as if they had been said especially for him, and he managed gradually to forget his feelings of guilt. When he snapped to attention, the procession was already turning down Calle Alcalá and starting its way back toward the palace. He jumped down from the tree and mingled into the crowd, advancing in fits and starts to try to catch up with the royal carriage. Reaching the Puerta del Sol, he went to meet back up with Ferdinando, who was yawning in the shade of a coach parked on a street corner.

"What a goddamn hassle, boy," he groaned. "And on top of everything, this sun burning like a thousand devils. You know what? I think I'll walk with you for a while. My knees, feet, and soul are getting tired of standing here."

Together, they went down Calle Mayor, the last leg in the royal procession's itinerary. The troops of the Wad-Ras Regiment formed two impenetrable lines on either side of the avenue, forcing the public to squeeze onto the sidewalks. Two bells rang out from the nearby church of Santa María, drowning out the rumbling of Pablo's stomach, which hadn't received any visits in several hours. Just then, someone collided with them, trying to push in the opposite direction of the procession.

"Whoa there, young man!" creaked Ferdinando, grabbing the youth's arm. "Be a little more careful, pal."

"Let me go!" shouted the lad, wrenching free from the grip, and beneath the brim of his hat glowed the steely eyes of Vicente Holgado.

"What the devil?" he murmured, recognizing Pablo. "Get away from here right now!"

And he continued off in the opposite direction from the procession.

"You know that guy?" Ferdinando asked, clicking his tongue.

"Yes, an old friend," said Pablo, distracted, his mind going a mile a minute.

"Well, your friend has lousy manners, boy. Alright, shall we go on, or what?"

Pablo hesitated for a moment. He observed the royal sedan continuing its path, and King Alfonso XIII waving at the crowd from the window. Then he had a premonition.

"No, Ferdinando. I think it's better if we don't go on."

Taking him by the arm, he led him back the way they had come. The reporter barely had time to protest, because at that instant there was a deafening explosion that made them jump in the air. Broken glass rained down on their heads, and the air filled with smoke, dust, shouts, and whinnies. An intense acidic smell seized the atmosphere and someone shouted:

"They've killed the king and queen!"

But the doom-crier was mistaken. Just as he had a year before in Paris, Alfonso XIII made it through unscathed, adding to the legend of his immortality. In all, five attempts would be made on his life, but not even the republic would manage to finish him off. At His Majesty's side, huddled inside the royal carriage, the newly proclaimed Queen Victoria Eugenia Julia Ena de Battenberg was trying to hold back tears as she assessed the bridal gown spattered with horse blood. Within an hour of her marriage, she had learned the price she would have to pay for being the wife of the king of Spain.

A few yards away, Ferdinando shook the dust from his waistcoat and looked at Pablo with his pupils more dilated than ever.

"Run and telephone the office," he said, his voice trembling, "and tell them that someone tried to assassinate the king. Then hurry back here, because you have some explaining to do."

And before the boy took off running, he added:

"Oh, and Pablo, I must say. Nice work."

It was the first time he had called him by his name.

−8−

When word got around Paris of the revolutionary stance adopted by Blasco Ibáñez, all the malcontents flocked to him—well-meaning fanatics, revolutionaries who romantically believed in his radicalism. And one evening, in a Spanish-owned restaurant up on Montmartre, the conspiratorial cabal was held.

EL CABALLERO AUDAZ,
El novelista que vendió a su patria

OUTSIDE NUMBER 8, RUE DANTON, A stone's throw away from Île de la Cité, a rather large group of people throngs together, trying to get inside the building. Today is Friday, October 31, 1924, and there is a capacity crowd at the Salle des Sociétés Savantes: within a few minutes the much-anticipated meeting between Blasco Ibáñez and Miguel de Unamuno is going to start, in another attempt to raise public awareness about the need to overthrow the authoritarian government of Primo de Rivera. There are more French citizens in attendance than there were at last month's meeting at the Community House, where Blasco came out to the acclaim of a multitude of Spanish exiles, because this latest meeting has been organized with the help of Parisian leftists from the League of the Rights of Man, including a few distinguished members of the French freemasons. The people complain loudly and incessantly outside the building, despite the concierge's polite insistence that no one else can enter the hall for safety reasons, and that he has just been informed that the meeting has already begun. Despite having taken the metro here from the printing house, Pablo is among those stuck outside. Seeing the situation, he decides to turn around and

THE ANARCHIST WHO SHARED MY NAME

go home. After all, he doesn't have much desire to be shut in to listen to those two paper revolutionaries, after everything Robinsón told him at lunchtime. As he makes his way through the crowd, a French militant tries to sell him a stamp: "Pro-liberation of Spain." He makes an excuse and breaks away from the youth and starts walking along the sidewalk toward the Pont Saint-Michel, and at that very instant a side door of the building opens and someone grabs his arm, dragging him inside.

"You didn't think you'd get away so easily, did you?" Robinsón smiles at him in the darkness. "Your Lordship always has a seat reserved at the Salle des Sociétés Savantes."

And Robinsón leads him via steep stairs to a loge from which he will be able to hear the speakers. A luxurious hanging chandelier illuminates the baroque salon and the hundreds of attendees, including many members of the Committee of Anarchist Relations. Below, next to an obscure door at the back of the room, Pablo recognizes Durruti and Ascaso, accompanied by two women with haircuts à la garçonne: Ramona Berri and Pepita Not, the only two female members of the Committee, former members of Los Solidarios. He also thinks he sees, among the people in the first few rows, Juan Riesgo, Massoni, and Vivancos with his arm in a sling, as well as the elder Orobón brother. Alone, next to the entrance, Recasens stands guard, his mien Napoleonic. Neither Jover nor Caparrós is present, of course, having left this morning for the border. There are also a good number of communists and syndicalists, many of whom have been recruited by Robinsón to take part in the revolutionary expedition. And in the press area, Pablo discerns the scrawny writer from *Ex-Ilio*, his hair pomaded and mustache recently trimmed, ready to take notes for the feature that will appear in next Monday's issue.

"Pablo," says Robinsón, stepping into the loge, "I think you know Anxo, Carlos, and Baudilio."

These are the three vegetarians Robinsón recruited at the restaurant on Rue Mathis.

"Yes, of course, how are you?" Pablo greets them, shaking hands.

Below, on the stage, the evening has just been opened by Charles Richet, an old and well-known professor at the Sorbonne, a mason, spiritualist, and expert in metempsychosis. His words are punctuated by shouts from the audience, railing against fascism, against Mussolini and Primo de Rivera, and even against the French government led by the Cartel des Gauches. After him, a Portuguese orator takes the stage, dressed in a tuxedo, and makes a brief but sincere homage to the memory of the tragic, unjust death of Ferrer Guàrdia. Then it is Ortega y Gasset's turn. He delivers a bold, uncompromising speech. But the main course arrives when the former professor of the University of Salamanca, Don Miguel de Unamuno, takes the stage, with his close-trimmed, bright white beard, and he inflames the audience with a passionate speech, an equal mixture of wrath and irony, such as this very moment when he provokes a wave of laughter with this superb attack going right for Primo de Rivera's jugular:

"You will have to excuse my language, but this stupid idiot says I'm a wayward son of Spain. Me, a wayward son? But what if I'm not a son of Spain? What if, like any good professor, I am its father?"

Aged by exile, the septuagenarian Unamuno appears to be reinvigorated by the audience's laughter and applause.

"Not that that drunken, whoring general is totally empty, no: it's that he's full of emptiness, which isn't the same thing. And now that other epileptic pig, with blood on his hands"—here he is referring to Martínez Anido—"Now he wants to call me a conspirator. But I do my conspiring in the light of day, gentlemen, not like them. I want everything I say to be known. And if I say it, it's precisely because I want it to be known…"

He goes on with attack after attack on Primo, relishing the well-known anecdote about Caoba, the dictator's goddaughter, whom he ordered to be set free after she was arrested for cocaine possession.

"A fine example of the little charlatan Buddha's professed respect for law and order!"

Then the slings and arrows rain down on the monarchy:

"And what do you think about that big-nosed idiot fate has given us for a king? Alfonso XIII is a wicked man and the main person responsible for what's happening in Morocco. You can't go to war as if you were challenging someone to a duel! Do you know what the Moorish king Abd el-Krim said after our audacious monarch accused England and France of selling arms to the Moroccans? He said why would they need to buy weapons from the other European countries, since they get plenty from the retreats and defeats of the Spanish army! We're the laughingstock of Europe!"

Unamuno has gotten hot under the collar, so he takes a breath and drinks some water.

"And what can we say about his spawn?" the diatribe against the monarchy goes on. "The prince of Asturias inherited his mother's hemophilia, the second son is deaf-mute since birth, and who knows what'll be wrong with the third. The Republic is the only alternative! And if it takes a revolution to get it, then I say there will have to be a revolution!"

A deafening wave of cheers and applause fills the room. The professor, emboldened, continues his jeremiad against the dictatorship and the monarchy. He leaves the stage to a standing ovation, waving like a bullfighter. It is then that Pablo sees Luís Naveira enter the hall, accompanied by the concierge, who appears to have begrudgingly allowed him in, but only to give someone a message. Must have been a handsome bribe. Naveira looks very out of sorts, and he erupts into wild gesticulations when he finds Recasens, who gestures to follow him to the back of the hall to talk with Durruti and Ascaso. The two men elbow their way through the packed crowd and finally reach the anarchist leaders. They exchange a few words and disappear through the rear door. Robinsón, who hasn't missed a thing, suddenly stands up.

"I'm going to go see what's going on," he tells Pablo, and he exits the loge, leaving Pablo sitting there with the three vegetarians.

After Unamuno, it is Blasco Ibáñez's turn. Blasco goes up to the podium straightening what's left of his hair, which is that flat black color of cheap vegetal dyes; he settles in behind the rostrum, fills a glass of water, and winds his Roskopf pocket watch as he waits for the applause to die down. The Valencian writer has not prepared his speech very much, because he has spent the last few days revising the French translation of his incendiary pamphlet, done by a young philosophy student and regular at his discussion group at the Café Americain. But although it is merely a hasty rehash of what he said a month ago at the Community House, his eloquence and his presence will be enough to inflame the audience's spirit, and they will not think twice to interrupt him constantly with shouts of "Anarchy!" and "Down with the bourgeoisie!"

"Republicans," Blasco begins, and a few protests are heard, "or maybe you are monarchists?" he asks, with obvious irony, leaving more than one person in confusion. "Spaniards, then," he continues, but once again he can't please everyone, for many in the audience are not Spanish, "Fine then, friends: I want to start by telling you that I don't like to beat around the bush. I aim straight at the trunk. And my axe chops right into the tree until it falls!"

A chorus of shouts and applause breaks out to echo his every phrase, pronounced with such belligerence that the more moderate audience members are shocked. We shall not reproduce them all here, for we've already heard them, *mutatis mutandis*, at the Community House, but we cannot resist recording his exchange with a heckler who, taking advantage when Blasco pauses for a sip of water, shouts:

"When you people take over, you'll shoot us just like the ones who are in charge today!"

To which Vicente replies in an energetic voice: "We will shoot those who rebel against the Republic, whether they're right or left, but we're especially going to shoot agents provocateurs," and he points an accusatory finger at the heckler.

And between the audience's bursts of applause, the Valencian writer rounds out his speech with a declaration of intentions that raises the temperature of the room by a few degrees:

"I'm not here for my health, nor to have a good time with you all. No, no, absolutely not. You want to know why I'm here tonight?" and after an expectant silence, he concludes by raising his fist: "I'm here to start the revolution!"

After the wild applause from most of the audience, a young communist from the front row climbs onto the stage and shouts, "Long live the social republic! Long live Russia!"

To which Blasco responds, inviting the young man to get off the stage, "Yes, my boy, long live the social republic indeed. But let's start with the democratic republic…"

The famous author's words are followed by chaos as the meeting breaks down into a heated debate, with some defending the Bolshevik revolution, others advocating democratic revolution, still others espousing anarchist revolution, and the craziest of the lot calling for capitalist revolution. When the meeting ends and Blasco comes down from the podium, an aged Spaniard from the front row reproaches him for endorsing Bolshevik communism. The writer looks at him kindly, steps closer, and whispers in his ear: "Don't worry, grandpa. A communist republic will never triumph in Spain. Let's let these young people help us achieve a democratic republic, and then we'll sweep the rug out from under them."

As Robinsón has not returned, Pablo exits the loge with the three vegetarians. In the street, he says goodbye to them and starts walking home. Crossing the Pont Saint-Michel, he hears a loud discussion between two tramps fighting over a spot that both claim to be their own. It appears that the ideology of private property has taken hold even among the least fortunate. Fifteen minutes later, arriving at the hovel, he tumbles into bed without taking off his shoes and falls into a deep sleep.

Robinsón wakes him up after a while, but Pablo doesn't know if he's been asleep for one minute or for hours.

"What, what is it?" he asks, stunned, as he sits up in bed.

"Take your shoes off, man. That's no way to sleep."

Pablo groans, takes off his shoes, and throws them at Robinsón, who miraculously dodges them.

"Come on, man, don't be that way. When all I'm trying to do is help you sleep better. You know what?" the vegetarian asks.

"What?" barks Pablo, covering himself with his blanket and hiding his head under his pillow.

"Nothing, nothing. Well, actually," he finally says, "I'm going to miss you."

But Pablo has fallen asleep and his only reply is a long, sibilant snore. When he wakes up in the morning, Robinsón will be gone.

SATURDAY'S WORK SHIFT PASSES UNEVENTFULLY. At noon, Pablo takes the risk of having lunch at the Point du Jour. After all, he reasons, he personally has nothing to fear, and perhaps he'll find a way to talk with Dubois and ask him to withdraw his complaint against Leandro. But the proprietor is not in, because he's already found a replacement for the Argentine: a quiet, ethereal Japanese waiter who floats between the tables like the shadow of a samurai. Pablo tries to convince some of the patrons to go talk to Dubois, and they all appear ready to help the young Argentine, who is well liked by the clientele. But when he proposes that they should take up a collection to mollify the elderly proprietor, they all turn their attention back to their meals.

The afternoon passes even more peacefully than the morning, all except the last hour. Julianín has made good progress in a short amount of time, and he's beginning to be more of a help than a hindrance. The strategy of five cents per error appears to be working, and now he corrects the proofs with such zeal that Pablo has to be very careful when typesetting if he doesn't want to break the bank. You might say that the boy has taken to heart the motto of the great typographer Firmin Didot, posted above the door: "An erratum injures the eye just as a false note in a concerto injures the ear." The truth is, Pablo is starting to grow fond of the lad, despite his meek, taciturn personality. That's why he does a double take when, at the end of the day, while diligently cleaning some plates, the boy breaks his usual silence to mumble, "I'm going to sign up for the expedition."

"What?" asks Pablo, jarred.

"I'm going to sign up for the revolutionary expedition. I don't want to spend my whole life standing by, waiting for them to let me go back to my country."

"But do you have any idea what you're saying?" Pablo reproaches him. "You're still just a boy."

"I thought you might be on board as well."

"Me? On board for this suicide mission? Who gave you that idea?"

"I don't know, I see you all the time with that joker in the bowler hat, the guy in charge of recruiting people, and I thought maybe—"

"Well, you think too much, Julianín. Get those crazy ideas out of your head."

"I've made up my mind. I'm going," replies Julianín, with aplomb.

"What do your parents have to say about it?" is all that Pablo can think to say, surprised at the boy's courage.

"They can say what they want, I'm not a baby."

"Listen, why don't you go home, and take tomorrow off. Maybe you can use the time to think calmly about whether or not it's a good idea—"

Julianín thanks him, gathers up his things, and leaves. As soon as he is gone, Robinsón enters.

"Ah, just the man I was hoping to see. The illustrious corruptor of youth!"

"Listen, Pablo, I don't know what you're talking about, but I need to tell you a lot of things and there's no time to lose."

"No time to lose, you say!" Pablo exclaims, somewhat irritated. "That's exactly what I've been doing ever since you got here: losing time. And now, on top of everything, now you're filling the kid's head with your revolutionary ideas!"

"If you're talking about that kid who just left, it was him who came to me. And you should follow his example. It seems you don't grasp the seriousness of the situation. We're trying to save Spain, goddammit!"

"You're trying to save shit!" and he throws the plate Julianín has just cleaned onto the floor. The metallic clang reverberates for a few seconds as the old friends stare into each other's eyes. Then, Pablo plops into a chair. "I'm sorry, Robinsón, I don't know what's come over me, maybe I'm getting old. You know that ten years ago I would have been the first in line to take up arms and run off to liberate Antarctica if necessary. But I just don't see it. I have a feeling that Primo de Rivera *wants* us to do something like that. If we cross the border and fail, there will be no way to get rid of him. He'll repress the rebellion and it'll give him more legitimacy, because he'll say Spain needs to treat rebels with a heavy hand."

Robinsón weighs his friend's words.

"If that's really what you think," he says, finally, "why are you helping us? Why did you take the letter to Amiens? Why did you agree to print the posters?"

Now it is Pablo who meditates on his friend's words.

"I don't know. I suppose my heart admires what you're doing, but my head disagrees. Although maybe what's really happening is simply that I'm afraid and I'm making excuses so I won't have to admit it."

Robinsón smiles:

"Afraid, you? I don't believe it," he says, squatting down next to Pablo. "And even if it were true, you know what my father used to say: only the brave can feel fear. I don't know, it's possible you're right and we're putting the cart before the horse, but that's a risk we have to take. It's our dignity at stake here, Pablo, as individuals and as a people ... Come on, let's go, it's your turn to buy me a drink."

And as they walk down Rue Belleville looking for a discreet bar that serves soft drinks, Robinsón tells Pablo everything that has happened since he left the loge at the Salle des Sociétés Savantes. Because things are coming to a head.

Last night, when Ramón Recasens asked Naveira if he would join him at the meeting of Unamuno and Blasco Ibáñez, Naveira replied that he was busy printing, that he would stay a while longer at the safe house on Rue Vilin, to see if he could develop the latest set of photographs for false passports. Fifty minutes later, as he was working in the darkroom they had set up in what used to be a bathroom, there was a knock at the door. Naveira thought for a moment that it was Recasens coming back for something he'd forgotten, but it wasn't the agreed-upon code knock. He dried his hands and came out of the darkroom just in time to escape through the window when the police started breaking through the door. He didn't have time to gather up his materials. And there on the table were the photographs of the best-known members of the Group of Thirty, those who absolutely had to have false passports to avoid endangering the mission: Durruti, Ascaso, Vivancos, Massoni, Recasens himself, Teixidó, and several others. Naveira hid on the roof, shivering with cold and praying the gendarmes wouldn't find him.

Only after he could no longer hear their voices did he abandon his hideout and run to the Salle des Sociétés Savantes. He had to argue with a concierge to let him in, but the man wouldn't let him pass until he heard the applause signaling the end of Unamuno's speech. Only then was Naveira able to talk with Recasens and meet with Durruti and Ascaso to tell them what had happened.

"It's a real blow," says Robinsón, attacking a raspberry juice. "Now nobody trusts anybody. The French authorities are supposed to turn a blind eye to us, because after all we're their political refugees, but now the gendarmes won't leave us in peace. Someone said they saw Fenoll Malvasía in Paris—the head of security for Primo de Rivera's government. Some people think he came to negotiate with the French police, others think he came to consult with one of his many informants. Wow, this is good juice."

"What's the plan?"

"Everyone has a different idea. We can't start slipping now, we have to keep pushing forward and working while we wait for word from Jover and Caparrós at the border. But people are starting to get nervous, 'cause it doesn't seem normal that they're taking so long to give a sign of life. In any case, Recasens and Naveira will get back to work as soon as we find another safe house where we can set up the counterfeiting equipment."

"And what if the telegrams finally come, saying it's time to enter Spain, but the passports aren't ready?"

Robinsón clicks his tongue and takes another sip of juice.

"In all likelihood, that's exactly what's going to happen. Then we'll have to make a decision. I think it's too risky for people like Durruti and Ascaso to travel with their real passports along with the rest of the expedition, because they might put it in danger. But there are others who think it's not fair for the masterminds to stay in Paris and send the rest of us to do the dirty work."

"And what's happening with the guns?"

"We spoke with Blasco Ibáñez today. It's very likely that he will give us money to buy them."

In fact, last night while Luís Naveira was explaining to Durruti and Ascaso that the police had discovered the counterfeiting lab, Pedro Massoni had placed himself in a strategic position to catch Ibáñez when he finished his speech. A little old man beat him to the author, and reproached Ibáñez for flirting with Bolshevik communism, but the novelist settled him down by whispering something in his ear. Only then was Massoni able to talk with him and accompany him to a private booth, where Unamuno was already sitting, talking with Marcelino Domingo and Ortega y Gasset. There, he tried to explain to Ibáñez why they needed his help.

"Listen, kid," Don Vicente cut him off, "any other day and I'd have told you to go fly a kite. But in times like this, you have to support even the craziest causes. On Saturdays I usually eat at my friend Pepe's restaurant on Montmartre, between the Lapin Agile and Place du Tertre. If you want, you can swing by around two, and we'll have a cognac while you tell me all about it. This is not the place to talk about certain things. My friends might be shocked."

Letting out a cackle, he went to sit with the shockable trio.

So it was that today at midday, after eating, Durruti and the limping Massoni and Vivancos walked to the top of the hill of Montmartre. The city was dressed in its best finery to celebrate All Saints' Day, and throngs of Parisians were out visiting Montmartre and the garish Sacré Coeur (whose construction was just completed five years ago) to pay their respects to their ancestors. The sun was shining timidly, and from the door of the basilica there was a magnificent view of the city, which extended like a dense forest, dotted here and there by various species: on the left, the Bois de Vincennes; Notre Dame and the Pantheon straight ahead; and the Eiffel Tower on the right, forming a sharp peak between the surrounding trees . . . When the three anarchists reached Place du Tertre, a zeppelin crossed the sky, attracting the attention of everyone below, who hadn't forgotten the German bombardment during the Great War. "Look, a flying whale!" shouted a child, eliciting some laughter from the crowd. But the three men ascended the hill for less festive reasons: to meet with Blasco Ibáñez and ask him for fifty thousand francs so they can buy weapons from a Spanish smuggler working in Paris.

Shortly before reaching the Lapin Agile cabaret, Durruti, Massoni, and Vivancos found the restaurant owned by Ibáñez's friend Pepe. Blasco, elegantly dressed and wearing a Legion of Honor medal on his lapel, looked surprised to see these three bandit-looking men enter the restaurant and walk toward the table where he had been smoking a cigar, amusing himself by blowing smoke rings while looking out the window at the many passersby. Most likely he had forgotten the appointment. Or he was only expecting Massoni. Whatever the case, he greeted them courteously one by one and invited them to sit down at the table. But the restaurant was still full and it didn't seem appropriate to discuss certain things, so, after a few minutes of small talk, Blasco picked up his glass of cognac and stood up:

"Wait for me here, gentlemen. I'll be right back."

The three anarchists watched him approach a short, portly man, whose thick mustache and bushy eyebrows gave him the appearance of a walrus. After exchanging a few words, he returned to the table.

"Don José has kindly agreed to let us have his best private room to talk for a few minutes. Don't forget to tip him well when you leave."

And he led them to the rear of the restaurant, where, after parting a red velvet curtain and going through a glass door, they entered a small room with a rough round table in the center, surrounded by a few worn-out, shabby armchairs. Who knows where revolutions would have been planned if it hadn't been for private rooms?

"*Voilà!*" exclaimed Blasco, making a theatrical gesture with his arm, and inviting them to sit down.

Durruti was the first to speak. He gave the writer a rundown of the activities that the Committee is conducting in Paris, before laying out the matter that brought him to Montmartre today: the revolutionary expedition that they are organizing to enter Spain and overthrow the dictatorship.

"And what would you like me to do for you, gentlemen? You don't expect me, at my age, to take up arms and run off to liberate Spain?" asked Blasco, rubbing his enormous belly with glee.

"No, of course not," Massoni chimed in, "we have human resources taken care of. There are a hundred men ready to cross the border. But we need weapons."

"Ha! We can talk to Don José, see if he'll loan us some steak knives," Blasco laughed, releasing a cackle that made him shake and cough violently.

"This is no time for joking," Vivancos interjected with unexpected firmness.

THE ANARCHIST WHO SHARED MY NAME

"There's always time for joking," Massoni replied in a conciliatory tone, "but I'm convinced that Don Vicente is much more than a comedian. After hearing him speak last night and the other day at the Community House, I don't think there's any doubt you're one of us. We've heard your Russian friends have given you a huge amount of money to finance a pamphlet that you're planning to distribute for free. I'm sure that, even if it was only a fraction of what people say, you'll have enough money to cover all of Europe with your words—"

"Hey, let's not exaggerate," Blasco interrupted. "If that were true, the pamphlet would already be in circulation. Oh, so I've been thinking about calling it *A Nation Kidnapped*, what do you think?"

"Magnificent," Durruti replied, "But if you give us the money maybe you'll be able to start writing the sequel, *A Nation Liberated*. Of course, we would be sure to wait until the first pamphlet has sold out before we enter Spain to start the revolution."

The writer hesitated a moment, surprised by the response, and finally cackled:

"You're very kind, my lad. Tell me, how much money are we talking about here?"

"Forty or fifty thousand francs."

"*Mon dieu!* That's no chump change."

"We want to do things right," Durruti interjected.

"Of course you do, lad, it goes without saying. Look, I'll see what I can do. Spain doesn't deserve to be run by those morons, and I will always support any plan to kick them out. It's a lot of money, but if I can arrange a few things, you can count on it. But you have to promise me you'll wait until my pamphlet comes out before you start the revolution, of course!" he exclaimed, bursting into another strenuous fit of laughter.

"Of course, Don Vicente, of course," Durruti replied without hesitation, almost giving the impression that he meant what he said.

"If you want, we can meet here on Monday at the same time. With a little luck, I'll have rounded up the money by then. In any case, *vive la bagatelle*, as that so-and-so would say ... Here's to the Republic!" Blasco panted, raising his glass.

"And to liberty!" added Durruti.

"To liberty!" said Massoni and Vivancos in unison, lifting imaginary glasses, since the rotund writer was the only one who had entered the private room with a drink. They say it's bad luck to toast with an empty glass, so imagine the disaster courted by toasting with no glass at all.

After saying goodbye, the three young men exited the restaurant, leaving an appropriate tip. Outside, the sky over Montmartre had grown overcast. They started walking downhill, each absorbed in his thoughts, and when they reached Rue des Martyrs they were surprised by the sound of a car horn.

"Need a lift anywhere, gentlemen?" asked Blasco with a nouveau riche grin from the backseat of his Cadillac, driven by his trusty Ramón.

The three anarchists looked at each other for a moment, then shook their heads. Blasco's Cadillac disappeared down the hill on the way to the Hôtel du Louvre.

VIII
(1906–1908)

THE PERPETRATOR WENT BY THE NAME Mateo Morral. He was twenty-six years old, a native of Sabadell. The dynamite-laden bouquet of roses he tossed from the balcony of house number 88 on Calle Mayor took the lives of more than twenty people, injuring several dozen more. Graphological investigation found that Morral was the very man who had carved the death threat on the tree in the Retiro, perhaps as an act of self-denunciation to escape his destiny. Two days later, he was found in Torrejón de Ardoz, having taken his own life with a bullet to the heart, but not before sending one of his pursuers to the great beyond. Another seventeen anarchists would soon be detained, but two intellectuals ended up paying for the mess, accused of conspiring in the failed regicide: the aged José Nakens, director of the weekly *El Motín*, whose office gave Morral refuge after the failed attack, and Francisco Ferrer Guàrdia, founder of the Modern School of Barcelona, where the would-be assassin had worked as a librarian during the months prior to the attacks. Nakens was sentenced to nine years in prison, while Ferrer was acquitted due to lack of evidence, after spending several months behind the iron bars of Madrid's notorious Modelo prison. Vicente Holgado's name never came up.

Pablo and Ferdinando stayed an extra day in Madrid to cover the news of the attack from the scene, and then they returned to Salamanca.

"Who was that fellow we ran into?" asked Ferdinando for the umpteenth time as the train crossed the fields of Castile.

"I already told you, I barely know him, Ferdinando."

"Didn't you say he was an old friend?"

"That was just a manner of speaking."

"But you must at least know his name, right?"

"No."

With this obstinate denial, Pablo's inner revolutionary was beginning to win out over his ambitions as a journalist. When they got back to Salamanca, he began frantically reading Bakunin, Proudhon, Kropotkin. His mother shook her head to see him reading such things, and she longed for the days when he used to devour the novels of Jules Verne or Emilio Salgari. But it was the death of Julián Martín that ultimately unleashed his anarchist spirit. One foul day, as Pablo was working at the office of *El Castellano*, the telephone emitted a fateful, baleful ring:

"It's for you, Pablito," said Obdulia, relishing the diminutive.

"For me?" Pablo was surprised, because it was the first time he had received a telephone call.

At the other end was his mother's sobbing voice. She was calling from the Hospital of the Holy Trinity, where they had had to bring Julián. Apparently, two men had attacked him as he was walking toward a school on the outskirts of Salamanca, stabbing him several times in the gut to rob him of the four pennies in his pocket.

When Pablo arrived at the hospital, he found his mother and sister crying inconsolably outside the room, while the doctor tried to convince the chaplain that his services would not be necessary. Julián barely had the strength to speak, and had lost a great deal of blood.

"Come closer," he said when he saw his son, his voice threadbare, nearly inaudible. Apparently, he had been waiting for Pablo's arrival to die, because he only had time to stroke his hair, leaving his final sentence half-said: "Don't forget..."

Pablo bit his knuckles so hard that his mouth filled with blood. The killers' lawyer said at court that they had been driven to crime by hunger. The two wretches had gone five days without eating when they lost their senses and assaulted the inspector. From that point forward, hunger became Pablo's worst enemy, and Peter Kropotkin's *The Conquest of Bread* became the book he lived by. Two months after the tragedy, María and Julia moved back to Baracaldo, but Pablo remained in Salamanca (now more than ever the city of death) and quickly came into contact with the anarchist and syndicalist groups of the area, feeling that he was honoring his father's memory with an increasingly fervent ideological commitment. He moved out of the apartment he'd been living in, which was too large and expensive for him alone, and rented a room near the university, in a guesthouse full of stuffy students, run by an irritable old lady popularly known as "Madam Crow."

His ideological commitment evolved into anarchist activism, and in early 1907 he was arrested for vandalizing the local cathedral with the iconic words of Josiah Warren: "Every man should be his own government, his own law, his own church." This arrest very nearly cost Pablo his job at *El Castellano*, where he had been emptying fewer wastebaskets and covering more stories, filling fewer inkwells and correcting more errata with each passing week. Luckily, thanks to Ferdinando's intervention, he managed to keep the job, with a serious warning: at the first sign of any more hijinks, he'd be out in the street.

But Pablo was not ready to give up his ideals, neither in politics nor in love. So, while his mouth filled with terms like "direct action," "self-determination," and "propaganda of the deed," his heart kept on drinking from the same source: the letters Angela sent him twice a month, which she lovingly perfumed even though she knew Pablo was unable to enjoy the scent. And even though they hadn't seen each other since that farewell so long ago at the train station in Béjar, the exchange of correspondence was so intense that they were convinced that sooner or later they'd be able to resume their relationship as if no time had passed. Sometimes, they made plans for their future; Pablo fantasized about traveling the world on a honeymoon, and Angela told him that she no longer wanted to be a spelunker, but an anthropologist, and that they would go off to live together in Africa, or America, or Oceania, where she would study the customs of the Jivaros or the cannibals. His correspondence with Robinsón was also regular in the beginning, but was interrupted when Robinsón made good on his pledge to run away from home and struck out on a life of wandering from village to village, all over Spain, sending letters and postcards with no return address, to which Pablo could not reply. On the last one he sent, Robinsón announced his intention to become a vegetarian for good and join a naturist commune on the Catalan coast, where he was planning to be isolated from the rest of the world until further notice.

Between one thing and another, Pablo turned eighteen years old, let his beard grow, and took to smoking cigarettes, holding them between his ring and middle fingers, with a somewhat dandyish affectation. One day he looked at himself in the mirror and felt like an adult, enough of an adult to start a family. Being an anarchist is one thing, he said to himself, but being a proponent of free love is something else altogether. So he wrote a letter to Angela asking for her hand in marriage. He didn't specify that his idea was to have a civil wedding, an aberration that Pius IX had decried as concubinage, but the details could wait. He awaited her response with a certain nervousness; a week went by, then another, and then another, and still he had received no reply. Pablo blamed the postal service and wrote another letter, again bringing up the question of marriage. And this time he did receive an answer, though not from Angela, but from Don Diego Gómez, ex-lieutenant colonel of the Spanish army in the distant war overseas. They were barely five lines of elegant calligraphy, but they cut like a mugger's knife:

Señor Martín,
I don't know if your father (God rest his soul) taught you such manners, but before making a marriage proposal to my daughter Angela, you should have spoken with me. Know this: I already have plans for her marriage, quite different from those you

propose. Therefore, I ask, nay, I demand that you stop importuning her with your letters. I hope I have made myself abundantly clear.

Sincerely,

Don Diego Gómez Arqués

Pablo spent three sleepless nights trying to convince himself that Angela's wishes had nothing to do with her father's plans. At his most delirious, he imagined her sequestered high in a tower, waiting for her vampire to come rescue her. At dawn on the fourth day, he sent a telegram to *El Castellano*, announcing that he would be taking his first vacation in four years. Then he went to the train station and bought a ticket for Béjar, prepared to kidnap Angela if necessary. Even if he had to face the whole Spanish navy.

He was welcomed by a sky rippling with big black clouds portending storm or disaster. The birds were practically skimming the ground in nervous, erratic flight. Between the station and the Gómez house, Pablo passed several familiar faces, but no one returned his greeting, as though the four years since his last visit had rendered him invisible or or as though his sparse beard had formed a mask impenetrable to those who remembered him with the smooth face of an adolescent. Whatever it was, feeling more estranged than ever, he arrived at Calle Flamencos and rapped with conviction on the Gómez's front door. But the only answer was silence. When he was getting ready to knock again, he heard a voice behind him:

"I wouldn't insist if I were you."

Don Veremundo Olaya, Robinsón's father, was avidly puffing on a pipe and smiling sadly.

"I almost don't recognize you, Pablo. How you've changed."

"For the better, I hope, Don Veremundo," he replied, returning the bitter smile. "Why shouldn't I insist?"

"Because tempers have been a bit unsettled in the Gómez family lately. And it seems to me that you've had quite a bit to do with it. Come, let's go inside, don't keep standing there."

The inn was the same as ever, with its arthritic wooden stairs that complained at every step and the large oak table dominating the dining room, the same table that had hosted their improvised Christmas dinner ten years before.

"You know how the old Colonel is," Don Vermundo continued, "when he gets an idea in his head, no one can shake him from it—"

"When ideas are unjust, they are defeated by facts," Pablo interjected, sounding like an anarchist pamphlet.

"You'll see what you'll do, but be careful. Don Diego Gómez is not to be trifled with. He wants to marry Angela to her cousin Rodrigo…"

Pablo felt those words like a deadly blade poised to pierce his chest. Fortunately, as Don Veremundo finished his thought, the sword changed course at the last second:

"But she flatly refuses to accept the marriage. She says that her heart is already promised."

The deadly blade transformed into a gentle lambskin caress, and Pablo could not suppress the proud smile of a winning suitor.

"Don't get your hopes up too high," warned the innkeeper, more versed in such battles, "Don Diego has locked her up in her room until she comes to her senses. The poor thing has been shut in there for weeks now."

"That son of a bitch," muttered Pablo between clenched teeth. "I'm going to talk to her right now."

He left the inn and headed back to the Gómez house, against Don Veremundo Olaya's warnings. If there was anything that could rile Pablo's ire, it was injustice perpetrated by the strong against the weak.

"Open up! Open the door!" Pablo shouted over and over, pounding on the door with the brass knocker.

He finally heard the voices of Angela's parents talking in the hallway. Then he heard a slap and the sound of footsteps going up the stairs. When the door opened, its aperture held the silhouette of Don Diego Gómez's imposing figure, which stepped out into the street preceded by the menacing eye of a Remington shotgun brought over from Cuba.

"If you don't leave this place right now," he said in a tone you might expect from a defeated old ex-colonel, "I'll buy you a ticket to the other side."

Pablo didn't budge, so Diego pointed the rifle between his eyes.

"Did you hear what I said?"

"It doesn't take much of a man to make a girl suffer," Pablo wanted to say, but his brain was going a thousand miles an hour, which always happened to him in times of danger, and the words that came out of his mouth were quite different:

"Don't be that way, Don Diego," he said, stepping back and putting his hands in the air, "I only came to tell you that I'm giving up on my proposal to your daughter. I'm sorry to have bothered you."

He spun on his heels and ran to the station, where he boarded the next train for Salamanca and, making sure that everyone around would hear him, he shouted goodbye to Béjar: "May we never meet again, you foul city!"

But Pablo had no intention of going very far. At the next stop, he discreetly exited the train and made his way back to Béjar on foot. When he arrived, night was coming on and it was getting quite cold. He turned up the collar of the old Sherlock Holmes raincoat Ferdinando had given him after Mateo Morral's attack and took a detour to Veremundo's inn to avoid walking in front of Angela's house. He waited until the dead of night, then knocked softly on the door of the inn. When Robinsón's father saw him appear again, he shook his head and said, "As stubborn as your father, may his soul in hell forgive me. Come on then, inside with you, you're going to freeze out there."

"Do you have any rooms free tonight?" Pablo asked, taking a bill from his pocket.

"Keep your money, son. Roberto would give me hell if he found out I took it. You can stay in his room. You know he ran away from home, right?"

"Yes."

"Let's not speak of it again. Just understand that I take no responsibility for what happens to you now."

After dining with Robinsón's parents, Pablo went to bed early, or at least pretended to. In reality, he didn't even undress. When the midnight bells rang from San Juan Bautista's, he got out of bed and stealthily left the room, lighting his way with the stub of a candle.

The attic was just as he remembered it, although it did seem smaller, as if it had been shrinking with the passing of the years. The decrepit old trunk was still sleeping in the corner, but it was no longer necessary to drag it over to the skylight: Pablo could easily poke his head out the window without even having to stand on tiptoes. He pushed the window open with a squeak, and discovered that the last thing lost is not hope, but habit: Angela still slept with the light on. He couldn't see into her room because of the closed curtains, but he thought he detected a shadow moving from one side of the room to the other, despite the late hour. He didn't know if she had been informed that he was in town, but in all likelihood his knocking and shouting had reached her room. No lock or key in the world can stop love from crossing a jail cell's walls, Pablo thought, paraphrasing Bakunin, who had less carnal forms of love in mind. Carried by this thought, he pushed the upper half of his body through the window and whispered as loud as he could:

"Psst, Angela!"

But the only reply was the stirring of the wind, which penetrated into the loft and snuffed out his candle.

"Angela, it's me, Pablo…"

Barely four yards separated one building from the other, but a whole world seemed to be intent on keeping them apart. I wish I really were a vampire, thought Pablo, so I could fly over to your room. Then, as if that thought were the password to the door of Ali Baba, the light in Angela's room suddenly went dark, and the window hinges creaked. Leaning out of the skylight, Pablo held his breath. In the darkness he could make out the sparkling of those eyes he had spent so many years imagining in dreams.

"Pablo..." whispered Angela.

"Angela..." whispered Pablo.

A shiver ran down his spine.

"How did you..." she tried to ask, somewhat upset.

"Why didn't you tell me?" he tried to respond, his voice faltering.

The shiver turned to a choking feeling.

"I can hardly see you," she said, reaching out her arm.

"Same here," he said.

An angel passed through the alley as the two youths tried to discern the outlines of each other's faces.

"I'm going to turn on the light," said Angela, "so we can see each other better."

"Won't that be dangerous?"

"Not at all. I always sleep with the light on," she said as she disappeared. When she returned to the newly lit window, she said, "Hey, you look good with a beard."

"So do you," Pablo replied.

"I look good with a beard too?" she teased.

"Yeah, I mean, no. Eh—you know what I mean," he said, his blush imperceptible in the faint light.

A second angel passed through the alleyway, even slower than the first.

"Pablo," Angela finally broke the silence, her voice trembling.

"What?"

"How far are you prepared to go for me?"

The inspector's son contemplated for a moment before answering:

"To infinity."

"Alright then. Get me out of here, in the name of all you hold dear, and let's run away together as far as we can get from here, to Africa, or to America."

"You know what I've been dreaming about these last few days?" Pablo asked.

"No, what?" sighed Angela.

"That you were a princess trapped in a tower and that I was coming to rescue you. It seems I wasn't too far off."

"And what happened?"

"When?"

"In the dream, dummy. Did you rescue me, or not?"

"I don't know. Every time I woke up just when we were about to climb out the window."

"Well then, this time we'd better wait a little longer before we wake up," said Angela firmly. "I can't handle it here anymore, this town, this family, this life. I want to go away from here, Pablo, and I want to go with you."

"Alright," he said, noticing that his mind was starting to run at a thousand miles an hour again. "Wait a minute."

Pablo stepped away from the skylight and relit his candle. His eyes scanned the attic like a tiger in search of prey. His heart started racing when he found what he was looking for: in a corner, covered with dust and time, a pile of planks appeared to be languishing in exile. Trying to make as little noise as possible, he dragged one of these long beams into the light, leaned it against the windowsill, and poked his head through the window again.

"Angela," he whispered.

"Yes?"

"I'm going to try to reach your window, but I'm going to need your help."

"Are you crazy?"

"No, listen. I found a plank I can use as a bridge. It's in good shape and it's long enough, but it's very heavy."

"And what do you want to do?"

"I'm going to push it over from here, but it'll reach a point where I won't be able to hold it any more. Then you'll have to lean out and grab the other end of the plank. You got it?"

"Yes."

"Alright. Here goes."

Pablo stepped away from the skylight and picked up the other end of the beam, pushing it with both hands. The sill creaked with the friction, and Angela bit her nails, her heart in a knot, fearing that the noise would wake her parents. The plank was now resting on its midpoint like a scale. There were still two yards to go, and it was growing more and more difficult. Angela reached out her arms, and Pablo kept pushing, straining more and more, the weight increasing exponentially with every inch gained. Finally, when he couldn't push anymore, he had to hang from the beam to keep it from crashing down to the street. But there was no going back, it was only a matter of time before his strength would give out and the plank would slip from his fingers. Just then, he felt the weight subside: it could only mean that Angela had caught the other end! He tried pushing again, and again the sill creaked loudly.

"A little further," he heard Angela whisper.

After a final effort, all the weight of the plank was supported. Pablo put his head through the skylight and could see Angela's broad smile illuminating the night: they had done it. Now all he had to do was cross this narrow wooden bridge suspended above the abyss.

"I'll come across," said Pablo.

"Wouldn't it be better if I went that way?" Angela replied.

"Are you crazy? What if you fall?"

"What if you fall?"

"It was my idea. I should take the risk. If I find out that it's safe, then we can both cross back to this side."

"Wait a second," said Angela, disappearing from the window.

When she reappeared, Pablo asked, "What did you do?"

"Nothing, I just blocked the door with a chair."

The two youths stared at each other in the darkness, perhaps thinking that this was a more exciting game than *hinque* or hopscotch. And a much more dangerous one, of course.

"Hold it tight on that end," said Pablo, clambering up onto the windowsill.

"Pablo ..." whispered Angela.

"What?" he said as he sat astride the plank and hugged it like a koala.

"Be careful."

"You got it," he said, and he started inching his way across the expanse, hugging the beam.

But Angela had not finished her sentence:

"Because if you fall, I'm going to follow you."

More pressure on poor Pablo.

"Don't tell me that. Just hold on tight."

When he was halfway across, there was a strong gust of wind.

"Pablo," Angela whispered again, her nerves apparently having triggered a case of acute verbal incontinence.

"What?" Pablo asked, lifting his head.

"I love you."

It wasn't the best moment to say it, of course, but she didn't know if she would get another chance.

"I love you too, Angela," Pablo responded, hanging over the void. And he thought that after this, even death would not matter.

Then a noise broke the spell and he saw the night watchman's light appear at the end of the alley. "Shit," muttered Pablo. He looked at the ground and felt a wave of vertigo. He clung tightly to the beam and held his breath, while Angela turned off the light in her room, and the night watchman started mumbling incoherent phrases; it was no secret that he had a penchant for doing his rounds with a belly full of port wine. At some point, he looked up and didn't seem to believe his eyes; he shook his head and slapped his bald spot a few times before wandering off mumbling nonsense.

"D'you think he saw us?" asked Pablo, when he recovered from the vertigo.

"I don't think so," replied Angela, "he's not just nearsighted, he's also always drunk."

And Pablo finished crossing that improvised bridge linking the two houses, the two hearts. When he reached the other side, Angela reached out her hand and helped him into the room. Their embrace was the sort that stops time and melts ice. Their mouths searched for each other, and found each other; their tongues recognized each other; their hands went adventuring, and got lost; their lips murmured and were quiet; their throats trembled and panted; their hearts pounded and raced; their skin grew damp with sweat and pale with excitement; their bodies struggled and succumbed; their clothes opened and fell away; their organs grew fluid and engorged; their minds went cloudy; and they lost all notion of time and space.

When they came to their senses, the light of dawn was coming through the window and a fist was pounding on Angela's door.

"Angela! Angela! Open the door, Angela!"

It was the voice of Don Diego Gómez, lieutenant colonel of the Spanish navy.

—9—

When the telegram arrived giving the go-ahead to start the operation, at a tumultuous meeting held at the Labor Exchange office of Château-d'Eau, some members of the organizing committee proposed sending a representative to Spain to confirm the actual preparation and rule out the risk of a police provocation. No one listened to them, and the expedition was set in motion. A project so loudly announced that some of the groups even had a public farewell party at Paris's Gare Saint-Lazare.

JOSÉ LUÍS GUTIÉRREZ MOLINA
El estado frente a la anarquía

IT WAS THE DEAD OF NIGHT by the time Robinsón finished telling Pablo about what had happened at the restaurant on Montmartre. The vegetarian left the bar in a huff because he had stained his shirt with raspberry juice, and nothing gets raspberry juice out. They walked home and, after smoking a ritualistic cigarette, said goodnight. Robinsón nodded off instantly, but Pablo had trouble falling asleep.

They got up early in the morning. Both of them had things to do. Outside, it was raining as it always rains in Paris: imperceptibly, until it soaks you through. They walked up toward Belleville together and parted ways at the metro station, Pablo to the right to go to the print shop, Robinsón to the left to go to the International Bookstore on Rue Petit. The morning has been passing uneventfully at La Fraternelle, until Robinsón appears at the last moment, unable to control his excitement.

"Pablo! Pablo!" he shouts from outside, pounding on the door.

"What's going on, have you gone crazy?" he asks, letting him in.

"The telegram, Pablo, the telegram."

"What about the telegram?"

"It came, we received it this morning at the end of a meeting of the Executive Committee."

"And what does it say?"

"'Mama, serious. They're operating this week. Come immediately. María.'"

Pablo let a whistle escape his lips.

"And what are you going to do now?"

"I don't know, there's an emergency meeting today at the Labor Exchange. There'll be a plenary assembly to make a decision. That's why we need the largest possible number of people to attend. We'll probably have to leave for the border as early as tomorrow, and wait there for the definitive order to enter Spain. However, some Committee members aren't convinced, because the content of the message isn't exactly what had been agreed. In addition, apart from the telegram, we don't know anything about Jover and Caparrós, which is pretty strange, after all. Well, Pablo, I have to run. Got to try to let everyone know. Hey, can I borrow your bike?"

"Yes, of course, take it."

"We still haven't gotten our hands on the paper for the broadsides..."

Pablo says nothing. Robinsón insists:

"You can't make a revolution with guns alone, and you know it. Words are as important as firepower."

"I'll see what I can do," says Pablo dryly. "I still haven't finished editing the weekly, and it has to come out tomorrow."

"If you're worried about the letterhead, just cut it off and presto."

"I told you, I'll see what I can do, Robin."

The two friends look each other in the eyes for a few moments, intensely.

"Sure you don't want to come with us, Pablito?" Robinsón finally asks.

"Here's the bike," is his reply.

A LITTLE AFTER SEVEN, PABLO HAS finished printing all the copies of *Ex-Ilio*. He takes out his tobacco pouch and rolls a cigarette parsimoniously, thinking about what Robinsón said. He puts a little tobacco in the palm of his hand, carefully shreds it along the length of the paper, licks the glue and delicately twists it. Deep down, he knows that he's going to end up giving in to his friend's request, but if the expedition is leaving tomorrow, he needs to start printing the posters right away.

Only then does he realize that they have not yet given him the text for the posters. So he smokes the cigarette, closes the shop, and heads home on foot, because Robinsón has not returned the bicycle. It's almost better this way, he thinks, because although it has stopped raining, there is now a strong breeze, surprisingly chilling for this time of year. Pablo wraps himself tightly in his overcoat and tries to keep warm by blowing on his hands. He wants to get home as quickly as possible to drink something hot, but when he reaches Place de la République his feet suddenly decide to turn right and start carrying him down Rue du Château d'Eau. The Labor Exchange building stands majestically, crowned by a clock that seems to encourage revolutionary hopes: "Fluctuat Nec Mergitur," is the message displayed on the sphere (and even though this is the motto of the city of Paris, Pablo can't help but interpret it as an allegorical key: you may be beaten by the waves, comrades, but they shall not sink you). At least it's warm inside the building, especially in the great hall, where three hundred revolutionaries have congregated this Sunday evening and are heatedly discussing the strategy to take in the next few hours.

Pablo stops at the entrance to the hall. The room is full of smoke and tension in equal measure. Ascaso, standing on a table, is trying to moderate the ad hoc assembly, but everyone wants to speak at once and impose his own point of view. Some suspect that it was the police who sent the telegram, and they suggest that the expedition should not set off until word is received from Jover and Caparrós. It is not an outlandish suspicion, because with all the commotion the Spanish exiles in Paris are making, it's quite likely that word of the conspiracy has reached the ears of Martínez Anido. And everyone knows that the best way to make a conspiracy fail is to provoke it yourself, and thus keep it under control. For this reason, some members, including Gíbanel and Pedro Orobón, propose sending a representative to Spain to confirm the validity of the telegram. But the group in favor of caution is overwhelmingly in the minority, and they lose the debate for good when the persuasive Durruti takes Ascaso's place at the table and pronounces the following words, surrounded by attentive silence:

"Comrades, believe me, I understand that many of you have misgivings. How can we be absolutely certain that the thing is ready? How can we be sure that the telegrams—both the one we received today and the one that came Thursday—weren't sent by the dictator's henchmen? In my opinion, there's only one way: we go to the border to see what's going on with our own eyes. We're not going to solve anything by staying here. What we do know for sure is that the conditions for carrying out a revolutionary action have been created. In Barcelona, the dictator has offended Catalan pride, and in doing so all he's done is give us new allies. He's taken the luxury of exiling intellectuals such as Unamuno and Soriano, sowing discontent among the middle class, and practicing the most shameless nepotism. The war in Morocco continues unabated, and our soldiers don't want to go off to die in Africa. Do you not see in all of this, comrades, the positive signs calling us to revolution? Of course, there are also negatives, but isn't it the shock between positive and negative that produces the spark? If anyone accuses me of adventurism, I say that there has never been a revolution that wasn't led by adventurers! It's possible that this time we are wrong, and we will pay with our lives, or end up with our bones in jail; it is possible that after this defeat there will be others, but what I know is that every time a situation like this arises, we take another step toward general revolt, and that our actions will never have been in vain."

Applause suddenly erupts throughout the hall, but Durruti still wants to add one more thing:

"Make no mistake, friends: I'm not trying to convince anyone, because an act of this kind can only be the work of people who are already convinced of the fundamental principles that I have just spoken of here tonight."

After Durruti's decisive speech, it is resolved to set out for the border immediately and wait for further developments. Tomorrow, first thing in the morning, before eight o'clock, all those who are ready to enter Spain to start the revolution are to show up at the Gare Saint-Lazare bringing only the bare necessities. There they will be given a train ticket and, if possible, a bit of money. They will receive their weapons at the border to avoid problems during the trip. So two groups are formed, those who will go to Saint-Jean-de-Luz, and those who will go to Perpignan.

"Everyone who wants to go to Perpignan, stand to the left, the others on the right," Ascaso orders them, resuming his position on top of the table, "Those with no preference, stay in the center for now. Remember that knowledge of the terrain is important and so are whatever contacts you might have in the interior. Logically, Catalans should go to Perpignan and Basques and Navarrans to Saint-Jean-de-Luz."

The crowd begins dividing up, including some members of the Group of Thirty, such as Juan Riesgo, Luís Naveira, Gil Galar, and Bonifacio Manzanedo, who stand off to the right. Robinsón is also among those going to Saint-Jean-de-Luz, together with Anxo, the vegetarian they call "El Maestro." In the group on the left, Pablo can identify Augustín Gíbanel and the brothers Orobón. Once the first distribution is made, the men in the center divide themselves evenly. Seeing that the movement's main ideologues do not join either of the groups, someone asks:

"And you fellows? Where are you going?"

"Well," Ascaso replies, "Some of us will stay here until tomorrow afternoon to handle the weapons purchase and to finish organizing the plans.

We can't go with the bulk of the expedition because the French police have records on us and we would jeopardize the success of the rebellion. But if it's at all possible we'll meet you at the border. In any case, tomorrow at the station we'll finish putting the groups together. Surely there are people who couldn't come or who didn't hear about the assembly. Also, you'll be adding reinforcements along the way, and in Saint-Jean-de-Luz and Perpignan they'll be ready to welcome you. Comrades," he says, raising his voice, "There's no time to lose: in Spain, the Revolution is ready to explode and we can't abandon our brothers now. Go spread the word, and everyone come to Gare Saint-Lazare tomorrow. Spain's future is in our hands. *¡Viva la revolución!*"

"*¡Viva!*" the crowd shouts, some with more enthusiasm than others. Most start to leave the room, some thinking about how they will explain to their wives that tomorrow they are going to liberate Spain, others with the fire of revolution burning in their stomachs.

Pablo stays to wait for Robinsón by the door, detachedly observing the faces of the men walking out. Many reflect the excitement of the moment, some have a distant gaze, some are engraved with a look of fear, still others just look tired. Judging by some of their expressions, Pablo figures that they will not show up at the station tomorrow, in others, on the contrary, he thinks he sees the sincere reflection of idealism about to be realized. When Robinsón sees Pablo by the door, he walks up to him accompanied by Teixidó.

"Thanks for coming," says the propaganda manager in a gravelly voice.

"How many do you need?" Pablo cuts him off.

"The ideal would be ten thousand. Five thousand for each group. But we can get by with half of that. I assume they've been able to print a few copies clandestinely in Spain."

"Fine then, I'll try to reach ten thousand, but I can't promise it. Tomorrow I'll bring what I have to the station. If you'll give me the text, I'll go to La Fraternelle right now. But listen, try to cut the letterhead off during the trip, I don't want old Faure to fire me. I'll have enough work trying to explain the disappearance of a few thousand quartos..."

"Consider it done," Teixidó promises firmly. "Wait a minute, I'll go get you the text right now," and he walks toward the table Ascaso stood on, which is now surrounded by Durruti, Vivancos, Recasens, et al. in heated discussion.

"In any case," Pablo says to Robinsón, taking advantage of Teixidó's absence, "I still think this is madness. Even worse if the main directors are staying here in Paris."

"What are you insinuating?"

"I'm not insinuating anything, Robin. I'm just saying that if things go awry, they're not going to take the fall, but if the revolution succeeds, they'll be the first to put on medals."

"You're starting to think like the goddamned bourgeois, Pablito. You should come with us to get the rubbish out of your head."

Teixidó returns.

"Here you go."

"It's not very long," Pablo notes as he looks over the text.

"We prefer to keep it concise as Don Miguel always says: what's good, put briefly—"

"—is twice as good," Robinsón completes his thought.

"And what's bad, if it's long, is twice as expensive," adds Pablo, quoting old Faure. "Well I guess I'll be seeing you in a few hours at the train station."

"Thank you very much," Teixidó extends his hand. "For Spain."

"For freedom," Pablo prefers.

And he leaves the place accompanied by Robinsón. Kropotkin is waiting under the stairs, jealously guarding the old Clément Luxe bicycle. After crossing the frigid Parisian night, they get back to the printing house.

"To be honest, I don't know who exploits me more, my boss or the proletariat," Pablo remarks sarcastically as he restarts the machines.

"Surely both do equally," Robinsón laughs, "but one does it to bring out the worst in you and the other the best."

"Right, but one puts food on my table and the other costs me sleep."

"Fine, you've got me there," Robinsón concedes, "but you could think of it another way: one buys your soul while the other gives you the gift of friendship."

"You ever thought of becoming a poet?" Pablo asks with a smirk as he lines up type in the tray. "But then again, what good is friendship if I don't have a soul?"

And so they go on philosophizing for a long while, Robinsón running the old Minerva and Pablo operating the Albatross. When three in the morning rolls around, they decide to call it a day. They have about eight thousand copies, and they are exhausted.

"How are we going to carry all of these?" asks Robinsón.

"In your shirt pocket if you like," Pablo replies, going down into the cellar. He returns with two big sacks, and they put the posters inside. The bags weigh twenty pounds each. "You want to come rest a bit before you start your revolution?"

"Of course. What time does your train leave for Marly?"

"Nine o'clock. I'll help you carry the bags to Gare Saint-Lazare and then I'll go the Gare du Nord to catch my train."

They tie the two bags together, drape them on the bicycle like saddlebags, and walk the bike home. They barely open their mouths on the walk. Events have sped up so much in these last few hours that the time for farewell has caught them unprepared. It doesn't occur to them that these could be the last few moments they will ever spend with each other; they are too tired for such bleak thoughts. In any case, fate still has a surprise in store for them.

When they reach home, they haul the heavy sacks up the seventy steps to Pablo's hovel. It is about four o'clock now, and they'll still be able to sleep for two or three hours before they have to get up to go to

Saint-Lazare. This time it is Robinsón who has trouble falling asleep. Pablo, on the other hand, is out like a light, and he dreams. He dreams about someone he hasn't seen in a long time, someone for whom he was ready to lay down his life: he dreams of Angela, whom he has long been trying to forget. But everyone knows that the desire to forget someone just engraves them deeper in the memory. Angela is wearing a night gown of blinding white, a whiteness contrasting with the brown of her skin. She is on a lonely road in the middle of a flat terrain that spreads out in all directions, with no sign of life anywhere. Suddenly a man appears out of thin air wearing a linen suit and a Panama hat. He grabs her waist and throws her over his shoulder. Angela screams and pounds on his back with her fists, but the man doesn't say a word, just starts running away down the road. Then Angela lifts her head and stretches her arms out to someone: "Come help, come help," she says again and again, as her face changes into that of María, Pablo's mother, and then to the face of Julia, his dear sister, and then to that of little Teresa, his ten-year-old niece, before finally turning back into Angela's face, still shouting "Come help, come help!" though no one goes to rescue her. Only when he hears his name does Pablo realize that he is the one they are calling:

"Come help, Pablo, come help, come help, Pablo, Pablo, come help, Pablo…"

"Pablo, Pablo!" Robinsón is shouting, shaking Pablo awake. "You alright, Pablo?"

"Huh? Yeah … I was dreaming, sorry."

"Don't worry, I couldn't sleep. You were dreaming out loud. Looked like you were having a rough time. I woke you up when you started shouting and waving your arms."

"Thanks. What time is it?"

"It's still early, Sleep a little more. In fact, I was thinking maybe I'd go look for Naveira, who lives just down the street, and have him help me with the bags so you can sleep a little longer."

Pablo says nothing, but he sits up on the bed and opens the drawer of the bedside table. He takes out an iridescent object that gives off a greenish glow, and observes it carefully. It is his good-luck amulet, a crystal eye made into a necklace that has accompanied him everywhere since it saved his life many years ago. He squeezes it in his hand, stands up and opens the hovel's lone window. Dawn is coming on, and the cold air strikes him in the face.

"Robin."

"What?"

"I had a dream."

"I know. And?"

But Robinsón's question is almost rhetorical, because he can read the answer on Pablo's face.

"I'm going with you to Spain."

IT IS EIGHT IN THE MORNING on the third of November 1924 when Pablo and Robinsón arrive at the Gare Saint-Lazare, carrying thousands of flyers and a pair of suitcases full of clothing and personal effects. Kropotkin, the faithful wiener dog, is happily leading the way, intuiting that this excursion will be longer than most. A few hundred people have come to meet outside the station, although not all of them are going to board the trains to Perpignan or Saint-Jean-de-Luz: word has spread like wildfire among the community of Spaniards living in Paris, and many have come here to bid farewell to the two parties, who are leaving at almost exactly the same time. There are some tearful women saying goodbye to their husbands, and clinging, bleary-eyed children kissing their fathers. There are also old Republicans who have come to the station to try to convince the revolutionaries that this is a fool's errand, but no one listens to a word they say. Most of those who have come have done so to pay homage to and cheer on these men who are willing to give their lives for the liberty of their beloved country, some of whom, doubtless the most fearful, carry pistols wrapped in newspaper, jeopardizing the whole mission. But who's going to tell them what they ought to do at this late hour?

Most of them are anarchists, although there are also some communists, various syndicalists, and miscellaneous revolutionaries. It is true that not everyone who was present last night at the Labor Exchange has shown up, but other unexpected people have joined the ranks: emigrants who see the improvised adventure as a good excuse to return home, deserters hoping to benefit from the recently declared amnesty, and even a few rough sorts who have gotten on board hoping to receive a little food and a bit of money, or at least a free train ticket to the warmer climes of Southern France, now that the autumn chill is starting to make itself felt in Paris. But what is to be done? The revolution needs as many hands as it can get. All the more so considering that just a month ago, optimists were talking about a few thousand men ready to cross the border.

The main organizers of the movement are also at the station, trying to bring order to the slapdash expedition and selecting the leaders of the two groups, who make their way to their respective platforms after having said goodbye to their family and friends. Eighty or ninety revolutionaries and one wiener dog load onto the train for Saint-Jean-de-Luz, with not a woman among them. The train for Perpignan takes on over a hundred, including Ramona Berri and Pepita Not. The adventurers, laden with suitcases, duffel bags, and rucksacks, spread out in the train car cabins, hoping to attract less attention. Some of them even try to sit in first class, but they are quickly ejected by the inspector, who hits the roof when he catches them spitting and tossing cigarette butts on the carpeted floor. Augustín Gíbanel and Valeriano Orobón are the ones responsible for handing out the tickets to the group headed to Perpignan, while Robinsón and Naveira are doing the same with those going to Saint-Jean-de-Luz. Pablo stuffs a few bundles of posters into the bags of his two companions and gives the other bag to Teixidó, so that he can distribute them among the leaders of the other convoy. Pedro Massoni, with his miserly mien, distributes a few francs to the men onboard the trains, watching to make sure no one gets off board after having received the measly stipend.

At 8:35, a long whistle announces that the Perpignan train is about to depart. The intrepid Gíbanel is the last to board, dragging a heavy suitcase which he claims contains several hams but which is in fact full of Winchester rifles. Scarves wave from windows and the air fills with fleeting kisses. Ten minutes later, another whistle announces the departure of the train to Saint-Jean-de-Luz. More scarves wave in the air; more desperate kisses fly. When the train starts rolling the parties who have come to see the liberators off begin to disperse, until the only people left on the platform are Durruti and Ascaso, watching the train disappear out of sight.

"Don't you get the feeling we're sending them directly into the lion's mouth?" Ascaso asks, his voice hoarse, not daring to look at Durruti, who takes a moment to respond.

"You know what, Francisco?" he finally replies, not taking his eyes from the spot where the train disappeared. "If I've learned anything in the last few years, it's that the struggle can be won without heroes, but not without martyrs."

Pablo doesn't know it yet, but he has just boarded a train bound for the gallows.

PART TWO

— I0 —

To the Spanish people:

Spain is going through a moment that is so absolutely critical, so great has been the number of crimes and injustices suffered by our disgraced citizenry under the thumb of swine in frock coats, spurs, and cassocks, that it is about to explode like a steam engine under too much pressure.

If we truly love justice and progress, if we have not lost that precious garment called dignity, if we have, finally, the very least a people can have—a sense of shame—we must take advantage of these good circumstances and march, all together as one man, to unleash the axe of vengeance on the Alfonsos, the Anidos, the Riveras, and all the swine who have covered us in blood and insults before the eyes of the civilized world. Should we fail to take action, we would deserve to be called cowards, accomplices to all the misfortune that weighs upon us, and worthy of the bitterest disdain of the whole educated world, which will consider us impotent to escape the quagmire we are drowning in.

Let us save Spain, my friends! Long live liberty!

Revolutionary poster printed at *La Fraternelle*

BOARDING A TRAIN TO START A long journey almost always produces a rumbling in the stomach. So we can imagine what a person feels when boarding a train along with eighty companions determined to start a revolution to liberate a whole country.

But Pablo's head is still elsewhere, a bit groggy from lack of sleep and the early departure. The train has left the Gare Saint-Lazare right on time, and the revolutionaries have spread out discreetly through the cars, although the large farewell party didn't exactly help them go unnoticed.

Of the Group of Thirty, only five boarded the train for Saint-Jean-de-Luz: Robinsón, who is repeating the same trip he made a week ago; Luís Naveira, "*El Portugués*," with his thick Galician accent, strident voice and elegant Catholic manners; Juan Riesgo, who appears to be a hoarder of physical abnormalities: hunchback, lazy eye, harelip; Enrique Gil Galar, who is missing a finger from his left hand, like the good carpenter he is (despite his appearance, which is rather that of a romantic poet); and Bonifacio Manzanedo, an affable explosives expert from Burgos, who has something in common with Pablo of which neither is aware: they were both among the 150 men detained three years ago in Bilbao for the much-talked-about murder of the director of the Altos Hornos foundry in Biscay.

Each of the leaders boards a different car and takes responsibility for a group of about fifteen men, distributed in various compartments. Pablo is in the group led by Robinsón, and almost without trying he's been promoted to something like lieutenant (if such a term can have any meaning in anarchist jargon). But as his body travels southward, his mind is going in the opposite direction: as he settles into his seat, he can't help thinking about the Beaumonts, whom he neglected to tell about his sudden decision to return to Spain and quit his job as caretaker of their estate. As soon as he arrives in Saint-Jean-de-Luz, he will send them a telegram. While he's at it, he will also inform old Faure, who will surely foam at the mouth. As luck would have it, Pablo hasn't come across Julianín amongst the revolutionaries, and he is hoping that the young apprentice will take the reins at the print shop. With these pragmatic thoughts, which you might call unworthy of a revolutionary, the now-ex-typesetter of La Fraternelle falls asleep. Let us take this brief rest as an opportunity to go over a few events unfolding in Paris as the group of revolutionaries passes through Orléans, Tours, and Poitiers.

At about the same time as the conductor of the train to Saint-Jean-de-Luz was shouting "All aboard," back in Paris at Flammarion publishing house, 26 Rue Racine, box after box began to emerge filled with pamphlets by Blasco Ibáñez, who finally settled on the title *Alphonse XIII démasqué: La terreur militariste en Espagne*. The print run is staggering, because the Valencian author has ceded his author's royalties to the publisher to be spent on propaganda and distribution, and that is what the brothers Max and Alex Fisher, editors in chief of Maison Flammarion, have done, launching an initial print run of 150,000 copies, which will be spread all over Paris within a few hours. For the Spanish edition, titled *Una nación secuestrada*, under the responsibility of editor Juan Durá, another Valencian exiled in Paris, the idea is to do a mind-boggling run of one million copies, which Blasco Ibáñez is planning to sneak into Spain. "Using airplanes if necessary," he is reputed to have said. The little book is over seventy pages long, and in it, Blasco takes a decidedly anti-monarchic (even more than anti-dictatorial) stance, howling for a remedy to the tyranny misgoverning Spain. It is planned to translate the pamphlet into most of the languages of Europe, as well as Hebrew, Arabic, and Japanese. The Valencian author's gesture will end up being compared to Zola's seminal *"J'accuse … !"*.

But if we dwell for a moment on this event it is not merely to kill time with literary chitchat while we wait for Pablo to wake up on arrival in Saint-Jean-de-Luz along with the rest of the comrades, but rather because the commotion that will arise in Paris in response to Blasco Ibáñez's incendiary pamphlet is going to have a very particular impact on the development of this story. We recall that today at noon, the trio of Durruti, Massoni, and Vivancos were supposed to meet with the Valencian author at Chez Pepe on Montmartre, to receive the money Blasco has agreed to give them to buy firearms for the incursion. But of course Blasco will not show up for the meeting. Who knows if it's because he forgot, or is too busy enjoying the success of his pamphlet, or because he was unable to get together the money he promised. The fact is that when the young anarchists enter the restaurant on Place du Tertre, the host will tell them that Blasco Ibáñez hasn't made an appearance there all morning. In the evening they will go looking for him at the hotel, but will only find his secretary, Carlos Esplá, who will explain to them that the publication of the pamphlet has led to the author receiving a few threats (including one challenge to a duel to the death) and he has decided to retire to his house in Menton on the Côte d'Azur. So farewell to arms, and another defeat for the Committee of Anarchist Relations. But there is no going back now.

When Pablo wakes up in the train, the first thing he sees is a furtive hand retreating from his backpack.

"Hey, what are you doing?!" he barks at the hand's owner, a bald, toothless man in the facing seat. Robinsón has disappeared, and the compartment is filled with cigar smoke.

"Easy there, comrade, don't get bent out of shape, we're in the same boat. Perico Alarco, at your service," the man says, extending his hand and smiling like a broken piano. "And this guy here is Manolito Monzón. Say hello, Manolito," he says, nudging his companion's ribs with his elbow. "He's deaf and dumb."

"Fine by me," Pablo replies, "what I want to know is what you were doing rifling around in my bag."

"Nay, compadre. Whatcha mean rifling around? We weren't rifling around. We just wanted to see those li'l papers we heard ya got in there. If we're gonna go to Spain and hand 'em out, we at least wanna know what they say…"

With a sour face, Pablo reaches into the bag and takes out a couple of posters.

"Here, take them. When you finish reading them, pass them onto other comrades. But with discretion, eh?"

"Well, thing is, see," says this Perico, his eyes bulging like a slaughtered sheep. "This here Manolito knows how to read, but he can't talk. When it comes to shooting the breeze I'm an expert, but with the whole reading thing, I sort of can't…Would you mind reading it for me, pal?"

Just then Robinsón arrives, with Kropotkin nipping at his heels, and sits next to Pablo.

"It seems there's been some trouble in the first car," the vegetarian explains, a bit worried. "Apparently a few guys started playing mus and a lady put up a big fuss. They don't understand that the whole thing could go to shit because of stupid stuff like this. Well, let's cross our fingers and hope the gendarmes don't show up during the trip."

The men playing mus are four Zamorans from Villalpando who had been inseparable back in Paris, earning the nickname "the Villalpando clan."

"Robin," Pablo stands up, taking advantage of the chance to make an escape, "Would you be so kind as to read the broadside to our friend here? I need to see a man about a horse."

"Sure, no problem."

Pablo gets up, giving a copy to Manolito Monzón the deaf-mute and another to Robinsón. As he squeezes past him, he whispers:

"Keep an eye on the bags. I don't trust these two one bit."

"Perico Alarco, at your service," the toothless man introduces himself, standing and perfuming Robinsón's beard with breath that reeks of rancid bacon. And the poor vegetarian begins to read the poster as quickly as he can, hoping to get rid of the interloper as soon as possible.

"It says, 'Spain is going through a moment that is so absolutely critical, so great has been the number of crimes and injustices suffered by our disgraced citizenry under the thumb of swine in frock coats, spurs, and cassocks, that it is about to explode like a steam engine under too much pressure—'"

"*Olé!*" shouts Perico, and his attention wanders out the window until he hears Robinsón read the final "*¡Viva la libertad!*" whereupon the toothless man shouts "*¡Viva!*" with vehemence, eliciting an echo from two anarchists passing through the corridor. "Thank you very much, my friend. Of course, you wouldn't happen to have a little wine to wet our whistles, would you? This here Manolito and me sure get thirsty on long trips."

"Sorry, I don't drink."

"Aye yay yay, it's me who feels sorry for you. So nothing, nothing to improve our lot!" and elbowing his companion's ribs again, they take their leave, just as Pablo returns.

"Quite the pair," Robinsón murmurs.

"You can say that again. Can we blame the dictatorship for them, too?"

"No, for them we have the local governments and the Church to blame. If those two had gone to Ferrer's school, they'd have turned out differently, and you know that better than anyone. But we need a revolution for them too."

"For them and with them."

"Well, yes. What can you do? Hey, do you want to work on removing the letterhead from the broadsides?" Robinsón suggests, noticing that the posters still bear the printer's mark, with La Fraternelle's logo (two outstretched hands) and the inscription "Imp. La Fraternelle, 55, rue Pixérécourt."

"It doesn't matter now, Robin. Mr. Savage can take his print house and shove it. If the revolution succeeds, I'll stay in Spain. And if we fail, we won't have to pay any rent in jail. Or in the grave."

Robinsón smiles bitterly. Shortly, the train stops its progress, and all of the passengers are ordered off with their luggage. A few of the revolutionaries cast worried looks at each other, fearing the worst. Those carrying firearms hesitate between hiding them and ditching them. But when they step onto the platform they are relieved to learn that it's just a transfer to a different train. Most of them take advantage of the occasion to eat the food they've brought from Paris: a hunk of bread, a slice of cheese or ham, a few boiled eggs, or a bit of fruit. The leaders step aside for a brief talk, exchanging opinions. It seems that two of the revolutionaries who had been riding in the last car got off in Tours and did not get back on. In Poitiers, another two said they had motion sickness, and that they would spend the night there and complete the journey the next day, but no one is betting on seeing them again. Five more will disappear at the Bordeaux station.

When they arrive in Saint-Jean-de-Luz, it is already the dead of night and there have been another ten desertions. Saint-Jean is a fishing village just a few kilometers from the border, and its Basque name, Donibane Lohizune, refers to the legend that the town was built on a swamp. The population is not quite seven thousand, and it is separated from Ciboure (Ziburu, in Basque) by the gash of the river Nivelle, which has its mouth at the Bay of Saint-Jean-de-Luz, an anteroom of the Bay of Biscay and the tumultuous Cantabrian Sea.

On the platform in the station, a group of about a dozen anarchists is waiting to welcome them discreetly, and the gesture seems to boost morale. Among the welcoming committee is the unmissable giant from Argentina, wearing a beret appropriate to these latitudes.

"Leandro!" Robinsón and Pablo shout in unison, as they fall into a three-way hug, Kropotkin circling frantically. The Argentine looks at Pablo as if wanting to say he knew Pablo would end up coming along.

"Che, I thought you guys would never get here. These French trains are slower than a gaucho dismounting from his horse."

They leave the station together with the rest of the group. They are a motley crew, an army of ghosts moving through the night. The leader of the welcoming committee appears to be a man in his forties, with a gray mustache and hair, bright eyes, and an intelligent gaze. He goes by the name of Julián Santillán. Some say he used to serve in the Civil Guard and that they threw him out for his rebelliousness, and with the advent of the dictatorship he had to go into exile in France. It is he who leads the group toward Place de Louis XIV, conversing with the leaders of the expedition, all except Robinsón, who is bringing up the rear with Pablo and Leandro.

"We thought there'd be more of you," says the former civil guardsman. "We heard talk of thousands of revolutionaries."

"Well," Naveira responds, "remember that more than half went to Perpignan, and that more comrades will be arriving on the next few trains. The idea is to try to round up volunteers at the border and wait for the signal from Spain to cross over. And how many men do you have here?"

"Not many, to tell the truth. A few from Bayonne, another handful from Biarritz, a few from Bordeaux, and the group of us from Saint-Jean-de-Luz who came to meet you. In all, about thirty, I'd say."

"Some is better than none," murmurs Juan Riesgo, unable to hide his disappointment.

"Have you thought of any place we could stay while we wait for the right time to cross the border?" asks Bonifacio Manzanedo.

"The local comrades can host three or four people per house. The rest will have to look out for themselves, maybe stay at an inn. There are several cheap, decent hostels near the central plaza."

At the opposite end of the group, lagging a bit behind, Pablo, Leandro, and Robinsón are catching up on the latest events, while Kropotkin runs around depositing turds all over the village.

"So old Dubois replaced me with a Japanese fella, huh? Well, it's his loss!" murmurs Leandro, spitting on the ground and furiously stomping the sputum.

"I hear that business is way up since then," Robinsón jokes, and Pablo takes the baton:

"Plus, you can finally see through the glasses."

The Argentine giant grabs them both by the collars:

"See if I don't make you bastards sleep in a ditch tonight!"

Kropotkin yips and tries to bite Leandro's leg, but the big man doesn't even flinch. Someone in the group tells them to keep their voices down and shut up that damn dog. They finally reach the plaza and Santillán goes into a restaurant. A few seconds later, he pokes his head out and tells them to come inside, that there's room for everyone if they squeeze together. Indeed, the place is enormous. It reminds Pablo a bit of the bistro in Marly-les-Valenciennes where Madame De Bruyn makes such delicious *hochepots*. The owner, a Biscayan from Guernica with a certain resemblance to Charlot, sets about serving them beer and wine, while an uproar of pots and pans erupts in the kitchen to answer the massive wave of hunger that has just rolled in. The revolutionaries spread out among the tables and start to warm their spirits and stomachs. A little group of vegetarians led by El Maestro sits apart from the others next to the door, and quickly becomes the butt of jokes among the general population, who view their table covered in salads and fruit juices with incredulity as they stuff their faces with roast beef. The leaders of the mission from Paris have convened at a table in the rear, where they are exchanging opinions with their comrades from Saint-Jean-de-Luz.

"So when do you think the thing is going to be ready?" asks Julián Santillán, the former civil guardsman. "We can't stay here very long without arousing suspicions."

"We have to wait until we receive the signal," warns Juan Riesgo, whose prudence contradicts his name. "Tomorrow we'll make contact with the leaders of the Paris Committee so they can inform us how things are going there and how it's been for the Perpignan contingent. In the meantime, all we can do is keep waiting and stay calm."

"Hey, Santillán," Robinsón interrupts, "why isn't Max with you guys?"

"Max who?"

"Max Hernández, the one they call El Señorito, the fellow in charge of recruiting in this area."

"Oh, him. The truth is, it's been days since anyone's seen him, the last time was when he appeared with a couple of Army officers, who confirmed that the regiments of Bilbao, Zaragoza, Lérida, and Barcelona are ready to rebel. Some say he went to Paris to speak with Rodrigo Soriano and Unamuno."

"And why in God's name did he want to talk to those two dreamers?" interjects Gil Galar, pushing his Romantic-poet hair from his eyes.

"I don't know, man," argues Santillán, "they're only the top leaders of the movement—"

"Who the fuck told you that?" Gil Galar erupts, standing up from the table, his eyes—the only lively part of his corpse-like face—bloodshot and bulging.

"Whoa, there, laddie boy," responds the ex-guardsman, cool as a cucumber. "Do us a favor, sit down and calm down. I heard Max say that the movement was organized from Paris by Soriano, Unamuno, Ortega, and Blasco Ibáñez."

"That must have been a diversion," interjects Naveira, conciliatory. "Maybe Max thought there was an informant listening. Or maybe he thought they could recruit more volunteers by name-dropping those pencil pushers. After all, that was his job, right?"

"Yes," Robinsón avers, "but the end doesn't always justify the means, Luís. You can't trick people into joining the revolution. We have enough hassles with the traps the cops lay for us, we don't need to go lying to each other as well."

They carry on these discussions until the Charlot of Guernica tosses them out into the street. In the middle of the central square, deserted at this hour, there is a kiosk. It is an old hexagonal gazebo open on all six sides where the village orchestra plays on Sundays. The revolutionaries huddle in it to finish getting organized. More than half find lodging with comrades who live in Saint-Jean-de-Luz. The rest of them head toward the flophouses in the blocks surrounding the plaza, to spend the few francs Massoni gave them when they boarded the train. Before going their separate ways, they agree to meet at lunchtime tomorrow right back here at Place de Louis XIV, when they will be joined by comrades from nearby villages who are ready to go liberate Spain.

Pablo and Robinsón are among those who will enjoy free lodging, as Leandro has assured them that at "his house" they would be honored guests and could sleep like angels. But the Argentine's enigmatic smile has failed to convince the two friends.

"Do we dare ask where you're taking us?" Pablo inquires as they start to leave the village.

"*Pas de souci, mon ami*," Leandro reassures him with his horselike smile. "We're almost there."

And indeed, after a couple of minutes Leandro stops before a cemetery gate and, bowing, invites them to enter:

"*S'il vous plaît*," he says, and leads the way nonchalantly.

IX
(1908)

"ANGELA, OPEN THE DOOR, FOR THE love of God!"

The voice of Don Diego Gómez sounded metallic and menacing, and the chair blocking the door seemed about to succumb under the strain. Pablo and Angela looked at each other in terror and hurried to dress.

"Let's go!" shouted the girl.

But it was too late. The chair went flying as the door blasted open like the mouth of a raging dinosaur, framing the distorted figure of the lieutenant colonel, still in shirtsleeves. Seeing them there together, he froze, turning into a pillar of salt, barely a tremble on his blanched face. Behind him appeared Angela's cousin Rodrigo Martín, dressed in street clothing.

"You see, Uncle? See what this sewer rat is capable of?" he shouted, glaring at Pablo with an explosive mixture of hatred, jealousy, and disdain. He had let his hair grow long, and a little mustache underlined his nose.

"Shut up!" ordered Don Diego, without moving his lips, like a perfect ventriloquist, "And do your duty."

Rodrigo entered the room, took off his kid glove and tossed it at Pablo's feet, in a gesture that everyone understood.

"No!" shouted Angela, her eyes wide with fright.

"Don't worry," Pablo tried to calm her with tragic aplomb. "If this is the price we have to pay for freedom, we'll pay it willingly."

And he went to pick up Rodrigo's glove.

"No!" Angela shouted again, stepping on it with her bare foot.

"He doesn't have a choice, my dear," said Don Diego Gómez, not changing his hieratic posture. "He can accept the challenge, or he can leave this room feet-first."

THE ANARCHIST WHO SHARED MY NAME

"I hate you!" Angela shouted, leaping on her father and striking his chest with her fists.

The lieutenant colonel didn't even blink. If anything, his pallor increased, as did his emaciated appearance. When he grew weary of the blows, he grabbed his daughter by the waist, threw her over his shoulder, and carried her out of the room.

"No, Pablo, nooooo!" Angela shouted, relentlessly striking her father's back.

But there was no choice.

"We consider this a very serious offense," said Rodrigo Martín, defiantly. "For the dueling weapon we choose pistols. Tomorrow at the break of dawn I will be waiting for you at the Fountain of the Wolf."

"Understood," said Pablo.

And he bent down to pick up the glove.

DUELS WERE FORBIDDEN IN TURN-OF-THE-CENTURY Spain, but the authorities tended to turn a blind eye, an indication of the atavistic respect they held for certain traditions. The Penal Code could prohibit the challenge, but a few dozen duels still took place here and there in the country every year. The president of the government could call it the "outdated institution of affairs of honor," but hotheaded gentlemen kept right on using pistols to cleanse their names. Eminent minds could demand harsher punishments for the seconds, but they continued to get off scot-free. Some people even suggested prohibiting newspapers from reporting on duels, arguing that most duelists were fighting *pour la galerie* and that if there were no press to spread word of their prowess, most of them would give up trying to pull their honor out of a hat. Obviously, it was more often than not just empty posturing, ending with shots fired in the air and reconciliation feasts; however, sometimes, in rare cases, the bullet found its mark, and in such cases public opinion would get up in arms. This was precisely what had taken place in the recent cases of the young Marquis de Pickman and the journalist Juan Pedro Barcelona, who ended up paying with their lives for a fit of unbridled honor, the first at the hands of Captain Paredes and the second to a bullet fired early by the director of the Catholic seminary El Evangelio, Don Benigno Varela, who paid poor homage to his forename. The response to this absurd bloodshed was the creation of the *Liga Nacional Antiduelista*, founded by prominent individuals who aimed to do away with the archaic affairs of honor. Among them, significantly, were several politicians, military officers, nobles, and reporters—precisely the sorts of people who had the strongest tendency to resolve their differences at twenty paces.

But these were not the duels that came to Pablo's mind as he left the Gómez house, but rather another that had taken place a century before, starring a young French mathematician. "Have I told you the story of Évariste Galois?" he thought he heard his father's voice say.

But Don Julián was dead, and now it was Pablo who was about to gamble his life. At the age of eighteen, he had never even fired a damned pistol, because he hadn't yet been called up for military service. The anarchists of Salamanca had also failed to train him in the use of a firearm, most likely because they didn't have any. In fact, his closest brush with a Browning semiautomatic was in Madrid on the night before the royal wedding, when Vicente Holgado lifted his hand to his side, smelling danger. And now his life depended on his dexterity with a revolver! How absurd, thought Pablo, how utterly ridiculous. But he could see no other way out of the imbroglio. What was he supposed to do, leave Angela in the lurch? Let Don Diego have his way? Sacrifice his love to save his skin? No, no way. Especially after that night, after the *nox mirabilis*. After all, he had come to Béjar ready to face the whole Spanish navy, and fate was now pitting him against a single adversary, so what did he have to fear? Of course, he would have preferred not to have to go to such an extreme, but what else could he do? This military family adhered to a code of honor that allowed no choice but to pick up the thrown glove. For them, there was no other possible solution: he had entered their house and dishonored their daughter. Now he could only hope that everything would be resolved by a shot in the air; or in the worst case, that the blood spilled would not be his own.

With these somber thoughts, Pablo left the village via the Carretera de Candelario. He needed to clear his head and stretch his muscles. The little road snaked uphill, while the sun struggled to find a path between the mountaintops and the low clouds. Dew glowed pearly on the grass along the road. The blackbirds were warming up their voices in the woods. A small carriage passed alongside him and stopped.

"Are you going to Candelario, young sir?" asked the friendly local. Pablo heard the words, but did not understand the question: his mind was far away.

"What's that you say?"

"I say if you want a ride, I'll take you to Candelario."

Pablo shook his head and stepped off the road. He had no desire to talk to anyone. He wandered into the woods, lost in his thoughts. He crossed rivers thinking of Angela, climbed hillsides thinking of his father, skirted ravines thinking of Angela, blazed trails thinking of his mother, clambered over a fallen tree thinking of Angela, rested a while thinking of his sister, stumbled a bit thinking about Rodrigo, caught his balance thinking about Angela, slipped and fell thinking about Don Diego, got up thinking about Angela, got covered in mud thinking about Évariste Galois, lost his way thinking about Angela. And when he wanted to go back to Béjar, he was completely disoriented. He had no idea how much time had passed, but the daylight was already waning. He started walking northward, guiding himself by the moss on the trees as his father had taught him, but the inevitable night caught up with him. He weighed the possibility of starting a fire and sleeping outdoors, but he settled for sitting on a rock and rolling a cigarette in the dark. Just as he was about to light the match, he saw something glowing in the distance. He stood up and walked toward the glowing dot, which grew larger and larger as he approached. Finally, he could make out a small stone structure, perhaps a woodsman's hut. Smoke was rising from the chimney, and there was light inside. He walked to the door, but he didn't have time to knock, because just as he raised his fist he heard a voice saying:

"Come in, young man, the door is open."

Pablo turned, surprised, but saw no one. Surely the voice had come from inside the hut. Timidly, he pushed on the door and found himself face-to-face with a bent old woman attending to a boiling pot in the fireplace; only then did he realize that he had gone a whole day without a bite of food. The woman looked a shambles, wrinkles competing with warts for the conquest of her face.

"Sit down, please," said the old woman, dragging out the syllables, "I was just about to take up my dinner."

"I don't mean to bother you," Pablo apologized. "I lost my way in the woods, and I haven't eaten in hours."

"I know. That's why I invited you to sit down," said the old woman, using the informal address as though his entry into her abode was all the permission she needed.

"Thank you very much," was all that Pablo replied, as he sat down on a stump that served as a chair. The hut was illuminated by an infinitude of candles, populating the corners like trembling fireflies. The walls, covered with shelves, offered a spectacle of flasks, jars, and bottles filled with salts, ointments, concoctions, and medicinal herbs with fantastic names like "lungwort," "bone knit," and "maidenhair." Here and there, an unexpected object interrupted the series of containers: a stuffed owl, a horseshoe, a boar's tusk, a wax doll, an astrolabe, an anatomy book, and even what looked like a bust of Pliny, missing its left ear. In a corner, beneath a cot, various feline eyes observed the interloper.

"You're not from around here, are you?" asked the old woman after taking the pot from the fire.

Pablo shook his head, and his guts tightened in anticipation of the repast.

"And yet, something brought you to Béjar, am I wrong?"

Pablo nodded as he watched his plate fill with a thick, brownish stew dotted with garbanzo beans.

"And I'll bet that something goes by a woman's name."

"How did you know?" Pablo asked, lifting the spoonful to his lips.

"You don't have to be an oracle to see that much, young man, it's written all over your face. All the same, they do call me Anita, 'the Fortune-teller.'"

"Why?"

"Because I can see the future."

Pablo's spoon halted its course halfway between his plate and his mouth.

"How far into the future?" he asked.

"As far as you like. A day, a year, a whole lifetime if need be. All you have to do is show me your palm."

Pablo dropped his spoon and looked at his hands.

"But I also know how to do other things," said the old woman, smiling beneath her mustache.

"What kinds of things?" asked Pablo, picking his spoon up again.

"Cure the ills of the body, for example."

"How do you do it?"

"It depends. Depends on the illness. To calm spasms, I press on the wrist with a strip of palm leaf. To bring down a fever, I place a flayed pigeon on the forehead. To stop bleeding, I let the drops of blood fall on the center of a cross made of two pieces of straw."

"And that works?"

"Of course."

They finished eating in silence. The stew tasted awful, but it warmed the stomach. From outside came a pained sound, like someone crying or moaning.

"It's just the weather vane," said the woman, "battling the wind."

Pablo drained the last spoonful, and in the brass bowl he could see his own face, inverted and warped by the concavity. Then he felt slightly dizzy, and a strange feeling of intoxication dulled his senses, as if the old healer had slipped some narcotic into the stew. He looked again at his reflection, and thought he saw an upside-down skull. The bowl slipped from his hands, bounced against the table and fell to the pounded dirt floor.

"Are you alright?" the fortune-teller asked.

"I'm a little dizzy, that's all," Pablo replied, without daring to pick up the bowl. "Would you please read my future for me?"

The elder examined him, squinting her eyes, which were like two pinpoints.

"Are you sure?"

"Yes."

"Come what may?"

"Yes."

"You know, sometimes it's bad news."

"I know."

"Then give me your left hand," said the woman, clearing the pot and the bowls.

As though that were a signal, the cats came out from under the cot and crept closer to the table. The weather vane on the roof continued to strain against the wind.

"Everyone wants to live to old age," sighed the fortune-teller, looking at her cats, "but nobody wants to be old. Let's see what we have here."

She took Pablo's hand and started palpating it as if she wanted to make sure it was made of flesh and bone.

"You have the hands of a pianist," she said after the inspection. "And your fingers bend back easily, a sign of loyalty and integrity."

Then, against all logic, she closed her eyes and slid her fingertips around the palm of his hand offered up like an open book, interpreting the wrinkled life map of the lovestruck youth according to the arcane rules of chiromancy. Grooves, planes, and bumps formed a topographical map that Pablo observed with care, surprised by the multitude of lines interconnecting like rivers, roads, and train tracks. Upon inspection, he noticed that the four main lines formed an M, as in Martín.

"These four lines that form an M," said the fortune teller, as if she had read his thoughts, "are the mother lines: the heart line, the fortune line, the life line, and the head line. Let's look first at the heart line, that's surely the one you're most interested in."

Pablo listened attentively, biting his lower lip.

"The heart line is deep and pronounced. This means that there is a great love in your life. But be careful, because it will be a love that will make you suffer, as with all great loves: the line is also winding and twisted."

So the first was an ominous sign.

"Now let's look at the fortune line . . . Aha: thin but continuous. This means that you won't have much money, but you will have enough to lead a decent life."

So the second was more benign.

"Now let's look at the life line."

And the third left the fortune-teller dumbstruck. Her hands began to shake, and when she opened her eyes, Pablo could see in them a strange mixture of fear and disbelief.

"What is it?" he asked.

Her horrified gaze conveyed her fingertips' findings.

"What is it?" Pablo asked again, his voice trembling.

"You had better go," the old woman said, throwing up her hands. "I'm just a crazy old lady who can't even mend her own skirts."

"You can't leave me like that!" Pablo exclaimed, standing to his feet.

The cats arched their backs and hissed menacingly. The woman got up and staggered to the bed. She took off her shoes and lay down.

"Tell me what you saw!" Pablo demanded, falling to his knees at the foot of the bed.

"Fine then, if you wish," she averred after a long silence. "But I have to tell you that even I don't fully understand it. I've never seen anything like it."

Closing her eyes with an ancestral weariness, she murmured:

"Your hand says you will die twice."

Pablo stood to his feet, thinking that this poor woman had lost her mind.

"Don't go yet," the woman bade him, without opening her eyes, "I told you that I don't fully understand it myself. But I want to give you something. If you have to die twice, it might be good for you to have it. Go, fetch me that little box from the mantle."

Pablo did as he was told. It was a small wooden box, the size of a fist, riveted with tacks.

"You open it," said the fortune-teller.

When he did so, a green light shone from inside, emitted by a small, spherical object.

"It is a good luck amulet," said the old woman. "It has saved many lives."

Only then did Pablo realize that it was a crystal eyeball, mounted on a thin chain to be worn as a pendant.

"It will help you escape danger," added the good woman. "And now, do me a favor and leave me alone. To get back to Béjar, follow the road that goes along the river."

Pablo placed the amulet in the inside pocket of his gabardine coat and left the hut in a state of shock. Then he went back and slid a few coins under the door. The sky had opened up and a bit of light was filtering through the branches, enough to be able to follow the river downstream. After a while, there appeared before his eyes the factory of Navahonda, and he heard the whistle announcing a shift change. I know this place, thought Pablo, and shortly he found himself at the foot of a majestic oak tree crowned with a wooden cabin, also known as "the hideout." It was cold, and his feet were wet, so he didn't think twice. He climbed up the trunk and entered the tree fort. He felt along the wall and found the candleholder, which still had a bit of candle left in it. When he lit it, he was pleased to see that the place was still in decent condition: surely Robinsón had taken good care of it right up to his departure. And best of all, the sackcloth blanket was still there in a corner, next to the old canteen. Pablo took off his wet shoes and socks, wrapped himself in the blanket as best he could, and little by little fell asleep, settling into an uneasy slumber filled with dark premonitions. He dreamed that the world was the palm of his hand and that the duel was taking place on this intricate map full of prophetic lines. An expectant crowd was gathered on the five phalanges, and on the wrist they had set up a gallery for the family and friends of the combatants: there was Angela, with her festooned blue dress, and there was Lieutenant Colonel Don Diego Gómez, decked out in his dress uniform, and the provincial inspector Julián Martín, accompanied by his wife and daughter Julia; and there was Robinsón, sitting next to Ferdinando Fernández, the writer for *El Castellano*, who was looking at Miss Obdulia, indolent as ever, and there in a corner was Vicente Holgado, trying to pass unnoticed. When the duelists leapt into the circle, the crowd erupted in raucous laughter, because Pablo had shown up for the duel in his underwear. But there was no going back: Rodrigo was moving closer along the fate line, forming a stark silhouette and pointing his pistol at Pablo. When he tried to raise his own sidearm, Pablo discovered that his shirtsleeves were stitched to his waist.

He was awakened by the strident call of a rooster. The candle had burned up, his mouth was dry, and his throat hurt. He opened the hideout's door, but the forest was still submerged in a thick darkness. He climbed down the tree, drank some water from the river, and emptied his bladder, finding a bit of comfort in the heat given off by his urine. He crossed the wooden bridge and went up to the Carretera de Candelario, which received him with the first rays of dawn. Then he took the Ruta del Castañar and made his way toward the Fountain of the Wolf, seeing no one on the way; it being Monday and still very early, only crazies and troublemakers could have the foolish idea of venturing to that desolate location. The fog was descending from the mountain, and it obscured the contours of the oaks and chestnut trees, as the cries of the more indolent roosters arrived from the village, sometimes echoed by the howling of wolves. When he reached the fountain, they were already waiting for him.

"Where are your seconds?" was Don Diego Gómez's greeting, as his blurry, herculean figure emerged through the fog, flanked by four other men: Rodrigo Martín, as pale and distinguished as a counterfeiter; Don Arturo Gómez, younger brother of the lieutenant colonel, who had come directly from Salamanca; Dr. Mata, the family's personal doctor prepared with a first aid kit; and a young priest with an aquiline nose who looked like he had been dragged there against his will.

"I have no seconds," Pablo responded.

"But that can't be," said Angela's father, irritated. "It violates the most basic rules of the duel."

"That's what we get for dueling with sewer rats," muttered Rodrigo, working from an apparently impoverished repertoire of metaphors.

Don Diego clicked his tongue, thought for a moment while looking at the sky, and finally said, in a menacing tone:

"You won't get off the hook that easily. Father Jerónimo and Dr. Mata can serve as your witnesses."

"But, Don Diego," the priest tried to protest, clearing his throat at regular intervals, as if he had a nervous tic. "My agreeing to come here in case there was a need for spiritual rites is one thing. Serving as a witness is quite another. Surely you know His Holiness Pius IX has laid out in the *Apostolicae Sedis* that these practices are to be punished by excommunication..."

But Don Diego's murderous look was enough to silence him. He seemed to be eager to get the thing over with.

"The duel will be at twenty-five paces," he continued, "with five bullets in the revolver and thirty seconds to shoot after the signal is given. The opponents may advance up to ten paces. Do the seconds accept these conditions?"

So, thought Pablo, there will be no shots fired into the air. This duel was completely in earnest.

"This—this is madness!" shouted Father Jerónimo.

"A man's affair is what it is," replied the lieutenant colonel. "And if there are any chickens here, let them dare to raise their hand."

This sounded like a real threat, and the priest crossed himself three times in a row, perhaps lamenting the failure of the divine injunction to love thy neighbor.

"Doctor," continued Don Diego, "the letters, please."

"Here they are," replied Dr. Gumersindo Mata, solicitously, giving one to each of the combatants.

"And what is this?" Pablo asked.

"What do you think?" Rodrigo replied with disdain. "The suicide note."

Indeed, in order to exonerate the surviving combatant of legal liability in case of death, duelists usually signed a note attesting their intention to commit suicide. Rodrigo scrawled a hasty signature, folded the paper carefully, and tucked it into a pocket of his dress coat, with a sardonic smirk. In that moment, Pablo could see that all hope was lost. What an idiot, he thought, they'll never let me leave here alive. But there was no way out. He signed the letter and placed it in the pocket of his gabardine coat, next to the good luck amulet, which was going to have to work all of its magic if it was going to save its new owner's skin.

"And Angela?" he asked.

"Don't worry about her, she's in good hands," replied Rodrigo, still smirking.

"Coin toss for choice of weapon," said Don Diego Gómez, opening a velvet-lined case holding two old but gleaming Gastinne Renette pistols with which he had fought three duels and lost one pinky finger. Now it was his nephew's turn to choose. "Heads or tails?" he asked, holding up a silver coin bearing the image of Isabel II.

"Always heads," said Rodrigo.

"Tails for me," said Pablo, as if there were any choice.

And Isabel II flew through the air before landing in Don Diego's hand.

"Heads," he said as he pocketed the coin.

Angela's cousin took one of the pistols from the case and gave it to his uncle Arturo to load. Pablo took the remaining pistol and gave it to Dr. Mata, who did the same.

"Coin toss for choice of position," Angela's father announced. "Heads or tails?"

"Always heads," Rodrigo insisted.

"Tails for me," Pablo again deferred.

This time, Isabel II did a few pirouettes and landed face down on the ground. The path to the Fountain of the Wolf was straight and flat, delimited on one side by a stone wall covered with moss. That was where the duel was meant to take place, and Pablo chose the point farthest from the fountain. The fog was starting to dissipate, and the sun seemed to be about to crest the mountains, eager to witness the illicit spectacle. The two young men went to the appointed spot and stood back-to-back, exhaling mouthfuls of heavy breath which mixed with the morning mist. When the seconds handed them the loaded pistols, their hearts began to pound like war drums.

"Turn up your lapels," whispered Arturo Gómez to his nephew as he passed him the weapon. "So he can't see the white of your shirt."

The seconds stepped away a safe distance and lay belly-down on the ground to take cover from stray bullets. Father Jerónimo was trembling like jelly and reciting a string of prayers. Then Don Diego's voice thundered, echoing off the mountains.

"Ready?"

"Yes," shouted the young men, bending their right arms and bringing the pistols to their noses, pointing at the sky.

"Advance!"

Don Diego counted off their paces out loud, like an inexorable drip. One, two, three, four ... twenty-two, twenty-three, twenty-four ... when he reached twenty-five, Pablo felt a shiver go down his spine. He turned to face his opponent, and then froze. The first of three handclaps was heard, and Rodrigo started walking toward him with short but decisive paces. At the second handclap, Pablo's mouth went dry. And when the third clap came, both combatants stretched out their pistols as two shouts were heard in unison:

"Fire!" shouted Don Diego.

"Nooo!" shouted Angela, running up the road.

Pablo turned his head just as a shot rang out.

The owner of the café thought the meetings would attract the police's attention, and he said so. It was decided to go to the golf course near the beach, where they would discuss and prepare the action. At this meeting, the prudent faction spoke up, saying it would be best to send two or three emissaries to the border to find out what was going on in Spain.

PÍO BAROJA,
La familia de Errotacho

THE CEMETERY OF SAINT-JEAN-DE-LUZ is larger than one might expect for such a small village. It spreads out behind the city wall, crowned by a smooth hill, and next to the wall of the north wing, the ancient house of the crypt keeper is nestled, out of use since the end of the Great War. The structure nonetheless appears to be well preserved, at least as far as one can tell in the moonlight, as though someone had been working to keep it in good condition. Next to the dwelling there is a crumbling crypt. Leandro reaches his hand between the bars and pulls out a handful of keys, which he illuminates with a pocket lighter. With a flick he spins the ridged wheel, and the spark ignites the cotton wick. Then he chooses one of the keys and opens the padlock that protects his hideout.

"Are you afraid of getting robbed by corpses?" Robinsón asks, trying to joke to calm his own nerves. The place is not what one would call comforting. But when Leandro enters the shack and lights the kerosene lamp hanging from the door frame, the vegetarian finds some comfort in the light. The place is more spacious than it appeared from outside, and it seems that someone has taken care to clean it recently. There is even a fireplace, with coals still hot, a shabby double bed, and a decent mattress stuffed with cornhusks. In the center is an oval table topped with a jar filled with chrysanthemums. Pablo and Robinsón look at Leandro in puzzlement, but the Argentine pretends not to understand.

"So," he says after a few seconds, "What's the matter, cat got your tongues? You don't have anything to say about my new home?"

"Man," says Pablo, "The truth is it's not bad … except for the neighbors, of course."

"And these flowers, Leandro?" asks Robinsón after chuckling at Pablo's witticism. "Surely you didn't steal them from some poor dead soul?"

Then, unexpectedly, the big man blushes and becomes as sheepish as a child.

"Well, thing is, the cottage isn't exactly mine—"

"No, obviously," says Robinsón. "This is the Lord's house."

"No, I mean, it's not *just* mine, it belongs to … to …"

"Who?" shout Pablo and Robinsón in unison, losing patience.

"Antoinette."

"Who??"

"Antoinette, the crypt keeper's daughter."

A smile starts to form on the two friends' faces.

"She's the one who put these flowers here," Leandro reveals, growing more and more agitated.

"Fine, so this Antoinette," Pablo presses wickedly, "who is she? I mean, apart from being the crypt keeper's daughter, would she be, I don't know, something more? Your housekeeper, perhaps? Or your personal assistant?"

"Your Latin teacher?" Robinsón contributes to the razzing.

The two friends crack up with laughter. Robinsón puts a chrysanthemum in his hair. "*Bonjour, mon petit coucou!*" he says, blowing kisses in the air. "*Je suis ta petite Antoinette*, you want to join me for a stroll amongst the dead?"

They go on this way for a while, joking at Leandro's expense. When they are finally done teasing him, Leandro manages to explain his situation: when he arrived in Saint-Jean-de-Luz barely ten days ago accompanied by Robinsón and fleeing the Parisian police, he quickly made the acquaintance of Antoinette. It was love at first sight, and a case of opposites attract, you might say, as Leandro's six-and-a-half-foot stature contrasts starkly with little Antoinette's four and a half. Within three days they were strolling hand in hand through the graveyard. But the Argentine hasn't been able to keep it a secret that he intends to accompany his friends to liberate Spain, and even Antoinette is not going to be able to change his mind. Finally, the three friends lie down to sleep with a strange mixture of joy, nervousness, and respect for their neighbors.

It is Monday, November 3, 1924, and the first day of the revolutionary adventure has come to an end.

"*BONJOUR!*" SAYS A SOFT FEMALE VOICE from outside the cottage in the morning: Leandro leaps out of bed and rousts the other two with kicks.

"Get up, get up, ya lazybones! Get up and get dressed, we have a visitor."

His tone is totally different from last night. It seems that Antoinette's presence has robbed him of his courage. When Pablo and Robinsón have dressed, the crypt keeper's daughter enters. She is a tiny but robust young woman, carrying a pot of milk and a basin for the morning's wash and shave.

"*Buenos días,*" she repeats her greeting in Spanish.

"*Buenos días,*" the two men reply, somewhat embarrassed. It has been a long time since either of them has woken up to a woman's face.

Leandro lights the fire and sets the milk to warm up, while Antoinette advises them to dress warmly, because it's cold enough to frost a beard out there. She then uses tongs to pick up a round stone from next to the fireplace and holds it over the fire for a few moments before dropping it into the milk, which quickly boils. "My grandmother always did it this way. It gives it a nice toasty flavor," and she smiles in a way that leaves Leandro literally drooling. The four of them drink their milk around the table. An awkward silence sets in. Pablo starts to get the sense that he and Robinsón are third wheels at this party. The vegetarian does not seem to catch on, and is contemplating Antoinette with the cherubic smile of one who feels himself in harmony with the entire universe.

"Well, you lovebirds, we'd better be going. Things to do, right, Robin?"

"Ah, yes, yes, we should go. Where?"

"First of all we'll go buy berets, because that's what people wear around here. We attract too much attention looking like this."

"Ah, no. Nothing doing. The bowler stays."

"Fine then, come with me to send a telegram."

"As you wish."

"Come on then."

"Let's go."

And the two friends leave the cottage, thanking Antoinette and reminding Leandro that they are to meet the others at the square at noon.

"See you there," says the Argentine.

"Yes, see you then," says Pablo, and he and Robinsón make their way through the labyrinth of graves and tombs, a path that they will retrace several times over the next three days of anxious waiting before they launch themselves into the revolution.

In Saint-Jean-de-Luz, time seems to slow down. The minutes seem like hours, the hours like days, and the days like weeks as they wait to receive the signal to cross the border. In the meantime, the most sensible thing would be for the revolutionaries to avoid being seen too much in the village, stay hidden in houses and inns, try to go unnoticed. But who is going to manage to box in this troop of angry men? Thus, early in the morning, the village of Saint-Jean-de-Luz fills with dozens of Spanish anarchists and syndicalists, excited and anxious, trying to kill time until lunch by shopping for berets and knives, emptying glasses of wine in the taverns, or catcalling the few young women who dare to cross the square alone. Some of them stand in circles, imprudently discussing the best way to carry out the revolution, each sure he knows the key. Others prefer to hole up in taverns playing mus, such as the four ruffians of the Villalpando clan, who with their dog-eared cards earn their reputation as incorrigible gamblers. There are also those who engage in more lucrative but less honorable pursuits, such as Perico Alarco and Manolito Monzón, who get kicked out of a butcher shop for trying to put a chicken in their bag.

Pablo takes advantage of the morning to send two telegrams, one to the Beaumonts and the other to old Faure, who will surely hit the roof when he reads it. Mr. Savage will not yet have realized that his Spanish typesetter has gone behind his back to print several thousand pamphlets on La Fraternelle letterhead. He also will not have found out what Pablo is about to discover as Robinsón is trying on a beret in a hat shop run by a Basque man named Mendiburutegia.

"I'm only trying it on to kill time," says Robinsón as Pablo smiles to see how the beret changes his friend's appearance. "I'm not giving up my bowler for one of these floppy rags."

And then it is Pablo's face that changes, and he goes running out of the shop.

"Hey, it's not that ugly, is it?" Robinsón asks the haberdasher, contemplating himself in the mirror.

But what gave Pablo a jolt and sent him running into the street was not the effect of seeing his friend in a beret, but the appearance of someone familiar through the window.

"Julianín!" he shouts. Julián Fernández Revert, the young typesetting assistant from La Fraternelle, turns on his heels. He holds one of the revolutionary flyers in his hands.

"There's an erratum here, Pablo. You owe me five cents," he says, with all the innocence in the world. "And please, don't call me Julianín. I'm not a kid. In fact, it's my birthday today..."

Pablo stands there not knowing what to say, looking at him with an impossible mixture of confusion, anger, and joy.

"Well then, happy birthday, big man," he finally exclaims, "but I assume you didn't come here to celebrate with me, or to collect your five cents."

"Of course not, I told you before that I wasn't going to stand around doing nothing. I've come to liberate Spain. Thing is, I fell asleep and was a bit late getting to the station," he says, lowering his gaze, ashamed, "but last night I caught another train with two other fellows who also missed the first train. We arrived a couple hours ago."

Pablo doesn't know whether to hug him or slap him, so in the end he opts for cursing:

"Goddammit, holy shit, Julián," he backs down, dropping the diminutive. As a welcome gift, he brings him into the shop and buys two berets, one for each of them. Robinsón, for his part, walks out wearing a sleek new bowler, wanting to be presentable for his return to the mother country.

WHEN THE REVOLUTIONARIES CONVERGE AT THE dining lodge for lunch, the man from Guernica advises them to stop meeting at his restaurant because they are starting to arouse suspicions, despite their many newly purchased berets. He has no problem serving them food, of course, but if they want to keep organizing conclaves and conventicles (his words verbatim), it would be better if they met somewhere a little out of town, maybe at La Nivelle golf course on the other side of the river. Some revolutionaries try to protest, asserting that they shouldn't draw much attention in a village like Saint-Jean-de-Luz, which was used to seeing lots of Spanish laborers looking for work, especially since the coup d'état that brought Primo de Rivera to power. But they have no choice but to heed the Basque's wishes, and they end up heading to the golf course, about five minutes by foot from the central square. Some of them, spurred on by wine or the cold, sing obscene or revolutionary songs as they leave the village. El Maestro ambitiously tries to sing "*La Donna è mobile*," and a choir of whistles accompanies him. When they finally arrive at the golf course, it is Juan Riesgo who speaks first, his hunch exacerbated by the cold.

"I managed to speak with Durruti this morning," he says. "But the telephone signal was terrible. You can imagine, during the first call there was a crossed signal, and I was listening to a conversation between a theater agent and his lover, a young actress who wouldn't stop crying. So Durruti didn't tell me much, we can't run the risk of police intercepting our calls."

In fact, what Juan Riesgo has been able to learn is that the weapons deal has failed, though he prefers not to tell the others so they don't lose hope. What he does tell them is that the Committee of Paris is asking for patience, and confirms that the comrades in Perpignan are also waiting for the signal. Someone asks if it's true that Caparrós has been arrested, to which Riesgo replies that he cannot confirm that rumor. On the other hand, he can say that Jover has succeeded in finding refuge in Barcelona, from whence he will be able to lead the internal insurrection, and it is to be assumed that when the thing is ready he will send the coded telegram (whose secret code words, "Mama has died," have been inevitably spreading among the men gathered in Saint-Jean-de-Luz). Also, insofar as possible, the members of the Group of Thirty who have remained in Paris will join the rest of them at the border; the plan is that Ascaso will go to Perpignan and Durruti will come here to Saint-Jean-de-Luz. It is then that someone proposes sending an emissary to Spain to investigate the situation firsthand. But Juan Riesgo opposes this.

"That's an unnecessary risk. Also, we'd have to consult with the Committee of Paris first. They've insisted we not make unilateral decisions. You know that coordination between the various groups is essential."

"Look, Juanito," replies Gil Galar, his Merovingian mane blowing in the breeze, "we're the committee now. We're the ones here in the trenches.

We can't keep consulting the Three Musketeers about everything, they have enough problems back in Paris."

"*El Chino*'s in Barcelona," Riesgo reminds him.

"He could be on the moon for all I care," replies Gil Galar. "We can't even speak with them safely! I think the comrade's idea isn't so silly. I'll go if nobody else has the balls."

"It's not a matter of balls," says Santillán, the former civil guardsman, "but of brains, although some of you seem to think with your gonads. If we decide to send an emissary, it makes sense to send someone from around here, someone who knows the terrain, don't you think?"

Gil Galar says nothing, biting his tongue in the face of such an indisputable argument. After a few more speeches, they come to a compromise: if they still have not received a telegram after twenty-four hours, they will send three emissaries to the other side of the border, chosen among the revolutionaries from Saint-Jean-de-Luz who know the area best: one will go to Irún, one to Vera, and one to Zugarramurdi. Also, that will leave time for Juan Riesgo to get in touch with the comrades in Paris to find out what's going on, though their opinion will not be considered authoritative in any way. Then, since it is starting to rain and there is no shelter to be found on the golf course, the revolutionaries return to the village and disperse.

However, all of that talk will have been in vain. They will not need to send anyone across the border, because a character many of them have been waiting for is about to arrive: Max Hernández, known as "El Señorito," who will make his entrance in Saint-Jean-de-Luz wearing a top hat and leaning on a cane with a mother-of-pearl grip, the type that often conceals a knife inside.

X
(1908–1909)

THERE ARE TIMES WHEN LIFE GOES by in slow motion. Especially as the line between life and death grows thin. Such was the case that winter morning at the Fountain of the Wolf: when the gunshot rang out, time seemed to slow down, as if it wanted to postpone the fatal outcome. Angela's unexpected arrival, her heartbroken scream at the sight of the duel, caused Pablo to turn at precisely the moment that Rodrigo's weapon gave its fiery report. The bullet emerged from the Gastinne Renette, carved a path through the mist, and struck Pablo in the left breast. The brutal impact sent his body flying, and it hung there, suspended in midair as though the earth had a momentary lapse of gravity. Then, little by little, he fell downward, leaving his hat and pistol still floating. When he hit the ground, the scene snapped back into clock time.

"Noooooo!" Angela was still wailing.

Pablo's body lay supine, a trail of blood streaming from his mouth. The girl fell on him and lifted his face, kissed his lips, and overflowed with tears of rage, suffering, and pain, and he had time to caress her face, smile, and say, "Don't cry," before losing consciousness. Rodrigo stood paralyzed, his arm extended and the lethal weapon exhaling smoke from its mouth as the seconds leapt to their feet like jacks-in-a-box and ran to the spot where Pablo lay motionless. Angela cursed them, tearing her hair and beating her breast. Then she saw the pistol that had fallen at her beloved's feet, and she grabbed it with both hands.

"Don't come any closer!" she shouted.

But Don Diego kept coming. When he reached out his arm to snatch the pistol from her, Angela pulled the trigger, but no shot was heard—only the smack of her father's hand—showing once and for all that this had been a mock duel, a foul ruse, a murder dressed in the guise of a gentleman's challenge. The lieutenant colonel's gloved hand struck Angela with such force that she crumpled to the earth, slack-jawed and semiconscious. Don Diego went to Pablo's body, verified that the wound was sufficiently mortal, and placed a cheap revolver in Pablo's limp right hand, a Velo-dog model made in Eibar, of the same caliber as the Gastinne Renette. Then, taking Angela in his arms, he abruptly ordered:

"Let's go. Let someone else discover this accursed suicide."

Father Jerónimo pushed Pablo's eyes shut and gave him his last rites as the other men hurried off down the road, not knowing that the scion of the Martín family did not have his heart under his left breast.

WHEN HE REGAINED CONSCIOUSNESS, THE FIRST thing he noticed was that he was lying in a bed. The incantatory litany of the *Tantum Ergo* reached his ears. He made an effort to open his eyes and thought he saw a shadow gliding out of the room, which was small and austere like a monastic cell. From a niche on the wall, a figure of the Virgin Mary observed him with a pious gaze: it was the Virgin of El Castañar, appearing to be keeping vigil over him. He swallowed and noted the bittersweet taste of blood. Then he remembered Angela's crying eyes and the acute pain that had made him lose consciousness. He didn't know if it was hours, days, or weeks that had passed, nor how he had gotten here, and he wondered for a moment if perhaps he was dead—maybe this was Heaven or Purgatory. Surely it was not Hell, because why in God's name would there be a Virgin presiding over the room if it were? But when he tried to sit up, a tremendous stabbing pain in the chest reminded him he was still alive. He touched the painful spot and discovered that his torso was wrapped in bandages. He had difficulty breathing, his head hurt, his mouth was dry, and his strength failed him, so he closed his eyes and went back to sleep.

He was awakened shortly thereafter by the sound of a man clearing his throat, quietly but incessantly, like a nervous tic. He tried in vain to remember where he had heard that cough before. He opened his eyes halfway, and Father Jerónimo's aquiline nose entered his field of vision, accompanied by a Franciscan monk with a sharply pointed beard.

"Praise God," exclaimed the priest when he saw Pablo opening his eyes.

"Yes, praise God," echoed the Franciscan.

"Where am I?" Pablo asked. And then: "Where is Angela?"

The two holy men exchanged a knowing look, and the monk left the room, as silent as a cat or a shadow.

"It is best if you do not excite yourself, my son," Father Jerónimo tried to calm him. "The worst has passed. The important thing now is for you to recuperate. Here, take this," he said, stirring the contents of a cup with a spoon.

"What is it?" asked Pablo, wary.

"Quinine, for the fever … with a few drops of laudanum for the pain. Are you hungry?"

Pablo nodded his head as he drank the potion, which tasted like bitter almonds.

"I'm not surprised. You've been in a delirium for a week and haven't eaten a bite."

The priest left the room and returned a little while later with a steaming bowl. It was a vegetable soup, bland but comforting, and Pablo ate it in little sips, under the incredulous gaze of Father Jerónimo, who was babbling expressions of lament peppered with latinisms that he himself translated, somewhat loosely:

"Aye, *amantes amentes*—lovers gone mad," he sighed, turning his eyes upward and adjusting his collar. "A miracle. It is a miracle. It is written in the scriptures: *Mors certa, hora incerta*—death is certain, but its hour is not. A miracle, truly a miracle."

Hearing the priest's words, Pablo remembered the fortune-teller in the woods and wondered if his good luck amulet had saved him from this first death. But he quickly pushed the thought from his mind, tormented by more pressing doubts. When he finished his soup he felt better, and had the strength to launch a volley of questions:

"Where am I, Father? Where is Angela? What happened to me? Who brought me here? Who knows—"

"Shhhh," the curate cut him off, lifting his index finger to his lips. "Do not overexert yourself, my son, it's not good for you. And give thanks to God for saving your life. When you recover, you will be able to ask any question you like. You are in the Sanctuary of El Castañar, but Brother Toribio and I are the only ones who know, so you needn't worry about anything. Please rest, and remember what Seneca said: *pro optimo est minime malus*—the best is the least bad…"

These words did nothing to calm Pablo, indeed had the opposite effect. He closed his eyes and waited for the cleric to leave the room. When he heard the door open and shut again, he tried to stand to his feet, but he fell to the floor like a man struck by lightning: another terrible pain in the chest nearly knocked him unconscious. He managed to stumble back into bed and settled in as best as he could. He had to admit it: the damned priest was right. After all, he thought, if I'm alive I suppose it's thanks to him.

"When I served your last rites and closed your eyes," explained the priest the next day, as Brother Toribio changed his dressings and cleaned his wound, "I noticed that there was still warm air coming from your mouth. I wanted to call Dr. Mata, but he had already gone off down the road. Then I thought it would be better to say nothing, so I came to seek help from my good friend Brother Toribio, doctor of medicine."

"And of theology, Father. And of theology," the Franciscan clarified.

"So between the two of us, we carried you here," continued Father Jerónimo. "But we still do not understand how you were able to survive a bullet in the heart."

"And Angela?" was Pablo's reply.

"She is in good hands, don't worry about her," the priest lied. "But rest, my son, rest, there will be time to speak of her."

And the two clergymen left the room.

Over the next few weeks, Father Jerónimo went up to the sanctuary every day to see the convalescent, and not a day passed that Pablo did not ask after Angela. But the answer was always the same:

"She is in good hands, do not worry. The sooner you recover, the sooner you will be able to see her."

And so, in hope of seeing his beloved again soon, Pablo turned into a model patient: he obeyed Father Jerónimo's instructions, took the medicine administered by Brother Toribio, and controlled his urge to smoke, since the injury had seriously affected his left lung. When he had enough strength, he asked for some paper and ink, and wrote a letter to his mother saying that he was doing well, that she shouldn't worry, but that he was very busy with work and would not be able to come to Baracaldo for Christmas.

"How much longer do I have to rest?" was the question Brother Toribio had to field every time he came to treat the "impatient patient," as he started calling him.

"As long as your body needs," the Franciscan invariably replied.

And the young man's body appeared to need much more care still, because as soon as he got out of bed and tried to walk he would start to asphyxiate, his head spinning, and he would have to get back in bed, exhausted and pale as sea foam. Christmas Eve arrived, and then Christmas, and then New Year's Day; on Epiphany, Father Jerónimo went up to the sanctuary, entered the cell, and gave Pablo a parcel wrapped in brown paper. The pale, cool January sun came in through the little window, illuminating the room with diffuse light.

"What is this, Father?"

"A gift, what do you think? Go ahead, open it."

It was a jointed wooden puppet with a thick string hanging from its waist, like a miniature reproduction of the rope holding Brother Toribio's habit. When Pablo pulled the string, the doll's arms and legs flailed up and down.

"I made it myself," said the priest, a smile on his lips.

Pablo pulled on the string three times, absorbed in the puppet's movement, until he finally lifted his gaze and looked at the man with the aquiline nose, of whom he had started to grow fond:

"Thank you, Father, but... I'm not a child. If you really want to give me a gift, tell me where Angela is."

The cleric furrowed his brow and his smile turned into a sigh:

"Aye, my son," he deflated on the only chair in the room. "It will never be doubt that drives us mad, but certainty. But, after all, I had to tell you sooner or later..."

A shadow of anxiety covered Pablo's eyes.

"Angela loved you... loves you very much—" Father Jerónimo continued, looking at his hands, the fingers of which were writhing on his lap like a collection of small white worms.

"How do you know that, Father?"

"Because I was... I am her confessor," said the priest, looking up to see the effect of his words. "And when she spoke of you, her eyes glowed with the flame of the purest love I have seen in my life—"

"Father, you're frightening me," Pablo interrupted him, his voice trembling, skeptical. "Why do you keep talking about Angela in the past tense?"

The fingers stopped their writhing and a thick silence took over the scene, interrupted only by the chaplain's nervous throat-clearing. Almost a minute passed until he managed to open his mouth again, a minute that seemed an eternity to his interlocutor.

"Because Angela has disappeared," he finally said. "She ran away from home on the day of the duel and no one knows where she is."

Pablo sat up suddenly in bed, his face twisted by suffering both physical and spiritual.

"But she knows I'm here, right?"

Father Jerónimo shook his head.

"Only Brother Toribio and I know that you are here. Angela most likely thinks you died in the duel."

"Goddammit!" Pablo lost his temper, jumping out of the bed and then doubling over in pain. "Why didn't you tell me before?" he squealed.

"It wasn't the right time, my son."

"The right time? What do you mean the right time? Who knows where she'll go now, if she's even still alive! Where are my clothes, Father?" Pablo asked, making his way toward the door.

But he had only taken two steps before his eyes clouded over and his knees gave out. the last thing he saw before he fell to the ground and lost consciousness was the jointed puppet waving goodbye from the foot of the bed.

PABLO WAS NOT ABLE TO LEAVE the Sanctuary of El Castañar until Saturday, February 13, 1909, the feast day of Saint Stephen and Saint Hermenegild. Back on Epiphany, when he had first regained consciousness late in the night, Brother Toribio and Father Jerónimo had convinced him that it would be no use to throw himself into the search for Angela in his current physical condition. It had been more than a month since her disappearance and, although her family, the police, and the neighbors from Béjar had combed the whole area and alerted the nearby villages, they still had no information about the Gómez daughter. The possibility of a suicide was growing ever more remote, because sooner or later the body would have shown up somewhere. The most likely thing was that she had managed to flee on her own, perhaps taking a train to some random destination. On the other hand, the fact that no one had found Pablo's lifeless body had left Don Diego and Rodrigo Martín disconcerted. When they commented on the strange situation to Father Jerónimo, the priest ventured, "Maybe the wolves ate him," but he did not manage to convince the duelists.

Now, after five more weeks of convalescence, Pablo's health had improved considerably and Angela was still missing. If anyone in the world can find her, he thought as he rose from bed on a frigid February morning, it's me. And he decided, despite the snow that had fallen in the last few days, that the moment had come to begin the search. Although in truth he did not have the slightest idea where to start.

"Be very careful," Father Jerónimo advised him, seeing that his decision to leave was firm. "If Don Diego finds out you're still alive, God help us. Bundle up, and take the medicine Brother Toribio gave you."

"Yes, Father, don't worry about me. And if you hear anything about Angela, write me right away. Who knows, maybe she'll end up coming back to Béjar."

"Angela? I'd be surprised. You know better than anyone that she was sick and tired of this village, that she was only waiting for the day when you would come take her to live far away, the farther the better. Do you know what she once told me? She said if dreaming of you was a sin, she was sinning every night—"

"I have to find her, Father, so she'll know I'm alive," said Pablo, his voice shaking.

"Yes, my son, yes. *Ite cum Deo.*"

And the two men embraced. Outside, Brother Toribio was waiting in a wagon to take the young man out of the village hidden under some blankets.

"Pablo," Father Jerónimo stopped him before he left the sanctuary.

"What?"

"I think you should keep this," he said, taking from under his robe a small parcel covered in the same brown paper as the Epiphany gift.

"Another gift, Father?" Pablo asked, smiling.

But a shadow of worry was covering the priest's face:

"I only hope it's not a poisoned gift."

Inside the parcel, cold and heavy like a corpse, there was a pocket revolver, the one Don Diego Gómez had slyly placed in Pablo's hand when he left him for dead on the day of the duel.

IT WAS DINNERTIME WHEN THE TRAIN stopped in the station of Salamanca. It had been three months since Pablo had left there ready to face a whole army, and now he was returning injured and defeated. He had asked Brother Toribio to leave him in Ledrada to buy a third-class ticket to the provincial capital. Not that he thought he would find Angela wandering around the bleak streets of Salamanca, but for the last few weeks of convalescence he had been imagining a thousand ways to start the search, and he had reached the conclusion that the most reasonable thing was to go first to the guesthouse where he had lived since his father died: he held out the hope that he had received some letter there, if not from Angela then at least from someone who could put him on the right track; and, in any case, he had to get his belongings... including the money he had saved and hidden under the mattress. Later there would be time to visit the office of *El Castellano*, where he had almost certainly lost his job, and ask for Ferdinando's help; maybe he would be able to publish an article in the newspaper announcing Angela's disappearance, however belatedly.

When he arrived at the guesthouse of Madam Crow, the old wrinkled one was exhorting the last diners to clear their plates and go to bed. Seeing Pablo enter, she made a sour face.

"Lord have mercy," she murmured, and crossed herself repeatedly.

"I know I owe you three months of rent," Pablo blurted out suddenly, approaching her, "but if you give me the key to my room I'll pay you every penny."

"You don't have a room anymore, little sir," the old woman grunted, pointing her finger like a pistol. "Do you think you can just appear and disappear as you please? Well you're wrong."

Two students stood up and left the room.

"Then just let me go in to get my things. Have any letters come for me?"

"I have your things and your letters in storage, little sir. But if you want them back you'll have to pay me for the two months you left the room empty."

"I'll do just that, if you'll only let me go in," Pablo insisted, suggesting with his eyebrows that the money was in the room.

The owner seemed to hesitate a moment, then finally walked over to one of the diners, a young man with bulging eyes who was drinking an herbal tea in little sips.

"Mr. Gregory Cook," the woman asked in a dripping tone, "would you be so kind as to allow this gentleman—"

"Not a worry, my lady, I shall accompany him myself," the man said with a distinct English accent, taking charge of the situation. And after finishing his cup, he got up from the table and approached the new arrival with a certain affectation. "Follow me, please."

They went up the stairs to the second floor and, upon entering the room, Pablo was petrified. Not because it stank of mothballs; nor because the room had been rearranged by the new occupant, giving it a decidedly bourgeois look; and also not because the top blanket (monogrammed G.C. in gold letters) was turned down with irritating care, ready to receive the prince of the pea; and also not because the proprietress had let the Englishman place hot water bottles under the sheets, something Pablo had never been allowed to do. Rather, it was because the old straw mattress hiding all of his savings had been replaced by a brand-new wool mattress.

"What happened to the old mattress?" Pablo managed to ask, his voice trembling.

"I asked the owner to throw it out, it was full of, oh I don't know the Spanish word. *Bedbugs*," the little man said with a very British combination of disgust and apathy.

"Holy goddamned shit…"

But the dandy was not at fault, so Pablo left the room, slamming the door. In the stairwell he ran into Madam Crow, who was coming up to collect her rent.

"So?" she asked, mistrustfully.

"What did you do with the mattress?" Pablo replied.

"What mattress?"

"The one I used to use before the Englishman moved into my room."

"I sold it for four pence to a family of gypsies. So what?"

"So, what you sold them, goddamn it, was all of my savings and your two months' rent! Now give me my things and stay here with your Mr. Cook."

"Nothing doing, little sir," the old harpy responded. "No money, no luggage."

That's when Pablo finally lost it. He took out the pistol Father Jerónimo had given him and pointed it at the innkeeper, though knowing it was not loaded:

"No more funny business, Madam Crow. Give me what's mine."

The old woman seemed more offended by the nickname than by the threat, but she did as she was told. She went to the reception and opened a double-doored closet. Inside was Pablo's suitcase, full to the brim, and everything that had not fit inside: his books, his umbrella, and his father's felt hat, as well as three letters that had arrived during his prolonged absence.

"I knew with those books you'd end up a bandit," the papery old woman spat, pointing to a book by Bakunin.

But Pablo wasn't listening. He leapt on the letters and inspected the return addresses, with growing frustration: one was from his mother, another from *El Castellano*, and the third from the Provincial Government of Salamanca. None of them appeared to carry any news of Angela, so he put on the felt hat, picked up the suitcase and left the guesthouse, not suspecting that the third letter was going to decide his path for him. He was badly injured, out of work, and the love of his life had disappeared, but the patria does not listen to excuses: Pablo had just turned nineteen years old, and he had been placed on the military draft list. The Provincial Government wished to inform him: the draft lottery was set to take place on the fourteenth of February—the very next day.

— 12 —

This Max was a svelte man, with a pale, bLuísh face. He had a heart condition, he said, and was at risk of dying at any moment. He had a union card from Barcelona, and he was an astute, friendly man. He always seemed to be amused by everything; he had seen many things, and he was an aficionado of cocaine. Max, it was said, brought some of the syndicalists to a brothel, where they drank and created quite a scandal.

PÍO BAROJA,
La Familia de Errotacho

MAX HERNÁNDEZ, "EL SEÑORITO," MUST BE over age forty, some even say he's over fifty, but he doesn't look it in the slightest: his white, clean-shaven skin, his meticulously combed blond hair, his thin, surgeon's fingers, his impeccable dentition, and his glowing smile, his turquoise blue eyes, his white, pin-striped suit, and his patent leather shoes make him appear younger than he really is. And while he claims that his heart is failing, he treats his suffering as a pretext to announce far and wide that he doesn't give a damn about danger, which gives him a certain rejuvenating vitality, amplified perhaps by his fondness for cocaine. He is also distinguished by his loquaciousness and an uncommon gift for languages, which together with his disarming looks give him an extraordinary ability of seduction. He appears in Saint-Jean-de-Luz on Wednesday, a little before lunchtime, looking like a perfect dandy and sporting a cane with a mother-of-pearl handle. "It's the best way to go unnoticed," he says with a certain cynicism to the men who come to greet him and ask how things are going. His reply only exacerbates their impatience and nervousness:

"The thing's just about ready, boys. Any minute now it'll be time to cross the border."

Yesterday, after the improvised meeting at the golf course, the revolutionaries returned to the village and dispersed into the twilight. The crypt keeper's hut again showed its hospitality, playing host to another lost soul, just turned eighteen years of age, who curled up with Kropotkin next to the fire. Today, the morning went more or less the same as yesterday, and when El Señorito arrives in the village at noon, the leaders of the movement are gathered around the music gazebo choosing the three emissaries they will send across the border tonight to find out the actual situation in Spain, against the stubborn opposition of Juan Riesgo, who still thinks the idea is useless and dangerous. But Max's arrival will completely disrupt his plans.

"It's coming to a head," Max repeats, faced with Juan Riesgo's distrustful sideways glance. "I've just arrived from San Sebastián, where the soldiers are ready to rise up when they receive the order. It seems that tomorrow Rodrigo Soriano will arrive from Paris to take charge of the matter."

"And what the hell does Soriano have to do with all this?" barks Gil Galar, who considers all politicians to be potential dictators.

"Hey friend, it's always good to have a politician on our side," responds El Señorito, taking off his white leather gloves. "We cannot underestimate the influence politicians can have on society, and on the army, who are always more cooperative if they know there's an 'authority' behind a movement like ours. Some even say that Romanones would be willing to take charge of a revolutionary government that overthrows the Directory, and that's an option we can't rule out—"

"That's an option you can shove up your ass," Gil Galar rants on, "We're not going to risk our lives just so some damned duke can step in and take the reins. This is an anarchist proletarian revolution, get that into your head!"

"Fine, listen, fine," Luís Naveira tries to calm their spirits with his fluty voice, "Let's not get excited. The important thing is starting a revolution and overthrowing the dictatorship, we can talk later about how we'll rebuild the country. In any case, Max, we are waiting to receive word from the interior to cross the border, because coordination is vital in cases like this. Now at least we know that things are about to heat up in San Sebastián."

"And not only in San Sebastián, I've heard also in the better part of the Cantabrian coast, from Bilbao to Santiago de Compostela. And from what I've seen, most of the villages of Navarre and the Basque Country are ready," El Señorito forcefully asserts. "The ideal would be to go to Hendaye and enter Spain via Irún, where we can meet up with the comrades from there, who are very well organized, so that we can all go together to San Sebastián."

"Very good, but what we don't know is if the thing is ready in other parts of the peninsula, especially Catalonia," says the ever-cautious Juan Riesgo.

"Indeed," Naveira concedes, "and that's why we need to wait until the telegram comes giving the green light for the incursion."

"Clearly," Max agrees. "I suppose it will be a coded telegram."

"Of course," confirms Riesgo. "And the less people who know the key, the better."

After a discussion that protracts until stomachs start to groan, it is agreed to abandon the plan to send three emissaries for the time being, because now they have an idea of the situation on the other side of the border. Provided that Max is telling the truth, of course. Because although the majority of them succumb to the charms of this curious revolutionary disguised as an aristocrat, not everyone trusts him. Including Pablo, who doesn't miss a detail of what El Señorito says and does, trying to remember where he has seen that face, observed that demeanor, heard that velvety voice before. And so it is that, instead of going to eat with Robinsón, Leandro, and Julianín (sorry, Julián), he mingles into the group surrounding Max, which also includes the four gamblers from Villalpando and the curious pair formed by the toothless Perico Alarco and the deaf-mute Manolito Monzón, who hope to cash in on El Señorito's aristocratic airs. But they are quite mistaken, as he not only takes them to eat at a wretched shack, but he won't even pay for cigars. But then, after a few glasses, he offers to take them to a portside brothel with an outlandish wager, improper for a man in a silk scarf and top hat:

"I'll pay for a whore for any man who's got a bigger one than me."

Some of them cheer at the notion and follow him out, who knows whether out of confidence they'll win the bet or spurred by the dark presentiment that this could be the last chance they have to embrace a woman. Pablo lets himself be dragged along with the group, more obsessed with trying to remember that turquoise gaze and velvety voice than with attending to venereal urges.

The brothel is a nondescript establishment located on the far side of the port of Saint-Jean-de-Luz, classier than one might think, frequented by melancholic sailors and traveling salesmen, workers from the nearby Portland cement factory, and police on their rounds. From outside, visitors can perceive the lattices of the wide windows with their slats discreetly lowered. Entering the vestibule, which stinks of camphor, the building's elderly porter has them wait a few minutes, because there is a respectable client coming down the stairs at this very moment, who doesn't want to be seen by anyone. He also informs them that guns are not allowed upstairs, and Max gives him his pistol, setting an example for the others, although apart from him, the only one who's armed is Casiano Veloso, one of the Villalpando clan, who reluctantly hands over his Browning. When an electric bell sounds, the old porter allows them in, pocketing a gratuity from Max. The group of some ten-odd revolutionaries flock up the stairs, dazzled by such decadence, accustomed as they are to the bedbug-infested bordellos of old Spain or the Parisian *quartier chinois*.

Upstairs, they are welcomed by Madame Alix, an obligatory coquettish mole painted on her upper lip, who greets them with a panache that would inspire envy in many a queen, giving Max a wink of complicity as if he were an old friend. She invites them into a shadowy salon, where a handful of half-naked young women are mingling with clients who are drinking beer and covering their crotches with their hats as they try to decide which one they will take. Madame Alix seats the group around a large table at the back of the room and pops a bottle of champagne on the house. The revolutionaries, unaccustomed to such luxuries, receive the generosity with hurrahs and kisses, and empty the champagne within a few minutes drinking straight from the bottle. Max takes a few condoms from the pocket of his blazer and offers them to the others, but most of them refuse, despite El Señorito's arguments that they are made of latex and not lambskin, that they are the only sure way to avoid syphilis, and that this is the latest model from Bell & Croyden, one of London's top brands. But indifference or ignorance carry the day and, one by one, the incautious revolutionaries let themselves be dragged away by the ladies, most of whom are French but some of whom are Antillean mulattas, probably from the French overseas territories, who strut their exuberant exoticism with colonial pride. One of them appears to be sending Pablo insinuating looks from the next table, where she is seated between the legs of a boxer-looking chap with whom she ends up disappearing, but not without locking her gorgeous almandine eyes with those of the disconcerted typesetter. There is also a Spanish girl, from Guadix, with peroxide-blond hair in the latest fashion, who makes up for her paucity of teeth by flaunting her Andalusian charm among the tables, and finally snags the toothless Perico, perhaps drawn together by their symmetry of gaps.

After a short while, the only ones left at the table are Max, Pablo, Casiano Veloso (with his musketeer's mane neatly parted and bags under his quarrelsome eyes), and Anastasio Duarte (a sideways-looking man from Cáceres, former chairman of the United Syndicate of San Sebastián, from which he was expelled for being constantly drunk).

"What are you waiting for, boys?" asks El Señorito, lighting a Khedive cigarette, one of his many snobbish habits. "You're not fairies, are you?" And he lets out a raucous laugh that brings Pablo to the brink of remembering where he has seen him before.

"On the contrary," replies Casiano Veloso, a bit offended, "what I'm hoping for is some free pussy."

"Me too," adds Anastasio.

"Oh, my little devils," Max muses, half-smiling, and he gestures with his hand to catch Madame Alix's attention. "What about you?" he asks Pablo, staring steadily into his eyes. And the typesetter is again just at the brink of remembrance, but his memory fails him at the last moment and hunkers down in some corner of his hippocampus.

"Heh? No, I'll pass," he says, as if he were playing poker.

And the others observe him with quizzical eyes, thinking maybe a fairy has slipped in with them after all. But before anyone can say anything, Madame Alix arrives to save Pablo from their hazing. El Señorito whispers something in the madam's ear, and she silently nods and gestures for them to follow her. Max, Casiano, and Anastasio stand up, leaving Pablo seated at the table.

"Sure you don't want to play?" El Señorito asks laconically before he leaves the room, obscenely caressing his cane's mother-of-pearl handle.

Pablo merely nods his head, as he watches the trio depart with Madame Alix, who gestures to a few of her girls to join the group. The party disappears through a scarlet curtain on the other end of the room, and the former typesetter of La Fraternelle remains for a few minutes wavering, trying to fight off the obsession that has been tormenting him ever since he first saw Max this morning in Saint-Jean-de-Luz, because there is no greater torture than the feeling of a remembrance that grazes the memory, yet refuses to crystallize in it. But you're not really going to give up, are you, Pablito, just when you've almost remembered? Consider this: the best way to get rid of an obsession is to dive straight into it, so let the alcohol carry you away, get up and walk toward the scarlet curtain, you still have time to lift up your head and see the three men cross through the double-framed door at the end of the hallway, preceded by as many half-naked young women.

Madame Alix closes the door from the outside and disappears down a stairwell at the end of the hallway, leaving it empty and in shadows. Pablo abandons his refuge behind the curtain and enters the hallway, flanked on both sides by thick doors that do not quite stifle the moans and sighs. He stealthily makes his way toward the last room. And as though in a novel by the Marquis de Sade, he crouches and peers through the keyhole at the obscene scene inside. But he only has time to see three male backsides in a row and hear a chorus of female laughter at the curious competition of weights and measures, because suddenly he hears at his back a soft Caribbean voice, very much like Angela's when she would put on her Cuban accent:

"What are you doing down there on the floor, my child?"

Pablo stands up, surprised, and turning, discovers that the reprimand comes from the young mestiza who had been giving him the eye in the salon and whom he had assumed was a native of Guadeloupe or Martinique.

"Come here, sweetheart, and stop snooping in other people's business."

Pablo can barely put up a fight as she pushes him into the room across the hall. This room is decorated with dubious taste, darkened with flower-print curtains, a motif repeated on the bedspread and on the upholstery of the chaise longue, as well as that of the easy chair next to the bed. The floor is covered with a fringed rug, and a clock on the wall appears to mark the rhythm of fleeting amours. Under the bed, although Pablo cannot see it, there is a washbasin for intimate hygiene. But the surprised revolutionary does not have time to amuse himself admiring the landscape, because the mestiza has already tumbled him into bed, with no more warning than a wink rehearsed a thousand times, and has started to strip off his clothes, after removing her peach-colored satin knickers. Her teeth glow white in the darkness, and her generous breasts oscillate arhythmically as she removes Pablo's boots, with him barely participating in the operation.

"But, my love, you have to do your part, I can't do it all by myself," says the Cuban girl, not losing her good humor, as she removes his trousers. As she tosses them on the flowered armchair, a few francs tumble out of the pockets and scatter on the carpet. "Don't worry, sweetie, I'll give them all back to you," she whispers in his ear as she removes his shirt, revealing his good luck amulet. "My goodness, what are you doing with this peeper around your neck?"

The crystal eye stares steadily at the young woman, who is spellbound by its greenish light.

"It's my good luck amulet," says Pablo, opening his mouth for the first time.

The girl presses her lips to Pablo's and kisses him with the kisses of her mouth, as if in an impious version of the Song of Songs. When their mouths separate, the amulet is around her neck and the crystal eye appears to have found lodging between her breasts. No, it's not magic or enchantment, it's the art of the street, studied under the tutelage of Master Hunger and Mistress Poverty.

Then, hypnotized by the glass eye swinging to and fro with the Cuban girl's thrusting, Pablo's body starts to abandon him, loosening up until he completely loses all notion of time and space. Then, without knowing how much time has passed, he returns little by little to reality.

"Well, well, kid," the girl's distant, quiet voice reaches him. "No one's ever fallen asleep on me like that before. How old are you, my sweet?"

"How old do you think?" Pablo answers with a question, still a bit groggy.

"No more than twenty-five, you must be a child of the Cuban War, like me. Want some, love?" she asks, showing him a small Moroccan leather case containing a small bottle and a hypodermic syringe.

It is then that Pablo finally sees the light that he's been looking for all day: his mind does a backflip to the past, bangs against the walls of the tunnel of time, and lands fifteen years ago in the city of Barcelona, during the violent events of the Tragic Week. In a fraction of a second he sees churches burning. He sees people running and screaming. He sees people dead on the barricades. And he also sees himself, barely nineteen years of age, hiding on a rooftop and refusing the morphine offered by a syndicalist with turquoise blue eyes, a sculptor with a velvety voice and thin fingers going by the name of Emilio Ferrer, who will turn out to be a police informant. The same eyes, the same voice and the same hands as this man who now goes by the name of Max Hernández, "El Señorito," and uses Bell & Croyden condoms.

Pablo leaps out of bed and runs from the room without putting on his pants, before the dumbstruck gaze of the Cuban girl, who is surprised by her client's sudden burst of energy. Pablo bounds across the hallway and opens the opposite door, provoking screams from the three girls inside, twisted between the bodies of Casiano Veloso and Anastasio Duarte.

"What the fuck is going on?" asks Casiano, his eyes all glassy. "Don't you see you're frightening the ladies?"

"Where's Max?" asks Pablo.

"Why? Has the revolution started, or what?"

"Where is he?" Pablo insists.

"He left."

"What do you mean he left? Where?"

"How should I know, buddy? I'm not his mother," responds Casiano, returning his attention to the plump blonde in his clutches. "Come on, relax and enjoy yourself with us, there's enough to go around."

But Pablo is in no mood to party.

"You're sure he didn't say where he was going?"

Neither man answers.

"And you didn't ask him anything?"

Again, silence.

"What a couple of idiots," Pablo mutters as he leaves the room and goes back for his pants. But the beautiful mulatto girl has disappeared, not without taking her fee in the form of the francs scattered on the floor, and, by way of gratuity, the crystal eye, the good luck amulet that has accompanied Pablo for over fifteen years.

"Shit!" he exclaims, putting on his pants in a hurry.

He returns to the salon, gathers up his overcoat and beret, and runs down the stairs, surprising the sleeping elderly doorman. When he emerges into the street, night has fallen, and there is no sign of El Señorito.

"Shit!" Pablo howls again, and he doesn't even know that Anastasio Duarte has told Max the telegram key in exchange for an injection of cocaine.

XI
(1909)

HE WOKE UP TO SHOUTS OF "Long live this year's conscripts!" He looked at the wall clock hanging on the glass door of the director's office, the same door through which the plump Obdulia had led him years before to steal his virginity: it was a quarter past seven in the morning. He went out on to the balcony and saw a group of young men walking toward the Plaza Mayor amid songs and jokes, trying with booze-soaked revelry to exorcise the dire future that awaited more than one of them.

The night before, after leaving Madam Crow's inn, Pablo had headed for Calle Zamora looking for Ferdinando Fernández. But halfway there he realized it was Saturday, and that there would probably be no one at the office, because the law prescribing a weekly day of rest had been adopted by some newspapers, including *El Castellano*, which no longer came out on Sundays. So he stopped in a cantina to fill his stomach with a bland, reheated stew. It was there that he read the letter from his mother, who lamented her son's absence during the Christmas holiday, and the letter from the newspaper, informing him that he had been fired for missing work with no excuse; and also the form letter from the City of Salamanca, convening him to the lottery slated to take place the next day. Just what I needed, thought Pablo, crossing his fingers in the hope that destiny, for once, would cut him some slack.

The Constitution of 1876 had decreed mandatory conscription for all Spanish lads (an obligation lasting a mere twelve years: three years of active service plus nine more in the reserves), but not all young men were condemned to leave their families in their nineteenth springtime, since the government set a quota for recruiting for each province, and it was the infamous lottery that determined who would be chosen. There were also other options to get out of recruiting (not counting more drastic measures such as fleeing or mutilating oneself): to start, almost anyone under five foot three was excluded, as well as anyone suffering from any disease or physical defect that would prevent him from fulfilling God's command to protect his sacred homeland. However, Pablo's anosmia was not on the list of pardoning disorders, and although he had still not entirely recovered from the bullet wound, that too would not get him out of service. It would have been easier to claim that he was the son of a widowed mother and the only support for his family, but the time had already passed for such excuses. Of course, he also didn't have the money to afford the so-called "metallic exemption," the legal bribe that well-heeled lads used to dodge their obligations, so legal in fact that it was even announced the same day on page 3 of *El Castellano*, as Pablo could read on a copy in the cantina: Previsión Andaluza (a simplified shares corporation specializing in credit and insurance) offered parents a military exemption for their sons, for the modest price of eight hundred pesetas, with no hidden costs, to be rendered in two, three, or four payments.

"Sons of bitches," murmured Pablo, feeling the revolutionary blood rush to his head.

And he wasn't the only one thinking that way, as he would soon discover. He paid for his dinner with the little money he still had, and set out for the office where he had worked for the last five years, with the remote hope of finding Ferdinando. Someone had taken the sign down from the door, but he could see light in the writing room, so he tapped gently on the door with his curled middle finger.

"It's open!" shouted an unmistakable voice.

Not even three months had passed since he had been there. However, Pablo felt like it had been an eternity: the furniture was in the same place, and so were the spittoons, and even the stuffed owl was still watching over the room from its corner with the same undaunted look as ever, but he had the impression that a patina of time had covered everything. Ferdinando himself, alone and bent over the typewriter, appeared to have put on a few years. It must have been the effect of surviving by a miracle; returning from the gates of Hell, the world always looks different.

"I'll be damned!" exclaimed the journalist as Pablo entered, with the face of someone who has just seen a ghost. "Come to my arms, boy, so I can see that you're flesh and blood." And he began to palpate Pablo's body as if frisking a thief. "We heard you were dead."

"Well, now you see I'm not—" smiled the revenant.

"Come on, let's go to the casino, we have to celebrate. I got left alone setting Monday's little poem, and later I'm going to the cabaret to see that beautiful little American gal ... But hell, you know my motto: Never do today what you can put off till tomorrow!"

When they had two glasses of cognac in front of them, Pablo started to explain to Ferdinando what had happened, leaving the reporter stunned and muttering:

"That's better than the feature on Manzoni we ran a few years ago ..."

After a few glasses and more explanations than he would have preferred to give, Pablo floated the possibility of putting a notice in the newspaper announcing Angela's disappearance.

"It won't do any good," said Ferdinando.

"Why not?"

"Because her parents already ran one."

In fact, while Pablo was recovering from the terrible injury suffered at the Fountain of the Wolf, Don Diego Gómez had searched heaven and earth for his daughter, whose disappearance had been announced in all of the newspapers of the province, including *El Castellano*.

"If you put out another announcement now saying that you're looking for her, she'll probably think it's her family trying to trick her into coming home. What's more, it would let her father know that you're alive ..."

The truth is that this world-weary man was totally correct, but Pablo was not ready to give up:

"Unless we put out a coded announcement."

"A coded announcement?" asked Ferdinando, raising his eyebrows.

"Yeah, an announcement in a code that only she will be able to decipher."

"You've read too many novels, boy. Fine, give me an example of a coded announcement," said the reporter sarcastically.

"I don't know, something like, 'Heartless vampire desperately seeks cannibal anthropologist.'"

Ferdinando nearly choked on his cognac.

"Yeah, buddy," he said when he had recovered, "and underneath we can put: 'Please meet at the printing office of *El Castellano.*' Have you lost your mind or what? Maybe the newspaper is run by a blind man, but he's not an idiot. An announcement like that would attract everyone's attention!"

A few patrons of the casino looked curiously at the strange pair formed by the journalist and his protégé.

"But wait, let me think," Ferdinando continued, seeing Pablo's desperate face. "Next week is Carnival, right? Maybe we can make it look like an advertisement for costumes for the masquerade ball ... What if we put: 'For sale by owner, vampire and cannibal disguises for Carnival?'"

Pablo's face lit up:

"Great idea! Or, just put: 'For sale by owner, heartless vampire costume for masquerade ball.' That will be enough. If Angela reads that, she'll know it was me that posted the ad."

"If you say so ... I don't know if I want to know what vampires have to do with all this, but I'll see what I can do," said Ferdinando. "Oh, and let's not forget: this makes us even Steven for the time you saved my ass in Barcelona."

Pablo smiled like a heartless vampire:

"Thanks, Ferdinando. So, do you know anywhere I could spend the night?"

"Do I know, man, what is knowing?" the reporter started philosophizing, his spirits lifted by drink and chatter. "Alls I know is I don't know nothin', and that there are only two types of people in the world who are interesting: those who know absolutely everything and those who know absolutely nothing... But since you asked, I'll tell you that you can stay at my house. Only thing is, I only have one bed."

"I don't want to bother you, Ferdinando."

"Then stay in the office, if you like. Tomorrow's Sunday, and no one will come in until the afternoon. Also, if you get up early you can go to the town hall to see the lottery."

"Oh, it's true. If they send me to Africa, I swear I'll desert."

"That sounds like a shoddy future for dear Angelina, if you find her, that is," Ferdinando remarked.

"Angela, her name is Angela," Pablo corrected him.

"Angel or devil, what's the difference, at the moment of truth they all drag us to hell."

The conversation ended after midnight, and Pablo wasn't the only one who gained from it; Ferdinando got his own benefit by finding the inspiration for the poem for the front page of *El Castellano*: "Fidel has been called up / so he curses his cruel luck / and complains. / Me, however, what I'd give / To swap and have his life to live!"

AT A QUARTER PAST SEVEN IN the morning, the shouts of the conscripts disappeared down the road on the way to City Hall. Pablo washed his face in a washbasin he found in the director's office and left the headquarters of *El Castellano* wearing his backpack. As he reached the Plaza Mayor, a few groups of youths were crowded around the doors of City Hall, smoking their last cigarettes before they submitted to the whims of the goddess

Fortuna. The good humor that had trickled through their singing a few minutes before now seemed to have melted like snow on the ground: now they were all sighs and worried faces. A maintenance worker in spotless livery came out to announce that the drawing was about to begin, in a solemn public session.

Pablo dragged his bag up the stairs, grunting with the exertion, and came to a standing rest in a corner of the spacious room where the draft lottery was to take place. A man with a shining bald pate was presiding over the drawing. At the time of Pablo's arrival, he was filling a kettle with balls marked with the names of the 224 conscripts, before the watchful gaze of those brave or mistrustful enough to attend the lottery. Once the process was complete, the time came to fill a second kettle with the 224 numbered balls corresponding to the total number of conscripts. It was then that the "innocents" were brought in: two boys, no more than ten years of age, dressed as if to receive their first communion. One of them, the darker one, went to the kettle containing the named balls; the other, a blond-haired little cherub, stood next to the kettle of numbered balls. Then, the shiny-pated man rolled up his sleeves like a magician or a butcher, and placed one hand in each kettle, stirring their contents with the pomp and circumstance of one who knows that he is shuffling the cards of fate. A few people in the crowd thought they read his lips saying, "*Alea jacta est*," and before you knew it the dark boy pulled out the first ball and gave it to a man with an ample mustache who was acting as stage manager:

"Miguel Sáez Aguña," the man read aloud, in an unexpected tone of pity.

"Number seventy-seven," the president responded after receiving the numbered ball from the cherub.

"Shit!" exclaimed a young man, who then stormed out of the room as the municipal secretary wrote his name and number in a ledger with a red cover.

"It could have been worse," Pablo heard someone near him say. "At least he won't be sent to Morocco."

The commentator was right: the balls determined not only who would have to pay the so-called "blood tax," but also their final destination: the lower numbers would be deployed to the overseas territories, the middle numbers somewhere here on the peninsula, and the higher numbers to the training corps, which is to say, the reserves. Therefore, the lower the number on the ball, the greater the likelihood of not returning home, as the popular wisdom went circulating all over the village that morning: "A boy conscripted, not yet married / he'll soon be dead and left unburied," a mother would recite, her heart full of worry. "Ten lads drafted, but only five / lucky ones come back alive," her neighbor would reply. And so on, enough to fill a book of proverbs.

After ten minutes of drawings, ball number one was pulled, corresponding to one Ángel Preto Beltrán. The unlucky lad left the room pale and stiff as a board, as some tried to cheer him up and others made the sign of the cross, as if he had been condemned to death. A half hour later, the highest numbered ball came out, number 224, and Agustín Arenzana Morán let out a cry of joy as he ran out and down the stairs to go celebrate at the nearest tavern.

"Unpatriotic swine!" shouted a shriveled neighbor who saw him crossing the square leaping for joy.

Pablo's ball was one of the last to come out, and it corresponded to number 66. A number that got him out of going to Africa, but not out of military service. As he was leaving City Hall, someone invited him to join the lottery celebration, but he declined the offer with no further explanation. Three weeks later, there would be the classification procedure for new recruits, but actual enlistment would not take place until August, and he would not know his final destination until October or November, so Pablo still had a few months to look for Angela before he had to fulfill his duty.

For the first few days, he wandered the streets of Salamanca with no fixed objective, hoping to run into her around every corner, while he waited for the announcement posted in *El Castellano* to bear fruit. Sometimes he found himself yelling his beloved's name on the banks of the river Tormes, or on the outskirts of the city, or even at the doors of the cathedral, until a neighbor threatened to call the police. Some nights he slept in the newspaper office, some at Ferdinando's house; he also spent some time at a print shop belonging to some anarchist friends, and he even slept a few times under the Roman bridge, his desperation growing ever worse. When he had spent his last penny, he decided to pawn his few belongings, including his suitcase. The only things he didn't hock were his father's hat, his revolver, and the good-luck amulet that the old fortune-teller had given him in the cabin in the woods.

So it was that the first Sunday in March arrived, and Angela still hadn't shown any sign of life. If she had seen the announcement, she hadn't deciphered it. But the most likely thing is that she hadn't even come across a copy of the paper. In fact, *El Castellano* was distributed only in Salamanca, and no one could be sure that Angela was still in the province. She could be in Madrid, or in any other city in Spain. Or even farther, Pablo thought—in America, in Africa, or in Oceania, surrounded by Jivaros or cannibals. There was also the possibility, though it made him sick to think of it, that she was at the bottom of the sea with a sunken clipper ship for a tomb. It was more to get these dark thoughts out of his head than because he had abandoned the idea of deserting that he showed up to fulfill his obligations as conscript number 66. They measured his height and weight, gave him a physical examination and found the wound on his left chest, freshly scarred over. Pablo said that it was a recent injury, and the two technicians appeared to be satisfied. They only asked him if he felt any discomfort, to which he replied that he saw stars when he sneezed and that he had difficulty breathing when climbing stairs. "That happens to everyone," they said, laughing. "Quit smoking and you'll see how much better you feel." Of course, if he had had money to bribe them, it wouldn't have been difficult for them to declare him unfit for service.

After the examination, Pablo was definitively enlisted in the draft of 1909. And although he still had a few months left to find Angela before he'd be called into the ranks, he realized that if he wanted to find her he would have to do more than wait in Salamanca for a miracle to happen. If only Robinsón were here with me, he thought. And a light went on somewhere in his brain.

"You're going to Barcelona?" Ferdinando asked when he heard the news. "When?"

"Tomorrow. Well, first I'll go to Baracaldo to see my mother and sister, to make sure they're well. But then I'm going to Barcelona."

"And what's going on with Angelica?"

"Angela, her name is Angela."

"Fine, whatever her name is. You're not hoping to find her in Barcelona?"

Pablo smiled for the first time in many days, because a glimmer of hope had appeared on the horizon. He did not understand why he hadn't thought of it before, but now it seemed clear that if Angela had left Béjar thinking him dead, she would have gone to look for Robinsón without thinking twice. And where was Robinsón? Until further notice, in a nudist commune on the Catalonian coast. However, he preferred not to share his thoughts with Ferdinando, and merely answered with the force of a poet or a conqueror:

"If she's not in Salamanca, I'll have to go look for her, even if I have to go to the ends of the earth."

−13−

We waited impatiently for the telegram. A man who has lived through such moments of shared fever can never forget them. We all knew that when the telegram came, we would have to amass at the border and battle our way across against the border police. Deep down, everyone knew that we were going to be up against numerous, well-organized forces, better armed than ourselves, and that many of us would end up paying with our lives for our revolutionary deed, even if it succeeded. But what did we care? Liberty is worth many a life.

VALERIANO OROBÓN,
statement recorded by Abel Paz in *Durruti en la revolución española*

WHEN PABLO LEAVES THE BROTHEL, NIGHT has already fallen. The neighborhood is deserted save for a stray cat mewling on the sidewalk next to the street's lone working gas lamp. Pablo walks in that direction and takes out his pouch of tobacco. A damp breeze comes in from the sea, deadening his muscles and making even the mechanical task of rolling a cigarette difficult. He buttons his overcoat and tugs his beret down over his ears. He hears a distant gramophone, its music arriving muffled and laconic. For a moment he considers going to the square to see if he can find Max, but he suddenly feels tired. Also, the clear image that had appeared to him as the mulatto girl offered him drugs is starting to dissipate, and he no longer feels so certain that El Señorito is the same apocryphal syndicalist he met in Barcelona in 1909. He takes a few drags from his cigarette as he observes the cloudless sky, amusing himself by picking out the major constellations, as his father had taught him in the fields of Castile. There is Ursa Major, the great bear, looking like a wheelbarrow; a little further is Ursa Minor, a twin of her mother but smaller; and at the apex of the celestial dome, Pablo's favorite: Cassiopeia, with her zigzagging silhouette forming a slightly exaggerated M. "M for Martín," his father would say, and Pablo believed him. With these nostalgic thoughts, he finally makes his way toward the cemetery along inhospitable streets. He feels a strange emptiness in his stomach, but it is not hunger. The scene in the brothel, which now seems blurry and decomposed, has left him ill at ease and without his protective crystal eye.

As he reaches the cemetery, the moon illuminates the niches and crypts, creating a disquieting atmosphere. Pablo sees that there is light in the decrepit crypt keeper's hut, and he crosses the maze of graves hastily. But when he approaches, he hears shouting inside: one male voice, another female. It is Leandro and Antoinette in a heated argument. Pablo hangs back, not knowing what to do. Then something strikes the back of his neck, something small and round. He turns around and sees no one, but another projectile strikes his arm: it is a cypress cone, known to botanists as a "galbulus," though the dead don't know that. And neither does Pablo, who can only scoop the hard, smooth berry from the ground and ask in an anxious voice:

"Who's there?"

But the only reply is another volley of galbuli. Pablo's eyes dart left and right in the moonlight, and he is on the verge of a panic attack when he hears Kropotkin yipping.

"You fuckers! Bastards!" he shouts at Robinsón and Julián, who emerge from behind a large tomb, dying from laughter.

"Shhhh! Don't shout, there are people sleeping," Robinsón snickers, gesturing at the array of graves.

"Will you tell me what you're doing out here?"

"Playing hide-and-go-seek, if you will," Robinsón answers. "Killing time while those two sort out their problems, which they've been at for almost an hour. And where the hell did you run off to, you rascal? We were looking for you all afternoon."

"Around."

"Around?"

"Yeah, around, following El Señorito to see if I could remember where I recognized him from."

"And?"

But Pablo has no time to respond, because the door of the shack opens and Antoinette stomps out, slamming the door behind her. Seeing them standing there, she runs in the other direction, sobbing. The three men and the dog enter the hut to find Leandro hunched over in a chair, plucking the petals from a chrysanthemum.

"Come in, boys, come in," he says without looking at them, letting out a sigh. Since none of them dares to ask, he offers the explanation: "Heart or revolution ... *c'est tout!*"

And judging by how Antoinette left, it is clear what the Argentine has chosen.

TIME CAN DILATE, BUT NOT ETERNALLY: if it stretches too far without contracting, it can break. And something has broken in Saint-Jean-de-Luz when Robinsón, Leandro, Julián, and Pablo arrive at noon to the music gazebo in the center of the square. Last night, they stayed up talking until dawn, but Pablo never found the right moment to share his suspicions about Max "El Señorito" Hernández, overwhelmed by the labyrinthine discussions about whether soccer would eventually beat out bullfighting as the national sport, whether ombre is more or less bourgeois than bridge, or if wooden pipes are superior to clay ones. Only when they put out the kerosene lamp and started to hear Leandro and Julián snoring did Pablo work up the nerve to whisper to Robinsón:

"Hey, Robin."

"What?" replied the vegetarian, half asleep.

"I think I know who El Señorito reminds me of."

"Who?"

"A police informant I met in Barcelona a few years ago."

"No kidding? Are you sure?"

"Yes. Well, no. I don't know."

"Which is it?"

"It was a long time ago—"

"Look, the best thing would be for us to get some sleep and gather our strength," Robinsón yawned. "Tomorrow we'll talk to him and ask him for some explanations, what do you think?"

"Yes," Pablo responded, though unconvinced, while his friend's snores joined the off-key chorus.

So this morning, the four night owls have had a hard time getting out of bed and have arrived at the square later than usual, finding it occupied by seventy or eighty very nervous Spanish revolutionaries. But El Señorito is not among them, as Pablo soon discovers.

"It's about time, Roberto!" blurts Luís Naveira, one of the few people who call Robinsón by his real name. "We thought something had happened to you, for Christ's sake!"

"What's going on?"

"The goddamn telegram arrived, man."

And the four young men's hearts all skip a beat. Even Kropotkin starts wagging his tail compulsively.

"Come on, let's get away from here," suggests Santillán, the former civil guardsman. "We're drawing too much attention."

The sky has started to fill with dark clouds, and the posse starts off in a hurry toward La Nivelle golf course, though nobody feels like singing this time. Some of them talk in small groups, but in quiet voices, as though at a funeral or trying not to bother an ailing elder. Others walk in silence, rendered mute by the knots in their stomachs or by who knows what pangs of conscience, such as Casiano Veloso and Anastasio Duarte, who sometimes look over at Pablo with eyes full of resentment, perhaps remembering his sudden outburst at the brothel. When they finally arrive at the golf course, the men unleash their passions and begin shouting at one another.

"Calm down, my friends!" Juan Riesgo pleads in vain.

"Silence, Goddammit!" howls Gil Galar, more corpse-like than ever.

It takes a portentious thunderclap to momentarily quiet their spirits.

"Friends," shouts Luís Naveira, taking the floor, flanked by the other members of the Group of Thirty and Santillán, the eldest man present, "it's been three days since most of us arrived from Paris, where we left our homes, our jobs, and even our families. Others have come from Bayonne, Biarritz, or Bordeaux, making God knows what sacrifices. And those of you who live here in Saint-Jean-de-Luz have welcomed us and let us sleep alongside your wives and children. But the moment of truth has finally come, my brothers. The time has come to see if all this sacrifice was worth it. The time has come to cross the border and liberate Spain from the yoke of dictatorship!"

"Hear hear! Down with the dictatorship!" some shout.

"Down with the monarchy!" others roar.

"*¡Viva la revolución!*" the most excited blurt out.

"The situation is," Naveira continues when the voices die down, "the telegram we were waiting for finally arrived this morning in Paris, and from there the Committee has sent it along to us and to our comrades in Perpignan."

A nervous murmur spreads among the revolutionaries.

"In fact," El Portugués continues, "the comrades who had stayed in Paris are going to take the train down this afternoon. Most of them will go to Perpignan, because we expect to need more reinforcements in Catalonia. But a few will arrive here tonight around dawn, including Durruti."

"So," someone asks, "are we going to have to wait around with our thumbs up our asses until they get here?"

"Right, that's what we've come here to discuss," replies Juan Riesgo. "I'm in favor of waiting for Durruti and the rest, because though there won't be many of them, it seems they're bringing some rifles."

"But it's also possible that they'll never arrive, if they're discovered with the contraband," argues Bonifacio Manzanedo, the affable explosives expert from Burgos.

"I think the best thing to do is cross the border as soon as possible," opines Gil Galar, always eager to make a display of his courage.

"Yes, but with what weapons?" asks one of the contingent from Paris. "Nobody's even given me a damn handgun yet. What am I supposed to do, start the revolution with my dick?"

Murmurs of agreement.

"Calm down, brothers," says Naveira, searching the faces of Juan Riesgo and Julián Santillán for approval, knowing that yesterday they traveled to Bordeaux to pick up a trunk full of guns, courtesy of the Spanish Syndicate. "There will be pistols for everyone who knows how to use one, whether or not we ultimately receive the rifles from Paris. We'll distribute them before we set off, and also ammunition, though I understand that some of you are already armed. Then, once we are in Spain, it won't be difficult to get our hands on more weapons, especially if the military is in rebellion, as Max said—"

"Of course," Pablo interjects, unsure whether or not to make his suspicions known, "why isn't Max here with us?"

"He took the night train to San Sebastián last night," Naveira informs him. "Right, Bonifacio?"

"Right," says the man from Burgos. "I ran into him on the street by the train station. He said he prefers to wait for us in Spain, and that once the conflict breaks out it will be more difficult to cross the border by train. Because, of course, he can't cross the mountains on foot, with his heart condition..."

Another thunderclap booms overhead, as if the sky were growing impatient with all of this hemming and hawing. But revolution is not something that can be taken lightly, and the men who have convened at the golf course are not about to take a rain check when the future of Spain hangs in the balance. So they keep discussing for a good while, despite the drops that begin to fall. When they finally finish their deliberations, a vote is taken by show of hands. And the result is indisputable: only Juan Riesgo and a handful of other men are in favor of waiting until dawn for the arrival of reinforcements from Paris. The rest, including the leaders of the expedition, vote to depart immediately for the border. After all, if the revolution has started, there is no time to lose.

"So let's meet up again in a couple of hours," proposes Naveira. "Right here. Those who voted to wait for the group coming from Paris, you can take orders from Juan. For the rest, take advantage of this time to get some rest or eat something if you haven't yet, because it's going to be a tough crossing. Don't fill up your bag with nonsense, pack only what's necessary. If you've got a gun, bring it. Do bring maps, compasses, flashlights, first aid kits. Courage, my brothers!"

And so, without further ado, the revolutionaries return to the village to gather up their belongings and eat something before departing, although many of them have a knot in their stomachs that makes eating difficult. In an even more nervous state than usual, Pablo, Robinsón, Leandro, and Julián, led by Kropotkin, walk toward the cemetery in silence, each thinking about his own worries. Once they reach the crypt keeper's hut, they set about packing their bags and suitcases, trying to pack only what is essential for the project of the revolution.

"Let's not forget the broadsides," Robinsón reminds Pablo.

"Or the tobacco," Leandro adds, ever the pragmatist.

However, since everyone has a different idea of what is essential, they end up packing a little of everything: personal documents, passports, and birth certificates; coin purses, billfolds, and wallets; switchblades and double-bladed knives; hip flask, cigarette case, matches, and a lighter (Leandro); underwear, sandals, pocket handkerchiefs, undershirts, a leather belt, a waistcoat (Robinsón); a silk scarf (Leandro); a pair of suspenders and a metal shoehorn (Julián); as well as hygiene items: combs, a small mirror, a bar of Heno de Pravia soap, pocket scissors, a shaving kit, a towel, and even a tube of perfumed pomade for hairstyling (Julián); an umbrella, a canteen, and personal items such as photographs, letters, notebooks, a pencil from the German brand Staedtler (Leandro), a Parker writing pen (Pablo), a pocket watch, chain missing (Julián); a tenth share in a lottery ticket from the French National Lottery of the eleventh of July (Leandro); etc. etc. etc.

Pablo is the first to finish packing his backpack, and he sits next to the fire to wait for the others. As he observes them, he realizes that at thirty-four years he is the oldest of the group: Robinsón is a year younger, Leandro is coming up on twenty-five, and Julián is still Julianín, having recently completed his eighteenth springtime. Actually, except for El Maestro and the ex-civil guardsman Santillán, Pablo must be one of the oldest of the whole expedition. And suddenly a fear enters him, a vague fear, a foreboding: something tells him that, if things go wrong, being one of the seniors of the group will not exactly work in his favor. Unconsciously, he lifts his hand to his chest, where his lucky eye should be, and not finding it, his fear grows even more acute. Then, while the others finish packing, he takes out his passport and his Parker pen and, with the subtle, precise stroke of a publishing professional, draws a tail on the zero of the year of his birth, and as if by magic his birth date changes from 1890 to 1899. Not even Han van Meegeren, the up-and-coming counterfeiter of paintings who will soon sell a fake Vermeer to Hitler's very own lieutenant, Hermann Goering, would have done better. This is no exaggeration, because tomorrow no one will realize the trick, unlike what will happen with other, sloppier revolutionaries.

"Robin," says Pablo after completing his artwork, "what year were you born?"

"Ninety-one," the other responds as he tries to close his kit bag.

"Give me your passport."

"Why?"

"Just do it, trust me."

And the one transforms into a seven, presto chango.

Having finished packing, the four friends eat a bit of bread and cheese, washed down with some sour wine that nevertheless manages to warm up their bodies and hearts. Except for Leandro's, which is oozing sadness from both ventricles and both atria. When they are about to leave, backpacks hefted, the Argentinian says:

"Wait for me outside, I beg you."

And in the solitude of what has been his dwelling since he met Antoinette, he tears a sheet from a notebook and, with his shiny Staedtler pencil, he draws a heart with an arrow through it. Underneath, he writes this terrible epigraph: "I'll come back to find you when Spain is free." And as a seal of love, a tear leaps to its death and serves as a signature.

Before leaving the shack, Leandro takes the photo of Antoinette from his left shirt pocket. This is the photo she gave him the first night they spent together. He lifts it toward the sky, like a priest with communion bread, and brings it to his lips to kiss it. Then he slides it back into his pocket, the image facing inward, and leaves the cabin. Outside, his three companions are waiting, and without saying a word, they set off in the rain.

XII
(1909)

WHEN PABLO ARRIVED THERE, BARCELONA WAS known as the "City of Bombs." It had been steadily earning this nickname ever since the first device exploded in 1884, announcing the new strategy of anarchism's radical wing: propaganda by the deed. A series of replicas of that inaugural blast shook the foundations of Catalan society, whose comfortable bourgeoisie was finally discovering the risks of a system that shamelessly rewards the powerful and punishes the powerless. Barcelona at the turn of the century had half a million inhabitants (half of whom were illiterate) and an economy based on industry and trade. But labor conditions tended to be subhuman: ten-year-old children working fifteen- or sixteen-hour days in dark, unsanitary factories at the miserable wage of one peseta a day. So the more rambunctious elements of the working class finally said enough is enough, it's time we start answering exploitation with explosions, degradation with detonations. *Dit i fet.*

After a long decade of attacks against the army, the church, and the Rossinian bourgeoisie, the authorities tried to patch up the matter, and almost succeeded with the so-called Trial of Montjuic, which the European press followed with enormous interest between 1896 and 1898: four hundred anarchists (or scapegoats, who cares?) were detained, fifty exiled, twenty incarcerated, and five ended up walking the steps to the garrote. The subsequent lull in violence was only an illusion; while it's true that for a moment no more bombs went off in Barcelona, when they finally started again they did so with a vengeance, to the point that Antoni Gaudí ended up paying homage to the very popular Orsini bomb (that spherical, spiked explosive used by Mateo Morral and named in honor of the Italian anarchist who attacked Napoleon III) by placing a replica in the claws of the pisciform demon trying to seduce a worker on the rosary chapel of the Sagrada Familia. In fact, when Pablo arrived in Barcelona on March 12, 1909, the city was still reverberating with the echoes of the fifteen bombs that had exploded in the last week, and the controversial Rull case was still fresh in people's minds—a case in which the authorities had executed an alleged anarchist accused of perpetrating several attacks, although in reality he was a police informant. The city's psychosis had reached such a magnitude that a royal decree had suspended constitutional rights for more than six months, notwithstanding the claims of Anselmo Lorenzo, a leading figure in Spanish anarchism, who said that "It cannot be sustained that anarchist terrorism exists, because anarchism represents the most perfect ideal of peace and economics, which is to say love and justice."

The antique Estación de Francia welcomed Pablo, who was coming from four days in Baracaldo with his mother and sister Julia, who had turned into a real lady, svelte and clever as a sphinx. But he was losing sleep over another woman, and he had no plans to give up until he found her. As he was leaving the station, an automobile nearly ran him down, and the driver shouted that he'd better be more careful if he wanted to live to old age. On reaching the other side of the street, the splendid sun shining in the sky compelled him to remove his coat, the same one Don Julián had worn as he traveled from town to town in Salamanca astride Lucero, and which he had just inherited at his mother's insistence. He took a carefully folded paper from its inside pocket, and for the umpteenth time he reread what Ferdinando Fernández had written when they said goodbye at the office of *El Castellano*: "Abelardo Belmonte. Plaza Urquinaona, 10, 3 I.a." It was the address of one of his cousins who lived and worked in Barcelona.

"He's the black sheep of the family," Ferdinando had told Pablo before embracing him for the last time and sliding a twenty-five-peseta bill into his pocket. "He's still a kid—a bit, you know. Excitable. He's declared

284

himself an anarchist but I don't know much more. But tell him what you wrote on the façade of the cathedral, and see if he doesn't help you out."

Now, following directions from a street vendor selling *barquillos*, Pablo was making his way through the construction work on what would become the Vía Layetana, and remembering the writer's words, clutching the piece of paper like a drowning man clings to a life preserver. Fifteen minutes later, he found himself in an open square, full of trees and surrounded by imposing buildings.

"Pardon me, grandfather," he said to an old man begging for alms, a black patch over his left eye, "Plaza Urquinaona?"

"You're standing on it, my lad," sighed the old man, and he shook the four coins he held in a coconut half-shell.

But you can't squeeze blood from a stone. Pablo merely thanked the man and departed. Door number 10 was manned by a concierge with the look of a lion tamer, one of the lucky ones who had received a job thanks to the last wave of anarchist attacks, after which the authorities had decreed that all of the buildings in Barcelona had to have a doorman to ensure the safety of the residents and to chase off criminals, with fines of up to fifty pesetas for any house that failed to comply with the order. And truth be told, this animal tamer appeared ready to thrash the first hooligan who dared to darken his door.

"Hello," Pablo got up the courage to say, "I'm looking for Abelardo Belmonte."

The man twisted his mustache while studying the new arrival.

"Third floor, number one," he finally conceded, his voice as flat as a gramophone.

And so it was that Pablo made the acquaintance of the nephew of Ferdinando Fernández, as well as his wife and his three children, a trio of hellions who tore through the house like a hurricane. The meeting was fruitful indeed: Abelardo not only found him a place to sleep (albeit in the municipal hostel on the Calle del Cid, in the middle of the Atarazanas district, which city governor Angel Ossorio referred to as "the most sinful quarter in Barcelona") but also put him in contact with La Neotipia, the anarchist cooperative of typographers, who ended up giving Pablo a little work here and there to live on. And, even more importantly: this saintly man was the one who told him of the Vegetarian League and put him on the path toward Robinsón:

"It was founded a few months ago by a Dr. Falp i Plana, who was the personal physician to the poet Verdaguer," he explained one day, seeing that Pablo was starting to get desperate because no one seemed to know anything about this alleged naturist commune where Robinsón had supposedly sought refuge. "It's not far from here, you can go ask. Didn't you say your friend is a vegetarian?"

Pablo went that same day to the Vegetarian League, located on the Rambla de las Flores, in the venerable Palace of the Vicereine. A secretary with frizzy hair, bearing a certain resemblance to Obdulia, asked him to wait a few minutes in a little room covered in spinach-green wallpaper. The walls were hung with paintings of bucolic landscapes and photographs of the league's public acts, and there was even a framed copy of the first menu the members had shared at the Mundial Palace restaurant to celebrate the founding of the league, a menu that seemed to Pablo like something out of a fairy tale: 1) amuse-bouche Brahma, 2) rice Pythagoras, 3) empanadas Esau, 4) beans à la Carthusian, 5) Tolstoy fruit salad, 6) lettuce Lahmann, 7) Kneipp bread, biscuit à la mode, fruits, cheeses, pasta, and malt. And to drink, grape juice.

"*Bon dia, què desitja?*" came a voice from behind him, giving him a start. It was Dr. Falp i Plana himself, founder of the institution.

"Hello," Pablo replied, somewhat uneasy despite the doctor's bonhomie. "You'll have to excuse me, but I've spent several days looking for a vegetarian friend of mine, and all I could think to do was to come here to see if you folks know him."

"If he's a vegetarian and lives in Barcelona, I'd be surprised if we didn't know him," responded the doctor, switching from Catalan to Spanish and glowing with a beatific smile.

"The truth is that I don't know if he lives exactly in Barcelona. The last news I had from him is that he was in a naturalist commune on the Catalan coast..."

Falp i Plana furrowed his brow almost imperceptibly, and observed the recently arrived young man with a certain suspicion:

"You must mean *naturist*. A very interesting trend, of course, although a bit shameless, don't you think? It's one thing to live in communion with nature and quite another to walk around in your birthday suit... But to my knowledge nudism has yet to arrive in Spain. What did you say your friend's name was?"

"Roberto, Roberto Olaya, but he goes by Robinsón."

"Very appropriate," the doctor smiled again. And then, as if he had suddenly remembered something, he went to the frizzy-haired secretary. "*Escolti, Eulàlia, no li diu res aquest nom?*"

"*Oi, it tant, doctor: és el que va dir aquella noieta tan mona de fa uns mesos i que a vostè li va fer tanta gràcia. Encara el dec tenir apuntat per aquí...*"

Pablo tried to understand what they were saying, but these fine people's Catalan was Greek to him.

"*Justa la fusta!*" exclaimed the founder of the Vegetarian League, clapping his hands together.

"What is it, doctor?"

"No, nothing," said the man, dismissively. "Just that two or three months ago a young woman came by here asking about a certain Robinsón. Curious, no?"

But *curious* was not the right word for how Pablo felt about it. His eyes opened wide as saucers and his lower lip started to tremble.

"Are you alright, young man?"

"Eh... yes, yes. What did she look like?"

"Who?"

"The girl."

"Oh, her. I don't know. What did she look like, Eulàlia?"

"Very pretty. A morena, rather dark. Big eyes."

It's her, Pablo thought, filled with joy, it has to be her.

"And what did you tell her?"

"About what?"

"About Robinsón."

"Oh, nothing. Told her I never heard of any Robinson other than Crusoe. She apologized, thanked me, and left. I didn't even have time to ask her name."

Pablo opened his mouth to say something more, but he decided to bite his tongue. This was the first news he had had of Angela in a long time, and although it was no guarantee that he would find her, at least it meant that she was alive and had been in Barcelona. It was even possible that she was still in the city.

"And now, young man," the doctor interrupted his thoughts, "you'll have to excuse us, we have things to do. Leave me an address where I can find you. If I hear anything about your friend, I'll let you know."

"Thank you, Doctor," Pablo said, filled with hope.

And the last thing he saw before leaving the room was the secretary's smile, as bright as a freshly sliced head of lettuce.

THE DAY THAT PABLO FINALLY EMBRACED Robinsón again, a bomb had exploded on the Calle de la Boquería. He heard the detonation as he was walking down Las Ramblas on the way to the Estación de Francia, and he saw the look of fear on the faces of the passersby. But he did not stop. Maybe on the train I can find out what happened, he thought. And he was not mistaken. At the entrance to the station, a group of workers was commenting on the event: a pipe full of dynamite had exploded next to Estabanell Orthopedics, leaving various clients injured, afflicting the already afflicted.

That same morning, Dr. Falp i Plana had summoned Pablo, who had spent a few days wandering all over the city hoping to find Angela, but with no results. It seemed that a member of the Vegetarian League had confirmed that a group of German naturists had taken up residence on the Costa Brava, hoping to proselytize in Spain the doctrines of Élisée Reclus and Richard Ungewitter:

"Who knows, maybe your friend is there," the doctor suggested when Pablo arrived. "What we don't know is the exact location of the camp, or commune, or God knows what it is. Near Blanes, apparently. You'll have to go there and ask. Let's hope it's not as hard to find as the Atlantis of *mossèn* Cinto."

Remembering the fallen poet, the doctor's eyes grew moist, and Pablo ran out of the Palace of the Vicereine to buy a third-class ticket to see his childhood friend.

Blanes was the first village of the Costa Brava, with its little stone houses that appeared to defy the name the Romans had given the place, *blanda* being Latin for "smooth." Since it was Wednesday, the village was filled with workday bustle, although the splendid sun that adorned the firmament tempted everyone to indolence. Pablo approached the little fishing port, but when he asked about the naturist commune they answered him with furrowed brows and suspicious looks, a hostile attitude that told him that he was on the right track. It doesn't matter, he thought, if I have to I'll stay on and live here until I gain their trust. But he did not have to go so far, because in the middle of the afternoon he crossed paths with the only person in Blanes whose tongue the cat had not gotten: the village idiot.

"Excuse me," Pablo inquired, "can I ask you a question?"

The man was seated on the sidewalk, trying to confound an orderly parade of ants scouting for food: he was licking his finger and drawing lines across the ants' path, erasing the scent trail left by those that had gone before, producing disorder among the followers. The idiot looked up and squinted in the sunlight.

"Whatchoo waaaan?" he said, stretching out the final syllable as he lifted his hand to his forehead to shade his eyes. His bottom lip was wet and drooping.

"I'm looking for a naturist commune."

"A whaaaaa?"

"A group of people who live in communion with nature," Pablo replied, quoting Dr. Falp i Plana.

"Ya gimme a kiiiiiiisss?"

The poor man was clearly not in full possession of his wits.

"Never mind. I'll leave you to your ants," Pablo gave up, turning around.

"If ya gimme a kiss, I'll brin' ya theeeeere," he heard the village idiot say behind him.

"What?" Pablo turned around.

"Tony'll brin' ya theeeere, Tony knows where they aaaare, but Tony wants a kiiiiiiiss."

"You mean if I give you a kiss you'll bring me to the naturist commune?"

"Tony don't know what that iiiiiisss, people says Tony is as good as bread and as dumb as a dried chestnuuuuut, but if you give him a kiss Tony'll brin' ya where you're looking fooooor."

Pablo thought about leaving the matter there, but then perhaps this dimwit really knew the location of the commune. And after all, he wouldn't lose anything by giving him a kiss; if it ended up being a wild goose chase, at least he would bring a bit of joy to this poor man, who was obviously starved for affection.

"Alright then," he said. "I'll give you a kiss, but only after you bring me there."

The man's face lit up like a child's on Christmas morning, and he jumped up from the sidewalk clapping his hands. Without another word, he started walking toward the outskirts of the village, with the sea to the right and the hills to the left. When they had passed the last houses, he took a path snaking into the woods above the precipitous coastal cliffs. They walked in silence for a while, with the song of crickets as background music. Finally, they stopped next to a massive rocky promontory, which surpassed even the tallest pines in height.

"This is iiiiiit, I wan' my kiiiiiss."

"What? I don't see anyone."

"Liiiisten," said the man. And standing there hushed, they heard children's voices in the distance. "They're on th'other side of the rooooock. Gimme my kiiiiss."

Pablo smiled like a proud father and gave the man a sincere hug, topped off with a loud kiss on the cheek. A cherubic glow came over the idiot's face, and a thin string of drool hung from his lower lip. It had been years since anyone had kissed him, as he stank like hell, where the greatest punishment the damned must suffer is neither burning pitchforks nor lakes of fire, but the putrid, nauseating stench of their own corrupt souls. Pablo did not realize it, but his left arm had emerged from the embrace stamped with the wet seal of happiness.

He climbed up the promontory with considerable effort and, reaching the top, he felt like the first discoverers of El Dorado must have felt: down below, in a bend in the coastline flanked by pine-covered hills and the crystalline waters of the Mediterranean, a group of about twenty people were sunbathing in the buff. There were even a few children, who were splashing about in the sea while their mothers did gymnastics on the beach. A few yards away, a piñon pine leaning precipitously over his head, an elder with toasted skin was addressing a handful of men wearing bowler hats. Among them, Pablo could make out his friend Robinsón, despite the latter having let his beard grow long, his chest now covered with red hair. The first thing he thought was that he should turn around and come back later, in the evening, when this uninhibited troupe would hopefully have occasion to cover up, be it only to ward off the cold. But then he remembered the reason that had brought him there, and he said to himself that if he'd gone through the ordeal of kissing a slobbering idiot, he wasn't about to become too prim to walk up on a gathering of unclad naturists. It was then that he saw Robinsón walking a few yards away from the group of men to play with a dog that had just emerged from the water. Suddenly and for no apparent reason, one of his father's frequent sayings came to his memory, something like "the shortest distance between two points, when there's an obstacle in the way, is a curved line." So he decided to walk around to try to reach Robinsón, taking care not to tumble from the cliffs and to avoid being discovered by the others. He skirted the steep cove in a C-shaped path and, coming near to the group, he could hear the tanned old man extolling the benefits of the sun for a long and healthy life, his Spanish pitted with gutturals:

"Why fill your body with dangerous drugs when you're ill, when the sun sends us the best remedy every day? When we offer up our naked bodies to the sun's rays for hours at a time, its fire burns off the thousands of invisible animals that live in our blood and on our skin, destroys the poison in our veins, and brings us health and strength—"

"So why did Homer say that one doctor is worth many men?" asked a gray-haired younger man with earrings in both of his ears, looking like a seventeenth-century pirate.

The old man clicked his tongue:

"You must know, Paco, that even Homer's genius dozed off from time to time. As Engels said, 'The proof of the pudding is in the eating,'" the old man quoted in English.

"What does that mean?" asked a stout, hairy companion.

"It means, Manel, that you can tell if the pudding is good by how it tastes. Wouldn't you all agree that you feel better since we started coming to sunbathe here at the cove?"

The men all nodded, and Pablo continued his way around the edge of the rubble, trying to get as close as possible to Robinsón, who was still playing in the sand with his dog. Getting a look at the creature, Pablo thought he recognized Darwin, the water spaniel his friend had had in Béjar the last time they saw each other.

"Pssst," he tried to get Robinsón's attention, but the sound was lost in the sea breeze and the crash of the waves. Not even Darwin turned to look, hypnotized by his master's caresses. Finally, Pablo picked up a pebble and tossed it with perfect aim, hitting Robin's bowler hat. Robinsón looked at the sky, took off his hat, examined it with confusion, and muttered a few words, just when another pebble hit his back. Then he turned around, perceived his childhood friend, recognized him, opened his mouth in astonishment, leapt to his feet, and shouted at the top of his lungs:

"Pablo!!"

Twenty heads turned at once, first toward Robinsón and then to where he was looking. And although it may be hard to believe, the truth is that Pablo felt more naked than ever before in his life.

—14—

On the night of November 6 of this year, a few groups of peasants crossed the French-Spanish border, comprising a total of around seventy, coming from Saint-Jean-de-Luz, where they had convened, with a handful among them leading the way, carrying automatic pistols and a good deal of ammunition, with the aim of starting a revolutionary movement.

La Voz de Navarra, 5 December 1924

IF IT IS TRUE THAT IT is possible to have a revolution without heroes but not without martyrs, right now at the golf course there are seventy-odd men destined to join the pantheon of revolutionary martyrs, although most of them would prefer to think of themselves as heroes. Not all the revolutionaries are present; several have abandoned ship at the last moment, such as Perico Alarco and Manolito Monzón, who have mysteriously disappeared. Furthermore, not all present are revolutionaries, because the group has been joined by more than one man whose only aim is to get into Spain without going through customs, due to not having his papers in order or being wanted by the police, such as Francisco Lluch, a deserter from the regiment of Sicily who wants to reach Eibar to see his dying father. It may seem outlandish, but most of them are dressed in suits and ties, as though even the business of revolution called for presentable dress (just ask Robinsón, who persists in wearing his bowler hat). Only those gifted with foresight or pragmatism have traded their suit for a corduroy jacket or a thick, high-necked sweater. But all of them do have a good coat to keep out the cold, and some have even brought a raincoat, because although the rain appears to have stopped, an army of black clouds is still arrayed menacingly across the sky.

The group of men has gathered in a circle around a large trunk and two crates, recently opened by Juan Riesgo, who has arrived to distribute guns and to bid the expedition farewell. The smaller crate contains a shining assortment of about fifty semiautomatic pistols, mainly Stars, Brownings, and Astras, although "shining" might be putting it a bit too poetically, because some of them are older than the men who are going to use them. The other crate, slightly larger, is full of packs of bullets of various calibers, mostly 9 or 7.65 mm.

"Anyone who's never used a gun before, wait till the end," says Gil Galar, starting to distribute the pistols, while Bonifacio Manzanedo takes care of distributing the corresponding ammunition, and Pablo takes advantage of the opportunity to distribute a few bundles of broadsides among the revolutionaries.

By his side, Luís Naveira opens the trunk and takes out two full doctor's kits containing plasters, antiseptic gauze dressings, small bottles of iodine tincture, bandages, packets of cotton, thread, needles, scissors, and a few pills and creams. Since he used to practice medicine, he keeps one of the kits and gives the other to Robinsón, who in turn gives it to El Maestro, his vegetarian friend, arguing that he only believes in medicine from mother nature. Naveira also takes a few electric flashlights from the trunk, as well as five or six compasses, various Michelin maps of Southern France and Northern Spain, two or three spools of rope, and even a few opera binoculars, which he distributes among the leaders of the expedition.

It is almost six in the evening when the distribution process is done. Since some of them were already carrying, it turned out that there were enough pistols for everyone, except for four or five who prefer not to take them because they don't know how to use them; on the other hand, some receive a double ration, such as the ex-civil guardsman Santillán. Juan Riesgo and those who are staying behind to wait for Durruti say goodbye to their companions, along with those who are hoping to meet up again tomorrow on the other side of the border, and depart carrying the empty trunk and crates. The regiment then divides into five small groups of twelve to fifteen men, each led by one of the leaders of the incursion: the exalted Gil Galar, the veteran Santillán, the explosives expert Bonifacio Manzanedo (who some say is carrying a pineapple bomb in his duffle bag, which is untrue), the doctor Luís Naveira, and an Aragonese snake-oil salesman known as "El Maño" (a nickname that rhymes with his real name: Abundio Riaño), who will lead the group from Bordeaux, where he used to earn his living selling various elixirs and hair-growth tonics. Ideally, they would have formed even smaller squadrons, and if they only formed five it's not due to a lack of men willing to lead them, but rather because there were not many who know the way into Spain. In fact, out of all the revolutionaries who spent those anxious days in Saint-Jean-de-Luz waiting for the telegram with instructions to cross the border, only three have stated that they are capable of guiding the expedition across the mountains, so at the last minute they have had to convince two smugglers from Ciboure to act as guides, in exchange for a small sum of money. So the plan, as Luís Naveira explains once the groups have been formed, is the following:

"Here's the plan, comrades. The departure of each of the five groups will be staggered, but we won't head toward Irún, as some have proposed, because it would be almost impossible to cross through Hendaye without being noticed. What we'll do is go up Mount Larrún and cross the border at different points that are less closely watched, between markers 10 and 48, and then we'll meet up again at the towers of Napoleon's Pass in Spain. From there we'll all go down together into the first village, which is called Vera. Don't get separated from the guides, always follow their directions, and walk in silence, in tight groups. It's possible that one of the groups will

run into a stray pair of carabiniers who are unaware of the popular uprising and are still guarding the border. If this happens, we'll invite them to
join the group and come with us to liberate Spain."

"What if they don't want to?" someone asks.

"What if they attack us?" asks another.

"If they seem resistant, or if they try to stop us," Naveira concedes,
"we'll subdue them with blades. Only in case of absolute necessity do
we use the firearms, so we don't draw attention from any other carabiniers that might be on the mountain. Once we get to Vera we'll have
to assess the situation. If the uprising has already started in the village,
we'll join the revolutionaries and follow their instructions. If not, we'll
go to the foundry there and distribute the posters among the workers,
and try to convince them to join us. Then we'll go to the Civil Guard
barracks and invite them to join the revolution, or to give up and hand
over their weapons; if they resist, we'll take the barracks by force,
which shouldn't be too difficult since it's unlikely that there will be
more than two or three pairs on duty."

"And then?" asks El Maestro, holding the doctor's bag.

"Then we'll head toward Irún, where it's to be hoped that the
comrades from the interior will already be organized and we can combine our forces. From there we'll go to San Sebastián to consolidate the
victory of the revolution. Any other questions?"

Since no one answers, someone shouts at the top of his lungs:

"*¡Viva la revolución!*"

"*¡Viva!*" most of the men shout back, with a level of enthusiasm
that will gradually wane with the passing of the hours, for while revolutions always start with a profusion of hurrahs, they usually end with a
profusion of blood, as the gathering dusk seems to be trying to tell the
would-be heroes, bidding them farewell with a violent salvo of crim-
son and orange rays, in a spectacular battle against the enemy darkness.

The first group sets off, commanded by Luís Naveira and guided by one of the two smugglers on the revolution's payroll; this group also includes the Villalpando four, led by Casiano Veloso. A few minutes later, Gil Galar's squadron departs, infected with their leader's zealous, romantic spirit, singing "La Internationale" and whooping with more vivas to the revolution; serving as their guide is a carpenter named Piperra, a native of Zugarramurdi with intimate knowledge of the area. A little later comes the group led by Abundio Riaño, "El Maño," mostly comprising anarchists from Bordeaux, Bayonne, and Biarritz, and guided by a nephew of the priest of Lesaca, a tiny village adjacent to Vera. The second-to-last to leave is the squadron commanded by Bonifacio Manzanedo and guided by the other smuggler from Ciboure. Finally, when the full moon is starting to peek through the clouds in the sky, it is time for the departure of the group led by the ex-civil guardsman Santillán, to whom Robinsón has turned over leadership, knowing that he has a tendency to lose his reason when surrounded by nature. "You'll have to tie me up like Ulysses," he told Pablo and Leandro when they arrived at the golf course. "Otherwise I'll start climbing trees." Of course, the typesetter and the Argentinian are also in this last squadron, as is the greenhorn Julián and the group of vegetarians led by El Maestro. The guide is a young man from Lizarraga in Navarre, with red hair and a freckled face, named Martín Lacouza, who works as a bread baker in Saint-Jean-de-Luz and is known for his affinity for war stories. But the improvised squadron will increase its ranks at the last moment, when they start to skirt the golf course to get on the road to Oleta:

"Hey, hey, wait for us!" shouts Perico Alarco, panting, followed a few paces behind by Manolito Monzón, who arrives flapping his arms. "Weren't we supposed to meet at seven?" asks Perico, feigning ignorance so as not to have to explain that the only reason they decided to join the expedition at the last moment was because they've been caught stealing chickens in Ciboure and have had to flee like a soul bitten by the devil.

And so the toothless Perico and the deaf-mute Manolito join up with the last group of luminaries setting off to liberate Spain with a handful of old pistols and a decent supply of revolutionary posters.

XIII
(1909–1912)

AFTER THE ENCOUNTER IN BLANES, ROBINSÓN made the decision to move to Barcelona. He had spent more than a year communing with his group of libertine naturists, who advocated vegetarianism and nudity as the paths toward a more just society, in which the ingestion of meat would be considered barbaric and clothing an unacceptable sign of class discrimination. In fact, the members of the commune all wore bowler hats simply as a means of subverting bourgeois sartorial codes: if the habit makes the monk, they reasoned, we'll all wear a tailcoat so its privileges disappear. Or, even better, let's all go naked as long as the body can handle it.

But Pablo's arrival was a turning point in Robinsón's life: for his soul brother, he would have worn a frock coat and cravat if necessary. That afternoon in early April, after their happy reunion, Pablo was invited to partake in a vegetarian dinner with the members of the commune, who did wear clothes for the occasion, not out of deference to the new arrival as he thought, but because sundown brought a goosebumps-raising chill to the air. The camp was located in the middle of the pine forest above the cove and it was there, over a crisp salad of radishes and carrots, that Pablo explained to Robinsón that Angela had disappeared:

"You haven't heard anything from her, have you?" Pablo inquired.

"No, nothing."

"Then you're going to have to help me look for her," he told him.

Robinsón did not think twice:

"You can count on me. Whatever it takes."

After dinner, the two of them went alone to the beach and, smoking his first cigarette in ages, Pablo told his friend the story of the duel at the Fountain of the Wolf.

"What was the first thing I told you when we met?" Robinsón asked, hardly believing his ears. "Stay away from Angela or her cousin will kill you."

"And I'll be damned if he didn't almost do it," Pablo avowed, showing him the scar near his left nipple. "It's a good thing we vampires don't have hearts."

The two friends smiled, as the sunset painted the sky with color. And, the next day, they caught the train from Blanes to Barcelona.

Their first project on arrival in the city, after convincing the management of the municipal hostel on Calle del Cid to give Robin a bed, was to formulate a search plan. If they wanted to find Angela, they had to be methodical. They only knew that she had fled Béjar in November and had appeared shortly thereafter in Barcelona, asking after Robinsón at the Vegetarian League. Because there was no doubt that it was she who had spoken with Dr. Falp i Plana. Who else could it have been? Therefore, there were two possibilities: either she was still in Barcelona, or she had left. If she was in the city, they would find her sooner or later. If she wasn't in the city, there were two more possibilities: either she was still in Spain or she had gone abroad. If she was in Spain, they would find her eventually, even if it took a lifetime. If not ... if not, it was better not to think about it. In any case, the first thing they had to rule out was that she had returned to Béjar, which was unlikely but easy to test: Pablo wrote a letter to Father Jerónimo, and Robinsón sent a telegram to Don Veremundo and Doña Leonor, his beloved progenitors. And the responses were rather similar: no one in the village had heard anything about Angela, although gossip held that she had gone abroad with Pablo, since some of the neighbors had seen the former inspector's son hanging around the Gómez house the day before she disappeared.

"If only!" Pablo mused as he read Father Jerónimo's letter, written in elegant gothic script. "Too bad gossips always lie."

Once they had ruled out that remote possibility, they set about the task of doggedly searching for Angela all over Barcelona. Robinsón, who had not given up his fondness for painting, sketched a faithful portrait of the young woman with the big, sparkling eyes that had dazzled Pablo in the Church of Saint John the Baptist so long ago. At La Neotipia, the anarchist cooperative of typographers, they made some copies which they distributed in the busiest parts of the city: Las Ramblas, the Plaza de Cataluña, the cathedral, the markets, the cafés in the city center, and even the modern, elitist neighborhood of Ensanche, in case Angela had taken work as a servant to a rich family. Below the drawing, there was a brief text explaining that the woman in the portrait was Angela Gómez Nieto, eighteen years of age, from Béjar in Salamanca, and asking anyone who had seen her to contact La Neotipia, Rambla de Cataluña, 116. And just in case Angela herself came across the flyer, Pablo added his signature to the bottom of every copy, along with some words in his unmistakable handwriting: "I'll be waiting for you every Sunday at five p.m., at the Fountain of Canaletas." Once they had distributed the first copies in the central parts of the city, they took a map, divided it into twenty parts and spent their time running from one to the next, combining their search for Angela with a search for work, which they badly needed. A few days after arriving in Barcelona, Robinsón managed to find a job as a busboy in the kitchen of a restaurant called El Dropo, where, despite its name (a Catalan word meaning "vague," "slovenly," or "lazy"), he was driven to work like a mule. The one most pleased by this arrangement was surely Darwin, the spaniel that accompanied Robin everywhere and had spent a year eating turnips and spinach. For his part, Pablo continued doing piecework for the anarchist typographers' cooperative, hoping that someday they would see fit to offer him a regular job with a steady salary. If he didn't run off, that is, which was also possible.

For the next three months, Pablo never once missed his Sunday appointment at the Fountain of Canaletas, and he impatiently waited for someone to show up at La Neotipia with good news. But Angela only appeared in his dreams and his thoughts, and he grew more and more desperate, as if he had been infected with the growing political and social unrest that was blowing around the country, felt even more acutely in the City of Bombs. The origin of the conflict, however, was more distant: Morocco, to be precise. The Spanish economic interests in the region had been threatened for a while now by the hegemonic ambitions of Moroccan potentates and by the colonial aspirations of neighboring France, but Antonio Maura, the president of the conservative government, had for the time being declined to engage in any sort of military intervention. However, pressured by bankers with holdings in the mines of the Rif, as well as army officials and King Alfonso XIII, who was getting bored collecting slippers and wanted to get into action, the president finally dissolved the courts at the beginning of June to prevent parliamentary opposition to the bellicose operations that were about to take place in Morocco. The Council of State authorized an extraordinary line of credit of more than three million pesetas, intended to reinforce the army in North Africa, and hostilities began.

But public opinion was not keen to repeat the colonialist adventures that had led Spain to the disaster of 1898, still fresh in the memory of the working class, tired of risking their lives in wars organized by and for the bourgeoisie. The unfair recruiting system, which allowed moneyed young men to get out of military service by paying eight hundred pesetas, had only fed the anti-military sentiment among the proletariat. So, when the reservists started to be mobilized, along with recruits who had nearly completed their three years of active service, the people came out into the street to protest the war. And in Barcelona the revolt was most fervent, because the port of Ciudad Condal was the point of embarkation for the boats headed toward Melilla—boats that, ironically, were exactly the same ones that had gone into the inferno of Cuba eleven years beforehand, owned by the aristocratic clergyman, the Marquis of Comillas, who must have been rubbing his hands together thinking of the profits.

On the afternoon of Sunday, the eighteenth of July, while Pablo made his way under a scorching sun to his weekly appointment by the Fountain of Canaletas, an event occurred that would have a great impact on Barcelona's immediate future. A group of soldiers passed in front of the Palace of the Vicereine on their way to the port to embark for Africa: this was the Hunters' Battalion of Reus, one of the last to be mobilized by the minister of war, the steel-nerved General Arsenio Linares y Pombo. Then, unexpectedly, as if the sun had unleashed the spirits of the people watching the parade of troops, the soldiers were surrounded by the crowd, hugging them and cheering them, violating protocol. The recruits joined in the celebration, breaking ranks and following the avenue of the Ramblas in the embrace of family, friends, and other citizens of Barcelona opposed to the war. Even Pablo was swept up in the fervor of the crowd: a young woman walking by grabbed his elbow and dragged him into the middle of the peloton before he had a chance to protest. When their eyes met, he saw that the girl's eyes were two different colors: one was blue like chinaware, the other as gold as a doubloon. And although it meant running the risk of missing his Sunday appointment for the first time, he ended up following the battalion down to the port.

At the wharf they waited for the civil governor of Barcelona, Don Angel Ossorio, and the captain general of Catalonia, Don Luís de Santiago, flanked by a host of police. Seeing the battalion arrive in such an informal manner, they ordered the recruits to immediately board the *Cataluña*, which was to take them to the battle front. But the straw that broke the camel's back was the behavior of a group of aristocratic women who surrounded the gangway and distributed little Catholic good luck patches called *detentes*, along with medallions and cigarettes, in an act of hypocrisy so flagrant that some of the soldiers defiantly threw the gifts into the water.

"Throw your guns in too!" shouted one mother.

"Let the rich go off to war!" proposed another.

"Or the priests, they've got no mouths to feed!" a third woman shouted desperately.

"Yes, exactly!" the crowd shouted, all worked up.

The captain general gave the order to heave the gangway, and the security forces fired shots in the air to disperse the crowd. The girl with the bicolored eyes bid Pablo goodbye with a kiss on the cheek and ran off down the jetty, leaving him standing there like a statue. Tears as thick as mercury erupted from his eyes, tears of impotence, rage, and desperation, tears for the injustice committed against those unfortunate young men whom he would perhaps soon have to join, tears fit to silence forever the viperous tongues that, back in Baracaldo, used to say that the Martín boy was incapable of crying, tears that were perhaps also those of a hopeless lover, tormented, consternated, downcast, defeated, wracked with pain for having lost his one true love in the most foolish, idiotic, outlandish, absurd way possible. Tears that would have pushed him to take out the handgun he always carried, to unholster the pocket pistol that had been placed in his nearly dead hand by the hateful lieutenant colonel of that other overseas war, and to manifest his anti-authoritarian rage through violent vengeance, if Abelardo Belmonte had not appeared out of nowhere to drag him away from there before the police read him his rights.

Arriving on Las Ramblas, having barely recovered from the emotion, Pablo looked at the time: it was almost five thirty. He thanked Ferdinando's nephew and took his leave, crestfallen. Arriving at the Fountain of Canaletas, he thought he saw a young brunette run off in the direction of the Plaza de Cataluña and disappear among the crowd enjoying a leisurely Sunday stroll in the city center, despite the sweltering sun. He only saw her for a moment, from behind and at a certain distance, but her hair and her gait reminded him of Angela. His heart skipped a beat as he set off running up the Ramblas.

"Angela! Angela!" he shouted with all his might, weaving his way through the crowd, who looked at him as if he were mad or suicidal.

But when he arrived at the square the young brunette had disappeared. Pablo scanned in all directions, then gave up and tossed his coat on the ground in rage and guilt. Only then did he catch sight of the young woman getting on a tram. When she sat down next to the window, he could see her face.

She was beautiful, but she wasn't Angela.

AFTER SUNDAY AFTERNOON'S UNREST, MAURA'S GOVERNMENT decided that no more boats would depart from Barcelona. However, the fuse had been lit. Over the next few days there were repeated protests, with people shouting "Down with war!" "Death to Comillas!" and "Send the priests to Morocco!", growing more and more violent as the news arrived of the large numbers of Spanish losses in the Rif. There was also unrest in Madrid: at Atocha Station, women threw themselves on the tracks to prevent their sons or husbands from leaving the capital. On Wednesday, a large meeting held in Sabadell ended with the drafting of a text that left no doubt about the position of the working class with regard to the conflict in North Africa. It read:

> Considering that war is a fatal consequence of the capitalist system of production, and that, given the Spanish system of army recruiting, it is left to workers to fight the war and the bourgeoisie to declare it, this assembly energetically protests: 1) against the action of the Spanish government in Morocco; 2) against the methods of certain aristocratic ladies, who insult the pain of the reservists, their wives, and their children, by giving them medals and scapulars instead of granting them the means of subsistence which the departure of their breadwinners has deprived them;

3) against sending useful, productive citizens, most of whom are indifferent to the triumph of the cross over the crescent, off to war, while the regiments could just as well be populated by priests and monks who not only have a direct interest in the success of the Catholic religion, but also have no wives and children, no households, and no usefulness to the country; and 4) against the attitude of the Republican representatives, who have not made use of their parliamentary immunity to stand up for the masses on the front lines of the war protest. And it promises the working class that it will focus all of its efforts, if a general strike is declared, to compel the government to respect the rights of the Moroccans to maintain their country's independence.

IN RESPONSE TO THAT MEETING, THE government prohibited any public protest against the war, whether in the street or in the newspapers, even issuing a proclamation in Barcelona banning the formation of groups and prohibiting telegrams and long-distance telephone calls, with the obvious aim of preventing the organization of a strike anywhere on Spanish territory. But the worst was yet to come: the Friday morning newspapers carried the news that ten soldiers from the Reus battalion had been indicted on the boat to Melilla as a consequence of the disturbances that took place on the wharf that Sunday afternoon. And when the rumor got around that they had been condemned to death, the people went up in arms.

Pablo followed all these events in a state of shock. The first week of August he was supposed to go to Salamanca for enlistment and to find out where he would be deployed, but after the commotion on the wharf and the subsequent disappointment at Canaletas Fountain, he was plunged into a trancelike state from which not even Robinsón could rouse him. It was as though he had given up the fight. He stopped going to work at La Neotipia, he stopped eating, stopped sleeping at the municipal hostel on the Calle del Cid, and stopped paying attention to what was going on around him. He merely wandered around the city looking lost, his ears deaf, and his face more and more crestfallen. It took a blood-soaked man dying in his arms for Pablo to open his eyes and look around himself: Barcelona was in flames, and an infinity of barricades had turned the city into a battleground, in what would go down in history as the Tragic Week.

The pressure cooker had definitively exploded on Monday, July 26, when a spontaneous general strike devolved into street battles against the forces of order and the government decreed a state of war. The Strike Law, amended three months later, required unions to announce any work stoppage eight days in advance; and, if that weren't enough, it also prohibited strikes for political reasons, which condemned to failure any attempt at a workers' protest aiming for real change. But that sweltering July Monday dawned with the city captured by the workers, and the announcement of a twenty-four-hour general strike spread like a dust storm: months later, the civil governor of Barcelona, Don Angel Ossorio, would state that the strike "did not go off like a bomb, but ran like a string of fireworks," a string that would last an entire week. The first day, they closed the factories and businesses, the taxicabs stopped running, and the trams—the last bastion against the general strike—had to be escorted by Civil Guard forces on horseback, and occupied by security guards armed with short rifles; and so, what had started as a peaceful strike ended up leading to a semblance of a revolution: the police patrols monitoring the streets and attending the trams were attacked by hordes of men and women who thought they saw an opportunity to avenge centuries of poverty and oppression. Governor Ossorio, overwhelmed by the events and unhappy with his superiors' methods, submitted his resignation that same day and made a backstage exit for his summer home in Tibidabo. The next morning, the city had been cut off, the press muzzled, and telegraph services shut down, which merely fed the wrath of the protestors, who attacked the police stations, stole weapons, and tore up the cobblestones to build barricades; and, without really knowing how or why, what had started as an anti-military protest spi-raled into an anticlerical revolt: the city filled with voices calling to burn churches, convents, refectories, any building that smelled of incense, and soon Barcelona turned into a sea of fires illuminating the starry sky at nightfall. From his summer residence in San Sebastián, King Alfonso XIII signed a decree suspending constitutional rights in Barcelona, while the city's politicians, whether Catalanist, Republican, or socialist, ended up distancing themselves from this amorphous, acephalous workers' rev-olution that had exploded in their hands. On the third day, the convents' tombs were desecrated, and a protest led by women made its way toward the doors of City Hall, bearing as a flag the shrouds of fifteen dead nuns, supposedly tortured and buried by their own cloistermates for having hidden illegitimate fetuses from the world. One person had the audacity to pull one of these mummified nuns from the sepulchre, and proceeded to dance through the streets with her corpse in a grotesque, delirious spectacle that finally made the ruling classes understand that the workers were not toying around. The bourgeoisie locked themselves inside their homes, hoping the torment would subside, and the clerics left running, scattering like ants, tearing off their cassocks and collars. And thus, as if it couldn't be any other way, on the twenty-ninth of July, ten thousand soldiers arrived in Barcelona from Zaragoza, Burgos, and Valencia, ready to reestablish law and order in the name of God and country. It was then that Pablo discovered himself cradling the blood-soaked head of a man in agony. And it was as though the contact with the hot viscous blood snapped him back to reality, and he looked around and took stock of what was happening.

"Get me out of here," said the injured man in a feeble voice, "for the love of God."

He was in a barricade made of paving stones, tramway rails, sewer lids, lampposts, gratings, mattresses, tables, and even straw chairs, protect-ing a group of men firing rifles and trying to stop the soldiers' advance.

He didn't really know how he had gotten there, but that question would have to wait: the important thing just then was to save this poor bleeding man. A few yards down the street, an overturned streetcar was serving as a parapet for another group of workers struggling to resist the fury of the police. A bullet tore through the air and struck the bare earth of the torn-up street, with a surprising oblique trajectory that could hardly have come from the other side of the barricade.

"Up there, on the terrace," the injured man creaked, pointing his finger, as a stream of blood escaped his mouth.

Then Pablo saw him: silhouetted against the sky, on top of a bell tower that had been spared the flames, there was the brick-red hat of a sniper priest, one of those *pacos* who in the last few hours had taken up posts on rooftops to help the military finish off the rebels. With no time to lose, he hoisted the dying man by the armpits and dragged him to the sidewalk as bullets whistled overhead. The first door he tried to open was immovable, as were the second and third, but finally the fourth door opened and they found refuge in a large, dark hallway. Pablo lay the man down on a tightly woven rug next to the windowed door. But it was too late: the dying man placed his hand on his shirt pocket, opened his mouth to say nothing, and exhaled his last breath. If he had been able to carry out the gesture, he would have taken from his pocket a sepia-toned photograph of a little girl with long braids and a mischievous smile, the back of which bore the inscription: "To my dear father on the day of my First Communion. Elena." "Do me a favor, tell her I love her," would have been his last words. But death took him away without time to say goodbye.

"*Requiescat in pace,*" Pablo heard someone whisper behind him as he closed the dead man's eyes. Spinning, he saw something moving in a corner of the hallway, shrouded in darkness.

"Who's there?" he asked.

"Emilio Ferrer, sculptor and syndicalist," the voice introduced itself, coming out of the darkness. It was a man of about thirty years of age, tall

and thin, who moved with a certain affectation and wore a red handkerchief on his head, tied at the four corners, vaguely resembling a cardinal's
hat. "Sorry about your friend."

"He wasn't my friend."

"Well, I'm sorry all the same."

A tense silence filled the hallway, while the gunshots and the howls of
anger and pain continued outside.

"And you? What are you doing here?" Pablo finally asked.

"Nothing, my Mauser seized up and I hid in here to try to fix it."

Pablo looked at the man with distrust.

"And who gave you fellows the rifles?"

"Joan Castells, the janitor of the Centro Radical. He had a whole arsenal, that guy. But it seems like a lost cause now. Did you see the cannons?"

Pablo shook his head.

"And that smell?" said the man, twisting his face in disgust. "I think
the dead guy took a shit on us, don't you smell that?"

Pablo didn't have time to answer: a massive mortar shell exploded in
the street, a few yards away, and the floor shook under his feet. Immediately,
as if they were waiting for a sign, the neighbors started coming out of their
apartments and running down into the cellar. Seeing the dead man in
the hallway, some of them made the sign of the cross, others whispered,
most averted their eyes and continued their way downstairs. Another shell
exploded a bit farther away than the first.

"Should we go?" Pablo asked, pointing at the door.

"Are you crazy? It's over, kid, if I were you I'd think about saving
my skin," said the sculptor. Laying his jammed rifle next to the cadaver,
he added, "You're young, you have a whole life ahead of you and a lot of
things to discover. But never forget that the paths of discovery are more
important than the discovery itself. If you'll accept my advice, that is."

That said, the sculptor with airs of a philosopher made his way toward
the cellar door; but then he thought better of it and ran upstairs instead.

Pablo stood there, not knowing what to do. In the shadows of the hallway, he looked at his hands, where the dried blood had started to flake off. "What am I doing here?" he thought. "What happened to me?" Then he started to remember everything: the scene at the port, the vision of Angela, the confusion, the foul turn, the city in flames, the barricades … At least I'm still alive, he said to himself, looking at the dead man; and he sat down on the floor, his back against the wall, his arms on his knees, and the lucky amulet hanging against his chest. Only when the cannons went silent and the shouting subsided did Pablo dare to open the door a crack, and saw the barricade empty: except for two men strewn on the ground, immobile and covered in blood, the rest had disappeared. A few gunshots still rang out, intermittently now—maybe the sniper priest was still imparting divine justice from the rooftop, shooting at traitors trying to flee or hide in doorways. A voice was heard calling to cease fire, and soon came sounds of boots and rifle butts pounding frenetically against doors: they were probably searching houses to make sure no rebels were hiding inside. The knocks kept getting closer and closer, and a murmur of voices started up in the cellar, as though the neighbors were discussing the possibility of coming up from their refuge. Now or never, thought Pablo. And he made his way upstairs with catlike agility.

When he reached the roof, the sun was beating down, and the sculptor had taken refuge in a small wooden shed.

"Want some?" the man asked as Pablo entered, pointing to a small brown glass bottle labeled Merck. His face bore a strange look of happiness, and his turquoise blue eyes glowed intensely.

"We have to leave, they'll arrive any minute," Pablo replied.

"And how do you plan to get out of here? Fly? There's nothing to be done, boy, so you might as well try this stuff, and really learn to fly."

Pablo looked at the vial attentively. Next to it, there was a cigar box containing a syringe with a bit of blood. It was the first time he ever saw such a thing, but he could deduce that it was an ampoule of morphine, or perhaps cocaine, the new drug that was starting to circulate, and which would lead the government to issue a royal order prohibiting the illicit trafficking of alkaloids in pharmacies, boutiques, bars, and brothels. Strange that a syndicalist can afford such vices, thought Pablo. And he observed him curiously. Despite his proletarian dress, his body appeared to have aristocratic aspirations: beneath the red handkerchief, he had smooth blond hair, a perfect match to his porcelain skin; and his hands, thin and bluish, were more those of a surgeon than of a sculptor.

"Sure you don't want any?" the man insisted, and in the silence that followed his question they heard military boots stomping up the stairs.

"Let's run across the rooftops," Pablo proposed.

"You go ahead and escape if you can. You're young and have your life ahead of you ..."

Pablo shook his head, looked at the man one last time, and left the shack running, not knowing that he would meet those eyes again years later. When the soldiers reached the rooftop, they found only the dope fiend Emilio Ferrer, supposedly a sculptor with a union card, in reality a low-level informant working on the payroll of the Civil Guard.

– 15 –

The night of November 6, 1924, fifty men were struggling across the mountains of Vera del Bidasoa waiting for the dawn. They were fifty young, strong men; in isolation, each of them meant nothing, was nothing, could do nothing; together they constituted the soul of a faction: a faction which, when it drags more and more men along, can turn into an army of salvation for a people; but which, when it does not have such luck, is nothing but a horde of bandits, doomed to die on the gallows if not already killed by a hail of bullets from the defenders of order.

EMILIO PALOMO,
Two Essays on Revolution

ALL ALONG THE PYRENEES MOUNTAIN RANGE, joining the Cantabrian Sea to the Mediterranean, numbered from west to east, there are a total of 602 markers (or *mugas*, as they are known locally) that delimit the border between Spain and France, from the Endarlatsa Bridge to Cape Cerbère. The squadron led by the former civil guardsman Julián Santillán has been assigned to cross the border at marker number 18, traveling along Inzola Creek and ascending Mount Larrún after leaving the neighborhood of Oleta. Anyone who knows the terrain (and the group's guide, Martín Lacouza, knows it intimately) knows that the best route to get from the golf course La Nivelle to marker 18 is the old Camino de Vera, which some call the Camino de Napoleón, convinced that it was the path taken by Bonaparte's army when they crossed the border in 1808 to conquer Spain. But most of the fifteen revolutionaries on their way to Oleta don't know anything about all that, and the men take their first steps on the banks of the Nivelle River without suspecting that they might be retracing the steps of Napoleon's troops a century before. More accurately, they know nothing of this until Lacouza, who is co-leader of the mission with Julián Santillán and proves to be particularly loquacious over the first few kilometers, starts to recount the historical failed incursion to the ex-civil guardsman, also reaching the ears of those walking just behind, but not the ears of the group formed by Pablo, Robinsón, Leandro, and Julianín (we can keep calling him that behind his back, to avoid confusion with the other Julián in the group), who trek at the rear of the squadron trying to convince Kropotkin to keep his barking down.

"If that mongrel doesn't shut the hell up," Santillán threatens from the front of the pack, "we're going to have to get rid of him."

And though the wiener dog has no commitment to the success of the revolution, when he hears the guard's tone a sixth sense tells him to quiet down.

Night has fallen completely when the men arrive at the neighborhood of Oleta, composed of a few scattered houses, although one can make out two main clusters. At the entry of the first there is a pelota court and a tavern with a letterbox proclaiming "Maison Landabururtia." The rebels huddle up next to the pelota wall and decide to make a brief stop at the tavern to escape the cold and rekindle the revolutionary fire before they make their way up the mountain. But not all of them ask for wine or brandy—Robinsón and the vegetarians prefer a fruit juice.

"We don't have any," says the barman in Spanish.

And so they have to be satisfied with sugar water, which is hilarious to Perico Alarco and Manolito Monzón, who are in a rambunctious mood.

"Water for the frogs, ribbit, ribbit!" jeers the toothless one, and Manolito follows the insult by puffing up his cheeks and opening his hands, imitating an amphibian.

But the vegetarians pay no mind; Perico is on the offensive and moves on to a personal attack:

"Hey Robinsón, you sure you're going to be able to cross the mountain with that lame leg?"

"You sure I won't cross your ugly snout with a left hook?" the vegetarian threatens with sudden violence, destroying all remnants of a festive mood.

"Hey, hey, don't be like that," says Perico Alarco, who as a barfly knows to keep his nose clean, so he changes tables to drink instead with Santillán, whom he tries to convince to give him one of the pistols he's carrying, because he and Manolito missed the distribution.

"After we cross the border," the ex-civil guardsman replies dryly, distrustfully.

The barman brings out some food, and the rebels start devouring it as if they had been starving for days (or, if you like, as if it were the last meal of their lives). It seems that the knots in their stomachs have loosened up with the walk and left them with an appetite. The owner recognizes the guide Martín Lacouza and asks him where he is headed at this hour, but someone from the group interjects and imprudently responds:

"To behead the king of Spain!"

When they get back out in the fresh air, clouds have obscured the moon, and it is starting to drizzle. Bad omen, more than one man thinks. The revolutionaries put on their berets and start walking again, following Martín Lacouza, whose usual loquaciousness seems to be dampened by the rain, as he says nothing until they reach a clearing at the foot of the mountain.

"Now the hard part starts," he warns, and he starts ascending, barely giving enough time for some of the men to cut some branches to use as walking sticks.

The Camino de Napoleon follows the ancient Roman road, which leads to Vera along the bank of Inzola Creek, and some say that chariots passed here during the Roman Empire. The ancient road, though it disappears completely in some stretches, emerges here and there along the way, with larger stones at the shoulders and a line of long, narrow pebbles down the middle. But the revolutionaries, slogging along in wet clothes under uncomfortable backpacks, are not interested in an archeology lesson: all they see is a steep, dark, snaking path, full of stones good for nothing but rolling ankles and making Robinsón's limp imperceptible among the whole group's unsteady gait. Indeed, even to say they can see the path is an exaggeration, because the oaks and alders that populate Mount Larrún barely let through any light from the shrouded full moon, and Santillán has ordered them not to turn on their flashlights unless absolutely necessary.

So, trudging through the darkness and ensconced in a silence disturbed only by the burbling of Inzola Creek and the twittering of the occasional sleepless bird, the revolutionary squad ascends the ancient Roman road. The initial enthusiasm has given way to a certain anxiety, and more than one man's liberator spirit has started to wane, although no one wants to admit it. But, as though to clear the dark thoughts from the rebels' minds, an unexpected event interrupts the ascent.

"Shhhh!" Martín Lacouza hushes them, suddenly stopping at a bend in the path.

The rest also halt, as though frozen by a magic spell. Even Kropotkin stills his tail and chokes back a bark. Over the noise of the water, they can just make out the sound of the footsteps of someone coming hastily down the path, in such a hurry that he nearly crashes into them when he comes around the bend. Seeing them, he drops the package he was carrying on his shoulder and runs back the way he came, as though he has seen a ghost. Only then does Kropotkin start barking, despite Robinsón and Pablo's attempts to muzzle him.

"Hey, hey you!" shouts Santillán, running after the fugitive, unholstering his pistol. But the guy seems to know the terrain, because the darkness swallows him before the ex-civil guardsman has covered ten yards.

"Easy, boys," says the baker from Saint-Jean-de-Luz, shining his flashlight on the parcel the man dropped. "Just a smuggler."

Perico Alarco draws near, takes out a knife and scratches the canvas covering the package. Kropotkin writhes free of Robinsón's arms and comes to sniff the parcel, receiving a kick in the ribs as a reward for his petulance. The inside is full of packets of sugar and coffee. But when Perico prepares to put them in his backpack, Santillán steps in with his pistol drawn.

"Don't even think about it," he says, pointing his gun at Alarco, "This could be the means of sustenance for an entire family."

Clenching his gums for want of teeth, Perico leaves the parcel on the ground, and the group sets off again, not knowing that the smuggler is crouching in the undergrowth and thanking God that they thought of his family.

Half an hour later, reaching a point where the stream widens a little, Martín Lacouza nearly trips over marker 18. He lights his flashlight, and the party can see the stone's inscription: "R-18." The baker shines his light across to the other side of Inzola Creek and finds marker 19 covered in moss. It is not yet ten o'clock and they have reached the border. Everything seems calm.

"From now on we have to be more careful," warns Santillán. "If you haven't loaded your pistol yet, load it now. We'll rest here for ten minutes and then we'll keep going till we reach the towers at Napoleon's Pass, where we'll meet up with the other groups."

"Excuse me, Julián, but the Inzola Inn is just up ahead," Martín Lacouza interjects, "Maybe we can warm up there for a few minutes and find out what's going on in Spain, before we continue on to the towers."

But the ex-civil guard snorts and answers abruptly:

"This isn't a honeymoon, Lacouza. It's a revolution. If your dick is cold you should go home. I mean it, go home now, 'cuz once we've crossed the border, I'll put a bullet in any deserters. Get me? Anybody who wants to cut out, do it now!" Santillán barks, directing his words to Perico and Manolito.

But both men stay steadfast. On the other hand, the two vegetarians Carlos and Baudilio, after a moment of hesitation, step away from the group, mumbling "Sorry," and "Good luck, comrades," and retrace their steps down the mountain with their tails between their legs. Robinsón looks at Anxo, "El Maestro," and though the darkness obscures his face, he can sense his smile.

"Nobody else?" asks Santillán, annoyed. "Alright then, we'll rest here for ten minutes. Martín," he says to the guide, "go to the inn and find out what's going on."

The rest take off their backpacks and sit down on the side of the road, surprised at the two vegetarians' desertion, which has only increased the general feeling of confusion and anxiety among the revolutionaries. It has stopped raining, though the leaves that remain on the trees are still letting treasonous drops fall. Some of the men load their pistols, others take the opportunity to smoke a cigarette. Leandro jumps over to a little islet in the middle of the creek, where a majestic alder tree is growing, halfway between the two markers. He takes out his knife and starts scratching into the tree's bark. Pablo feels tempted to shine his flashlight on the tree to see what Leandro is writing, but he opts instead to take out his Astra 9mm and give Julianín a quick lesson on the function of a semiautomatic pistol (although he would have preferred not to have to do it). If he had chosen to shine the light, he would have seen that Leandro has inscribed the tree with an L and an A, both separated and united by a heart.

"Look, this is the butt," Pablo says to his former assistant, who takes out the Star pistol that luck has granted him and follows the instructions. "You insert the clip in here, give it a good smack so you hear the click. Like this, see? Once the pistol's loaded, release the safety and hold the grip firmly with your right hand. If you want more stability, hold your wrist with your left hand. To aim, you have to line up this front sight with this notch at the back here, but don't spend too much time aiming or they'll blow your brains out before you can get a shot off," Pablo warns Julianín, who seems apprehensive or intimidated. "When you pull the trigger, it activates the hammer and it strikes the bullet in the chamber, and it shoots out. Release the trigger and aim again. If you're still alive, that is. Any questions?"

Julianín shakes his head, somewhat bewildered by the ballistics tutorial Pablo has just delivered with the tone of a trigonometry lesson. There is a tense silence, which Robinsón breaks by changing the subject:

"What does the R mean?" he asks.

"What R?" replies Pablo, confused, thinking Robinsón is referring to the pistol.

"The one inscribed on the marker, before the number 18."

"Oh, yes. R-18 ... I don't know, actually."

"It means 'raya,'" says one of the revolutionaries at his side, a native of Lanuza, in the Pyrenees of Aragon. "At least that's what I heard a civil guard say once in my village—"

"It can't be," says Pablo. "We share the markers with the frogs, so it has to be a word that starts with an R in both Spanish and French."

"So what does it mean?" Robinsón insists.

"Reference," interjects El Maestro, making an effort to join the conversation and forget the departure of his two friends. "It means reference."

But there is no time for more digressions, useful as they might be for calming the nerves and crowding out bad thoughts, as the guide has just come back:

"The inn is closed and there was no light in the windows."

"Fine then, let's go on ahead," says Santillán, in a tone that does not invite reply. He decides to bring up the rear of the troop, just in case anyone else gets cold feet.

The group moves on, and once they are on Spanish soil, one of them kneels and kisses the ground, another clutches a fistful of earth. The contact with the homeland seems to lift the spirits of the party, which shortly reaches the clearing around the Inzola Inn. From here, the road to Vera splits: the left fork goes to Peña del Águila and the straight path goes up to Usategieta (also known as Napoleon's Pass in memory of the failed incursion), where they have arranged to meet with the other revolutionaries. While they make their way to the pass, Martín Lacouza tries to tell El Maestro about another battle he knows like the back of his hand, but Santillán barks from the back of the platoon demanding silence. So El Maestro never learns about the story that took place here almost a century ago, in the time of the despot Fernando VII, when General Mina reached Napoleon's Pass at the head of hundreds of Spanish exiles with the aim of overthrowing the monarch and installing a liberal government. Had he heard the story, El Maestro would have thought that Hegel was right when he said that history always repeats itself and that great events always happen twice. Although perhaps it is better that Martín Lacouza does not get the chance to recount the fate of General Mina, because it would be a shame to dampen the revolutionary spirit with past failures. Because Mina did fail, although he managed to save his own skin: when the king's forces repelled the attack, the general took refuge in a mountain cave before finally reaching the border. Also, what Hegel did not say but Marx added is that history repeats itself, first as tragedy and then as farce.

When the platoon reaches Napoleon's Pass, the other groups have not yet arrived. Although Pablo's group was the last to depart, it is the one that has taken the shortest route: the Usategieta ridge is not far from marker 18. The men sit down to wait, leaning against the *palomeras*, wooden towers designed for the peculiar Basque art of pigeon hunting by net, which offer a modicum of shelter from the frozen wind blowing up here. Shortly, the first group from Saint-Jean-de-Luz arrives, led by Luís Naveira. It has been only a few hours since they parted ways, but it seems like years, to judge by the effusiveness with which some of them celebrate the reunion. The sky has started to clear up, and the full moon faintly lights up the men's tired faces as they slap each other's backs to chase away the cold or the fear. Far below, the village of Vera is hidden among the mountains, which hide the few lights still lit in the village. If Leandro could see them with opera glasses, he would make out one light that was redder and brighter than the others: that of the foundry, where the night shift must be on by now.

"Well, I'm going home," says the smuggler from Ciboure who has served as guide to Naveira's group.

"Thank you," says the Galician, giving him his fee.

"We had two deserters," Robinsón informs Naveira when the man disappears.

"We had three," the Galician laconically replies.

And they will not be the only ones; as the other groups arrive they will report more desertions. Always the same story: someone stopped to piss or to drink from a spring, or to remove a stone from his shoe, and the moment the others were a few paces away he took off running the way they had come. It appears that the rumor has gotten around that no one is waiting for them in Spain. The night's darkness, fatigue, and fear did the rest. The last group to arrive is the one commanded by El Maño, but the word "group" is exaggerated, because other than Abundio Riaño, only the nephew of the priest from Lesaca who has acted as guide and two other brave men have managed to reach Napoleon's Pass. Not all of the groups had a Santillán to keep the faint of heart in line.

"Don't get discouraged," says the former civil guardsman around midnight, hoisting one of his pistols overhead as he starts his way down toward Vera, "You'll see, this day will go down in history. ¡Viva la revolución! Down with the dictatorship! Long live free Spain, goddammit!"

"¡Viva!" shouts someone, without much conviction.

"From here on out," Santillán repeats his threat in front of everyone, "I'm going to shoot anyone who turns back."

Among the seventy revolutionaries who set out from the golf course, only around fifty start the descent to the village of Vera. Well, as the poet said, it's better to be few and brave than many and meek. Anyone who has come this far must be a true revolutionary.

XIV
(1909–1912)

QUESTION: WHAT IS THE SAFEST WAY to avoid being very miserable in the future?

Answer: Don't expect to be very happy in the first place.

This was the thought that crossed Pablo's mind as he leaped from one rooftop to another, fleeing the soldiers—a thought that might seem out of place in these circumstances; nevertheless, given the vagaries of the human spirit, where there is no straight line, it turned out to be a blessing: curiously, this thought snapped him back to his senses and saved his life. If he had not had it, he probably would have been caught by his persecutors or tossed himself into the abyss from one of those rooftops. Because that thought led him to another, and the second thought led on to a third. In the end, he said to himself, happiness is to human beings as home is to the drunkard: he doesn't know how to find it, but he knows it exists. Pablo knew what happiness was, but he had lost it: therefore, it was a matter of having patience, not losing his nerve or his mind, hoping without despairing. Starting now I have to focus on surviving—he promised himself—that's the best way to honor Angela. And that was how he managed to get out of this adventure he had gotten himself into without really knowing how or why: leaping from rooftop to rooftop, he reached the other side of the block, forced open a door, descended the stairs, and emerged onto a narrow, empty street. He fled the conflict zone as a few scattered gunshots continued to ring out behind him.

The entry of the troops into the city brought an end to the revolutionary hopes of the thousands of dreamers who thought they were changing the world by burning churches and raising barricades. They held out for just two more days, but that was merely the death spasm. On Friday, two more infantry companies arrived with three hundred civil guards as backup, which practically put an end to the street skirmishes. The people started timidly coming out of their houses, some public services were restored, and, symbolically, a trolley resumed its usual itinerary in the working-class neighborhoods. The captain general, emboldened, gave the order to resume embarkations to Melilla, and that same day an infantry regiment marched down Las Ramblas on the way to the port, under the docile gaze of some of the locals, who appeared to have forgotten the origin of the terrible disturbances that had brought the city to its knees.

"We've seen how you strut with your guns, but you let them drag you to the slaughterhouse!" was the only anti-military shout that was heard among the crowd. The heckler was arrested, and no one came to his defense.

On Saturday the shops reopened, the barricades were taken down, the paving stones put back into place, and communications reestablished. There were even a few dozen German tourists, who had no trouble as they visited the main attractions of the Catalan capital, though they were accompanied by an escort from the urban guard and by the soundtrack of a few gunshots still whistling from the rooftops. The last bloody episode took place in the ruins of a Lay Dominican convent, on whose fire-damaged walls the rebels had pasted posters with these strange words: "We have great respect for religion and great respect for atheism. What we hate is agnosticism, those who do not choose. Long live the revolution and the schoolteachers of Catalonia!" A morbid multitude gathered at midmorning inside the building, and the Civil Guard gave the order to disperse; the people paid no mind, and the guard lost their patience, a shot rang out, panic set in, the crowd left the building in a whirlwind, and the stampede devolved into a gunfight, leaving six dead and many injured—the bloody epilogue to a tragic week. The next day not one shot was heard in Barcelona, and the florists of Las Ramblas reopened their flower shops, definitive proof that order had been restored.

Since the municipal shelter on Calle del Cid had closed its doors when the troubles broke out, Pablo spent the last few days of the week in the house of Abelardo Belmonte. Ferdinando's nephew had suffered a leg injury at the start of the troubles, and so he had no choice but to stay home caring for his three rebellious children, while his wife went out into the street and joined the group of "red women," who attacked police stations and convents under the leadership of Juana Ardiaca, a young member of the Radical Party whose father had been condemned in the Trial of Montjuic. On Sunday morning Robinsón also appeared, after having participated in the last throes of the rebellion.

"It's over," was the first thing he said upon entering the house on Urquinaona Square, accompanied by Darwin, his steadfast spaniel. "The way it was is over."

And he was not mistaken: in the morning, the reprisals started. On Monday, a military tribunal condemned the first rebel it came across to life in prison, as an example and a warning. Then, almost two thousand individuals were prosecuted, one thousand jailed, fifty sentenced to life in prison and seventeen to capital punishment, although only five were finally executed; of them, the first four were mere participants in the rebellion who drew the short straw: the union organizer José Miguel Baró, accused of having rallied the mobs; the delinquent Antonio Malet, alleged to have organized an enormous bonfire of religious objects; the security guard Eugenio del Hoyo, condemned for firing on an army patrol; and the idiot who danced with the nun's skeleton, Ramón Clemente, prosecuted for building a barricade. In a certain sense, a complete sampling of the crimes committed over the course of the week. But they still had yet to find the mastermind of the revolution. And Maura's government took advantage of the situation to get rid of its own pest, Francisco Ferrer Guàrdia, founder of the Modern School, whom many already considered guilty since the attempted regicide by Mateo Morral. The educator was shot dead in the castle of Montjuic on the thirteenth of October in that year, 1909. By that time, Pablo was dressing in the uniform of a recruit.

After spending a few days holing up with Robinsón at Abelardo's house, talking about the human and the divine and waiting for the situation to calm down, Pablo wound up convincing himself that it was not worth the hassle to desert: it would have forced him to live a life of secrecy or to live in exile in a foreign country, making the search for Angela even harder. The way things were, absentees and deserters had a rough time of it: most of them ended up getting caught and sent to Morocco to fight on the front line, as punishment for cowardice and treason. It would be better to stay in Spain, accept whatever peninsular destiny fate had in store for him, and not lose hope, never lose hope, because sometimes the drunkard finds home by falling asleep on the first porch he comes to. Also, Pablo's sympathies for anarchistic ideas had been gathering strength again, perhaps as a result of (or a palliative for) his heartsickness. And, contrary to what one might think, anarchists at that time were not in favor of military desertion, but favored instead a very different tactic: anti-military proselytism in the barracks as a tool to undermine the army from within. The theory could not be more obvious: since the soldiers are workers obligated to serve the country according to an unjust system of recruitment, at times of crisis they will stand beside the people to defend the revolution, provided they are sufficiently educated. A sample of this could be seen during the events of Tragic Week: the army had barely gotten into action by the fourth day of the rebellion, while the Civil Guard had drawn their pistols right away. In fact, the rebels applauded and cheered the soldiers, until the latter were finally given no choice but to quash the rebellion: after all, the people had come out in the street precisely for them, to prevent them from being sent off to a war invented by the ruling classes.

So, on the night of August 3, 1909, as the legally prescribed time ran out, Pablo Martín Sánchez, draft number 66 in the district of Salamanca,

left the City of Bombs to return to the City of Death, to fulfill his patriotic duty. Robinsón, excused from military service for his limp, accompanied him to the station. He promised to meet back up with Pablo a
few months later in Ciudad Condal, in case Angela ended up giving a
sign of life, although he was convinced that it would be in vain: he was
growing ever more skeptical that the young woman who had asked after
him at the Vegetarian League was in fact their childhood friend. Basically,
his idea was to stay in Barcelona to earn a little money and then travel
to France or Germany, where naturism and vegetarianism enjoyed more
respect than they did in Spain. But he had not yet mentioned any of this
to his soul brother.

"Listen, Pablo," he said when they were about to arrive at the Station
of France.

"What?"

"Can I be honest with you?"

"Of course."

"Blood brothers shouldn't beat around the bush. We have to call a
spade a spade, right?"

"Spill it, Robin. At this rate they'll be discharging me before you've
managed to say anything."

"Fine. Do you really believe that a man should be tied for life to the
first woman he loves, and have eyes for no one but her?"

Pablo stopped walking abruptly, but said nothing.

"I don't know, it seems to me like you ought to enjoy life a little more
and stop dragging your ass like a penitent. Don't think so much about the
sad stuff, focus on the pleasures within our reach. Have you ever heard of
free love?"

"Drop it, Robin," Pablo interrupted, beginning to walk again.
"Thanks for the effort, but you're not going to get Angela out of my
head. You do what you like. I'm going to make the search for her the
meaning of my life."

"Very well, very well, sir. But what will happen if someday you find out she's married someone else?"

Pablo stopped again, looked at his friend, and said only six words.

"Then the search will be over."

PABLO ENTERED THE RECRUITING OFFICE ON Wednesday morning and turned himself over to military jurisdiction, but the final deployment of the regiment did not take place until the end of September, a few weeks earlier than the scheduled date because of the flaring war in Morocco. In a twist of fate less random than it appeared, his voyage followed the path of a boomerang: the position he was randomly assigned was the old barracks of Atarazanas, in a Barcelona depleted of soldiers after the recent deployments. All he had to do was take a step forward during the recruit screening process to be assigned to Ciudad Condal, before the speechless stare of the other recruits, who thought he must be crazy because no one wanted to go to the City of Bombs after the recent events. What they didn't know is that this young man had a powerful six-letter motive for stepping forward: Angela. It was no accident that Barcelona was the last place she had been seen, because she preferred it over Cádiz, Santiago, Burgos, or Zaragoza, where she would most likely have been consumed by nostalgia or desperation. So it was that Pablo ended up spending three long years in the barracks of Atarazanas, believing that sooner or later he would end up finding Angela. While hope is the last thing to be lost, it is often the only thing one has.

The first few weeks were the most difficult, because the mood was still very tense due to the war in Morocco. The air was full of the fear of being sent to Africa, and although it was unlikely that the new recruits would be deployed immediately, the veterans punished them for their fear and anxiety by inventing the most humiliating practical jokes, with the tacit permission of the higher officers. On the first day, as a welcome gift, the "newbies" were led to the "royal latrine," the filthiest of all, where the soldiers had been accumulating excrement for days in anticipation of the new crop's arrival. The stench was so unbearable that some of the instigators covered their noses with scarves soaked in cologne as they laughed and shoved the newbies into the latrine; the most delicate of them vomited as soon as they were inside, and those who withstood the first impact had their heads shoved into the foul pit toilet, to shouts of:

"Look in there and tell us if you can find any damned Moors!"

Ten times Pablo was subjected to this humiliating punishment, but even if he had wanted to he could not have vomited. This earned him the respect of the veterans, who had never seen anyone with such endurance. Of course, he never let on the secret to his success, that for him there was no difference between the smell of a fart and a rose, a rotten egg or freshly mown grass, a putrid latrine or the sparkling toilet of the queen of England.

To make matters worse, the barracks of Atarazanas had been chosen as the place to incarcerate and judge many of those arrested for the events of Tragic Week, which did not exactly help to calm people's nerves. Within its walls the military tribunal was convened, and various summary war trials were held, including that of José Miguel Baró, the first rebel executed at the castle of Montjuic. However, when Pablo arrived in the barracks, the case that was on everyone's lips was that of Ferrer Guàrdia, who in a cruel irony was condemned to death for being the leader of a leaderless revolt. Perhaps fearing that some altercation might take place during his execution, the authorities decided to increase the number of military personnel guarding the fortress, and on the morning of October 13 they stationed a number of soldiers there, including several newbies from the nearby barracks of Atarazanas, which many interpreted as the latest in the series of practical jokes. "So they'll learn," said Sergeant Hansen. And among those in for a lesson was Pablo Martín Sánchez.

They had to wake up at four in the morning to walk to the military fortress. It was a chilly night, and at El Paralelo they crossed paths with various nighthawks who came staggering out of brothels and other dens of iniquity. At Calle Carrera, Pablo lifted his head and had a strange feeling, like a premonition of the future: through the curtains of an illuminated balcony, he saw the graceful silhouette of a female body. From there, laden with heavy rifles and unwieldy belts of cartridges, they ascended the road that winds its way to the top of the mountain, where they joined other companies assigned to guard the fortress. The firing squad was chosen at random from among the soldiers of the Infantry of the Constitutional Regiment, and they were given the customary ammunition mixed with blank cartridges. The rest of the group was spread out over the mountain, in the areas surrounding the fortress and in the gorge of Santa Amalia, the chosen location for executions. This was where Pablo was stationed. Shortly before nine o'clock, he saw the morbid procession emerge through one of the fortress's posterns, led by Ferrer, looking haggard but dignified. He was wearing a gray flannel suit and a tie, with his head uncovered and an arrogant goatee pointing forward. Curiously, the laces had disappeared from his shoes: they had removed them lest he be tempted to suicide. When they passed near, Pablo heard what the founder of the Modern School was saying to the leader of the firing squad:

"I can see, lieutenant, that you are very young. How long have you been an officer?"

"One year."

"Only? Oh, what a sad way to start a military career!"

"Sad? Why?" the lieutenant shot back indignantly.

"Because when you give the order to fire, you'll be taking an innocent life."

The procession continued on slowly toward the chosen spot for the execution, immersed in tragic silence. As they came to a halt in front of the governor of the fortress, the latter shouted a question, barely audible to Pablo:

"Do you have any last wishes?"

Ferrer hesitated an instant, and then said in a firm voice:

"My only request is that you don't make me kneel or turn my back to the firing squad. And no blindfold."

The officers exchanged opinions under their breath and finally agreed to concede to half of his request: he would die on his feet, and facing forward if he wanted, but with his eyes covered and his hands tied behind his back. Pablo saw them bring Ferrer to the end of the ravine, next to the wall, saw Ferrer resign himself to being blindfolded and handcuffed, as the firing squad lined up in front of him and the soldiers made the sign of the cross. Finally, after the order to "Aim," he could clearly hear the last words shouted by the anarchist educator:

"Boys, you're not the guilty ones. Aim well and shoot without fear! I am innocent! Long live the Modern School!"

Pablo winced at the roar of gunshots. When he dared to open his eyes, the body of Francisco Ferrer Guàrdia was lying on the ground, the skull perforated with bullet holes, ready to be buried in a mass grave for being an atheist and an impenitent. It was one minute past nine in the morning.

The people of Barcelona responded to the execution immediately but timidly, because they were still fresh from the calamity of Tragic Week. The most notable events were street disturbances and a handful of bombs, to one on Calle del Cid, a few yards from the municipal inn that had given Pablo shelter when he had first arrived in Barcelona. The more progressive political class let its displeasure be known, and at a meeting in Valencia the Republican representative Rodrigo Soriano said the following prophetic words:

"When they shot Ferrer, the government signed their own death sentence."

And he was not mistaken: on October 23, the liberals took power again, with Segismundo Moret at the head. A few days beforehand, Pablo had made a promise, inspired by the deep impression that the legal assassination of Ferrer had produced in him: as soon as he found the love of his life, he would dedicate all the strength he had left to fighting against the government that sent its most brilliant men to the firing squad. I'll believe it when I see it, Prime Minister Maura would have said if he had been privy to Pablo's intentions: while Maura only had ten days left in office, Pablo was in for three years of service, three long years with no news of Angela.

16

The dense shadow of the night was thinning out into the first lights of the dawn, the cold, hostile dawn that stabbed them with frosty winds, these men spurred on by political ideals and chance. They began to be able to make out the silhouettes of the humble homes of Vera de Bidasoa. The revolutionaries advanced in silence, as though they sensed something unclear but threatening. Bonifacio Manzanedo, in front, immediately behind him Pablo Martín Sánchez and Julián Santillán, two of the most dedicated of this group of ad hoc warriors.

JOSÉ ROMERO CUESTA,
La verdad de lo que pasó en Vera

NEXT TO THE MAIN ROAD THAT descends from Napoleon's Pass to Vera, back in the thick woods, there is a weed-choked path unworthy to be called a road, impassible to mules, donkeys, or horses. But Piperra, the guide from Zugarramurdi who helped Gil Galar's group cross the border, insists on taking this path, and no one has the energy to argue at this point, unaware that the only reason the guide wants to avoid the main road is that it passes next to the farmstead of Eltzaurdia, where some of his relatives live. However, more than one of them comes quickly to regret not having put up a fight, because the footpath proves to be almost impossible: the rain has turned it into a mud bog, slippery and dangerous in the dark, and not even their walking sticks prevent them from falling down over and over as they slide in the mud like filthy pigs. Those who are carrying electric flashlights have no choice but to light them. On both sides of the path, fallen oaks appear to laugh at the partisans' pitfalls, as they mutter strings of blasphemies and curses before the silent audience of ash, holly, and beech, wild hazelnuts and ferns. Only Robinsón, who miraculously still has his bowler hat unsullied on his head, feels in his element, in a sort of spiritual osmosis with nature, and he even takes time to harvest a few herbs growing at the edge of the path, plants called horsetail that are supposed to be good for the circulation and for healing poultices.

When the platoon gets past the heart of the woods the trail finally becomes more manageable. A dog barks nearby, but Kropotkin, having learned his lesson, does not respond to the provocation. The strange dog is guarding a stable full of animals, which the revolutionaries skirt in silence to continue their descent toward Vera. Starting here, the road improves noticeably, corresponding to the final length of the old Roman road. The rain has given way to clouds, indistinct from the smoke rising from the sleepy chimneys of the first houses, signs that they are approaching the village. It is not yet one in the morning when the road opens onto the Carretera de Francia and the first houses of Vera can be seen in the darkness, triggering a flood of adrenaline among the revolutionaries, who stop their progress, not knowing exactly what to do next, disconcerted by the silence and calm reigning in the village. Did they expect to find the people in arms, the streets filled with barricades?

"Now what do we do?" someone asks.

"There's no light in the Errotacho mill," says Piperra, who knows the village well.

"Nor at the Itzea house," adds Martín Lacouza, not to be outdone.

Indeed, the mill is the first building on the left, followed closely by the farmhouse of Itzea, the residence the Baroja family has kept in Vera since 1912. But Don Pío, contrary to what some will later claim in a spirit of malice or betrayal, is not at home at this moment, and cannot see the group of forty-some-odd men (and one wiener dog) about to pass beneath the window of his study.

"What we do is go into the village and find out what's going on," suggests Gil Galar, always ready for action. "From here everything seems calm, but who knows."

"That's true," avows Luís Naveira. "We'll walk all together, in formation, and cross the village with weapons ready. If the revolution hasn't broken out here yet, we'll have to be the ones to make the first move. If we find anyone in the street, we'll invite him to join the uprising, and then we'll head to the foundry to inform the comrades. Then we'll attack the barracks of the Civil Guard and contact the revolutionaries from Irún and San Sebastián. Does anyone know how to get to the foundry?"

"Yes," responds Piperra, "it's just on the other end of the village, on the Carretera de Lesaga. Follow me."

And the revolutionaries take out their pistols, stepping straight into the wolf's mouth.

The picturesque hamlet of Vera, as the newspapers are wont to describe it when they bother to mention it at all, consists of two main neighborhoods: Altzate, which the revolutionaries have just entered, and the neighborhood of Vera proper, home of Saint Stephen's parish, City Hall, and the Plaza de los Fueros. There are two possible ways to get from one neighborhood to another: either by following the Carretera de Eztegara, which runs parallel to the Zia River, now swollen with the autumn rains, or by taking Calle Leguía, which goes directly to City Hall, as Piperra is well aware.

"If we take Leguía, we'll pass in front of the barracks of the carabiniers and the Civil Guard."

"Then let's take the main road," suggests Santillán, knowing that a barracks is not such an easy thing to take by force. "If we have to face the Civil Guard, it will be better to do it with the foundry workers at our side."

But in order to reach this point of bifurcation, the group has had to make their way along the Calle del Altzate, where a dog barked in one of the houses, perhaps alerted by the smell of Kropotkin or by the uncertain footsteps of the insurgent battalion. This is not a negligible fact, as it is the barking of dogs that will light the fuse that will ultimately inflame newspapers all over Spain. The dog's owner is the village constable, Don Enrique Berasáin, known as "the Dandy" for his feeble demeanor or for his habit of overgrooming. He has just gone to bed after finishing his nightly round, and is in the process of affixing his snood—which keeps his meticulously maintained mustache in place overnight—when he hears the urgent barking of his old mastiff, who this time is not barking at nothing: when he gets up from the bed and looks out the window, Don Enrique Berasáin still has time to see a large group of ragged-looking men wearing backpacks disappear down the street toward the neighborhood of Vera. "Too many to be smugglers," the constable thinks, unsure whether to call the mayor or the Civil Guard. But what else could those men be up to at this ungodly hour?

As Berasáin gets dressed, the revolutionaries continue forward, advancing in a tight group, except for Pablo and Robinsón, who have taken out the subversive flyers and are placing them in doorways. When they reach the intersection, they unanimously agree to follow the suggestion of the former civil guardsman Santillán, so they set off on the Carretera de Eztegara toward the foundry. Thus, the Dandy does not spot them as he makes his way out his front door, cursing his bad luck, and fearfully walks up Calle Leguía toward the barracks, having taken the precaution of bringing his late grandfather's spear along, just in case. He had thought when they offered him the job of constable that his most difficult task would be making sure that people didn't toss papers on the ground and that the children were all at home by ten o'clock at night. On the other side of the river, the band of revolutionaries is advancing through the shadows with halting steps, finding not a soul on the streets save a black cat arching its back from the abandoned driver's seat of the streetcar that runs between Altzate and Vera. Just after that, the alley enters a tunnel of leafy trees, and the sound of the water makes the unexpected silence surrounding the group seem even denser by contrast. The revolution has clearly not broken out in this village, where the people seem to be sleeping like angels.

"Why the devil aren't the men of this damned village out in the street?" Gil Galar asks, speaking loudly. When someone tells him to lower his voice, he gets angry: "The sooner they know that we've arrived, the better, am I right?"

But the group continues advancing, silently and steadily like an army of ghosts.

The Carretera de Eztegara enters the neighborhood of Vera and ends shortly thereafter, opening onto the main avenue, which splits to the right and left depending on whether you want to go to Irún or to Pamplona via Lesaca. On the instructions of the expedition's guides, the posse turns to the left and soon they can make out the lights of the foundry, whose machines apparently never get tired, working day and night. As the revolutionaries approach, the sound of the motors becomes more audible, and the light of the ovens glows through the large windows, illuminating the path. The smokestacks exhale smoke peppered with sparks that crackle as they come into contact with the cold, wet night. A stone wall separates the pavilions from the street, and the revolutionaries hug close to this wall until they reach the entrance, firmly locked at this hour. On the façade of the main building, engraved in stone, the name of the factory appears in large letters: "Fundiciones de Vera."

"Hey! Hello! Does anyone hear us?" shouts Julián Santillán with all his might.

"Comrades! Is anyone there?" Bonifacio Manzanedo shouts in turn.

But the noise of the machinery prevents anyone inside from hearing them.

"We'll have to wait for a shift change," someone proposes.

"Or for the foundry's security guard to go on his rounds," suggests a man who knows the drill, because he worked as a watchman at Renault in Boulogne-Billancourt.

"And why don't we jump the gate and force our way in?" says Gil Galar.

"Maybe if we walk around the factory we can enter through the back," offers another.

But no one takes the initiative. Just in case, Pablo throws a bundle of pamphlets over the wall and slides a few more under the main door.

"Che, what if we stop and rest a while, while we decide what to do?" proposes Leandro, ever the pragmatist, saying out loud what many are thinking.

Of course, we should not forget that these men have spent hours trekking through the mountain forest, while most of them have spent many months only walking on the paved streets of Paris or other cities in France. Santillán and Naveira again try to get the attention of the laborers working inside the factory, but when they fail, there is nothing left to do but accept the Argentinian's idea and follow the group walking away from the factory, again hugging the wall in the direction of the Bidasoa River, where they can rest and have a bit to eat or drink while a decision is made. But before they reach the river, on the other side of the street, there is a quarry that promises better shelter than the wet banks of the Bidasoa, so that is where the troop heads, already removing their backpacks.

And what has Don Enrique Berasáin, the well-groomed constable, been up to all this time? He exited his house as the church's bell struck one, and, cursing his luck, followed Calle Leguía until he reached the barracks house of the Civil Guard. The door was locked and he had to bang the knocker insistently. Finally, a female voice came from inside:

"Who's there?"

"The constable, Don Enrique Berasáin," the Dandy replied, bundling himself in his overcoat.

The woman opened the peephole.

"What's going on?"

"I need to talk to the guardsmen on duty."

"Come in," the woman said begrudgingly, closing the little window and opening the door. "They must be about to arrive from the patrol office to change shifts."

Indeed, not five minutes passed before the arrival of the pair formed by the corporal Julio de la Fuente, a native of Tiebas, Navarra, and the guardsman Aureliano Ortiz, born in Espinosa de los Monteros, Burgos, both unmarried, both twenty-six years old. The corporal's thick, nervous mustache, with points like battering rams, is the first to enter, followed by the corpulent Aureliano, panting like a bulldog before its prey.

"What's going on?" asks the corporal when he sees the constable, losing no time with niceties.

"A troop of forty or fifty men just passed through the village via the Calle de Altzate, sir," says the Dandy, solicitously. "Perhaps they are smugglers."

"Smugglers?" barks de la Fuente, charging at the constable with his Kaiser mustache. "Have you ever seen smugglers travel in a herd?"

"No, sir," Don Enrique practically apologizes, "that's exactly what I thought, but seeing them pass right under my window, at this hour, and what with the looks of them—"

"What do you mean, 'the looks of them'?" the corporal cuts him off.

"I don't know, there wasn't much light, but they had a bad look about them, so I came to inform you immediately."

"You didn't stop to inform the carabiniers on the way?"

"No, sir, the truth is that no, I thought it best to come straight here—"

"Fine. Come with us," the man orders, not taking off his puttees, and with a tone that suggests that he is thinking that the constable might have had the decency to arrive ten minutes later, after the shift change. "Which way did they go?"

"I don't know, it seemed like they were coming from the direction of Itzea," the constable replies uncertainly.

"I didn't ask you where they came from, I asked where they were going," the corporal says gruffly, slinging his rifle over his shoulder and going back out into the street.

Don Enrique takes a few seconds to reply.

"I would say that they must have taken the Carretera de Eztegara—"

"Then they must have gone toward Lesaca or toward Irún," the guardsman Ortiz speaks up for the first time, satisfied to have made this utterly obvious deduction.

"What time did you see them pass by?" asks de la Fuente.

"Couldn't have been more than fifteen minutes ago—"

"Well, then they've probably already left the village. Let's go."

The three men make their way in the darkness, guided by Ortiz's flashlight, and go up Calle Leguía toward the church. They stop when they reach the Plaza del Fuero, where the street splits toward Irún or Pamplona.

"And now what?" asks Ortiz, but Corporal de la Fuente only raises his mustache as if trying to sniff out his prey. Ortiz continues, "Should we split up?"

"Not a chance!" barks the corporal. "Have you forgotten regulations, Ortiz?"

The hulk from Burgos shrinks before his superior's reprimand.

"We'll head toward Lesaca," orders the corporal, "because if they took the road to Irún, they'll be detained in Endarlatsa."

But Julio de la Fuente would have been better off if the herd, as he called it, had headed toward Irún. Because sometimes the distance between life and death depends on a decision as trivial as choosing whether to go right or left at a crossroads, and the reality is that the three men took the same route that had been taken moments beforehand by a group of revolutionaries who had come to Spain bearing the hatchet of war. In the distance they can already see the lights of the foundry, the sparks that erupt from the smokestacks like fireworks, and the glow of the ovens in the large windows, and soon they hear the sound of the machines, growing louder and louder as the men approach. When they reach the main entrance, not noticing that the ends of the seditious post-ers left by the rebels are still poking out from beneath the door, Corporal de la Fuente says to the constable:

"Go home, Don Enrique, we're leaving the village and this is out of your jurisdiction. We'll take a look around and ask the carabiniers from the post in Lesaca if they've seen anything. Thank you for your cooperation."

"I wish I could have done more," replies the Dandy, as he turns on his heels and gives thanks to God.

De la Fuente and Ortiz continue on and have barely taken a few steps when they think they hear voices coming from the quarry of Argaitza. Then, as if a spell has been cast, they switch roles. The corporal halts, filled with doubt, and it is the stocky subaltern who takes the initiative, advancing without hesitation. De la Fuente has no choice but to follow his colleague, until, suddenly, twenty or thirty yards off, a light turns on and shines on them. The first to react is Aureliano Ortiz, who lifts his Mauser rifle and shouts in a voice worthy of Isidoro Fagoaga, the famous tenor born in Vera:

"Halt in the name of the Civil Guard!"

And the echo bounces off the walls of the quarry, surrounding the revolutionaries.

XV
(1912–1913)

IF THE BARRACKS IS THE SCHOOL of life, Pablo would have preferred to go uneducated. Because as for learning, what most people call learning, there was much he did not learn in those three years that he spent serving the country. All he learned was that when you enter the barracks, you leave your balls outside (Sergeant Hansen's favorite saying). On the other hand, he became an expert in getting used to things: sleeping on straw mats and having his head shaved; the chalky taste of mess and the farcical idea that a man could get by on potatoes, chickpeas, lima beans, rice, bacon, and butter; eating from tin plates and drinking from tin cups; washing pots without soap or a scrubber, using only hands, water, and sand; wearing the clothing of a new recruit, as stiff as mummy wrappings, with his cape, his army hat, and his puttees; the metallic voice of the trumpet playing reveille, retreat, silence, mess, squadron, section, company, battalion, or troop; the hysterical shouts of "Formation!" and "Present arms!"; punishment and the fear of punishment, hitting before being hit, robbing before being robbed; fixing shoes and cartridge belts, pointlessly polishing his rifle, his leathers, and his combat boots; eternal patrols, imaginary patrols, rounds, counter-rounds, and watches; guarding the munitions depot without resting on his laurels; treating his feet with salt and vinegar after military marches; the monotonous rhythm of one-two-three-four, one-two-three-four; loading and unloading a Mauser, the clip, the hammer, the trigger, the chamber; military music in general and the "Marcha Real" in particular; learning to sing "Girl, don't fall in love with a soldier, / a sergeant or an officer, tra-la-la, / a sergeant or an officer, tra-la-la, / Because when they march off to the front, / You'll be left all alone, tra-la-la, /You'll be left all

alone, tra-la-la"; taking advantage of Sundays and leave days to visit anarchist hangouts, or to catch up with his old love, the movies, or to go to
the Fountain of Canaletas to wait hopelessly for a miracle, or to write to
his mother and Father Jerónimo with the vain hope of receiving news of
Angela, or to walk along the beach with Robinsón, before the latter ran
off to live in a commune in Lyon, from which he would send him various
books "to counteract the harmful effects of military instruction," as he will
write in one of his dedications: the *Manual of the Perfect Anarchist*, author
unknown; the *Catechism of a Revolutionary* by Sergey Nechayev; *Free Love*
by Carlos Albert; and various books by Nietzsche and Schopenhauer; living in fear of being sent to Morocco, although the order never came, or of
being arrested and losing his mind, as happened to a conscript from Teruel
who took his own life by smashing his head over and over against the wall
of his cell; going to the fortress of Montjuic for periodic shifts, never forgetting the defiant goatee of Ferrer Guàrdia in the ravine of Santa Amalia;
or listening to the green recruits swearing allegiance to the flag after the
standard question: "Do you swear to God and promise the king that you
will always follow his flag until the last drop of blood falls, and never abandon the one who orders you into battle or in preparation for it?" In sum,
becoming a better soldier and a worse person with each passing day.

And so, by the time he left the barracks, Pablo was twenty-two years
old and more lost than ever. Not only had he not heard anything from
Angela, but he had no station, no pension, and had just wasted three years
of his life, years during which the world kept up its old tricks: while hostilities continued in Morocco, a republic was proclaimed in Portugal, revolution broke out in Mexico, and the European powers were carving up
the cake of sub-Saharan Africa. Even the skies had started to be colonized
by airplanes, and the fashion for automobiles had become so widespread
that it was not unusual to see dogs and cats mowed down by the side of
the road in the big cities. A few proper nouns had made their way into
the newspaper headlines, leaving readers stunned at their epic or tragic

acts: in 1910 Luigi Lucheni, the anarchist who had assassinated Empress Sisi, committed suicide in his jail cell; at the end of 1911, the Norwegian Roald Amundsen reached the South Pole, one month before his British rival, Robert Scott; and in 1912, the transatlantic ship the *Titanic* sank after crashing into an iceberg, turning the Atlantic Ocean into an aquatic mausoleum with over one thousand corpses. But the fact that would change Pablo's fate was going to happen much closer to home.

A cold, disagreeable wind was blowing the Sunday morning when the doors of the barracks of Atarazanas were opened to release the discharged soldiers who had completed their three years of active service. Waiting outside were the girlfriends of some of those lads with whom Pablo had spent the endless, useless hours, without ever really developing a friendship with any of them. Then, the scene filled with kisses and hugs, reunions and goodbyes. Not really knowing what to do, with no one there to greet him, Pablo stood, his bundle under his arm, like someone waiting on a train platform for a visitor who will never arrive. He leaned against the wall of the barracks and closed his eyes, letting the wind caress his face, while the people started to disperse, leaving him there alone. Twice he told himself that he would count to ten and then open his eyes, but both times he counted and both times he did not dare to open them. The third time he counted, he felt a cold, smooth, feminine hand on his face. For a moment he believed that miracles exist, and he quickly opened his eyes. However, it was not Angela, but a young woman with an athletic figure and catlike features.

"Don't you remember me?" the girl asked, with a tentative smile.

Until Pablo stared directly into the eyes that were looking at him, his memory did not recover the remembrance of that summer afternoon: the left eye was blue like Chinese porcelain, the right gold as a doubloon.

"Sorry, I didn't recognize you. It's been a long time …"

"Well, I have thought a lot about you," said the girl, with candor that sent blood to Pablo's cheeks. "You're blushing," she smiled again.

"Who, me?"

"Who else? But don't worry: they say a blush always fades within a minute and a half—"

"What are you doing here?" asked Pablo, trying to change the subject.

"I came to look for you."

"For me?"

"Who else?" she repeated. Seeing Pablo's surprise, she added, "Just kidding. I was passing by on my way home."

"Oh, I see. And where do you live?"

"Hey, that's not something you just ask a proper young lady."

"I'm sorry. Barracks life makes boors of us."

"It's alright, I'm an emancipated woman," she said proudly. "Haven't you read Soledad Gustavo?"

Pablo shook his head.

"Well, you should . . . I live right over there, on Calle Carrera."

"And may I ask your name, or is that also something one shouldn't ask a lady?" Pablo tried to joke.

The girl thought about her answer, then replied:

"Call me Cuzanqui."

"Cuzanqui?"

"You don't like it?"

"I don't know, it's strange."

"I like it."

"What does it mean?"

"Nothing. Does Pablo mean anything?"

The wind appeared to stop suddenly.

"And how do you know my name is Pablo?"

The girl made a contrarian face:

"I'm sorry, I'm late getting home," she said, and began walking toward El Paralclo.

"Wait, wait," Pablo stopped her. "How do you know my name?"

"You told me the other time."

"Are you sure?"

"Completely."

The two young people looked into each other's eyes, cut off from their surroundings. He observed her curiously and she returned a burning look. Pablo then understood that life is a storm governed by chance, a storm in which everyone ends up drowning, even the smart ones, although they might manage to stay afloat a bit longer. And without really being aware of his words, he heard himself saying:

"We are toys in the hands of fate, aren't we?"

The girl (let's cooperate and call her Cuzanqui) took his hand and dragged him toward El Paralelo. When they reached Calle Carrera, she stopped:

"Wait for me a moment. I'll be right back."

And she ran up into her house. When he looked up, Pablo had a déjà vu moment: three years beforehand, he had made the same movement in the same place, on the way to the fortress of Montjuic. The girl soon appeared on the balcony of the second floor, as if to make sure that Pablo was still down there, and waved to him. Five minutes later, she came back out the door, with her eyes shining and her hair tied in a bun.

"Let's go," she said. "I'll take you to a place where you can see all of Barcelona."

They went up the piney slopes of Montjuic, until they reached a promontory on the north face of the mountain.

"Wait," said Cuzanqui, covering Pablo's eyes with her hands, "Don't look yet."

They walked another few paces, like a blind man and his guide dog, until the girl took away her hands and said joyfully:

"Now you can look!"

The image seemed like the work of an urban landscape painter: all of Barcelona unfolded at their feet, making them feel like the king and queen of the world. They sat down on the grass and stayed there until the sun set, talking and contemplating this spectacle without noticing their hunger or the cold.

"We should be getting back," he finally said.

"Yes," she said begrudgingly. "But wait a second. Close your eyes again."

Pablo did as he was told, asking:

"Are there still more things to see?"

"Of course," she said.

And taking him by surprise, she kissed him on the lips. Pablo felt a shiver go down his spine and an acute pain in the pit of his stomach.

"I can't," he blubbered, his eyes still closed. And when he dared to open them, Cuzanqui had disappeared.

PABLO PROMISED HIMSELF HE WOULD NEVER see that girl again, but the episode at Montjuic wormed its way into his consciousness. "Do you really think a man should be tied for life to the first woman he loves?" Robinsón had asked him shortly before going into seclusion. "I'm going to make the search for her the meaning of my life," Pablo had replied. But after four years without any word of Angela, his conviction was starting to waver. It was then, as he walked down from the mountain with an unsteady gait, that an unexpected solution started to take shape in his mind: if I can't manage to find her, maybe I can get her to find me. How? By doing something crazy, something that grabs the attention of half the world, even if I have to risk my life doing it. After all, he thought, for Angela I'm already dead, so it doesn't make much difference. With such errant thoughts he reached the house of Abelardo Belmonte, Ferdinando's nephew, who received him with open arms and invited him to stay in his house as long as he needed. Two days later, Don José Canalejas was assassinated in Madrid, and Pablo found the way to get his name in all the newspapers.

Canalejas had been prime minister of the country for almost three years and had made enemies on the right and the left. So in those tense, hair-triggered times, no one was surprised when an anarchist from Aragon named Manuel Pardiñas fired off three rounds in the middle of Puerta del Sol, as the prime minister was on his way to the Ministry of Governance in the middle of the morning, wearing a frock coat and traveling with no bodyguard. Canalejas had stopped in front of the window display of the San Martín bookshop, and the pale, mustachioed anarchist with one bad eye took advantage of the distraction to draw near to him and to secure his place in the bloody history of Spain with the cry, "Long live anarchy and death to tyrants!" After that, finding himself surrounded, he repeated the cry and shot himself in the temple. The next day, Pardiñas was front page news in all the major papers, and no one in the country went unaware of the anarchist's "deplorable act." It was said that the perpetrator ate no meat nor fish, and that his only vice was books about anarchism—he didn't drink or smoke, didn't even play cards; it was also said that he had traveled to Argentina to dodge his military service and that they had expelled him from that country after the assassination of the police chief of Buenos Aires. Among his personal effects they found an anarchist pamphlet, a fountain pen with a golden plume, a section of Flammarion's *Astronomía popular*, and a photograph of a woman with the dedication "To my unforgettable Manuel," showing that even assassins can be mama's boys. His personality caused such a sensation that a motion picture was produced, called *The Assassination and Burial of Don José Canalejas*, with the fresh, young Pepe Isbert in the leading role.

"Now for the king," said Abelardo when he read the article in the newspaper.

And more than one took him literally.

•

PABLO REACHED MADRID AT THE START of April 1913. Atocha Station was the same human boiling pot as North Station had been twenty years earlier, but now the carriages were not just competing against each other: they also found themselves in a constant battle of insults and swindles against the onslaught of automobiles threatening to steal their business. Pablo had spent the last few months working as a boilermaker in a metallurgy plant in Pueblo Nuevo (he needed to save up some money before he could carry out his crazy plan), all the while establishing ties to the most radical elements of Barcelonan anarchism, even being tempted by the anarchist writer and lawyer Ángel Samblancat (a native of El Grado, like Pardiñas), to write an article in the weekly *La Ira*, which he was planning to publish with Federico Urales. Samblancat, a friend and mentor of the poet Salvat-Papasseit, would have been shocked to learn that years later his name would be used for a brand of trousers. But Pablo had in mind other ways of realizing his ire, more direct than writing little articles.

He had decided to go to Madrid because there he could kill two birds with one stone. Bird number 1: the vulture, Alfonso XIII, who had shown no hesitation in sending Ferrer Guàrdia to his death. Bird number 2: the dove, Angela, who had taken off flying and gotten lost in the firmament. The plan: attack the first to catch the attention of the second. The weapon: the pocket pistol that a certain lieutenant colonel had placed in his hands. (No question of using bombs as Mateo Morral had, lest he risk taking innocent lives. A precise job. One point-blank shot, and a passport straight into all the newspapers.) The justification: though the life of a tyrant may be very respectable, the life of the people is more sacred, as Saint Thomas Aquinas himself once said. In the worst case he would end up in the garrote, passing into posterity as the regicide who put an end to the tyranny of Alfonso. In the best case, the shot would miss and the monarch would come out unharmed, and capital punishment would be commuted to life in chains (in an act of royal magnanimity), and when the Republic was reestablished in Spain, he would be pardoned with full honors, and free to spend the rest of his life with Angela, who would be proud to be the wife of a national hero. Such were Pablo's thoughts as the train crossed the central plateau toward Atocha Station. No doubt about it: he had come completely unhinged.

However, attacking the king would be no easy task. The rumor was going around that Pardiñas had shot Canalejas out of sheer opportunity, while his real objective had always been Alfonso XIII. In fact, a few days after the assassination, the Spanish ambassador in Paris sent a dispatch to the minister of state informing him that the prime minister's death had emboldened anarchists to action, many of them residing in France and ready to complete the task that Pardiñas had left halfway done. So when Pablo reached Madrid, the capital was infested with revolutionaries, and security was tighter than ever. He took a room in an inn called the Amelia on Calle Montera, near the ever-widening wound of Gran Vía, the vast project of urban demolition that was changing the face of the city. The innkeeper was a female version of Don Quixote: tall, gaunt, and with that absent gaze unique to the adventurous and the mad.

"Do me a favor and show me your identification papers," she muttered in greeting.

"This isn't exactly the Ritz," Pablo grumbled as he took out his documentation.

"Express orders of the government," replied Doña Quixote.

So Pablo had no choice but to sign the registry with his real name. Then he was taken to his austere room, with an iron-framed bed, a bedside table topped with marble, an armoire of blackened wood, a slightly greasy easy chair, and a small washing station with a mirror and a ceramic basin. He unpacked his bag and hid his revolver under the mattress, but then changed his mind and decided to find it a safer hiding spot—he did not want to risk having that scarecrow innkeeper find it as she was making the bed and then report him to the police, ruining all his plans. So he felt around the back of the armoire until he found a protruding nail from which he could hang the pistol, securing it with a piece of twine from his bag; then he slid the easy chair over to the balcony, took down the curtain and filled its hollow rod with the five bullets he had purchased before leaving Barcelona. Only then did he decide to go out into the street, with the idea that he would find Vicente Holgado, the newsboy-cum-anarchist who had saved his life during the attack by Mateo Morral.

It took him a few days to find him, looking everywhere: in cafés, in meetings, in libertarian gatherings, and even in movie theaters, which had been proliferating like rabbits since the last time Pablo visited the capital. But he ended up finding him in the most unexpected way: at dusk on the fifth day he returned to the Amelia hostel and went out onto the balcony to smoke a cigarette. He leaned on the railing, took a deep drag, and exhaled the smoke, thinking that if he didn't find Vicente soon, he would have to plan the attack by himself. And at that moment, he saw him, on the balcony of the hotel next door, leaning on the railing and smoking a cigarette, as if it were his own image reflected in a mirror.

"Vicente!" Pablo exclaimed.

"Pablo?" Vicente exclaimed in return.

And they looked at each other in surprise.

"What are you doing here?" asked the Madrileño, whose appearance was still vaguely gypsy, vaguely gangster.

"I came to—" Pablo started to say but bit his tongue. "Can we talk?"

Vicente looked him in the eyes, trying to decipher his intentions, and then looked around at all the balconies nearby.

"I think it would be better if we went somewhere else."

And he brought him to the same bar they had been to seven years before.

"I want to thank you," said Pablo after sitting down at a discreet corner table.

"Why?" asked Vicente, though he already knew the answer.

"For saving my life on the day of the royal wedding."

"It was nothing," he said. And then added: "But you didn't want to talk to me just to thank me, did you?"

"No … I came to ask you to help me kill Alfonso XIII."

Vicente said nothing, but his nostrils flared in reflex, as if at the smell of danger. He gazed steadily at Pablo, then took out his pouch of tobacco. After rolling a cigarette, he said:

"You know you are the fifth person to propose that idea to me this year?"

"Wow," Pablo said, surprised, "apparently the work of regicide is in high demand."

"But now is not the time."

"What do you mean, it's not the time? Any time is a good time to get rid of a tyrant!"

"Shhh, don't talk so loud," Vicente whispered, looking suspiciously at a pair of men who were leaning their elbows on the bar. "Look, Pablo, in my mind, the success of any revolutionary act depends largely on whether it's committed at the right time. And this isn't it: after what happened to Canalejas, the waters are really choppy and the cops are watching us closely. Actually, it's better we stop talking about this. How do you know I'm not one of them? How do I know you're not?"

Pablo remained silent, trying to get used to the situation: he had been sure that Vicente Holgado would help him plan the regicide, and now he felt somewhat betrayed by this revolutionary and his strategic pretenses. Although, when he really thought about it, perhaps this was only a pose, a distraction tactic on the part of the anarchists, who had probably already chosen the candidate destined for the front page of every newspaper: they had most likely been planning an attack for months, and it was even possible that Vicente himself had been assigned to the gruesome task, which is why he now had to dissuade all of the visionaries who might jeopardize his plan in their haste to do away with the king. So if Pablo wanted to shoot His Majesty, he would have to do it alone … and make sure nobody beat him to it.

"Alright, Vicente, I understand what you're saying," he finally conceded, "but I still think that there aren't good times or bad times to get rid of the cancers of our society. That's what I think and that's what I say, because I've always preferred to have the world disagree with me rather than disagree with myself. But you have more experience in the matter than I do, and I respect what you say. When the right moment comes, I'll be ready if you need me."

"You promise you're not going to pull some damn fool prank?"

"I promise," said Pablo.

And he did not intend to go back on his word, because what he had in mind was no prank.

17

The Directory, desirous that public opinion should have true information preventing any confusion and establishing the importance of the facts, avoiding conscious and unconscious exaggerations by sources, finds that it must make known the following events, which seem to be revolutionary in character, instigated by anarchist elements coming from France, doubtless in relation to advanced Spanish syndicalism.

On the morning of the seventh day of this month, the municipal authorities of Vera (Navarra) observed suspicious individuals, who had doubtlessly crossed the border recently, and who, being thirty in number and armed, clashed violently in the vicinity of the village with a pair of civil guardsmen on duty, and then dispersed.

ABC, November 9, 1924
(official memorandum from the Office of the President)

THE GROUP OF REBELS IS RESTING in the darkness of the quarry, while the leaders stand next to the road discussing whether it is better to wait for the workers to come out of the factory or to assault the Civil Guard barracks immediately, when Manolito Monzón, who has gone over by the corner of the factory wall to empty his bladder, comes back running in a state of panic, gesticulating wildly. Only Perico Alarco, who is used to interpreting his accomplice's flying hands, understands:

"Somebody's coming," he translates. "And they're armed."

After which both men disappear into the darkness.

The alerted revolutionaries instinctively go quiet, placing their hands on their holsters, but they have already been discovered: two silhouettes are visible against the illuminated wall of the factory, and these silhouettes are walking toward the quarry, topped with the unmistakable tricorn hats of the Civil Guard. The first to detect them are the leaders standing by the road: Bonifacio Manzanedo, Luís Naveira, Gil Galar, Julián Santillán, El Maño, and Robinsón, who quickly go from having their hands on their pistols to having their pistols in their hands. The rest of the expedition does the same, and some huddle closer to the cluster of leaders, including Pablo, Julianín, Leandro, and El Maestro, whose teeth have begun to chatter, who knows if from cold or fear. It is then that Luís Naveira, as if trying to keep the silhouettes at bay, lights his flashlight and shines it on them, causing them to stop in their tracks. The fat one lifts his gun to his shoulder and shouts:

"Halt in the name of the Civil Guard!"

To which the revolutionaries respond by pointing their own pistols in turn:

"Halt!" some of them shout.

"Who's there?" demands the guardsman Ortiz when he hears their voices.

"Spanish citizens," respond some.

"Where are you going?" Ortiz insists, as if reading from the manual.

"To liberate Spain!" responds Gil Galar, and he takes two steps forward.

"¡Viva the Republic!" exclaims Manzanedo, naively believing that his cry will be the magic words that make the guards lower their rifles.

"Halt!" shouts Corporal de la Fuente, his voice wavering, and he fires a warning shot into the air.

Chaos ensues: young Julianín's hands begin to shake at the sound of the gunshot, his vision blurs, and as he is trying to pass his pistol to one of the comrades in the front line, the gun goes off in the direction of the guards. Pablo jumps on him, trying to avoid catastrophe, but the time for prevention has passed and the guards now feel threatened and start shooting. A bullet strikes Pablo's thigh. The courageous guard Ortiz is kneeling to fire as per his training; with the fog and the darkness he cannot see that he is facing more than forty armed men, or perhaps the rapture of heroism has compromised his judgment. Corporal de la Fuente, more perceptive or more cowardly, is also pulling his rifle's trigger, but in retreat, as he shouts to his partner, "Come on, Ortiz, let's go!" a shout which collides in the air with that of Santillán, more concise and peremptory, "Fire!" and a hail of gunshots rings out in the night. Not even the barking of Kropotkin can be heard over the roar of battle.

Corporal de la Fuente does not have time to say anything else, because several bullets catch him in his retreat. One of these severs his carotid artery, and he falls on the ground twitching, while Ortiz defends himself like a titan. Of the five bullets in his magazine, at least four find their mark: two strike Bonifacio Manzanedo, one in each of his legs, and he falls to the ground howling in pain; another grazes Gil Galar in the right temple as he is trying to reload his pistol, though the wound is not quite fatal; one catches El Maestro in the kidney just as he turns to escape. But the valiant guard's resistance is futile against the many-headed enemy before him. As he tries to reload his rifle, his body is riddled with bullets. Seeing that his cause is lost, he launches himself in desperation into the fray of gunfire, brandishing his bayonet as his only threat, until a bullet hits his chest and punctures his heart. The brave guard collapses like a sack of cement, his body a sieve pierced with sixteen bullet holes. Gil Galar, bleeding and stumbling, approaches the guardsman and tries to take his Mauser, but Ortiz does not seem to want to give it up, as though clutching his rifle were his last act of resistance. Then Galar takes out a knife and stabs him twice in the neck, just in case. But the guardsman is already a corpse.

"Let's get out of here," someone says.

"No, it's better if we go on together," advises Santillán in vain, as several have already started to run, such as Casiano Veloso and his crew from Villalpando, and the buffoons Perico Alarco and Manolito Monzón, who took off running at the first gunshot.

Of the injured, the worst off is Bonifacio Manzanedo: the bullets have destroyed his left knee and his right tibia. Gil Galar is also in bad shape, with a concussion, although it could have been much worse, considering that it was his temple. Pablo has also been lucky, despite the seriousness, as the bullet went clean through his thigh, without hitting the femur. We know nothing of El Maestro, who disappeared into the woods with a handful of other revolutionaries and a bullet in his back. But thankfully they left behind the satchel, which Robinsón now approaches to find the first aid kit, also looking around for the bowler hat he lost in the fray. The rest of the men surround the injured ones, panicked in body and soul. Naveira takes the other first aid kit from his backpack, but he changes his mind at the last second:

"We'd better go to the river, we can use the water to clean the wounds," he says with conviction that surprises even him.

Leandro and Santillán, the two largest men, hoist Bonifacio by the shoulders and bring him to the bank of the Bidasoa, while Pablo and Gil Galar make it with the help of Robinsón and Naveira, respectively. Two or three men, without anyone really knowing why, drag the corpse of the guardsman Ortiz and throw it in the water, still clutching the Mauser. But no one remembers Corporal de la Fuente, who reposes a hundred paces up the road, his head bathing in a pool of his own blood.

"Pass me the scissors," says Naveira, who being a former doctor takes charge of the operation, and tears open the trouser leg of poor Bonifacio Manzanedo, who cannot contain his painful shrieking. "Give me your tie," says Naveira, and he ties it around the man's upper thigh as a tourniquet. Someone rolls up a handkerchief and puts it in Bonifacio's mouth to bite, to help manage the pain.

During this time, Pablo has taken off his own trousers and is letting Kropotkin lick his wound, knowing that there is no better disinfectant than saliva, even dog saliva. Gil Galar, kneeling at the river's edge, plunges his romantic-poet head into the icy waters of the Bidasoa, trying to control the bleeding. Robinsón takes out the linen compresses and soaks them with iodine tincture, while Naveira finishes disinfecting the wounds by applying an antiseptic ointment, seeing by the flashlights of El Maño and Santillán. Then he bandages Bonifacio's and Pablo's legs with astonishing speed, taking a little more care with Gil Galar's head.

In the meantime, the rest of the group discusses what to do next. Their victory in this first battle is indisputable, but the skirmish has chilled the spirits of the partisans, who appear finally to have understood the dangerousness of their mission, and are seriously starting to doubt the likelihood of its success. Few have faith that another encounter with the forces of order will transpire without fatal casualties among the rebels.

"Now is the time to attack the Civil Guard barracks," hisses Santillán, "because they're short two men."

"Or the time to escape before it's too late," says Martín Lacouza.

"Weren't we told that the revolution had already broken out in Spain?" asks Anastasio Duarte, who still unquestioningly believes what Max told him when he was plying him with cocaine.

"We'd best get the hell out of here," someone adds. "They must have heard the gunfight from the village, and they're sure to send reinforcements any minute."

Not even Gil Galar, with his newly bandaged head, dares to disagree. They all seem to have finally realized that no one was waiting for them on this side of the border. Although there is one who does not want to admit it:

"Let's try to make it to Lesaca," Santillán proposes, "maybe the comrades from the interior are already organized there."

And since no one has a better idea, the group makes its way down the Carretera de Pamplona, which runs parallel to the Bidasoa, anguish written on their faces, dragging Bonifacio Manzanedo, who is starting to grow delirious with the pain and to ask for a pistol to blow his brains out, until he loses consciousness. As they try to wake him, they send three men ahead to look for any signs of trouble, but these three come running back:

"Two carabiniers are coming down the road!" says one.

"It looks like they arrested one of our men!" says another.

Indeed, hearing the exchange of gunfire, the pair of carabiniers from the outpost at Lesaca, named Santos Pombart and Emilio de Inés, interrupted from their night watch on the Carretera de Pamplona, came running toward the source of the gunfire. They quickly came across José Antonio Vázquez Bouzas, one of the revolutionaries who took off running at the first shots and who, unlike those who ran into the woods, opted to stick to the road with no idea where he was going.

"Halt in the name of the carabiniers!" they shouted, pointing their rifles and flashlights at him. "Who's there?"

"Just a worker, headed to Bilbao to look for a job," Vázquez Bouzas blubbered, raising his arms and starting to shake.

"Then you've got the wrong road, because this is the way to Pamplona," Santos Pombart informed him. "What were those gunshots?"

"I don't know ... I saw a few men quarreling on the way out of Vera, but I kept my distance."

"You're under arrest," said the carabinier Pombart; and after taking down his information and making sure he was unarmed, he said: "Come with us."

That is when the rebel lookouts spotted them and came running back to inform the group.

"Everyone into the ditch!" orders Luís Naveira, apparently taking charge of the situation. "You three," he says to the group that spotted the carabiniers, "let's go see what they want."

The road curves to the right a few paces ahead and they can see the carabiniers' lights as they approach the bend. Naveira and the other men huddle down in the ditch, hiding behind a telegraph station. When the pair comes near, Naveira shouts:

"Stop or we'll shoot!"

To which Santos Pombart responds in turn, pointing his carbine:

"Halt in the name of the carabiniers!"

But Naveira is already firing the three bullets left in his magazine at point-blank range, but with such poor aim (the aim of a doctor's assistant, no more and no less) that he only manages to perforate Pombart's cap, while the latter only needs to pull his trigger once: the bullet enters Naveira's body just below the nose, crosses the superior maxilla, and exits via the occiput, exploding out the back of the skull. Naveira falls to his knees on the ground, his eyes already lifeless. The three men next to him take off running, and the carabiniers' shots do not find their marks. A little further on, hearing the gunshots coming from the direction of Lesaca, the group of revolutionaries feels surrounded, and there is a general flight into the woods, despite Santillán's efforts to keep the group together. But even he ends up accepting the situation and, with Leandro's help, tries to hoist Bonifacio Manzanedo, who has regained consciousness and is vehemently resisting:

"Leave me, leave me, comrades! For God's sake, save yourselves if you can, I'll only be a burden!"

Faced with his insistence and the gravity of the situation, they have no choice but to leave him there in the ditch, hoping someone will find him before he bleeds to death. Robinsón helps Pablo get up and they trudge off into the woods, struggling to find balance between their respective limping, followed by Kropotkin, Leandro, and Julianín, whose eyes are bulging out of their sockets. Joining them are Santillán and the guide Piperra, though the group will be quick to fragment. So when the carabiniers advance a little further, accompanied by the detainee Vázquez Bouzas, all they hear are voices and footsteps in the woods, so they decide to turn back, fearing an ambush, without ever discovering Manzanedo lying seriously injured in the ditch. They go back to the bridge of Lesaca and take refuge in an electricity plant, the Electra Bidasoa, where they telephone the outposts of Vera and Lesaca to ask for backup and to report what has happened.

In the meantime, the constable Don Enrique Berasáin, who had already fled a hundred yards homeward when the clash erupted in the quarry, came running back into town at the first sound of gunfire to alert the other pair in the barracks, the guardsmen Silvestre López and José Oncina. So the three take off in the direction of the quarry of Argaitza, and before reaching the foundry they can hear the carbine shots coming from the road to Pamplona. Guardsman Silvestre López knocks with the butt of his gun on the door of the factory, and this time the watchman hears and quickly opens. When asked, he replies that he just heard the shots, but that they are the first he has heard all night. "Come with us," they say, and the watchman comes out with an acetylene torch to light the way. A short distance ahead, they discover the body of Corporal de la Fuente, in the middle of the street, lying face down and shrouded in his cape. After checking that he is indeed dead, they drag him back toward the corner of the factory wall. As they seem to hear noises in the forest, they decide not to keep advancing, but they call after the guardsman Ortiz by name, once, twice, thrice. Receiving no reply, Silvestre López says to the constable:

"Go back to the village and tell the civil and military authorities: the mayor, the municipal judge, the head of the Somatén, the captain of the carabiniers, and whoever else you damn well have to. We'll stay here and wait for reinforcements."

And Don Enrique Berasáin, "the Dandy," retraces the path he has already covered four times over the course of this long, horrible night.

XVI
(1913)

PABLO SLID THE ARMOIRE AND BEHIND it wrote: "On April 13, 1913, Alfonso XIII will die." He used a piece of gypsum, which left his fingers chalk-stained. Then he took down his Velo-dog revolver and tossed it on the bed, with the twine still tied on. He slid the chair over to the window, climbed up with catlike agility, and took down the bar containing his five bullets. It was then that the door of the room opened unexpectedly, and in marched the proprietress, Don Quixote in skirts, broomstick at the ready. Seeing him perched up there, she made a nasty face and muttered "Sorry, I thought you'd already left," and she exited, giving one last look at the pistol lying on the bed. "Shit," mumbled Pablo, regretting that he had not locked the door on his return from breakfast. But now it mattered little: in a few hours all of Spain would know of his act. His fingers felt hot as he slid the bullets into the cylinder of the revolver, and then he used the twine to hide it, as he had learned to do during his flirtation with the anarchists of Barcelona: he tied it to the button that held his suspenders in place, put a hole in the right trouser pocket and let the weapon slide down until it almost reached his ankle. If he were to be patted down, no cop would go that low: duty first, but it's not worth the risk of throwing out your back. Later, all Pablo would have to do to use the pistol is put his hand in his pocket and pull the string. Before leaving the inn, Pablo took his lucky amulet from his suitcase, kissed it, and hung it around his neck. Then, in the street, he breathed deeply.

A magnificent spring sun was shining in the sky, and many Madrileños were taking advantage of the Sunday morning to attend the event of the day: the great military parade of allegiance to the flag, presided over by

His Majesty Alfonso XIII. After the military ceremony, the monarch was to travel to the palace in front of his Presidential Guard, departing down the Paseo de La Castellana, turning onto Calle Alcalá, crossing Puerta del Sol, and finally taking Calle Mayor—an itinerary very similar to the one he had taken on his wedding day. Pablo thought that if the anarchists were planning an attack, they would do it toward the end of the parade, as Mateo Morral had done seven years back, since the narrow streets of the old town were more propitious for escape than the big avenues. So he went to Calle Alcalá and walked toward Plaza de Castelar—dominated by the statue of the goddess Cybele—to get a jump on any other would-be assailants. The main buildings were covered with garlands, colored banners were hung from the streetlamps, and the streets were starting to be taken over by zealous visitors, journalists, and peddlers, looking forward to a boom in sales of peanuts, lupin beans, and other treats. Next to the door of the casino, a man on his knees was begging for alms, holding in his hands a sign that said: "To err is human, but to blame it on someone else is even more human." Pablo kept thinking about this phrase until he arrived at the palace of the Marquis de Casa Riera, all locked up as it had been ever since, as legend had it, having suffering an amorous slight in his gardens, the marquis had planted a cypress tree, making his descendants promise that, until that tree died, his palace would remain uninhabited and his garden untended.

"The king is gonna come this way, right? He's gonna come this way?" a madwoman suddenly erupted in Pablo's face, muttering hysterically. Her eyes were bulging, her gums bloody.

"Yes, Señora, he'll come this way, don't worry," Pablo said soothingly, when he had recovered from the initial surprise. And then, in a lower voice, he added: "Unless somebody stops him, of course."

The woman made a surprised face and lifted her hand to her mouth. Pablo took advantage of the opportunity to get away from the encounter and continue his way through the crowd. A little farther, he saw a man exiting the bar La Elipa wearing a strange camel's hair cape: their eyes met and the man half-closed one eye, giving Pablo a little wink of complicity. Since he didn't know the man at all, Pablo turned around, surprised, but the man kept going without a word. Damn, he thought, people are getting crazier all the time. And his own thought surprised him: maybe he too was off his rocker? What would his father have said if he knew what his son was about to do? And what would his mother and sister say when they saw him on the front page of all the newspapers, having committed regicide? He had a moment of hesitation, and he stopped walking. For an instant, he thought this was all a huge mistake. But then he remembered Angela's eyes and Ferrer Guàrdia's defiant goatee, and he recovered his courage. He put his hand in his pocket, tugged on the twine and noted the heft of the revolver; then he lifted his gaze, saw that he was standing in front of the Bank of Spain, and decided that that was the right place to wait for the passage of the military procession. Before making his way to the front row, he bought a cone of lupin beans. As the first bean crunched between his teeth, he thought of Robinsón, who used to call them *chochos*, and he felt strangely calm.

The front of the procession appeared in the square under the goddess Cybele shortly after one thirty in the afternoon, and a cool breeze picked up quickly, as though Aeolus wanted in on the party. Alfonso XIII, in an impeccable dress uniform and gleaming tall boots, was riding his beautiful Alarún, flanked by the count of Aibar and the chief of the Cazadores, followed a few yards back by the minister of war, the captain general of Madrid, and a good number of officers. On his usual expressionless face, the Bourbon smile seemed drawn on to dissimulate his underbite. Several riders led the procession, opening a path on the left side of Calle Alcalá and obliging the public to step back onto the sidewalk in front of the Bank of Spain or onto the tramway rails running down the center of the avenue. When the monarch saw that his path was open, he clicked his spurs gallantly, striking out ahead of his entourage, and the impassioned crowd shouted. Pablo understood that this was the moment, and for the first time he felt butterflies in his stomach. He put his hand in his pocket and started pulling up the twine little by little. He felt the butt reach his hand just as the king was approaching, and took a step forward out of the throng to get a clear shot. Just then, something caught his attention in the crowd before him. He stopped, completely petrified, frozen, stunned, almost dead: a few yards away, in the front line of people on the opposite side of the road, there was a woman watching the royal procession. And although her eyes had lost the glimmer of yesteryear, Pablo recognized her in an instant.

It was Angela.

He felt time stand still. He stopped hearing the shouts of the multitude. His fingers relaxed, and the revolver slid back down his leg. He fastened his gaze to Angela's face, and the world around him disappeared for a moment, erased or blurred by the hand of God or the devil. At first he could only see her in parts, as if he were incapable, after so much time, of taking in her whole existence: first he saw her eyes, then her lips; a moment later, her nose, her cheeks, and her hair, held in place with pins; then he became aware of her whole face, her neck, the black dress hugging her body; then his gaze fell on her arms, and traveled the length of them: the left was extended to hold a parasol, the right was bent, enlaced with another arm. And it was at that moment that Pablo understood that the line that separates happiness and doom can be razor thin. It was at that moment that Pablo felt something in his heart break forever. It was at that moment that Pablo discovered that the arm enlaced with Angela's arm was that of another man, a man whose other arm was holding a little girl, a little girl who was looking at Angela and moving her lips, lips that were saying: "Mama, when is the king coming?" and it was the man who responded, moving his lips in turn, and anyone paying attention could see that they were saying: "But, sweetie, he's already here." And the man and Angela looked at each other, and in that look there was love, or affection, or complicity, and he smiled and she returned the smile, a sad smile, it is true, but a smile nonetheless. And so the procession passed between them, like a solar eclipse, leaving that image engraved forever in Pablo's memory and choking his throat, at the epiglottis, like a rope around his neck. A few seconds passed in which he couldn't breathe, and perhaps he would have died of asphyxiation right there if fate had not held another surprise for him: suddenly, two gunshots rang out and everything turned to confusion and shouting and rioting.

The noise of the gunshots released Pablo's throat and a blast of cold air flooded into his lungs. When he came to his senses he still had time to see, a few yards away, the pistol in the hand of a man with glassy eyes, spellbound by his own audacity, before two guards jumped on him to subdue him. He had just shot at His Majesty Alfonso XIII, who appeared to have snapped out of his trance. And from the ground, the would-be assassin pulled the trigger of his Puppy-Velo-dog for the third time: there was a flash and a bang without smoke, and the man was buried under a human avalanche ready to lynch him, as various soldiers from the Royal Guard drew their swords to protect the Bourbon, and the air was filled with an acrid, dry, unnerving smell. Pablo did not get as far as thinking that such might have been his own fate, despite how closely his own weapon resembled the assassin's; instead, he looked immediately to the opposite sidewalk, as the crowd erupted into cheers for the king and hurrahs for the monarchy. He got down on his knees to try to spot Angela between the horses' legs, but Angela was not there. So, on all fours like a dog, he broke out in a convulsive sob, from which he couldn't even be rescued by the consoling words of a girl at his side who said to him:

"Don't cry, sir, the king is alive. Look."

In fact, while the guards and agents of order moved on the anarchist (no one had any doubt that the author of the attack was an anarchist), Alfonso XIII once again smiled, and corrected the official who had ordered the procession to resume at a gallop:

"No, General. At a pace! As if nothing happened."

Later it would be known that the would-be assassin was named Rafael Sancho Alegre, a member of the anarchist group known as Sin Patria who had come directly from Barcelona to attack His Majesty. But all he accomplished was to increase Alfonso XIII's reputation as indestructible, letting him come unscathed through the umpteenth attempt on his life, and to boast to the journalists when he arrived at his palace: "I saw him step away from the group," he would say in reference to Sancho Alegre, "and start walking toward me; for a moment I thought it was to praise me, but at the same time I thought he might be an evildoer, and I prepared to defend myself. I could have killed him, but I did not care to."

But among the crowd there was one man distant from all of this, although he had been ready to commit the act himself. His eyes were overflowing with uncontrollable tears and the pocket revolver was digging into his shin. He had spent the last four years of his life chasing a ghost, and now that he had found it, he had discovered that it was in vain. The ghost had left him for dead. The ghost had found a new life. The ghost had even managed to start a family. He stood up and left that place, walking robotically. He disappeared up the old Calle del Turco, where a group of agents of order had set up a checkpoint to catch any accomplices to the attempted regicide. They patted him down and let him go, proving that the twine trick was a sure bet. But Pablo, at that moment, didn't even remember that he was carrying a pistol. If he had remembered, he might have done something crazy. He simply started wandering the streets of Madrid until he lost track of time. Only when his footsteps reached Calle Montera and he found himself in front of the door to the Amelia Inn did he come to his senses: through the frosted glass of the door, he could see that the proprietress was talking with two civil guardsmen. A survival instinct told him that it was better not to enter, and so he hid in the adjacent doorway until they came out. As they were leaving the inn, Pablo could hear their parting words:

"Be sure to let us know, ma'am, if that man shows up here again."

Then they disappeared down the street and Pablo waited a few minutes before going into the inn. When he did so, he took out his revolver and ordered the proprietress to open the door to his room. He put his things in the suitcase and ran down the stairs. Before leaving, he paid his bill and left a good gratuity. Stepping out into the street, he almost ran smack into Vicente Holgado, who was leaving his own hotel in a hurry.

"Where are you going?" they both asked in unison.

"North Station," they both replied.

And that is where they went, with only one idea: to get out of the hornet's nest as fast as they could.

18

The municipal constable, all told, showed praiseworthy zeal in accomplishing his duty. With his warning, and the services offered by the captain of the carabiniers and his forces, the Civil Guard, the local Somatén, and the harmonious and effective cooperation of the neighbors, the matter was resolved admirably, and the insurrection was quashed as soon as it arose, a bitter memory for this village due to the tragic deaths it caused, but also an occasion of glorious satisfaction because, through their fulfillment of the duties of citizenship, and inspired by love of country, the villagers were able to disrupt the perverse plot hatched against our Spanish Homeland, which arose in this peaceful village, not hesitating to face those who sought to disrupt order in the Nation, at the very moment when peace is most needed to continue the era of progress led by the current Directory that we are fortunate to have in charge of our government.

Minutes of the City Hall of Vera,
November 16, 1924

"IT'S BETTER IF WE PART WAYS," admits the former civil guardsman Santillán, when he can no longer see the road behind him, "that's the only way we'll have a chance of escaping, now that all is lost."

The others nod in agreement.

"There are a few ways to try to reach France from here," explains Piperra, knowing that this is the only hope to save their skin. "The shortest way is to go over the butte of Santa Bárbara and cross the border at Labeaga peak, but it is also the hardest way and I think some of us are not in shape to make it," he says, looking at Pablo.

"And what other options are there?" Robinsón asks, not ready to leave his friend in the lurch.

"Going back the way we came. That's the most accessible way."

"Crossing the village?" asks Pablo.

"We can skirt the edge of it."

"Too risky," declares Santillán.

"Would you be able to accompany us, Piperra?" Robinsón asks.

The guide takes a few seconds to respond.

"Let's go," he finally says. "We'll try to make it to the Eltzaurdia farmstead without being seen. I have some relatives there. Maybe we can hide out there until things blow over."

"Alright then," says Santillán, who has come to terms with the situation and is starting to get nervous. "Let's split up and leave right away, before the carabiniers alert the border patrol and cut off our escape. I'm going to go by Labeaga, who's with me?"

There is a moment of indecision, because Leandro and Julianín are hesitant to abandon their friends. But they do not appear to have a choice if they want to have any hope of saving themselves.

"Go on, boys," Pablo resolves the situation. "I'll see you in France, one way or another."

And they say goodbye quickly, containing their emotions, embracing for what could be the last time, as Piperra explains to the ex-civil guardsman how to reach Labeaga. Then Santillán, Julianín, and Leandro head off up the hill, leaving the glow of the foundry behind. Pablo holds onto Robinsón, doing his best to handle the pain, and both follow Piperra and Kropotkin, who seems to know the way. They go around the butte of Santa Bárbara and make their way toward Vera through fields and prairies, dotted here and there by Basque farmhouses, most with their lights on: clearly, the sound of the gunfire has awakened the inhabitants. The sky is growing clearer, and a few stars are keeping the moribund moon company as it cuts the horizon of the majestic Mount Larrún, so close and so far away at the same time, as if proclaiming the border between salvation and damnation. For Pablo every step is a sacrifice and each stumble is mortifying, but he continues onward, biting his tongue. A stream lies in the fugitives' path, and Robinsón proposes throwing away the pistols and ammunition, too incriminating in case of arrest. After a few moments of indecision, they end up throwing them into the turbulent water, which quickly swallows them. Shortly thereafter, before reaching the main road, Piperra stops:

"Wait for me here, I'll go see if the coast is clear," he says, and disappears for a few seconds.

"Robin," Pablo whispers in the darkness.

"What?"

"Do you think we'll get out of this?"

And since the vegetarian does not respond, he continues:

"How could we have been so foolish, Robin? How did we let ourselves get tricked like this?"

But again he does not respond, because the guide comes running back.

"Let's go, follow me," he says under his breath. "The road is clear."

The three men and the dog cross the road connecting the neighborhood of Altzate to the old village of Illecueta, where no one appears to be aware of what has happened. However, there are unmistakable voices coming from Vera sounding the alarm. As they pass behind the farmhouse of Zelaia, a light comes on inside and the three revolutionaries hit the dirt, and Pablo has the misfortune of knocking his injured leg against a rock. The former typesetter cannot contain a shriek of pain. Someone opens a window and a figure appears above the sill:

"Who's there?" asks a worried, elderly male voice.

The three men hold their breath.

"Who's there?" insists the old man.

And this time it is Kropotkin who saves the situation, barking at just the right moment.

"Get out of here, you mutt!" the old man shouts, and slams the window shut.

When the light goes out, the men continue on their way, with Pablo more hobbled than ever. Shortly they arrive at the farmstead of the Baroja family, which is still shrouded in silence and darkness, as is the Errotacho mill, a little further on, where the road to France splits off from the main road going up to Napoleon's Pass. Piperra knows that there is no choice but to go to the mill, although it lies dangerously close to the road, and they are nearly discovered by an approaching automobile, aggressively revving its engine. The three revolutionaries hide among the bushes, and after a few seconds the headlights illuminate the street. The car passes like a sigh of relief, because they cannot see that traveling inside it are three members of the Somatén of Vera, who are going up to the border to report what has happened and to give the order that no one should pass. It seems that the civil defense corps formed by Primo de Rivera as soon as he took power is acting as a sentinel and living up to its supposed Catalan etymology, "*som atents*"—"we are vigilant." But although the three fugitives cannot see them, they can sense them:

"They're going to the border to alert the carabiniers," snaps Piperra, a carpenter by trade and a pessimist by nature. "Let's go!"

They take the main road toward Usategieta, but shortly Pablo lets himself fall to the earth, gasping:

"Save yourselves, fellas. I give up. I have no right to make you lose more time—"

"Not a chance, Pablo. It's not much farther," says Robinsón, who, despite his sickly complexion and the limp he has suffered since his bout of juvenile polio, lifts Pablo onto his back and drags him as best he can, until they reach the Eltzaurdia farmstead.

"Wait for me there," says Piperra, pointing at a little thatched hut next to the house, and he goes to the door and pounds on it energetically.

After a few minutes that seem like hours, someone opens the little window and the light of a kerosene lamp illuminates the young man's face.

"Auntie, it's me, Pedrito. Open the door, please."

The woman does as her nephew asks, and he slips inside the house without waiting to be asked in. It is half an hour before he comes back out to fetch Pablo and Robinsón, who by now are desperate and chilled to the bone. Kropotkin has to wait outside.

"Ay, by the name of the Blessed Virgin!" the woman complains as she sees them enter, while her husband looks suspiciously at the longhair and the wounded man who have just disturbed the tranquility of their dwelling. "I knew that this boy would bring us nothing but trouble!"

"Calm down, Auntie," says Piperra, "and give these men something warm, you can see what shape they're in."

The woman prepares them a café con leche. Robinsón gives her the horsetail, prized for its hemostatic properties, that he collected on the way into Vera, and she puts it on to boil. The vegetarian takes the opportunity to change Pablo's dressings, now completely soaked with blood, and applies a healing poultice made of the medicinal herbs. When he finishes the process, the man of the house opens his mouth for the first time:

"You can stay here until tomorrow," he says to his nephew, in a dry tone that invites no discussion. "But your friends have to leave now."

"But, Uncle," Piperra tries to protest.

"Not another word. If they're not gone in five minutes, I'm going to inform the carabiniers."

The three men leave the house. Decidedly, the people of Spain are not ready to start a revolution.

"Don't worry," says Robinson to Piperra, buttoning his overcoat, "we know the way, it can't be much farther."

"No, listen," the guide replies hanging his head, "I'd go with you, but . . . Napoleon's Pass is up that way, and then straight ahead you'll reach the Inzola Inn. You can't miss it. Good luck, comrades!"

The three men say farewell, as Kropotkin nips at the pant cuffs of the man who is staying behind, as if reproaching him for his cowardice. It is not a great distance from the Eltzaurdia farmstead to Napoleon's Pass, but the going is steep, and Pablo suffers unspeakably with every step. Also, as if that were not enough, the road soon splits to the right and left, and neither Robinsón nor Pablo knows which way to go. Finally they decide to follow Kropotkin, who opts for the road to the left, but after a short distance the path disappears into a thick forest.

"This doesn't look familiar to me," Robinsón laments.

"Me neither," Pablo moans.

And they decide to go back to the fork in the road. In the valley below, the village of Vera appears to have awakened, as many lights are lit. The two friends take the road to the right, and the first glow of dawn is starting to rise behind the mountains when they finally reach the pigeon towers of Usategieta, the same place where a few hours ago fifty revolutionaries, bent on liberating Spain, convened before making their descent. But Pablo can go no farther, and asks Robinsón to rest for a moment.

"It's alright, stay here and don't move," the vegetarian agrees. "I'll go see if the road to the inn is clear."

And then Pablo commits a fatal mistake, a beginner's mistake, as if the devil himself had set a trap for him in the form of a cigarette whispering *light me, light me and smoke me*. Because Pablo, his mind addled by pain and fatigue, takes out his tobacco pouch as Robinsón is disappearing down the road toward Inzola, and he rolls a little cigarette and lights a match, not on the first try, nor on the second, but finally on the third, and the brief glow catches the attention of a pair of carabiniers patrolling the area, a pair comprising a corporal and a sergeant who have been informed of the revolutionary insurrection and who are approaching Pablo's location, following a tiny ember that blinks to life with each successive puff, a pair that hides behind a rocky outcropping and then shouts "Halt!" at Pablo, who is unarmed and missing the good luck amulet that used to accompany him through thick and thin, and he has no choice but to raise his arms and curse his bad luck, and hope that Robinsón is not on his way back, that he will take some time to return, so that he can at least save himself.

"Halt there!" orders one of the carabiniers, while the other searches the surroundings, with his rifle at the ready. "Stand up! You're under arrest!"

And Pablo stands up, trying his best to hide his infirmity, because he knows that he will be considered guilty if they discover that he has a bullet wound. And he lets them search him, and tie his hands behind his back with a wire, not seeing that Robinsón has returned just in time to hide in some bushes and curse himself for having thrown his pistol in the river, leaving him unable to face down the carabiniers, unable to do anything but watch, crouching in the foliage as they take Pablo away, and bite his tongue, and wipe his tears on Kropotkin's back, tears that flow like Inzola Creek a few yards away, tears of pain, rage, and impotence, tears of fear that he will never again see his friend Pablo Martín Sánchez, the anarchist with no sense of smell, the vampire with no heart, the kindred spirit he has entangled in this failed adventure. And not far off, he hears two gunshots, and Robinsón has no choice but to jump into the creek along with his trusty wiener dog, to try to reach the border before daybreak.

So, little Pablo, you look at the sky and think you see the constellation Cassiopeia, which seems to form an M, an M as in Martín. But it is probably just a hallucination, brought on by fever or exhaustion, because the light of morning is already starting to cause the stars to fade. In the meantime, what has faded for good is the revolutionary hope of ending the dictatorship of Primo de Rivera.

PART THREE

−19−

Forces of the Civil Guard from the outposts near the Bidasoa River and of the carabiniers (about 150 officers) from Vera, Echalar, and Lesaca, went into the forest, strategically deployed by their commanders, as soon as they learned of the painful events that had taken place in Vera, with the aim of capturing the criminals. Their praiseworthy work immediately began to yield excellent results. By noon, when we arrived in Vera, eleven syndicalists had been rounded up.

Diario de Navarra, 11 November 1924

IT IS OFTEN SAID THAT HISTORY IS written by the victors, but we sometimes forget that it is journalists who take the notes. The first gazetteers arrive in Vera de Bidasoa at midmorning, most of them coming from Pamplona and San Sebastián, as the holding cell at the carabiniers' barracks is already starting to swell with revolutionaries captured in the mountains. But no one dares to transfer them to the barracks of the Civil Guard, with two guardsmen's bodies still warm:

"If they bring them there, they'll be pistol-whipped to death," the constable Don Enrique Berasáin, who has become the unexpected star of the day, tells the journalists. "Don't doubt that for a second."

It takes the arrival of Patricio Arabolaza, the famous, valiant, recently retired soccer player, to divert the reporters, unseating the Dandy as the center of attention. The former forward of the Real Union Club of Irún, who in the Olympic Games of Antwerp made the first goal in the history of the Spanish soccer team, was one of those who most fervently participated in the search party to capture the rebels:

"No, I was driving from Irún to go hunting in Echalar," the renowned athlete deliberately explains, "and passing through Vera I stumbled into all this mess. So I made my car and my person available to the forces of order, that's all."

"But, isn't it true that it was you who dragged Corporal de la Fuente out of the river?" asks a junior reporter from *El Pueblo Navarro*, repeating the rumor that has been circulating among the journalists.

"No, no, absolutely not. I only saw the trail of blood leading down toward the Bidasoa, and I let the authorities know. They put a boat in the river to look for the guardsman's body."

"But then, you might say that it was thanks to your cooperation that the body was found," insists the reporter from *El Pueblo*.

"Man, if you want..." concedes Patricio, used to being the star of the best plays.

And so, with the inestimable help of the Dandy, the footballer, and many others who participated in the search, the reporters manage to reconstruct the broad strokes of what has happened. They have converted the plaza next to the City Hall of Vera into a center of operations, where throughout the day more news reports and authorities arrive in equal measure. So it soon becomes known that a large group of armed men has littered the village with subversive literature and had a skirmish with the forces of order in the early morning. So it is that the village comes to be filled with civil guards and carabiniers, some of high rank, such as the colonel subinspector of the Civil Guard, Don José Rivera, who appears to be crammed into the sidecar of a motorcycle driven by his assistant, Captain Don Nicolás Canalejo, both of them coming from San Sebastián. So it is that they learn of the death of the corporal de La Fuente, the guardsman Ortiz, and Luís Naveira, and that their bodies have been transported on pallets like merchandise to the cemetery of Vera, where the judicial morgue is located. So it is that they witness the pompous disembarkation of the Civil Governor Don Modesto Jiménez de Bentrosa, arriving in his automobile from Pamplona. So it is that they are informed that in the area of the skirmish, one rebel was found with injuries to both legs, and was transferred to the Hospital of Mercy, where Dr. Gamallo is trying to spare him from an amputation that by all reckoning looks inevitable. So it is that they see descending from his horse the elegant, haughty lieutenant of the carabiniers of the dispatch of Lesaca, Don Augusto Estrada, who this very day will be promoted to the rank of captain and selected to organize the border patrol, in coop- eration with the French forces of order. So it is also that at lunchtime they catch wind of the rumor that another rebel has been captured in the forest (this is Abundio Riaño, "El Maño," laid low by gunfire near border marker 10) and that a carabinier has been transferred to Vera with three bullet wounds of uncertain prognosis. So it is that they see the mayor of Vera, Don Antonio Ollo, constantly entering and leaving City Hall, declining time and again to make any comment. And so it is that in the first hour of the afternoon they observe an automobile passing on the way to the hospital, in which they can spot the long, romantic, blood-soaked mane of Enrique Gil Galar, half-dead, because it seems that the bullet did not merely graze his right temple but lodged behind the ear. And so it is indeed that, as night falls, the journalists return to their homes, ready to write out their piles of scribbled notes and to cook up the chronicles that will fill the pages of the newspapers in the days to come. As long as the state censor gives them permission, of course. But let us not get ahead of the events; let us pick up the story where we left off, with the former typesetter of La Fraternelle looking at the sky, thinking he recognizes the flattened M of Cassiopeia, the M for Martín, as his father used to say.

They drag Pablo at gunpoint along the Carretera de Francia, his hands tied behind his back and his jaw clenched as he tries to hide the secret of his injury. At least he has been spared the humiliation of having the buttons torn from his pants, as happened to some of his other comrades, forced to walk with one hand on their neck and the other holding up their trousers. Entering the village, the first lights of dawn are already climbing up the mountains, and the windows of the houses are filled with the drowsy, worried, or curious faces of those villagers who are still at home. In the Calle de Altzate, a little girl steps out onto a balcony and salutes one of the carabiniers, who tells her to go back inside. But the child does not obey, and she keeps looking agog at the limping gladiator, as if seeing some unexpected greatness in his downfall.

Shortly thereafter they arrive at the barracks of the carabiniers, which welcomes them with the familiar motto "Morality, loyalty, valor, and discipline," engraved on the door, over the insignia of the rising sun that is the emblem of the house. In the receiving room, the corporal and the sergeant sign the admittance sheet, deposit the detainee's confiscated backpack, and lead him to a waiting room, where they replace the wire digging into his wrists with a pair of rusty handcuffs, leaving him in the charge of two youths recently graduated from the carabiniers' academy. In the waiting room there is a bench covered with a filthy, worn-out oilcloth, but they require Pablo to remain standing with his face to the wall, and he does not even have the spirit to protest. To his back he feels two rifles pointing at him, as well as the steady gaze of one of the carabiniers, the younger of the two, still beardless, with his eyes wide open so as not to lose sight of him for a single instant. This makes Pablo think of Julianín: who knows what has become of his former assistant? And from Julianín his thoughts jump to Leandro, the Argentine giant... Maybe they managed to cross the border together, and are now safe on French soil. And Robinsón, what has become of Robinsón and Kropotkin? What would his friend have thought when he came back to the *palomeras* and found him gone? But a shout distracts him from these digressions, a stentorian shout that suddenly resonates from the room next door:

"Bring me the new one!"

Pablo turns his head and the two young carabiniers gesture with their rifles to tell him to walk, and bring him to the interrogation room, somewhat bigger than the last room and less decrepit, though no one would think to call it comfortable. In the center of the room there is a wooden table with a rickety chair on the side closer to the door, and a plush green easy chair on the other side, in which sits Feliciano Suárez, lieutenant of the carabiniers of the section of Vera, who has recently been appointed as the military investigating judge. Next to the window, breathing out mouthfuls of smoke from a recently lit Partagás cigar, is Don Veremundo Prats, the captain of the carabiniers who has spent the night coordinating the search and capture of the seditionists, with the cooperation not only of over one hundred civil guards and carabiniers having arrived by automobile from the nearby settlements of Sunbilla, Lesaca, and Santesteban, but also members of the local Somatén militia, including a good number of the inhabitants of Vera and of the neighboring farmsteads. In the back, on the right, half-hidden behind a typewriter, a typist indolently observes the entry of the detainee.

"Sit down," orders the investigating judge, without even bothering to look him in the eye. "Take off his handcuffs."

The beardless boy does as he is told, with nervous and terribly cold hands, while his companion never stops aiming his rifle at Pablo. The lieutenant takes a little tin from a box and with a gesture tells the detainee to dip his index finger in the black, gelatinous mass it contains, and then place it on a sheet of paper on the table.

"You can wash, if you like," he tells him, pointing to a rag above the spittoon, a burlap rag that appears to have already cleaned several hands today. But Pablo prefers to wipe his finger on his pants, though he does not have time to be too thorough, because they quickly put the handcuffs back on him. "What is your name?"

"Pablo."

"Pablo what?"

"Martín Sánchez."

The stenographer records his words like a mechanical echo. A fan hangs from the ceiling, its blades woven together with spider webs.

"Age?"

"Twenty-five," Pablo replies without hesitating for an instant.

"Profession?"

"Typesetter."

The stenographer lifts his eyes from his machine, trading his usual indolence for a brief moment of curiosity.

"Religion?"

"None."

"Ay, another one. Put 'lapsed Catholic,'" Don Feliciano says to the secretary. "Place of origin?"

"I come from Paris."

"But you are Spanish."

"Yes, from Baracaldo."

"Aha. And what business do you have in Vera?" asks the lieutenant, leaning over the table and looking the detainee directly in the eyes for the first time.

"You're the ones who brought me to Vera."

"Listen, don't be a wise guy," Don Veremundo Prats suddenly interjects from over by the window, pointing his cigar at Pablo. "You're being asked what you were doing when you were arrested. Answer!"

"I had just crossed the border, on my way to Bilbao, where I was going to visit my mother and my sister, who live there."

"Fine, you can take him away," the investigating judge orders. "Put him in cell number 6." Turning to Don Veremundo, he muses, "At this rate we'll have to start putting them in two by two."

Passing in front of the waiting room, Pablo can see two men facing the wall, monitored by two carabiniers, and while a shove from his guard keeps him from double-checking, he would swear that one of the detained is Casiano Veloso, the leader of the Villalpando clan who barely two days ago was happily frolicking at Madame Alix's brothel. Pablo is led in silence down a long corridor, after which a few stairs descend toward the cells, from which emanates an unpleasant smell of sewer or latrine that he cannot detect. It is surely the gloomiest, dankest part of the building, barely lit by a dirty lightbulb that hangs from the ceiling in the main room, around which separate cubicles are arrayed, according to the claustrophobic penitentiary system of cell distribution. Under the light there is a table, where a guard sits nodding off. Hearing the three men enter, he suddenly snaps to attention, showing a scar running from his left cheekbone to his right jowl. It is not for nothing that they call him Splitface.

"Empty your pockets and put the contents on the table," he says to the detainee with unnecessary vehemence, using the informal address in a condescending manner, as the beardless boy removes the handcuffs. "The belt and the shoelaces too. We don't want you getting any stupid ideas."

Pablo has no choice but to obey, although for a moment he imagines taking off his belt and using it like a whip to attack the carabiniers. But it must be the fever, which has already started to cloud his judgment, because otherwise why would he have such fantasies when it is obvious that there is no possible escape?

"The money too?" Pablo asks, after putting his passport, pen, tobacco pouch, and matches on the table.

"The money too!" barks Splitface, whose countenance seems to confirm the theories of physiognomy.

The beardless lad then proceeds to search him, and, feeling his pants pockets, discovers the blood soaking his right thigh.

"This man is injured," the novice carabinier announces, somewhat surprised.

"It's nothing," Pablo snaps. "Just a scratch."

"We should get a doctor," insists the lad.

"I said it's nothing," Pablo cuts him off, staring into his eyes. "Just finish searching me and leave me in peace with my scratches."

"Whoa there, we're the ones giving the orders around here," the sentinel warns him, brandishing a rubber truncheon. And, after a few seconds of hesitation, he instructs the young carabinier: "Hurry up and finish searching him, then into the hole, jelly roll. If the wise guy wants to bleed to death, I won't be the one to stop him. Which cell does he go in?"

"Number 6," blubbers the beardless boy.

"Signed, sealed, and almost delivered!" exclaims Splitface, with a chuckle.

Having completed the operation, the jailer takes a rolled-up mattress and a filthy blanket from beneath the stairs, and hands them to the detainee along with an outdated newspaper, not to cultivate his wayward soul but to wipe his bodily waste. Then he opens the grilled door of cell number 6 and with a gesture invites him to enter, if one can speak of invitations in such a situation. The door creaks loudly and the key squeals as it turns like a rusty garrote. The cubicle is even smaller and narrower than Pablo had imagined, and the darkness is nearly total, because the only light it receives comes from the dirty lightbulb out in the room passing through a tiny peephole in the door, three thin slits in a row. There is also a hatch in the lower part of the door, through which the prisoner can receive his food without needing to open the cell, but this hatch is closed and can only be manipulated from outside. As his only company, in a corner, he can barely make out the inevitable commode, which others call a crapper, made of thick, curved planks of wood held in place with iron rings, where the incarcerated may deposit his number ones as needed, and also number twos, without risk of leakage. When the footsteps of the two carabiniers fade away up the stairs, Pablo hears a sob in the adjacent cell, but before he has the presence of mind to try to communicate with his neighbor, Splitface's voice resounds:

"You! If I hear you grumble again, I'm gonna make mincemeat outta you, you hear me? And the same goes for the rest of you!"

A thick silence falls over the inmates, and Pablo has to stifle his desire to know who his companions in captivity are. However, even if he were able to speak with them, in all likelihood he would not even try, because the most sensible thing is surely to give the impression that he does not know any of the five revolutionaries who were detained before him and placed in cells identical to his own. The first to arrive was José Antonio Vázquez Bouzas, whom we saw flee the skirmish and who was captured by the carabiniers responsible for the death of Luís Naveira. A while later they brought in Francisco Lluch, the deserter of the regiment of Sicilia who came to Spain to see his dying father (cell number 2). The roosters were waking up as Tomás García and Justo Val arrived, both natives of Aragon living in Biarritz, the only brave men from the group of Abundio "El Maño" Riaño who dared to cross the border, aside from the unfortunate Abundio and the nephew of the priest from Lesaca (cells 3 and 4). And shortly before Pablo's arrival, Eustaquio García was brought in to keep the rats company. This is the young man from Soria unable to control his weeping (cell number 5). Unaware of this information, but perhaps suspecting it, the former typesetter of La Fraternelle unfurls his sleeping mat, leaving one of the ends rolled up to serve as a pillow, and he stretches out on it, covering himself with the blanket and trying to control his shivering. Despite the wound, which is starting to get infected, and the roaches and lice creeping all around him in the cell, and his anguish before the uncertain future that awaits him, and the discomfort of the dungeon in which they have just locked him, he quickly falls asleep, not even waking up a few minutes later when Casiano Veloso and Ángel Fernández arrive, both from the Villalpando clan, and are both placed in cell number 7, the last free cell. And he barely wakes up when, after a few hours, they bring him a refreshment in the form of a cup of re-brewed coffee (with a flavor somewhere between chicory and dishwater, but with the virtue of being something hot to drink), whereof he takes a few sips before falling back asleep. It will not be until midmorning that he finally comes to consciousness, with his body stiff and his injured leg numb, when a familiar voice in the central room wakes him:

"Che, don't bust my balls! The photo goes with me to the grave—" but Leandro cannot finish his sentence, as a rifle butt to the kidney brings him to his knees.

Pablo struggles to arise, and goes to the peephole, but the three narrow gaps are angled up toward the ceiling and he cannot see what is going on.

"I don't know how it works in your country," says Splitface's voice, "but here rules are meant to be followed. Let's see that photograph ... Mmm, not a bad looking little lady, she can keep me company while I guard you scumbags."

"Son of a bitch," this time it is the voice of the former guardsman Santillán that Pablo hears on the other side of his cell door, followed by another blow of a rifle butt and a shout that is not so much of pain as of wrath.

"Alright, alright, party's over," the sentinel says loudly, "Finish searching them and let's finally throw these rats in their goddamn pigsties. No blankets or mats for them, we've run out."

It is then that Pablo's cell door opens and they shove Santillán inside. He has just enough time to catch a glimpse in the bare bulb's dirty light of the silhouettes of Leandro and Julianín, guarded by half a dozen pissed-off carabiniers.

XVII
(1913)

THERE ARE VARIOUS STRATEGIES FOR ENHANCING memory, but techniques for the cultivation of forgetting are poorly understood. Time heals all wounds, some say. Including heartbreak. Sure. And in the meantime? In the meantime, Pablo said to himself, the best thing to do is to put some distance between yourself and your sorrow. Especially if you are also being pursued by the police.

In Madrid, Sancho Alegre was going to be interrogated, incarcerated, judged, sentenced to death, and pardoned by Alfonso XIII, but by the time that happened, Pablo Martín and Vicente Holgado would be ten thousand miles away. After the failed regicide and the chance encounter at the door of the Amelia Inn, they seemed to have developed a silent agreement: if fate insisted on uniting them, the most reasonable thing to do would be to follow its plans. At North Station they took the train to Irún, where they arrived near dawn, with just enough time to hire a smuggler who would help them cross the border. Once in France, they had no problem reaching Bordeaux, whose port was the point of embarkation for various ships, merchant boats, and transatlantic liners.

"I'm going to America," said Vicente, gazing at the sea. "And you?"

Pablo took a few moments to reply. They had sat down at the end of the pier, and it was starting to get dark. The idea had crossed his mind, too, but it seemed crazy. It's one thing to forget, and another to travel to the end of the world. He tried to imagine what kind of life he could have in America, but he could not. Maybe it would be better to stay in France, to go looking for Robinson and become a naturist, or a vegetarian, or whatever; or maybe to stay right there in Bordeaux, why not, waiting for better days when he could go home to be with his mother and sister. But then, with no warning, he had a vision of Angela in the arms of another man, and a knot formed in his throat. Madrid was still definitely too close. He needed to gain some distance in order to cleanse himself thoroughly. In the fog that had started to lift, Pablo looked at Vicente, who was still staring at the horizon, and remembered the old proverb his father used to say: in case of doubt, movement is always better than stillness, because if you hold still, you might just be on a scale being weighed with your sins. He stood up, sighing, gripped the Velo-dog pistol he had been planning to use on the king of Spain, and threw it as far as he could into the sea.

"I'm going too," he finally said, determined to start a new life.

Within a few days, they managed to find work as waiters on a transatlantic liner with a promising name, the *Victoria*, of the *Transamerikanische Linie*, which was transporting first- and second-class passengers, as well as third-class, reserved for the poorest immigrants hoping to find a better life in the land of opportunity. The imposing two-chimney steamship had come from Hamburg, weighed fifteen thousand tons, traveled at a speed of twenty-one knots, and carried an initial crew of eighty men, gradually increasing as they took on new passengers at port after port: Amsterdam, The Hague, Bordeaux, Bilbao, La Coruña, and Lisbon, then heading for New York and ending the trip in Buenos Aires. And although neither Pablo nor Vicente had ever been on a steamship, their stubbornness and courage finally convinced the captain, an old sea wolf who appeared to have leapt from the pages of a novel by Conrad or Melville:

"What languages you speak?" he asked them in macaroni Spanish, his head tilted forward as he took short, quick puffs from a foreign-smelling cigar.

"Any language you need," replied Vicente Holgado, audaciously.

"Have you ever worked as waiters before?"

"Since the cradle," Vicente assured him.

"Alright then," the captain conceded, wincing and stroking his intricate double chin, the faithful mirror of his soul. "I'll try you out. But if you don't work hard, your trip ends in Bilbao, understood?"

"Understood," they both said at once.

And so it was that they became crew members of the *Victoria*.

The first days were calm, except for the first few hours, during which Pablo stumbled more than walked, his handkerchief constantly pressed against his mouth. But once he had adjusted to the smooth rise and fall of the waves, a strange calm came over him, as though all the distasteful things he had been through in the last few years were being dissolved by the stirring of Neptune. The waiter's uniform made him feel as though he were acting in the theater, and he set out to play his role to the best of his ability. Arriving in Bilbao, the captain informed them that they would be kept on until the end of the voyage, and Pablo took advantage of his leave time to go to Baracaldo to see his mother and sister, despite the objections of Vicente, who preferred to remain onboard to avoid unwanted encounters with the police. When his family saw him come through the door, they smothered him in kisses. Then his mother said, with tears in her eyes:

"The Civil Guard came by looking for you. What have you done, my son?"

"Nothing, mother, don't worry," Pablo tried to calm her. "If they come back, tell them I'm on vacation in America."

But the joke was only funny to Julia, who smiled with a sweetness that Pablo remembered from long ago. However, she was no longer a child: she had turned into a woman, no doubt about it, and she must have had plenty of suitors. So Pablo was not surprised to be met by silence when he suggested that, if they could, they should come to meet him in America. They looked at each other, and a smile came to Julia's face, this time more knowing than sweet.

"Did I miss something?" Pablo asked, pretending to be offended.

"Oh, dear brother, don't you think we have our own lives?" Julia replied with a certain sarcasm. "You think that while you've been out gallivanting all over the world, we've just been at home sewing and waiting for your return?"

"Don't tell me you've both taken lovers—"

"No, not me, for God's sake!" exclaimed María, smiling for the first time. "But your sister ... well, you tell him yourself, Julia."

It turns out Julia had gotten engaged to a young man from Bilbao, a student in his last year of law school who was planning to take her to the altar as soon as he was done with his studies, because he had a job lined up as a lawyer in his uncle's firm.

"Well, well, my little sister," said Pablo. "Now, maybe she'll lift us all out of poverty."

The three laughed heartily and, for the first time in a long time, Pablo felt a glimmer of happiness. He was not even thinking about Angela, but about Julián, his long-lost father, the fourth leg of this table, which has been rickety since his death: how the humble inspector would have liked to share in these brief moments of familial joy.

"Pretty, pretty, pretty," said Pablo in the end, stroking his sister's hair and quoting himself.

Then he embraced them for the last time and went running back to the *Victoria*—he was not about to stay on land, all dressed up with nowhere to go. The journey lasted twenty-one days, and apart from coming to terms with his own life and admiring the infinity of the ocean, Pablo used the time to get to know a fascinating character: a young Pole who went by the name of Meister Savielly, traveling in first class with his wife. He was a thin fellow with a robust build; he usually wore a bespoke black suit, replete with various folds, pockets, buckles, and buttons. He was neither an adventurer, nor an eccentric musician, nor a politician trying to go unnoticed, but a famous chess player on his way to participate in the international tournament in New York. Every night, after dinner, he sat at a table in the game room and had a magnificent alabaster board brought out, on which, with the firm delicacy of a watchmaker, he placed his marble chessmen, black and white, beautifully carved. Behind him formed a line of gentlemen eager to bet a bit of money to challenge the master, knowing that the more they wagered, the more time he would spend on them. Throughout the whole trip he never gave up more than a handful of pawns, and that was merely to avoid discouraging his rivals completely and leaving himself without clients. He also offered simultaneous games, including some he played blindfolded, leaving the onlookers dumbfounded. If that were not enough, he also acted as an impresario, seducing passersby, uttering quips and clever phrases like a gallant at court, in exquisite French: "The winner is always the one who makes the second-to-last mistake," he warned one of his rivals before starting the game. "If they ever outlaw chess, I'll become a criminal," he said to another, vehemently. "You can't live from chess, but you might die from it," he sighed from time to time. "Castling is the best path to an orderly life," he usually declared before saying goodnight and going to bed. During the day, he locked himself up in his cabin with a travel board and spent his time analyzing papers covered with glyphs, while his wife entertained herself in the first-class dining room or in the party room talking with the other passengers and with crew members, especially Vicente Holgado, who at thirty years of age and with his dapper garb produced sighs among the young (and not-so-young) ladies onboard.

"Keep an eye on your friend," Savielly said to Pablo one day, after ordering his umpteenth vodka. "My wife is very dangerous."

Savielly had chosen Pablo as his personal waiter since the night when a more-than-usual rocking of the boat had scattered his chess pieces while he was waging an interesting game against a little old man with a white beard bearing a certain resemblance to Sigmund Freud. Pablo had just served him a vodka and had grown absorbed watching the game, when the boat gave a sudden lurch, scattering drinks and pieces. Savielly's pants were soaked, so he retired to his cabin to change in order to continue the game. When he returned to the lounge, he was surprised to see that the pieces were set up in exactly the same position they had been in before the upheaval:

"I see that you have a good memory," he said to the old man with the white beard.

"It wasn't me," confessed the man, pointing to Pablo, "It was the youngster."

Indeed, Pablo had picked up the spilled glasses and ashtrays, as well as the chessmen, putting them back in their spots on the board.

"Commendable," the master nodded, looking at him with curiosity. "Do you know how to play chess, or do you have a photographic memory?"

Pablo did not really understand the question, so he merely replied:

"I learned to play when I was a boy, with my father."

From that day forward, Savielly requested that it should be Pablo who brought his vodkas to his cabin, and, in addition to good tips, he plied him with a few master lessons in chess, adorned with this and that memorable aphorism. And when they finally spotted Long Island, and the Statue of Liberty greeted them with her torch held high, Savielly gave him his travel chessboard, with a dedication scrawled on the back: "Someday, if I become world champion, this board will be worth its weight in gold. Warmly, S.T." Under the signature he had stamped his particular ex libris, a little coffee mill, a symbol of how he planned to grind up all of his rivals.

The *Victoria* was moored for three days at the mouth of New York's East River, to resupply before it continued on its way to Buenos Aires. At that time New York was a city seething with life, receiving constant arrivals of boats stuffed with Italian, Jewish, and Eastern European immigrants brought to Ellis Island, where, after a Darwinian selection process, their fate was decided: only the strongest could stay, while the elderly, the lame, and the nearsighted were marked with a stamp bearing the humiliating initials L.P.C. ("Liable to become a Public Charge"), to be sent home as quickly as possible. While the government was wasting its jail cells on campaigns against public spitting, the country was filling up with wretches and beggars. Thus, the third-class passengers of the *Victoria* were loaded onto pontoon boats bound for Ellis Island, while those in second class were interrogated by officials of the immigration service and inspected by doctors to certify their health before they were allowed to disembark; the first-class passengers, on the other hand, merely had to give their word that they met the legal requirements. Finally, those crew members of the *Victoria* who wished to get off the boat had their papers confiscated just in case they got the idea to stay in New York, in the spirit of the old saying: opportunity makes the thief.

When Pablo and Vicente finally set foot on terra firma they felt something like the opposite of seasickness: the impressive equilibrium of the concrete blocks holding up the gangway nearly pitched them to the ground. Then, little by little, they got used to it and walked toward the center of Manhattan. The imposing skyscrapers of Wall Street, the dangerous streets of Chinatown, and the immensity of Central Park left a great impression on them. But Vicente Holgado did not come to America for sightseeing, and it did not take him long to make contact with the central core of the American anarchist movement, which had grown markedly since the nineties, after the arrival of many European immigrants with radical tendencies, people whom President Theodore Roosevelt had called "enemies of humanity," forbidding them entry into the country shortly before leaving office. That same afternoon, after the depths of the island to experience for the first time the wormlike feeling of riding in a subway, they went to Greenwich Village, where an old friend of Vicente's was living after having fled from Madrid following the attack by Mateo Morral. When he opened the door, Pablo recognized in this man the pocky, pale journalist from the Café Pombo, the former writer from *Tierra y Libertad* whom he had met the night before the royal wedding.

"My dear Vicente Holgado!" the man exclaimed, sticking out his neck like a plucked duck.

"My dear Pepín Gómez!" replied Vicente.

And they embraced. Then they had a glass of wine to celebrate the reunion and went to the Café Boulevard, in the East Village, where that night the Sunrise Club had invited the famous activist Emma Goldman to give a talk. Goldman was the former lover of the equally famous Alexander Berkman, the same man who years before had awakened the anarchistic conscience in an adolescent named Pablo Martín Sánchez. When they arrived, she had already started her speech, and Pablo was surprised by the vitality of this tiny bespectacled woman who spoke with equal passion about the dramas of Ibsen, the anarchist commitment, and the hypocrisy of puritanism, flying the banner of sexual freedom as the standard of the feminist movement.

"Marriage and love have nothing to do with each other: they are as distant as the poles," she was saying at that moment, as Pepín Gómez translated for his Spanish friends. "It is friendship, not marriage, that should govern human relations. Two of my former lovers are in attendance here today, and what is it that still binds us all together? The love of humanity, the ideal of a better future in which men and women no longer establish relationships of servitude. Yes, yes, I said servitude: the prostitute who puts a price on her services is more free than the downtrodden wife who marries to serve her husband for a lifetime!"

The silence in the café turned into a buzz more exciting than applause.

"Why is it that you cannot accept your own freedom?" she continued. "Why do you have to chain yourself to another person to survive?"

But this was the last bit that the former contributor to *Tierra y Libertad* could translate, because the people nearby hushed him. In any case, Pablo was no longer listening, because the final words had stirred up two distant memories: on the one hand, Robinsón's ideas about free love, and on the other, what Ferdinando Fernández had said at the office of *El Castellano*, quoting Berkman himself: The only love that a revolutionary can allow himself is the love of humanity. And between one thing and another, he could not keep himself from thinking about Angela. Only when the speech was finished did he emerge from his reverie.

"Come on," Pepín said, standing up, "I'm going to introduce you to Emma Goldman."

When they reached her, "the most dangerous woman in America" (as FBI founder J. Edgar Hoover would later describe her) was already surrounded by friends and admirers, enjoying the glaring absence of the blue coats of the police. But when she learned that two anarchists recently arrived from Spain wanted to meet her, she excused herself and went to greet them:

"Welcome to the USA, amigos!" she gushed, extending her chubby hand for a vigorous handshake. Under her arm she held several copies of her book *Anarchism and Other Essays*, which sold like hotcakes after these gatherings, and a little treatise in French titled *Petit manuel anarchiste individualiste*, by Emile Armand, because she was so used to being arrested after her speeches that she came prepared with quality reading for the jail cell. Emma Goldman had closely followed the trial of Ferrer Guàrdia and never missed a chance to bring up the subject whenever she met someone from Europe.

"What news do you bring me from the land of Ferrer?" she asked in English, and Pepín translated for her.

"The last we heard before we left," responded Vicente, "was that someone tried to assassinate the king as revenge for what they did to Francisco."

"Very good," Goldman replied.

"I saw them shoot Ferrer with my own eyes," Pablo started to say, but at that moment an elderly Alexander Berkman appeared and swept the star attraction away, under the pretext that they had to travel to Denver the next day. Two years later, at the same venue, for the first time in America, Emma Goldman would explain to an audience of six hundred how to use a contraceptive, earning herself an arrest and several days in jail.

"You never told me about the Ferrer Guàrdia thing," Vicente reproached Pablo as they were leaving the Café Boulevard, while Pepín led them back home. "Did you really see the firing squad?"

"You and I really don't know much about each other, Vicente," Pablo defended himself. "I only know that you once saved my life, and that we once went to see the Lumière Cinematograph together, back when nobody knew what it was."

They both smiled, and Pablo's mind started reliving the scene at Montjuic Castle, until Pepín Gómez stopped in front of a building lit up with red lights, its façade plastered with a poster bearing an image of a young woman with golden curls, under a sign proclaiming "America's Sweetheart." Pablo looked up and wondered what Emma Goldman would think about these new film actresses who were starting to light up the torrid dreams of the American male.

"What say we check out Mary Pickford?" he ventured.

But the other two were already gone from his side, at the ticket booth digging coins from their pockets.

20

One of the detainees was brought to the barracks of the carabiniers. He did not mention that he was injured, but over the course of the afternoon it was discovered that he had a bullet wound in his leg. He was brought to the hospital, where he was examined. His thigh had been pierced by a bullet.

El Pueblo Navarro, 11 November 1924

THE INTELLIGENT GRAY EYES OF Julián Santillán, the gray-haired former civil guardsman, take some time to adjust to the darkness of the cell. When they finally do, he recognizes his cellmate. They greet each other silently, and Pablo offers him his spot on the bedroll so that he can relax for a bit, but Santillán declines by shaking his head.

"Those sons of bitches didn't take you to the hospital?" he asks, remembering the bullet Pablo took in the skirmish. But it is Splitface who responds:

"Silence in there, goddammit! The next one to open his mouth gets it shut permanently!"

And the two men have to wait until lunchtime before they are able to exchange a few words, though silence in company is doubly unbearable. It is two in the afternoon when they hear footsteps on the stairs, followed by the smell of burnt food that somehow overcomes the reigning stench, permeating through the cracks in the doors.

"Royal fare for these rats," protests the guard when he sees a pair of his colleagues enter with a large steaming pan, following two others armed with rifles. "I'd give them nothing but bread and water to teach 'em a lesson."

The carabiniers talk amongst themselves while the mess is served on plates made of peeling iron, the rust mixing with the food in those spots where the original enamel has flaked away. Pablo and Santillán take advantage of the noise and chatter to exchange a few words in hushed voices:

"What a goddamn disaster," Pablo murmurs.

"Don't lose hope," Julián tries to console him. "When the revolution succeeds, they'll come get us out of here, you'll see. Do you know if more of us have been arrested?"

Pablo nods in the darkness:

"There were already people in the cells when I arrived, I assume that they're our guys. And I thought I saw Casiano upstairs. Also, if they've started putting us two to a cell, there must be a reason—"

"Clearly."

"Not to mention that they might be bringing some of us to the Civil Guard barracks."

"Let's hope not," whispers Santillán knowingly, having seen how his former colleagues tend to treat prisoners, sometimes shackling detainees to the wall with cruel, short chains so that the prisoner cannot lie down on the ground, can barely change position at all.

Soon they hear the sharp sound of a trapdoor opening and the jailer's voice ordering the prisoner in the first cell to step back from the door. It seems they are starting to distribute lunch.

"Hey, it was Leandro and Julián who came with you, right?" Pablo asks rhetorically.

"The Argentino and the kid, yeah," nods Santillán.

"Did they catch you all together?"

"Yeah, we were about to cross the border when two pairs of carabiniers showed up. We hid in an abandoned mine, but the bastards saw us go in and waited outside to hunt us like rabbits—"

"Silence, I said!" bellows Splitface, as cell number 6's mess hatch opens. "Get back from the door!"

Two plates enter, one after the other, sliding along the floor pushed by a rifle barrel and accompanied by bread crusts and rusty spoons. Still steaming on the plates is a stew of indiscernible color, holding various chunks vaguely resembling cabbage and potato, which the prisoners devour with insatiable voracity.

"You can keep the plates and spoons in your cells to keep you company," the guard tells them, growing hoarse with so much shouting. "You shitbags are gonna start thinking we're your maidservants. Oh, and I recommend you hold your bowels until tonight, because we only empty the latrines once a day around here. Wouldn't want you thinking this is the Ritz."

The prisoners empty their plates in silence, wiping them with the last little bits of bread. But while many of them are still hungry afterward, no one dares to protest, not even Leandro or Santillán, who are not used to biting their tongues. Maybe they think that it won't do any good, maybe they're still smarting from the rifle butts and they don't want a second helping of kidney pain. Some try to sleep to regain their strength, but despite their fatigue, their digestion, and the darkness, few of them manage: it is a well-known fact that Morpheus does not gather those with a troubled conscience into his arms.

Not even a half an hour has passed when another detainee is brought in, under the charge of the same two young carabiniers who brought in Pablo this morning.

"You missed lunch. Should have been more punctual," Splitface sneers at him, barely able to hide how much he enjoys tormenting the prisoners.

The new one is one of those who crossed the border with the group led by Bonifacio Manzanedo, Juan José Anaya, a baker from Madrid with a certain resemblance to Douglas Fairbanks, who just starred in the American film *The Thief of Bagdad* and is already a celebrity, especially after marrying Mary Pickford.

"Empty your pockets and put everything on the table," the guard recites begrudgingly or grumpily, tired of repeating the same thing over and over and annoyed that no one has come to relieve him. "Look at Mr. Revolutionary," he appears to cheer up when he sees the detainee put a silver cigarette case on table. "I'd like to know who you stole that from. And what's this? Let's see ... *Oh là là!*" he exclaims à la française when Anaya takes from his pocket a newspaper clipping showing a photograph of the Italian anarchist Mario Castagna with a patch over his eye. But his joking mood suddenly evaporates when the carabiniers frisk the Madrileño and discover in the lining of his coat a recipe for making explosives. "Well I'll be damned! Where should we put this son of a bitch?"

"In cell number 3, with prisoner Tomás García," replies the beardless carabinier, after consulting some papers collected in the interrogation room.

"Put him in the hole!"

But the unexpected voice of Lieutenant Feliciano Suárez, investigating judge of the facts, leaves them all petrified:

"One moment!" he says, entering the guardroom, the stench of which turns his face to a disgusted grimace, followed by the stenographer and a short, tubby man buried under a tripod and various pieces of photography equipment. "We are going to proceed to the anthropometric profiles," he explains snootily, "and, given the circumstances, we decided it would be better to do it here so we don't have to bring the prisoners up and down. Any objections?"

"No, sir," mutters Splitface, "whatever you say."

"Understood, then. And you?" he asks the chubby little man, who has already started to unload his gear. "Can you shoot them in these conditions?"

"I guess so, if there's no other way—"

"Then get on with it, get to work. Start with this one," he says, pointing at the newcomer, "and then go on to the others. And you, Gutiérrez," he finally says to the stenographer, whom he is leaving in charge of monitoring the operation, "come up and tell me when they're done. If any other prisoners arrive in the meantime, I'll send for you."

Having spoken, he leaves the dungeon quickly, like a pearl diver returning to the surface after a few minutes holding his breath underwater, trusting that the photographs, once developed, will be the finishing touch on the brilliant anthropometric profiles, in which, after noting the detainees' names and those of their parents, as well as the date and place of birth, profession, and current address, Don Feliciano will write the description that he finds most fitting for these men: "*Pistoleros*."

The short, chubby photographer removes his beret and places it on the table. His fingers, marked with magnesium chloride burns, show surprising dexterity as they mount the tripod and set up the photographic camera, a German Voigtländer from the Great War. Then he takes out a leather pouch and pours some flammable white powder on a metallic strip, which has a handle and a tinder starter.

"Stand with your back to the wall," he says to Juan José Anaya, who with his Hollywood leading man looks is the most appropriate to start the photography session, despite being in the sights of two carabiniers who would be glad to gun him down. "Very good, don't move."

And then, as he pushes the button triggering his Voigtländer with his right hand, he activates the tinderbox with his left, igniting the magnesium powder and producing an intense flash, which penetrates through the cracks in the cell walls, followed by a cloud of smoke and the strong smell of burnt magnesium. A few ashes float in the air, falling gently like black snowflakes.

"Very good. Turn for a profile shot," says the portly little man, unperturbed and with unquestionable professionalism, as he reloads the film. And barely giving Douglas Fairbanks time to strike a prisoner's pose, the camera shoots again. The plates will memorialize him with his hair smooth and short at the temples, fleshy lips, a regal nose, and pointed chin, dressed in a thick coat hiding a blood-soaked shirt.

Ashes are still floating when they put Anaya in cell number 3, without a bedroll or a blanket, and at the same time bring out his cellmate, Tomás García from Zaragoza, who appears with his hair disheveled and his lips puckered, bundled in a jacket and with a handkerchief around his neck. He is immortalized in two photos before being returned to his cage. After him, starting with cell number 1, the process continues: Vázquez Bouzas, who will pass into posterity stooping, his gaze distant, with his pencil-thin mustache and his incipient baldness, dressed in a pale waist-coat and tie; Francisco Lluch, the deserter from Asturias, with prominent jaw and nose, furrowed brow, dark suit and tie; Justo Val, a wiry, lazy-eyed laborer from Huesca, wearing an overcoat and a knit sweater, sharing a cell with Leandro Fernández, our hulking Argentine, who cannot stop himself from provoking Splitface when they take him out of his pigsty, with his preternatural cheekiness:

"If it turns out good, you'll have to send me a copy at home," he says to the photographer, perhaps knowing that the guard will show some restraint in the presence of Don Feliciano's secretary.

After Leandro comes the young Eustaquio García from Soria, who has caught the contagious sadness and affliction of his cellmate, the even younger Julián Fernández Revert, Julianín to his friends, whom the camera captures with his head tilted, perhaps under the weight of his pain. Then comes Pablo, more pallid than usual. After him, Julián Santillán and the two from Villalpando: Casiano Veloso, with his musketeer's coiffure, his goatee and eyebags ever more pronounced, and Ángel Fernández, who will give the photographer his clear eyes, aquiline nose, and an unbelievable toupee that appears to be trying to leap from his head. But by this time, Pablo will no longer be in the prison, because he has suddenly fallen to the floor with the second magnesium flash.

"And now what's got into this one?" a surly Splitface demands, approaching with disdain. "Hey, you," he says to the beardless carabinier, "bring me a pitcher of cold water, I think this one's fainted."

"I told you he needs a doctor," the youth dares to respond.

"Shut your mouth and bring me some water!" shouts the guard.

And so it is that they discover the bullet wound through Pablo's right leg, which, although it will get him out of the dungeon to be transferred to the Hospital of Mercy, it will also end up being the straight line that is the shortest distance between his fate and the scaffold.

THE HOSPITAL OF MERCY IS AN aging, dilapidated building, located right next door to the Civil Guard barracks and run by selfless nuns who serve as nurses. It has limited resources and lacks modern facilities, but at least the rooms give onto a small garden where the song of starlings gives hope to the hearts of the convalescents. It is almost five in the afternoon when Pablo arrives at the hospital, having recovered from his fainting spell but obviously limping, in handcuffs, and in the charge of two carabiniers. Passing through the main entrance, he immediately hears bloodcurdling screams in a voice he recognizes, coming from the opposite wing of the building, like a delayed echo from the quarry of Argaitza:

"Give me a pistol to blow my brains out!" Bonifacio Manzanedo is shouting over and over, unsoothed by the nuns' morphine or gentle smiles.

They bring Pablo through the building toward the source of the shrieking. On the way he passes various carabiniers, and one of them tries to throttle him, taking the law into his own hands; this is the brother of Pedro Prieto, the carabinier injured this morning between markers 40 and 41 when he tried to arrest four of the revolutionaries who finally managed to cross the border. Prieto survived by the skin of his teeth—three bullets hit his body: one in the thigh, another in the stomach, and a third in the left nipple, which, entering obliquely, was miraculously stopped by the tobacco tin in his breast pocket after tearing through his uniform. The carabiniers take the enraged brother away, and Pablo continues his way toward the spacious room where Bonifacio Manzanedo is howling for a pistol. It seems that they want to put all of the injured insurrection-ists together, either to be able to control them better or so that they will drown together in their misfortune.

When the former typesetter of La Fraternelle enters the room, Bonifacio's shrieking suddenly stops, but only for a fraction of a second. Their eyes meet just long enough for them to recognize each other and to tacitly agree that it is better if they do not speak. Although at this point, both of them injured by rifle bullets courtesy of Spain's finest, they have little left to hide.

They lie Pablo down in a bed with sheets so white that he almost feels bad dirtying them with blood and mud and grime and sweat. They free one of his hands from the handcuffs only to attach the other to the head of the bed, and a guard remains to keep an eye on him. The contact between his body and the mattress, despite the hardness of the latter, appears to alleviate the pain while he awaits the arrival of Dr. Gamallo, to the background music of the wailing and lamentations of Bonifacio Manzanedo. On the wall next to the bed, an onlooking figure of Christ acts as a watchman, leaning over Pablo as though he were trying to leap down from his cross to cure all of his ills with his holy embrace.

"Good afternoon," says Dr. Gamallo entering the room, followed by two sister nurses dragging and shuffling their feet. But before he examines Pablo, the doctor goes to Bonifacio's bed, and without mincing words tells him the terrible news: "Listen well, Manzanedo: we have no choice but to amputate your right leg. The bullet has shattered the bone and it risks becoming gangrenous, which could kill you."

Contrary to what you might think, the doctor's words quiet the man down, as though the news were a form of anesthesia. Meanwhile, the actual anesthesia is in the hands of one of the nurses, in the form of a hypodermic needle about to be injected.

"This is what's best for you," Dr. Gamallo continues, placing his hand on the injured man's shoulder in an affectionate farewell, as is customary.

"Also, you should thank God that we were able to save your other leg."

Bonifacio releases a sob as the nurse jabs his thigh. Dr. Gamallo then goes over to Pablo's bed. He is an elegant man, with a friendly, intelligent look, an ample mane of white hair, and a yellowing beard. The fatigue of a long day of hard work is visible on his face—the mayor of Vera dragged him from his bed in the middle of the night to tell him that a posse of revolutionaries had entered the village and had battled the Civil Guard.

"Let's see, what have we here," he says in greeting, gesturing to the nuns to remove the patient's trousers and underpants. "Well, well, it looks as though you've already been treated."

Judging by Dr. Gamallo's grimace, there seems to be an unpleasant odor emanating from the wound when they remove the dressings from Pablo's leg.

"Mmm. So they made a poultice of horsetail, did they? Apparently your companions knew what they were doing. It's a marvelous plant for stopping bleeding. But it was not enough. The wound is infected," says the doctor, clicking his tongue. "Let's see, bend your knee. That's it. Aha. Good, good, it looks like you're in luck. The bullet went through your thigh without hitting the bone, otherwise you'd be singing a duet with Manzanedo. Why didn't you come sooner, good man?"

But Pablo makes no reply.

"Wash the wound thoroughly and put extra ointment on the exit wound, here in the inguinal region—the infection is worse there," Dr. Gamallo instructs the nuns. "Change his dressings every two hours and give him morphine if necessary. I'll come by after dinner to see if we can release him. Oh, and also treat those sores from the handcuffs on his wrists."

The two women assent solicitously and the doctor says goodbye to Pablo by placing his hand on his shoulder, then starts to leave with the intention of going to the operating room to prepare for the amputation of Bonifacio's leg. But before he can make it through the door, shouting is heard from the yard, and two carabiniers burst into the room dragging a man with a dirty, bloody bandage on his head that fails to hide the unmistakable romantic coiffure of the corpse-like Gil Galar:

"*Ne me touchez pas! Ne me touchez pas!*" he rants in French. "*Je suis un citoyen de la France, moi!*"

"Come on, move along, you liar," a walleyed brute of a carabinier urges him forward. "A dog, a dog is what you are," he says, giving him a smack.

"There, there, calm down, please," Dr. Gamallo intervenes. "What's wrong with this man?"

"It's another one of the rebels, Doctor," explains the walleyed guardsman. "We found him in Echalar, hiding in a shed. Apparently the dimwit somehow managed to cross the border, but not knowing the terrain he accidentally crossed back into Spain. Now he wants us to believe he's a Frenchman, the dirty dog—"

"It's fine, it's fine," Gamallo cuts him off. "Put him in this bed over here, and I'll examine him right away. And treat him with some decency, for God's sake. He's not an animal."

The doctor goes out and then after a few minutes he returns accompanied by two men with a gurney who take Bonifacio Manzanedo away, clinging to the hand of one of the nuns, whom he begs not to leave him alone while they saw off his leg. For his part, Gil Galar continues ranting and raving in French, trying to explain to the walleyed carabinier that he has nothing to do with the attack, that he has come from France to look for work and that he doesn't even know these two injured men next to him. In the midst of this chaos, Pablo remains silent, as a nun treats his injury and Christ keeps looking down from his crucifix, wondering how he got wrapped up in this mess.

After dinner, with Gil Galar sedated in the bed (they had to remove the bullet that was lodged behind his ear, not without some difficulty) and Bonifacio Manzanedo recovering in the operating room, Doctor Gamallo approaches Pablo's bed, ready to discharge him.

"How are those injuries?" he asks him quietly in greeting. Pablo answers with a question:

"Fine, thank you, but do you think I could stay the night here, Doctor?"

And although Agustín Gamallo has received specific orders not to keep injured rebels in the hospital unless absolutely necessary, either humanity or the deontological code outweighs the military orders:

"It's fine, you can stay, I'll write a report asking permission to keep you tonight under observation. But you should know that in a few minutes we're going to bring Manzanedo back in here, and that Gil's sedation will soon wear off, so I don't know how well you're going to sleep with two howling roommates. In any case, get some rest while you can, because I'm quite afraid you have some difficult days ahead."

Pablo thanks him with a sincere smile, and thinks that maybe with such men, all is not lost in his dear embattled Spain. Then he notes the devoted nuns and remembers Friar Toribio, the Franciscan who cured other injuries of his so many years ago. Ironies of life, he says to himself, that the salvation of an atheist lies in the hands of the clergy. And before falling asleep, he thinks about the places he has spent the recent nights: a cemetery, a brothel, a jail cell, and a hospital.

XVIII
(1913–1914)

AFTER THE STOP IN NEW YORK, the *Victoria* continued southward, with Pablo and Vicente onboard making future plans. Both of them would have liked to stay in New York, but the immigration service would not have made it easy for them. So they consoled themselves thinking that Argentina was a land full of opportunities:

"The comrades of the FORA are based in Buenos Aires," said Vicente as soon as they embarked, showing off his mental world map marked with black flags.

"What's the FORA?" asked Pablo, less versed in international anarchism.

"The *Federación Obrera Regional Argentina*," Vicente recited. "Pepín told me to go there and ask for a Spanish fellow by the name of Rocafú, who can introduce us around in the movement and find us some work."

Their first stopover was in Havana, the second in Puerto Cabello, and shortly thereafter they crossed the equator, a pretext for a raucous party among the first-class passengers, with a dance and a masquerade ball, which nearly ended in tragedy: Vicente Holgado seduced the daughter of a wealthy rancher from Rosario, and he couldn't think of anything better to do at the end of the party than to consecrate the flirtation in one of the lifeboats. But the ring bolt fastening the aft of the dinghy gave out under the strain, and they nearly fell into the sea to be swallowed by the waves. The young woman's cries caught the attention of those few passengers who were still on deck, and the stunned lovers were rescued, but were not spared punishment for their outrageous behavior: the girl was confined to her cabin for the rest of the trip (under the pretext of a terrible headache) and Vicente was demoted from the first-class waitstaff, assigned to clean the latrines in third class for the rest of the voyage.

Before arriving in Buenos Aires, they made stops in Recife and Rio de Janeiro, where Pablo tried to find out if what his father had told him was true: in the Southern Hemisphere water spirals down the drain in the opposite direction as in the Northern Hemisphere. Unfortunately, he found it impossible to test it, because he had forgotten which direction water spirals in Spain. Then, as they grew nearer to Río de la Plata, they started to feel the onset of the austral winter. And when the tugboats dragged the *Victoria* toward the wharf at Puerto Madero, Pablo and Vicente went up to the bridge to tell the captain that they planned to stay in Argentina. The man took a few quick puffs on his Cuban cigar, while rubbing his hands together for warmth and shifting his weight from one foot to the other.

"I knew it," he sighed. "You little Spaniards always do this to me."

He paid them what he owed them and wished them good luck.

IT WAS NOT EASY TO GAIN the trust of the anarchists of Buenos Aires. The Argentinian government had conducted a brutal policy of repression three years beforehand in response to the assassination of the police chief, Ramón Lorenzo Falcón, at the hands of the young Ukrainian Simón Radowitzky, who was seeking revenge for the bloody repression of the so-called Red Week; but now, after a period of clandestine operation, the Argentinian anarchists who had not landed in the prison of Ushuaia were starting to surface again, little by little, and did not want to have to go back into hiding on account of the arrival of more trigger-happy European exiles. What is curious is that Pablo's disembarkation in Buenos Aires was the end result of a chain reaction set off by the tossing of the bomb at the chief of police: 1) emergency order requiring the deportation of nearly three hundred foreigners under the Residency Law; 2) among the deportees is the Spaniard Manuel Pardiñas; 3) Pardiñas returns to Spain; 4) Prime

Minister Canalejas is assassinated by Pardiñas in Puerta del Sol; 5) Pardiñas gets his name in all the newspapers and inspires the film starring Pepe Isbert; 6) Pablo discovers the way to get Angela's attention and decides to go to Madrid; 7) Pablo sees Angela, with daughter and husband, on Calle Alcalá, which interrupts his planned regicide; 8) Pablo flees the capital with an old acquaintance, Vicente Holgado; 9) after crossing the border into France, they decide to travel to America; and 10) they arrive in Buenos Aires and the anarchists of the FORA receive them with suspicion, because the Radowitzky mess is still fresh in their minds, and everyone knows that in Spain someone has (once again) tried to bump off Alfonso XIII.

Nevertheless, when Pablo and Vicente disembark in Puerto Madero, they have an ace up their sleeve that will ultimately open the door to the inner circle of Argentine anarchism: a letter signed by Pepín Gómez and addressed to the attention of Ataúlfo Fernández, aka "Rocafú."

Rocafú had been born in a farmhouse on the Catalan coast, in the municipality of Premiá, but very close to Teiá, where he shared a school desk with the one and only Ferrer Guàrdia, in one of life's little coincidences that are not so coincidental after all. At eighteen years of age, fleeing an arrest order issued against him in Barcelona, he filled his suitcase with more ideals than clothing and managed to cross the Atlantic as a stowaway on a cargo ship. And although he was now living as a retiree in the town of General Rodríguez, together with his wife and the youngest of his five sons, among the anarchists of Argentina he still enjoyed the prestige that he had earned as one of the founders of the first anarchist journal in the country, *El Descamisado*, and as a member of the group of the mythical Errico Malatesta, who a quarter of a century before, during his exile in the New World, had organized an expedition to the south of Patagonia to find gold and foment the anarchist movement. The undertaking ended up a fiasco, but at least it served to propagate anarchist ideals and to lay the necessary groundwork for the birth of the FORA, Argentina's largest labor federation, dominated by anarchists, the general secretary of which was now looking at the two Spaniards who had entered his office asking for Rocafú. The walls were hung with a great number of newspaper clippings, and Pablo could not keep from smiling when looking at one of the most yellowed of them, documenting Malatesta's arrival in Buenos Aires: underlined in graphite, there was a sentence that the Italian had borrowed from Josiah Warren, the same saying Pablo had scrawled on the cathedral of Salamanca, earning him his first arrest: "Every man should be his own government, his own law, his own church."

"So you have a letter for Don Ataúlfo," said the secretary of the FORA looking at the envelope that Vicente was holding. "He doesn't come here very often. His health has been a bit precarious lately. But if you give me the letter, I'll make sure it gets to him."

"We prefer to give it to him in person," Vicente declined the offer.

"As you wish, but in that case you'll have to go to Once and take the train to General Rodríguez."

"Is that very far?" Pablo asked.

"About fifty kilometers."

The station of Once was a neo-Renaissance-style building, new and imposing, with an opulence that contrasted with the pack of "whelps" hanging around outside, those shoeless, half-naked boys stinking of the orphanage and crying out to sell newspapers. Vicente, seeing them, remembered his childhood as a newsboy in the streets of Madrid, and he shook his head bitterly. They boarded the train and crossed the suburbs of Buenos Aires, until the landscape opened up to countryside. When they reached General Rodríguez, they asked around for directions to the house of Don Ataúlfo. His wife, Graciela, opened the door for them and invited them into the bedroom, where they found Rocafú smoking in bed, wrapped in a wool sweater that he wore to keep from catching cold, although the weave was so thin that tufts of white hair poked out everywhere. He wore glasses without frames and a beard in the style of Proudhon, jumbled and unruly like a swarm of bees. Seeing them enter, he welcomed them with a few lines of revolutionary poetry:

"'What a joy to listen / to the anarchist troubadour / who gives a sideways glance / with a certain look of horror. / If joy comes to your face / when he tells you who we are / then in the name of anarchy / he greets you with amour,'" he recited in a hoarse voice and a peculiar Spanish accent, getting up from bed to extend to them a withered, chapped hand with elephantine skin. "Do you know those verses?"

Pablo and Vicente shook their heads, but it was Graciela who spoke:

"These men are from Spain, Ataúlfo. They have come to see you."

"Oh, what an honor! So they will want to know how the poem ends: 'We are those anarchists / that they call assassins / because we urge the worker / to seek his liberty. / Because when they oppress us / we turn against the tyrants / and we always rebel / against all authority.' Let's see, let's see. What news do you bring me from my dear Spain?"

There were two photographs over the head of the bed: in the first, a young Rocafú was embracing Errico Malatesta, who was holding in his free hand an enormous block of ice; in the second, he was looking proud with Graciela on their wedding day, in one of the first civil weddings ever performed in the country. Though surely Emma Goldman would have made a disapproving face.

"Not much from Spain," said Vicente, "but we have a letter for you from New York."

"A letter? From New York? Let's see, let's see … Well would you look at that, it's a letter from Pepín! His father and I were great friends … Says here you boys want to try your fortune here in Argentina. I'll see what I can do. But first, we have to celebrate this meeting, that's what I say."

He went to the window, poked his head out and shouted:

"Leandro! Come here for a minute!"

A lad entered who couldn't have been more than fifteen years old, but tall and built like a brick house.

"Go get some firewood and stoke the fire. Let's brew up a nice bitter yerba maté for these Spanish friends."

So it was that Pablo and Vicente got to know the mythical Rocafú, who was soon able to find them some work: Pablo joined the linotype operators' union and within a few weeks started working at La Belladonna, an anarchist-leaning press directed by the Catalan Xavier Nicolau; Vicente, for his part, found work at the port as a stevedore and soon became one of the leaders of the union. They rented an apartment together on Calle Cayena, on the corner of San Martín, and for an entire year they actively participated in the debates held at the FORA, in the general strike of October, and in the protests against the new mandatory voting law, but they never stopped going up to General Rodríguez to visit Rocafú and his family. Well, at least Pablo never stopped; at the onset of spring, Vicente fell sway to the charms of a tango dancer and started spending his Sundays in more lustful pursuits.

"Why do they call you Rocafú?" Pablo asked Ataúlfo during one of his visits, when he finally had the confidence to speak to him personally.

Rocafú looked at him disconcertedly, as though he did not remember the origin of his nickname. But then his smile returned:

"It's been so long since anyone asked me, that I'd nearly forgotten... Do you see my son Leandro? When I arrived in Argentina I was like him: strong as a rock and full of fire. So they started calling me Ataúlfo Rocafuego; but these Argentinos are lazy, so it wasn't long before they had shortened it to Rocafú."

On another occasion, Pablo asked him, "Tell me about the expedition to Patagonia."

"Haven't I already told you about that?" Ataúlfo wondered, starting to doubt his own memories.

"Yes, but I like that story."

And then Rocafú told him for the umpteenth time about that adventure, which seemed like a story from a novel by Emilio Salgari: the surprising events of the ill-conceived expedition led by Malatesta, which ended at the Cape of the Virgins, where they built a hut and lived on seafood for a few weeks before returning to Buenos Aires with their tails between their legs and a story to tell until the end of their days.

"And did I already tell you the one about Quico?" he would usually ask.

Quico was Francisco Ferrer Guàrdia, his former schoolmate, whose death led Rocafú to perpetrate one of his great acts: the idea of declaring a general strike in Argentina in protest against Ferrer's assassination. And see if he didn't do just that: the FORA convened a meeting the very day of the execution, and some twenty thousand people attended, and the following day they began a general strike that would last for four days.

"It was the least we could do for a fellow worker," Rocafú would jest, before asking Pablo to recount the great educator's last moments.

On certain occasions, if Rocafú was feeling exuberant, he would take out his treasure chest: an old wooden trunk full of news clippings, including articles he himself had published in *El Descamisado* and in *La Protesta Humana*, under various pseudonyms. He would spread them out on the table and look at them like one looks at a newborn child, and then let out a sigh of nostalgia, followed by one of those questions that implicitly contain their own answer:

"Isn't anarchy a philosophical theory, Pablo? Isn't an anarchist simply one who believes that it's possible to live without the principle of authority?"

But sometimes it also happened that Pablo would arrive at General Rodríguez and Rocafú would be indisposed or still sleeping, and then he would chat with Graciela, who had been one of the first schoolteachers in Argentina to teach about anatomy and sexuality in her classes, or he would play soccer with Leandro in the courtyard, a sport that was already inspiring fervent passion in Argentina, and which they played by making balls out of old, rolled-up underwear, throwing their shirts on the ground to serve as goalposts.

And so summer came, and then autumn, and little by little Pablo found his place in this family which had welcomed him like a son, as he tried, though it was impossible to forget Angela, at least not to get a knot in his stomach every time he thought about her. Sometimes he received happy news from Spain, but as often as not it left a bad taste in his mouth, such as the day he received a letter from his sister announcing that the law student had kept his promise, and she was now a married woman. Not that he wasn't glad, but that he regretted not being able to share those happy moments with her. So sometimes he felt like what he was: an exile, a refugee, a fugitive. And when he received news that Julia was pregnant, he started to think about going home. Perhaps it was too soon to be able to live in Spain without the risk of being arrested, but he could settle in France and make a quick trip to see his family. Surely Robinsón would welcome him with open arms to his commune in Lyon. Also, it would sure be nice to see him, by God.

However, it was the death of Rocafú that pushed him over the edge in his decision to return to Europe. The old anarchist's health had been deteriorating recently, especially with the arrival of winter; he had a hard time breathing and developed worrisome gaps in his memory. One morning in early July, Pablo went up to General Rodríguez and found Graciela in a state of despair: her husband had gone out for a walk the previous afternoon and still had not returned home. Just when they were ready to go to the commissariat to report his disappearance, it was the police who came knocking on the door, bringing (as always at that house) bad news: Rocafú had been found dead in a hotel in Buenos Aires, from a bullet to the temple. He had left a fifty-peso bill on the bedside table, along with a note saying: "For the management, in case the bullet goes through my skull and damages the wall." And in the pocket of his blazer, on the heart side, they found a long letter written to his wife and children, in which he asked them for forgiveness for any harm he might have caused them in his life or in this final act of liberation, which he hoped they would understand:

Someone once said that all that is necessary for evil to triumph is for good people to do nothing. Since I can no longer do anything and I've become nothing but a burden, I leave way for the youth who want to take the reins of this struggle, which belongs to me and to all humanity. I love you, like no one has ever loved anyone before, your husband and father and friend:

Ataúlfo Fernández, "Rocafú"

The day of the burial, Pablo spoke with Vicente and told him he was going back to Europe. A week later, he boarded a steamship of the Hamburg America Line, the *König Wilhelm II*, after going to General Rodríguez to say goodbye to the distraught Graciela and her son Leandro, who since the death of his father seemed to have suddenly become a man:

"Che, don't forget to write us," said the youngster, taking Pablo aside. "Now I have to take care of Mama, but someday I'll come see you in Europe."

Pablo smiled and ruffled his hair, not imagining that Leandro would end up keeping his word. Then he took from his pocket an envelope with the FORA's handshake emblem and gave it to the lad.

"What's this?"

"See for yourself."

Opening the envelope, Leandro's eyes glowed: it was a photograph of his favorite soccer team, the Argentinos Juniors, signed by several of the players. The club was not yet playing in the first division, but it had many followers among anarchists, because it had been founded ten years before-hand by militant socialists and left libertarians who gave it the weighty name "The Chicago Martyrs" in homage to the five workers executed after the protests of May 1, 1886, to demand an eight-hour workday. When the lad lifted his eyes from the photograph, Pablo had disappeared.

On the wharf, he said goodbye to Vicente, and neither of them really knew what to say.

"Have a good trip," said Vicente.

"Take care," said Pablo.

With no further words, they embraced, each with a lump in his throat, perhaps suspecting that they would never see each other again. And they were not mistaken.

21

The expedition assigned to invade via Catalonia had no better luck: arriving in Perpignan the anarchists reunited in the outskirts of the city, and some of them crossed the border. It was at that time that the Gendarmerie, who had been informed of the plot by the Spanish police, decided to act: they detained twenty-two men from a party of thirty-eight insurgents armed with pistols, while the rest chose to disperse in disorder, and approximately fifty of them managed to reach the Pyrenees, where they were forced to retreat by the presence of various regiments, stationed all along the border with machine guns and artillery.

EDUARDO GONZÁLEZ CALLEJA,
El Máuser y el sufragio

IT IS STILL PITCH BLACK IN the picturesque village of Vera when, in the cold a.m. hours of Sunday, November 9, 1924, the shouts of Splitface awaken those prisoners who have managed to fall asleep. Today, the two civil guards who died in the skirmish, Aureliano Ortiz Madrazo and Julio de la Fuente Sanz, are going to be buried in graves 19 and 20 of the first parcel of the cemetery of Vera, but neither Pablo nor his thirteen fellow inmates are going to be here to hear the bells of the Church of Saint Stephen ring out in mourning, because Splitface's shouting is to announce that they will shortly be transferred. And we would do well to note that there are fourteen rebels, because in addition to those who had their photos taken on Friday afternoon, there are also two more who were arrested yesterday: Gregorio Izaguirre, a carpenter from Santurce residing in Paris, with a beard and a surly expression on his face, and Anastasio Duarte, whom we know from his participation in the revelry at Madame Alix's house, and for having sold himself out for a measly hit of cocaine. So only the most seriously injured (Bonifacio Manzanedo and Enrique Gil Galar, dutifully cared for in their beds at the Hospital of Mercy) will hear the tolling of the funeral bells which nearly the whole village of Vera will hear. Once the funeral is over, the Bishop of Pamplona, Monseñor Múgica, will come to the hospital with his miter still at the ready to give the holy sacraments to Manzanedo, who is in critical condition after the amputation of his leg. However, Bonifacio and Enrique will hear no bells for their friends Luís Naveira and Abundio Riaño, who will spend two more days in the municipal morgue, sleeping the eternal sleep on blocks of solid ice, until the undertakers undertake to give them a burial. The bells will not toll for them, because God's heart does not beat for those who commit suicide, nor for murderers, nor for unbaptized children: his clemency only offers them the shameful shelter of the commonest of graves.

The death of Abundio Riaño was especially controversial. After fleeing into the woods alone after the skirmish, El Maño wandered all night and part of the morning looking for refuge in the farmhouses he found along the way, where he offered money to anyone who would shelter and hide him. But they all turned him away, and some even refused to tell him what direction to go to get to France. Around noon he was found near marker 10 by the chief of the Civil Guard of Sunbilla, Trinidad Gastériz. Riaño tried to hide among the ferns, but when he heard them shout "Halt!" he had no choice but to raise his hands and surrender. However, the chief did not trust him and, thinking that it was a ruse (or maybe taking revenge for the death of his colleagues), he fired his Mauser rifle several times, with good aim, and the defenseless revolutionary took a bullet directly in the heart. Which does not explain why, to the forensic examiners' surprise, the body also had several injuries from hunting pellets. In any case, the bullet that pierced his heart first passed through a letter that Abundio was carrying in his breast pocket, a short letter addressed to his mother but never sent. It read:

Dear Mother, how are you? I'm doing well, don't worry about me. God willing, we will be able to see each other again soon, in a Spain that is new, different, free. Take care of yourself and my brothers, tell them that when I come to Zaragoza I will bring them lots of presents. With love and devotion, your son, Abundio.

The letter was written on the back of an advertisement for hair-restoring ointment.

For his part, Pablo was returned to the jail yesterday morning, after a night in the hospital that was much calmer than Dr. Gamallo had predicted, and he was placed back in cell number 6 with Julián Santillán. The day passed without incident until the arrival of the two new detainees, whom Splitface treated with the same disdain as all the others. The first to arrive was the carpenter Izaguirre, who was placed in the cell with Vázquez Bouzas, and then Anastasio was put in with Francisco Lluch, who lost his mind in the middle of the afternoon and started shouting that he was innocent, that he had done nothing, that he was being held in error. Splitface quieted him in his own manner, taking him out of the cell and giving him a thrashing that disburdened him of the desire to open his mouth, offering a perfect example of how problems are solved in this Spain of Primo de Rivera:

"Jesus Christ was innocent too, you son of a bitch, and he ended up on the cross kicking his feet!"

The sad thing is that if there is anyone innocent among the detained, it is precisely Francisco Lluch, the deserter who joined the revolutionary group with the sole aim of getting across the border in time to see his father's last breath.

After the evening ration and the emptying of the latrines, the fourteen inmates try to sleep, but in the middle of the dark, cold night, surprising even the sleeping roosters, they are roused from their cots and brought in pairs to the arches of the square in front of City Hall, where two Civil

Guard trucks are waiting to transfer them to the Provincial Prison of Pamplona. It is then that Leandro and Julianín discover that Pablo is also among the detained. As they are arriving in the square, they are loaded into the two vehicles like pigs to slaughter, their feet shackled to the benches and their hands to the metal bars supporting the canvas top of the paddy wagon. Three civil guards get into the cabin of the first truck, while only two get into the second, because they are also transporting a box with the weapons seized from the seditionists and the destroyed rifle of guardsman Ortiz, as legal evidence for the pretrial hearing that will soon be held. A vehicle full of carabiniers brings up the rear of the caravan, which sets out for Pamplona in the darkness, allowing the prisoners to talk to each other for the first time since they were arrested, with their voices partially hidden by the rumbling of the engines. The first truck contains those who were in the odd cells, and the second those from the even cells, but at the last moment, to even out the groups, Julianín has been transferred to the second wagon, where he finds his friends Pablo and Leandro, as well as the former guardsman Santillán, the deserter Francisco Lluch, the scrawny Justo Val, and Anastasio Duarte, who as soon as the journey is underway begins to cuss and try to bend the metal bar to which he is cuffed.

"Don't waste your energy," warns Santillán, who knows these trucks well. "It would take the strength of fifty men to break it."

Pablo and Leandro search for each other's eyes in the darkness, but it is their voices that find each other, separated only by the gaunt frame of Justo Val.

"Che, Pablo, I had hoped that at least you..." the Argentine starts, but leaves the sentence unfinished. "And Robinsón?"

"I don't know, I think he managed to escape, we were very close to the border when they caught me."

"Yeah, we almost made it, too. How's your leg?"

"Well, it could have been worse. And how are you, Julianín?" Pablo asks, unable to keep from feeling responsible for the boy in front of him.

"Fine," is all that his former assistant can respond, not bothering to protest the diminutive name.

"Does anyone know where they're taking us?" Justo Val chimes in, so emaciated that he looks like a ghost visiting from a two-dimensional world.

"I heard one of the guards saying that we're going to Pamplona," says Lluch.

"Then they're taking us to the Provincial Prison," Santillán deduces. "And not even God escapes from there."

The silence falls again like a heavy weight on the inmates, with the background music of the truck engine. Freezing air comes in through the gaps in the canvas, causing more than one man's teeth to chatter. Unexpectedly, it is Julianín who breaks the silence:

"If they are taking us to Pamplona it's because they're afraid someone will come to rescue us," stammers the former erratum hunter, who ever since he shot at the guards in the quarry of Argaitza had been unable to recover the courage that made him leave Paris.

"No, if they're transferring us to Pamplona it's because we didn't fit in that shithole anymore," opines Leandro, ever the pragmatist.

"If they're taking us to Pamplona," Santillán clarifies, "it's because they want to judge us as quickly as possible. And our only hope is that the revolution has been successful in Catalonia and is spreading throughout Spain."

"Ah, but haven't you heard?" pipes up Anastasio Duarte, who was the last detainee to arrive at the carabiniers' barracks. "The Perpignan party didn't even get across the border, and several of our boys were picked up in Saint-Jean-de-Luz, including Durruti."

"But what kind of crazy talk is that?" Leandro gets excited, and if his hands and feet were not tied he probably would be leaping on Anastasio, as he did when he was a child in his neighborhood of General Rodríguez when one of his friends insulted his mother.

"Are you sure about that?" asks Santillán.

"It's what I overheard from one of the officers who caught me yesterday in the woods."

"Then we're fucked."

Hopelessness falls like a guillotine on the prisoners, cutting off their desire to speak for the rest of the journey, because what Anastasio said is not far from the truth, both with regard to Perpignan and to the arrests in Saint-Jean-de-Luz. He does not know any more details, but what is sure is that the attempted revolution has been a total failure. To start, when Durruti, Vivancos, and another eight anarchists got off the train on Friday at dawn, the news that something serious had just happened in Vera had already made its way across the border and the police of Saint-Jean-de-Luz were at the ready, so they had to abandon the box of rifles they had checked from Paris. Durruti got angry when Juan Riesgo told him about what had happened, because by jumping the gun they had violated the most sacred, most fundamental rule: maximum coordination between the different rebel groups. But he did not have much time to complain, because as he was talking with Juan Riesgo and the other fellows who had arrived from Paris, they were discovered and detained by the French police, giving up without a fight. That same Friday, many of the rebels who fled after the skirmish and managed to cross the border before dawn were detained in the outskirts of Saint-Jean-de-Luz and other nearby settlements, such as Sarre, Ascain, and Hendaye. In all, more than twenty insurgents have fallen since then into the hands of the police and are waiting to be repatriated, although with a bit of luck they will convince the French authorities to deport them to Belgium before the Spanish government sends the extradition order. Among them is Robinsón, who was arrested tending to the ulcers on his feet at a spring near Ascain, but his greatest pain was having to be separated from his faithful Kropotkin, with whom he was already plotting another incursion into Spain to try to free Pablo. However, El Maestro is not to be found among the detainees; although he managed to cross the border with his bullet wound, he was discovered by the police next to a path between the stations of Urrugne and Saint-Jean-de-Luz; he lost his nerve, and tossed his life away beneath the rattling wheels of the express train from Paris.

Meanwhile, at the other end of the Pyrenees, in Perpignan, the news of what happened in Vera has come as a shock to Francisco Ascaso and the nearly two hundred men (and women) who were waiting for the definitive signal to cross the border to liberate the anarchists held in the penitentiary at Figueras. But it was probably them who acted too late, because that very Friday morning, while Pablo was being taken to the holding cell in Vera, there was a failed attempt to attack the Atarazanas barracks in Barcelona, perpetrated by Catalan anarchists, including Gregorio "El Chino" Jover. Various revolutionary groups met up around the fortress, waiting for some military men on the inside—men supposedly cooperating with the plot—to open the door for them. But no one opened the door, and the rebels started to get nervous, and then the police arrived and there was an intense firefight. The security guard Bruno López lost his life in the battle, and the anarchists Josep Llàcer and Juan Montejo were captured and are now waiting in the Modelo jail in Barcelona for their summary judgment scheduled for tomorrow, Monday the tenth of November, although we may as well skip ahead and mention that it will end with Llàcer and Montejo's necks in the garrote right there in the jail courtyard, the first spitting on his executioner and shouting "¡Viva la revolución!" and the second clutching a crucifix.

All this being the case, with the French and Spanish police alerted to what has happened in Vera and Barcelona, the hundreds of revolutionaries who arrived in Perpignan have to disperse to keep from attracting attention. Most of them decide to stay in France, where a few dozen anarchists and syndicalists have been detained by the gendarmes, accused of illegal possession of firearms and falsification of personal documents. However, a group of about fifty brave ones go to the border and wait in the foothills of the Pyrenees for the contact who was supposed to guide them into Spain.

But the comrade brought them bad news: several army regiments, with machine guns and artillery, were waiting for them along the border, in a show of rapid coordination never before seen in the Spanish armed forces. Unless, of course, they had prior information. In addition to Francisco Ascaso, among the fifty brave men who had to retreat with their tails between their legs was Valeriano Orobón, who apart from translating the "Song of Warsaw" into the anarchist anthem "*A Las Barricadas*," will also leave the following heartfelt words for posterity: "That day, in the middle of the mountains, a thousand meters above sea level, I saw many of those fifty men weeping because they could not offer their lives to the revolution. Ascaso was one of them. Durruti with the Vera group. Jover was in the group who attacked the Atarazanas barracks in Barcelona. It was a naive, clumsy attempt, whatever you like. But there was a great revolutionary passion in these men. They deserve everyone's respect for that. They failed, that's all. We have failed so many times! But, in the end, we will triumph." You win some, you lose some, Valeriano. After Primo's dictatorship, the Republic will come, and then Franco's dictatorship, which you will not live to see, and after that democracy, which you could not even imagine, though your song's lyrics will outlive you.

XIX
(1914–1916)

WHEN PABLO DISEMBARKED IN THE HAGUE, one thing was on everyone's lips: Jean Jaurès had been assassinated in Paris. A nationalist student aptly named Raoul Villain fired three rounds at him at the Café du Croissant, thereby eliminating one of the greatest proponents of French pacifism. But the news would not last long as the hot topic, because the following day Poincaré's government decreed a general mobilization and all hell broke loose. Fortunately, the *König Wilhelm II*, under a German flag, had departed that very morning from The Hague and was now on its way to the port of Hamburg. That was a close one, thought Pablo when he heard the news. Because ever since leaving Buenos Aires, many passengers (especially the French) were afraid that armed conflict would break out during the trip and that they would not be able to reach their destination. In fact, the Austro-Hungarian Empire had declared war on Serbia the same day that the transatlantic of the Hamburg America Line berthed in the Port of Lisbon, producing a devastating domino effect of international alliances that would lead Russia to mobilize its troops, Germany to declare war, and France and Great Britain to do likewise. And to think that it all started when Gavrilo Princip, another young nationalist (Serbian, this time), dispatched the heir to the Austro-Hungarian throne, the Archduke Franz Ferdinand—along with his controversial wife Sophie Chotek—as they made their way through the multitudes of Sarajevo aboard their garish Gräf & Stift motorcar, bathing in adoration before being bathed in blood.

But even as the world at large raged with violence and war and destruction, in the personal sphere there was reason for joy: when the ship docked in Bilbao, Pablo learned that he had become an uncle. He approached

Baracaldo with the imprudence of a man who feels that the happiness that awaits him merits the risk he is taking, which paid off when he arrived at his mother's house to find Julia there nursing an adorable baby girl named Teresa. When he took the child into his arms, he held her by the ribs and rubbed his nose against hers, as Rocafú had told him the Eskimos kiss. And when the child started crying, Pablo unwrapped the present he had brought from Argentina, like a magician taking a rabbit from a hat: a tin rattle, which put the infant to sleep with its rhythmic sound. Only then did Pablo have a moment to speak with his mother and sister.

"And where is my brother-in-law?" Pablo asked. "Don't I have the right to meet the father of this precious baby?"

"Oh," Julia replied, "he's working all day at the lawyer's office. We'll see, he might yet get us out of poverty!"

"Let me know when we're rich, I'll come back," Pablo joked.

"Why don't you stay in Baracaldo, son?" María interjected. "They say that France is going to war—"

"I can't stay, Mama."

"Why not? Are you still wanted by the police? They never come by asking about you anymore."

"That's a good sign, but you never know. They could come at any moment. And I don't want to make you suffer for no reason."

"Don't you think we're suffering as it is, knowing that you're going to live in a country at war?" Julia snapped.

"France hasn't entered the war yet," Pablo clarified, "and if it does, it won't mean anything for the Spanish, they can't make us fight in their ranks. Unless Spain joins in on one side or the other, obviously. But in that case, things will get bad around here, too—"

"I don't think so," said Julia, who, ever since learning that she was bringing a new being into the world, had started to take an interest in politics. "Prime Minister Dato implied that in case of a conflict, Spain would remain neutral."

"Well, that's better for everyone," Pablo replied with a certain vehemence. "Wars only serve to keep rich people rich and poor people poor. And to distract workers from the real struggle, of course."

"Shhh," went the recently promoted grandmother, "you'll wake the baby."

But the baby had already started crying again.

A few hours later, Pablo was again on the high sea, on his way to The Hague.

After Jaurès was assassinated and France entered the conflict, the hostilities erupted on an extraordinary scale: half of Europe was involved while the other half watched in horror, a conflict that would leave ten million dead. But it would be four long years before such a tally could be made. Spain, just as Julia had predicted, preferred to stay on the sidelines and proclaimed its neutrality from the very outset: the same day that France mobilized its troops, *La Época* (one of the newspapers closest to Prime Minister Dato's government) ran the editorial section under the headline "*Neutrales*," and made a staunch argument for noninvolvement in the conflict, inviting public opinion to stand behind this stance. Even former Prime Minister Maura decided to come out in favor of neutrality, with these words: "Spain cannot, will not, should not go to war." And this is not surprising, because it would have been a nasty mess for Alfonso XIII, having a British wife and an Austrian mother.

Recently disembarked, Pablo witnessed the outbreak of the conflagration with a mixture of rage and stupor. France, a country that had seen the birth of men like Proudhon and newspapers like *La Révolte,* had always been an emblem of struggle to anarchists, an example for the working class to follow. Its participation in a capitalist war could only be seen as a failure of the revolutionary ideas inherited from the Jacobins, and irrefutable evidence that chauvinistic nationalism was winning out over proletarian internationalism. So Pablo decided that the best thing he could do was to stay in France and try to spread the pacifistic ideas of the cruelly assassinated Jean Jaurès, even at the cost of putting his own life in danger. And he could think of nowhere better to go than Paris, the city where he had been conceived, reasoning that the anarchists there would be better organized than in The Hague. The first thing he did was to contact two old friends: Robinsón, who was still living in his commune in Lyon, and Ferdinando Fernández, the old writer for *El Castellano*. He wanted to convince the former to join him in his anti-war crusade, and to the latter, he wished to offer his services to the Salamanca-based newspaper as a correspondent, a position that was beginning to come into fashion at that time, and which the Great War would help to establish. After all, it could be a way to make a living and a perfect soapbox to denounce the horrors of the war. The idea was less far-fetched than it might sound; those days saw a rise in classified advertisements posted by young men who were willing to go to the scene to cover the conflict, and the Spanish were no exception: "Intelligent, educated young man," reads one ad that appeared in *La Vanguardia* in August. "Speaks French, English, and Italian, with experience traveling in Europe, offers service as war writer for major newspaper." The Barcelona-based newspaper itself was the first in Spain to send correspondents to the capitals of the countries involved in the war.

However, ever since the war broke out, the postal and telegraph services were compromised, so the letters that Pablo sent to his friends took some time to receive replies. When they finally arrived, at least they brought good news. The first was from Robinsón. It closed with, "You know what? I will come as soon as I can. It has gotten unbearable around here lately." The letter from Ferdinando took even longer, but for good reasons: *El Castellano* had been published on a weekly basis for several years, and the old blind poet Don Cándido was no longer the editor, but with the outbreak of war it was now possible to start publishing daily again, because readers were avid for fresh news. Ferdinando passed Pablo's offer on to the new owners of the press and waited for them to make a definitive decision, which did not come until the Battle of the Marne, when the French troops repelled the German offensive on Paris and disrupted the Schlieffen Plan, a sign that the military campaign would last much longer than had been expected. Finally, *El Castellano* resumed daily publication starting on the first of October, and Ferdinando himself wrote the editorial, with his usual inflammatory, emphatic style: "For some time now," he started, "we have been ruminating on the idea of making *El Castellano* a newspaper worthy of our beloved Salamanca. Finally, today, the first of October, we have fulfilled these longstanding, passionate dreams, allowing us to be in daily communication with our dear subscribers, to whom we remain ever indebted and whom we must defend and serve in their legitimate aspi-rations, regardless of what it may cost us." And he concluded with a lofty proclamation, in keeping with those bellicose times: "We shall fit into its columns all that is propitious to the wellbeing of our dear forgotten Salamanca and all of its inhabitants, in accordance with the motto that we have been shouting far and wide since the very first issue of *El Castellano*: Independence, Order, Progress, Morality, and Justice. And now to fight for this creed, as there is plenty of fighting to be done."

By then, Pablo had already obtained his credentials from the school at Quai d'Orsay as a war correspondent on the Western Front, although the conditions imposed by *El Castellano* were more than spartan: the sal-ary would be the same as if he were working in Salamanca, but he would have to pay for his own lodging, and he would not even have his name in the byline, as his job would be to send the information so that others could put it into shape. "That's the best we can offer," read the telegraph from Claudio Gambotti y Ragazzi, the new director of the press. "Take it or leave it." And he took it, because what else could he do? He was no Edwin Weigle, and *El Castellano* was no *Chicago Tribune*. In Spain, a small handful of men would divvy up the glory: men such as Gaziel, Salvador de Madariaga, Ramiro de Maeztu, Julio Camba, Corpus Barga, and Armando Guerra, the cynical pseudonym of Francisco Marín Llorente, a lieutenant colonel and a Germanophile historian. The vast majority, however, would have to be satisfied with struggling to fulfill the duties of a journalist in conditions of poverty and anonymity.

In any case, Pablo never liked to brag about his ordeals during the Great War, or to talk about his experiences as a correspondent. Indeed, in the captivating tales of his life that he recounted to little Teresa years later, he would speak very little of those dark times. "I could barely make out Mars's face," he would say with a certain poetic irony, dismissing the significance of the matter. But reading the articles in *El Castellano*, you can perfectly imagine the horrors that he must have witnessed. Luckily, he had his best friend Roberto Olaya near at hand. Olaya had let his hair and beard grow out even longer, so his nickname was all the more appropriate. Toward the end of October, he arrived in Paris and between the two of them they managed to keep their feet on the ground and their heads on their shoulders. That is, between the three of them, and not because Robinsón was accompanied by Darwin, his faithful water spaniel who had gone on to a better world, but because he appeared arm-in-arm with his "emotional companion," as he called her:

"Pablo," he said after their perfunctory boxing-match greeting, "I'd like to introduce you to Sandrine, my emotional companion."

"*Enchantée*," said the young woman, extending her hand and giving a slight curtsy, very theatrical. Her eyes were of that dull blue the English call gray, with hair the color of fire and a strange, deep, velvety voice, probably because she had been born with two uvulas, or really one uvula that split into two when she spoke, but Pablo knew nothing of that.

"Come in, come in, don't just stand out there."

Pablo had rented a squalid little room in a hostel near the Victoria Palace Hotel, the center of operations for foreign journalists who had arrived in Paris to cover the war. He invited them to sit down on the two mismatched chairs in the room and he sat on the iron bed flanked by an old pine bureau and a shelf with a few books. Completing the scene, a table and a washstand with a basin, a water pot, and a soap dish.

"*Avez-vous eu des problèmes pour arriver?*" Pablo asked in halting French.

"You can speak Spanish," said Robinsón.

"Yes, my grandfather was Galician, from O Grove," said Sandrine in Spanish, with a more than acceptable accent.

"*Ah, muy bien,*" said Pablo with relief, because his French was still not as fluent as he would have liked.

"Problems, buddy," Robinsón replied to the question, "We didn't have any problems per se. But, not being French, they did check our bags several times. Seems there's quite a bit of freelance espionage going on among citizens of neutral countries—"

"Oh, so you're not French?" Pablo asked Sandrine.

"No, I'm Swiss."

Sandrine's story was a juicy one. The daughter of a rabbi from Geneva, she ran away from home when she was just a teenager and, after traveling through half of the world, she finally ended up in Lyon. Without a franc in her pocket and with more hunger than hope, one night she decided to end her life by jumping off the Pont de la Guillotière into the black waters of the Rhône. But Robinsón, who at that time was earning his living as a portrait artist in the Alpine city, caught her by the belt at the last second. That same night, Sandrine went with him to the vegetarian commune where he had been living since he left Barcelona. But the outbreak of the war had finally disrupted the group of naturists: some fled France, others hid out in the Alps, and one of them even enlisted in the army, arguing that one can only live freely in a free country. Even Robinsón, despite his obvious limp, had been pressured to enroll as a foreign volunteer in the offices of the Amitiés Françaises, which saw a wave of enlistment during the first few days of the war. So when he received Pablo's letter, he didn't think twice: he discussed it with Sandrine, they packed their bags and took the next train to Paris.

"And have you found out anything about Angela?" Robinsón asked.

Pablo had been expecting that question, as he had never mentioned the subject in his letters from Argentina. But it had to come up sooner or later. Without going into much detail, he recounted the scene in Calle Alcalá, and then dropped the subject for good. Angela had turned into a dangerous memory.

That same day, Robinsón and Sandrine rented a room in the same hostel, and they soon found a way to earn a living; Robin continued to take advantage of his knack for drawing by setting up in train stations and outside recruiting offices, where young soldiers had their portraits done for a few francs, to be immortalized together with girlfriends, mothers, or sisters before being sent to the slaughterhouse, and Sandrine started serving drinks in a cabaret on Rue de Montmartre, until one day they heard her singing as she mopped the floor, and she became a real *vedette*, with the very provocative and Jewish-sounding stage name Sanhédrine.

During the first few months of the conflict, Pablo learned his new job in a trial by fire. The battles of the Somme and Yser, which he had to cover without being able to leave Paris, taught him that the war correspondent's worst enemy is not fear, nor powerlessness, nor fatigue, but the censorship imposed by the countries in conflict. In order for the war to be able to continue its course, the patriotic spirit among the citizens had to be kept aflame, and this could only be done by hiding the truth of what was going on in the battlefields, especially on the Western Front, which rather seemed like an extermination camp. The newspapers of the neutral countries soon understood the game, and many of them agreed to accept money from the propaganda ministries of one side or the other. Despite everything, foreign journalists were prohibited from going near the front, but instead were given the special privilege of access to the telegraph services that had been established, provided that they wrote their dispatches in French so they could be reviewed by the censors. So Pablo had no choice but to improve his skills in the language of Rabelais, and to accept that he would not be able to do much to support the cause of pacifism with the official communiqués that journalists received twice a day and the strict press laws of the French government, which prohibited "any information or article containing a message that could support the enemy or exert a harmful influence on the morale of the army or of the populace," under penalty of fines or even incarceration. And given that advocating for anti-war positions could only be interpreted as an unequivocal sign of harmful influence, Pablo had to learn to write between the lines.

It was not until mid-November that he was able to participate in his first "excursion" to the battlefield, organized expressly for a group of international journalists by the foreign minister, Théophile Delcassé, one of the primary architects of the pacts that culminated in the Triple Entente, the alliance between the French, Russians, and British. But there was a hitch: they would not be covering active engagements, but visiting the aftermath of the Battle of the Marne, on territory safely in the hands of the allies. The gates of Paris were still decorated with barbed wire and steel parapets, vestiges of the days when the German army had nearly taken the French capital. Six sentinels scrutinized the reporters' papers before letting them get into the military vehicle which would take them to the crime scene (war being nothing but a state of generalized crime). The first few kilometers were strangely peaceful, the deceptive calm before the storm, but arriving in the vicinity of the Marne, the view changed dramatically, from the picturesque string of villages to houses in ruins, ransacked homes, charred roofs. The inhabitants had been caught off-guard like the victims of Pompeii by the volcanic onslaught of the Germans, leaving whatever they were doing suspended, halfway done: food in the oven, clothing on the line, a rag doll by a washbasin ... At first, very few people, here and there an elderly woman with the dazed, sullen look of one who has lost everything overnight. Only arriving in the more densely populated areas, such as Meaux or Montmirail, was he finally able to talk with witnesses of the events, who were eager to tell the journalists about what had happened during the days of the German occupation, probably to exorcise their demons. It was then, hearing the brutal tales of those poor people, that Pablo understood that war is the greatest poison mankind has invented.

"I thank God," said a former schoolteacher from Meaux, who had been blinded years before, "that I was unable to see the horrors of this war. If I had, I would have gouged my own eyes out like Oedipus." Two thick tears ran down his cheeks as he continued: "I wish they had taken all my senses, because wine now tastes like blood to me, and bread tastes like death, and the rooster's crow sounds like the screaming of women being raped." He took a crumpled handkerchief from his pocket, blew his nose noisily, and his voice trembled as he took his leave with these bitter words: "When he was a young man, Montaigne believed that philosophy should teach you how to die. But when he was older, he discovered that no, it was just the opposite, philosophy should teach men how to live and let live. I wish the men in power had read more Montaigne and less Napoleon."

These words rang in Pablo's ears during the rest of the trip, not only when looking at the valleys riddled with holes by artillery or when counting the innumerable miniature French flags signaling the dead buried under the wet earth of the trenches. At that moment, more than ever, he was certain that the black flag of the anarchists, the flag that is the negation of all flags, is the only one that deserves to be raised in this life. And from that day forward, for nearly two years, he woke up every morning with the old man's words ringing in his ears. Until, that is, the Battle of Verdun.

After that, words failed.

22

In the early dawn hours on Sunday morning, in two automobile trucks sent expressly to Vera and duly guarded by the forces of the Civil Guard, the detainees arrived at the city's penitentiary. The prisoners were put into cells in the third gallery of the ground floor of the prison, and were visited by the chaplain, Don Alejandro Maisterrena, who learned that ten of them professed the Catholic faith and four of them professed no religion.

El Pueblo Navarro, 11 November 1924

WHEN PABLO AND HIS THIRTEEN COMRADES are incarcerated in the Provincial Prison of Pamplona, popularly known as the "Triple-P," the predominant penitentiary system in Spain is what is known as the "progressive system," tried for the first time in the prison of Ceuta in 1889, generalized throughout the national territory at the turn of the century, and confirmed after the recent decree of 1923. This system is based on a gradual improvement in the prisoners' situation as they approach the end of their sentence, taking into account their behavior and the seriousness of the crime, and includes four phases: first, the phase of solitary confinement, when the prisoner is kept under strict control and surveillance; next, a phase of communal living with other prisoners, with educational and vocational activities aimed at reintegration; then a phase of preparation for release, during which the prisoner enjoys temporary passes to leave; and finally, a phase of conditional or probationary freedom. And so, in keeping with standard procedure, all of the detainees from the incident at Vera will receive the first degree of punishment at Triple-P, placed in individual cells while they await their trials. Although some of them will never see the end of the first phase.

It is still nighttime when the two paddy wagons arrive in Pamplona, slowing down to twenty-four kilometers per hour, the citywide speed limit. Five minutes later, the trucks pass through the black steel gates of the prison and enter the large yard, waking up the prisoners sleeping in the south wing of the building. The night watch has been reinforced with fifteen soldiers, and there is an increased police presence along the avenues and roadways leading to the jail. A few civil guards, wrapped in their black cloaks and with their chinstraps quivering beneath their jowls, assist the soldiers and prison guards in removing the prisoners, arms cramped and wrists bruised, from the trucks. In silence they lead them at gunpoint, hands and feet in chains, to the booking room on the ground floor of the prison, where the well-mannered prison warden, Don Daniel Gómez Estrada, is waiting to greet them, leaning on his cane. He opens with an allusion to his counterpart in Burgos:

"I will not say, as some of my colleagues do, that one prisoner is shit, two prisoners are two shits, and more than two prisoners is a shit storm, although that may be true in some cases. You boys just keep in mind that this detention center is governed based on three fundamental principles: the discipline of a barracks, the seriousness of a bank, and the austerity of a monastery. If you can behave accordingly, we'll get along just fine."

The fourteen arrivals listen in silence, internally cursing the director for his air of superiority.

"If you have money, you can buy food and clothing at the concession booth. If not, you will have to be satisfied with the common mess and the prison uniform."

Having spoken, he exits the room with an arrogant stride like an opera lead, and yet he cannot hide the limp caused by his prosthetic leg, and he leaves the revolutionaries in the hands of the administrative staff for booking. Before the morning trumpet sounds, the prisoners are led to an adjacent room where the "shearer" shaves their heads, and then to the shower station, where they are required to disrobe and bathe. Being shorn and showered, they are ready to put on the prison uniform, which feels rather like a hair shirt on their skin stripped of undergarments. The least unfortunate receive new uniforms of thick cloth, while others are given old suits of white denim with gray stripes, as thin as cigarette paper and hardly more insulating. But no one protests for fear of being put in a pine pajama once and for all.

"You can bring your coat to the cell, but the rest of your clothing stays in the depository until you leave or till someone comes to get it for you," says one of the prison guards to Pablo when his turn comes. "But you should know, if no one comes to get it, when you leave here the moths will have made a feast of your rags. If you ever get out, that is—"

"I don't think my old clothes are of any interest to anyone," Pablo answers dejectedly, "except maybe for the cooks to add flavor to the mess. Do what you like with them."

Once in uniform, the prisoners are given two stiff blankets (but no sheet, lest any of them should get the idea to tear it up and braid it into a noose), a bowl, a tin spoon, and as always, an old newspaper. Then they are each assigned a three-digit number, to strip them of any shred of identity they might have left, and they are taken to the individual cells in the third gallery of the lower level of the jail, dedicated to the most dangerous criminals. The Provincial Prison of Pamplona is built according to the latest Spanish prison design, with a panoptic structure of four radial galleries in the shape of a Christian cross, as Daniel Gómez Estrada likes to boast every time an official visitor deigns to visit the building. With this arrangement, both the common rooms and the individual cells have natural light, and Pablo's cell, number 31, is no exception, as it borders the large courtyard, where the prisoners entertain themselves by playing soccer or betting cigarettes on impossible flea races. It is slightly more spacious than the cell at the carabiniers' barracks in Vera, and although it's not big enough to launch a rocket (only about six by ten feet), at least it has a wooden cot, half-hidden by a dirty bedroll of milled straw, and a latrine located just below a tiny window letting in the faint light of the courtyard. There is no running water, of course, but a full bucket in a corner serves both for the morning hygiene and to help wash detritus down the urinal, which doesn't stop the cell from stinking of mildew and urine, although Pablo does not notice. On the damp walls are phrases scrawled in pencil and chalk, and obscene drawings scratched in with the handles of spoons.

"I advise you to do some soul-searching," says the jailer as he removes Pablo's handcuffs. "It's Sunday, and Father Alejandro will be here to hear your confessions."

Without further ado, he slams the iron door and turns the lock with a squeak, leaving Pablo alone with his thoughts, as soldiers pace up and down the corridor of the third gallery, marking the slow passage of time with their metronome steps.

The first thing Pablo does is inspect his new abode—who knows how long it will be his home? High up the wall there is a small window, its glass so dirty that it is almost opaque. By standing on the commode the prisoner can open it and enjoy a narrow slice of sky. Also, by gripping the bars and hoisting himself up, he can see the large cobblestone courtyard. On the windowsill, Pablo is surprised to find a trembling starling. The bird does not take flight. The faint light of the dawn shines into the cell and illuminates the graffiti-covered walls, and clinging to the bars, Pablo surveys the courtyard, empty at this early hour. Then he lowers himself down from his vantage and busies himself trying to decipher the shaky handwriting of the former tenants. There are phrases and sentences for all tastes and in all colors, from "Take pity on me, Lord, I beg you," to "Fuck you all," along with some of a more political bent, such as the following found next to the commode: "You can shackle our hands, but never our ideas." Over the head of the cot some-one has written "There are two types of men: those who choose life and those who choose death," and, next to the door, another prisoner (or maybe the same one, who knows) scrawled his last words: "Soon they will come to take me to the garrote. I die an innocent man and all I bring with me to my grave is the memory of your face: October 31, 1921." A shiver runs down

Pablo's spine, and he decides to quit reading. So he closes the window and stretches out on the cot, his fingers interlaced beneath his nape. The darkness turns the water stains on the ceiling into mythological monsters, continents from lost worlds, faces of unknown or forgotten people, and Pablo is transported back to a moment from his childhood, lying on the grass in the fields of Castile, looking at the clouds, his father telling him about Leonardo da Vinci and his theory of marvelous inventions that emerge from the imagination of open minds when they stare long enough at clouds or puddles, or glowing embers, or stains on walls. And so, watching the moisture stains play across the ceiling, he drifts off to sleep.

And he dreams, he dreams like one who has not dreamed in days. He dreams that the stains turn into black cloaks, and the black cloaks into civil guardsmen, which then turn into prosecutors, and then into priests giving the holy sacrament, and then into executioners, and then into coffins, which turn into pits, bottomless pits into which he will fall forever, until the end of days, amen.

Pablo wakes up falling off the cot and landing hard on the cement floor. Shortly, the prison chaplain, Don Alejandro Maisterrena, will arrive to ask for his confession, but he will be disappointed. "Don't despair, my son, Jesus Christ and the apostles were also prisoners." When the prisoner refuses, he will have no choice but to abandon cell 31 with some parting advice: "Try not to masturbate," he will say with a reproachful look, "it weakens the body, and the semen falls on the ground, and turns into dust, and who knows where the dust will end up …"

And so, from the moment the priest disappears through the door until the next Wednesday, when the interrogations and pretrial procedures will start, the only company that Pablo will have will be the starling, which inexplicably lingers on the windowsill, shivering from cold or fear or nostalgia, and his only contact with the outdoors will be the daily half-hour walk around the little courtyard allotted to the prisoners in solitary confinement. But between today and Wednesday many things will be happening outside the prison, some of which will reach the prisoners' ears despite their isolation, because news crosses prison walls like radio waves or nosy ghosts. For example, tonight Gil Galar will go on hunger strike at the Hospital of Mercy in Vera, in protest against the doctors' claims that his head injury was caused by a pistol rather than a rifle bullet, suggesting that it was his own comrades who shot him. Tomorrow, Monday, the French newspaper *Le Matin* will run a statement by Blasco Ibáñez denying accusations of having helped organize the attack and calling the revolutionary movement absurd and criminal. On Tuesday, rumors will arrive that Bonifacio Manzanedo removed the bandages from his amputated leg and bled to death overnight in Vera, and the story will even be picked up by a few newspapers in Pamplona, but will be corrected in later editions: the truth is that he remains alive, but his stump is developing gangrene and will need to be operated on again. And on Wednesday morning, Enrique Gil Galar, having abandoned his hunger strike already, will arrive at the Provincial Prison of Pamplona to be admitted directly to the infirmary, where he will be examined by the doctors before being locked up in a cell on the third gallery of the lower level, in conditions of heightened security and solitary confinement, like the rest of his comrades. Almost at the same time, coming from San Sebastián, three more detainees accused of participating in the Vera incursion will arrive, and it will be then that the pretrial procedures will begin, once the military tribunal has been set up there at the prison, presided over by Infantry Commandant Manuel González de Castejón, who will take over as special investigating judge to continue the proceedings initiated by Don Feliciano Suárez in Vera de Bidasoa; Sergeant Ortega of the regiment of Sicilia will serve as secretary.

AT SIX IN THE EVENING ON Wednesday, November 12, 1924, Pablo is brought for the third time in one day to the interrogation room, located on the first floor of the central building of the prison, from which the four galleries radiate like the arms of a stone octopus. The room's windows have not been opened, and the air is thick with soporific smoke, through which the investigating judge emerges. At his side stands the prison warden Don Daniel Gómez Estrada, decked out in livery and wearing the falsest of smiles, which he learned at the School of Criminology under Don Rafael Salillas. In a corner, perched behind an old Underwood no. 5, the secretary cleans his glasses with his jacket tail for the thousandth time, ready to miss nary a comma of the prisoner's statement.

"Sit down, please," the investigating judge says to Pablo, without asking the guard to remove his handcuffs. The warden shakes his hand in parting, and he says, "You sure you don't want to stay, Don Daniel?"

"No, no, thank you, I'll leave you to your work," he excuses himself, and walks out dragging his orthopedic leg and looking at Pablo like a parent reproaching a naughty child.

"First name?" asks Castejón.

"Pablo, same as last time."

"Surnames?"

"Martín Sánchez, once again."

"No wisecracks!" barks the judge, his friendly demeanor breaking into a threatening abruptness. "Just answer the questions, with no more comments."

But it is the third interrogation Pablo has had to endure in the past ten hours, and he is starting to lose his marbles hearing the same refrain over and over and seeing that the sincerer his replies, the more ludicrous they seem to the judge. That is the real torture: asking the same question again and again, for hours and hours, until the prisoner's mouth goes dry and his brain throbs, and he ends up saying anything it takes to be able to go back to his cell and drink a gulp of water and shake his head free of the endless hammering of repeated questions. Perhaps the old methods were more effective, such as tearing out fingernails with pliers or administering electric shocks to the scrotum, but they left marks and were unpleasant.

Also, considering how easy it is to forge the quaking signature of these miserable creatures, who would want to get blood on his shirt just for a lousy declaration? So it is that Pablo has finally admitted to participating in the shootout at the Argaitza quarry, since the Mauser wound is indisputable evidence, but he insists that he did not fire any shots or lead any group. Nevertheless, Judge Castejón carries on with the same litany:

"What was your intention entering Spain?"

"My intention was to see with my own eyes whether the revolution had started, as they told us in France before we crossed the border."

"Did you fire at the civil guards at the quarry?"

"No, on the contrary, I tried to prevent the shooting, by tackling one of our men when he drew his pistol."

"You don't need to write that down," Castejón says to the secretary, who is pounding away at the typewriter in the corner; before Pablo can protest, the judge continues: "Were you one of the leaders?"

"No, I've already told you a thousand times."

"You'll tell me a thousand more if need be!" the judge shouts virulently, surprising even the secretary, who gives a start in his seat. "Who was commanding the excursion?"

"No one, we had no leaders."

"But someone must have been the brains of the operation, I would think—"

"I imagine so, but I don't know who it was. All I know is that in Paris it was Blasco Ibáñez, Unamuno, and Soriano who were spreading the idea that revolution was about to break out in Spain," Pablo declares, knowing that none of the three have anything to do with the incursion.

"Very good, you see how you start remembering things when you really try? And if you were to see your fellow adventurers, you think you would recognize them?"

"It's possible," Pablo concedes.

"Bring them in, one at a time," Castejón orders one of the two guards, initiating a sequential lineup. But Pablo will stubbornly refuse to recognize anyone, as Leandro is marched in, followed by Julián, then Julianín, and all the others, even Casiano Veloso and Anastasio Duarte, whom he resents ever since the episode in the brothel. Unfortunately, not all the interrogated men will have such nerve or such sense of loyalty. Indeed, just this morning Casiano declared that he had seen Pablo fall down injured in the skirmish, and that he considered Pablo one of the main leaders of the expedition, and Anastasio even claimed that the man with the thigh injury was one of the most merciless participants in the death of the guardsmen.

"Do you have anything to add to your statement?"

"No."

"Fine. Read your statement and sign down here."

"This is not exactly what I said," Pablo replies after looking over it, with the resignation of someone who is inured to having his words twisted.

"If you don't want to sign, we'll do it for you, don't worry," says the secretary cynically, getting up from his chair with his pen in his hand.

Only then is Pablo allowed to drink some water and go back to his dungeon, where he will sleep for the last time in solitary, because tomorrow night, shortly after the bedtime bell, they will return to bring him to the interrogation room.

Pablo is surprised to find the room also occupied by the ex-guardsman Santillán, the lunatic Gil Galar, and the feeble Vázquez Bouzas, under the watchful eye of several civil guards. The special investigating judge, Don Manuel González de Castejón, accompanied by his secretary, the prosecutor, and the court speaker, gives them the worst possible news: when the review of the facts is completed, having been approved in Burgos by his honor the senior captain general of the Sixth Region, Señor Burguete, the four of them will be tried by a summary military tribunal which will be held without fail tomorrow morning, Friday, November 14, 1924. The rest of the detainees will have an ordinary trial once the summary tribunal has been completed. The secretary then proceeds to read the entire list of charges, in which Pablo figures as one of the main leaders of the revolutionary incursion and as the perpetrator of the shots that killed the two civil guardsmen, as demonstrated by the bullet wound in his thigh and corroborated by the accusations of multiple other detainees. The prosecutor is seeking capital punishment for the four accused men, and they shall have their choice of defense counsel from among a commandant of the carabiniers, a captain of Artillery, and a sergeant of the Civil Guard. The accused are informed that their solitary confinement is hereby lifted, as the law prescribes. While they must remain in their solitary cells, they henceforth have the right to maintain contact with the outside world, and to receive visits from their parents, children, or wives, if they wish. It is even possible that the press will visit the prison to ask them a few questions. May they sleep well, and may they meet God with their sins confessed.

XX
(1916–1918)

HEMINGWAY WROTE THAT WORLD WAR I was "the most colossal, murderous, mismanaged butchery that has ever taken place on earth." And he went on, from firsthand knowledge: "Any writer who said otherwise lied, so the writers either wrote propaganda, shut up, or fought." This rang true with Pablo's experience as a war correspondent; little by little, he found himself without paragraphs, without sentences, without words, without letters. Until, finally, he went mute. Especially after the Battle of Verdun, the famous Battle of Verdun, which lasted for ten interminable months and turned into one of the most inhumane and useless conflicts in history. Journalists called it "the hell of Verdun" and the "meat grinder of Verdun," but for Pablo it was always the "futility of Verdun," because not only did it lead to hundreds of thousands of deaths on both sides, but it also left things, militarily, about the same as they were before.

The battle had started in February, when the troops of General Falkenhayn, the chief of the German General Staff, launched a massive offensive on Verdun, bombarding the city and the enemy lines for nearly ten hours straight, turning the front line into an atrocious spectacle of fire and shrapnel, where the bloodcurdling screams of the soldiers could barely be heard over the deafening sound of explosions. No mere rain of shells, it was a deluge of 1,500 bombs a minute, an incessant pounding of artillery, which the Germans—in a pique of exaggerated lyricism—referred to as *Trommelfeuer*, or "drum-fire." The storm was not followed by calm, but by a surge of German infantry ready to roast any injured survivors with hellish flamethrowers, but they forgot that a wounded lion is even more dangerous: the French fought tooth and nail to defend Verdun long enough for reinforcements to arrive, and it turned into the longest battle of the war.

But Pablo would not see the magnitude of the tragedy with his own eyes until the end of the year, when the top brass of the French army realized that after nine long months of gestation, the Battle of Verdun had come to term, and they cordially opened the trenches to foreign correspondents, as if wanting to boast of their imminent, pyrrhic victory. By then, fourteen nations had dug up the hatchet of war, and the conflagration was taking on apocalyptic proportions.

The morning they left Paris started out cold and unpleasant, a morning made for staying home by the fire, not for going to look for it in the trenches. The journalists loaded onto the military vehicle at dawn's first light, and despite the excitement of the moment, they barely opened their mouths until they were on the Via Sacra.

"This is the famous road they call the Via Sacra," the officer driving the vehicle informed them.

"Why?" asked the Swedish correspondent from the *Rockbalius Triduojer*, more out of deference than anything else, because he knew the answer quite well.

"Because it's the route we used to supply our army with weapons and food, and to stop the Germans from taking Verdun."

There were shacks erected on both sides of the road, as well as stables and aviation hangars, while vehicles from the French High Command, artillery convoys, and uniformed soldiers on bicycles circulated on the highway. A railway built for the occasion ran alongside the main highway, indifferent to the many cemeteries flanking the road, with their crosses and flowers and mounds of still-fresh earth. They passed a truck going the other direction, carrying German prisoners from the front, their faces red and trembling like rose petals.

"How young they are," mused the Russian reporter from the *Novoye Vremya*.

And they all agreed, through the most explicit of silences.

"I can't understand," said Pablo a few minutes later, after they passed a Red Cross truck overflowing with injured soldiers, "what's the point of defending Verdun?"

The astonished officer jerked the steering wheel and they very nearly careened off the road.

"I mean," Pablo clarified, "it's not such a strategic location. It's surrounded by German forces, so the French army has to maintain a wider front line, but if you were to cut your losses and give up Verdun, the battle front would be shorter and a lot of lives would be saved, don't you think?"

No other reporter dares to open his mouth, although they know that the Spanish correspondent has a point. In fact, the obvious proof that Verdun did not have any real military value (although it was a historic symbol of Gallic pride) was that when it was attacked by the German army, it barely had cannons to defend itself, because they had all been sent to more crucial units. But it is one thing to be aware of it and another to say so to an officer driving you to the front line after several months of battle and hundreds of thousands of deaths.

"People," said the officer, trying to maintain his composure, "see what they want to see. And sometimes what people want to see doesn't match up with reality."

"But isn't it true," Pablo insisted recklessly, "that General Joffre is of the same opinion, and that he only accepted the situation due to political pressure?"

The officer's face took on a sudden look of fear, which lasted only as long as the flutter of a butterfly's wings.

"Gentlemen," he said as he stopped the vehicle abruptly, "we have arrived in Souilly. You will have the honor of being greeted by General Nivelle."

And he exited the vehicle, slamming the door behind him.

General Nivelle, despite the cold, came out to receive them in shirt-sleeves, like a feudal lord going out on horseback to contemplate the magnitude of his territory. He was wearing high boots and spurs, and his face showed the steely determination of the chosen and the mad. He greeted the journalists in a friendly manner, although with a certain haste, and showed them a map of the trenches and sites that they could visit during their tour. He finished by reminding them that it is forbidden to speak with the *poilus* (infantrymen, in French military slang) and shook each of their hands before retiring to rest in the general barracks.

"Let's move on, gentlemen," ordered the officer driving the military vehicle.

From that point forward, security was increased: between Souilly and Verdun they had to stop a half-dozen times, intercepted by sentinels who stepped out of their guard posts and stood in the middle of the road, holding up their arms in a form of a Y with a rifle in the air and demanding their clearance papers or the password. "Racine," the officer would say, or "Rivoli," or "Argona," and they would then be allowed to continue on. Finally, in the distance, they could make out a brownish stain in the middle of the valley.

"That's Verdun," the officer informed the correspondents, who were left agog.

Verdun. Pablo had been hearing about Verdun for months. He had written the word hundreds of times and now finally those six letters were incarnated. Incarnated in ruins. They entered via the Port of France and parked the vehicle to better contemplate the atrocious spectacle. The city had been razed by German bombs, a scene from a horror story or nightmare, houses in ruins, streets destroyed. A banner of surrender made from an old sheet still hung from a balcony, as though the abandoned buildings were the only ones able to fly the white flag of peace. A bit farther on, in the door of a café, one could still read the faded poster of the last evening show hosted there, before the bombs brought about an unplanned change of schedule: "Tonight," it said, "at eleven o'clock, the debut of the beautiful Paquita with her famous Spanish dances." A rotten debut my compatriot had, thought Pablo, just as several distant explosions snapped him back to reality.

"Those aren't explosions," the officer informed him, "that's cannon fire."

"And what's the difference?" asked the Dutch reporter from the *Nieuws van den Dag*, still green on the subject.

"Almost the same as between life and death," responded the officer with delight. "Cannon fire is the sound that our cannons make when they're firing, explosions are the sound that German bombs make when they fall. You'll soon learn to tell the difference, don't worry."

Shortly thereafter, the group of reporters left the city with hearts clenched, and went out to the countryside toward the trenches. The countless artillery craters were sometimes fifteen feet deep, giving the landscape a surreal, lunar, phantasmagoric appearance. They found themselves just a few kilometers from the enemy, but the rear guard troops seemed immune to the screeching sound of German grenades careening through the air nearby: a few men were washing clothes in a stream, others were cooking mess, brushing horses, transporting bags of supplies, sawing boards, eating, drinking, sleeping, or doing gymnastics on a horizontal bar erected between two large posts stuck in the ground. Soon, they saw about twenty pack mules coming from the front, their short stature helping them carry bread, rice, and meat to the soldiers without being hit by the German artillery fire, although more than one of them did not make it. When they finally arrived at the entrance to the trenches, there was a tense calm, disturbed only by the cannon fire from the front line. The commanding colonel of the area came out to greet them—one of those old French military men with a Van Dyke beard, energetic and cheerful, a lover of wine, women, and bad jokes. On their arrival, he greeted them with effusive impatience:

457

"Come along, men, take a helmet and a gas mask, we have to take certain precautions. We're going to the most advanced trench, twenty yards from the enemy. I hope none of you has a heart condition."

On the ground was a pile of helmets, heavy and dirty, which the reporters went through and tried on until they found the right size; then they put on the gas masks, a fabric sack that covered the face completely, along with dark isinglass lenses that fit poorly over the eyes. Finally, the colonel had them put on a metal hood that made them look like displaced deep sea divers. It was then that the old officer let out a great laugh which remained hanging in the air until it was drowned out by a pair of explosions.

"All right, that's enough, you can remove your costumes, ladies," he laughed at his prank. "I only wanted you to know how a grunt feels going into combat. I hope you can use that in your articles. Now follow me, please, I have many things to show you," and he hurried them off with the enthusiasm of someone organizing a camping trip.

Somewhat burned by the joke, the reporters set out through a labyrinth of trenches toward the front line. They made their way, ducking and huddling, despite the depth of the trenches, not realizing that a German grenade hitting them there would have been like shooting an arrow through an arrowslit in a castle wall. What really got to Pablo was not the distant roar of cannon fire, but the roar he saw in the faces of the soldiers along the way. Because what he saw in their eyes was neither fear nor dread, neither hope nor madness. Rising from deep within their hearts and metastasizing on their faces, it was hatred. Not for Germany, nor for the war, not even hatred toward their superiors, no: hatred for the reporters themselves. Because the war had begun two years before, and the daily chronicles still insisted on portraying life in the trenches in a positive, even sympathetic light. No. Life in the trenches was hell, however much the officer liked to joke about it. See if anyone ever dares to publish the truth.

"*A veure quan us atreviu a publicar la veritat, colla de cretins,*" murmured a soldier in Catalan as the reporters passed. Pablo was the only one who understood him, and, pretending to tie his shoe, he lingered behind. Since he was not authorized to speak with them, he waited until the colonel disappeared around the corner, and asked in Spanish:

"Is there a Spaniard here?"

Leaning against the trench walls, four soldiers gave him surly looks, warming their hands with their breath.

"Yes," one finally said, touching his muddy visor. "Ramón Tarrech, at your service—yours and God's."

"Pablo Martín," Pablo introduced himself, overlooking the soldier's sarcasm. "So there are Catalan volunteers here at Verdun."

"Of course. Five of us came from my village, and I'm the only one left. The other day there was a journalist from Barcelona and he said that a few thousand Catalans have already died in this accursed war. Oh, General Joffre is from Rivesaltes, we said, and we ran here like rabbits into the foxhole. You can write that in your paper, and you can print my name, if you want."

"Why don't you go home? You're one who can, after all."

The youth thought about his response while he cleaned his nails with the tip of his bayonet.

"Because you get used to death, just like hunger or cold," he said at last, "and because when you've seen certain things, you can't just go home and relax. You want to know how a man dies in the trenches? You want me to tell you how two of my friends died yesterday? You want to know the truth about this fucked-up war? Maybe you guys will finally stop printing that we spend our days playing cards and joking around while whistling 'La Marseillaise.'"

Pablo shot a glance to where the other reporters had disappeared. Apparently no one had noticed his absence.

"Yes, of course I want to know, that's why I came," he said, looking back at his compatriot. "But it's not our fault. With the censorship—"

"Censorship? Censorship is a coward's excuse. You can always choose to keep silent."

The other three nodded their heads, although they didn't understand a word of Spanish.

"At six in the morning I went out with two others to inspect the terrain," he started to recount, trying to contain his emotion. "There was total stillness in the German trenches. So much stillness should have made us nervous, but we were too tired to realize it. Thing is, somebody saw us go out, or discovered us when we were drawing close, because when they had us in their sights they started to shoot. We jumped headfirst into a shell pit and got drenched in mud. Then grenades started exploding all around us. One to our left, another to our right, and the third exactly where we were standing. After the explosion, I opened my eyes, but there was only darkness and dust and smoke, the acrid smell of powder, and I choked. Am I injured? I thought. And then: Am I dead? I moved my arms and legs, touched my face and chest. Nothing. All fine. But then I saw my two friends, one on top of the other, bleeding. Philippe's guts were out, like he was giving birth to his own guts, his eyes already lifeless. The explosion had torn Benjamin's leg off, and there was a red stain across his chest, and he lay there looking at me, begging me for help. I went to him, knelt down, took his hand. It was very cold. He tried to speak to me, but nothing came out. Then, not knowing what he was doing, he unbuttoned his pants and died pissing on Philippe's open wound."

Ramón's voice shook, and a guillotine of silence fell in the trench. One of the French soldiers made the sign of the cross and the other blew his nose on a dirty, stiff handkerchief, perhaps to hide a sob. They had only understood two words of the story, but those had been enough: Philippe and Benjamin.

"We couldn't get their bodies until tonight," Ramón added.

All Pablo could say was, "I'm sorry."

"If you really mean that, do me a favor—" was the soldier's reply.

"I don't think anyone would dare to publish it," Pablo interrupted.

"Not that."

"What then?"

"Benjamin kept a diary since he arrived here. He said that he was writing it for his girl, so she would know how brave he had been during the war in case he died. But she lives in Marly, near Valenciennes, in occupied territory. So we can't send it by mail."

"And what do you want me to do?"

"Just keep it until this rat hell of a war is over. Then send it to the girl. We don't know if we'll get out of here alive…"

"Alright," said Pablo, "Just give it to me."

Ramón exchanged a few words in French with his companions, and they all nodded.

"Come with me," he said to Pablo, and they went down a passageway between two trenches. Shortly thereafter, turning a corner, they found themselves in a broader space, enclosed with a roof, where several soldiers were finishing lunch by the faint light of oil candles. Ramón went to a corner and put his hand between two boards.

"Here it is," he said to Pablo, giving him the little journal with its worn-out, muddy cover. "Read it if you want. We read it. Maybe it'll help you understand this damn war better."

Pablo opened the diary and looked at the small, precise lettering, like a reflection of life in the trenches: "Here you live outside time and the world," said the first sentence. But that was as far as he could read, because then came a thundering voice:

"Monsieur Martín! Monsieur Martín!"

He barely had time to stuff the journal in his jacket pocket before the officer who had brought them to the trenches appeared, pointing his finger like a pistol:

"You have committed a very serious infraction," he barked, spittle flying into Pablo's face. "Come with me immediately."

And Pablo's only goodbye to Ramón was a brief but unmistakable look.

After recovering the stray correspondent, the expedition continued the planned tour: they arrived at the frontline trenches, with their cannons vomiting fire, their periscopes and their earthquakes, before then retreating to visit an aviation field, with its fighters, reconnaissance planes, and bombers. But it was during the return trip to Paris that Pablo would see the true face of Mars. Less than fifteen minutes had passed since they got into the vehicle meant to return them to the capital, when they came across three military trucks on the side of the road. A few yards away, in the woods, a platoon of dejected soldiers appeared to have turned to stone, helmets in hands and breath bated. The officer stopped the vehicle and let the reporters out. Without a sound, they made their way over to the circle of soldiers. For the first time in his life, Pablo had an experience resembling smell: when he breathed, the air stifled his throat, made his mouth bitter and turned his stomach, producing a sort of suffering he had never known. It lasted only an instant, but he would never forget it: it was the smell of death, acrid and sticky, almost tangible, palpable, even for someone whose nose can't tell a turd from a rose, a rotten egg from freshly mown grass, a foul latrine from the toilet of the queen of England.

"Are you alright?" the correspondent from *Novoye Vremya* whispered to him.

"Yes, yes, thank you," Pablo replied. "I was just a bit dizzy."

At the feet of the circle of soldiers there was a deep hole piled with dozens of corpses, dismembered and incomplete bodies, bloody and swollen, with torn uniforms, in a jumble of legs, arms, and faces twisted in macabre grimaces. Fortunately, when the journalists arrived, the first shovelfuls of earth were already beginning to fall, like a curtain drawing shut to hide the worst debasement. However, the worst was yet to come. Because death, the smell of death, the taste of death is inevitable in war, and all the more so in a generalized butchery like this one. But, just as there is something worse than finding a worm in your apple (finding half a worm in your apple), there is something worse than dismembered dead bodies: dismembered live bodies.

Back on the road from Verdun to Châlons, they saw a dark building with the flag of the Red Cross waving from the rooftop. It was an old convent converted into a hospital, the last stop on this tour of horrors. An army medic came out to greet them, and somewhat forcefully bade them to enter, with the sadism of certain butchers or surgeons. On entering the building, the distant echo of bombs was superimposed with the bloodcurdling screams of one of the patients, setting everyone's (except the medic's) hair on end. In the large room of the old refectory, ensconced in disquieting shadow, one could make out the outlines of a multitude of beds and hear the gasping and moaning of their current occupants.

"Sometimes it's not so easy to know if a soldier is dead," the hosting medic was saying in an unpleasantly loud voice, "because the shock from a mortar shell can kill you from the inside, without apparent injuries. In that case, we either wait for obvious signs of death (rigor mortis or putrefaction) or we do a cardiopuncture. What is cardiopuncture, you might ask? It's the definitive test: we insert a very thin needle into the area of the heart until it reaches the cardiac muscle. If the needle moves, the man is still alive. If not, he has passed on."

They'd count me dead, thought Pablo, and his heart started beating faster in his right breast. But the excitement did not last long, or rather it transformed, because suddenly someone opened one of the curtains and the light poured in, revealing the most monstrous and terrifying spectacle imaginable: some of the dead lying on beds did not even have human form, they were fragments, pieces, chunks of bodies, incomprehensibly still alive. Pablo had to make an enormous effort not to avert his eyes; by his side there was a man with his lower jaw torn off, his face turned into a ball of rags holding two astonished eyes that looked ready to jump out of their sockets; a little further on, writhing in agony, was a man with only one arm and only one leg, on opposite sides, looking like an unfinished puzzle; and on the next bed, a man without legs was howling at the sky and stretching his neck like a jack-in-the-box. The journalists left the room with heavy hearts. Some managed not to vomit.

A few days later, the Swedish newspaper *Rockbalius Triduojer* carried the following headline: "He who has not seen Verdun has not seen the war."

AFTER THE "VERY SERIOUS INFRACTION" COMMITTED in the trenches, Pablo Martín Sánchez had his press credentials revoked, preventing him from practicing the profession for the rest of the conflict. He only avoided deportation or a war trial because the military had more urgent matters to attend to. In any case, the annulment was unnecessary, because on arriving in Paris, Pablo was determined not to go back to work as a journalist as long as the censor board was the measure of all things, and he prepared to look for work that would allow him to survive until the end of the conflict. Whatever there was. Whatever he found. Whatever he had to do.

"I'll sing in a cabaret if I have to," he said to Robinsón on return from Verdun.

The City of Light had transformed into a surprising, paradoxical spectacle; perhaps the penury of the soldiers at the front had excited the epicurean spirit of those who had the good luck to remain in the rear guard. The theaters, cafés, and casinos, which had been shuttered at the start of the war, were now fuller than ever. Absinthe, which had been prohibited by the French government in an attempt to crack down on alcoholism and avoid the degradation of the race (in the verbatim words of the ordinance), was now again wetting the whistles of those who knew where to find it. What's more, the famous fortune-teller Madame de Thèbes, in a fit of optimism or blindness, recently predicted that the war would end in the spring, and triumphant airs were blowing through the streets of Paris:

"I tried to rent a balcony on the Champs Élysées," Pablo heard one man saying to another in the middle of the street, "to watch the troops go by in the victory march."

"And?" the other man asked.

"Too late, they were all taken."

In these circumstances, Pablo had little trouble finding work in Paris: within a few days he was emptying ashtrays and bussing glasses at the Cabaret du Père Pelletier, where every night an artist named Sanhédrine delighted clients with her velvety voice and voluptuous curves, while at the back of the room a young man with a bowler hat and an unwieldy beard never took his eyes from her.

"What was all that about free love, Robin?" Pablo would whisper as he passed.

"*Va te faire foutre,*" his old chum would mutter, his eyes glued to his "emotional companion" until she gave up the stage to the incredible, the fascinating, the renowned hypnotist Sergio Antunes. Then, Robinson would leave the room to go wait for the artist at the Café du Croissant, where just a few years before, Raoul Villain had shot and killed Jean Jaurès, wiping out all traces of prewar pacifistic ideals in one fell swoop.

So went the days, weeks, and months. The United States joined the fray, and then the Bolshevik Revolution swept Russia. Just when the war's end was finally in sight, Paris was bombarded, and Sandrine was left voiceless and out of work.

23

Then the captain general of the Sixth Region, in accordance with Article 652 of the Code of Military Justice, declared that a summary trial would be pursued only against the four suspects whom he deemed had been caught in flagrante delicto, that is: Pablo Martín Sánchez, Enrique Gil Galar, Julián Santillán Rodríguez, and José Antonio Vázquez Bouzas, and that the rest of the detainees and suspects should be appropriately tried in ordinary military court.

CARLOS BLANCO
La Dictadura y los procesos militares

SOMEONE ONCE SAID THAT MILITARY JUSTICE is to justice as military music is to music, and this dire aphorism will be put to the test today. Ever since word got around, the bars of Pamplona have been abuzz with the events of Vera and nothing else. Some people mutter under their breath that the Rivera dictatorship is looking for a distraction to make the people of Spain forget about the disasters of the war in Morocco, and what could be better than the heads of a few bungling anarchists to burnish the reputation of heavy-handed justice and savoir faire, as Don Miguelito likes to say in his amorous prancing with La Caoba. A summary war tribunal is the right venue, others say, but how to choose the victims from such a large band of revolutionaries? Best not to be excessively cruel, the authorities seem to think, lest the people accuse us of hubris or disproportionality, like the ancient Greeks. Let us be magnanimous, and leave Bonifacio Manzanedo in the care of the nuns in Vera, since it would be poor taste to bring a case against a recent amputee. But the other two injured men will receive no such mercy. For them, we shall seek capital punishment, because God has accused them with his infallible finger! While we're at it, let's also throw the book at the former guardsman for having bitten the hand that fed him, and that little lamb Vázquez Bouzas, who after all is the only one who was arrested in flagrante at the scene of the crime ... So let's get going, open the proceedings.

IN THE PROVINCIAL PRISON OF PAMPLONA, the harsh trumpet call rings out at seven in the morning, but it awakens none of the four defendants, as they have already opened the curtains of their eyelids so as not to miss the prologue of the play they are about to star in. Last night, after hearing the bad news, they were visited in their cells by the illustrious commandant of the carabiniers, Don Nicolás Mocholi, whom they have all chosen to defend their case. While they are aware that he is not a lawyer; there were not many choices, after all, and at least he appears to be a good man, this dapper Mocholi, which is already something, all things considered. The defender did not even bother to ask them if they were innocent or guilty, but only tried in his soothing voice to encourage them, and invited them to remain calm, advising them not to say anything during the hearing unless absolutely necessary. This morning, at first light, the jail was filled with the commotion appropriate to the solemn occasion, with all necessary precautions, increased safety measures on the exterior, and the prison staff reinforced with civil guards and soldiers from the artillery command. It is not yet seven thirty when the four accused men are brought their usual morning meal, though this time breakfast is accompanied by a tough, sweet bun, as if to tell them they had better gather their strength, for they will need it. Shortly before eight, a few guards enter the cells, frisk them again absurdly, and instruct them to put on their coats—who knows if this is because it's freezing cold in the hearing room or so they won't have to appear before the tribunal in their ridiculous pajamas. Then they are led, hands cuffed in front, to the penitentiary's auditorium, where their trial is about to begin: a summary war council where they will not be judged as members of a revolutionary movement but as the perpetrators of the crime of armed assault on the forces of order, resulting in the death of two civil guardsmen.

The footsteps of the prisoners and their guards are heard in the third gallery of the lower level, where some of the other political prisoners dare to cheer them along. "Chin up, che!" comes from one of the last cells, and Pablo recognizes the speaker and thanks him in his heart. The footsteps continue into the entrance of the main building housing the hearing chamber, and they stop in a small, dark anteroom for the admittance of the tried, where prison chaplain Alejandro Maisterrena is waiting for them. In a tone that suggests he already knows the answer he asks the guards, "Listen, is it not possible to remove the handcuffs from these poor wretches?"

"You know we're following orders from higher up, Father."

"What about loosening them a little?" he asks, gesturing at the injuries on the prisoners' wrists.

"You're too good, Father. If it were up to me we'd tighten them."

Don Alejandro chooses not to insist, lest they think he sympathizes with these impious anarchists. A few muted voices are heard from inside the room, this being a public hearing, and the more impatient spectators having already found their way in, hoping to beat the crowd. Santillán asks if anyone has a cigarette, but just then the bell rings announcing the start of the tribunal and an assistant opens the door of the anteroom, instructing the prisoners to enter in single file. Santillán is first in line, held by two civil guards, his gray hair and mustache contrasting with his dark brown eyebrows. Next is José Antonio Vázquez Bouzas, diminutive compared to the former civil guard, his low stature having gotten him out of military service. After that comes Pablo, with a few days' scruff and an inquisitive look, and then finally Gil Galar, leaning on the chaplain's shoulder, pale, emaciated, and with his head carefully bandaged, perhaps to inspire compassion among the judges. The entry of the four inmates raises the first murmurs of the morning, despite the fact that there are not many spectators yet, except for the numerous journalists who have congregated at the tables set up for them.

The four men are brought to the center of the room, where they are made to sit down on the defendants' bench. It is colder than one would have expected, graveyard-cold, but luckily the prisoners are wearing their coats. Presiding over the tribunal is Colonel Antonio Permuy of the Infantry Regiment, still absent from the head table opposite the accused, already occupied by the chairman, Don Manuel Espinosa, and another five captains acting as judges. To the right, at the prosecutor's table, lieutenant Don Adriano Coronel adjusts his uniform, showing signs of impatience. Defense counsel Don Nicolás Mocholi's athletic figure is seated on the other side of the head table, rubbing his vitiligo-addled hands and casting soothing looks at his clients. From a dais behind the accused men's bench, the investigating judge, Castejón, is serving as rapporteur, leafing nervously through various pages as if looking for some lost document; next to him, serving as assistant secretary, Sergeant Ortega places on the table the damaged rifle of Corporal de la Fuente and a box containing weapons, munitions, French money, and other articles confiscated from the insurgents which may be used as evidence in the hearing. The scene is completed by various transcribers, bailiffs, and assistants, as well as soldiers and security guards positioned at strategic points around the room.

At eight o'clock sharp, as the bells toll from a nearby church, the president of the tribunal, Don Antonio Permuy, enters the room with all the pomp he can muster, adjusts his glasses, and does the perfunctory three bangs of his gavel:

"Sit down gentlemen, please. The session has begun."

A shiver runs down Pablo's spine. With no warning, a retching feeling surges from his stomach up his throat, leaving a bitter taste in his mouth that will remain there throughout most of the hearing. The acting rapporteur, special investigating judge Señor Castejón, opens the military tribunal by reading a hundred pages of legal briefings to the backs of the accused, while the public section of the room gradually fills with spectators. First he explains the facts of the case and the investigations that led to the detention of the culprits, highlighting the inestimable assistance offered by the residents of Vera and the forces of order. The journalists take notes compulsively, following the rhythm of the stenographer's typing, as he sits on the other side of the room, facing them like a conductor. Occasionally the crowd breaks out in murmurs, especially at the mention of the possible involvement of celebrities such as Miguel de Unamuno, Ortega y Gasset, Rodrigo Soriano, and Blasco Ibáñez, although the investigating judge makes it quite clear that their participation in the attack will not be considered in this summary hearing, but in the ordinary hearing that will take place later; but the most noise occurs at the description of the death of the two civil guards at the quarry of Argaitza, producing murmurs of indignation among the audience. After the narration of the facts, there is a reading of one of the posters found under the entry door of the foundry of Vera:

"You yourselves may judge the intentions of the traitors," intones the officious voice of the rapporteur Castejón, "who distributed these statements in an attempt to recruit the assistance of the incorruptible people of Vera: 'Spain is going through a moment that is so absolutely critical, so great has been the number of crimes and injustices suffered by our disgraced citizenry under the thumb of swine in frock coats, spurs, and cassocks, that it is about to explode like a steam engine under too much pressure...'"

PABLO KNOWS THE TEXT BY HEART, and his attention wanders outside the room, where he hears the distant sound of pounding, probably of a hammer. Maybe it is coming from the prison workshops, where they make the espadrilles that cover the feet of half the workers in Spain, bearing the label of Almacenes Ruiz, a company that has made a killing by exploiting prison labor.

"'Let us save Spain, my friends! Long live liberty!'" the investigating judge finishes reading the pamphlet, raising murmurs around the room.

"Silence, please," demands the president of the tribunal, hammering his gavel against its sounding block.

When order has been restored, the time comes to hear the statements made by the insurgents during the interrogations. These are recited by Judge Castejón and followed keenly from the bench by the four accused, who cannot keep from making faces of surprise and disbelief hearing what some of their comrades have said. Soon, the former guard Santillán stands up from the bench and tries to protest, but Mocholi signals to him from his table to sit back down, because there will be time for arguments later. The court also hears the statements of the carabiniers Pombart (whose hat Naveira perforated just before he died) and Prieto (who was seriously injured in the forest), as well as of the corporal who fatally shot Abundio "El Maño" Riaño. The proceedings continue with the reports from the autopsies and burials of the civil guards, which provoke a wave of signs of the cross among the crowd. Next, the judge reads the indictment against the detainees, including Francisco Lluch, who has not managed to convince the tribunal that he had nothing to do with the attack and that he was only crossing the border to visit his dying father. Finally, amid great expectation, they announce the provisional findings of the prosecutor and the defense attorney, followed by the reading of charges by Judge Castejón, after which presiding judge Antonio Permuy is ready to give the floor to the accused, if they wish to expand on their statements.

"One moment, Your Honor," says Mocholi. "Considering that my client Enrique Gil Galar has suffered serious head injuries, I wish to request the temporary suspension of the hearing so that a medical examination can be performed to determine if he is in full possession of the physical and intellectual capacity to speak for himself."

"Request granted," agrees Don Antonio Permuy, after exchanging a few whispered words with the court speaker. "The session is suspended for the time necessary to perform a medical examination of the accused."

The exam will only take twenty minutes, during which Gil Galar is led to the prison infirmary and examined by two military doctors, Commandant Eduardo Villegas and Captain Angel Bueno. Once they have finished, they return to the chamber and the hearing resumes with the doctors' declaration that the prisoner is in full possession of the mental and physical capacity to speak on his own behalf.

"The accused have the right to expand on their statements if they wish," repeats the president of the tribunal.

But the four prisoners have little to add, and only wish to clarify a few points. Julián Santillán, for example, denies having been detained in flagrante delicto, because he was captured the day after the events in question and put up no resistance. Vázquez Bouzas speaks up to assert that he hadn't been fleeing when he was arrested, but was going along his way far from the events. Gil Galar, struggling to stand, states that when he heard the civil guards shout "Halt!" he made a half-turn and started running, as demonstrated by the bullet he received behind the ear. Finally, Pablo stands, opens his mouth, and says nothing. He looks at the defense attorney Mocholi, and, before sitting back down, says:

"I have nothing to add to my previous statements."

And then it is the prosecutor, Don Adriano Coronel, who asks for another suspension in the session:

"Your Honor, the prosecution considers that, since the Code of Military Justice places special importance on expert tests performed before the trial, and since we are so fortunate as to have Drs. Villegas and Bueno in the room, it would seem appropriate to have the rest of the accused men in this summary trial undergo a medical examination to determine the origin and nature of their injuries."

"Does the defense accept the prosecutor's request?" asks Don Antonio

Permuy in a begrudging tone that suggests that it would have been simpler to make such a request at the same time as the previous expert intervention.

"Of course, Your Honor, the only reason I didn't make the same request myself was to avoid unnecessarily interrupting the process of the trial," says Mocholi.

"The session is suspended again," the presiding judge proclaims as he stands up, annoyed.

This time the interruption will take half an hour, and when Pablo, Santillán, and Vázquez Bouzas return to the room and the procedure resumes, the doctors state that the bruises on the prisoners' wrists were caused by the handcuffs. With regard to Pablo Martín's injured thigh, they declare that it was caused by a firearm, with the entry wound on the posterior side and exit wound on the anterior side, with an upward trajectory. However, the injury is not considered serious, as there is no bone damage.

"Tell me just one thing, Commandant," the prosecutor says to the military doctor who provided the report. "Can you specify what type of firearm produced the injury of the accused Martín?"

"Everything seems to indicate that it was a bullet from a Mauser rifle, such as those used by the Civil Guard."

"Thank you," the prosecutor says, sitting down, as another murmur spreads through the room.

"However," says Don Nicolás Mocholi, not losing any time, "you claimed that the entry wound was found on the posterior side of the defendant's thigh. Would you be able to determine through expert analysis the position of the injured man in relation to the shooter?"

"Objection, Your Honor," the prosecutor interrupts. "The purpose of the medical examination was to determine the origin of the injuries, not to assess how they might have been produced."

"Objection overruled, the question is relevant. Please respond, Commandant Villegas."

"Well, it seems clear that the injured man had his back turned to the shooter at the moment of impact, and was located at an elevated position or leaning forward."

"Does this mean that he could have been injured from behind, while fleeing?"

"It is possible, yes."

"Just like Gil Galar. No further questions, Your Honors. The defense rests," says Mocholi, returning to his seat looking satisfied.

The president of the tribunal again whispers something in the ear of the speaker, and gives the floor to the prosecutor:

"The prosecutor has the floor. I ask him to be as brief and clear as possible in his accusation report."

"Thank you, Your Honor," responds Don Adriano Coronel, standing from his seat. "I will be as brief as I can. But first allow me to again remind the members of the tribunal of the essential characteristics of this trial, to avoid any confusion. We must remember, Your Honors, that, given that this is a summary trial, we cannot reasonably weigh and examine all of the evidence with the scrutiny and meticulousness that we would use if it were an ordinary trial, because quick processing and exemplary punishment are the elements that characterize this type of trial. This has been taken into account here, Your Honors, along with other reasons of a patriotic nature that require immediate sanctions …"

The prosecutor's monotonous spiel continues unabated and the first yawns start to proliferate in the room, spreading from one person to another like the Spanish flu that just five years ago devastated half of Europe. Pablo loses the thread of the prosecutor's speech and is surprised to observe the procession of silent mouths opening and closing among the audience, transformed into a choir of timid singers covering their mouths before a deaf audience. Only when he sees them stand up after a long while does he turn his attention back to the presidential table and discover that all of the members of the council have also stood up to listen to the prosecutor's request:

"For this reason, Your Honors, with conscience vested in our just God, the prosecution asks that the arraigned Pablo Martín Sánchez, Enrique Gil Galar, and Julián Santillán Rodríguez, for the crime of armed assault without circumstances mitigating their responsibility, receive capital punishment, and in case of pardon, life in prison, as well as a fine corresponding to indemnity of the families of the victims, in an amount no less than ten thousand pesetas."

The three prisoners merely look at their defense attorney, trying to control their emotions, but an intense murmur courses through the audience, which now spills out into the hallway, obligating the president to call for order again:

"Order, order, or I shall have to clear the room!" he barks, trying to be heard over the buzz of the audience and the bang, bang, bang of his own gavel.

"In the case of the accused José Antonio Vázquez Bouzas," the prosecutor goes on as the murmurs die down, "the prosecution sees no problem in modifying the wording of its initial request, and now wishes to request six years of correctional prison, for the crime of engaging in armed acts disturbing the peace, it being unproven that he participated in the aggression against the civil guards. That is all, Your Honors."

Seated at the press table, the cub reporter of *El Pueblo Navarro*—the very same who a week ago tried to convince the famous footballer Patricio Arabolaza to confess his participation in the discovery of the body of the guardsman de la Fuente—scribbles these hurried lines: "The accused men listened to the prosecutor's requests with apparent calm. Perhaps Pablo Martín grew slightly more pale, Gil Galar a touch more corpse-like, his facial injury flattened and bloodless, his eyes always closed, like a tragic puppet, broken and wobbling on the bench..." Tomorrow, when these words are published, he will smile with satisfaction at the poetic inspiration that seizes him when he least expects it.

"Thank you, Mr. Prosecutor," says the presiding judge. "The defense has the floor."

Don Nicolás Mocholi, who barely slept last night preparing his plea, does not read his statement but instead recites it, showing off a rhetorical skill he learned in the manuals of Quintiliano, starting with the recommended *captatio benevolentiae*:

"Your Honors, gentlemen of the commission, members of the general public: considering that the prosecution is represented by an official of the prestigious legal corps of the army, and the defense by a man who does not have the good fortune to hold even the license to practice law, it is natural that the inevitable prejudices that you may have formed should produce an environment propitious to the opinions of the former. But I do not lose hope at this, and neither do I consider my handling of the case a failure. While there is great skill and talent on one side, on the other side, from this defense, lie the true orientations that should serve as a compass for this respectable council when the time comes to deliberate on the verdict..."

Perhaps Nicolás Mocholi does not have his attorney's license, but his words have a hypnotizing effect on the attendees, something we did not see during the prosecutor's speech, nor that of the speaker of the court. The affable commandant of the carabiniers knows how to provoke the audience, aiming his verbal darts directly at the listeners' nerve fibers:

"To you," he says, speaking to Pablo and his three benchmates, "I ask you not to increase my suffering, which is great, by resenting my inability to defend you. I have seen you weep much over the past night. Keep crying, my sons, because your tears give me the courage to complete the thorny mission I have been assigned..."

Pablo listens to the defense attorney's words carefully, especially when he finally gets into the substance, and tries not to get lost in his fancy legalese:

"Your Honors, we have before us a case of collective delinquency, but not co-delinquency, which is not the same thing. Because for the former, all that is necessary is a group or assembly, while the latter requires communication of desires or intentions to realize a common plan..."

A draft of cold air momentarily distracts Pablo from Mocholi's speech. He adjusts his coat and looks in the direction of the draft: one of the room's high half-windows has a broken pane. Scanning the room, he catches the eye of a girl sitting in the first row of seats reserved for the public, one of the few people not raptly absorbed in the defense attorney's speech. The girl's eyes remain fixed on him, with a strange mixture of apprehension and fascination, as if two inner forces were engaged in an arduous battle between her heart and her brain. Only then does Pablo recognize this gaze to be that of the girl who came out onto the balcony in Vera, just one week ago, when he arrived in the picturesque village via the France Road, injured and bound with wire. The woman sitting next to her pulls on her sleeve and instructs her to listen to Señor Mocholi, who continues his complicated peroration:

"The outcome of the proceedings will convince you, Your Honors, that my clients are not complicit in the act in question, because it is clear that such complicity can only apply to those who cooperate in the execution of an act through other actions, whether prior or simultaneous, and it is a fundamental principle of penal law that only those acts of which such a person is aware can be considered prior, and that complicity by simultaneous actions only corresponds to such a case as when said person assists another by deliberate and manifest action..."

Pablo again loses the thread, unable to find any relationship between the defense attorney's speech and what has happened in his life since Robinsón appeared in the doorway of La Fraternelle. Isolated from his surroundings, as if it were not him being tried but someone else, Pablo lets his gaze wander over the diamond pattern of the tile floor, and he rubs his hands together in a state of distraction, gently massaging the bruises left by the handcuffs. Only when he hears his name issuing mushily from behind the mustache of Commandant Mocholi does he snap to attention:

"...and thus a summary trial is being imposed on these four poor men even though none of them was caught in flagrante delicto, as required under Article 650 of the Penal Code: José Antonio Vázquez was doing nothing but walking along the road, and did not flee when apprehended; Pablo Martín was not even armed; Julián Santillán was detained in the forest the day after the events, and put up no resistance; and as for Enrique Gil, it cannot be confirmed exactly when he was injured, nor has it been established which law enforcement officer injured him, which proves that the serious injury he has suffered was caused by what is commonly known as a stray projectile."

Don Nicolás's words seem to elicit an effect, and a quiet murmur goes through the room.

"In addition, if that were not enough, the lineup was conducted in an unlawful manner, which means that, given that all of the detainees had met each other either before or after crossing the border, it was not difficult for the accusers to indicate whomever they wished, in order to redirect suspicion away from themselves—"

"Yeah, exactly!" interrupts Gil Galar from the defendants' bench, suddenly awakening from his lethargy, and receiving a reprimand from Mocholi in the form of a dirty look. Mocholi continues his defense.

"It can therefore be concluded that none of my clients took part in the armed aggression, or at least that such participation has not been demonstrated, and to impose such a serious punishment based on mere suspicion would be an affront to the conscience. Tell me, Your Honors, how can you write their sentence if it is to open with a declaration of 'proven facts'? Can you conclusively confirm in your findings that my clients caused the deaths of the guards, or the injuries of the carabinier? No, plainly no, if I dare speak for you. This is why, gentlemen of the council, considering that there is insufficient proof of the criminal responsibility imputed to them, I ask that my clients Pablo Martín Sánchez, Enrique Gil Galar, and Julián Santillán Rodríguez be punished with incarceration in the medium-security prison, according to the first rule of Article 82, as mere participants in a crime of rebellion against the form of government and not as the leaders or direct perpetrators of the bloody deeds in question: ten years and one day to twelve years in prison. With regard to the other prisoner, José Antonio Vázquez Bouzas, this defense seeks his acquittal, considering that he was not part of the armed uprising."

More whispers run through the room, and Don Nicolás Mocholi takes advantage of the interruption to drink a bit of water, bolstering the effect of his words with a calculated dramatic pause before delivering the coup de grace:

"And now, gentlemen of the council, allow me to digress a moment, because it would be ridiculous to seek any other punishment, and yet, given the seriousness of the penalty sought by the prosecutor, it is an appropriate conclusion to my defense. Have no doubt, Your Honors, all of Pamplona will shed tears if the gallows are raised in the region of Navarre. These pious people will feel deep commiseration with these men, who are not professional criminals. Draw near, gentlemen of the tribunal, to the piety that emanates from the God of Calvary, and away from the implacable justice of the God of Sinai. Remember the principle of *in dubio pro reo*: in the absence of clear evidence, it is better to absolve a guilty man than to condemn an innocent. And if you are still not convinced, consider that it is pointless to punish the stone that injures, better to look for the hand that threw it. Who knows if, after some time has passed, honorable hands will unwittingly shake that criminal hand!"

That said, Don Nicolás Mocholi sits back down, casting a soothing glance at his clients, while the whole room seethes with chatter, passions unleashed.

XXI
(1918–1921)

BOMBS HAD RAINED ON PARIS AT the outbreak of the war, and the trickle continued for the rest of the conflict. Airplanes, zeppelins, and long-range cannons launched their payload onto the City of Light, despite the French army's efforts to preserve the capital. But in a metropolis of nearly three million residents and more than twenty thousand acres, the likelihood that ordnance would hit one's own roof was rather slim, so the Parisians learned to live with the air raids just as a person learns to suffer in silence through dyspepsia or hemorrhoids.

One splendid spring evening, with the full moon playing a starring role in the sky, Pablo, Robinsón, and Sandrine left the Cabaret du Père Pelletier and strolled home. They walked in silence, wrapped up in their thoughts. Only Sandrine opened her mouth from time to time to sigh.

"Is something wrong?" Robinsón asked after the third sigh.

"No, nothing. I was thinking."

"About what?"

"About happiness. And unhappiness. About whether it's possible to be happy in the middle of a war. Sometimes I think yes, other times no."

"And what do you think right now?" Robinsón asked, grabbing her waist.

"Right now I think I don't know."

"You know what I think?" Pablo interjected. "I think people looking for happiness are like a drunkard looking for his home. He doesn't know how to find it, but he knows it exists."

Robinsón and Sandrine had a good laugh.

"That's why I don't touch alcohol," said Robinsón, pressing up against Sandrine, "because that way I always remember where home is."

The three friends were about to laugh, but the sound of a siren interrupted them. It was the signal announcing that enemy planes were near, telling Parisians to hide in their cellars and basements. It sounded like the lament of an animal going to slaughter.

"They sure love a full moon," whispered Pablo.

And although they were getting used to it, they quickened their pace across the Jardin des Tuileries, while the luminous rays of the searchlights explored the celestial dome, and the violent curtain fire of the anti-aircraft artillery was starting to crackle. For a few days the German Gothas had been trying to fly over Paris, in a desperate attempt to change the course of the war, which had taken a definitive turn in favor of the Allied Powers since the United States joined the fray. But the defensive artillery had managed to repel the attacks, leaving the bombers to scatter to the outskirts. That night, however, was going to be different.

"Listen!" said Pablo, pointing at the sky.

The drone of an airplane, like the buzzing of a colossal bee, seemed to be drawing nearer the spot where they were standing. Within seconds a tremendous explosion reached their ears.

"That bomb fell in Paris!" exclaimed Robinsón.

Then another ordnance exploded even closer.

"Get down!" shouted Pablo.

And the next bomb fell just a few yards away, leaving them deaf and covered in dust. Two more explosions rang out as the droning sound disappeared into the distance.

"Are you alright?" Pablo asked, spitting dirt.

"Yeah," responded Robinson by his side.

"And you, Sandrine?"

Sandrine said nothing. They saw her stand up from the dust and rubble, eyes wide, as still as a ghost. She was not injured, but when she opened her mouth, no sound came out: she had been left mute. From the impact, the doctors would say. From the shock, the neighbors would say. From the fear, the clients would say at the cabaret. And what do we do now? Robinsón would ask. She makes her living by singing. All we can do is wait, while they diagnose the goiters, rest, and hope her voice comes back. And if possible, get a change of scene. Get out of Paris if the war allows it. Quit hearing the sound of explosions, the whistle of the siren, the sound of a light switch clicking but no light coming on.

A week later, Pablo bid farewell to his friends at Gare d'Austerlitz, where the workers were finishing up fixing the destruction produced by one of the bombs dropped during the night raid. Regularly, every fifteen minutes, there was a violent, dry explosion, and Sandrine would shudder: it was Bertha, the German long-range cannon, which had been spitting its shells every morning for a week, from six to eight o'clock, with strict German punctuality, at a distance of more than sixty miles.

"We're going back to Lyon," Robinsón had said to Pablo the night before.

And then, at Gare d'Austerlitz, they embraced, not knowing that it would be years before they saw each other again.

PABLO STAYED IN PARIS UNTIL THE end of the war, deep into the autumn. Only then did he decide that the time had come to return to Spain, to rejoin his mother, his sister, and little Teresa. Hopefully the police had stopped looking for him; after all, more than five years had passed since the failed attempt on the life of Alfonso XIII. If I don't go home now, I never will, he said to himself.

But first, he had a promise to keep. He rummaged in the bottom of a drawer for a black leather diary, with a date engraved on the upper left corner: 1916. He had not opened it since leaving the trenches of Verdun. He hadn't dared. He ran his fingertips over the rough, cracked leather of the cover. Finally making up his mind, he opened the diary to the first page, looking for an address where he could send it. Nothing. "Here, one lives outside of time, outside of the world," said the first sentence. And then he could not stop reading Benjamin Poulain's words composed for Annabel Beaumont, his fiancée, his *chérie*, his *fifille*, his *petite chouchoute*, words that displayed the soft side of a man who had shown nothing but obstinate courage at the battlefront. By the time he reached the last page, he had a lump in his throat. Later that night, he quit his job at the Cabaret du Père Pelletier. The following morning, he filled a knapsack with his scant possessions and settled his bill with the owner of the inn. He made his way to Gare du Nord, bought a ticket for Lille, and boarded the train, setting out on a trajectory that he would repeat many times in years to come.

When he reached Marly, he asked at the bakery for Annabel Beaumont. The elderly baker woman told him that the Beaumonts were living on a farm outside the village, near a beautiful pond where the German troops had bathed after the conquest of Valenciennes.

"Why are you looking for Annabel?" the woman asked.

"I have something for her from Benjamin Poulain."

"Ay," sighed the baker. "That poor boy."

And she came out from behind her counter to point him the way.

"Wait, young man," she said before he left, entering the pantry and then coming back out. "Bring them this loaf of bread for me."

Pablo walked for about ten minutes with the hot bread under his arm, until reaching the Beaumonts' farm. He could see that before the war it had been a beautiful house, with the character of the old bourgeoisie, but the four years of German occupation had taken their toll: the large garden looked like a jungle, and part of the rear eaves had fallen down. On top of the roof, a young man in a French army uniform was inspecting the damage, while a bald, stocky gentleman held the ladder for him.

"Good afternoon!" shouted Pablo through the fence.

But the greeting was drowned out by the barking of two boxer puppies, excited by his presence, and the only person who seemed to welcome him was one of those clay gnomes that had come into vogue before the war, which Madame Beaumont insisted on keeping in the garden even though the trend came from Germany. Pablo rang the doorbell and a servant came out to open the gate, invited him in and left him standing in the hallway while she went back to the kitchen, where something was burning that should not have been.

"Who is it?" came a voice from upstairs.

And then at the top of the stairs, Annabel Beaumont appeared. Because that young woman with white skin, blond hair, and long eyelashes, who was wearing black velvet slippers and grimacing with her large, bright mouth, could be no other than Annabel Beaumont, the *nenette*, the *petite chouchoute* that Benjamin Poulain had invoked over and over in his diary.

"Annabel?" asked Pablo, although he already knew the answer.

"Yes," said the young woman, coming down the stairs, two question marks shining in her pupils. Pablo took the black notebook from his knapsack, saying only:

"This is for you. It was written by Benjamin Poulain."

Annabel covered her mouth with both hands and came running down the stairs, tearing the diary from Pablo's hand.

"*Ah, mon cher, mon cher!*" she exclaimed, falling to her knees while kissing the notebook as if it were a crucifix, tears running down her doll cheeks.

Hearing the shouting, the maid came running spatula in hand, and a powdered woman appeared at the top of the stairs, just as the stocky man and the young soldier entered the house, while Pablo remained in the middle of the hallway, a loaf of bread in his hands, enduring the accusatory gaze of four pairs of eyes:

"This is for you," is all he thought to say. "The baker gave it to me."

And he stretched out his arms, offering up the bread.

PABLO SPENT THE NIGHT IN MARLY, in the Beaumont's house. When he explained to them that he had come from Paris with the sole aim of delivering Benjamin Poulain's diary, they invited him to partake in the delicious *hochepot* the maid was making. It turned out that there was one empty seat, because Annabel had locked herself in her room to cry and read the diary of her dear departed Ben. After clarifying that he hadn't gotten to know him, Pablo had no choice but to spend the evening telling the family about his experiences as a war correspondent and conversing with Joseph Beaumont, a lieutenant aviator in the French army. The young airman had been part of the famous squadron GC-12, *Les Cigognes* (the Storks), alongside the recently deceased Roland Garros, who between tennis matches had invented a timed trigger system allowing fighter planes to shoot across their own propellers. And the young Beaumont was very proud of that:

"Roland was a genius," he said. "Reckless, yes, but aren't all geniuses reckless?"

"It's an unfortunate country that loses its geniuses because of war," Pablo attacked.

"Better to be without geniuses than without country," Joseph counterattacked.

"But what kind of country sends its sons to slaughter?" Pablo dug at the wound.

"And what kind of sons let the neighbor rape their mother?" Lieutenant Beaumont parried.

But it never boiled over. Quite the contrary. When the dessert course was served and Pablo confessed his intention to return to Spain, Joseph Beaumont made him an offer:

"Tomorrow I'm going to Lille, in order to fly from there to Bordeaux. That's a stone's throw from the Spanish border. Would *monsieur le correspondant* like to accompany me on my journey?"

"Former correspondent," Pablo corrected him.

"As you like it, but you only have one minute to decide," the aviator pressured him, standing up and taking a strange hourglass from a bookcase. It was made of two empty, sawed-off lightbulbs, joined by a twenty-cent piece. The hole in the coin let the sand (which Joseph Beaumont had collected in one of his journeys to the Sahara) pass from one lightbulb to the other. "One minute," he repeated, turning the hourglass over.

But Pablo did not let the time run out.

IN LILLE THEY HAD TO WAIT three days until the weather conditions were propitious to start the voyage. The vehicle was a single-propeller military biplane, three hundred horsepower and three seats in the cabin: Joseph Beaumont, with his leather helmet and gloves, took the front seat; Pablo sat in the rear seat, his heart ready to jump out of his mouth; and the mechanic went to the front of the plane, adjusting a black wool balaclava.

"Contact?" he asked, standing on tiptoe and holding a propeller blade.

"Contact!" exclaimed Joseph after activating a motor switch.

The mechanic then gave the blade a push and ran to jump into the second seat, while the motor started to rumble and the wings shook like those of a newly hatched sparrow. As the biplane left the earth, Pablo couldn't repress a shout of glee:

"Woooow!"

The wind blew in his face and stifled his nose, so he had to turn his head to breathe. From the sky the earth looked like a carpet, with its fringes of pastureland and its roads like the veins of a great multicolor leaf. The plane had stopped shaking, and if it weren't for the cold, the wind, and the roaring of the engine—and the hole in the floor that reminded him that this machine had been designed as a tool of death—he could almost have said that flying was a gift from the gods. After a few hours, the mechanic pushed half of his body out of the hole and leaned toward Joseph Beaumont, trying to tell him something. He tried one, two, three times, but there was no way to be heard. Finally, he took off a glove, dug around in his bags, took out a pencil and paper and wrote: "We have 1/2 hour of fuel left." The lieutenant turned his head, smiled, and gave a thumbs-up with his gloved hand. Only then did Pablo realize that his fingers were aching from clutching the plane's shell.

In short order, they landed at the first clearing they came to. It was a military training field, outside a provincial city, not far from a popular picnic area. A sentinel armed with a rifle came to greet them and then stood at attention when he saw the three-starred war cross pinned to Lieutenant Beaumont's lapel, but this did not prevent a crowd of curious people from approaching the plane and pestering the heroes at the helm with questions. Finally, a military truck appeared, finding its way through the crowd, and filled the fuel tank. The motor came to life again, and the plane disappeared into the sky, leaving behind a chorus of gaping admirers and an intense smell of burned gasoline.

That same afternoon, Pablo and Joseph said goodbye forever at the aerodrome of Bordeaux: the lieutenant aviator would die a few years later in the most unexpected way. He, who had plowed the skies at an altitude of twelve thousand feet; he, who had crossed enemy lines under the thunder of grenades; he, who had landed in impossible conditions, finished his days on earth by being struck by lightning during a picnic. His sister Annabel, *la chouchoute, la cocotte, la petite mimi* of Benjamin Poulain, could not cry for him: during the winter she had caught the Spanish flu, which would end up burying more people than the war itself. And Pablo would not take long to find out.

In Hendaye, while waiting to cross the border, he wrote a postcard to Robinsón, telling him that he was going to live in Baracaldo. On a corner of the postcard he drew an airplane, with three passengers onboard and an arrow pointing at the third: "This is me, I'll tell you later," he wrote, not suspecting that it would be many years before he would be able to keep that promise. Then, once in Spain, he bought a newspaper. He opened it at random and read: "The epidemic is spreading in a fast, virulent manner. The

Public Health Authority has held a meeting and decided to close all public gatherings as well as public and private schools. The flu is making great gains in rural areas. There have been many deaths in the population. Today it happened that the bodies of a father and son were driven to the cemetery together, victims of serious flu infections." The news was from Jerez, on the other end of the peninsula, but it was worrisome nonetheless. Pablo got into the train to Baracaldo with a dire feeling of foreboding, which would be confirmed as soon as he arrived at his mother's house and saw the Chaplain Ignacio Beláustegui coming out, the same priest who had baptized Pablo at the Church of San Vicente Martir thirty years beforehand.

"Ay, my son," the cleric sighed, recognizing him.

And he gave him four pieces of bad news: the first, that his mother had the flu; the second, that his sister had the flu, the third, that his niece had the flu; and the fourth, that his brother-in-law had just died from the flu.

But the Sánchez line was not going to succumb so easily: mother, daughter, and granddaughter all survived the epidemic. In a certain sense, Pablo filled the void left by his brother-in-law. He moved into Julia's house and became like a father to little Teresa. He gave his mother the care and attention he had never been able to show her. He tried to convince her to come live with them, but the good woman did not want to abandon the house where her two children had been born. He went back to work as a boilermaker, as he had done in Barcelona, this time at the foundry of Altos Hornos de Vizcaya, one of Spain's biggest metallurgical companies. He joined the Sindicato Unico, almost as if automatically. And he even started going out with a young woman named Celeste, a friend of his sister Julia: they saw each other a few times, strolled through the central streets of Bilbao, went to the movies, and even shared a kiss, under cover of darkness and without premeditation. Life was finally starting to adjust to normalcy (or at least to what mortals generally understand as normalcy).

Then the manager of Altos Hornos was murdered, and normalcy went to hell.

24

It became obvious that the highest authorities of the dictatorship were not disposed to let the crimes go without immediate and exemplary punishment, not only the killings of the civil guards but also the opposition's attempts to overthrow the dictatorship. The fact that the guilt of the accused was not sufficiently proven was considered a secondary matter, as was the ridiculousness of the notion that a former minister of Alfonso XIII, the Count of Romanones, a representative of the most rancid despotism of the Restoration, could have been the leader of an extreme left revolutionary movement.

JOSÉ LUÍS GUTIÉRREZ MOLINA,
El estado frente a la anarquía

"SILENCE IN THE ROOM!" THE PRESIDING judge shouts desperately. "I'm warning you for the last time, ladies and gentlemen, if I have to interrupt this session again it will be to eject you all."

And he bangs the gavel with such fury that the head breaks off, then bounces off the presidential table and ricochets toward the bench of the accused, tracing through the air a parabola worthy of a ballistics manual. The crowd ducks to dodge the projectile, mouths agape like spectators at a tennis match, watching the object fly dangerously toward the injured, bandaged head of Gil Galar. But Pablo, seated at his side, lifts his handcuffed hands at the last second and catches the gavel head in mid-flight, provoking gasps in the audience. He stands, the guards do nothing to impede him, and he makes his way across the room to place the object on the presidential table. But before he reaches it, a bailiff blocks his way and orders him to return to his seat.

"Thank you," rasps Don Antonio Permuy, though it is unclear if he is speaking to Pablo or to the bailiff, who leaves with the broken gavel to fetch a new one. "Let the session continue. The accused have the floor, if they wish to make any further statements in their own defense."

This time it is Pablo who speaks first, hoping to capitalize on the effect of his gracious gesture. He stands and his voice fills the room:

"Gentlemen of the tribunal, too much ink has been wasted in this summary trial. Half of what has been said about me is untrue. The statement that I brought harm to the guards has no basis, for the simple reason that I threw myself to the ground as soon as I heard the first shots and it was then that they injured me. The man who said that I fired is a liar, and he inculpates himself, because if his accusation were true it would mean that he was at my side when the events took place and he did nothing to prevent it, and would therefore be just as guilty or innocent as me. Let the man who said that come here and show himself, and see if he can prove it!"

The two guards in charge of Pablo force him to sit down, and then it is Gil Galar who takes the floor, standing up with great effort and talking haltingly, almost raving:

"Yes, yes ... Let's find out who said that I fired at the Civil Guard ... Let him come here and say it to my face ... let him swear it before God if he's got the guts ... Come on, now ... Who said it, eh? Let him come forward and repeat it—"

"Anything else?" asks the president of the tribunal, seeing that the bandaged head appears to have gotten stuck in a never-ending loop like a scratched gramophone record.

"No, nothing else, why bother?" responds Gil Galar in a voice from beyond the grave as he sits back down.

Vázquez Bouzas rises to speak. Even standing he's not much taller than Pablo or Santillán are seated. He only confirms the words of Mocholi, delighted that the counsel is seeking his acquittal:

"I have nothing to add to the words of the defense counsel, which are a faithful reflection of the truth," and he sits back down.

When it comes to Santillán's turn, he rises to his feet, staring at the president of the tribunal, and declares in the voice of a man accustomed to giving orders:

"I want to formally protest against whoever accused me of being the inciter and leader of the group, because it is a lie and it is slander, and I want my protest to be legally processed."

"Such protest cannot have any legal effect," responds Don Antonio Permuy, "because the way to exculpate yourself is by proving your innocence."

"Alright then, let the individual who accused me come here and explain where he saw me, who I was with, and how I was dressed," Santillán insists.

The president holds a brief private dialogue with the chief auditor, before speaking for a final time:

"There are no grounds to grant the accused man's request, because the presentation of evidence is sufficient and needs not be corroborated with further discussion following the reports of the parties. In any case, the statements of the accused will be documented in writing. This tribunal will now withdraw to deliberate. The case is ready for sentencing and the session is closed."

Three knocks with the new gavel serve as colophon to the act, and the public starts to leave the room little by little, chatting excitedly about the spectacle. It is eleven thirty in the morning and outside the Provincial Prison of Pamplona the mercury in the thermometers has not quite hit six degrees Celsius. But the tribunal's deliberations will take longer than expected, to the point that at dinner time the journalists are advised to go home, because it is very likely that a sentence will not come down until the end of the day. Some of them insist on staying, but they have to give in to reality when there is still no decision at seven o'clock in the evening.

In any case, the sentence (regardless of the verdict) will not be totally firm, because it will have to be sent to Burgos to be approved by the captain general of the Sixth Region.

Meanwhile, the four accused men have been returned to their cells, where they are anxiously awaiting the result of the deliberations. It appears that Gil Galar has definitively lost his judgment (pun intended—how foreboding!), and is incessantly sobbing and calling out to God and the Holy Spirit. Pablo, in the next cell, tries to kill the time by reading the newspaper that they gave him along with the latrine basin. It is a copy of *La Voz de Navarra* from two weeks ago—back when he was still in Paris and planning to stay there for a long time. Who would have thought that fifteen days later he would find himself in a Spanish prison awaiting the decision of a tribunal seeking to give him "*la pepa*," the prisoner's euphemism for capital punishment? Seated on the cot, as he hears the general population cheering on their fleas in the yard, he distractedly turns the pages of the newspaper, thinking more about the trial than about what is before his eyes, but one article catches his attention: it is called "The Almanac of Omens," and its author is Eduardo Carrillo. Pablo reads the first sentence, because it appears to describe his own state of mind: "For the past few weeks, my life has turned into constant anguish," and he moves to the light of the small window to see better. "The one responsible is a friend," the text goes on, "who, knowing how superstitious I am, has sent me a copy of the *Almanac of Omens*, with a dedication that says: 'So you know what to expect every day, in all of the circumstances of existence, from every object and from all people.' Because, indeed, in this book everything is predicted to torment us at all times."

"Plate!" someone suddenly shouts in the corridor, and Pablo, so absorbed in his reading that he did not even hear the trumpet refrain announcing lunch, gives a start beneath the window.

The menu is the same as yesterday and the day before and every day: two hundred grams of bread and a stew of garbanzo beans, lentils, or fava beans, as hard as stones, followed at seven in the evening by a cloudy broth or a purée of uncertain flavor. So it is throughout the year in the Triple-P, except for Christmas and September 24, the day of the Virgin of Mercy, patron saint of prisoners. Then the prison doctor complains that there are more prisoners suffering from constipation than from tuberculosis! But Pablo will not be around long enough to taste the Christmas menu, and for the moment he chokes down the broth, trying to trick his palate with the help of the newspaper, as reading helps distract from the distasteful flavor of the ration: "And it is in vain to pretend to be indifferent and smile after having read," the article goes on. "The poison remains in our spirit, and when the moment arrives when we need to know whether the lessons of magical science are true, we feel a profound disquiet. I am not saying that fortune-telling is an exact science. Perhaps it is nothing more than a millenarian fantasy, but it is also possible that it is a thing quite worthy of being taken into consideration. What was of concern to such as Socrates could very well concern us all. History itself is an unending study of the Occult: if Caesar had only listened to his wife's dreams, we tell ourselves, he would not have succumbed to the dagger of Brutus. And little by little, as we turn our gaze backward, we stop smiling."

The article goes on for a few more paragraphs, and when Pablo finishes reading it, he remains pensive for a while. He looks at the palms of his hands, remembering the fortune-teller who years ago told him he would die twice, and wonders if he would have the courage to open the *Almanac of Omens*.

In the middle of the afternoon, the four prisoners receive a visit, no less unpleasant for being foreseen: a few journalists, taking advantage of the lateness of deliberations, have asked the warden's permission to visit the prisoners. The first to appear, with his little mustache and his pomaded hair, is the cub reporter from *El Pueblo Navarro*, who reminds Pablo of one of the writers from *Ex-Ilio*, the one who asked him to cover the meeting of Blasco Ibáñez in the Community House so he could go see Raquel Meller:

"Good evening," he says as he enters the cell, preceded by an armed guard. "Cigarette?"

Pablo accepts the offer in silence.

"It seems that the council is inclined to benevolence," the reporter tries to cheer him up. "At least that's what the rumors say."

"Rumors are rumors," Pablo replies laconically, stretching out on the cot. And the poor reporter won't get more than a few bitter monosyllables out of him.

Half an hour later, another journalist arrives, but Pablo doesn't even bother to look at his face. Only when he hears his unmistakable voice does he lift his head in surprise:

"Good morning, boy," says Ferdinando Fernández, editor of *El Castellano* from Salamanca.

"Ferdinando! I can't believe it!" says Pablo, recognizing in this aged man his journalistic mentor.

"I can't believe it either."

And they look into each other's eyes, trying to see a glimmer of hope, as Pablo is attacked by memories, images racing before his eyes as if on a sped-up Lumière Cinematograph, visions of moments experienced with this journalist with his perpetually dilated pupils: the corpses floating in the river Tormes, the churros that they ate at Café Pombo, the bomb tossed by Mateo Morral which nearly blew up under their noses, the old Sherlock Holmes-style gabardine coat that Ferdinando gave him after the attack, the advertisement that *El Castellano* agreed to run when Angela disappeared . . .

"Were you in the courtroom?" Pablo asks, trying to shake the flood of memories from his head.

"No, I didn't arrive in time. But I managed to talk to one of the jurymen, Captain Granados, a friend of an old acquaintance of mine."

"And?"

"Well, it appears that the defense was brilliant and there's disagreement among the tribunal. They've been in the meeting for hours and still can't agree on the verdict. And the longer it takes, the better for you."

"Why?"

"Because there won't be unanimity on the sentencing. And this is good. It will be one more reason to protest if they find you guilty. Active forces, especially here in Pamplona, have already started to mobilize in case they need to ask for a pardon, God forbid. And you can be sure that I'm going to do whatever I can to get you out of this mess you've gotten yourself into."

"Thanks, Ferdinando."

"It's nothing, my friend." And he adds, letting out a sigh: "If anyone had told me when I first saw you walk into my office that you, of all the reporters, would end up on the front page—"

"Well, when I wrote the Josiah Warren quote on the front of the cathedral, more than one newspaper mentioned it."

"Yes, even then you were finding ways," smiles Ferdinando. "What was the quote again?"

"Every man should be his own government, his own law, his own church."

"Look where being so much your 'own' has gotten you."

The guard at the door clears his throat to let them know that the visit has come to an end.

"Thanks again, Ferdinando."

"It's nothing. I'll keep you informed ... if they let me."

And the two old friends shake hands in goodbye.

At ten o'clock that night, the four accused men are taken from their cells and brought to the attorney conference room, where Nicolás Mocholi is waiting for them, his six-foot-three frame crowned with a face that is tired but comforting:

"I had you called here to inform you, unofficially, of the result of the deliberations. I don't want you to have to wait all night. You should know that about twenty minutes ago, after spending over eight hours in deliberations, the members of the tribunal finally left the prison, and tomorrow the sentence will be sent to Burgos—"

"And what's the verdict?" asks Santillán, impatiently.

Mocholi hesitates an instant and then says:

"You've been acquitted for lack of evidence."

The four men look at each other in emotion and surprise.

"But," Mocholi notes, pointing his index finger at the sky, as if pointing to the crucifix on Calvary, "the sentence means nothing unless it is approved by the captain general. If he disagrees with the verdict, the case will move on to the Supreme Tribunal of War and Marine. If he approves it, the sentence will be firm and not subject to appeal, but you will still be subject to possible prosecution in civil court."

"Thank you so much, Commandant," says Santillán, aware of the great effort the defense counsel has put into the case.

"Don't thank me yet," Mocholi warns. "To be honest with you, I have a feeling that the captain general is going to overturn the sentence."

Don Nicolás Mocholi's feeling is well founded: the verdict was not unanimous. Both the president of the tribunal, Don Antonio Permuy, and the speaker, Señor Espinosa, disagreed with their colleagues' findings, formulating a dissenting opinion on the grounds that there is indeed sufficient proof, at least to condemn Pablo Martín and Gil Galar.

"Don't jinx us now," Santillán implores as they are led out of the conference room and back to their cells.

Pablo is the last in line down the cement floor of the third gallery, and on entering his cell he is seized by the desire to find a copy of the *Almanac of Omens*. Maybe it would indicate whether the stars will align favorably in the office of the captain general of the Sixth Region of Burgos.

THE END OF THE WEEK APPROACHES with exasperating slowness. Those who have never been locked up have the false impression from bad novels that the prisoner eventually loses all notion of time. Nothing could be further from the truth. In prison, one is aware of every passing hour, every minute, every second. The trumpet refrains, as precise and reliable as a cuckoo clock, announcing muster, latrine, yard, mess, shift change, head count, bedtime, or silence, regulate the prisoners' rhythm of life such that, if one day the trumpets were to disappear, they would be completely lost. Even the prisoners in solitary confinement, who are not very much affected by the alerts, end up depending on them to order their daily life.

But apart from the trumpet music that reminds him of his years of military service, the only company Pablo has in his dungeon is the faithful starling in the window, who is still there between the rusty bars, despite the cold and damp. Pablo knows that it is the same bird, not by the beautiful glints of green on its chest, nor by the elegant white marks on its throat, nor by the cheerful song that announces its waking, which after all are nearly identical traits in all starlings, but by the veil that clouds its eyes: the starling is blind. Perhaps some cruel prisoner poked its eyes out with a pin, and the poor little bird had no choice but to live in this place from which everyone wants to escape. Ever since discovering its blindness, Pablo has taken care of it and gives it bits of bread, lentils, or the occasional half-chewed chickpea, and as the hours become interminable toward the end of the week as he awaits the verdict of the captain general of Burgos, Pablo passes the time by building a nest for the little bird. He has read the outdated newspaper twice in its entirety, and meals and walks in the yard are but fleeting distractions, only taking up a fraction of the time. Not even Sunday with its mandatory mass, shower, and change of clothing offers respite from the heavy daily routine. So Pablo, using pieces of straw from the threadbare bedroll and the splinters of wood from the old rickety cot, spends the weekend weaving together a tiny nest for his cellmate, following the technique his father taught him for building castles out of toothpicks.

On Sunday night, the nest is finished. Pablo climbs up on the latrine and opens the filthy lattice, causing the little bird to lift its head in expectation of its ration. He places under its beak a handful of bits of bread and water, and gently slides the bird to the other side of the sill so he can deposit the agglomerate of wood and straw in the bird's favorite corner, between the left side wall and the first of the three vertical bars. But the starling seems annoyed when it returns to its spot and finds it occupied. It pecks at the object, as though trying to fend off the forces of an invader, so furiously that its fragile weave starts to come apart.

"Hey, don't do that," Pablo whispers, standing on the latrine.

But the blind starling will not listen to reason, and within a couple of minutes the much belabored nest is in tatters. Pablo closes the window cover and lies down on the cot, covering himself with his blankets. He hides his head beneath the blanket corner and starts to cry, releasing the tension built up over these many days, until, curled and whimpering, he gradually falls asleep. When the trumpet plays muster in the morning, he will get up and find that the starling has proudly resumed his preferred spot on the windowsill. Starlings are not nest dwellers, little Pablo; it's hard to believe you forgot the ornithology classes your father gave you in the fields of Castile.

ON MONDAY AFTERNOON, TWO GUARDS COME to take Pablo out of his cell and bring him to the conference room, together with the three other men facing summary trial. There waiting for them are the investigating judge, Castejón, and Don Nicolás Mocholi, with an expression on his face that does not foretell good news:

"The captain general has dissented on the verdict," Mocholi tells them without ado as they enter the room, averting his eyes. "The case has been sent up to the Supreme Tribunal of War and Marine, which will have to hand down a firm and definitive sentence within fifteen days.

Neither Pablo, nor Julián, nor Enrique, nor José Antonio knows what to say. Only Gil Galar speaks up, muttering a stream of incomprehensible syllables.

"The hearing will be in Madrid," says Judge Castejón, "but you all will stay here, so I advise you to choose a defense attorney as soon as possible."

The four men look to Mocholi, who again averts his eyes:

"I'm sorry, gentlemen, but I have to take a different case ... I have some health problems that prevent me from traveling to Madrid ... I advise you to choose Commandant Don Aurelio Matilla, who lives there and is an expert defense attorney—"

"Tell us the truth, Commandant Mocholi," Santillán interrupts him. "I beg you."

Don Nicolás hesitates for a moment, clears his throat, and concludes:

"That's all I have to say. Commandant Matilla will put together an excellent defense, no doubt about it. If you've been acquitted once, I don't see why you can't be acquitted again."

But you don't have to be very perspicacious to hear the deep indignation in Mocholi's words, disguised as false hope. Sometimes even God's plans follow higher orders.

XXII
(1921–1923)

"OPEN UP, OPEN UP IMMEDIATELY!" SOMEONE shouted as Pablo lay in bed, while a rifle butt rapped insistently on the front door .

Two years had passed since his return to Baracaldo, two years since he had decided to end his life of exile, two years of normalcy which the knocking of that rifle butt would put an end to once and for all. It is well known that we are all slaves to our past, and ghosts can appear at any time: even at three in the morning of a freezing winter's day, while we are sleeping tranquilly, cheek nestled snugly in the pillow. Or perhaps not so tranquilly, in Pablo's case, as he had been having nightmares for the past several days.

"Open the door or we'll tear it down!" the shouting on the landing came again, menacingly.

Pablo jumped out of bed, put on pants, and went out to open the door. In the hallway, he passed his sister and niece, also awakened by the disturbance.

With a gesture, he instructed them to go back into their bedroom. When he opened the front door, two civil guards grabbed him and put him in handcuffs, while two others searched the room: the judge had ordered his arrest for involvement in the assassination of the manager of Altos Hornos.

Things had started to get complicated a week before, when the company fired thirty-eight workers and threatened the Sindicato Unico to sack another five hundred if they did not stop their attitude of passive resistance, asking for pay increases that the management was not inclined to grant. The union men met at the Casa del Pueblo in Sestao. Tempers flared in the assembly, and they ended up divided into two camps: on the one hand, those in favor of teaching a lesson to that "son of a bitch who started out as an intern and now thinks he's the king of the world," as someone said, and, on the other hand, those of the opinion that violence would do nothing to improve the situation (and would probably have the opposite effect). Among the latter there was, curiously, one member who had tried to end the life of Alfonso XIII, though no one knew it. It was not that Pablo had lost faith in the struggle, nor that the responsibility of taking care of his family made him fear for his job, but that in the end he had understood what Cicero wrote about Julius Caesar: it is not wise to kill a tyrant, it is preferable to let him fail so he does not become a martyr. And the authorities would surely take advantage of any attack to carry out ruthless repression against the unionists, no doubt about it.

The next day, the automobile of Don Manuel Gómez Canales, general manager of Altos Hornos de Vizcaya, was shot as he left his offices in Baracaldo, and that same night the detentions began. For several days, the screams of the tortured were heard in the barracks of the Civil Guard of Sestao, and many workers stopped coming in to work: some because they had been arrested, others because they had skipped town. Some even managed to board a boat bound for Mexico or Argentina to avoid the *canario*, that torture device that made even those with the steeliest resolve sing like a bird. But Pablo kept coming in to work, despite the dark premonitions of his sister Julia:

"Ay, brother dearest, one of these days Spain's finest are going to come for you …"

"I have nothing to fear," Pablo would reply. "This time I didn't do anything, and I can prove it."

In fact, he has the best of alibis: at the time of the attack, he was in the factory cutting steel beams. But then, three days after the shooting, Don Manuel Gómez died as a result of his wounds, and the police discovered a terrorist plot led by Hilario Oliver, José Manzaner, and

Francisco Hebrero, alias Malatesta, colleagues of Pablo's in the boiler-maker shop. At the first man's home they found a dozen bombs, fifty anarchist books, and the well-known Browning pistol, signature of the anarchist tribe. Another wave of arrests began, ending up with 150 syndicalists infesting the jail cells.

"Leave my sister and her daughter in peace," Pablo begged as they forced him down the stairs. "It's not their fault."

"Then it must be yours, right, cretin?" asked one of the guards, delivering a kick to his behind. "Go on, shut your mouth and keep movin'."

In the street there was a police wagon waiting to transport him to the barracks of the Civil Guard of Sestao. But when they tried to open the rear door of the vehicle, the lock was stuck.

"Goddammit, not again," murmured the driver, and he took from under his seat a hammer and a chisel. "There," he said after smashing the lock with three blows, "you can put the birdie in his cage."

But the cage was not empty: inside the wagon, his eyes met the frightened eyes of Jesús Vallejo, a syndicalist and boilermaker like him at Altos Hornos de Vizcaya.

Arriving at the barracks, they locked them in a cell where blood-curdling screams could be faintly heard. On the wall of the cell someone had written over and over: "I love you, Mama," until his pencil or his patience broke. In the next cell, a woman in a white chemise and wet hair started murmuring "the rain, the rain, the rain," in a monotonous dirge.

"Shut up, you crazy bitch!" shouted the sentinel, before turning to the new arrivals: "You know what this filthy whore did? She threw one of her clients' clothes out the window! And then she went to the cemetery to eat dirt from the graves…"

The first they called was Jesús, who came out of his cell trembling and with a look of terror on his face. Half an hour later, they came to fetch Pablo. Then, as if reluctantly, they took him to the interrogation room, taking a little tour of the yard: there, naked and hanging upside down from a stairwell, Jesús was being whipped with a riding crop.

"That's what'll happen to you if you don't tell us what we want to hear," the guard who had previously kicked Pablo said menacingly.

But Pablo would have better luck than his friend. Not because he was less guilty, nor because he was more intelligent, nor because they had already gone through their whole repertoire of tortures that night, but because he was the son of Julián Martín, a former professor of Captain Lorca, who was in charge of the interrogations.

"Pablo Martín Sánchez," said the captain, ruffling some papers and parsimoniously stroking his prominent chin, "son of Julián Martín Rodríguez and María Sánchez Yribarne. Let's see, let's see … I had a teacher at school in Baracaldo who went by that name. He wouldn't be your father?"

"My father died a long time ago," Pablo responded, sitting in the chair that the captain offered, "but he was a teacher in Baracaldo before becoming an inspector, yes."

"So he reached inspector? Very good, I'm happy for him. It's a shame he died. He's one of the few teachers I remember fondly. What was it he always used to say?" Captain Lorca made an effort of memory, biting his lower lip and rubbing a hand over his shaved head. "Oh, yes: when you find a good move, look for a better one! This is something I've always tried to put into practice in all facets of my life. And it hasn't hurt me any, I assure you … You, for example, you're a good move, Pablo: I have here a warrant for search and capture that reached this office a few years ago, on the thirteenth of April 1913. Let me think … Wasn't that the day they attacked His Majesty in Madrid, right in the middle of Calle Alcalá? But that was a case that closed quickly. We're not going to dig up the past, surely there's a better move …"

Pablo looked at him with eyes as cold as the steel beams he had been cutting in the factory.

"Don't look at me like that, friend," the captain blurted, smiling. "You remind me of your father when he used to scold us. I'm ready to believe you, young man, all you have to do is tell me the truth. Being the son of Don Julián, you can't be bad people. Look, I'm going to be sincere: this is a matter of teaching the anarchist riffraff a lesson about what happens when they take the law into their own hands. But of course you don't have anything to do with those scum, right? I'll bet anything they force you to pay union dues, like so many others, am I right? You would be surprised at the number of honest workers who end up joining because of threats. I don't want to elaborate, but the other day I ran into a neighbor, his eye looked like ground meat. And I stopped him and I asked him, 'Tomás, by God, what happened to you?' and he goes and tells me, as if it were the most normal thing in the world, 'Nothing, I didn't pay my dues.' We can't let these kinds of things happen, Pablo. That's where all the trouble starts. It starts with beating up the guy who doesn't want to pay union dues, and it ends with killing the manager. You get me? That's why you have to nip it in the bud, crush these vermin, cut off the hands of anyone who rises up in arms. Don't you agree?"

From the yard came a long, acute, howling lament.

"Of course you agree," the captain replied to himself, taking out a list of names. "But let's get down to brass tacks. Let's see, let's see ... Macías, Madero ... ah, here: Martín. Martín Sánchez. It says here that at eighteen o'clock on the eleventh of January, which is the time at which Don Manuel Gómez was shot, you were working in the factory La Vizcaya belonging to Altos Hornos, because that day you had the afternoon shift. Is that correct?"

"Yes."

"Perfect, that's all I wanted to hear. You see how it wasn't so difficult, Pablo? Your father always said: when you find a good move, look for a better one! Go on, sign here and get out of here before I change my mind."

Outside the station, he could still hear the screams of Jesús Vallejo coming from the yard. Pablo clenched his teeth and tried to pull himself together, not suspecting that a few days later the poor man would try to commit suicide by throwing himself repeatedly to the floor from the window of his cell. But Pablo had too many of his own problems to think about to be able to worry about others. Because although he had gotten lucky on this occasion, he suspected that everything had started to get tangled. When he got home, his mother opened the door, having been notified by Julia. She took him into her arms, crying, and when she recovered her composure she said:

"From now on I'm going to live here with you. And if they come to get you again, first they'll have to drag me away by the ankles."

Pablo kissed his mother, hugged his sister, and sighed to see little Teresa, who had fallen asleep next to the fire and appeared to be having a nightmare, to judge by the expression on her face.

"She didn't want to go to bed," explained Julia. "She kept asking, 'When is Uncle Pablo coming back?'"

Uncle Pablo took the child in his arms and gave her his special goodnight kiss, rubbing noses. The girl woke up and, after seeing her uncle, fell back asleep, but now without the worry in her brow. Pablo brought her to the bed and then told the two women about all what he had been through.

"So you might say," he said in conclusion, "Papa saved me from Heaven."

"Thank the Lord," exclaimed María, putting her hands together.

"Yes, for once," Pablo conceded. "Hopefully he'll be just as merciful with the rest of my workmates."

Spain had turned into a powderkeg and sooner or later it would explode. The unions and the owners were at each other's throats and every day the newspapers greeted the morning with a slew of obituaries. Just one day before the manager of Altos Hornos was riddled with bullets in Baracaldo, a cork boss named Enrique Barris had been assassinated in Sevilla, and the next day it was the metals magnate Juan Abelló who went on to meet his maker, in Tarrasa, where the violence of nearby Barcelona was spilling over. The situation in Barcelona was really nasty: there the bosses had managed to turn the Sindicato Libre into a nest of paid gunmen, aiming to wage war on the anarcho-syndicalist groups that were predominating in the working class. And as if that weren't enough, General Martínez Anido, the military governor of Barcelona, had pulled from his top hat a poisoned rabbit that would end up provoking another assassination: the so-called *Ley de Fugas*, or "Flight Law," according to which a policeman had the right to shoot freely at any prisoner who tried to escape. And use turned into abuse: if a man didn't want to run, all they had to do was give him a little shove.

On the eighth of March, almost two months after the Altos Hornos attack, three men riding a motorcycle and sidecar in Madrid shot at the automobile of the prime minister of the government, Don Eduardo Dato, who that same day had said to his wife: "If they kill me, that's just an occupational hazard." Three bullets proved his fears: the first lodged in the chest at the seventh rib; the second destroyed the mandible; and the third pierced the cranium, the meninges, the cerebellum, the annular protuber-ance, the medial ventricle, and the frontal lobe of the left hemisphere. And although the investigation was more difficult than expected, it was finally found that the perpetrators of the attack had been three young Catalan anarchists who came to Madrid with the sole intention of ending the prime minister's life. One of them, Pedro Mateu, would end up confessing: "I didn't shoot Dato, I didn't even know him. I shot a prime minister who authorized the cruelest and bloodiest of laws, the *Ley de Fugas*." Decidedly, the rabbit in Martínez Anido's top hat came out scorched.

Learning about the assassination, Pablo feared the worst. Madrid was very far away, it is true, but as an old saying goes, the scalded cat fears even cold water: he also had had nothing to do with the death of the manager and he had nearly ended up tied upside-down. When he returned to the factory, he thought about his mother, ready to be dragged off by the ankles if anyone wanted to take away her son. He thought about Julia, who still hadn't recovered from the fright of two months ago. He thought about little Teresa, who was still asking who those men were who had come into their home so late at night. And the thought of exile occurred to him. But reaching home, the three women wouldn't hear of it. Don't leave, said his mother. Don't even think about it, said his sister. If you leave, his niece threatened, I think I'll never speak to you again. So he opted to create a hiding place. For this purpose, he chose the little dressing room at the back of Julia's bedroom, sliding the armoire over so that it would hide the entryway, and making a hole in the armoire's rear panel, a sort of human doggie door. In case of unexpected visits, he could simply open it, slide the clothing out of the way, and crawl through the trap, which would only take a few seconds. His chance to test it would arrive sooner than he thought. The next day, in fact.

They were having dinner in the dining room when the doorbell made them jump. Pablo leapt from his chair and ran to Julia's room, opened the armoire, pushed on the panel and disappeared into his hiding place. He held his breath in the darkness until he heard the voice of his niece saying:

"You can come out now, Uncle Pablo."

The three women waited for him, seated on the bed, with their hands on their knees, and could not keep from laughing when they saw him come out from between the clothes in the armoire, like a mole poking its head out of a molehill:

"False alarm," said Julia. "It was the neighbor bringing Easter eggs."

"To hell with those eggs," grumbled Pablo.

And the three women all laughed heartily again, breaking the tension. When they went back to the dining room, the soup was cold.

"Next time," said Pablo, "don't forget to hide my plate before you open the door. The police know how to count to four."

But there would be no next time. The trial for the assassination of the manager of Altos Hornos did not begin for another year and a half, and would end in the middle of 1923 with the pardon of the four accused (including

Jesús Vallejo, who in the meantime had tried to commit suicide again), as the jury was given to understand that the confessions had been obtained under torture. Even so, the trial had an effect on Pablo's spirit, and he gradually became more and more distant, focused, taciturn. He stopped going to union meetings. He stopped walking along the banks of the Nervión. He stopped going to the community library. He stopped drinking wine with his workmates. He even stopped going out with Celeste, his sister Julia's friend, giving a lame excuse: I have to take care of my family, otherwise I'm not the man you deserve, but to do so I'm probably going to have to leave the country soon. Deep down, for all those years, the greatest joy in his life was a child, curious as no other, who never stopped asking about the divine and the human, putting him in more than one predicament:

"Uncle Pablo, if God is everywhere, is he also in Hell?"

Damn kid.

"Uncle Pablo, is it true that fish don't sleep?"

Her curiosity had no limits.

"Uncle Pablo, Grandmother says that you can't smell flowers. Is that true?"

That's how the personal questions started.

"Have you ever been in love, Uncle Pablo?"

And Uncle Pablo had no choice but to tell her his whole life story.

"Well, I'd say that if God exists, Hell must be where he spends most of his time," answered the anticleric.

"I don't know if fish sleep, but I know they dream. Because you can live without sleeping, Teresa, but you can't live without dreaming," replied the romantic.

"Of course it's true, don't you know that Grandmother never lies? I can't smell smells, good ones or bad ones, not the smell of a rose or the smell of a fart," responded the anosmic.

"I only fell in love once and I almost didn't live to tell about it," replied the vampire with no heart.

So it was that by age nine Teresa knew her uncle's story better than the tale of Little Red Riding Hood.

"Uncle," she asked him one night, "what's your first memory?"

"The Lumière Cinematograph," replied Pablo, after thinking for a moment.

And the next day he decided to take her to the movies, in the hope that the Lumière brothers' invention would do a bit to slake her unquenchable thirst for knowledge. The hard part wasn't convincing his niece, who jumped for joy at the idea, but rather her mother, who had never been able to forget the tragedy of the Teatro Circo movie house in Bilbao, where a false fire alarm had led to the death of forty children, smothered under the stampede. But that was many years ago, and the halls were better prepared now. So they left the house at dusk, a peaceful mid-September twilight. And the film that they went to see was *Nanook of the North*, by Robert Flaherty. *El Noticiero Bilbaíno* had published an enthusiastic review that morning: "This is a film shot at the North Pole, with interesting and curious scenes of the life of the Eskimos. The viewer will surely be astonished at the labors and tasks that Nanook the Eskimo performs in order to hunt walrus, seal, and bear and to catch salmon, as well as seeing the hunter hack apart a harpooned walrus and eat its raw flesh with apparent pleasure. *Nanook of the North* is one of the best reels being projected this season."

"What do you say we all go to see the Eskimos together?" Pablo had said. His mood had improved a bit since his colleagues from Altos Hornos had been pardoned. "Maybe that way you'll believe me when I tell you that they kiss by rubbing noses."

When the lights went out, Pablo again felt the same emotion as that day long past when he went with Vicente Holgado to Madrid's avenue of San Jerónimo and paid two *reales* to see the magnificent, the incredible, the extraordinary invention of the Lumière brothers. Now the movies lasted an hour instead of a minute, but the emotion that one felt when the lights went out was still the same. The first reel left them gobsmacked, especially little Teresa, who had to snap her mouth shut to keep from dropping the caramel her uncle had bought her at the concession: a kayak approached the camera, conducted by Nanook handling a double-bladed oar with the skill of a swordsman. A five-year-old boy was traveling on top of the boat, clutching tight to the prow to keep from falling in the water. But the best part was when Nanook got out of the canoe and started pulling members of his family out through the narrow hole, as though the kayak were a great monster spitting up Eskimos: the mother, Nyla, with her weeks-old infant; Cunayou, the bright-smiling teenager; and Comock, a husky puppy with feet white as snow.

"Close your mouth," Julia told the girl again and again.

But there was no way. Especially not when Nanook and the other men hunted a walrus and cut it up to eat it raw. Nor when they discovered a baby polar bear hidden in a cave. And even less when they all started building an igloo with large blocks of snow cut out with sharpened walrus tusks: and the best thing was that the igloo had windows made of ice to let in light! But Pablo started getting worried, because the film had been running for almost an hour and he still hadn't seen what he wanted to see.

"Look!" he was finally able to exclaim, overjoyed. "There you have an Eskimo kiss!"

Indeed, the beautiful Nyla and her little were rubbing their noses together in a gesture of tenderness. And little Teresa looked at her uncle and smiled beneath her nose.

When they left the theater it was night. And although the film had ended with a frightening snowstorm, there was a big smile on Teresa's face, and another, fainter, on Julia's, and a third, barely perceptible, on Grandma María's; and Pablo looked at them, unable to keep from cracking a smile himself, a glimmer of joy or hope. But soon their smiles would turn to clenching teeth, because at that moment, at Ciudad Condal, a military coup was being planned.

That same month of November, the case was in the hands of Attorney General Don Carlos Blanco. And he saw something terrible in those documents, as ten days later he resigned from the case on the pretext of illness. Did it seem monstrous to him to accuse a few innocent men, a few poor abused men, perhaps turned over to the government by agents of the government itself who were themselves involved in shady, unspeakable dealings? Carlos Blancos did not say. But he resigned from the prosecution, and abandoned that commission that would have to issue a sentence sure to be excessive and unjust.

JOSÉ ROMERO CUESTA
La verdad de lo que pasó en Vera

TWO WEEKS, TWO LONG, INTERMINABLE WEEKS will pass until the next trial begins before the Supreme Tribunal of Madrid. Two weeks in which more detainees will continue arriving at the Provincial Prison of Pamplona, accused of having participated in the revolutionary insurgency in Vera: among them, a pair of indigents named Perico Alarco and Manolito Monzón. Two weeks in which Pablo will continue choking down the mess, which seems to be some sort of concrete, and suffering fleas like leeches, and the shouting and singing of the general population prisoners in the yard. Two weeks in which the former typesetter of La Fraternelle will have time to think about what has happened and what has not happened, and what could happen if the Supreme Tribunal finds in his disfavor. Two weeks imagining a thousand and one ways of escaping, without ever trying any. Two weeks listening to the dull hammering of footsteps in the corridor and enduring it when the trap door of the cell opens suddenly and his privacy is invaded by the eyeball of the guard. Two weeks shivering just thinking about the remote possibility that the absurd American fashion had arrived in Spain of offering guided visits to ladies who want to see the prisoners. Two weeks confessing his fears to the blind starling in the window and patiently listening to the prison chaplain Alejandro Maisterrena, who insists on speaking to him of God and the Holy Trinity.

"Look, Father," Pablo finally says, "I've always thought that the best Christian is not the one who talks most about God, but the one who offends Him the least."

Two weeks also unintentionally memorizing the obscene phrases and drawings that decorate the walls of his six-square-meter cell. Suffering from prisoner's syndrome, in which the mind travels continuously to the past and future but avoids as much as possible dwelling on the present. Reading outdated newspapers to learn that Charlie Chaplin is going to marry Lita Grey, the teenaged fellow actor he has already impregnated, and a few others, not so long outdated, that Ferdinando Fernández manages to sneak in for him, such as this copy of *Le Petit Parisien* in which Blasco Ibáñez continues to deny any involvement in the events, although at least now he is showing solidarity with the accused: "My heart is with those involved in Pamplona and Barcelona. They were victims of their own good faith and enthusiasm, and there is no doubt that they will be avenged." Two weeks hearing the sounds of Gil Galar slamming himself against the wall of the adjacent cell, and remembering, despite himself, comrade Jesús Vallejo, who tried to commit suicide in Sestao by tossing himself from the window of his cell, with his hands in his pockets. Two weeks, finally, in which Pablo will receive two letters that will further deteriorate his already shattered nerves.

The first arrives on Monday, November 24, and it is from his sister Julia, writing from Bilbao. The missive is brief and a few parts have been censored. It says:

Dear Pablo,

I don't know if these words will reach you, but I trust that my immense sisterly love will cross the stone walls of the prison. The newspapers say that you boys killed two civil guards, and you can't imagine the fit Mother raised. [Sentence redacted]. But even if it were true you know that I would give my life if it meant I could get you out of there. I can't bear it any longer shut up in the house all day waiting to find out about you in the newspapers. One of these days I'm going to take the girl and come see you in Pamplona, even if I have to get on my knees and beg them to let me in, because they only accept visits from parents, wives, and sons and daughters. [Sentence redacted]. Take good care of yourself and don't do anything foolish.

Love,

Julia

Pablo reads the letter under the window of his cell, to the song of the blind starling, which lately has been chirping incessantly. When he finishes reading it, eyes moist, he punches it into the bedroll over and over until his knuckles bleed.

Three days later, at nightfall, he receives another letter, but this time it is the prison chaplain who delivers it to him personally, to Pablo's surprise.

"It came addressed to me this morning, but it is for you," says Don Alejandro, somewhat consternated. "Just this once, I'm letting it slide, because it has come from Béjar with the seal of the Church of San Juan Bautista. But if it happens again, I'm going to inform the director so he can apply the appropriate censorship."

Pablo thanks him with a look and opens the envelope with trembling hands, recognizing the unmistakable gothic calligraphy of Father Jerónimo, who after the first words of encouragement and the inevitable exhortation to trust in the mercy of Our Lord and Savior, writes the following:

…and thus, dear friend, arriving at the end of this epistle and given the exceptional circumstances in which you find yourself, I find myself obliged to confess something that might further stir the turbulence of your spirit. It regards Angela, again, but this time they are not rumors. After all these years, she has returned to Béjar. She appeared yesterday for the sacristy, accompanied by a girl who must be her daughter. She came to see me directly, brandishing a newspaper clipping describing the events in Vera. She looked me in the eyes and asked only, "Is it him, Father?" And as I lacked the strength to answer, she left the sacristy uttering blasphemies, so it is very likely that she is planning to come to Pamplona to see with her own eyes if the prisoner is the very same Pablo she knew in her childhood…

At this point, Pablo is unable to keep reading. The letter falls from his hands, his eyes get blurry, and he collapses on the cot, under the worried eyes of the prison chaplain, who asks him if he wants to call a doctor. Pablo shakes his head and hears Don Alejandro stumble over the food bowl on the way out of the cell. And so, staring steadily at the stains of moisture on the ceiling, which are starting to blur and take the form of Angela's face everywhere, Pablo spends the night in vigil, reinterpreting the last fifteen years of his life, ever since a bullet pierced his chest and permanently estranged him from the fate that had been awaiting him. At the first light of dawn he will fall into a strange stupor, and when he wants to read the letter again he will not be able to find it anywhere, leading him to imagine that perhaps it had all been a dream. But in a corner there will be the overturned bowl, blurrily reflecting his deranged face, to remind him that sometimes reality takes the form of a nightmare.

•

FINALLY, AFTER TWO WEEKS OF TENSE waiting, in Madrid on Monday the first of December, 1924, at eleven in the morning, the trial commences before the Supreme Tribunal of War and Marine, without the presence of the four men on trial and in glacial cold, chilling to ears and hearts: "Cold, very cold," announces the morning newspaper: "a real ice storm. It is said to be a wave of ice coming from the United States: if it pays import tariffs, maybe we should raise them!" Considering that the case has been turned over to the Supreme Tribunal, the trial should have lost its summary status and hence its urgency. But such is not the case, because the government of Primo de Rivera is anxious to complete the process and strike a blow that will teach the rebels a lesson. And if it did not happen sooner, it is only because of a polemical report written by the high prosecutor, Don Carlos Blanco, claiming that a summary trial is absolutely inappropriate in this case, because it would not provide the necessary conditions to guarantee a fair and evenhanded sentence, putting the war council in the terrible dilemma of condemning without total certainty or acquitting without a full argument, which could be avoided if the four accused men were judged through an ordinary trial together with the rest of their co-conspirators. At the beginning of the week, Blanco sent a letter to the tribunal, saying "if, for reasons of a higher order, I am compelled to seek a guilty verdict against the dictates of my own conscience, I shall be forced to resign my post with the government." In the face of this intransigence, Council President Gabriel Orozco counterattacked, saying that if Prosecutor Blanco was foolhardy enough to stand behind his statement before the tribunal, Orozco too would resign. The imbroglio ended on Friday morning and was resolved as things so often are in this country (to use an expression from the pamphlet of Blasco Ibáñez, which has finally found its way secretly into Spain) of gluttonous, cowardly Sancho Panzas: with two weeks' sick leave for Don Carlos, who will end up being suspended indefinitely in the exercise of his duties.

.

So, at eleven in the morning at the Hall of Justice, the hearing commences to decide the fate of the four accused men acquitted in the summary trial. The procedure is rather similar to what we already saw in Pamplona, as though the same set designer has been hired again, and the same actors but with different names. The public audience also looks almost identical to that of two weeks ago, although slightly more numerous, and the journalists are there as well, pens and notebooks at the ready. Presiding over the tribunal is the veteran General Gabriel Orozco (so hard of hearing that he keeps an old ear horn on his desk), flanked by the generals Picasso and Gómez Barber, who are acting as spokesmen, and the robed counselors Trabada, Alcocer, Valcárcel, and González Maroto. To the right of the tribunal is the freshly shaven, surly countenance of Lieutenant Angel Noriega, who has had no qualms about stepping in to replace Don Carlos Blanco. To the left of the presidential table is the defense attorney, Commandant Aurelio Matilla, who has the difficult task of following the magnificent Mocholi and his eloquent reading of jurisprudence in the summary trial. Finally, in front of the tribunal, the reporting secretary Don Antonio Méndez sits at his table, ready to call the court to order on the arrival of the president of the tribunal. In glaring absence from the defendants' bench are Pablo, Enrique, Julián, and José Antonio, who are in their cells at Triple-P, smoking the cigarette butts that the general population prisoners have tossed from the yard, nervous in the knowledge that their fates are being decided four hundred kilometers away.

The hearing starts with the reading of the minutes of the summary trial, the statement of facts, and the statements of the accused. Allusions are made to the possible participation of prominent Spanish political and cultural figures residing abroad, as well as to the unfortunate conduct of the War Council of Pamplona, which was unable to maintain the procedural formalities for the inception of the summary trial and the establishment of criminal liability. Finally, the time comes for the statements of the

prosecution and the defense, which break down into a dialectical battle
that will surely upset the balance one way or another. However, as a historian will point out years later, the cards were stacked against the defense
from the start.

"Your Honors of the tribunal," Prosecutor Angel Noriega takes the
floor with his starchy voice, "it is the duty of this prosecution to serve
justice, truth, and society. And such high values would be offended if, having heard the account of the facts, the statements of the accused, and the
findings of the summary trial, we were to allow the men guilty of such
atrocities to go without punishment."

The silence in the room is now absolute, and only the spasmodic
clicking of the typewriter dares to react to the prosecutor's hard words.

"This is why," Noriega goes on, "although the evidence may appear
somewhat incomplete, as is often the case in summary trials, and while
there may have been a few minor formal defects in the conduct of the
summary trial, this prosecution will only attend to the fundamental issue
in the matter, which is nothing less than the crime of assault by deadly
weapon resulting in the death of two civil guards acting irreproachably
in the line of duty. And thus in moral terms the prosecution considers
the acquittal issued in Pamplona to be totally unjust and asks that it be
overturned, requesting this in accordance with the holy law requiring the
punishment of the guilty, the need for exemplary penalties in such cases,
and the need to defend Spanish society from the wave of destruction that
threatens it today."

One of the elderly men in the front row of the audience bursts out
in a violent coughing fit, and Don Angel Noriega interrupts his speech
until an orderly appears with a glass of water to soothe the convulsing
grandfather.

"Although it is not possible to determine as a scientific fact," Don
Angel continues without losing his composure, "precisely who was the
actual perpetrator of the shots that killed the two civil guards, it is the duty

of justice to make an example to society and impose the death penalty on those who with the greatest likelihood must have been the perpetrators, because that is what is called for by the heroic guards' right to justice, in due reparations to the *Benemérito Instituto*, knowing that the inconceivable travesty of an acquittal would surely cause these revolutionary bandits to think they can try again with impunity. For all of these reasons, Your Honors, the prosecutor believes that his dutiful course of action is to ask that the death penalty be imposed on Pablo Martín Sánchez, Enrique Gil Galar, and Julián Santillán Rodríguez, with the method of execution according to the Ordinary Code, as well as damages of five thousand pesetas for each of the families of the murdered guards. As for José Antonio Vázquez Bouzas, we seek a punishment of six years in correctional prison for assault with a deadly weapon."

Now indeed the public is unable to keep quiet, and a stifled murmur spreads through the crowd. But presiding judge Don Gabriel Orozco does not have the hearing of Antonio Permuy and lets the murmurs die out on their own without reaching for the gavel.

"Gentlemen of the jury, Mr. Prosecutor, members of the public," defense attorney Don Aurelio Matilla begins his statement, his forehead beaded with sweat despite the cold, "the prosecutor's words can only be understood as the result of the pain and astonishment that we are all suffering. But it is the duty of justice not to follow the reasons of the heart, but the dictates of reason, and the proven facts. And here the only evidence indicting my clients is the dubious claims of some of their fellow rebels, surely made with the vain hope of exculpating themselves. Regarding the injuries suffered by Pablo Martín and Enrique Gil, they only prove that they were part of the group, but they absolutely do not demonstrate that they were the actual perpetrators of the deaths of the civil guards. Also, the events, Your Honors, as is well known, took place at night, and the guards shot at the men with long rifles that could have injured even those who fled."

The prosecutor Noriega clicks his tongue and gestures disdainfully with his hand, showing that good manners are not acquired by daily shaves at the barbershop.

"Even if you are completely correct, esteemed colleague," Matilla points his finger at him, "you yourself recognize that the evidence is somewhat incomplete, as always tends to happen with summary trials, and I agree: in fact, Your Honors, the evidence is totally incomplete, and the countless formal problems that occurred during the investigation, problems the prosecution calls 'insubstantial,' are lamentable and shameful. Let me give you just one example, which is less banal than it might seem at first: the accused were required to swear on their statements, instead of being instructed to tell the truth … and such was the very reason that this same court once annulled a case on the third of June, 1908!"

General Picasso shifts uncomfortably in his seat, having been part of that tribunal.

"Surely you will agree with me, Your Honors: in order to determine who were the leaders of the insurgency, the age of the accused men should be known. The injuries that some of them have suffered should be documented technically. The acts of cruelty which Mr. Duarte alleges were committed by Mr. Martín should be verified concretely, as should the leadership role attributed to Mr. Santillán; all of this should be done with deep respect for procedural formalities, having the prisoners stand in a simultaneous lineup, not a sequential one, and reading the accused their own statements before they are signed. But none of this was done as it should have been. And even so the prosecutor brazenly dares to ask for three death penalties based on mere hypotheses and moral convictions!"

Don Aurelio's final salvo produces a few exclamations in the audience, but the prosecutor Noriega remains unperturbed in his seat, a smug look on his face.

"But since when do we make appeals to 'moral conviction' as the basis for a request for the death penalty? No, Your Honors, no: the moral conviction of the guilt of my clients cannot be sufficient for the court to issue a death sentence. It could perhaps be the justification for an acquittal, if it involved the certainty of the innocence of a defendant, but it can never serve to tear a human being's life away. Evidence, Your Honors, evidence is what is needed, not moral convictions. And, to tell the truth, this defense does not find in the entirety of the summary trial a single piece of evidence, neither sufficient nor even merely indicative, that three men should suffer the most irreversible of punishments."

The volume of the murmurs now increases considerably, to the point that even Don Gabriel Orozco can hear them without needing to use his ear trumpet, and for the first time he grabs his gavel and gives three raps with unexpected violence.

"Silence in the room!" he shouts, turning red with rage and producing immediate silence in the audience, surprised by the judge's sudden fit of anger.

"Let us, then," continues Don Aurelio Matilla, also somewhat intimidated by his colleague's outburst, "leave haste and exemplary justice for those clear-cut cases that do not require contrasting evidence. And let us remember that the code requires that the accused must be caught in flagrante delicto in order to be tried in a summary trial, a condition that was not met in the case at hand, defined in Article 237 of the Military Justice Code. This is why this defense considers and asks that all of those detained for the deeds in question should be processed together, combining the summary trial against my defendants and the ordinary trial being pursued against the others."

Don Aurelio sits down again at the table, drying the sweat from his brow with a yellowed handkerchief and silently giving thanks for the daring applause of one spectator, who is advised by a bailiff to curb his enthusiasm or leave the room. The president of the tribunal exchanges a few words with General Picasso, seated just to his right, and the latter responds by speaking into the ear horn, obliged to raise his voice so much that his words reach the last rows of the audience.

"The prosecutor now has the floor for his rebuttal," Don Gabriel Orozco announces, a few decibels louder than necessary.

"Thank you, Your Honor," Don Angel Noriega clears his throat and continues. "The defense is either mistaken or lying when he puts words into the mouth of the prosecution that the prosecution never said. It is one thing to acknowledge that there have been minor procedural irregularities, which are understandable in such a trial, and quite another thing to say that there is insufficient reason to apply capital punishment. It is enough to note the aggravations of the crime, such as the aggressors' moral milieu and the meetings of a revolutionary nature that took place in the neighboring country, as is expressly stated in the summary. They are all bandits," he says, chewing every letter, "anarchists, and communists, with criminal histories, who had no qualms about viciously attacking two committed defenders of law and order, under dark of night and amassed as a mob—"

"I object, Your Honors!" interrupts Commandant Matilla, rising to his feet. "Not all of my defendants have criminal records—"

"What did he say?" the president asks General Picasso, putting the ear trumpet to his ear.

"He objects, Don Gabriel."

"Well, objection overruled," he shouts vehemently, "You will have time for rebuttal against the prosecution, be patient, sir."

Don Aurelio sits back down, and the prosecutor Noriega continues his speech:

"And what further proof is needed to condemn the guilty? Is their guilt not sufficiently established by the injuries suffered by the guards and the aggressors themselves, as well as the autopsy results and the statements of their own co-conspirators? Of course, Your Honors, the defense does well to maintain the innocence of his clients. Indeed, that's his duty and his promise. But my job is to accuse, and so I accuse, taking a position that is very different from that of the defense, knowing that the poet was right when he wrote: 'In this world of betrayal / nothing is truth, nothing is a lie / but all takes on the color / of the lens that guides the eye.' And clearly Señor Matilla looks at the matter with rose-colored glasses, while I look at it through the lens of the law and divine justice. Thus I insist and say to whoever claims that there is insufficient proof, that I can provide the most irrefutable proof there is: that which we achieve through moral conviction. I have it, Your Honors, and thus I sustain the accusation."

A burst of applause resounds in the room, and no bailiff dares repress it. Apparently the claque is not just for the theater.

"I cannot help but regret, Your Honors," defense attorney Matilla begins, "that the prosecutor has neglected to respond to the fundamental argument made by this defense—"

"The defense attorney has the floor for his counterargument," the president of the tribunal interrupts him, not having heard that Don Aurelio has already started his speech.

"Eh, thank you, Your Honor. I was saying that it is regrettable that the prosecutor has not seen fit to respond to the allegations made by this defense and has insisted on basing his accusation on reasons of moral delinquency. In any case, I would like to make it quite clear that I did not ask for acquittal and neither did I assert the innocence of the accused. What I said was that based on the case files it is not possible to deduce sufficient evidence, nor even indications, on which to base the imposition of a punishment so serious and so irreversible. Because the fundamental question still cannot be resolved conclusively: Who actually killed the guards? Could it not have been the rebels who also lost their lives in the gunfight, or perhaps Bonifacio Manzanedo, who is still recovering from his injuries in the hospital of Vera?"

The prosecutor again makes an ostentatious gesture of disdain from his desk and observes how the public reacts to the defense's words. In the last rows he notices his wife, who waves to him with her fingers.

"And it is not true, Your Honors, that the defense sees the case through rose-colored glasses of benevolence, but through the crystal-clear lens of conscience. And it is also not true, gentlemen of the tribunal, members of the public, that the defense maintains the innocence of the accused, for the simple reason that it is not known if they are innocent or not, just as it is not known if they are guilty or not. But what I do know is that it is my duty to ask for and require sufficient guarantees of the manifest guilt of the accused in case the tribunal decides to apply the ultimate punishment."

Don Aurelio Matilla takes a dramatic pause, leaving the room in expectant silence, slowly looking around at the faces of the public, and then at the members of the tribunal, and concludes:

"Your Honors, I would finish by asking for mercy for these poor, unhappy men, if I were convinced of their guilt. But as I am not, all I ask for is justice."

And he sits back down, convinced that his argument was irreproachable.

"Very well, gentlemen," the president Don Gabriel Orozco stands, seeing that the defense attorney has completed his speech, "if no one else has anything to add, we will proceed to suspend the session and start deliberations."

"One moment, Your Honor," the prosecutor Noriega stands, "I would like to speak one last time."

"What does he say?" Don Gabriel asks General Picasso, lifting his trumpet.

"That he wants to say a few final words," says the general, bringing his lips close to the instrument's bell.

"I really don't see the need, Mr. Prosecutor," the president says, a bit irritated, "But I grant you one minute."

"Thank you, Mr. President. I only wanted to remind the members of the tribunal, and also especially the members of the public, that in case any of the accused are condemned to the death penalty, Article 2 of the Penal Code could always be applied, seeking the government's pardon."

Even the furniture in the room, accustomed to hearing the greatest barbarities, appears to tremble before such a subtle display of cynicism.

Two hours have passed since the start of the hearing, and Don Gabriel Orozco declares the end of the session, as the first flakes of snow begin to fall on Madrid. The Superior Tribunal of War and Marine will have eight days to issue a sentence.

XXIII
(1923)

THAT NIGHT PABLO DREAMT OF THE bare breasts of the beautiful Nyla and woke up thinking they were living together in an igloo. But the dream would unravel quickly. As soon as he saw the newspaper hawker surrounded by a half dozen passersby, he knew that something serious had happened.

"Page 18, sir," the urchin said, handing him *El Liberal*.

Pablo opened the newspaper with a sigh and a premonition. "Late Breaking," he read in the second column, and below, in large, menacing letters, the fatal question, "A coup d'état?" A rhetorical question, in truth, because the answer followed, in the form of a manifesto issued at two in the morning by the captain general of the Fourth Region, Don Miguel Primo de Rivera. "To the Country and the Army," the Marquis of Estella started his harangue, in the baroque prose that would be a hallmark of his junta: "People of Spain: A moment has arrived, more feared than hoped (because we would have preferred to live forever in legality and let it dictate Spanish life in perpetuity), a moment to gather our yearnings, to attend the calamitous duty of every man who, loving his country, sees no other path to her salvation than by liberating her from the professional politicians, from men who for one reason or another offer us a picture of misfortunes and immoralities that started in '98 and that threaten Spain with the looming prospect of a tragic and dishonorable end."

Standing there on the street corner, Pablo read the first sentence and turned to stone. Then, still reading, he started to walk slowly, dragging his feet with the caution of a boxer in the ring, making little leaps, swallowing saliva, shaking his head when he came across phrases such as: "This movement is one for men: as for any man who does not feel his full masculinity, let him sit in a corner and make no disturbance while awaiting the good days that we are preparing for the country." Or: "We do not want to be ministers, we feel no ambition other than to serve Spain. We are the *Somatén*, of legendary and honorable Spanish tradition, and as such our motto is: 'Peace, peace, and peace.'" And after the pompous prattle came the key part, where the devil showed his horns: "Declaring ourselves to be in a state of war in every region, the captain general or his deputy will dismiss all of the civil governors and entrust their duties to military governors and commanders. Places suspected of being centers of communist or revolutionary activity will be occupied, as will train stations, jails, banks, electric utilities, and waterworks, and all suspected and known criminal elements will be arrested. Otherwise, citizens should go about their lives, normally and peacefully."

When he finished reading the seditious proclamation, Pablo's mouth was dry and he was as pale as death. He stopped pacing, lifted his head, and arched his eyebrows. His legs had carried him back home, cleverly. Must be a reason, he thought, and he decided not to go to the factory. In the end, if the coup prospered, the repression of syndicalists was more than assured.

"What's going on?" his mother asked as he entered.

But Pablo did not have the strength to respond; he merely left the newspaper on the table, open to page 18, and prepared himself to wait at home for the situation to develop. That same night the doorbell rang, and the room filled with a silence thick enough to cut with a knife.

"Who is it?" Julia finally asked, her voice trembling, as Pablo ran to the hiding place and disappeared behind the clothing in the armoire.

No one answered.

"Who is it?" Julia asked again, more firmly, but the only response was the sound of footsteps going down the stairs. Ten minutes later, Pablo came out of the hiding place like a mole from his molehill, and this time no one dared to smile.

They could barely sleep that night, and Pablo stayed at home again the next day, waiting for his sister to return from work with a good supply of newspapers. The *ABC* arrived from Madrid with front-page photos of the mustached leaders of the military uprising (Primo de Rivera, Cavalcanti, Saro, and Berenguer), while *La Libertad* carried the headline "Total crisis. The King accepts the resignation of the Government," and *La Correspondencia de España* left no room for doubt: "Primo de Rivera, President of the Council," reporting on the inner pages that the trade unionists were starting to flee Barcelona.

"I am afraid that they are showing us the way," Pablo murmured, thinking about exile, and María looked at her son and could not keep two hard, curdled tears from falling on the table with a slapping sound.

Reading the newspapers put Pablo in a state of deep consternation. General Primo de Rivera had decreed martial law and constituted a Military Directory, arguing that the "professional politicians," as he called them with unmistakable disdain, had brought the country down a dead-end road, and that it was vital once and for all to get rid of the stains of administrative corruption, separatist nationalism, and revolutionary terrorism. No one failed to see that this coup camouflaged another, more devious intention: to avoid the investigation open against various military officers (implicating even His Majesty Alfonso XIII) for the disaster of Annual, where the Spanish army had suffered one of its most shameful defeats at the hands of Abd el-Krim's troops. Of course, the anarchist and communist comrades had not stood idly by, and had even sent a note to the press informing them of the creation of an action committee against war and dictatorship. But the syndicalist movement was not having its best days, especially in Barcelona, where the military governor, Don Severiano Martínez Anido, and the top police chief, Don Miguel Arlegui, treated it with a policy of brutal repression, putting on the final touch one month before the military uprising by incarcerating the top tier of Barcelonan anarchism. And now, to add insult to injury, there were rumors that the new Directory planned to reward Anido and Arlegui for their vigilance by appointing the former minister of governance and the latter general director of public order. The message was clear: iron-fisted repression against union activism was the order of the day.

That night, as the Martín Sánchez family was eating and discussing the consequences of the coup, someone came to the door again, this time knocking rudely instead of using the doorbell. Pablo hid in the dressing room again, and Julia again asked "Who is it?" receiving the same terrifying response: dreadful silence.

"Tomorrow, I'll open it myself," Pablo sneered as he came out of his hiding place, "and let God's will be done. I'm tired of hiding like a lizard."

But the next night no one rang the doorbell or knocked on the door. They only slid a sheet of paper through the mail slot, scrawled with threatening words: "We know who lives here, and we don't want scum in this building. This is your last warning." Apparently the obsession with cleanliness preached by the tyrant had seeped into the neighbors' household.

"Sons of bitches!" shouted Pablo, opening the front door.

But there was no one on the landing.

THE PRIMOGENITOR OF THE MARTÍN FAMILY tossed and turned all night, and the first rooster's call made him jump from bed. From the bottom of a trunk, he rescued the satchel he had bought in Paris during the Great War, filled it with a few articles of clothing, and left the house without a sound, leaving a brief note on the kitchen table:

It's better if I don't stay here. I'm going to try to cross the border and wait for the situation to clear up, which will surely be soon. Spain can't let this barbarism triumph. I love you infinitely, Pablo.

   P.S.: Burn this note as soon as you're done reading it. I'll write to you from France signing "Aunt Adela."

A tense calm was breathing in the railway station. The crowd was smaller than usual and those who were there were trying not to look one another in the eye, so as not to see the deer-like fear of the refugee shining in each other's pupils. At the end of the platform, Pablo thought he recognized a fellow member of the Sindicato Unico, with a beret pulled down to his eyebrows and his shirt collar turned up like the ears of a stalking dog. But both of them acted as if they didn't know each other, and they boarded different cars of the train to San Sebastián. Pablo poked his head into the first compartment and pulled it out again: it was empty, and he preferred not to travel alone. He stuck his head in the second and took it out again: a priest did not seem like the best company either. He finally ended up taking a seat in the third, where there were three people, apparently a family: an old man with a gray mustache, who was peeling a banana with extreme care; a woman (probably his daughter) with an enormous wart between her eyebrows, where the bridge of the nose backs up for a running start; and a child with blond hair (probably the grandson) playing with a tin soldier. They appeared completely distant from the country's situation:

"Do you know how to divide a banana into three equal parts?" the grandfather asked the child.

"No," responded the grandson begrudgingly.

"Then watch," the man whispered like a sorceror, and he stuck his index finger in the tip of the banana, pressing downward until the fruit opened like a flower with three identical petals.

"Hello," murmured Pablo, interrupting the show.

"Hello," responded the family in unison.

And the train started off with a doleful whistle.

Pablo got off in San Sebastián and took the Topo, the narrow-gauge electric train that would take him to Hendaye, on the other side of the border. Ten years before he had crossed it on foot, in the middle of the night, with the help of smugglers and the company of Vicente Holgado, whom he had never heard from again since they said goodbye in the port of Buenos Aires. But this time was different: Primo de Rivera had opened the doors of Spain to let the rats out, following the old refrain that says if the shit will sweep itself away, we can save our brooms. And if some of them decline to leave, there will be plenty of time to chase them out, such as that library rat Miguel de Unamuno, rector of Salamanca, who would dare to call the general's manifesto "troglodytic" and who would sooner or later be exiled to the inhospitable Canary Island of Fuerteventura.

Even so, Pablo's heart started to beat full speed when they arrived in Irún, which would be the real trial by fire. They were required to get off the train with their luggage and to pass through customs, where a carabinier looked through their suitcases and a gendarme asked for their papers. Pablo greeted the first in Basque and the second in French, while they rifled through his satchel and scrutinized his passport, and seeing that he had lived in France during the Great War, the gendarme gave it back to him with a look of sympathy. Five minutes later, Pablo was again aboard the Topo, ready to cross the border, seated next to a pair of French newlyweds whose honeymoon had been interrupted by the military uprising:

"*Je t'aimerai toujours*," the man was saying, dressed like a musketeer from head to toes in black cap, scarf, and cape.

"*Contente-toi de m'aimer tous les jours*," she replied, in a game of words that Pablo would have appreciated if he hadn't been preoccupied with getting across the border as quickly as possible.

Setting foot on French soil, the first thing he did was write a postcard, with the image on the front showing a beach filled with children in bathing suits and ladies with parasols:

Dear family, I have been getting confusing news from Spain, it seems that the Marquis of Estella has taken the reins of the nation. Is this true? Oh, it was time someone dared to bring some order to our godforsaken country! When I get back we will celebrate the good day that has dawned for our dear homeland, but for the time being I will keep enjoying my vacation here in the South of France, where the sun shines with divine radiance. A kiss to you from the coast of Hendaye, Aunt Adela.

He sighed with resignation, stuck a stamp in the top right corner of the postcard and slid it into a mail slot, which swallowed it with the eagerness of a Venus flytrap.

PABLO STAYED NEARLY A MONTH IN Hendaye, waiting for the situation to clear up on the other side of the border and chaining himself, like a shipwreck victim to a floating trunk, to the rumors that were going around amongst the exiles:

"Have you heard about the letter Blasco Ibáñez wrote to Lerroux?" someone asked, and they all gathered around to find out what the celebrated novelist had written at his Côte d'Azur estate to the founder of the Radical Party. "Seems Blasco was planning to do a world tour, but he wrote to Lerroux offering to cancel the trip if they need him in Spain."

"And did Lerroux reply?" asked someone, impatient.

"Yes, of course, he told him to go see the world if he wanted, but to stay in contact, because they are planning to take advantage of the coup d'état to flip the omelet one more time and proclaim a Republic."

However, the floating trunk soon proved to be rotten, and the drifting shipwrecked men would end up drowning with their naïve dreams: in the middle of October, the Sindicatos Unicos of Barcelona published in *El Diluvio* an open letter to all workers announcing the indefinite suspension of their activities, while the UGT and the Socialist Party dropped their pants and accepted the dictator's deal. This was the straw that broke the camel's back for Pablo, and he had no choice but to accept the fact that the Military Directory had taken power. He decided to move to Paris, because although Primo de Rivera would continue to claim that the situation was exceptional and transitory, he saw from a distance that there was no plan to stir the pot anytime soon. Doubtless in the capital he would have more avenues for finding work than in the cities of the Midi, where there was an ever-growing population of exiled Spaniards looking for work. On the last postcard written from Hendaye, Aunt Adela told her family that she had fallen in love with a wealthy Parisian businessman, and that she was going to live in the City of Light.

The first thing Pablo did when he arrived in Paris was head to the Cabaret of Père Pelletier to look for work. But the cabaret no longer existed; in its place was an orthopedic shop. Then he went to the hostel on Rue Lecourbe, where he had lived during the Great War, to see if they had any free rooms, but it had been converted into a brothel. Little by little the country was starting to recover from the damage of the conflict, and it was in the capital that people showed the greatest desire for a clean slate. Paris had been chosen to host the eighth Olympic Games of the modern era, and the motto *citius, altius, fortius* had seduced the Parisians, who were eager (and proud) to be the capital of the world. How else can one understand the infernal contraption that rose up proudly between the boulevards Saint-Denis and Sebastopol to regulate traffic? A total absurdity, to tell the truth, because people idled there slack-jawed, looking at the little red light, causing more accidents than it prevented—not to mention the bothersome, noisy whistle that announced clear passage for pedestrians. Finally, Pablo thought, looking at this primitive traffic signal, things of modern life. And when he turned the corner he suddenly collided with a pair of sexagenarians had also been gawking at the novelties.

"*Oh, pardon,*" they said.

"*Excusez-moi,*" said Pablo.

The man readjusted his top hat, which had slid down his bald pate, while his wife, covered with powder and gemstones, stood looking at Pablo with surprise:

"*Monsieur Martin?*" she finally asked, pronouncing his name à la française.

"*Madame Beaumont? Monsieur Beaumont?*"

Wonders of life, those two sexagenarians were the Beaumonts, whom Pablo had met at their estate in Marly at the end of the Great War. For a few seconds they did not know what to say to each other, until the woman proposed that they go have a coffee at La Petite Porte, which was close by. In fact, they had come down to Paris for the wedding of a nephew, and had nothing to do until the next day. It was then that Pablo learned that the lieutenant aviator Joseph Beaumont had died struck by lightning and that the ethereal Annabel, *la petite chouchoute* of Benjamin Poulain, had been carried off by the Spanish flu.

"We live in Lille now," said Madame Beaumont, dissimulating a groan, "and we only come down to Marly for the weekends."

They stood for a long moment in silence, until Pablo broke it by saying that he had arrived in Paris that very morning and was looking for work and lodging. Then the Beaumonts looked each other in the eyes, shook their heads in silence as if they had been expecting such a confession, and made him an offer: their caretaker in Marly had informed them that he was thinking of quitting, and so sooner or later they would need someone to take care of the estate during the week when they weren't there. Maybe that would interest you, they said, until you can find work more suited to your skills. They would give him lodging and a modest wage; a wage of any kind in those days was nothing to scoff at. He would only have to take care of the dogs and the garden, and maintain the house in good condition for when they came to spend the weekend. "Thank you, I will think about it," said Pablo, and before saying goodbye he wrote down the number of the Beaumont estate's recently installed telephone line.

But the day had yet more wonders to reveal. Leaving the café, Pablo bought *Le Quotidien*, the new leftist newspaper founded by Henri Dumay to fight against journalistic corruption, and the twenty cents he paid for it were well spent: not because the paper made a call of protest against the death sentence for two of the three anarchists accused of assassinating the Spanish prime minister, Eduardo Dato, nor because the front page carried a photograph of Eugenia Gilbert, "the most beautiful woman in Los Angeles," but because on the inside his attention was caught by two articles that would decide his fate. The first congratulated (not without a dose of irony) the inexhaustible imagination of the Parisian bourgeoisie, who, ruined after the war, had found an emergency solution to their economic problems by killing two birds with one stone: firing the domestic help and renting out their rooms, the so-called *chambres de bonne*, generally cold, miserable little hovels on the top floor, accessible only by the service stairs, ideal for poor students or penniless laborers arriving in Paris to look for work. For twenty-five francs a week, one could have a more or less dignified room, said the article, and Pablo suddenly imagined himself living up among the chimneys. It wouldn't be so bad, he thought, surely the views are excellent. And the idea made him smile, there in the middle of the street. The second article was even more interesting, announcing the plans of Sébastien Faure (a well-known anarchist writer and editor) to start publishing a weekly newspaper in Spanish, intended for the large Spanish community living in Paris, which was sure to keep growing in the wake of Primo de Rivera's coup. This Faure had been one of the main proponents of French pacifism during the European war, and Pablo had even written him a letter offering to collaborate on his anarchist newspaper *Ce qu'il faut dire*, just before it was permanently banned by the censors. I'll have to stop by to see him, thought Pablo, maybe he can give me some work. And he wrote down the address of the print shop, called La Fraternelle, located at 55 Rue Pixérécourt, in the middle of the Belleville neighborhood.

The next day, Pablo was renting a *chambre de bonne* on Rue Saint-Denis for thirty francs a week, and two days later he came to an agreement with Sébastien Faure to work as a typesetter at La Fraternelle, where he would be responsible for composing everything written in Spanish, especially the weekly *Ex-Ilio: Hebdomadario de los Emigrados Españoles*, the first issue of which was slated for early November. It mattered little that it had been nearly a decade since Pablo had set foot in a print shop, ever since his time as a linotypist at La Belladona in Buenos Aires: for Faure it was enough that he knew the job and he espoused the anarchist creed, the only faith worthy of being professed on the face of the earth. In any case, at first he would be under the supervision of Célerin Didot, an old typographer who would help him brush up on the tricks of the trade.

"One thing, though: I can only offer you work on the weekends," Sébastien Faure informed him, twisting the tips of his mustache, "because from Monday to Friday the Albatross and the Minerva are running at full steam. But two days is enough to compose a four-page issue, don't you think?"

"Of course," replied Pablo.

Leaving the print shop, the sky had clouded over. He looked at the time on his pocketwatch, but the hands had stopped moving: between one thing and another, he had forgotten to wind it that morning.

"Excuse me," he stopped an aged man who was walking down the street, "do you have the time?"

The man looked at him through thick spectacles and said only the following before continuing on down the street:

"There at the base of the clock, there is death. But fear not, lad."

A thunderclap tolled and the sky poured forth a heavy rain.

XXIV
(1923–1924)

PABLO SOON LEARNED THAT SÉBASTIEN FAURE was better known around the print shop as *Monsieur Fauve*, or "Mister Savage," for his hot and sudden temper. In any case, he would not suffer much from Monsieur Fauve's spontaneous fits of rage, because the old anarchist was very clear on two points: that God was an invention of the rich to keep poor people in line, and that Sundays were made for rest (something even the Lord acknowledged). And what goes for Sunday is good for the whole weekend. So Faure left La Fraternelle every Friday afternoon and did not return until Monday morning, leaving Célerin Didot in charge of the print shop. This Didot was an affable typesetter, advanced in years and proud of his snow-white mustache and illustrious surname.

"An erratum injures the eye like a false note in a concert injures the ear," was the first thing he said to Pablo, after giving him his typesetter's coveralls. And, so he would not forget that maxim of the mythical Firmin Didot, he had him compose the sentence, print it and hang it over the door as a test of his knowledge of the trade.

But the miserable salary of a part-time typesetter would barely allow Pablo to cover his rent, so he had no choice but to call the Beaumonts and accept the job as caretaker of the estate. Until I find something better in Paris, he thought, not suspecting that he would end up staying in Marly for a whole year. He went up on the first Monday of November, agreed to the terms of the contract with Mr. Beaumont, fixed up the shack next to the pond, and decided that he may as well enjoy the chance to breathe the fresh air, hard to come by in the capital. It was also a chance to resume a former pastime that he had completely forgotten:

writing letters to his old friends. The first he wrote was to Robinsón, with whom he had lost touch since the bearded one left Paris to live in Baracaldo. Then he wrote to Vicente Holgado, hoping that after so many years he would still be living on Calle Cayena with Luciana, the tango dancer. He also wrote to Graciela, the wife of Rocafú, and to their son Leandro, who must, by then, have been a full-grown man. He wrote to Ferdinando Fernández, with whom he had lost contact since his press credentials were revoked after the episode in Verdun. And he even wrote to Father Jerónimo, who had saved his life at the Fountain of the Wolf when everyone else had given him up for dead... But of all the letters he sent, only two received a reply: the one to Father Jerónimo and the one to Graciela. The priest in Béjar was happy to hear from him again and told him about the rumor that had been going around the village for a few years: that Angela was living in Madrid, where she had gotten married and had a daughter. Congratulations, thought Pablo, who couldn't help feeling a pang of nostalgia.

Graciela, for her part, gave him two bits of news, one good and one bad. The good news was that her son Leandro was now living in Paris, following in Pablo's own footsteps (Pablo's last letter, written at the start of the Great War, carried the stamp mark of the City of Light), and she included Leandro's address and asked Pablo to go by and visit him to see how he was. The bad news was that Vicente Holgado had died in Buenos Aires four years before, during the bloody events of Argentina's own Tragic Week. Following a metal workers' strike for an eight-hour work day, a terrible face-off had occurred between the forces of order and the workers, ending in hundreds of deaths and thousands of injuries. But Vicente had not been killed by the police, but by the boys of the Argentine Patriotic League, a xenophobic nationalist attack force that had shown that Mussolini's fascism had a twin brother on the other side of the Atlantic. He was riddled by twelve bullets in the doorway of his home and died in the arms of Luciana, the tango dancer, who heard the gunshots and came running down the stairs just in time to hear him say "I love you," followed by an agonized "Sons of…" which Vicente left unfinished.

A few days after receiving the letter from Graciela, Pablo went to see Leandro, taking advantage of having finished his work at La Fraternelle early in the afternoon. It was a sad, rainy Sunday, one of those Sundays that seem to be made for suicides and gravediggers. Leandro was living in a hostel on Rue des Beaux Arts, just across from the Hôtel d'Alsace, where Oscar Wilde had died toasting with champagne, leaving an unpaid debt of more than two thousand francs, after claiming that "in this world of ours, there is no spectacle more lugubrious than a rainy Sunday afternoon in Paris."

Pablo rang at the door, but no one answered. He tried again and heard a groan coming from the bedroom.

"Leandro?" he asked, speaking through the crack in the door.

"Who is it?" roared a hoarse voice.

"It's Pablo, Pablo Martín, your mother wrote to me to tell me—"

The door opened suddenly and the silhouette of a giant appeared:

"Pablo!" exclaimed the silhouette, leaping on the visitor, strangling him more than hugging him. "Come in, che, come in. A real pleasure to see ya…"

The son of Rocafú had turned into a big man, over six foot four, broad and strong as a windmill. He was wearing pajamas and his hair was mussed.

"Pardon the mess, I had a long night. Care for some yerba maté?"

Leandro brewed the bitter herb in a little gourd, and Pablo burned his tongue on the first sip. Then they caught up, and it turned out that the son of Graciela was working as a waiter at the Point du Jour, a bar near the print shop of Sébastien Faure.

"Don't tell me you're working for the old crank!" the Argentine wondered. "Did ya know he was friends with my daddy? Pen pals, really, because they never got to meet each other in person. But they wrote each other every month, Papa in Spanish and Faure in French, don't ask me how they did it, but they understood each other. I suppose that deep down they spoke the same 'language'—the language of Proudhon, Bakunin, Ferrer Guàrdia, and Malatesta. It was Malatesta who put them in touch with each other. So when I arrived in Paris I went to see him and said, 'Monsieur Faure, I'm the son of Ataúlfo Fernández and I'm looking for work.'"

"And he didn't give you anything at La Fraternelle?"

"Yeah, he did, he took me on as an apprentice, but I didn't even last two weeks. I'm not cut out for it, Pablo. Haven't you seen my hands? Look at these fingers! When I try to grab a letter I grab the whole tray!"

Over the head of the bed there was a photograph of a soccer team, framed and with a crack in the glass.

"Remember that?" Leandro asked.

"Of course," replied Pablo. "Argentinos Juniors, the proletariat team."

"Formerly known as the Martyrs of Chicago. Did you know they're playin' in the premier league now? This photo is a relic, 'cause the jersey's not red and white anymore, now it's green and white."

They filled their gourds again and went on talking.

"I imagine you've heard about Vicente," said Leandro.

"Yes, I learned from your mother's letter."

There was an uncomfortable silence.

"I came to Paris after they killed him," Leandro finally said. "I couldn't take it in Argentina anymore … My old man always said that a conservative is someone who prefers injustice to disorder. And my country is full of conservatives, Pablo. You know what? Those sons of bitches from the Patriotic League were fixin' to kill me too. Look," he said, lifting his shirt and showing a bullet scar: "I got out of there with this in my side, but there are two of them who will never forget my face … if they can remember anything at all! You know what I did to them?"

Pablo arched his eyebrows.

"I grabbed them by their necks and knocked their goddamned heads together, so hard their skulls split open like a couple of ripe watermelons. They left a hell of a mess on my shirt."

For a moment all that was heard was the sipping of the mate straws. When seven o'clock rang out from the nearby church, Pablo got up to leave.

"Wait," said Leandro, "D'you have a bicycle?"

"No," said Pablo, putting on his coat. It had started to rain.

"Then I've got a present for ya," said Leandro, with a giant smile. He shuffled through the junk in the corner until a handlebar appeared, then a seat and finally an entire bicycle.

"*Voilà!*" he exclaimed with joy. "It's old, but it's not just any bike. It's a Clément Luxe from '96, a real antique. So treat 'er gently, like she was yer granny. Also, the scrap dealer I bought her off of told me she used to belong to one of those famous bohemian painters or writers, I can't remember who—"

"But you're not going to need it, Leandro?"

"Me? You want me to smash it to bits? The day I tried it out I nearly killed myself. Tell the truth I only bought it 'cause I felt sorry for the scrap dealer…"

Pablo and Leandro embraced, or rather it was Leandro who embraced Pablo while Pablo let himself be squeezed by that soft-hearted giant.

"Come by the Point du Jour whenever you want. I work there every day except Sunday, because I told the boss my religion wouldn't allow it…We'll see if he ever finds out that I'm more of an atheist than Galileo! It's on Rue de Belleville, by Place des Fêtes."

"We'll see each other there for sure, Leandro. All three of us."

"Three?"

"Yeah, of course. You, me, and Clément here." He smiled and stroked the seat of the Clément Luxe.

He left with an old bicycle and a new friend.

THE MONTHS PASSED WITH THE PHLEGMATIC precision of a Swiss watch. The Military Directory went about consolidating its power in Spain, and for Pablo the idea of returning home seemed ever more remote. In France, on the other hand, it was the left that took power, and the new Cartel des Gauches turned a blind eye to the groups of Spanish exiles, ever greater in number, who were holding meetings to protest against the dictatorship of Primo de Rivera. The activities were well documented in the weekly *Ex-Ilio*, which Pablo was now solely responsible for editing, since the aged Célerin Didot had had to retire after suffering an embolism which left half of his body paralyzed. The print run was modest, but it got as high as two thousand copies during the Olympics, because many Spanish workers had worked on the construction of the shiny new Stade de Colombes and the Piscine de Tourelles, and they passionately followed the results of their compatriots in the contests of track and field, tennis, swimming, soccer, and boxing. And when the Olympic Games reached their end (without a single miserable medal in the locker room of the Spanish sporting army, as one journalist called it), it was the first anniversary of Primo de Rivera's coup d'état that filled the four pages of *Ex-Ilio*.

At that time, Paris had turned into a boiling pot of anarchists, communists, Republicans, and Catalan separatists, conspiring in broad daylight with the insolence and resolution of those who believe they have justice on their side. September was beginning, and La Fraternelle was invaded by groups, associations, collectives, and clubs of Spaniards who wanted to publish pamphlets, brochures, fliers, and posters announcing meetings, talks, colloquia, or theatrical performances to protest against the situation in Spain and to mark the upcoming anniversary of the military uprising.

"If this keeps going on, I'm going to need someone to help me at the print shop," said Pablo to Sébastien Faure, seeing that the work was starting to pile up.

And although Monsieur Fauve grunted and cursed and tugged his mustache, the next day he sent a beardless lad named Julianín, the son of immigrants from Álava, so Pablo could teach him the job. Smart move, because the work did not let up after the thirteenth of September. The commemorative activities stretched on for a few weeks, as though the indicated date had been only an excuse to stoke up the exiles, the starting gun for a protest movement that was bound to explode sooner or later. Pablo could not attend many of those activities, because he had to spend the weekdays at Marly-les-Valenciennes taking care of the Beaumont estate. But he did manage to attend some of the major meetings, such as the one organized at the Union Local by the politician Rodrigo Soriano, attended by more than six hundred people and criticized in a ferocious article in *L'Humanité* titled "Anarchists and Bourgeoisie Rub Elbows," which claimed that anarchists were nothing more than the bourgeois of the working class. But even more famous was the meeting that took place on the first Saturday of October in the Community House, with the participation of Blasco Ibáñez, who seemed to want to show Soriano—his sworn enemy—that he was able to attract a bigger crowd. Of course, on this occasion Pablo ended up attending in a professional capacity:

"Hey, you were thinking about going to the Community House tonight, right?" one of the writers of *Ex-Ilio* had asked him that same afternoon.

And Pablo had said yes, because he had been planning to pop in for a while after leaving La Fraternelle.

"Thing is, I have a date with a girl to see Raquel Meller tonight . . . You'd only have to take notes, and tomorrow I'll come in first thing and get them, and write the article . . ."

It was not the first time Pablo had been asked such favors and accepted, even though Sébastien Faure absolutely forbade it. He left La Fraternelle with a notebook in his hand, ate a bite at the Point du Jour with his friend Leandro, and then headed to the Community House pedaling the old Clément Luxe 1896. The place was packed, and Blasco Ibáñez had managed to beat Rodrigo Soriano not only in quantity but also in quality:

the cream of the crop of the Spanish intelligentsia exiled in Paris were all there. As soon as he walked into the assembly room, Pablo saw Miguel de Unamuno seated in a corner, in his usual posture, with his legs crossed and the toes of the top leg tucked behind the calf of the bottom leg, listening attentively to the words of José Ortega y Gasset, another illustrious intellectual who had had to abandon the homeland. A little further on, a group of renowned politicians was standing in a circle waiting for the speech to start, and Pablo was able to distinguish among them Francesc Macià and Rodrigo Soriano himself, who was grinning from ear to ear as if he wanted to prove to everyone that he had come to hear Blasco because this was no time for rivalry among peers. Pablo went to the back of the room and, passing by the circle of politicians, he could hear Macià saying in his Catalan accent:

"I already dealt with that issue ..."

Just then Blasco Ibáñez took the podium and the most riled-up members of the audience broke out in cheers and applause, which would end up peppering the whole speech. When he finished talking, he came down from the stage and left the Community House like a real music hall diva, waving at his admirers. As he recorded this image in his notebook, Pablo heard someone at his side:

"You want some?"

He lifted his gaze and saw a man with a pocked face offering him a little tin of snuff.

"No, thanks."

"Interesting speech, huh? Blasco knows how to hit where it hurts. I saw more than one person squirm to hear him criticize Spain. Some people would rather keep their blinders on, don't you think?"

"Well, nobody likes to hear a mother insulted, even if the one doing it is a brother—even if the brother is right."

"Yes, I think that's exactly what it is," the man conceded, before clarifying, in a quieter voice, "Especially if you're an infiltrator. That's why it's better not to speak of certain things here. Come by afterward to the café La Rotonde and join our discussion group …"

Pablo observed the man attentively as he snorted a pinch of snuff.

"I'm sorry, I can't. I have to wake up early tomorrow for work," he declined the invitation.

"A shame. What's the world coming to when not even *la France* respects the day of rest?" he lamented as he took out a card with the address of the Café de la Rotonde. "Come by one of these days, but don't wait too long."

Pablo took the card and headed toward the exit. The man's last few words had left him ill at ease. Leaving the room, he thought he heard someone shout his name, but he didn't turn around to make sure: he mounted his bicycle and pedaled away with all his strength until reaching his hovel on Rue Saint-Denis. Only then, arriving at home and looking at the card from the man with the pockmarked face, did he realize that there was handwriting on the back: "We need your help, friend. Contact us immediately."

That night he had nightmares and the next morning he went to La Fraternelle in a foul mood. To make matters worse, the writer who had asked him to cover Blasco Ibáñez's speech did not appear in the print shop all morning, and Pablo ended up having to write the article himself, swearing it would be the last time. When he finished writing the text, he lined up a set of characters and composed the headline that would appear on the first page of *Ex-Ilio*: "Blasco Ibáñez Stirs the Conscience of Spanish Immigrants in Paris."

But then there were two loud knocks on the door, and Pablo jumped, overturning the tray and spilling type all over the floor.

−26−

The death penalty, as states apply it today, certainly originates in a spirit of vengeance, vengeance without measure, as terrible as hate can inspire, or vengeance governed by a sort of summary justice, that is, punishment as retaliation: an eye for an eye, a tooth for a tooth, a head for a head.

ÉLISÉE RECLUS, cited by El Duende de la Cárcel

in *La tragedia de Vera: un crimen jurídico*

THE SUPREME TRIBUNAL ON WAR AND MARINE has eight days to hand down a sentence, but it only takes three to issue its verdict: on Wednesday, December 3, 1924, in the early evening, a captain of the Civil Guard departs from the offices of the Hall of Justice of Madrid and takes the train to Burgos, carrying under his arm a large binder to be given to the captain general of the Sixth Region. Few people know its contents, and at the Triple-P the defendants are biting their nails waiting for the disquieting rumors that have come across the prison walls to be proved true or false. And what these rumors say is that the verdict is unforgiving to three of them and amenable to the fourth. However, it will not be until tomorrow evening that the notice will be officially pronounced, revealing the entire contents of the sentence handed down by the Supreme Tribunal on War and Marine, including fourteen findings and seven conclusions, for a total of more than two hundred pages. Too much ink, as Pablo recently said, for a lot of balderdash and such a sad result: José Antonio has been acquitted for now, but he must tread carefully the rest of his days; as for Pablo, Enrique, and Julián, they must get ready to act in their final scene in this thankless theater known as the gallows.

The three prisoners receive the news in the attorney conference room at the Provincial Prison of Pamplona. They are taken out of their cells after dinner, the flavorless mush churning in their nervous stomachs. In the corridor of the third gallery, when they see that Vázquez Bouzas is not with them, they start to suspect that their worst fears are true. When they arrive in the conference room and find Nicolás Mocholi with bloodshot eyes, there is no room left for doubt. By his side Don Daniel Gómez Estrada smoothes his hair, shining with brilliantine.

"You can sit down, if you like," says the peacock of a warden, with feigned anguish that only betrays the hypocrisy of his politeness.

But the three men have no desire to sit, and they remain standing as they listen to the quivering voice of Don Nicolás:

"I won't beat around the bush. The three of you have been sentenced to capital punishment. Tomorrow you will be officially informed of the sentence and on Saturday it will be carried out at the break of dawn."

Mocholi's abrupt words have a paralyzing effect, freezing the scene and stopping time for a few seconds, until Gil Galar breaks the spell, collapsing to his knees in a fit of convulsions and sobbing. But Pablo cannot hear him, because a sudden fear has taken over his senses and he stops listening to what is going on around him. He can only see. And he sees Gil Galar fall to the floor and no one go to help him up. He sees Mocholi move his lips in an appeal for calm, his vitiligo-stained hands making wild gesticulations up and down. He sees Santillán kick a chair and two guards try to subdue him, under the disapproving eye of the warden, who pounds the floor with his cane. He sees paint flaking off the walls and wet cigarette butts in the spittoons. He sees the guards' uniforms, their bayonets, and the chinstraps pressing their jowls. He sees his own hands and the shackles binding them and his blown-out shoes and his prison uniform. And only when the guards take him out of the conference room does he begin to recover his hearing, just in time to hear Mocholi saying to Daniel Gómez Estrada:

"No, sir, the people of Navarra will not allow the blood of these poor wretches to fall on its soil!"

Don Nicolás's vehement assertion does not allay the anguish of the poor wretches, but it does accurately reflect the state of mind of the majority of the local population. Yesterday afternoon, the most pessimistic rumors began to circulate, and the machinery to seek a pardon began to turn, emboldened by the knowledge that it had been granted two months ago to Pedro Mateu and Luís Nicolau (condemned to death for assassinating the prime minister of the government, Don Eduardo Dato), so there is no reason it should be denied this time. The truth is that there is a certain discomfort among certain sectors of Pamplona's society, and although no one dares to justify the revolutionary attempt, there are many who would readily accept the overthrow of the dictatorship. The spectacle of the garrote, furthermore, would be the shameful culmination of a trial full of irregularities, which, to further the scorn, has ended with a severe punishment for those who voted in favor of acquittal in the first summary war trial: two months of imprisonment for the five speakers and one month of probation for the presiding judge, Commandant González de Castejón, for lack of zeal in the fulfillment of their duties. Of course, neither the president of the tribunal Don Antonio Permuy nor the rapporteur Don Manuel Espinosa, who issued dissenting opinions, were subject to any disciplinary action.

The three prisoners are returned to their cells, in tomblike silence, only interrupted here and there by the whimpering of Gil Galar. When Pablo enters his cell, he has the impression that it has shrunk. He flops onto his lousy cot and thinks about Angela, and about his sister Julia, and his niece Teresa, and his compassionate mother, and his deceased father, and he feels the need to see the sky and the stars and the constellation Cassiopeia, with its shape like an M, an M for Martín. And the prisoner in cell 31 gets up from his cot, climbs up on the toilet and opens the filthy portico, to see that the sky is still clouded over and not a single star is visible in the firmament. But what he can see is the blind starling, strangely motionless on its ledge. He pokes it with his finger and it doesn't move: apparently death, before knocking at his door, has had the courtesy to appear at the window.

PABLO HAS BARELY CLOSED HIS EYES when the trumpet blares muster. It is seven in the morning on the last day of his life, and drops of rain are splattering on the cobblestones of the courtyard, producing a dull noise like frying food which drowns out the bustle that has taken over the prison since dawn. The guards of the Provincial Prison of Pamplona have been reinforced with forty soldiers of the Regimiento de Infantería América, perhaps in fear of an unlikely assault by the revolutionary hordes to liberate their condemned comrades, and the special forces of the Civil Guard have also come to offer their services, securing the building and the nearby streets on foot and on horseback. Also, access to the prison has been strictly forbidden to anyone not having written authorization from the presiding judge.

Beyond the prison walls, activities are more frenetic than inside, as there are many organizations, associations, and personalities mobilizing to seek a pardon for the three condemned men. The mayor of Pamplona, Don Leandro Nagore y Nagore, is at the forefront, dashing off telephone calls to the Directory and to the mayorship of the palace, and personally visiting the Bishop of Pamplona, the vice president of the deputation, and the civil governor to ask them to intercede on behalf of the prisoners. Also doing their part are the Chamber of Commerce, the Press Association, the Osasuna Sporting Association, the Red Cross, the deputation, and the Athenaeum; even the Socialist Party will, at the last hour of the evening, join in the petitions for pardon, although with limited enthusiasm, because anarchists are not the saints of their devotion, per se. But the heart of Alfonso XIII does not soften with telegrams such as the one sent by the vice president of the Regional Deputation of Navarra to the mayor of the palace:

> Ruego Vuecencia hereby transmits to His Majesty the King fervent supplication of Deputation Navarra that, proving once again his noble sentiments, he grant if possible royal pardon to three unfortunate men condemned death High Council of War for reprehensible acts in Vera where two civil guards sacrificed life. With sincerest gratitude I reiterate to Your Majesties unwavering loyalty of Navarra and its Deputation. Vice President Gabriel Erro.

Up to a certain point, it makes sense that the proud Alfonso XIII would not compromise with the supplications of a handful of bureaucrats and a half-dozen bleeding-heart associations; but the fact that he also does not yield before the complaints of the Holy Church, considering the king's strong tendency to cater to the will of the clergy, is something that not even the Bishop of Pamplona can understand. But such is the caprice of the son of María Cristina. The prelate will have no choice but to order all of the temples of Navarra to direct their prayers to Heaven for the three wretches' pardon.

"I would like the Civil Guard to be grateful to me," the Bourbon will say, after claiming that the garrote is more humanitarian than the guillotine or the firing squad because it does not produce a release of blood. "In consideration of the *Benemérito Instituto*, I decline to grant a pardon to the assassins of two guardsmen."

But until the vile garrote starts to pierce the neck of the condemned, there will always be those who take refuge in popular wisdom: where there is life, there is hope.

Pablo does not move from his cot in cell 31, tucked into his blankets, not even when they bring him the morning's stale coffee. In the adjacent cell, Gil Galar breaks out in an agonized litany, interrupted here and there by sudden strikes against the wall. It is not unlikely that all three condemned men are entertaining the same dark idea, as would surely happen to anyone in their situation. Pablo, in any case, cannot help thinking about the conscript who committed suicide by tossing himself repeatedly against the wall of his narrow cell; or about Jesús Vallejo, the workmate from Altos Hornos who tried twice without success. And having crossed that line, his mind gets lost in dark thoughts, wandering toward those that succumbed to the sirens' song. And so he thinks about Mateo Morral, who shot himself in the heart. And about Leandro's father, Don Ataúlfo Fernández, who did away with his life by putting a bullet in his temple. And about a story that Vicente Holgado told him when they lived together in Buenos Aires, a story of a faraway country where they force the condemned to choose from among ten capsules of cyanide, knowing that one of them is empty … Pablo also thinks about the possibility that people will come to watch him die in the garrote, and the very idea makes him shudder from head to toes. He wonders if the prisoners will be taken to the barber before going to the killing square, so they will be presentable when their necks are crushed. An old wives' tale comes to mind: once upon a time, if a prisoner's noose broke twice in a row, he would be set free. Unfortunately, the garrote is made of unbreakable steel.

Suddenly, the door to cell 31 opens and he hears the nasal voice of a guard in the corridor:

"You have a visitor, Martín. Please come with us."

"Who is it?" Pablo asks as the guards put him in handcuffs.

"Your wife and daughter," responds the nasal voice, and Pablo is about to say that it must be a mistake, because he has no wife nor daughter. But then he thinks that maybe it will be his sister Julia, having come to visit him with little Teresa and having lied about her identity so they would let her in.

They go down the corridor of the third gallery and then up to the first floor of the central building, where the visiting room is located. It is a long, inhospitable room, and only the scant light from a tiny window makes it possible to discern the visitors' faces. Two large, parallel, vertical fences divide the room into three parts: on one side, the prisoners' section, on the other, that of the visitors, and in between, a dead zone occupied by a guard, to make sure that nothing but desperate words can cross the dense iron mesh.

But when Pablo arrives in the visitation room, it is not his sister and niece who await him:

"Angela?" he says with a thin voice that falters on its way out of his throat.

"Pablo?" Angela replies, her eyes filling with tears.

"How did you—?" Pablo starts to ask, but is unable to finish the sentence.

"Why didn't you tell me?" Angela murmurs.

"I thought—" he says.

"I thought you—" she replies.

But there are moments in life when words fail. Pablo and Angela clutch the iron mesh, looking at each other across the three-foot span that separates them, completely confused.

"Pablo," Angela finally manages, turning her head to the teenage girl at her side. "I want you to meet... I want you to meet your daughter, Pablo. This is your daughter, your daughter Paula."

And Angela's sobbing finally overcomes her like the opening of floodgates long locked shut, as Pablo opens his mouth, unable to articulate a word. He looks with an astonished expression at this fifteen-year-old girl, the living image of her mother, in every way except the eyes, because the eyes are his eyes, the eyes of Pablo on the face of an adolescent. And then she stands and pokes her thin fingers through the fence, saying:

"Hello, father."

What can Pablo say? He opens his mouth and says:

"Hello, daughter. Hello, Paula."

She becomes curious, and asks:

"Where have you been all this time?"

And then, without letting him answer:

"Did you do it, father? Did you kill those guards or didn't you?"

But then a bell rings in the room announcing the end of the visit. What? Already? That was over before it started, thinks Pablo. He says:

"No, of course not," looking at the two women.

And now it is Angela who speaks again, saying to Pablo before they take him away:

"You're still as handsome as ever."

Pablo looks at Angela, tears come to his eyes, and he mutters:

"If I get out of this—"

"What?" asks Angela, her voice broken.

But Pablo has a lump in his throat, and the guards are already taking him away.

"… I'll come find you," he manages to say before disappearing through the visitation room door.

However, apparently Angela has not heard him, because she clutches the grill and repeatedly shouts "What?" as her daughter Paula tries to calm her and a prison orderly approaches to lead them out of the room. The last thing that Angela sees of Pablo is his nape, bristling with shock or fear; a nape destined to bristle again tomorrow at the mortal cold of the irreversible garrote.

Half an hour later his sister and niece come to visit him, but they are denied entry. Perhaps it is better this way; Pablo is in no condition to handle any more emotion.

At quarter to one in the afternoon, shortly after the mess trumpet, the special judge, Lieutenant Colonel Don Bartolomé Clarés arrives at the Provincial Prison of Pamplona, to officially read the three condemned men their sentence. At that very moment one of the executioners who will preside over tomorrow's ghastly proceedings steps off of the express train from Madrid. He is escorted by the Civil Guard from the station to his room in the prison; the other arrived yesterday from Burgos. The accused listen to the judge's words, and their hands cannot keep from shaking as they add their signatures to the statement of condemnation. His thankless task complete, Don Bartolomé Clarés leaves the prison center, while Pablo, Julián, and Enrique are led to three small cells on the second floor, right next to the chapel, accompanied by the prison chaplain, Don Alejandro Maisterrena, and by various brothers of Peace and Charity, in habits and rope belts, tasked with keeping them company during their last hours in this vale of tears built by God in barely seven days. At the entrance to the chapel, a few soldiers stand guard with bayonets.

"A scoundrel!" shouts former civil guard Santillán before sprawling on the cot of his new and final cell. "Whoever accused me is a scoundrel!"

Santillán's cell is the farthest from the chapel. He can barely keep his hands from shaking, despite the bottle of cognac they brought him to warm up his body. The adjacent cell holds Gil Galar, his face a mess, muttering incomprehensible syllables. In the last cell, right next to the chapel, Pablo cannot shake from his mind the image of Angela and Paula through the bars. He sits down on the floor, with his back against the wall, and covers his body with a drab blanket and a plaid cap. No one knows where this cap came from, but it allows him to hide his face from unwanted gazes and concentrate on his thoughts. Now, for the first time since they arrived in prison, time starts to pass at a fever pitch for the three inmates.

Shortly after two o'clock, there is a visit from Dr. Joaquín Echarte, charged with the paradoxical task of supervising the health of prisoners, following the last-minute departure of the head medical examiner, Don Eduardo Martínez de Ubago, suffering from a poorly timed flu. Then Nicolás Mocholi arrives; he will stay with the prisoners for the rest of the day. He encourages them to receive the holy sacrament, knowing that it can help their pardon plea. Gil Galar is the first to let himself be convinced, in a sudden and final attack of faith, and he asks for the presence of Don

Alejandro Maisterrena to express his sincere desire to reconcile with God. Soon, Julián and Pablo also succumb to the Christian confession—in these circumstances, it would take quite a detachment from life not to try anything that might help get a pardon. At five in the afternoon, two barefoot Carmelite nuns come to the prison and place the holy scapulars of the Virgin of Carmen on the prisoners. Gil Galar will spend the rest of his remaining hours fervently and compulsively kissing his scapular.

At six o'clock, as a dull hammering sound starts coming from the outdoors, the prisoners receive a visit from the mayor of Pamplona, Señor Nagore, who updates them on the procedures being conducted to achieve clemency, and he assures them that he will not let up his efforts for a single instant. Along with the mayor, the bishop of the diocese has come, Monseñor Múgica, whom Gil Galar previously met at the hospital in Vera, so Múgica visits Galar first:

"How are you, Enrique?" asks the prelate.

"I have made peace with God, Monseñor," sobs Gil Galar, jumping to his feet.

"Very good, my son, very good. It takes courage to die as a Christian ..."

And, as if realizing his lack of delicacy, he adds:

"But I will keep trying to obtain the pardon until the bitter end, my son; I still have one more document to file, and perhaps it will have good results. *Nihil desperandum.*"

"Thank you, thank you, thank you. And, if not, I will go to heaven and see the angels ... Oh, my God ..." and he starts crying inconsolably when Monseñor Múgica leaves his cell to visit Santillán, who has polished off the bottle of cognac.

"Is there any hope?" the former civil guard asks without greeting.

"The dear departed Pope is praying for you in heaven," is all the bishop manages to say, somewhat surprised by the suddenness and intensity of the question.

"So, all is lost, isn't it?"

"Try to think about the sweet blessings of eternal life," he suggests, inviting him to kiss a cross given to him by Pius X. "And leave the worrying to us. We will keep trying for you until the end."

But Santillán rejects the invitation and plops down heavily on the cot, while the sound of hammering is now unmistakable and no one dares to ask what it is, lest their fears be confirmed.

When the prelate enters Pablo's cell, the former typesetter only lifts his face, without taking off the plaid cap, which seems to protect him from the inclemency of terrestrial, and even perhaps divine, justice.

"*Arratsalde on*," the Bishop Múgica greets him in Basque, knowing that Pablo is a native of Baracaldo.

"*Arratsalde on*," responds Pablo, also in Basque, although he has little grasp of the language.

"My good friend the parish priest of Baracaldo, Don Ignacio Beláustegui, wrote a letter asking me to look into your case," the bishop tells him, but Pablo barely makes a gesture of affirmation with his head hearing the name of the priest who baptized him. "I would like to be able to tell him that Christian sentiments have found their way into your heart, as you were taught by your pious fathers—"

"I already confessed, father," Pablo interrupts him.

"Very good, my son, very good. *Errare humanum est, perseverare autem diabolicum*," he misquotes Seneca. "I will come back to see you after dinner, perhaps by then we will have passed a hurdle for the pardon plea. But, just in case, prepare yourself to die as a Christian."

"*Bai, jauna*," Pablo responds, retreating back into his thoughts.

When dinnertime comes, none of the three condemned men has any appetite, so they only have coffee or eggnog, a humble treat that the Triple-P serves only on death row. The tension is growing more and more unbearable with every passing minute that the longed-for pardon does not come. The telephone rings over and over in the office of Don Daniel Gómez Estrada and the muffled bell can be heard faintly in the prisoners' cells, renewing their hopes every time. A few brothers of Charity walk from one side to another, carrying glasses of water or cups of coffee while the brothers of Peace try to comfort the men's spirits with kind words. At half past ten the Bishop Múgica returns, as promised, and after saying a few words of pious consolation, he shows them the crucifix given him by Pius X:

"Kiss it, my sons," he says to each of them, one at a time, "and come with me to the chapel, and let us pray the holy rosary together."

And the three men, more dead than alive, get up like ghosts and follow the prelate to the oratory, where the prison chaplain and a few other priests who have come together tonight are waiting for them, such as the canon Don Alejo Eleta, doctor of theology from the University of Salamanca, or the parish priest of San Lorenzo, Don Marcelo Celayeta.

"Keep it near the prisoners until the last moment," bids Monseñor Múgica in parting, handing Pius X's crucifix to Don Alejandro Maisterrena.

Leaving the chapel, they encounter Mayor Nagore, who has just sent—from right here at the jail—one last desperate telegram to the general director of the Civil Guard: "Behalf city Pamplona I beg Your Excellency intervene grant mercy pardon death penalty for Vera prisoners show sincere repentance." But at this hour, the general director is probably already in dreamland, unlike the three convicts, who understandably cannot close their eyes. Especially Pablo, who receives a telegram from his mother in the middle of the night.

"Please read it to me, Don Alejandro," Pablo asks the chaplain.

"Are you sure?"

"Yes, yes, please."

"Very well, it says: 'Dear son: Lost all human hope, your mother, consumed with grief and prostrated before Virgin of Sufferings, begs you prepare yourself to die as a Christian, just as she taught you to live as a Christian. Do not deny this final advice from your mother. María Sánchez.'"

Pablo hides his head between his legs and lets out a hoarse, convulsive moan, as he did the day he came out of his mother's womb. When he manages to recover, he says to Don Alejandro:

"Would you be so kind as to reply to my mother? I don't have the strength to write. Tell her that I die as a Christian."

"I shall," responds the chaplain. "Anything else, my son?"

"Yes, roll me a cigarette, would you? My hands won't stop shaking."

Gil Galar and Santillán also write to their mothers, although the former civil guard is still holding out hope for a last-minute pardon. Around two in the morning, the doctor, Don Joaquín Echarte, examines the prisoners, not finding them any worse than is to be expected in the situation. They do seem a bit cold, and he asks that they be brought another blanket and a glass of anisette. Shortly, Gil Galar falls asleep, and when his continuous lamentations fall silent, Santillán says to one of the brothers:

"He's at peace now, glad to be asleep. But he'll see when he wakes up…"

At half past three, Pablo appears to suddenly regain his spirits, and he asks to speak with the special judge, Don Bartolomé Clarés, who arrived at the prison at midnight, as an unequivocal sign of the improbability of a pardon.

"I would like to say goodbye to the two friends who helped me when I was injured," he says to Don Bartolomé.

"What are their names?"

"Leandro Fernández and Julián Fernández."

"I'll see what I can do," says the judge with a circumspect tone.

And after half an hour, Leandro and Julianín appear, their eyes red, who knows if from crying or from fatigue.

"Pablo!" Leandro exclaims, unable to repress the impulse to give him a hug. But the two guards hold him back, and the Argentine curses them in every language he knows.

"Boys," Pablo looks in their eyes, his own bloodshot as well, "thank you for everything. Say goodbye to everyone, and good luck in your trial.

Better luck than I had, at least." And he forces a weak smile, somewhere between a wink of complicity and a grotesque grimace.

"What really pisses me off," the Argentine dares to say, "is that those bastards condemned you unjustly."

"Maybe you'd prefer if I'd been condemned justly?" Pablo replies with Socratic irony.

An angel passes, leaving the question suspended in midair.

"See ya soon, che," is all Leandro can say by way of goodbye.

"See you soon," Julián repeats him, otherwise dumbstruck.

"See you never," Pablo says, before they drag his friends away. The last thing Pablo sees is Leandro trying to writhe out of the guards' grasp and receiving a hail of blows.

At half past four, the three prisoners are taken out of their cells and brought to the chapel, where Don Alejandro Maisterrena is going to officiate the first mass. Julián Santillán looks serene, as if he still trusts in the final coup de grace. Gil Galar won't stop kissing the scapular, as he stares at the image of the Redeemer crowning the altar and prays with trembling lips. Pablo keeps his head down, covering himself with his blanket and huddling under the plaid cap. It is almost five when the canon, Alejo Eleta, officiates the communion mass, and the three broken-willed puppets take the communion like automatons performing a ritual repeated a thousand times.

After the second mass, the director of the Triple-P, on express instructions from the judge, goes to his office and telephones the civil and military governor to find out if he has received the pardon order, because if not, the preparations for the execution will begin. When he returns, everyone can read on his grimacing lips that the pardon has been denied. The first light of dawn is beginning to come in through the chapel window, faintly lighting the pale, overwhelmed faces of those present, who appear unable to come to terms with what is happening.

Some of those men, probably hoping to escape punishment, invoked my name and even accused me of statements against the Spanish troops, and of organizing revolutionary work in Paris. That was true, but had nothing to do with the Vera incident. The prosecutor of that trial asked for I don't know how many years of jail for me and maybe the death penalty too. Blasco Ibáñez called those men dupes, said that they were a bunch of bandits. I took umbrage at that, and I stood up in their defense. Knowing that they were to be executed, I wrote a letter to the ambassador of Spain saying that I alone was responsible for what happened in Vera, even though this was not true, and asking to be tried by the Supreme War Tribunal, before they were executed. I offered to go to Madrid and risk everything. That letter was given to the ambassador. I waited in vain for his reply.

RODRIGO SORIANO,
España bajo el sable

ONE EXPECTS TO HEAR ROOSTERS to crow at dawn, but this cold morning of the sixth of December, 1924, they all appear to have been struck dumb, perhaps mesmerized by the pain of the people of Navarra as they waited to see the blood of three unfortunates fall on their soil. Even the sun seems to have succumbed to the reigning malaise, and is acting lazy, as if it wants to delay its appearance from behind the mountains and low clouds, leaving to the shadows the honor of waking up the executioners. Around the jail, immersed in a macabre silence, the early risers and mean-spirited among the curiosity-seekers are circling like buzzards that smell meat on the road to the slaughterhouse. Inside, a tragic breath spreads among the workers, guards, priests, brothers of Peace, and all those who will take part in the harrowing entourage. At six twenty-five, the judge Bartolomé Clarés gives the prisoners the order to prepare themselves for the ceremony.

The execution will take place outside the confines of the prison, on the so-called Vuelta del Castillo, located next to the moat of the north wing of the prison, where the perimeter road begins. This way, all of Pamplona will be able to witness the magnificent spectacle directly. Last night the carpenters built a wooden platform with two execution apparatuses, one of which will have to be used twice. The executioners, after a frugal breakfast, have come to the place with drowsy faces, listening to the grunts of the hogs at the adjacent slaughterhouse, in a grotesque game of mirrored fates. They are the same (the executioners, not the pigs) as those who barely a month ago were tasked with operating the garrote on Josep Llàcer and Juan Montejo at the Modelo prison in Barcelona. The one from Madrid is tall and gangly, jaundiced and with the surly demeanor you would expect from a man in his line of work. The one from Burgos, on the other hand, is short, fleshy, ruddy, and cheerful, and he boasts that in his long career as an executioner he has now executed fifty-one people.

"With my system, the skin does not tear, and there is not even a drop of blood," he says proudly to his colleague, as he takes a few pieces of polished steel from a case and sets about attaching them to the post.

The one from Madrid says nothing and proceeds to install his execution instruments on the other apparatus, while the onlookers begin to congregate.

"Smooth as silk," says the one from Burgos, satisfied, after greasing the axle and spinning the crank. He wipes his hands on the thighs of his trousers, ready to wait for the arrival of the procession.

Meanwhile, in the chapel, the three prisoners are getting ready to march in their last parade. Standing, handcuffed, they gravely await the arrival of the warden and the special investigating judge, who will lead the procession. A line of soldiers is standing guard in the corridor, bayonets at the ready. At six fifty-five Daniel Gómez Estrada appears, recently shaved, to organize the procession. Three minutes later, with an unequivocal gesture of his cane—his throat is incapable of emitting a sound—he orders the group to depart. The silence is absolute, and only the sound of footsteps in the corridor of the first gallery lets everyone know that they have not gone deaf. At the head is a squadron of soldiers; after them, walking at a funereal pace, are the prison warden, the investigating judge, the medical examiner, and the civil and military authorities, as well as the three local residents officially chosen to serve as witnesses to the execution; then, two or three yards back, comes Gil Galar, paler than ever and with a lost gaze, supported by two brothers of Peace and the chaplain Don Alejandro Maisterrena; he is followed by Julián Santillán, remarkably calm, flanked by the two obligatory brothers and by the parish priest Marcelo Celayeta; third is Pablo, his feet dragging as he is carried along by another pair of brothers of Peace, under the watchful eye of the canon Don Alejo Eleta; finally, bringing up the rear is another squadron of soldiers. Arriving at the end of the first gallery, the group turns to the right and follows a passage that is off-limits to common prisoners, reserved for offices and bureaus.

"Let me go," Pablo says to the brothers of Peace. "I have enough strength to walk on my own."

The two holy men grant his request, and shortly the group stops before a small door at the end of the corridor. Opening it, a footbridge crosses the ravine of the north wing to reach staircases that lead to the ring road, where the execution platform has been set up. The first squadron of soldiers goes out the door and crosses the bridge, followed by the authorities and the witnesses, then Gil Galar and Julián Santillán do the same, accompanied by their respective brothers and priests. And then, when it is Pablo's turn, something unexpected happens, which surprises the few people remaining on the landing: with a sudden, abrupt motion, he breaks free from the brothers accompanying him, violently shoves the guard behind him and runs into one of the offices. In two strides he reaches the first window he finds, opens it, and leaps out headfirst like an Olympic diver, his shackled hands pointed ahead.

The two brothers of the Peace and Don Alejo Eleta stand there paralyzed, waiting for the dull thud of the body hitting the ground, as a few soldiers enter the office shouting and leaning out onto the windowsill, their rifles at the ready. The commotion reaches the head of the procession and several come back across the bridge, including the warden and the investigating judge. They all lean out the window, but down below, in the gully covered with brush and shadows, they cannot make out Pablo's body.

"Go down and see what happened!" warbles Don Daniel Gómez Estrada, but several soldiers are already running downstairs.

"Let's go down too," suggests the magistrate to Dr. Echarte. "I'm afraid you might have some work to do."

Meanwhile, at the other end of the footbridge, Gil Galar and Santillán are surprised and disturbed by the commotion.

"What happened?" the former civil guard asks Chaplain Maisterrena, who returns from the office making the sign of the cross over and over.

"Martín Sánchez—he jumped out the window," says the priest, his voice afflicted. "May God have mercy on his soul."

"But, did he die, Father?" asks Gil Galar, his eyes like dinner plates.

"I don't know, my son, I don't know." responds Don Alejandro, making the sign of the cross again.

"Well done, Pablo," Santillán murmurs to himself.

Not three minutes have passed before Don Bartolomé Clarés removes their doubts, arriving accompanied by Dr. Echarte, who corroborates the judge's words with nervous nods, as if trying to play the drum of his sternum with his little beard:

"The prisoner has died. His skull is smashed. Continue on," he orders laconically.

And the group continues on, even more distraught, if such a thing is possible. A rooster finally crows in the distance and his cackle dimly reaches the procession, like an improvised elegy. A chorus of hogs replies from the slaughterhouse, completing the liturgy. It appears, little Pablo, that you've managed to get away with it. It appears you have managed with your last flight to keep the vile garrote from squeezing your neck and having your death serve as a morbid spectacle to this city of Pamplona and this Spain of Sancho Panzas, cowardly and gluttonous, incapable of grasping any idea from beyond its manger. Too bad your peers no longer have the courage of a Don Quixote to launch themselves into the void. But poor, poor Angela, Pablo, poor Angela when she hears the news, now that she has found you again. And poor Paula, also, who in a single day has regained her father only to lose him again. Although, as the Bishop of Pamplona would say, *pro optimo est minime malus*: the best is the least bad; indeed, the best is the least bad. In any case, it won't do any good for us to stand here looking forlornly through the window. Let us leave the brothers of Charity praying to Heaven for your impious soul, and follow the procession to learn the fate that awaits your partners in misfortune. Let's not miss the end of this magnificent farce.

At six minutes past seven o'clock, the procession reaches the base of the platform. It has been decided that Gil Galar will be the first to be executed, so they take Santillán to a nearby vacant lot so he will not have to witness the death of his companion. Unable to stand on his own, assisted by two brothers of Peace, Enrique ascends the steps to the platform, his eyes bugging out of his contorted face. Once they have seated him on the wooden bench, the chubby executioner from Burgos fits the iron band around his neck, while a guard comes up to remove his handcuffs and Don Alejandro Maisterrena prays, entrusting the wretch's soul to God. Most of those present respond to the incantatory prayer by kneeling on the ground. With a thick rope, the executioners tie the prisoner's hands and feet, binding him firmly to the apparatus and covering his head with a black cloth.

"Don't cover my face," Gil Galar sobs. "I'm a martyr."

But the executioner from Madrid pays him no mind, perhaps remembering the spit he received in the face recently at the Modelo prison of Barcelona, while his colleague is already starting to turn the handle and the prisoner repeats again and again, beneath the makeshift funeral shroud, "Dear Jesus, have compassion for me. Mother, forgive me." The sound of the vertebrae cracking is drowned out by Gil Galar's shrieking as he writhes like a leech on the chair. The terrible shaking and convulsions last a few minutes, until finally the body lies lifeless at seven twenty-one. The executioner from Burgos turns the crank in the opposite direction and releases the band that holds the dead man's head, and two brothers quickly take the body away and put it in a rough pine coffin behind the curtain. The executioner from Burgos wipes down the contraption with a yellow cloth, as he speaks with his colleague from Madrid about which of the two apparatuses to use for the next condemned man.

"If you like we can use this one again, it's smooth as silk," the man from Burgos offers, "that way we don't have to get yours dirty."

Just then a prison functionary comes running, waving a telegram. More than one person thinks it is the pardon, arriving fatefully late, including Don Daniel Gómez Estrada, who breathes a ridiculous sigh of relief when he reads the contents:

"It's from Gil Galar's mother," he says, and in response to the tense anticipation, he reads: "Having lost all hope, let my son pray to the Virgin of Carmen, as we are doing. Last hugs. Your mother and brothers."

But Enrique no longer has ears to hear the appeals of his venerable mother. Unlike the former civil guard Santillán, who hears the reading of the telegram as he is going up the steps of the platform, with a firm and sure foot, looking serenely at the people around him.

"Can I say a few words of gratitude?" he asks Judge Clarés as his handcuffs are removed and the executioners tie him to the post.

"You may speak," allows Don Bartolomé.

"I would like to give thanks with all my heart to the people of Navarra for their efforts to get us pardoned. And I want them to know that I die, that we die, victims of tyranny. Because that's what triumphed today, not justice, but tyranny!"

"Anything else?" asks the judge, visibly uncomfortable.

"Yes," he says, looking for someone among the crowd. "I would also like to thank our defense attorney, Don Nicolás Mocholi, who did everything he could for us." Not finding him in the crowd, he finishes: "Well, you can tell him for me. Oh, one last thing: I have a photograph of my family here in my shirt pocket. I would like you to place it over my heart in the coffin."

An emotional silence spreads through the crowd.

"And you," he says to the executioner disdainfully, "try not to make me suffer."

"No, sir, you won't feel a thing," says the executioner from Burgos, getting ready to cover his head with the black cloth.

"No, don't cover my face," Santillán complains energetically. "Why bother? Let the people of Navarra see what you're capable of. Long live the Revolution! Long live free Spain!"

But the last exclamation catches in his throat, because the executioner is already turning the handle and the former civil guard's face contracts in a rictus of terror in view of all of those present, who respond with shouts of horror or turn their heads not to see the awful spectacle that the justice of Primo de Rivera is offering us this morning. It is seven thirty-eight on Saturday the sixth of December, 1924, when the last awful scream passes Julián Santillán's lips. Shortly thereafter, his heart stops beating. The portly executioner unscrews the handle and releases the band, allowing the dead man's head to flop against the post and remain staring at the firmament with empty eyes, face turned purple, tongue out, mouth filled with white foam, in a posthumous gesture that seems to be asking who in heaven will pay for the injustices that men commit on the face of the earth.

"*Consummatum est*," says Chaplain Don Alejandro Maisterrena, making the sign of the cross.

And in the nearby slaughterhouse, a few hogs respond with their last grunts, ignorant of the fate that awaits them.

EPILOGUE

WHAT A GREAT IDEA, THE EPILOGUE, this port where ships finally arrive and can take stock of the journey. It is a chance to fasten the ropes and tie up the loose ends, and apologize to the passengers for the turbulence of the trip. And so the moment has arrived, dear reader, for you to breathe deeply and collect your luggage and get ready to cross the gangway to terra firma. I only hope you will not reproach me for the abrupt and tragic end of this adventure, because what else could I do but be faithful to the truth, as unpleasant as it may be? I too would have preferred a less cruel fate for my anarchist namesake and his unfortunate fellow travelers, but history is not an à la carte menu where you can choose whatever dessert catches your eye. It is true that I regret not having been able to hear from Teresa's mouth her own version of the dramatic ending, and that I cannot help but wonder what the semi-reliable old woman was referring to when she said she had a final "little surprise" for me. Who knows if it would have added a new twist to the whole thing? But hold me back, dear reader, don't let me go on building castles in the air. It is time now to take advantage of this final sigh, while the stevedores finish tying up the boat, to tell you a few details that you might want to know before you step onto the dry earth and disappear forever inland.

After the legal murder, as some called it, at the Provincial Prison of Pamplona, the lifeless bodies of Julián Santillán and Enrique Gil Galar were brought directly to the cemetery, in a hearse flanked by several civil guards and a good handful of onlookers. However, Pablo's body, according to official sources, did not leave the prison until the next day. It seems that he remained in the hospital room until the medical examiner,

Don Joaquín Echarte, proceeded to perform the autopsy on the evening of Sunday, December 7, 1924. Shortly afterward, a hearse accompanied by several pairs of mounted civil guards left the jail, transporting a rough pine coffin decorated with a cross made of tin foil. Throughout the weekend, as a sign of mourning, all soccer games in the capital of Navarra were suspended.

The more leftist elements of Spanish society did not hesitate to start issuing their criticism, albeit from exile. *Le Quotidien*, for example, offered this headline in its edition of December 7: "Alfonso XIII and the Directory commit a triple murder," and ended the article with a prophecy: "The civilized world can never forget this crime." The next day, several French newspapers printed the letter written by Don Miguel de Unamuno, Don Vicente Blasco Ibáñez, and Don José Ortega y Gasset to the Marquis of Magaz, the acting interim president of the government, because Primo de Rivera was in Morocco spurring on his troops. The letter was blunt and left no room for doubt about the anti-dictatorial stance of the three intellectuals, although they distanced themselves from direct participation in the revolutionary insurgency in Vera de Bidasoa. It read:

> In our name, and in the name of the many Spanish people who, deprived of freedom, cannot do so themselves, we protest the cruel travesty of justice that the Directory has just committed by executing the three men put on trial for the events of Vera.
>
> The statements made on the record were not read to the defendants so that they could confirm or deny them; the arrests were not made in flagrante delicto, but several hours after the fact; the detainees were not put through a lineup to be recognized by witnesses.
>
> The prosecutor of the Supreme Council himself, when formulating his accusation, understanding that it was based on

arbitrary evidence, recognized its deficiency, and built his argument on moral convictions as if in a medieval court; this same judicial authority sought to mitigate the terrible ritualism of the prosecution, and while asking for the death penalty, noted that a plea for pardon is applicable in such a case.

Finally, the defense counsel, in a very clear statement that should be an inspiration to even the most skeptical and passionate soul, ends by saying: "I swear to you on my conscience and my honor, after having meditated extensively on the contents of the briefs in this trial, that I do not find a single piece of evidence, neither sufficient nor even merely indicative, that three men should suffer the most irreversible of punishments."

The Directory found it convenient to foster belief in a revolutionary organization, and invented the absurd fable, which even a moron could not possibly believe, of a communist plot, instigated by Republican elements and with the purpose of giving power to a monarch, the Count of Romanones. To dress up this farce, they did not hesitate to throw around our names, and what is worse, to taint them with the blood of three innocents.

For our part, we consider legitimate everything that is done to overthrow a dictatorship that debases us and degrades us in front of the world, and when we believe that we have sufficient means for this purpose we will fulfill our obligation without ostentation and also without hesitation. But that is what will indicate to us our duty, not those who try to discern in us the disloyal faith of a few adversaries unchecked by justice or even respect for the honor of their fellow man.

Now we shall meet the obligation of the moment, by protesting as fervently as we can the death of the innocent; the facts lead us to call it murder. Given the prosecutor's petition for pardon, the blood falls entirely on the foreign government now oppressing our country. We also protest that such acts provoke the discredit of Spain in the eyes of civilization, and we beg the world not to judge our country for the work of a tyrannical minority, who are the least prepared and the least competent to govern it. Spain demands to be governed, like all modern people, by the sincere and spontaneous expression of the national majority.

Signed:

> VICENTE BLASCO IBÁÑEZ,
> MIGUEL DE UNAMUNO,
> JOSÉ ORTEGA Y GASSET

A few days later, Unamuno dedicated a poem to Pablo, Enrique, and Julián: Sonnet XCVIII of what would end up being his book *De Fuerteventura a París*, accompanied by a note strongly criticizing Alfonso XIII and all of his cohort of stupefied idiots, as he had begun calling them. These were the lines that he dedicated to them posthumously:

Gain, real gain, is all in vain
and its path will lead to nothing,
but understanding stops at 'but' ...
and everything is left for tomorrow.

"We have to act!" shout the sane:
"Stick! Stick!" looking at the slaughter.
Who cares if the cattle is a sheep
or a wolf? Our law treats all the same!

A few poor boys go to the garrote
"With no blood spilt," oh, such mercy!
in Vera they were caught, and the throat

of the village gave nary a groan; their patience
is waiting for the Riffian to overthrow
the vile dictatorship of our dementia.

Around the same time, Blasco Ibáñez managed to inundate Spain with his leaflet *Una nación secuestrada*, without managing to turn it into *una nación liberada*, as Durruti aspired. One hundred thousand copies were smuggled into the country during the month of December 1924, in an operation you might almost say was conducted by land, sea, and air. Since the pamphlets were distributed for free, they found their way into the houses of the bourgeoisie, the nobility, and even the churches. It caused a stir of such magnitude that the authorities ordered all plaques in honor of the Valencian writer taken down; all of his property was seized, his books were banned (some were even burned in public squares), and there were some who clamored to have his citizenship revoked. To all this, Blasco responded with a boast from his fortress on the Côte d'Azur: "The pamphlet was the artillery. Now we fire the machine guns." But, at the moment of truth, the renowned writer's powder got wet, and he ended up dying in 1928, one day after his seventy-first birthday, completely estranged from politics. So he did not live to see the advent of the Republic he so yearned for. However, he left for posterity the foreboding words of the executive Pablo Dupont, a character in his novel *La bodega*, which clairvoyantly predict what will end up happening to the rebels of Vera: "A little fright in the first moment, and then Boom! Boom! Boom! The lesson they need, the prison, and even a little touch of the garrote, so they remember to watch their step and leave us in peace for a while."

During the months following the revolutionary attempt, detainees kept arriving at the Provincial Prison of Pamplona, with a total of thirty-three defendants in the ordinary trial. Among them were Unamuno, Blasco, Ortega, and Soriano, who were declared rebels by association. But the trial would not begin until January 1927, so many of the detainees would end

577

up spending more than two years in prison despite their innocence. In the meantime, in April 1925 La Fraternelle published a minor opus titled *La tragedia de Vera: un crimen jurídico*, edited by the Comité Pro-Presos and signed with the pseudonym El Duende de la Cárcel, which would ultimately encourage another revolutionary attempt in Vera de Bidasoa on May 26, 1925, although with limited impact: twenty armed men tried to cross the border between markers 24 and 25, but they were discovered by the carabiniers, who welcomed them with a hail of gunfire and stopped them before they set foot on Spanish soil. Some claimed that it was a plot intended to avenge the death of the anarchist comrades; others said, without much basis, that the rebels' aim was to get revenge on constable Enrique "The Dandy" Berasáin, who had received many death threats since the events of November. But it is also likely it was a plot concocted by the police under Martínez Anido ("that epileptic pig with blood on his hands," as Unamuno called him). Such was the case in an incident at the end of 1926, denounced by the brave captain of carabiniers Juan Cueto: a group of police, apparently commanded by Luís Fenoll Malvasía, the director of security in the government of Primo de Rivera, bought some firearms in France, brought them up Mount Larrún and fired several shots into the air in the middle of the night; then they slept in a barn and the next morning went down to Vera to report that a large number of communists had tried unsuccessfully to cross the border, leaving behind two crates full of pistols (which were precisely those which the police themselves had just bought in France). The aim of the ruse was obvious: to maintain latent fear among the Spanish populace and thus legitimize an unpopular dictatorship.

Finally, on January 10, 1927, the ordinary trial began for the thirty-three men accused of having organized or participated in the bloody events of Vera. Despite the large number, I will list their names here, so as to leave a written document of all of them. We have already met many of the men prosecuted by the ordinary war tribunal: the four abovementioned intellectuals accused of sedition; José Antonio Vázquez Bouzas (who escaped the garrote by the skin of his teeth), Bonifacio Manzanedo (who was not brought in to the Triple-P until March 1925, when he had fully recovered from the two amputations that saved him from the garrote), Julián Fernández Revert (Julianín, who entered prison a boy and would leave it as a man), Casiano Veloso (the musketeer from Villalpando, whose statements condemned Pablo), Anastasio Duarte (the man from Caceres with an averted gaze, who sold his country for a shot of cocaine), Juan José Anaya (the Douglas Fairbanks of Madrid), Justo Val (the carpenter from Santurce who shared a cell with Vázquez Bouzas in Vera), Francisco Lluch (the deserter of the regiment of Sicily who wanted to return to Spain to see his dying father), Eustaquio García (the afflicted young man who shared his tears with Julianín), Angel Fernández (another of the Villalpando clan), Pedro Alarco (the toothless informant, better known as Perico), and Manuel Monzón (Manolito, the deaf-mute). The rest of the men prosecuted in the ordinary trial were: Francisco Jáuregui Tellechea (a native of Vera de Bidasoa, accused of concealing the fugitives), Manuel del Río Menéndez (from Órdenes, Coruña), Inocencio Clemente Ansó (from Santa Engracia, Huesca), Isidoro Lorente Delgado (from Tobillos, Guadalajara), Alejandro Díaz Gazco (from Getafe, Madrid), Mateo Palme Barranco (from Tudela, Navarra), Felipe Crespo Martínez (from Armañanzas, Navarra), Domingo Bocos Pernía (from Pampliega, Burgos), Ángel Ramos Pina (from Fitero, Navarra), Antonio Pingarrón Magaña (from Madrid), Ángel García Pellisa (from Monzón, Huesca), and Manuel Zulaica Caramés (from San Sebastián, Guipúzcoa). To these, we should add José Manuel López Martínez (from Castril, Granada, who died in prison before the trial was held) and Bienvenido Vázquez Gustiñas (whose case remained separate from the principal trial because the latter was already in plenary session by the time he was arrested). The majority of them were in prison when the trial took place, with the obvious exception of the deceased López Martínez and those who had been released on bail, such as the young Eustaquio García, the ineffable Perico Alarco (although the toothless one would end up going back to jail shortly thereafter on charges of robbery), and the deaf-mute Manolito Monzón (who would also be tossed back in the slammer for begging on a public street).

Is anyone missing from this long list? Yes, in fact: what about Leandro, the Argentine giant, son of Rocafú, who nearly killed old Dubois, and who fell in puppy love with little Antoinette, the crypt keeper's daughter? If he is not included it is simply because he does not appear on any official list of the men prosecuted in 1927. This is one of the great unsolved mysteries of this story: after the execution, he disappeared from the face of the earth. The last thing we know of him is that he went up to the chapel to say goodbye to Pablo. After that, the newspapers of the time do not mention his name again, and history books are silent about him.

In any case, in Leandro's absence, the ordinary trial began on January 10, 1927. Many of those prosecuted chose Don Nicolás Mocholi as their defense attorney, and the illustrious commandant rose to the occasion, managing to convince the tribunal to acquit all of them of the crime of armed aggression, due to lack of evidence. What he could not prevent was that some were accused of rebellion against the government: Bonifacio Manzanedo, Casiano Veloso, and Manuel del Río (each condemned to twelve years in high-security prison), as well as José Antonio Vázquez Bouzas, Anastasio Duarte, Julián Fernández Revert, Justo Val, Gregorio Izaguirre, Tomás García, and Ángel Fernández (ten years and one day of high-security prison). Inocencio Clemente and Gabriel Lobato were found guilty as accomplices and sentenced to two years, four months, and one day in jail. The rest were acquitted or declared rebels. However, none of those condemned for rebellion completed their sentences: between the twelfth and the fourteenth of April, 1931, they were released, some by the frenzied masses who attacked the prisons after the advent of the Republic and others by the amnesty decreed by the new government. Also, in September of that same year, the City Hall of Vallejo de Mena (Burgos), the birthplace of Gil Galar, asked the Congress of Deputies to review the trial in which their native son had been prosecuted. The petition was accepted, and investigations began, but the process took longer than expected and the Spanish Civil War cut short the chance to posthumously exculpate the three men. "So the men executed in December 1924," the historian José Luís Gutiérrez Molina would write, years later, "will remain stigmatized forever. It was never proved that they were the perpetrators of the killings, but they died for the dictatorship's need to mete out exemplary justice against its adversaries." Who knows if some day, now that the spirit to dig up the shadows of the past is starting to awaken, someone will engage in the magnificent madness of looking back at the dictatorship of Primo de Rivera and exhuming the files on that ludicrous trial. Who knows, indeed, if the last chapter of this story remains to be written.

For their part, those who were not detained by the Spanish authorities had mixed fortunes, although the tragic destiny that awaited many of them is surprising, as though the failed plot hatched in Paris had marked them with some sort of curse. We have seen how Anxo "El Maestro" García ended up crushed by a train between the stations of Urrugne and Saint-Jean-de-Luz, the day after the events in Vera. The next to fall was Recasens, aka "Bonaparte," guillotined in summer 1925 after an attempted robbery in Bordeaux. He was followed shortly by Teixidó, the man who handled revolutionary propaganda in Paris, with his snuff and his hoarse voice, shot down by the police in the bar Bruselas on Calle Urgell in Barcelona, in a settling of accounts that was not even investigated. The next to fall was Piperra, the guide from Zugarramurdi who could not convince his aunt and uncle to shelter Pablo and Robinsón: after spending nearly a month hiding in the farmhouse of Eltzaurdia, he started life over in Saint-Jean-de-Luz, where he found work as a bricklayer's assistant and was buried in a ditch after falling from the wall he was working on. Years later, during the Civil War, it would be Francisco Ascaso and Buenaventura Durruti who would die tragically, after spending more than a decade trying to change the world: shortly after being detained by the French police in December 1924, they managed to embark at the port of The Hague for America, where they began robbing banks for the cause of anarchy. They returned to Spain during the Republic and participated in the Civil War, becoming true revolutionary legends, which surely contributed to their legendary deaths: first Ascaso, who took a bullet square in the forehead when trying to suppress the fascist uprising of July 1936 at the barracks of Atarazanas in Barcelona; Durruti would die four months later, at the Ritz Hotel in Madrid, after receiving a bullet in the heart trying to stop the advance of the nationalist troops.

But not all of the men met so foul a fate. Gregorio Jover and García Vivancos, for example, lived to be old men, despite also participating in Durruti's American adventure and the Spanish Civil War, where they led the column *Los Aguiluchos* of the Twenty-Eighth Division of the Republican Army. Jover, the third of the three musketeers, would end up dying in Mexico during the years of Franco's dictatorship, in 1964, after having been secretary of the subdelegation of the CNT in exile. Vivancos, who had been in charge of obtaining weapons for the failed insurgency at Vera, would die shortly before the arrival of democracy in Spain, after having lived a cinematic life: after the Civil War, he fled to Paris, where he was imprisoned by the Nazi army and interned for four years in the concentration camps at Le Vernet and Saint-Cyprien, but he was finally rescued by the Resistance and went on to participate in the liberation of France, where he stayed to live. Postwar poverty forced him to make a living painting colorful scenes and landscapes on handkerchiefs and selling them to wealthy tourists. He ended up meeting Picasso in 1947; the master took him under his wing and found him a patron. From then on, he had considerable success as a painter, showing in famous galleries and selling paintings to celebrities such as Greta Garbo and François Mitterrand. He finally died in 1972, in the Andalusian city of Córdoba, enjoying a well-deserved vacation during the death throes of the Franco dictatorship.

Finally, Roberto Olaya, aka "Robinsón," childhood friend of Pablo

Martín Sánchez, mystical anarchist and bowler-hatted vegetarian, moved to Belgium after being deported by the French authorities in 1924. No one knows how Kropotkin, his faithful wiener dog, managed to convince them to let him come along, but it is certain that he did so, because he was with Robinsón on his return to Spain after the proclamation of the Republic in 1931. One of the first places Robinsón went after arriving in Spain was Baracaldo, where he spent a few days visiting Pablo's sister Julia, leaving a big impression on little Teresa, who would never forget the long red beard and the fascinating stories told in prophetic tones by this old friend of her uncle the anarchist. When the Civil War broke out, Robinsón declined to take up arms: his philanthropic anarchism had evolved into an ecumenical pacifism, and so he fled to Panama, where he would die of typhoid fever. Before he left, however, he wrote a letter to Julia to say goodbye, accompanied by a watercolor by his own hand, titled "Vera. Synthetic Vision?" The drawing was awkwardly surrealistic, depicting an old pedal-driven printing press (the Minerva at La Fraternelle?), with a drainpipe emerging from it, pouring into a barrel filled with blood and a jumble of severed heads, hands, and feet, anticipating Picasso's *Guernica* by a few years. A civil guard and a judge were overseeing the operation of the machine, while various prisoners with their hands tied behind their backs were waiting to be dismembered. The scene was completed by a nude woman, looking at the viewer from a window at the back of the room as she let a bird escape from her hands.

And what happened to Angela and her daughter Paula after their visit to Pablo at the Prison of Pamplona? They simply disappeared. They disappeared just as Angela had done fifteen years before: without a trace. Angela's husband, Paula's putative father, overturned heaven and earth looking for them, but he never managed to locate their whereabouts. Perhaps they fled abroad, to Africa, America, or Oceania, where Angela always dreamed of traveling with Pablo Martín Sánchez, her childhood friend, her eternal love, her heartless vampire.

AND THAT'S ALL, DEAR READER: THE stevedores have finished their work and the time has come to say goodbye. I only hope that the bitter taste that the tragic ending of this tale has left in our mouths will last long enough to keep us from making the same mistakes again and again. If these pages serve to save from oblivion a group of men whose lives were cut short by the desire for liberty, it will be one more reason to think that the time that I have dedicated to reconstructing their history has not been in vain. And if, in eighty or ninety years, somewhere in this immense world that keeps incessantly filling up with human beings, another Pablo Martín Sánchez stumbles upon the history of an anarchist who shared his name, he will always be able to put his hand on this book written by another namesake, which will perhaps give him some direction in the work of seizing a memory from where it lies glowing in the moment of danger. Although, truth be told, patient reader, I will be satisfied if I have managed to bring you to the last page and you have enjoyed the journey, because writing is nothing but a stroll you take with someone you do not yet know. Because if I am glad of anything, deep down, it is that I was able to share this story with you, the story of an anarchist who shared my name, the story of Pablo Martín Sánchez, a story I hope was worth telling.

ADDENDUM

I WISH TO APOLOGIZE TO MY editor, Jaume Vallcorba, and sincerely thank him for giving me the opportunity to include this final note, considering that the book is already in galleys. And if I apologize to him it is so I won't have to apologize to my conscience, which has been gripped by unease for a few hours now. Let me explain. A few months ago, after I finished writing this book, and when I had already signed the publishing contract, I had a few copies sent to various people, hoping that they would give me their sincerest opinion and help me clear up certain doubts that I still had not resolved: I sent the text to a couple of historians, a few trusted friends, and to a handful of people I had met during my fieldwork in Vera de Bidasoa, Paris, or Baracaldo, including the "geriatric bloodhounds." Many of them responded kindly to my appeal, giving me their opinion or pointing out certain geographical or historical errors. What I did not expect is that those copies would pass from person to person until they reached the one who has set my conscience ill at ease.

Last week I received an email from someone I do not know saying that he had read the draft of my novel. He claimed to know firsthand the story of what happened in Vera, and, although it was generally in keeping with my account of the facts, he didn't understand how I could believe the official version of the suicide of Pablo Martín Sánchez. At first I thought it was a joke or the delirium of a conspiracy theorist. But I could not keep a glimmer of doubt from persisting in my thoughts. And since it is always better to fret in doubt than to rest in error, I tried to contact the person responsible for this delirium, but in vain: he did not respond to any of my messages. So, since time is not on my side (the publication of the book is now imminent), I have decided to include this addendum before it is too late. And not because it seems necessary to me to air my last-minute worries, but because I consider it my responsibility to reproduce here the words of this message, even if only to avoid depriving the reader of the right to know another possible version of this story, as outlandish or fantastic as it might seem. Here, verbatim, are the words that have caused me such anguish:

Forget everything you've read about the last night the prisoners spent in the Prison of Pamplona. Don't believe a word of it: it's a sack of lies, a pathetic reproduction of the official version that the authorities gave of the facts. Everything was distorted and machinated so the hypothesis of Pablo Martín Sánchez's suicide would be believable. I don't know what actually happened, but what I'm sure of is that Pablo didn't kill himself, though everyone insists on claiming he did. Don't tell me you didn't see the number of incongruities that can be deduced from your own account of the facts. Do you really believe that a man condemned to death, properly guarded, can escape from his guards, enter an office, open a window, and launch himself into the void without anyone stopping him? Do you really believe this tall tale that Pablo Martín was last in line, at the rear of the pack, and that he started running just when there were almost no witnesses, flanked only by a chaplain and two brothers of Peace? And why is it that during the last night he always keeps his head down, barely talks to anyone, and covers his face with a cap and his body with a blanket? Doesn't it seem suspicious to you that the medical examiner Eduardo Martínez de Ubago was replaced due to illness by the doctor Joaquín Echarte the night before the facts? And doesn't it seem strange to you that Leandro, the Argentine, does not appear again among the defendants, that the last we know of him is when he comes to visit Pablo the night before the execution? And doesn't it seem even stranger to you that Pablo wanted to say goodbye to him and to Julián Fernández Revert, putting them in danger by revealing that they were together at the time of the shootout? Doesn't it seem odd to you that they set up two garrotes, considering that there were three condemned men? Doesn't it seem very strange to you that it only took them three minutes to pronounce the suicide and go on with the procession? And why was there any need to perform an autopsy on Pablo if we can assume that everyone had seen what happened? And, in the event that they actually performed one, doesn't it seem strange to you that no one mentioned that the victim's organs were on the opposite side from normal, due to his *situs inversus*? And, what's more, since when does it take two days to do an autopsy? And why do you think Pío Baroja repeats the rumor that it wasn't Pablo Martín Sánchez who was buried in his grave? And what will you tell me about the tremendous censorship imposed on Spanish newspapers during the days following the tragic events? Unfortunately, I do not have the answers to all these questions, but what I do have is the conviction that Pablo did not commit suicide in the Provincial Prison of Pamplona. And, if not, let me ask you one last question: Haven't you stopped to wonder about the identity of the "Duende de la Cárcel" who wrote the essay published by La Fraternelle in April 1925?

Now perhaps you will better understand my unease. And what if this message is true, as crazy as it seems? Shouldn't I consider postponing the publication of the book, following up on the new lead, and if it turns out to be correct, rewriting the truthful end of this story? Of course, that would be a bit ridiculous if it turns out to be the fantasy of a lunatic, the delirium of a madman, the ramblings of a would-be prophet. But then, why *did* Pío Baroja repeat the rumors that Pablo did not commit suicide? Why did he include, in the last few pages of *La Familia de Errotacho*, the statements of a certain Manish claiming that the one who committed suicide was not Pablo Martín Sánchez, but another man who "went to the grave with a name not his own"? Also, if that weren't enough, today I googled my name again after not doing so for a long time, and I stumbled on a new anarchist dictionary, published by the Asociación Isaac Puente, in which the entry dedicated to Pablo Martín Sánchez says: "Detained for his participation in the events of Vera de Bidasoa, was condemned to death, and committed suicide on the way to the garrote. *Some claim that he died many years later in Lavelanet.*"

But no, I tell myself, I can't get carried away by unfounded hearsay, nor by the personal wish that my namesake had had better luck: who knows if, deep down, I'm not feeding these rumors because they let me fantasize about a different fate for the anarchist who shared my name? No, definitely not, I tell myself, and I feel better for having been able to write a final addendum to make peace with my conscience, confessing these vague last-minute worries and covering my back just in case someone comes along to tell me that they heard someplace, that people somewhere are saying, that there's a rumor over yonder that it wasn't Pablo who jumped out that window ...

Now, as I hurriedly finish writing this note, I can't avoid the temptation to look again and again at the old photograph that Teresa gave me in parting, where Pablo appears with his arms around a woman and a teenage girl next to a delivery truck advertising the French cheese *La vache qui rit.* And then I think that the woman could actually be Angela, and the girl her daughter Paula, and then I think again about the letter I received last week, and suddenly I am struck by more doubt, and I go back to consult a few forgotten archives, and I ask myself with my body all racked by nerves how is it possible that Pablo appears in the photo next to a poster for *La vache qui rit*, if this advertising logo, designed by the artist Benjamin Rabier, wasn't used until 1925? And then the malaise starts to overwhelm me, and I finish this note in a great hurry so I can send it as soon as possible to my editor—at this final moment I'm not going to repent for having written this story and for doing what I'm already doing inevitably without wanting to.

Barcelona, October 6, 2012

Pablo Martín Sánchez was born in Reus, Spain in 1977. He graduated from the Institut del Teatre de Barcelona with a degree in dramatic art and from the University of Barcelona with a degree in literary theory and comparative literature. He received a master's degree in humanities from the Carlos III University of Madrid and a Ph.D. in French language and literature from the University of Lille-3 as well as a Ph.D. in literary theory and art and comparative literature from the University of Granada. He is the author a collection of short stories, *Fricciones* (E.D.A. Libros, 2011), and two novels, *The Anarchist Who Shared My Name (El anarquista que se llamaba como yo)* and *Tuyo es el mañana* (Acantilado, 2016). In addition, he has translated the works of authors such as Alfred Jarry, Raymond Queneau, and Wajdi Mouawad and teaches writing at the Ateneu School of Writing of Barcelona. In 2014 he was invited to join the Oulipo and is currently the only Spanish member of the group.

Jeff Diteman is a writer, painter, and translator from the French, Spanish, and Italian. Following a BA in literature from the College of Idaho and studies in linguistics at the Sorbonne-Paris IV and Portland State University, he is now completing a Ph.D. in comparative literature at the University of Massachusetts, Amherst, where he teaches international fiction and digital culture. He has translated and adapted works by Raymond Queneau, Eduardo Berti, Georg Büchner, and Sappho; these and other writings have been featured in *Drunken Boat, The Missing Slate, Nailed Magazine, Jacobin*, and *Inventory*.

Thank you all
for your support.
We do this for you,
and could not do
it without you.

DEEP
VELLUM

DEAR SUBSCRIBERS,

We are both proud of and awed by what you've helped us accomplish so far in achieving and growing our mission. Since our founding, with your help, we've been able to reach over 100,000 English-language readers through the translation and publication of 32 award-winning books, from 5 continents, 24 countries, and 14 languages. In addition, we've been able to participate in over 50 programs in Dallas with 17 of our authors and translators and over 100 conversations nationwide reaching thousands of people, and were named Dallas's Best Publisher by *D Magazine*.

Deep Vellum is a 501c3 nonprofit literary arts organization founded in 2013 in Dallas's historic cultural neighborhood of Deep Ellum. Our mission is threefold: to cultivate a more vibrant, engaged literary arts community both locally and nationally; to promote the craft, discussion, and study of literary translation; and to publish award-winning, diverse international literature in English-language translations.

As a nonprofit organization, we rely on your generosity as individual donors, cultural organizations, government institutions, and charitable foundations. Your tax-deductible recurring or one-time donation provides the basis of our operational budget as we seek out and publish exciting literary works from around the globe and continue to build the partnerships that create a vibrant, thriving literary arts community. Deep Vellum offers various donor levels with opportunities to receive personalized benefits at each level, including books and Deep Vellum merchandise, invitations to special events, and recognition in each book and on our website.

In addition to donations, we rely on subscriptions from readers like you to provide the bedrock of our support, through an ongoing investment that demonstrates your commitment to our editorial vision and mission. The support our 5- and 10-book subscribers provide allows us to demonstrate to potential partners, bookstores, and organizations alike the support and demand for Deep Vellum's literature across a broad readership, giving us the ability to grow our mission in ever-new, ever-innovative ways.

It is crucial that English-language readers have access to diverse perspectives on the human experience, perspectives that literature is uniquely positioned to provide. You can keep the conversation going and growing with us by becoming involved as a donor, subscriber, or volunteer. Contact us at deepvellum.org to learn more today. We would love to hear from you.

Thank you all. Enjoy reading.

Will Evans
Founder & Publisher

PARTNERS

SUBSCRIBERS

FORTHCOMING FROM DEEP VELLUM
_____

JOHANN WOLFGANG VON GOETHE · *The Golden Goblet: Selected Poems*
translated by Zsuzsanna Ozsváth and Frederick Turner · GERMANY

SERGIO PITOL · *Mephisto's Waltz: Selected Short Stories*
translated by George Henson · MEXICO

ZAHIA RAHMANI · *"Muslim": A Novel*
translated by Matthew Reeck · FRANCE/ALGERIA

KIM YIDEUM · *Blood Sisters*
translated by Ji yoon Lee · SOUTH KOREA

DEEP
VELLUM